PRAISE FOR "WHAT'S BRED IN THE BONE"

BOOK ONE IN THE XK9 "BONES" TRILOGY

What's Bred in the Bone is an exciting, highly imaginative science fiction thriller and police procedural. Whether human or canine, Gephardt knows her characters and breathes life into them. Her writing is taut, the plot intricate and fast-paced. This novel is a dog-lover's dream!
 --**Robin Wayne Bailey, author of the** *Brothers of the Dragon* **Series**

There were so many things to love about this book . . . besides from all the animal goodness, there is a good mystery going on. I think this can best be described as a police procedural in space - and with dogs. There's plenty of action and intrigue to keep the reader's attention.
 --**Booker T's Farm**

Gephardt does a fantastic job of putting us inside of these animals' heads. Every action they take makes sense for an animal, and you get the feeling that she truly understands what makes our canine friends tick. She also has a great sense of humor, with some pages making me giggle as I read them.

I found the story absorbing and I wanted to keep reading; the day I read it, our dinner was 45 minutes late because I didn't want to put the book down.

I really enjoyed this book. I stayed up way too late several nights as I wanted to read "one more chapter." The storyline was interesting, and I will be looking forward to other books in this trilogy.

Drawing on deep research into canine behavior, animal cognition, and sustainable environmental design, Gephardt gives us a world full of honor, intrigue, and betrayal, peopled with a cast of believable characters—both human and XK9—we care about, and enjoy spending time with, and filled with problems that are definitely worth talking about.

Please follow **Jan S. Gephardt** on your favorite online platform. She's on Facebook, Twitter, and LinkedIn. Her website https://jansgephardt.com/ includes her regularly-updated blog "Artdog Adventures."

Learn more about **Weird Sisters Publishing LLC** at https://weirdsisterspublishing.com/. The website features "The Weird Blog," and information about all of their book and story releases, from **Jan S. Gephardt, G. S. Norwood**, and (starting in 2022) **Warren C. Norwood.**

A BONE TO PICK

THE 2ND NOVEL IN THE XK9 "BONES" TRILOGY

JAN S. GEPHARDT

For my sister,
G. S. Norwood,
Even more mysterious and complex than we thought.
You made an indelible difference.

CONTENTS

A BONE TO PICK

By Jan S. Gephardt

CHAPTER 1

MIDNIGHT CROP INSPECTION

"What is that dark thing in Bonita's quinoa patch?" XK9 Shady Jacob-Belle dialed her vocalizer low, flattened her ears, and growled. Unease slithered in her gut. She drew back from the balcony's railing.

Her mate Rex had been gazing toward the starry nighttime sky-windows with a dreamy look on his furry black face. Now he crouched beside her in the shadows, tense and focused. He stared toward the quinoa. "I am not sure." Like her, he'd lowered his volume as far as it would go.

Together they peered through gaps in the trailing curtain of sweet potato vines that hung down from the rooftop garden on the level above them. The leafy vine tendrils provided a handy impromptu blind.

Through their brain link, Shady felt her partner Pam rouse from an exhausted sleep. Physically, Pam was at home, seven kilometers away in the Central Plaza District of Orangeboro. But their brain link gave her the ability to be aware of what Shady was doing. *Shady?* Pam's mental voice came across drowsy and disoriented. *You okay?*

For now. Stand by, Shady answered. Whatever lurked a hundred meters away in their neighbor's field, it was roughly human-sized. Shady's hackles rose with a prickle of foreboding. All she could see in the darkness was a lumpy shadow among the meter-high quinoa spikes. Veils of mist drifted on thermals up the clifflike terraces from the river far below. Some were too thick to see through. Air currents carried scents from the quinoa patch away, not toward her.

She stifled an urge to bark. Better stay silent until they knew more. It might be nothing. But it also might be a Transmondian agent, here to spy on Rex's Corona Tower home. Spy, or do something worse.

Shall I come out there to you? Pam seemed wider awake now.

Be ready to call it in but stay put for the moment. There may be a simple fix.

Shady activated the neural Heads-Up Display of her Cyber-netically-Assisted Perception equipment, then shifted to the ther-mal-imaging setting. A man's hot, white form blazed into view among the dark, much-cooler stalks. He'd positioned himself about a meter from Rim Eight Road. "Damn. Definitely a man out there."

At her side, Rex's deep growl rumbled like thunder. "Not. On. My. Watch." He rose from his crouch, then whirled toward his bedroom door. No light flicked on when he entered. He must've used the com in his CAP to disable the motion sensor.

She followed, of one accord with him. On a different night they might have been less alarmed, although no night was good for prowlers. But tonight their world had changed, very much against the Transmondian government's wishes. The humans of Orangeboro and Rana Habitat Space Station had publicly declared to the Universe that XK9s were not mere forensic tools, but sapient beings.

News feeds all over Alliance Space had broadcast a presenta-tion that Rex, Shady, and the rest of the Pack had given to demonstrate some of their capabilities. They'd designed it to show that XK9s were capable of sapient-level thought.

The government of Transmondia had tried to stop the presentation. They'd launched hot rebuttals the moment broadcasts began. Transmondian government officials, as well as the government itself, were the XK9 Project's major backers. They'd sold XK9s to agencies all over Planet Chayko, and planned expansions far beyond Rana Station. Premium dogs sold for millions of novi, a lucrative trade that would end if XK9s were declared sapient and shielded from trafficking by Alliance-wide laws.

I'm calling it in, Pam said. *I'm getting dressed.*

Shady's gut tightened. Her hackles prickled anew.

"Head for the garage," Rex said. "We can swing through the orchard. Approach from the back of the property. I imagine he will be focused more toward the road, with its potential traffic. He may not expect us to come from the other direction." Rex had lived here more than two months. He knew the layout of the two-hectare property far better than Shady, who'd only visited a couple of nights.

She and her mate moved silent as wraiths through the apartment, then six flights down. They passed rack upon rack of seedlings, bathed in blue light and fastened all the way down the leeward wall of the stairwell. The young plants' vigorous, fecund smell hung thick in the air, laced with faint, faded scent-trace from Family members—but not from Rex's human partner, Charlie Morgan. Charlie was currently in the hospital. The doctors had brought him out of his re-gen coma on Friday, but he still wasn't healed.

I alerted Dispatch, Pam reported. *Your backup's on the way.*

Thanks. Shady passed this on to Rex. Gratitude for Pam's conscious presence and backup through the link filled her with a warm swell of affection. Poor Charlie had worn himself out, staying up to watch the XK9s' presentation on the vid screen in his hospital room. He probably was deep asleep right now, unable to advise or comfort Rex.

Mist-borne odors of hours-ago supper and the big oak tree at the courtyard's center mingled with the other smells into Corona's unique mélange. Rex led her to the underground garage, then out on the spinward side of the tower, opposite their watcher's location.

They leaped up the embankment by the driveway. "He is crouched in a harvest-ready field, heedless of the damage he is doing to the crop." She hadn't been a Ranan for long, but angry disgust soured her throat. "Only an ignorant foreigner would do that."

Hot rage like charred coals burned in Rex's scent factors and deepened the menace in his growl. "Transmondian agent. Got to be. Probably thinks the crop is just tall weeds."

Her mate was right. No Ranan would make such a mistake. A stealthy foreigner, concealed, spying on Corona, almost certainly came from the Transmondian Intelligence Service. Rex had good reason to hate the TIS, and especially Col. Jackson Wisniewski, the spymaster who'd tried to make Rex one of his assets.

Shady followed him toward a grove of fruit trees. By now she'd phased into full guard-dog-on-the-hunt mindset, ready to deal with this trespasser. They'd learned as puppies how to quietly navigate thick, wild brush. Far easier to move in silence through Corona's well-maintained orchard, but better not get sloppy. Especially not if this guy was from Transmondian Intelligence. She kept her nose up, sorting through the night-smells. At last came a tendril of the stranger's scent, laced with a telltale touch of gunshot residue.

GSR? Alarm radiated through the link from Pam. *Is he armed?*

I don't think so, Shady replied. "Faint GSR," she texted to her mate, not daring any sound at this point. If only she and Rex had a brain link like the one she shared with Pam!

"GSR confirmed, but maybe a day old," Rex texted back.

Gunshot residue didn't wash off easily, although this man had tried. It was yet more proof that he was a Transmondian, or at least a dirtsider from Planet Chayko. Almost no Ranans had either access to firearms or any need for them on their space station home. Good thing this man didn't smell as if he had a gun tonight.

They crept closer, screened behind a trellised vineyard row on the leeward side of the tower, their footsteps muffled by clover. A quick dash across a short gap brought them onto neighboring Bonita Tower property, between two rows of leafy quinoa topped by heavy seed heads. Shady brushed carefully between the drying stalks, wary lest they crackle.

She and Rex moved upwind of the intruder, a couple of rows over. She'd already committed his personal odor profile to memory, but now she studied his scent factors. The involuntary exudations betrayed the dusty-smoky smell of fatigue. Perhaps a touch of shuttle-lag? She caught the faint *pa-pum* of his heartbeat, his careful, even breathing, and then his quiet yawn.

"Wait here," Rex texted. "I'll approach him from behind." He disappeared around the end of a row.

Shady halted, ears up. "How close is our backup?" she texted Dispatch.

"En route," the dispatcher replied. "ETA about five minutes."

"Good evening, sir," Rex said in a calm, moderate tone.

The man gasped. Dry stalks crunched.

"I do not believe I recognize you." Rex's robotic vocalizer-voice wasn't capable of much emotional nuance, but from the cadence she pictured him with ears up and tail wagging. Trying to look as non-threatening as an unexpected, enormous black wolf-dog in the night could. "May I please ask what brings you —" The *pop* of a trank-pistol cut him off.

Shady shouldered between the plants. "Shot fired!" she told Dispatch. "We are engaging!"

"Here, now! There is no call for that." Rex had dodged the trank bolt. A black blur of motion beyond a last row of stalks, he darted in, snapped his teeth onto—

The man twisted, faster than humans could move. His weapon popped again.

Rex stumbled backward into the quinoa, legs wobbly, then fell over.

Rex! Shady reached the intruder in less than a stride. She slammed against him at full gallop. Lunged for his weapon-hand.

"Officer down!" Pam yelled to Dispatch through Shady's connection. "Need backup! *Stat!*"

The man tumbled away from Shady with a yell, then regained his feet and swung the pistol toward her.

Still has two darts. "Stand down!" She zigzagged to evade his aim.

The pistol jerked back and forth, tracking her.

Dammit. She darted closer to the man, feinted right, then dodged left around a leafy stalk. Lunged from behind it to slip under his guard and go for his weapon-arm. She sank teeth into the muscle and bone of his brawny forearm. Coppery-metallic blood filled her mouth. She attempted the protocol throw-maneuver, a full-body twist. XK9s were so big and powerful, that always brought suspects down.

Except—this time it didn't work.

He swayed but kept his feet. "Damn you!" His left fist landed like a sledgehammer against her face.

Ears ringing, she flinched away from the next blow. Let go, then circled around. Darted in and latched on again. She bit farther up his arm this time, behind and just above his right elbow.

He yelled and tried to hit her, but he could only strike awkwardly across his body at her. She moved backwards with his motion when he attempted an elbow-strike. Jaws locked, she sidestepped a backward hammer-fist meant for her abdomen.

She clamped down harder on his arm. Her teeth sliced muscle and tendon, grated on bone.

He yelled, cursed, struggled against her.

She dragged him backward.

They rotated in a ragged circle. Quinoa stalks bent and shattered, but the man kept his feet.

She'd met one objective, anyway. She controlled his right arm —the one that clutched the trank pistol. He couldn't get an angle to point it at her. Her bites had half-disabled his arm, and he couldn't break her grip.

He screamed rage and pain. Wrenched his body back and forth.

She dug her teeth in harder and wrapped her front legs around his torso for a better anchor against his wild swings. With her hind feet still on the ground, she pushed or pulled into his every twist. Could she get him off his feet?

He staggered, spun. Stayed upright.

Her feet blundered over a knot of shattered stalks. She stumbled.

He threw all his weight into driving her into the ground with his shoulder.

She released her jaws. Pushed away just in time.

He landed like a load of bricks. Lay there on his side for a moment, stunned.

If only I could use handcuffs! She darted forward. Grabbed his trank pistol—but also sank teeth into part of his hand.

He raised his head with an agonized yell. Threw a desperate punch with his left fist.

She dodged away behind him, dragging his right arm, jaws still clenched on his hand and the trank pistol. His blow couldn't connect. She gave his hand a "kill shake," but maybe he couldn't let go. "Stand down!" she ordered. "Stop resisting! You are under arrest! "It is your right to say nothing, but it may—"

He rolled his body toward her, reached out with his left hand. Lurched upward with an angry grunt.

She powered backward hard and fast, teeth still locked on his hand. Yanked, but didn't manage to dislocate his shoulder. She dragged his heavy bulk about half a meter through the quinoa.

"As I was saying, it may harm your defense if you do not mention, when questioned—"

He gathered himself, drew his legs in toward his torso, then tried to kick her, but couldn't connect. Nor could he break her grip or regain his feet.

She pulled as hard as she could. Her 119 kilos couldn't match his weight, but she could keep him off-balance till backup arrived. "Let us try this again! It may harm your defense if you do not mention, when questioned, something you later rely on in court. Anything you do or say may be used against you in a court of law." She gasped and panted and drooled around his hand. This was exhausting. She paused for an instant.

He lunged at her. His fingers tore through her furry ruff, ripped a gouge in her cheek, then caught on her collar. He gave a triumphant yell and twisted. The collar tightened against her throat.

She choked … Strangled … Terror thundered through her. She clenched her jaws harder, ground her teeth into his pistol hand.

He roared in pain and fury, but he couldn't pull away.

Muscles and tendons shredded between her teeth. She tasted a new flow of blood. How was she not breaking bones?

They swayed back and forth. He twisted the collar with all his might.

Black spots gathered at the edges of her vision. Somewhere far away, Pam was yelling.

The collar broke. She could breathe again!

She released his hand and the pistol. Staggered back. Gasped gulps of air, lest she black out.

The man's cry of triumph turned to anguish. She'd shredded his right hand to gory ruins. The trank pistol fell to the ground. He collapsed with a cry and stared at his macerated hand. His whole body shuddered.

Shady drew in another deep breath, then licked her lips to clear them of blood. She found the pistol with a forepaw, passed it to a hind foot, then sent it spinning away into the field. *Nasty thing!* She snorted. *Still no sign of Rex.* That dart must've delivered a full load. He might be out for hours. *I'm on my own.*

No you're not! "Officer down! Officer down! Officer needs assistance!" Pam yelled into her com. "Rim Eight Road, Ninth Precinct, corner of Bonita and Corona!"

More sirens. These came from spinward.

The man's ragged cries grew quieter. He bowed his head and moaned.

Where was I with that arrest warning? Oh, yes. "It is your right to have an attorney with you while you are questioned." Her voice issued from the vocalizer, still attached to her collar on the ground near him. "If you cannot afford an attorney, one will be appointed to represent you before you are questioned. Do you understand these rights?"

He didn't answer. Didn't move.

Sirens wailed in the distance, far to leeward on Rim Eight Road.

"Subject apprehended!" she shouted into her com through the vocalizer, also texting the words to be sure they went through. "Need medical assistance! Need backup now!"

The man groaned. He laboriously pushed up onto his left hand and knees.

Shady eyed him. "You probably should stay down. You have lost a lot of blood. You will get dizzy, and bleed harder."

He hugged his ruined hand to himself. Rocked back and forth and glared at her. "You'd like that, wouldn't you?" Definitely a Transmondian accent. South-central piedmont, from the cadence and the half-swallowed "yud" for *you'd* and "wu'nt" for *wouldn't.*

"I would have preferred for you to stand down when I told you to, so I did not have to hurt you."

"I don't take orders from a bitch." His left hand cradled his wounded right arm. Now he pulled it harder against himself. A new, pungent, deceitful scent grew alongside the dark blood-smell of traumatic injury, the raw darkness of fear, and scorching stink of fury. The fingers of his left hand slipped inside his torn, bloodied jacket.

Shady growled. "Think twice about that."

He froze. Met her gaze, then bowed his head. "I didn't do anything."

Like you could fool me that easily.

The sirens drew closer.

His left hand slipped into his jacket again. Flashed back, then forward to throw—

Shady dodged it, circled right. A second knife. She kept moving. A third—but by then he'd twisted himself off-balance and she'd moved behind him.

She launched herself against his back and shoulders. Bore down with all her weight onto the man's burly shoulders and upper back. He fell on his face once again. Lay still for half a second, then his muscles shifted and tensed.

She grabbed his left triceps in her jaws. "Stop now, or I shall bite you hard."

He shook himself almost like a dog. Uttered a deep, gut-level yell and strove to rise.

She clamped down full-force. *Damn*, this creep was strong. And persistent! Cold, queasy fear coiled in her gut. *I'm not heavy enough. He's never going to give up.* Shady twisted to throw her body into the back of his head. *That's his third face-plant.* "Stop! What do you think you can do?"

She drove her weight down on him again, as fast and hard as she could. Through the link, she sensed Pam's yell into her com.

The man hunched his back. His body trembled with exertion. He must be in horrific pain.

Shady's teeth sliced into his triceps. "Stop! Stop! Now I am destroying your other arm!" Her voice yelled from the churned-up ground where he'd dropped her collar.

Hot blood flowed, but his back muscles bunched. Heaved.

How was he still moving? "Stop! Stop!" She bit all the way through to the bone. But it was like biting a steel girder.

A steel girder leaking blood. The ground reeked of it. His arm and back and body were slick with it. So was she.

His head bowed. His breath rasped. He shuddered, then collapsed.

CHAPTER 2

AFTERMATH ON-SCENE

S hady withdrew to the shadows at the side of Rim Eight
Road. Out of the bedlam. Out of the way. She shivered
and lowered her head.

She'd waited subjective eons for her backup to arrive while
she and the stranger fought. But once Orangeboro Safety
Services did arrive, they came in force. Emergency beacons and
police flashers transformed the darkness into a dizzying dance of
lights. An ambulance crew worked on the man she'd fought. But
where was Rex?

You saw him go down, Pam said through the link. *How long will
he stay tranked? Oh, I wish I could help you look!* Stuck four
Precincts away, it would take Pam at least twenty minutes to get
here by train. *If* all the connections went flawlessly.

The trank takes hours to clear. I need to find him.

Uniformed Police Officers intercepted all would-be onlookers
at the perimeter. Bleary-eyed, bathrobe-clad humans from the
nearby residence towers craned their necks to see. Voices lifted
in a babble of questions and speculations. Reluctant, they
retreated.

Shady cocked her head toward the sky-windows high above,
darkened for the night cycle. No journalists' cameras buzzed

aloft. Field ops must have civilian signal-disruptors like the ones deployed in sensitive areas at Central HQ. Reporters had police scanners and informants. If they weren't here already, they soon would be.

But she wanted all civilians—especially reporters and their cameras—kept far away from the bloody wreckage she'd made of the intruder. The paramedics stayed intently focused, so he must still be alive. Pretty amazing. It kept them too busy to look at her like she was a monster.

You are NOT a monster. It was a righteous use of force, Pam reassured through the link. *You did what you had to do, and the recordings will show you warned him. A lot.* She projected her anguished love, and how she wished she could be there in person.

Restlessness seized Shady. She paced blindly, panting dry-tongued. She must find Rex. Memories of the fight replayed unbidden. She shivered and licked her lips to rid them of blood. Then she began her search.

Thermal-driven mist flowed past. She gazed toward the quinoa patch, now trampled and wrecked. Where was he in that mess? What was in that trank dart?

Trank dart. That meant the stranger *must* be from Transmondian Intelligence, right?

That's my guess, Pam said. *That trank pistol kinda seals it.*

Was it the XK9 Project's usual mix, or something more deadly? No. Not thinking that. Shady shuddered.

No! Don't go there. Bad enough it's a normal trank dart! Asshole didn't even answer—just shot him. Pam's anger burned through the link.

Shady cast about, nose working, gut in an anxious knot. She couldn't smell Rex. Thermals flowed strong and steadily, up the hill from her toward him. *No sound of his movement. No scent of him.* She might have to circle the whole field to get downwind, but she'd *thought* he was right over here. Heart pounding faster than her exertion should warrant, she stopped to take stock of her position. Then she pushed through three rows of quinoa toward the back of the property. Shoved her anxiety aside and focused on the hunt. *There. Maybe now* if she quartered to spinward . . .

Another patrol unit pulled up, lights flashing. Shady glanced at it, saw a tall man get out. But she needed to find Rex. She moved down the row and lifted her nose. Had she circled far enough out?

"Rex! Shady!" a man's voice called.

That was—she looked back. Now his scent reached her. *Chief Klein!* Relief made her legs wobbly. Maybe things would be okay after all.

The Chief is there? Wow. But thank goodness! Pam said.

Shady returned to the edge of the field nearest the road, then activated her com. "Hello, sir. I'm in the quinoa field, looking for Rex."

"I'll be right there." His tall form turned toward the edge of the field and the sound of her voice, then stopped. He bent to pick up her broken collar. "Are you all right?"

"I am fine, but the subject tranked Rex."

He looked toward the remains of the quinoa field, but his posture signaled uncertainty.

"Over here, to your left." She stepped beyond the last row.

He straightened. "Ah! Yes." His long legs covered the distance quickly. "Let's find him."

Shady wagged her tail to greet the Chief, but she dodged his reaching hand. "Sorry, sir. I am covered with the subject's blood. You will not wish to touch me."

He hesitated, gave her a worried look. "You sure it's all the subject's?"

"I believe so. Excuse me, but I need to find Rex." Shady pushed through the shattered stalks. "I think he is in this direction. I must circle around to catch his scent."

Klein followed. He activated a bright hand-light that threw the surrounding area into stark light and shadow.

Shady returned to her earlier position. Klein's hand-light

threw harsh stripes of brightness and shadow across the field. It messed with her night vision, but Klein was a human. He probably needed it to keep from tripping on the bent and shattered stalks. She closed her eyes and followed her nose.

Pam stayed quiet. Shady sensed foreboding in her partner.

Shady had been tranked twice in her life. The bite and burn of the needle, the sinking dread as the drug took her—she shuddered. *That was bad enough.* Then came an achey, head-pounding hangover once she woke up. Back in captivity. In the Dark Crate, left to dread the beating that would come.

Why did they trank you and beat you? Pam asked.

We tried to run away. We were puppies. Didn't know they'd implanted trackers in us. She continued to cast about. Caught a fugitive whiff, then it dissolved.

Pam's troublement echoed through the link. *We had no idea when we came to Transmondia to meet you. K-9 training on Rana isn't anything like that.*

We didn't dare tell you. Not till we made it off-planet, and thought it was safe. She sighed. *Off-planet.* Away from the regimented hell, the cages and straps and prods of the XK9 Project's breeding and training facilities. Rana Station had offered them refuge, but clearly the Pack wasn't safe yet.

Too right! Pam's worry rang through the link.

Shady plowed back and forth through the quinoa, careless of additional damage. This crop was already a total loss. She hungered for Rex's scent. She sorted among the cacophony of odors. Broken quinoa had different scent-aspects from whole stalks. Torn roots, fresh soil, trampled soil, the recent smells of anger, fear, blood, the Transmondian, and her own odor-trail filled her nose. *Where is he? He's got to be here.*

Klein followed. His scent factors shifted to the sharp, edgy acid of worry. Then she walked through a waft of a different personal bouquet.

Her heart seized. *There! Rex!* She hurried to him.

Klein spotlighted him.

He looked oddly flat and inert. Because of the light?

But no deathly taint clouded Rex's beloved scent—only the loathsome trank. The *standard* trank, the one the Project always used. Its reek seeped from his hide, exuded from his breath— but he was breathing. Shady bowed her head. *It was only a trank. He's alive.* Then she lifted her head and her voice. "He is alive. But deeply sedated. It smells like the Project's usual formula."

Klein bent, touched Rex, then straightened. He spoke into his com to order an ambulance for Rex.

Shady shook her head. *What can the ambulance do for him?*

I'm sure Klein wants him under medical care, Pam replied. *Tranquilizers are powerful drugs. They can have weird effects.*

Shady flicked her ears. *The Project always just let us sleep it off.* She shied away from the other memories, then stood beside Rex.

Klein frowned. "This calls for a full investigation, and a strenuous protest. Wisniewski's gone too far this time. I'm not having this in Orangeboro!" He scowled down at Rex's inert form, then turned away. "Archy? Yes, I need to speak with Mayor Idris."

Exhaustion sapped Shady in a sudden rush. She lay down beside Rex, rested her chin on his shoulder. Listened to his steady heartbeat, his slow, deep breaths, and allowed herself a few minutes to rest.

A new ambulance arrived. Its crew approached with a stretcher.

"The Transmondian shot him with a trank pistol," Shady told them.

Her voice issued from the vocalizer on her broken collar. It still dangled from Klein's hand. He glanced down as if startled. "One moment," he said to whoever was on his com, then handed the collar to one of the paramedics.

"It is the Project's patented trank formula, from the smell of it," Shady added, then texted "Thank you!" to Klein.

One of the paramedics gave her a startled smile. "The same trank the Project sold the OPD? Great! We have the antidote!" He dug into his bag. "Got a supply from OPD Central HQ, just yesterday. I sure didn't think we'd use it *this* soon!"

Wow. Awed by their good fortune, Shady backed away. Better give the crew room to work. She shot a look toward Klein. He'd gone back to pacing in circles and talking on his com with someone—Mayor Idris?—a couple of meters away.

Klein must be the one who made sure the antidote was available. Pam's admiration surged through the link. *This has all the hallmarks of his doing. Especially after that nonsense with Virendra and Ordovich in Central Plaza, I bet he was worried about attacks.*

He certainly has been a friend to the Pack. Shady knew he'd taken a lot of political heat for changing his position, after lobbying all those years to acquire the expensive XK9s. That heat had included direct pressure from the Premier herself, just tonight. But once Rex convinced him, Klein had staunchly maintained that the OPD had been tricked. The XK9s were sapient beings, and the Project was breaking anti-trafficking laws by selling them.

"What did he use to deliver the trank?" a new voice asked.

A uniformed officer approached. Shady'd last seen this officer enforcing the perimeter, but now the woman fished a glove out of her pocket. "Hi. I'm UPO Marya Seaton, Ninth Precinct. I worked a mugging with Rex and Charlie a week ago. Seems like ages. You say he was shot? How?"

"Trank pistol. Just like the Project's dog wranglers sometimes used. I kicked it over this way. He also threw three knives." Sniffing them out helped steady Shady's nerves. "I did not dare let him trank me. One shot renders us helpless, but a second would kill us." An all-too-vivid memory flashed through her mind, of how a fluffy black-and-white three-year-old named Polly had died in convulsions.

She returned to Rex's side before Seaton got the last evidence bag sealed. The paramedic who'd told her about the antidote kept his fingers on Rex's pulse till the huge black dog began to growl and twitch.

The other paramedic peered at Shady with a worried expression. "We have orders to bring you both to the Sandler Clinic. Are you injured?"

Shady shook her head. "I do not think so." She'd been covered with blood to the point of dripping, but now it had begun to clot and cake. Parts of her body already had started to stiffen up from the fight, but she didn't think she'd gotten anything worse than strains, bruises and scrapes.

Regardless, their specialist veterinarian Dr. Sandler would probably want to scan and do tests for hours to make sure they'd sustained no lasting damage.

She yawned a wide stress-yawn. All she wanted was a nice, long drink, maybe an extra bowl of Master Mix for a snack, and then to fall into Healing Sleep. Her XK9 metabolism would take it from there. She'd awaken healed and rested.

Rex heaved up to lie on his stomach, head off the ground but unsteady. His ears drooped at asymmetrical angles. He shuddered, panting.

Shady moved in closer, chest tight. She sniffed him in detail.

He leaned against her, still shaky.

The lingering undertones in his scent alarmed her. *He doesn't smell right.*

Are they on it? Pam's alarm echoed through the link.

"We'll need to get a statement," Seaton said.

"Later!" The paramedic who'd administered the antidote eyed his mobile scanner, then glanced toward Rex with a frown. "Let's get you both to the Sandler Clinic. Right now!"

CHAPTER 3

COMMODORE CORNWELL GETS SCHOOLED

S hady dozed beside Rex on a double-sized dog bed at the Sandler Clinic. He'd plunged deep into Healing Sleep, once Dr. Sandler and her assistants had gotten him stabilized. Shady had refused to leave Rex, so they'd accommodated her with the double bed.

Once Klein confirmed that a "mate" was the same as a Girlfriend-of-Record, they'd also filled her in on their diagnosis. This entitled Shady to health information about Rex that otherwise would be privileged.

Dr. Sandler had explained that Rex's numerous previous exposures to the trank drug apparently had sensitized him to it. He'd told her once that between Ordovich and the dog wranglers he'd been tranked sixteen different times while growing up. Each exposure made the sensitivity worse, until this one caused a severe reaction.

"We could've lost him this time," Dr. Sandler had said. "It's thanks to you that we didn't."

Shady's stomach had dropped into an icy chasm. Remembering now sent a new shiver through her. *That was too close a call.*

Are you okay? Should I come back? Pam and Balchu had met the ambulance at the Sandler Clinic, and stayed with Shady through the night's ordeal. Only after Rex was stabilized, Shady was thoroughly washed and checked out, and the two XK9s had settled into their double bed, had Balchu persuaded Pam to go home.

You can't have made it home yet. Shady laid back her ears but welcomed the distraction. *You'll be a zombie in the morning.* She wasn't sure what a "zombie" was, but in the past both Pam and Balchu had assured her it was a bad thing to be in the morning.

I can come back.

Go to bed. I'm just worried about Rex. You can't do anything to help him.

Pam hesitated, her conflict easy to sense through the link.

Go. I love you. Sleep.

Pam hesitated a moment longer, then focused on her homeward path. Shady could still sense her living presence, distant in the background. The link never completely disconnected them, unless—as Rex and Charlie had discovered—one of them was under anesthesia.

Shady sighed. She snuggled a little closer to Rex's warm bulk. Closed her eyes. The painkillers Dr. Sandler had given her eased her. Healing Sleep lured her toward her own dreamless oblivion. It would be nice to relax for—

Somewhere out in the clinic, a door slammed. "Get Sandler in here," a man's voice ordered. "I've come for XK9 Rex."

Shady leaped to her feet with a growl. She stepped half-across Rex's somnolent form, hackles straight up. Her lips curled back. Her head lowered. She eyed the door, ready to strike. She'd done battle for her mate once already. She'd do it again, at need. *Don't you test me tonight, fool.*

Now what? Through the link, Pam's words felt like a groan.

Not sure. That's the story of tonight, isn't it? Shady opened the link wide enough for Pam to sense the situation more fully. Then she waited, taut and defensive, though she kept her ears up to hear better. Almost immediately the intruder tangled with Dr.

Sandler. They argued all the way down the hall to just outside Rex and Shady's door.

"My clinic. *My patient.* My. Rules." Shady'd never heard Dr. Sandler so angry.

"I have the authority to override you," the man retorted. "Stand aside."

"No."

Air currents through the cracks carried scent factors from both humans. Sandler's burned with defensive fury. The intruder's reeked of angry frustration.

Shady didn't relax her snarl, but she put in a call to Klein. "There's an intruder here, demanding to take Rex."

"I'm already on my way back. Don't let him."

"He must go through both Dr. Sandler and me, first."

"Good." Klein signed off.

"I can make things very uncomfortable for you, Sandler." The intruder paused. "I know about Howland."

Consternation warred with the fury in Sandler's scent. "Howland has nothing to do with this. I was not responsible for that mess. And I will not be bullied, Commodore."

Howland? Shady filed it for future investigation but did not relax her vigilance. *Commodore? Commodore of what?*

"Need I remind you of your civic duty?" Commodore Clueless-about-what's-waiting-behind-the-door-for-him demanded.

"Need I remind *you* of my legal position as the attending physician of a sapient being?"

"*Allegedly* sapient."

"*Officially* sapient in Orangeboro."

"In Orangeboro only."

"In *Orangeboro, where we are.*"

"Not for long. Stand aside." Shady's ears caught a soft swish of cloth, then the high-pitched whine of an EStee powering up.

Enough of this. She leaped off the bed, hit the door latch, and slammed it open. "Shoot her, and I will take you down."

The man in the SDF midnight-blue uniform drew in a sharp

breath, then turned his EStee on Shady. Dr. Sandler flinched away with a stifled squeak.

"Try it, fool. Give me a reason." Shady met his gaze straight-on and bared her teeth. His little pop-gun didn't worry her. An EStee's shock-prongs couldn't penetrate XK9 fur. Its tranquil-izing drug, though effective on humans, wouldn't give her more than a headache unless several of its short-needled darts pene-trated fully.

He let out a long, careful breath. Stepped back. Crucially, he also shifted the EStee, so it pointed at the ceiling. Not holstered, but it would do for now. "Where did you come from?"

"Transmondia. Same as Rex. Same as that agent I shredded to hamburger in the quinoa field, back in Precinct Nine." She underscored her words with a growl. "Did you get a good look at him?"

"Um." His expression went wary. "Yes." In the background, Shady's sharp ears caught the sound of the clinic's entrance door opening.

"Good." She growled louder. "Then you know what I am willing to do to defend my mate."

Footsteps with a welcome, familiar gait approached through the midnight stillness of the Sandler Clinic.

"Your mate?" The Commodore's gaze flicked to her right. Perhaps he glimpsed Rex's sleeping form through the doorway?

"Surely a man who has done enough homework to know about Howland has done enough homework to know that I am Rex Dieter-Nell's extremely protective mate." She stepped forward to more completely bar his access. "Did you do your homework, Commodore? Or do you need to be schooled?"

He took an involuntary step back, then grimaced and holstered his EStee. "I need information from Rex. I *will* have it. It's a matter of Ranan security."

"Perhaps you should take that question up with my boss." Shady nodded toward the approaching Chief Klein.

The Commodore turned with a cool, haughty expression to meet Klein, but he couldn't mask the dismay in his scent.

Shady wagged her tail. "Thank you for coming," she texted to Klein. "He is not pleased to see you."

Klein's smile quirked a bit broader. "Hello, Cornwell. Did your attempted end-run around me fail?"

"Call your dogs to heel, Klein. I need that information."

Klein grimaced. "My *officers*. Please! Show at least a little respect and you might get more cooperation."

"*Information* is what I need. If they're loyal to Rana Station, I shouldn't need to coerce their *cooperation*."

"And yet you walked in here and tried to do exactly that— coerce them." Klein shook his head. "Not that you'll get much information out of an XK9 in Healing Sleep."

"In what?"

"He did not do his homework, sir," Shady said. "You might have to explain it using small, simple words."

Cornwell shot her an irritated look.

She met his gaze. Answered with a tail-wag and a full-tooth snarl.

Klein's scent blossomed with the sweet-sour of sardonic amusement. "Let's talk further in my office. We should allow my officers to rest and restore themselves. SDF Military Intelligence does have a legitimate right to *ask* for their cooperation. But understand this from the start: I will not even try to compel them to speak with you."

SDF Military Intelligence. Shady snapped her ears flat. *Is the Station Defense Force's Military Intelligence parallel to the Transmondian Intelligence Service?* she asked Pam.

Um, maybe. I'm not up on —

"Cut the crap, Klein. You know that dog has information we need. There was also a second dog, as I understand it. I want both of them."

Tuxedo. Shady's chest tightened with foreboding. She texted Tux and his partner Georgia: "If SDF Intelligence agents come to talk with you or take you somewhere, make sure you are not available."

Good call. through the link, Pam's worry mingled with agreement.

"Understood," Tuxedo replied immediately.

"What's going on, Shady?" Georgia's text popped up a second later.

"I'll explain soon," she texted back to Georgia and Tux.

Klein shook his head at Cornwell. "No, you can't spirit him away, either. But there's an excellent, highly secure interview suite at HQ."

Cornwell scowled. "*My* facility."

Oh, hell no. Shady fluffed out her hackles and snapped her ears flat with a snarl. "That is not acceptable. I know Rex would never agree. Not after what Wisniewski put him through."

I'd like to know more about that, too, Pam said. *But maybe tomorrow?*

Shady moved closer to the doorway and Rex. He'd told her enough to know how little he trusted any intelligence service.

"Absolutely not!" Cornwell whirled to glare at her. "Klein! Make this—"

Shady growled. "Rex does not like what he calls "spooks." He does not trust them. He most certainly would never willingly place himself or any member of the Pack in their power without a great many safety assurances."

Pam's approval rolled through the link. *Good to make that clear.*

Cornwell stiffened. His scent factors boiled up with fury, while his gaze went cold as ice. He drew in a breath, but Klein raised a hand to stop him.

"Rex is a trauma survivor," the Chief said. "Like all trauma survivors, he has triggers. He may have a wealth of information to share, but I don't advise pushing him to defend himself."

Cornwell scowled. "The other dog, then."

"No!" Shady underscored the word with a snarl that put

every tooth back on display. She and Tux's mate Elle had talked many times about the ill-treatment their mates had endured at the hands of Col. Wisniewski. They'd struggled to help them cope with their reactions, even months—actually, now almost a year—later. She refused to propose that either Rex or Tux endure anything that might wound them all over again.

Totally with you there, Pam said.

"No." Klein used a calmer tone, but equally firm. "All Pack members are sapient beings. I can talk with them about the need for the information they know. We can arrange secure interviews, if they are willing."

Cornwell's eyes narrowed. "I *require* the information. I want to be optimally prepared, when the Transmondian we captured tonight can be interrogated."

"Who captured?" Shady asked.

On the other end of the link, Pam laughed.

Cornwell gave Shady a smoldering look. "The captured agent. I require the information!"

"And I truly believe you shall have it." Klein kept his tone reasonable and calm, even though his scent factors flared as hot as Cornwell's. "But not by trying to bully any member of the Pack. Or any of our associates, such as Dr. Sandler. Send me your best negotiator, *later this week*. After Rex recovers from the injury he suffered tonight, and once his partner has recovered more, he might be willing to talk."

Cornwell's jaws clenched. He exhaled a long breath, scent factors harsh with adrenaline-acid and scorch. "Monday. And I'd better get answers." He pivoted away from Klein, then stalked toward the Clinic's entrance.

Shady, Dr. Sandler, and Chief Klein watched him go.

Klein blew out a forceful breath. "Well. That could have gone better."

Shady's hackles still prickled, spiked out to the max. "It also could have gone worse. As it stands, there is no blood on the walls."

Dr. Sandler grimaced. "My housekeeping crew and I thank you."

"Unfortunately, this isn't over." Klein scowled in the direction the Commodore had gone.

Dr. Sandler turned to Shady. "But maybe now you can finally sleep."

Shady yawned a toothy yawn, then lowered her forequarters in a luxuriant stretch. "I would like some sleep."

You and me both, Pam said. *Here's to no more interruptions tonight!*

CHAPTER 4
CLEVER PLANS

Hildie Gallagher debated with herself the whole time her tea steeped: inner balcony with Abhik and Smita, or alone on her outer balcony? Her chest tightened.

What could she say to them?

What had she *started*?

She closed her eyes and let out a long cleansing breath. No, there really was no escape from her brother and his Significant. Their flat wasn't that big. Might as well park her ass on the inner balcony and make herself available for interrogation.

Who knew? Maybe they'd offer insights.

The timer dinged. She pulled out the tea ball, let it drip, then set it in its little blue bowl.

She scooped up grapes and cut papaya, grabbed a couple of luchis—blessings upon her little brother, who always made sure they had freshly-fried luchis—and yogurt. She carried her breakfast outside.

Her housemates sat snuggled against each other, drowsing over their own tea and empty breakfast dishes. Smita quirked an eyebrow at her. "Well? Did you finish things?"

Hildie's throat tightened. She set her tray onto the table, then sat. "No."

Abi laughed, damn him. "Told you she wouldn't! You owe me a kiss."

Smita sat straighter and scowled at him. "Later. Wipe that smirk off, first." She turned to Hildie. "What happened to your plans?"

Hildie shook her head. Avoided eye contact. "I—I just couldn't. Not—You saw the presentation."

Neither spoke.

"You at least saw the re-runs! Surely?"

"Oh, of *course* we saw it!" Smita laughed. "So?"

"That big black dog—Rex—that's his partner. They have some kind of mind-link. Cybernetic chip-to-chip. And Rex was pretty nervous."

Abi's look turned quizzical. "That dog seemed fully in charge and cool-headed to me."

"Because Charlie talked him through his nerves. He stayed focused on Rex the whole evening, except when he faded out at the end because he was exhausted."

"So, you couldn't talk?" Smita asked. "He was finally awake, and you *still* couldn't talk?"

Hildie shook her head. "It was a really bad time to try. Some of the Family was there. Mimi gave me her chair, next to his bed."

"Oh, Hils, you better watch yourself." Abi's dark eyes teased her. "She's got her eye on you! She's making plans already."

Got that right. There'd been a time when that would've seemed like all her prayers being answered. Five years too late now. No matter how smart and good-looking he was, she'd mapped out a new course since then. One that no longer included Charlie Morgan.

"So, okay." Smita sipped the last of her tea. "We get how the mother feels. How did Charlie react?"

"I think he was surprised to see me." The delight and wonder in his face when he first spotted her ... She frowned, throat suddenly tight. "But anyway, the timing was all wrong."

"Was he annoyed?" Smita asked. "Dismayed? Give us something!"

Hildie bit into a luchi. Abi's luchis were always flaky perfection, but this one could've been sawdust, for all she tasted of it. She studiously ate every crumb before she answered. "Not dismayed, not annoyed. Kind of—" *Overjoyed?* No, better not say that, or she'd never hear the end of it. And *no way* did she need to tell them she'd held his hand all evening. It had been so damned *easy* to slip back into … Damn it. What had she been *thinking?* "I don't believe he was sorry to see me. But surprised, for sure."

"Well, it's been years." Abi shrugged. "I guess anyone would be surprised."

"You have today off. Going back?" Smita reached across, then popped one of Hildie's grapes into her mouth.

Hildie nodded. "Best to get it over with. He's haunted me long enough."

Smita stood. "We expect reports from the field, you hear? But I'll miss the seven-thirty train if I don't get dressed." She shot Abi a come-hither look. "Bet-payments with interest, if you come right now!"

Her brother stood immediately. He scooped up dirty dishes but paused on his way inside. "Seriously, Hils. Good luck, today. You have to do what's right for *you*."

TAKING a piss should *not* be this complicated.

Charlie balanced on the edge of his hospital bed and let the dizziness pass. He hated needing to call for help. "RAMoD, assist me."

The Robotic Assisted Mobility Device came to life in the corner of his room with a twinkle of lights, then rolled to his bedside. A sturdy central column on a wide, C-shaped base, its adjustable robotic arms moved in slo-mo. They latched onto his cast in several places and hooked onto his IV pole. READY, it blinked. PLEASE ATTEMPT TO STAND.

Charlie eased himself off the edge of the bed. He clung to the handhold on RAMoD's near side, then pulled himself to his feet. At least his *right* arm still worked. He waited for a new round of dizziness to pass. Was it hot in here?

"Bathroom." Charlie had to verbalize, because he couldn't interface with the stupid thing through his CAP. Cripes, this was humiliating.

He'd been painfully up and down countless times since they'd brought him out of his re-gen coma early Friday. Too much inaction was against the Orangeboro Medical Center's Code of Honor, or something. He'd already started physical therapy. He and ol' RAMoD also had made several agonizingly slow, sweat-soaked trudges around the Re-Gen Unit.

Footsteps sounded in his doorway. His day-nurse Nanda eyed him with brows raised. "Need human assistance?"

"No. Thanks." Charlie focused on putting one foot in front of the other. Did his best to ignore the bone-deep ache in his cast-encased left arm and the pounding in his head. Tried not to think about what Dr. Zuni called "cascading failure of the muscle sheath integrity," or to visualize his left arm dissolving into bloody goo.

I wish I could help, Rex said through the link. Charlie's XK9 partner had gone through his own health issues last night. He'd spent much of this morning growling and grumbling through a long battery of scans and neurological tests at the Sandler Clinic.

I am fine. XK9s are tough. What is Sandler thinking?

Charlie grimaced. *I suspect she's thinking that you had a bad reaction, and she needs a new baseline.*

Rex just growled again. The sudden lower volume of input said he was trying to mute his side of the link.

Charlie managed his business in the bathroom. "RAMoD, take me back to bed."

Nanda was back in the doorway, if he'd ever left. "Do you feel up to a visitor? She's authorized."

His only authorized visitors were Family members. Had Zuni called them in for a consult? But—shouldn't Charlie be told if there was one? "Um, sure." Probably his mother, but why hadn't Nanda said that?

The nurse disappeared back outside.

Hildie stepped into Charlie's doorway.

Holy shit. He froze. Joy, shame, yearning—too many feelings clashed inside of him all at once.

"Hi. Have I come at a bad time?" She gave him a dubious look. "I guess what I really should ask is: am I welcome?"

Charlie made a strangled croak, dragged in a breath, and tried again. "Yes. Yes, of course! Come in."

She stepped inside but seemed ill-at-ease. Apparently, she *hadn't* been a wishful hallucination last night. In Charlie's half-remembered impressions, she'd worn her blue Safety Services coverall then, after working a watch with his former crew on the Emergency Rescue Team.

Today she wore civvies. Her lightweight, flowing dress wrapped around her torso to compliment her curves. Much more flattering than that jumpsuit. The pale dress accented her smooth, nut-brown skin. The fabric pattern had little red flowers that exactly matched the tiny sparkles of her red crystal earrings. On duty, she'd always tied her hair up in a no-nonsense knot, but now it swung loose. Thick, black waves rippled soft by her face and flowed long, past her shoulders.

Charlie closed his mouth and remembered to breathe.

"Sorry to just barge in like this, but—well, I had today off, and ... She frowned.

He never remembered seeing Hildie look quite so ... *beautiful.* Back before the *Asalatu*, back when she and he sometimes hung out off-duty with others from the crew, she always wore a loose-fitting kurta and churidar combination. That was a while back, but the stab of anguish that transfixed him hurt lots worse than his headache or his left arm.

For the past three years he'd been sure that he must've disgraced himself so badly their friendship could never be repaired. It didn't seem reasonable that she was here. "I figured I hallucinated you last night."

Her mouth made a sardonic twist. "I'm a little surprised you even noticed. You were focused pretty exclusively on Rex. And then you faded out at the end."

"I noticed, all right. I could barely believe it." He gulped. "How—why *were* you there?" *Ugh, that came out wrong.* Was the headache making him stupid?

She blew out a breath. "I wanted to talk with you, but I decided it wasn't a good time, with the Family there, and the presentation, and all. I'm not sure now's any better, though. You look like you're busy."

He did? He'd halted halfway to his bed. Semi-naked and covered with bruises, in this clumsy cast and supported by RAMoD, he must be quite the picture. "Oh, yeah. Bathroom runs are currently the highlight of my day." Memories rushed back, of joking around with her in better days, back in the "before-times." He attempted a grin. "Gotta push the envelope, you know."

She gave him a startled look, then sputtered a short laugh. "Yeah, that's you, all right. Always pushing—" She stopped short. Maybe remembering the last time he'd said that to her?

What had possessed him to say it now? "I'm sorry."

"This was a bad idea." She shook her head, but avoided his gaze. She spoke so softly he barely heard her. "I should go. This isn't going to work."

Panic seized him. "No! Please stay. I'm a jerk. I messed up. I'm sorry." He lurched in her direction, then grabbed RAMoD's handhold to ride out a dizzy spell. Hot embarrassment washed over him in a haze of black dots. When his vision cleared, she was gone.

❖ ❖ ❖ ❖ ❖ ❖ ❖ ❖

WE CANNOT CONTINUE THIS WAY. Shady underscored her words with a growl.

Pam hefted the riot shield from the patrol unit's rear storage compartment, then held it over Shady's short path from the vehicle to the entrance of LEO's Grill. *It would help to know what direction I should worry about,* Pam grumbled.

One bound propelled Shady a good meter past the doorway. *No direction. None. I am in no danger. These protocols are an overreaction. Remember, I won last night.*

Pam returned the shield to its storage place, thanked the UPO who'd given them a lift across Central Plaza, then followed Shady inside. She didn't try to hide her worry. *You won that round, but Rex didn't. I'm with the Chief on this.*

The bartender waved at them. "They're waiting for you. Third corner."

Shady already had a clear, recent scent-trail for Balchu and his parents. Two other people had accompanied them. *I didn't know Balchu has a sister.* She took a step in that direction, then looked back when Pam didn't follow.

Sarnai's here, too? Surprise and a sharp touch of anxiety colored Pam's scent. *Is she here with a companion?*

Shady'd already parsed the commonalities in the two younger women's profiles, as well as the familial markers among Balchu and his relatives. *Smells like the sister has a roommate or an intimate partner.*

Pam's anxiety-odor strengthened. *Wow. When they said a 'family meeting,' they meant everyone. Sarnai has an Amare named Rose. I've never met either of them. I only just met Tuya and Feyodor.*

Shady nuzzled her partner. *I know you're anxious, but it'll be okay.* Pam's family consisted only of "Mother." Pam never spoke or thought of her mother without an uprush of discomfort, both through the link and in her scent. Shady had never met her.

Pam's worry might be misplaced, but it seemed a natural outcome.

Tuya and Feyodor are lovely people. Shady had met Balchu's parents the same time as Pam, after the presentation last night. *They like you. Why wouldn't Sarnai and Rose like you, too?*

I don't know. It's just—She drew in a shaky breath. *Family. I don't know anything about families.*

Shady lolled her tongue. *Pack is family, and you know about us. Don't worry so much.*

Yeah, but the Pack is full of dogs, and dogs love more generously. Humans are pricklier.

The Pack is also full of humans. And Balchu's family has good reasons to like you. Shady circled behind her partner and gave her a gentle push. *Don't be a coward. Give them a chance.*

Pam scowled. *I'm no coward.* She squared her shoulders and strode forward.

Shady nudged her to the left. *This way.* She trotted on ahead, tail high, with Pam at her heels.

Balchu, his parents, and two young women about Pam's age had taken over a crescent-shaped booth in the semi-murky interior. They'd probably seen her and Pam coming. LEO's had been artfully designed for its law enforcement patrons. They'd managed to build all seating as corner booths, so no one's back was exposed, and they'd provided excellent sightlines with aligned aisles and well-placed mirrors.

Feyodor rose from his place next to Tuya, a broad grin on his face. He waved to them. "There she is! Hello, Pam! Hello, Shady! Welcome!"

Sarnai and Rose regarded Shady with startled expressions and anxious scent factors.

Shady greeted Feyodor and Tuya with a wriggle and a wagging tail, then turned to the two young women. "Yes, we XK9s always look bigger in real life. But even Balchu is used to me now."

Balchu grinned. "We have our moments."

"And, as it happens, you were correct all along," Shady said. "Your apartment really is too small."

Seriously. Again? Pam asked, but kept it to the link.

"Funny you should mention that," Feyodor said.

Tuya gave him an irritated look. "Not yet."

"It's good to finally meet you both." Sarnai stood. She stretched a hand across the table to Pam. "I've wanted to meet you since the first time Balchu said, 'I met this woman,' and we realized he meant someone *really* special."

Embarrassment bubbled up in Pam's scent, but she smiled and took Sarnai's hand. "I think he's pretty special, too."

Sarnai eyed Shady. "The vids sure didn't do *you* justice."

Shady dipped her head and fluttered her tail. "We were bred to be large and intimidating. It can cause fear, but we cannot help the way we were built."

Sarnai nodded. "You are what you are. Not so long ago, and still in some places today, society didn't accept people like Rose and me, either. I believe I understand, somewhat."

Oh, I like her. Shady sidled closer. Her tail shifted to full-wag. "My fur is soft, I just had a bath, and I like to have my ears scratched."

Sarnai and Rose laughed, then obliged her.

You're shameless. Pam parked herself on the opposite end of the booth's bench, next to Balchu. He wrapped his arm around her, and she snuggled close.

"I am delighted we all could meet like this for lunch today." Feyodor had not yet sat down. He lifted a glass of something that smelled alcoholic. "To this family!"

Everyone laughed. All humans who had a drink of any sort at hand, from water to a beer mug, lifted it. "To the family!"

Shady leaned in close to Sarnai and Rose. "He is up to something," she said quietly. "Do you know what it is?"

Sarnai's brow furrowed. "You think so, too?"

"Scent factors do not lie."

Rose chuckled. "Told you. He's got something up his sleeve."

"All right, Dad, spill it," Sarnai said. "What's up?"

Thump. Shady caught a furtive movement: Tuya kicked Feyodor's ankle and gave her husband a stern look.

Feyodor froze for an instant, then let out a cautious breath. "Is this not enough? We're all here, breaking bread together. Getting to know each other. Family members should also be friends. Get along. Grow closer, so we are always there for each other. That is a very good thing."

"He's been up to something ever since Pam became Balchu's Amare," Rose muttered to Shady.

Shady pricked her ears. "Being Amares changed things?"

"Well, that's a pretty big step." Rose smiled. "Going official, you know."

Shady tried not to let Pam sense too clearly how much this interested her. "No, I did not know. This makes a difference to Ranans?"

"You really *aren't* from around here, are you?" Rose gave a low chuckle. "Yeah, it's a big deal. A *really* big deal. It even changes your civil status. I mean, it's not as monumental as being Domestic Partners or something. But it changes your rights to make decisions with your lover, changes your tax status, changes lots of things."

"These status changes. What are they based on?"

"It's all in the Civil Code."

Shady blinked. "Oh. Thank you." When she'd come to Rana, she'd studied the Statutory Code, the laws that affected criminal justice. She'd neglected the Civil Code. Clearly, that was an oversight.

Rose grinned. "What do you think? Do Balchu and your partner have a future?"

"Oh." Shady eyed Pam, who was studiously ignoring her and smiling up at Balchu. "Pam and Balchu are mates. I realized that for certain last week."

"Mates?" Rose asked the question, but Sarnai focused on her, too.

Shady let her tongue slide out in a dog-smile. "Many couples are compatible, pleasant, companionable. They will stay together for a season, or until something goes wrong enough that they decide to part. But if I may judge by XK9s and my small experience of humans, some are mates. Unusually well-matched. Innately compatible. It is a deeper thing. I think Tuya and Feyodor probably are mates, although they are irritated with each other at the moment. That makes it harder to discern." She tested the two women's scent factors. "The two of you also smell like mates, if I have interpreted your scent factors correctly."

Sarnai and Rose put their arms around each other. Their eyes softened, their smiles widened, and their scent factors blossomed with fragrant pleasure. "You mean that?" Sarnai asked. "We're *mates*? For real?"

"Scent factors do not lie." Shady wagged her tail. "Neither do XK9s. What else would you like to know?"

CHAPTER 5

REX'S INTERVENTION

"Oh!" Rex halted in the middle of a hallway at Orangeboro Medical Center. He lifted his nose to the air currents. This might portend bad things for Charlie. Better investigate!

His friend Bill Sloane, who'd given him a ride from the Sandler Clinic, sidestepped quickly to avoid walking into him. "What is it, Big Guy?"

Rex laid back his ears. "Trouble, I think. I need to follow this. Do you mind going on ahead to check on Charlie for me?"

"Um, sure." Bill's scent shifted into the mid-tone, muddled odors of mild confusion. But Rex had seen his friend adapt quickly while sorting through confusion several times in the week he'd known him. Rex trusted him to handle this. After a moment's hesitation, Bill continued on their original route toward the Re-Gen Unit.

Now Rex could follow a new and troubling trace in the air. He recognized Hildie's scent profile, and he felt the reactive reverberations from Charlie through the link. Something had gone badly between them.

He tracked her to a small, tucked-away conference room. It

had a door, but she'd left it ajar. It also had a light, but she'd left it dark.

He stopped in the doorway. She stood near the farthest corner of the room, arms wrapped around herself, head bowed. "Hello, Hildie. We need to talk."

She gave a little gasp and looked up. Fear bloomed in her scent factors.

"Please do not worry." People often were frightened of him, whether he wanted to scare them or not. "I shall not hurt you."

"I don't want to talk." She bowed her head again.

"I can tell from your scent factors that you are feeling overwhelmed and frightened—not so much of me, I think. More about something that happened. I suspect that Charlie did or said something you did not anticipate."

She looked up. "Are you a mind-reader? How could you know that?"

"I do not read minds. I read and interpret scent factors and human body language. Scent factors never lie, and body language rarely does."

She frowned, but he noted promising shifts in her stance and bouquet: he had piqued her curiosity. "Scent factors?"

"Living creatures that experience emotions emit a variety of scents, depending on what they feel. Over the years, XK9s have learned to correlate many scent markers that signal particular human emotions. Since scent factors are involuntary reactions that humans cannot normally detect, they cannot be faked."

"That's ... terrifying." She stared at him. "And right now, I smell overwhelmed?"

"Perhaps a better description would be 'freaked out.'"

She gave a rueful laugh but relaxed a little more. "Yeah, that's a pretty good description."

"Perhaps you should sit down. Sometimes that helps." He cocked his head. "Do you know any breathing patterns? Whenever Charlie gets upset or frightened, he runs breathing patterns to calm himself."

She kept her gaze on him but felt her way to a chair and sat. "What frightens Charlie?"

He let his tongue loll. "Microgravity, mostly. I believe that reaction must have started with the *Asalatu* incident."

"Probably." Her scent turned sharply bittersweet with an ache of worry. "I can't imagine he has many good memories from anyplace in microgravity."

Should he share this? "On the contrary, some of his best memories seem to be of the time when he was working with the ERT at the Hub. But remembering also seems to cause him intense pain."

She bit her lip. "I know how that works."

He walked over to her, then sat beside her chair. "However, I do not believe those are top-of-mind for him at the moment. From the reactions I am sensing through our brain link, he also feels more than a little freaked out by whatever happened between you."

She groaned. "Yeah, I guess he would be. Probably doesn't have any idea what caused me to react that way." She hesitated. "He doesn't know what we're talking about, does he?"

"No. He can sense that I am in the hospital building. If he were able to walk through the corridors, he could find me if he wanted to search. But he cannot hear what you and I say, because I have not opened the link to him."

She gave him a rueful look. "I appreciate your discretion." Her closed, tense body language said she still wasn't sure she could trust him.

"It seems to me that this should be a private conversation." He met her eyes with what he hoped a human would read as openness and honesty. "Charlie may sense it if I have a strong reaction to something, but he will only receive a taste of my emotion. Nothing of our verbal interaction."

"You'll keep it between us?"

Rex nodded, human-style. "You have my word. In police work, we often must use care and discretion about what we reveal or keep confidential. Trust is hard to rebuild once broken, so I try never to break it." *Particularly in your case.* Unless things went seriously awry, Hildie might become a permanent part of his and Charlie's landscape. Better make no mistakes!

Her body relaxed some. "Thank you."

"May I ask, then? What did he say that caused your reaction?"

She hunched her shoulders, all tight and skittish again. Looked away.

Rex waited for her.

"He said *all* the things." Her voice came out a scratchy near-whisper. "Everything I've been wanting to hear for *years*. All in one burst." She hugged herself again. "You're right. I just—I freaked."

"What had you wanted to hear from him?"

Again, she didn't answer right away. Again, Rex waited.

"He apologized. Wanted me to stay with him. Admitted he was wrong." She sighed. "I guess there was one thing he left out, but I could hardly expect him to come right out and say the 'l-word,' after all those years of silence."

Rex wasn't sure what Charlie needed to apologize for, but if Charlie and Hildie both knew, he'd figure it out soon enough. "Did you decide to reach out to us now, so you could receive that apology?"

"No. Well, maybe. I don't know." Her hands twisted in her lap. "When I pulled him out of that bunker last week—Oh, God. What a gut-punch." She shuddered. "It was too much like the *Asalatu.*"

"Did it trigger a flashback?" Rex had been learning a lot about those, from dealing with Charlie.

Hildie shook her head. "Not … exactly. But I'm having trouble sorting out what's from then and what's from now."

Rex didn't push her. She smelled like she needed to talk, so he waited. The skills he'd learned in police training seemed to work just as well outside the interview suites.

"He just *had* to push that envelope. Just *had* to make one more run." She chewed her lower lip, kept her eyes averted. "Of course, that 'one more run' turned out to be one for the history texts."

Last week Rex had learned some of what had happened when the starship *Asalatu*'s wreckage had collapsed on Charlie's Emergency Rescue crew. They'd driven their Multipurpose Emergency Response Space-Vehicles, called MERS-Vs, in amongst the wrecked pieces of the ship to retrieve surviving victims—hideously dangerous work. But he only knew a few basic facts. Hildie'd actually *been there*.

"If it wasn't for Charlie, they all would've died, you know." One eyebrow lifted. "*Do* you know? I guess I should ask."

"Not as much as I would like to."

She closed her eyes and let out a long breath. "Tuuri's MERS-V ... Like a wineglass hit by a flagstone. The wreckage shifted *so fast*—" She shuddered. "Ellen and Charlie—it wasn't so complete with them, but we didn't know that right away. It was just ...."

A tear slid down her face. She opened eyes full of pain and brimming with more tears. Stared horrified into a vision only she could see. "Charlie started working the cutting tools and manipulators on T-1. That machine was his *baby*. He kept it in top shape, knew every trick to maneuver it, had an uncanny sense of where his edges were, right down to the last millimeter. Like it was part of him. How he managed to drive it one-handed, I'll never know. One whole side of his cockpit was crushed in on him. But he not only drove it, he found a way to make leverage. And once he found it, he went to work on it. Bullheaded, you know? Relentless." She laughed, half-crying. "The man just does *not* give up."

Rex thumped his tail on the floor. "Noticed that."

"It was like a miracle when they pulled free. I just—I couldn't believe it. We knew he was com-to-com with Ellen, but until they ran cockpit recordings later, no one realized how hard he worked to keep her conscious and responding. They both had a full load of passengers, so he wasn't just keeping *her* awake by force of will—he was keeping *all* of them *alive.*"

"Passengers?"

"People rescued from the wreck. They were sealed inside the MERS-Vs' Arms of Life, midway through transit to the *Triumph.* For Charlie, 'passengers onboard' was all you needed to say. He would've kept on trying till he bled out, if it came to that. There is no 'quit' in that man. He was *going* to bring his people home."

"And he did."

"Yeah. He did. He saved thirteen people that day, because he was too bullheaded to give up."

They sat together, silent for a while. Rex remembered the end-report well enough. Thirteen lives saved, not counting his own. Charlie'd sustained catastrophic injuries and almost bled to death. Ultimately his left arm, shoulder and part of his torso were too badly crushed to save. A few years later, the Ranan Government had awarded him its highest honor for courage, the Medal of Valor.

"You pulled him out of his MERS-V?" Rex figured he knew this answer, but he needed to ask.

She nodded, eyes closed. "I thought he would die." Her voice fell to a broken whisper. "I loved him so *much,* and I thought he would die right there in my hands." She drew in a long, ragged breath, then let it out slowly, just the way Charlie did when he struggled to control a strong reaction. "That's the moment my nightmares always return to. And last week—it happened all over again. For real."

Rex placed his head in her lap. He was large enough that his head more than filled it, but she stroked between his ears as if he'd activated a reflex. Maybe he had: humans and dogs had been influencing each other's evolution for millennia.

They sat that way for a while. She stroked and stroked. Gradually her scent factors calmed from turbulent upheaval and anguish to something cooler and more melancholy.

He dialed his vocalizer down. "What do you want now?"

She sighed, opened her eyes. "Are you a Listener, Rex?"

He kept his head on her lap but wagged his tail. "Not by training. But I have a sense that to some extent dogs are natural-born Listeners."

She answered with a low chuckle. "Yeah, my cat is, too."

"Except your cat can't talk."

Hildie gave a sharp laugh. "Oh, you think not? I assure you, she often gives me what-for. Or sings a sad song about something she wants."

Rex lolled his tongue, careful not to slobber on her leg. "I stand corrected. But I shall ask again. What do you want now?"

"I don't *know* anymore." She grimaced. "I came here determined to look him in the eye and clarify to myself that he's really just a normal, ordinary guy. That the romantic fantasy I'd built up in my mind was just that. A fantasy. No real human could live up to that. He's been haunting me this whole time. For five —well, actually almost seven years." She shook her head. "I fell in love with him the day we met. I don't know what it was—it just ...."

"I know exactly what you mean." Rex lifted his head. "It was the same way for me."

She gave him an incredulous stare. "What? How?"

Memories crowded in. "There was this whole big group. Thirty candidates, and we were each supposed to choose one. I could not imagine how I would figure out which one to choose. And then I saw Charlie."

Her eyes sparkled with amusement. "Game over, eh?"

"Decision made." Rex's tail thumped the floor. "It was a month until the formal Choosing, but every interaction just confirmed what I already knew. He was my choice."

She nodded. "Huh. I guess you do understand. I'd never experienced such an amazing, strong connection. Instantly. Except—in my case, he was already claimed. He had an Amare."

Rex snapped his ears flat. "Felicia. I have heard about her. The Family still despises her."

"Me too." The surge of fury in her scent factors made it clear how much. "But he stayed with her, despite our connection."

"Charlie has a loyal heart." Rex could imagine how it must've gone. He had enough distance by now to see this same pattern in the affair Charlie'd had with Pam during XK9 Training. Pam had been the one who broke it off. "Even when a relationship is not working out, he hangs on because he made a commitment. Bullheaded, as you say."

Hildie scowled. "I just figured he didn't find me attractive enough. Felicia was not only beautiful, she was full-on *glamorous.* Who could compete with that?"

"Charlie's grandma Carrie has a saying, 'pretty is as pretty does.' I think the Family agrees Felicia failed that test."

She shook her head. "After he woke up from re-gen, he didn't want to see anyone from the crew. We figured he thought we'd failed him."

That wasn't Rex's impression, but she and Charlie would have to sort that out for themselves. "So—you moved on?"

"I tried to. The whole team went through months of therapy. It was horrible. We lost the entire MERS-V crew, one way or another. Charlie and Ellen both had traumatic injuries. Tuuri died. George … I think he was a patrol officer for a while, but I heard he committed suicide a couple of years ago. He was locked on to the *Triumph,* delivering passengers when the rest of the team was crushed. He couldn't get past the feeling that he should have been with the others."

"Survivor guilt." Rex growled softly. "I know that one. Why was I spared, when they killed that other puppy? That is a tough question."

She stared at him. "Who killed *puppies?* That's horrible!"

He looked up at her. "The XK9 Project. It was not uncommon. A puppy who repeatedly failed a test—"

"With XK9 puppies? That's like killing *children!*"

Rex stood. He paced across the room, tongue out, panting. On the far side he stress-yawned, stretched, then returned to her side and sat. "I cannot stop them yet. I am still trying to save my own Pack."

"Pack Leader." She nodded. "I'm sorry. Of course you are."

"Did Charlie tell you about the Transmondian spy?"

She shook her head. "We've barely talked. I've been so ...." She grimaced.

"We have special security protocols." Rex ducked his head and fluttered his tail. "I do not believe there are Transmondian assassins behind every bush, but it is good to know that Chief Klein is determined to protect us. I think we will be okay."

"My God. Now I feel so self-centered and petty. We've done nothing but talk about me!"

Rex flicked his ears. "You were the one in the greater distress. You have been through a terrible ordeal. Do not minimize it. We are not competing to see who has more problems."

"No. I guess not." She gave him a rueful look. "But it's a pretty good reality check."

"Here is another. It seems to me that you and the others on your emergency team have managed somehow to come back together and be strong. You certainly did save us last week. I am very grateful."

"Thanks. We've worked hard to build back."

Rex cocked his head at her. "At the beginning of this conversation, you said you had been wanting to hear Charlie apologize for five or seven years. That latter is as long as I have been alive. I take it not everything went back to normal for you after the incident and your apparent recovery."

"Ah. No. Definitely not. The *rescue team* recovered. I ... My love-life didn't. Don't get me wrong. I went out with other guys." She gave a rueful chuckle. "My aunties and cousins and a dozen Family friends fixed me up with so many eligible men I could've gone on dates with three different guys every week for a year."

From the sour angst in her scent, none of those men had suited her. "A rich field of choices did not help?"

"No." She gave him a wry look. "I wanted the one who didn't want me. And nobody who did want me, suited me. It's the oldest story in the book."

"They were not Charlie."

"Exactly. It's so *stupid*! All my efforts to form a good relationship had the Ghost of Charlie looming over them. Not one of them made the same kind of magic for me." She clenched her fists. "I wanted the *magic*, damn it! Even after I figured out that I'd conjured up most of that magic out of my imagination, I still wanted it."

Uneasy doubt clouded her scent. Rex guessed she wasn't as certain the 'magic' was all in her imagination as she wanted to be.

"Eventually, I just gave up on dating." Hildie grimaced. "It's a damned waste of time. I haven't been out with a guy in more than a year now, and I haven't really missed it."

Uh-huh, try again. Rex lolled his tongue but didn't challenge her.

"I decided I needed to focus on my career. I've had success, so far, but I'm not planning to stop at sergeant. I love my work, and it loves me back. I'm going as far with my career as I can."

Rex nodded. "You appear to be quite intelligent, and I can attest that you are good at what you do. You should find much career success."

"Right! Thank you! So when I pulled—" She stopped. Took a calming breath and squared her shoulders. "What happened last week gave me an opportunity. Now I have a chance to confront my past and finally *deal* with it. I came here today to lay that ghost to rest. Once and for all. So I can get *on* with my life!" She stood. "So. Good. I said it."

"Except, you did not accomplish your intent."

She opened her mouth as if to object, then closed it again with a grimace. "No. I didn't. Instead, I freaked."

Rex let that thought resonate for a moment, distracted by new impressions via the link. He needed to get back to Charlie soon. His partner was in trouble. He looked at Hildie. "What will you do now? Do you think that if you try again, you will also freak again?"

"No, I'm done with that. Thank you." She eyed the doorway. "Now *I'm* the one who should apologize."

Rex stood, too, but he waited for Hildie.

She bit her lip. "You probably want to go see him. But thanks. It helped to talk."

"I had a sense that it was important. You are right, however. I do want to see Charlie now."

"Good. Okay." She drew in a resolute breath. "Let's go see Charlie."

CHAPTER 6

HILDIE'S PROMISE

"You're a really good sport." Charlie offered Bill Sloane a rueful look. The man had showed up at his door alone after Rex ditched him. The dog hadn't told either Bill or Charlie where he was going. Charlie'd received only the vaguest of impressions through the link, of a fairly intense conversation with someone he suspected might be Hildie.

The tall UPO shifted on his chair and rubbed his neck. "Rex asked me to check on you. Thank you for letting me in."

This man had stepped in to help Rex last week when Charlie couldn't—then he'd nearly paid with his life on Friday. Charlie was eager to welcome him in and thank him.

Bill shrugged off his thanks. "I like Rex a lot."

They'd chatted for a while about the big dog, but Charlie found it harder to think, the worse his arm hurt. Nanda had tried various means to mitigate his rising fever, but none seemed to work for long.

Nanda popped in again. "Dr. Zuni's on his way." He glanced over his shoulder. "Oh. And here come Rex and Hildie."

Claw-clicks and footsteps sounded outside his door. Rex crossed the distance from the door to Charlie in one stride, but Hildie stayed back. Lunch-plate-sized forepaws landed on Charlie's bed. By some miracle of dexterity Rex avoided all the wires and IVs. His big wet nose hit Charlie's overheated ribs like an ice cube on a hot stove.

"Oh! Oh! You are worse than I thought!" The enormous black dog commenced an urgent sniff-over, in intimate, forensic detail. His alarm rang sharp through the link. *What is happening? What is wrong? Oh, this is bad! You are too hot! I should have come sooner! You do not smell right at all!*

Charlie endured his worried examination and surges of pain from the bouncing it caused. *No, I didn't think I would.*

Rex wheeled. Made the door in a single bound. "Nanda! Nanda! What is wrong with Charlie?"

"Woah, take it down a couple-dozen notches, Rex!" Nanda scowled. "Dr. Zuni's on his way over here now. He's going to run some diagnostics."

Hildie didn't say a word, but she walked back over to Charlie's bedside and gently took his available hand. It was something Felicia would never have done. Before the Family even knew if he'd live through the procedure, Felicia had declared that she "didn't sign up to be hitched to a cripple." She'd walked away and never looked back.

The warm strength in Hildie's hand anchored and fortified him. Gratitude tightened his throat, left him awed and light-headed. He gazed up at her, squeezed her hand. "Thank you."

She frowned. "How do you feel? *Really?*"

"My arm's not good." He met her eyes and tried to keep the sickening, stomach-drop fear out of his voice. "*Really* not good. I'm gonna lose it again."

OH, this is SO not the time to tell him I'm finished with him. Hildie took a seat on the bedside chair. She didn't break eye contact. Didn't release Charlie's hand. He was clearly very ill, but somehow that old magic sizzled through her, just as powerful as ever. *Pretend he's your patient, damn it. Keep it professional.* His hand burned in her grip.

"I'm so glad you came back." Charlie's grateful smile thrilled her, but it also made her queasy with guilt. "We've barely had time to say anything."

She shook her head. "It's all right. We can talk later."

His eyes drifted closed, but he nodded. He was silent a moment, then spoke in a low, tired voice. "I really needed a Medicine Goddess. And here you are."

His words lanced like a spike to her heart. For a moment she couldn't breathe. He'd coined that nickname years ago, partly to tease her and the other paramedics, calling them Medicine Gods and Goddesses. Everything the Emergency Rescue Team did was challenging, but the MERS-V drivers got the "glamour" coverage whenever the team's work made the news. Hildie and her fellow paramedics might be the core of their operation. They might sometimes pull off near-miracles. But MERS-Vs were easier to photograph, so the paramedics rarely got much notice. "Medicine Goddess" was Charlie's way to make sure that she and the others knew that *he'd* noticed.

Dr. Zuni arrived with a cavalcade of assistants and diagnostic equipment. "Out! Out! Everyone out!" He hesitated. Eyed Hildie. "*You* can stay. The rest of you, all non-medical personnel, out!"

I don't deserve this. I'm such a horrible impostor! Zuni believed that she really *was* Charlie's girlfriend. She'd come by the ICU a lot last week. Each time, Mimi and Charlie's sister Caro had to argue with the ICU staff over whether Hildie was allowed in. She should've taken a hint and backed off, but instead she'd let Mimi put her on Charlie's formwork. According to the official record, she was his Girlfriend-of-Record.

Charlie had to release her hand for the scans but he kept glancing her way. He seemed reassured all over again each time he looked at her.

And each time he smiled with relief, her guilt burned hotter.

Zuni did his scans. He popped open access-ports on the cast and took samples. His scowl grew deeper and more grim with every reading.

Charlie shuddered, struck by a chill.

Hildie turned to Nanda. Perhaps a blanket over the area they weren't scanning could—

He was already there with a pre-warmed blanket, an undeclared "Medicine God" in his own right.

"Thank you." She tucked the blanket around Charlie.

Charlie relaxed with a sigh.

Zuni gave him a rueful look. "Charlie, you're moving irrevocably into that cascading failure sequence I described earlier."

Hildie thought Charlie'd fallen into a doze, but now he looked up with a soft groan. "I figured as much."

"We can act now, save as much of the arm as possible, and when you wake up, we'll talk about options." Zuni paused. "Or we can wait till it's a life-threatening emergency, and the luxury of options is gone."

"You already know my choice," Charlie said. "Do it."

"Give me a few moments to alert your Family. I have the forms ready."

Charlie turned to Hildie. His whole body went taut and anxious. "Hils? Will you be here? After they—will you still . . .?"

Oh, crap. She knew what he was trying to ask. Last week Caro and Mimi had made sure she knew his history with Felicia at the end. For years, Hildie had imagined that Charlie'd probably married the ungrateful user-bitch. The reality had instead been Felicia's ghastly betrayal. *There's only one answer.* "Do you *want* me to be here?"

"Please. Yes." He drew in a breath. "I know I only just found you again. And I'm so sorry we can't take more time—"

Damn it, I was always right there. You knew where I was. But last week she'd begun to understand why he hadn't reached out. She grimaced. What else could she say? "I'll be here, Charlie. Of course I will."

He relaxed with a grateful sigh. "Thank you. I knew I could count on you."

Oh, God. Way to twist the knife!

She looked up, and there was Dr. Zuni, beaming at her. He gave her a satisfied nod and a warm smile of approval that made her squirm inside with shame. "This could take a while, depending on how much tissue is involved. You'll need to take tomorrow off."

Tomorrow? Oh, crap, crap, crap! She'd been thinking they had enough time tonight. *What have I done? What did I just promise?* She was scheduled for work tomorrow. She'd have to take Annual Leave. This was such short notice! Captain La Rochelle would—

"Hildie? If I may?" Nanda quirked an eyebrow and forwarded a form to her HUD. "I know you didn't have a chance to get this one done last week, when we did yours."

She gulped. It was the formwork to make Charlie her Boyfriend-of-Record. But it required his conscious endorsement, which had conveniently precluded it last week. She'd never meant to finish the process.

However ... it would entitle her to unquestioned Emergency Family Leave for as long as Dr. Zuni declared it to be necessary. End of problem, no matter when she'd been scheduled for work. Captain LaRochelle was legally barred from disputing or denying it. Emergency Family Leave received the very highest priority on Rana Station.

It meant there'd be no ugly argument with Captain LaRochelle about her last-minute cancellation. And that argument *would* have been ugly.

But it also meant she couldn't hide her new status from her Family.

How far am I willing to go to keep a promise? Abi will never let me live this down. And what will Charlie believe about me, if I do this?

But she already knew what she would do. "Um, Charlie?" *I'm really doing this. Oh, holy crap.* But she most sincerely did *not* want to tangle with LaRock. And she had this one last opportunity to finally test out the old, beautiful fantasy. Even if it wasn't real, she could now say that she hadn't passed up her last chance. "While you're authorizing forms, could you, um, do one more?" She held her breath. Sent it to his HUD.

He froze. Gazed into the middle-distance "HUD stare" with awe and disbelief. Then he turned to give her a look of knee-melting joy. "Are you sure about this?"

Her chest tightened so much it was hard to speak. "I'm gonna need a good reason to be off work. And I'm ..." She gulped. "I'm, um, already on yours."

He extended his hand to her. His face, alight with jubilant love, was everything she'd ever fantasized. And more. *Oh, so much more.*

She took his hand. Her pulse raced. She let him draw her close. How many years had she dreamed of this? His lips were cracked and hot, but whole-hearted. His good arm encircled her in the embrace she'd ached long years to receive.

She answered with the kiss she'd yearned to give him since the day they met.

COLD. Charlie shivered under pre-warmed blankets. His throat ached. So did his head, his shoulders, his back. The groggy mental fog thinned, then shifted. Resolved into an all-too familiar view of monitors and masked medical staff.

Back in surgical recovery.

How many times had he been through this? He couldn't count them—still too fuzzy.

It was over. For well or ill.

He still couldn't feel much of his body. He glanced at his left —*oh, that looks so weird.* His head spun. He looked away.

Welcome back. Rex's subdued, careful greeting through the

link carried echoes of remembered regret for the pain his overexuberance had caused last time. *Did I do that better?*

Much better. Thanks.

A masked figure talked him through the basics: he was safe. The surgery was successful. He'd be back in his room soon. He coughed on cue, to take out the breathing tube. It hurt to talk, but he answered their brief questions.

They must have him on some powerful pain blocks. He couldn't feel much of his body, but he could see the shape of it under the covers. And also the place where his arm ... *wasn't.* So, why did his left palm itch?

I never woke up for this part, last time. They put me straight into re-gen. Everyone had feared he wouldn't survive, last time. His Family had made all the decisions for him. And Felicia had made her choice, too. By the time he'd been revived, he was weeks late to the party. She was long gone. Without a backward glance. After everything he'd done, trying to make it work.

I cannot say that I've formed a good opinion of Felicia. Rex's disapproving growl rumbled through the link.

Then you're right in line with the rest of the Family. The old heartache clenched its claws. Charlie grimaced.

The nearest nurse gave him a worried look. "Are you in pain?"

"Not—No. Unhappy memory. Sorry." A harsh whisper was all he could manage.

The nurse touched his right arm with a gentle, gloved hand. "We'll have you back to your room pretty soon. Then you can rest."

Back to his room. His melancholy deepened. What time was it, anyway?

It's 03:21, Rex said. *And yes. Hildie's there, waiting for you.*

I didn't ask. He'd been afraid to.

You didn't have to. I know you.

He let out a long breath. Soon enough came the floaty vibration of people moving his bed. Charlie kept his eyes closed.

Passing under ceiling lights wouldn't help his headache. His concussion was a week old, but the motion still made him dizzy. A door latch clicked. The bed stopped rolling. *Snap*, the lock engaged. He winced.

Someone took his hand. Startled, he opened his eyes.

Hildie smiled at him. Her eyes glimmered in the lights from the monitors in his darkened room.

He gazed up at her, breathless. She'd *stayed*.

"Oh, that look on your face was *so* worth waiting for." Her grin brought a rush of delight. Her hand closed a little tighter on his. She leaned forward to tenderly kiss him.

He reached up with his good arm, warmed beyond words. Pulled her nearer and returned her kiss.

For a sweet, lingering moment, nothing else existed. Then Hildie pulled back—but only a little.

"Thank you," he said, in his raspy voice. "Thank you for not being gone."

CHAPTER 7

MONDAY MORNING SURPRISE

orning. In an empty apartment. Again.

Rex lifted his head. He put his ears up, but his spirit sagged, forlorn. He reached out to Charlie, but his partner had only come out of surgery a few hours ago. No surprise he was sleeping.

At least I can feel that you're there. He spoke quietly through the link. No need to actually disturb Charlie. He'd have enough to deal with, enough decisions to make, when he woke.

Rex could have taken Emergency Family Leave today, like Hildie had. But even though the hospital didn't fight him about visiting Charlie anymore, there wasn't a lot of good he could do for the man by watching him sleep. Also—with all due apology where it should be offered—watching Charlie sleep was really boring.

So, he'd opted to go to work today. He rose with a yawn, then stretched fore and aft to limber up.

Auto-functions had opened pre-programmed windows for optimal ventilation. A soft breeze wafted through, rich with damp morning scents. It bore quiet whirrs, chitters, and chirps to his ears. Rana's carefully-controlled, closed ecosystem offered a pale whisper, compared with the early-morning hoots, cries and shrieks of the Transmondian hinterland where Rex had spent his puppyhood. Normally, the quiet reassured him. But the persistent, hollow silence of Charlie's bedroom echoed in his heart.

He stepped down from his XK9-size, custom-made orthopedic dog bed. The bed had been a "Welcome to Corona Family" gift when he arrived on-Station. Night before last, he'd looked forward to sharing it with Shady. That hadn't worked out too well. And even though he'd tried to sweet-talk her into coming back with him last night, she didn't feel free to come. So, this morning he'd awakened alone.

Shady said that Pam had abandonment issues. She'd reacted badly to the question of where Shady should live. To say Pam's relationship with her mother was "tense" minimized the situation. *A lot.* And Shady said she'd once caught a half-glimpsed memory through the link of a very young Pam, terrified and alone in a dark, scary place. Pam hadn't meant to share that with her and never would talk about it. All of this made Shady go slowly with Pam, working on it with her, Balchu, and a Listener trained in family counseling. They'd set up a schedule of regular sessions.

Maybe someday Shady could come to live with him in Corona Tower. But not yet.

So, other than him and some furniture, the place was empty. Rex would have to go to a different residence level to find other sapient beings this morning.

After a bathroom detour, he padded into the kitchen, hungry. Did all humans have psychological problems? Charlie had dealt with most of his post-traumatic stress from the *Asalatu* wreck that had almost killed him five years ago. But some nights he woke up yelling. He still grew anxious in microgravity, and sometimes had flashbacks when he went to the Hub. Maybe now that Hildie was back in his life, she could help him with those problems.

In the kitchen Rex stepped onto the sensor pad of Uncle Hector's Dog Food Dispenser. "Good morning, Rex," the appliance said in Hector's voice. "You have lost two-tenths of a kilogram. You might need a little extra food, to return to your optimum weight." The rattle of kibbles into the waiting metal bowl always made a special music to lighten his mood. Rex grasped the rim to remove it from the dispenser. Charlie's uncle Hector was a genius, for sure. And also free of psychological problems, as far as Rex could tell, so there went that hypothesis.

The corner elevator, on the far side of the living room wall, rumbled to a halt on Rex's level. Human footsteps approached: sounded like Ted's gait. A moment later, the friendly brown face of Charlie's father appeared at the kitchen window. "You haven't arranged a ride yet, have you?"

Rex wagged his tail politely, but he didn't stop till the last kibble was gone. Good thing his vocalizer worked, even when his mouth was busy eating. "I was about to call Precinct Nine."

"Don't. I have a surprise for you." Ted grinned. "Shall I wait for you, or meet you in the courtyard?"

Rex gave the polished empty bowl one last tongue swipe, then trotted out through the living room to join Ted on the inner balcony.

They took the elevator, in deference to Ted's knees. He punched the button for the garage. "It made no sense to us, to drag hapless UPOs all over Orangeboro, just so you could have a ride. So, we got you a ride of your own." Ted looked a lot like Charlie when he smiled.

The elevator doors parted. Charlie's mother, Mimi, stood next to an unfamiliar yellow auto-nav car, with aerodynamic lines and reflective silvering on the windows.

Rex darted forward, his ears and tail straight up, his lonely wake-up forgotten. *What is this?* It gleamed. Sanitized and prepped—for *him*. "Oh! This is wonderful!"

"I still think it's too conspicuous," Mimi said.

"Who would expect him to ride in something like this?" Ted asked. "It's the perfect disguise! And look how excited he is!"

"Mm-hmm. And *you'll* only need to borrow it *once* in a while, I suppose."

"Only when the need arises. It's *Rex's*."

Rex barely listened. He explored all around the car twice, sniffing every place on its polished surface where human hands might have touched it, then turned to Ted. "How do I control it?"

Charlie's father grinned. He went through the list of the standard vocal command protocols, thumbed the doors open, then showed Rex where to give the car a retinal scan and a noseprint.

A woman's voice sounded from the car's command panel. "Hello, Rex. You may call me Carmella. Please enter the vehicle."

Rex's tail fanned faster and faster. "This is so smooth! Thank you!" He leaped in through the open door, then looked around. "This will be very convenient." He swiveled an ear toward them. "May I use it to transport Shady or others?"

"You may use your car access however you please. It's an exclusive lease, so the car is always available immediately. You're a valued member of Corona Family. We want you to be safe." Ted eyed him—or was it the car?—with a lingering smile and a touch of delight in his scent. "I take it you approve?"

"Very much. Thank you!" Rex's tail fanned at top speed. His *very own* auto-nav!

"Carmella, close doors and lower windows," Rex said. To his intense delight, the doors promptly swung closed. Both side windows hummed open. Rex stuck his head out, his tongue lolling with excitement.

"Rex, remember you're not supposed to be visible!" Mimi called.

"Where would you like to go, Rex?" Carmella asked.

He wriggled with joy. "Carmella, take me to Orangeboro Police Department Central Headquarters." Then he sighed. "Roll windows back up."

Mimi nodded her approval. "Thank you!"

"Proceeding to Orangeboro Police Department Central Headquarters," the car's voice acknowledged. "Rolling windows back up." The vehicle performed a three-point turn. The windows rose.

Ted and Mimi waved goodbye.

The auto-nav rolled upward from the basement garage's sunken entrance, along the driveway to Rim Eight Road.

His very own auto-nav! This was *so amazing!* Too bad he hadn't had Carmella a week ago. He'd tried unsuccessfully to catch a train, then ended up walking the whole way to HQ.

Carmella rolled smoothly down Rim Eight Road. It gained speed.

Rex growled. He leaned against the inside of the window. The car's movement probably created a lovely breeze. But Mimi was right. It made sense not to risk being seen coming out of Corona Tower.

Carmella turned downward onto the on-ramp that flanked Glen Haven Station at the top of the switchbacks. Rex heaved a heavy sigh. No, it wouldn't be good if people saw him here, either.

The car commenced the first swooping downward glide, hugged the curve at the bottom, then started another downward plunge.

This was torture.

But no. It would be foolhardy.

He kept the windows up.

A second thrilling curve.

A third downward—"Carmella! Lower left window halfway."

He wouldn't put his head out. He'd just place his nose at the *edge* of the silvered glass ... oh.

Oh.

A marvelous onrush of odors swirled in past his nose, borne by currents of misty, cool morning air. *Fantastic!*

The car took the third tight turn. Rolled smoothly downward. Rex couldn't stop himself. He jammed his nose out through the half-opening. The wind in his nostrils tantalized and teased, a rich feast just out of full reach. He lapped at its edges, its hints and glimmers.

On the fourth turn, his resolve broke. "Carmella, lower windows."

Down they came. A brilliant extravagance of scents flooded in. Rex stayed low, but the final leg of the switchback gave a foretaste of ecstasy. At the bottom he groaned. "Carmella, windows up."

Enclosed once more.

Rex's hackles prickled, He clamped his ears flat. The car took the more crowded, level, Rim Seven Road at a safe, reasonable speed. It turned onto the ramp that passed by Crozier Gulch Station, then commenced its course down the next set of switchbacks.

Surely by now he was far enough from home.

"Carmella! Windows down!"

A sumptuous onrush hit him full in the face. He thrust his head and shoulders out. His ears fluttered. His jaws gaped to draw in more! And more! *And more!*

This was wonderful!

This was amazing!

Best! Transportation method! EVER!

THE SALLY PORT at OPD HQ offered its usual cacophony of smells both mechanical and organic, even at this relatively quiet, before-change-of-watch hour. Shady yawned. She leaped out, then waited for Pam and Balchu to step out of the police auto-nav that had provided their ride. They showed their badges to the reader, then entered through the gate.

Behind them, a sleek, yellow civilian vehicle pulled up to the sally port entrance. It halted at a checkpoint outside.

Balchu whistled. "Hot damn. Is that a Citron Flash?"

Warning lights oscillated. "This is a restricted area," a stern automated voice announced. "Civilian vehicles are not allowed. Please depart the premises immediately."

The yellow car did not move.

A UPO approached it.

The mirrorlike window lowered smoothly.

"You can't—" The UPO's jaw dropped.

A familiar, furry black head emerged, ears up. "Chief Klein has mandated that we must travel in closed cars," Rex said. "Lacking a patrol unit, I rode in this."

"The hell?" Balchu stared.

Pam laughed. Bemused, Shady stood back to watch.

"Um, okay." The checkpoint UPO treated Rex and the car to a second, wide-eyed examination, then gave an admiring whistle. "Nice wheels, Pack Leader!"

"Thank you." Rex's tongue lolled long. His eyes sparkled.

"Wait here, please." The UPO jogged away to consult with a supervisor.

Pam shook her head. *Bet he doesn't know he's got the hottest car in town.*

Shady lolled her tongue and texted her mate. "You caused quite a stir. Whose idea was the Citron Flash?"

"Is that what it is called? Ted got me this car," Rex texted back. "Mimi thinks it is too conspicuous, but I think Ted wants to borrow it frequently."

"That would explain it. It apparently is a desirable model."

"It has a smooth ride."

"I should hope so!"

The solution to Rex's access problem turned out to be a temporary ID-tracker and guidance device attached to the Flash's control module, and a parking slot in the Command Staff garage.

Rex stepped out, then watched it depart to park itself. He joined Shady, Pam, and Balchu with greetings for all and a wagging tail. "I now have my own car pass."

"You might need a less conspicuous auto-nav," Pam said.

Rex flicked his ears. "I have worried about that. But 'Carmella' is a very enjoyable car."

"What's it like, to ride in a Citron Flash?" Balchu asked.

Rex wagged his tail. "It is very nice." He described riding down the switchbacks with his head out the window after he thought it was safe. Neither Shady nor Pam thought this was a good idea, but too late now. Their discussion lasted through the halls of HQ until they reached the elevator and stairs that led downward to the investigative center in S-3-9.

Still-airborne scents by the doors gave silent witness there. Senior Special Agent Elaine Adeyeme and her two Lead Special Agents, Shiva Shimon and Shawnee Kramer, had taken the elevator only a few minutes earlier. A stranger had accompanied them.

Rex growled. Hot protectiveness filled his scent. "I do not know this new man."

The stranger's personal odor was intimately intermingled with Elaine's. Scent factor residuals made it clear that he and Elaine felt great affection for each other, and had, in fact, mated several times recently.

"Elaine seems to care about him," Shady said. "He is probably her Significant."

"I wish to judge him for myself. But why did she bring him into Headquarters? This is a secured area!"

CHAPTER 8

A PECULIARLY RANAN THING

S hady let her tongue loll. "Perhaps this new fellow also is an agent." She left Rex to growl over the SBI group's scent trace by the elevator doors and turned to Pam and Balchu. "Will you wait for the elevator, or take the stairs?" Did she really want them to join her? Would that help or hurt her plan?

Pam frowned. "I don't feel like waiting. Let's go." They began the three-level trek down the stairs to Elaine's investigative center for the *Izgubil* case.

"I suppose Elaine could have found a mate within the Bureau." Rex's ears had clamped flat against his skull, but now they lifted. He gave Shady a puzzled look. "What makes you think she has a Significant?"

Shady snorted. "Her ring, of course."

"Ring?" He stopped in the middle of the staircase, fore and hind feet on different levels. His eyes went distant: almost certainly, he was stepping back through that bred-for-perfection memory of his. In his place, she'd be doing the exact same thing. "Oh. What about her ring?"

"Do you mean to tell me you've spent all this time with SSA Adeyeme, but never even noticed her ring?" Pam asked.

Rex ducked his head and continued his descent. "It did not seem relevant."

Balchu chuckled. "Not into jewelry, Rex?"

Shady crossed the first landing to continue downward. "The double band means she is in a Domestic Partnership. Therefore, she has at least one Significant." SSA Adeyeme's ring had two golden bands intertwined, with a faceted gemstone set into an intricate knotted design. Even though Shady knew little about fine jewelry, she thought Elaine's ring was beautiful.

Rex flicked his ears, probably as confused as she had been when Pam first mentioned it. He followed her across the landing and down the next set of steps. "Our lessons on Rana Station culture said nothing about this."

"Maybe Dr. Ordovich did not think we would need to know," Shady said.

"More likely, he underestimated its importance to Ranans," Pam put in. "He misunderstood a lot about us."

Shady wagged her tail. "If he had known you better, perhaps he would not have sold us to you."

"Good point," Pam said.

Balchu nodded. "I think we're all lucky on that score."

"Anyway, Rex, the ring configurations are like a code." Hope lifted Shady's spirit. Rex was interested. But from the unsuspecting smell of Pam and Balchu, Shady'd better go cautiously. "It is a useful way to gauge human relationships or anticipate human reactions."

"I can see how it would work for you that way," Balchu said. "Never thought about it like that."

"What a peculiarly Ranan thing to do," Rex stopped again, this time on the second landing. He looked over his shoulder at Pam and Balchu. "Do your rings follow the code?"

"Yep, we're marked and categorized." Balchu offered his left hand for inspection, then grinned at Pam. "She's kinda spooky about commitments. Whenever I look at this ring, I feel like I won a championship."

Pam gave him a wry glance. "You sure did some champion apologizing to earn it, I'll give you that."

Shady proceeded down toward the third level, her tail now up and waving. "Pam and Balchu's single bands show that they are Amares in a Declared Relationship. Sarnai and Rose told me yesterday that it is a very important step in the progress of their relationship."

Balchu frowned. "You three were talking about *us*, yesterday?"

"For a little while." Shady lolled her tongue, teasing. "But I have been studying the importance of the various relationship-status levels, working on my human-psychology field studies." They reached the bottom of the steps. "The Civil Code is like a sort of key to the mysteries. It makes things a lot clearer."

"Is that what you were reading last night?" Pam asked. "You certainly seemed preoccupied."

"Yes. I learned a great many things."

Balchu frowned. "'Field studies'? Like—like a naturalist observing animals in the wild?"

"Humans and dogs are animals, too. I have been learning how a person's standing changes, both in society and in Ranan families, depending on what their relationship status is."

Rex nodded, human-style. "Charlie did seem to think that Hildie being his Girlfriend-of-Record—and asking him to be her Boyfriend-of-Record—is a big deal."

Shady led her little band down the hallway. "It is a big deal. But it is not nearly as big a deal as being Amares, like Pam and Balchu." They drew closer to S-3-9, where the SBI investigation had its headquarters, then stopped outside the entrance. "Before we go inside, Rex, I need to ask you a question. Would you be my Amare?"

Pam gasped. Balchu let out a startled "Woah!"

Rex halted, ears canted back. He gave her a sniff.

Shady glanced up at one of the surveillance cameras in this

hallway, monitorable in realtime from inside, and always recording. She made no move to go in.

Rex's ears went up. Understanding dawned in his scent
factors. "Certainly, I shall be your Amare. I love you, and I want
you to live with me always."

Yes! Triumph surged through her. She'd done it! She'd pulled
it off! And Pam hadn't stopped her!

Shawnee Kramer yanked open the door to the investigative
center. The tall Lead Special Agent beamed at them, excitement
strong in her scent factors. "Did we hear that right? Did you two
just become Amares?"

Amares. Pam's resignation echoed through the link. *Damn. I
did not see that coming.*

REX STEPPED past Shawnee into the S-3-9 war room, nose up, tail
wagging. What a brilliant mate he had!

"Yes! Yes, we did! Will you be our witness, too?" Shady's ears
stood straight up. Eyes bright, tail like a fan, the satisfaction in
her scent factors told Rex she had planned this in detail.

Shawnee laughed. "Oh, wow! Congratulations! This is exciting! Of *course*, I'll be another witness!" She turned to call back
into the war room. "All of us will be, won't we?"

Laughter and footsteps approached. Familiar smells rushed
ahead of them.

"Absolutely!" Tall, blond Shiv gave them both a wide grin.
"Congratulations!"

"What a wonderful development!" Elaine strode forward, her
face alight with joy. The stranger followed her. A man of medium
height in the uniform of a Senior Special Agent, he looked tall
next to his diminutive mate.

Rex's tail waved high and delighted, but he shot a wary
glance toward Pam. Balchu's scent bubbled with amusement,

though he struggled to keep a straight face. Everyone acted so pleased! Maybe this really was a big deal. Rex's hope soared.

But Pam's scent factors were all over the place, and she looked stunned. Would a few "magic words" sway her? He nuzzled Shady's ear. "How is Pam taking this?" he texted privately.

"With resignation," his mate replied, also by text. "She realizes this is checkmate. We would have been in family-counseling sessions for months, while she resisted facing her fears. I just accelerated the timeline."

"No more resistance?"

"Right now, she's still off-balance. She'll have plenty to say after she's stewed about it some."

"Lucky you." But now it was time to work. He focused on Elaine. This morning the distinctive odors of her dog-phobia had faded to near-nothing beneath the scent of her upwelling pleasure. She extended her small, dark brown hand toward him, a bold move. Better yet, her hand was steady. "Congratulations to both of you!"

Delight to see her again filled Rex in a happy rush. He couldn't contain a whole-body wriggle, a small squeak of joy. "Thank you. I am very pleased to see you again." Rex longed to rub his face against her, to drink in her personal aroma as he liked to do with Charlie, but that would terrify her. He confined himself to lifting his nose until it rested under her outstretched palm.

A strong surge of pungent protectiveness rose in the stranger's scent and body-language, but he held back, his gaze on Elaine.

She ran her hand across Rex's head to rest on his shaggy ruff and smiled. "Rex, Shady, I'd like you to meet Senior Special Agent Mike Santiago. He's the leader of SIT Alpha. As you appear to have deduced, he also is my Significant." She looked up at her mate with warm delight. "This is XK9 Rex Dieter-Nell, the dog who changed everything. And his *Amare*, Shady Jacob-Belle."

The man stared, eyebrows halfway to his hairline and mouth open. "When you said you were losing your fear—" He stared at her hand on Rex's neck.

"To be fair," Shiv said, "it would be hard to stay terrified of a creature who so obviously adores her. You should've been here a week ago, when Rex was rolling on his back at her feet, telling her she was legendary for her bravery and brilliance. I think Elaine has a deeply devoted fan."

Rex dared to brush his head gently against her side.

To his elation, she replied with a shy caress.

He met her Significant's gaze. "It is true. I do love Elaine. Even Charlie is jealous. I cannot explain it. I simply am happier when she is near."

That elicited a soft chuckle from Santiago. "Gotta say, I know how *that* feels."

The warmth in his scent and expression when he looked at Elaine reassured Rex. He might—*might*—be worthy of her, after all. Rex gave the man a more thorough examination.

His erect bearing suggested a military background, but the three pips and two golden stars of an SBI Senior Special Agent glinted on his collar. And no matter how straight he stood, he couldn't match Shiv's height. Probably older than Charlie, but his light brown face remained relatively free of lines. Only a few silver hairs glinted among the many black ones at his temples. His alert, dark eyes studied Rex, then he extended his hand.

Yes, he *might* do. Rex offered his forepaw.

The man shook it with a firm but not painful grip. "My pleasure."

Shady offered her paw next, which he also shook.

"Shady is not only Rex's new Amare, but she also often acts as his second-in-command." Elaine took a chair near a dormant workstation. Santiago settled into the one next to her. "Cinnamon and Tuxedo sometimes fill in as capable lieutenants."

"Not to mention flitter-reconstructors," Santiago said. "That demonstration on Saturday was absolutely amazing."

"Are any more XK9s coming to this meeting?" Elaine asked Rex.

He shook his head. "Not this early."

She turned to Shady. "So I can ask you about your encounter with Commodore Cornwell Saturday night, without risking a security breach?" She glanced toward Balchu. "Is there anything you're free to tell me?"

"I was right there with Pam while she was reacting to input from the brain link," Balchu said. "That makes me kind of a witness. The secrets are safe, but I'll go get coffee if you'd rather."

Elaine shook her head. "Thanks, but I think you're already in." She looked back to Shady.

Shady snapped her ears flat. "Cornwell was hell-bent on taking Rex and Tux right then, even though Rex was in Healing Sleep. Not that he knew what that was. But to get Rex, he would have had to go through both Dr. Sandler and me. And, within just a few minutes, Chief Klein, too."

Rex stifled a growl out of respect for Elaine, but hot anger pumped his pulse faster. Shady'd had to tell him about it later. He'd been so deeply asleep, he'd missed the whole thing. "You said he pulled an EStee on Dr. Sandler?"

Santiago stifled what sounded like a groan. His scent factors jumped into the high, sharp, off-notes of embarrassment.

"He did." Shady's hackles rose. "That was when I took over the conversation. I told him I'd shred him to hamburger, just like the Transmondian agent, if he tried to take you away."

"She wasn't bluffing," Pam put in.

"I think he realized that," Shady said. "He put the EStee away. Klein got him to accept sending a trained interviewer this week. Cornwell said he'd send one today, so expect an interruption, if he does."

Elaine shared a worried look with Santiago.

Her mate grimaced. "Rooq started out on the tech side of spycraft. He's a wonk and a nerd, with all the interpersonal skills that implies—which is why he's not *Admiral* Cornwell right now. Interactions with other people were, um, never his long suit."

"I imagine he has yet to think of Rex as 'other people,'" Shiv said. "That's got to be a big part of the problem."

Seething indignation brought a growl to Rex's throat. He mostly managed to choke it back. Shot a worried look at Elaine, then lowered his head and fluttered his tail. "Sorry. I detest spooks."

She gave him a wry look.

Santiago's scent factors shifted from his earlier embarrassment to a sludgy-prickly mix that mirrored his rueful expression. "You've dealt with Wisniewski. Of course you hate spooks. All I can say is, Rooq's more geek than spook. He's not as bad as you may think."

Rex eyed the man, suspicion rising. "You know him."

"We go back a ways." Santiago's mouth made a rueful twist. "I stood up in his wedding, so, yeah. I know him pretty well."

Oh, Elaine, who did you get tangled up with? Rex gave her a worried look.

"He has a legitimate national-security interest," Elaine said. "You'll have to talk to somebody from Intelligence at some point soon."

Rex clamped his ears flat. "As long as it is somebody *with* reasonable intelligence."

CHAPTER 9

"NO TARGET ACQUIRED"

C harlie could sit upright, although he leaned against a couple of strategically-placed pillows. He eyed the assembled group: Dr. Zuni, Gran Annie, his sister Caro, and their parents—plus Rex and Hildie.

He avoided looking at his left, um, stub. There was only a weirdly short, *wrong*-looking lump of bandages. The surgery had taken his arm off just below the shoulder. Off. Gone. Void. The sensation of his left palm itching had gone away, but now sometimes it felt as if he had a cramp, or part of a finger had gone to sleep.

He pulled out of that sucking mental vortex, but there could be no "not thinking about it." The plan was to use what remained of his left arm as stable tissue to build upon. But to build upon, with what? That was the question. "So. It all comes down to what I choose to stick onto my stub."

Dr. Zuni gave him a pained look. "That's not how I would have expressed it."

Hildie sat nearby. She was *still here*. That continued to feel like a miracle, but one that might be pushing some sort of "use by" date. She'd seemed more distant this morning. *Or was she?* Maybe that was his depression misinterpreting her exhaustion.

Rex slid his nose under Charlie's right elbow, cold and wet along the ribs. Then he leaned against him. This moved Charlie a couple of centimeters to the left, but the love Rex emanated through the brain link steadied him. Rex had come from work to join this midday briefing in person. Somehow, today Rex had acquired his own auto-nav. Even more startling, Shady was now his Amare.

There hadn't been much time to discuss any of it before Dr. Zuni started his briefing, but Gran Annie had promised a celebratory feast to welcome Shady tonight.

And Charlie would miss it. *Still stuck in here.*

Rex leaned in and pushed him another centimeter to the left. *I wish we could do it here, but the hospital isn't built for it.*

Got that right. Have fun, and open the link when it seems appropriate.

I shall not forget you.

But will you outgrow me? By the time I get out of here, will you even need a sidekick?

Rex gave a soft growl and clamped his ears flat. *You are my partner, not my sidekick!*

"Guys." Hildie frowned at them both. "Audible vocals, please!"

"Sorry!" He reached out to her, but she'd turned back toward Zuni.

Rex turned to Zuni, too. "The genetic augmentations you propose sound very much like Shady's description of the agent she fought on Saturday night."

Zuni nodded, but did not speak.

Ah. That means he's been consulted on the case and can't talk about it, Charlie told his partner through the link. *You're probably right to make the comparison.* Charlie wasn't sure how he felt about being transformed into something like that Transmondian agent. There'd been a short disclaimer in the raft of formwork about being considered an "available asset" by the SDF. That worried him, too. *What unexpected complications might crop up?* He frowned. Kinda futile to ask Zuni to predict unpredictable unknowns. "What might the augmentations do to my personality? Will that change?"

"No, certainly not." Zuni shook his head. "Don't worry about that. That's not what this would do."

Would refusing the augmentations leave you at a disadvantage? Rex cocked his head at Charlie.

Maybe I should ask. "If Rex ever encounters another such agent, I wonder if it would be better to meet him with equal strength."

Rex wagged his tail. "Exactly! Thank you!"

"It would involve another re-gen. How long would that take?" Hildie asked.

Charlie squirmed on his pillows. Cultured bones and tissues were created ahead of need, up to a certain stage. Once infused with his own stem cells, the re-gen part was an accelerated growth burst. That was the standard technology, anyway. But Dr. Zuni had finagled authorization for a different kind of "genetic augmentation" re-gen package that no one could even *access* without special clearance.

"Augmentations utilize a systemic treatment," Dr. Zuni said. "They're not focused on only one limb or organ, although the arm tissues also will need time to grow. Augmentations are a whole-body makeover. We're talking maybe four or five days, for what are essentially two parallel procedures."

Charlie exchanged a worried look with Hildie. "Coming out of a re-gen that long will not be fun." But the augmentations accelerated reflexes, multiplied muscle strength, and strengthened bones. He'd never have to worry about another fracture. Ironically, the biological augmentations offered levels of speed, strength and reflex reaction-time denied to those with police-approved prosthetics. Yet the government clearance meant the results were legal. "I wish I could talk with someone who's had the procedure done to them and lived with it for a while. Is that possible?"

Dr. Zuni smiled. "Actually, you might be in luck. I *do* know of one person who's currently here in Orangeboro. I'll see if he'd be willing to talk with you. I can't say more till I know how he feels about meeting you."

"Privacy restrictions. Got it." Charlie nodded. Were the situation reversed, he'd appreciate the precaution, too.

"Yes. But I'll try to reach him today." He activated a case pad on a side table, then bent over it.

Rex gave Dr. Zuni a speculative look.

What's that stare about, Rex?

The XK9 turned his speculative gaze on Charlie. *Because of patient privacy, he can't say. But I may know who it is.*

Charlie glanced Hildie's way to apologize for more link-talk, but she and Caro had their heads together. Hildie made a comment to his sister that he couldn't catch. Caro nodded and answered at equally low volume. *Well, okay, then.* He returned his attention to Rex. *You think you've met Zuni's mystery guy?*

Rex's tongue slid out in a happy loll. He wagged his tail. *Unless I'm very much mistaken, he lifted a shed off of me in the Five-Ten last week. I wondered how he was able to do that.*

Lifted a shed? Charlie gave him a quizzical look. *How big?*

Rex snorted. *Big enough, believe me. Too big for a normal human to lift.* "Need of the moment," he said. *I knew there must be more to the story!*

"Your expressions are something to behold when you're talking to Rex through the link." Hildie's low chuckle brought to mind memories of better days, but then she frowned. "And you're doing it again."

"Busted. Sorry!" Charlie gave her a rueful look. "I plead habit —and we didn't want to interrupt."

"It is my fault." Rex ducked his head, fluttered his tail, and gave Hildie his soulful 'puppy-eyes' look. "I distracted him. I shall try to do better."

Hildie's irritated look melted into a mollified smile. She

stroked the big dog's massive head and scratched behind one ear. "Okay, I get it. Forgiven."

Charlie grinned at them both. *Nice save.*

I'll always have your back, partner. Rex sidled a little closer to Hildie so she could reach the other ear.

Gran Annie eyed Rex, Charlie and Hildie with a satisfied look. She closed the cover on her case pad, then stood. "We'll do some research. Ralph has contacts at the Biosciences Department of Station Polytechnic. I know Hannah will want to look into the litigation histories in regard to both the police-approved prosthetics and this augmentation technique. We must decide whether the Family should approve of them."

"Of course." Zuni nodded. Charlie thought it was pretty clear Zuni believed they should pursue the augmentations, but Gran Annie always said a Chartered Family that didn't cover its due diligence was a Family built on shaky foundations. She wasn't the only Head of Household who thought that way.

Rex cocked his head at Charlie. *The Family needs to approve? Isn't it your decision?*

Either route involves risks and trade-offs. A Family has better resources for researching in depth than one lone guy in a hospital bed. Charlie gave him a rueful look, worn out by the very thought. *And especially since the augmentations seem to involve changes to my genome, it's something that might someday impact future generations. That makes it a Family concern. If I want to do that, I'll need their active endorsement.*

From the way Caro's brow furrowed and her arms hugged her torso, his sister was still grappling with Charlie's new choices. "I'm going to talk with Fatima about her friend with the interchangeable arms. I know about the OPD's limitations, but it can't hurt to explore that angle."

"I bet Mac and Yo-yo would give you their thoughts on prosthetics, if you have questions," Hildie said.

"Oh, no doubt." Charlie smiled. Fergus "Mac" Mac Dermott and Wu "Yo-yo" Guanyu were two grizzled veterans on the ERT base's maintenance crew. They'd been there forever. Mechanical geniuses in their specialty areas, they kept all of the base's equipment running. Both had interchangeable multi-tool prosthetics that they were always custom-modifying to outdo each other. Their "arms" race never ended, because where would be the fun in that? "Unfortunately, most of their whizbangs and cool gizmos are things a police officer can't have."

The citizens of Rana Station had opted not to authorize what the popular media called "cyborg cops." Domestic police officers on-Station could have none of the gadgets and armaments one often saw in a realiciné.

No interchangeable gun ports. No deployable knives, nor any other deadly weaponry. No less-lethal arsenal in a lockable shoulder-mount. No cyborg arms or legs programmed to move at hyper-speed or perform maneuvers a natural limb could not. Oh, and just to be total buzzkills about it—no chrome, no sparkly metalflake paint, and no onboard lights. That last one made no sense to Charlie. Every time he used a hand-light, he wished he didn't have to tie up a hand with holding it. Wouldn't onboard lights be a great solution?

Rex laid his ears back and gave Charlie a disapproving look. *Why would you even bother to consider prosthetics? You have a chance to be XK9-tough!*

Charlie raised his eyebrows. *Due diligence.*

Well, "due" it and get it over with. Then let's talk about how I wouldn't have to worry about accidentally killing you after you get the augmentations.

Charlie wished he could object to that fear, but they both knew it had almost happened last week. He sighed. *You do have a point.*

A few at a time, the rest of his Family members rose, picked up their own case pads, and said goodbye. Charlie welcomed the change of focus. They congratulated Rex one more time, and they all made sure to pat Hildie's hand or shoulder and tell her how grateful they were that she'd stayed to help Charlie.

Hildie made smiling but vague replies. She hid her worry pretty well, but Charlie knew her tells. His queasy foreboding returned.

He sensed Rex looking at him, met his partner' gaze. *I'm worried.*

You're not wrong. But remember she also is tired, and you still don't know each other that well in your current lives. I imagine she needs to rest and reflect some.

Charlie let out a soft sigh. *Probably. In her place, I'd need space, too.*

Dr. Zuni looked up from his case pad. "I am at your Family's disposal to answer any further questions. You know how to reach me. Call anytime. It would be best to make a decision within the next 36 hours. The sooner we can act, the better."

"I know. Thank you." Charlie rubbed his chin. Maybe his Family members' research—and perhaps a conversation with Dr. Zuni's augmented person—would give him clarity.

"We'll get you settled right, this time." Dr. Zuni nodded, as if things were already decided. Then he turned to Hildie. "Young lady, I cannot express how pleased I am that my patient actually has a worthy woman in his life, now. That other one actively interfered with his recovery. I have faith that you are a person of vastly superior character. Your care will greatly aid his recovery. Thank you." He picked up his case pad and departed.

Charlie, Rex and Hildie stared after him.

"Um, well," Charlie said. "No pressure, or anything, Hils."

Hildie sighed. "You think?" She still wore the pale dress with the little red flowers. It had wilted some since yesterday. Her hair was rumpled on one side, from when she'd caught a nap on the temp-bed in the family alcove of Charlie's room. The skin around her eyes had darkened, as it always did when she was tired.

He offered a rueful half-smile. "You look exhausted."

"That bad, huh?" She stifled a yawn.

"Still beautiful. All the more beautiful to me, because I know *why* you're exhausted. There's no way I can thank you enough."

"You'll have to owe me, I guess." This time the yawn wouldn't be stifled.

Rex rubbed his face against Charlie's side, then stepped away. "I shall be back. My new Amare has plans for tonight, so probably not until tomorrow—unless you mean to make your decision before then."

Charlie shook his head. "I need to learn more, before I decide anything. And you need to pay close attention to anything your Amare wants." He grinned. *Also, you're actually only a thought away,* he added through the link.

Always, Rex replied the same way, then switched back to his vocalizer. "Chief Klein asked me to stop by his office, and I need to get back to work. Elaine wants to discuss changes in staffing assignments. Meanwhile, I think you and Hildie need to talk privately."

Charlie and Hildie sat quietly till his claw-clicks faded away.

"That 'Pack Leader' title isn't ceremonial, I guess." Hildie gazed after him.

"No, it isn't. From what I've been able to gather, Klein and Adeyeme are taking the XK9s' sapience status seriously. Rex in 'admin mode' has been a very busy dog." The changes bemused Charlie, even though he agreed with them. He turned to Hildie. "Look, what Zuni said—"

"Let's talk about it later." She stood with a grimace. "You're right. I do need to go home. I ate a food-service sandwich, but I'd kill for some of Abi's bhaate-bhaat, a hot shower, and a long nap."

"I'd say you've earned them."

She didn't reply but walked over to the family alcove and retrieved her crystal earrings from a niche for personal belongings. Then she consulted the bathroom mirror to put them on again and run her fingers through her hair. She sighed at the result. Yawned again. "It'll have to do."

He eyed her, concerned. Like Corona, her Feliz Tower home was in Ninth Precinct, although it was on Port Hill, rather than Starboard. Long ago, they'd joked about being "hollering across the valley" neighbors. "Do you have a car pass?"

She shook her head. "I normally never need one."

"Let me get one for you. You're too tired for the train."

She gave him a worried look. "That's pretty expensive."

"Call it Medicine Goddess care. I can't fix you a bowl of bhaate-bhaat, but I can make sure you're delivered home in relative comfort." Thank goodness Corona Family maintained an account with Town Cars On Call. His CAP connected him. He made the arrangements, then pinged her HUD with the pass. She was right. On his salary, that *was* a bite. But she was worth it.

She walked back over to his bedside, took his hand. "Thank you." She kissed his forehead, hesitated, then adjusted her aim. It wasn't as ardent and heart-stopping as the kiss she'd given him before he went into surgery, but it sent a warm tingle through his whole body and lit fires in places he was in no condition to use.

She turned toward the door.

"Will you come back?" He blurted it out before he could stop himself.

She looked back at him, cocked an eyebrow. "Not bored with me yet?"

He couldn't read her expression. He gazed at her, throat tight. "I don't think that's possible."

Her mouth curved in a wry smile. Then she walked out.

What would he do if she didn't come back?

Charlie caught himself. *That's depression talking. She's my Girlfriend-of-Record, for pity's sake!* Mind-boggling thought, but factual truth. Surely that meant something?

But Rex had confirmed it. She'd held herself at a cooler remove once she was sure he'd come through the surgery okay. That wasn't just his imagination. Her manner had been subtly remote, and it wasn't just because she was tired. She'd put distance between them and kept it there most of the day. Now that the first rush of enthusiasm had passed, Hildie must be having second thoughts.

Events had moved so *fast* yesterday. Was she reconsidering? Or maybe just wondering *how did that happen?* If so, he couldn't blame her.

Hildie was—had been—a once-in-a-lifetime friend. They'd made an instant connection, and before the *Asalatu* they'd been fast friends. Rex was right, though. They *didn't* really know each other in their "current lives." They had some ground to make up, and nothing guaranteed they'd be as good a match now as they could have been then.

He rode out a spasm of heartsick regret. If he'd been smarter —if he'd allowed himself to actually *consider* life without Felicia? He let out a long, shaky breath. *Oh, God. How different things might have been!* An image of his old targeting range-finder rose in his mind to taunt him with blinking red letters: NTA, "No Target Acquired." In recent years it had become his personal shorthand for having no clear idea of his way forward.

What is that? Rex asked through the link. *I receive that mental impression sometimes when you're depressed.*

He grimaced. *An image from my past.* His old MERS-V, "T-1," had once been his workplace, his kingdom … and more tied up with his self-worth than he'd imagined. Until it almost became his coffin.

Your MERS-V? From the dog's tone through the link, he pictured Rex's head cocked, ears up.

My targeting readout. Charlie released a soft breath. *When my sensors locked on, it told me how close I was to the person I needed to rescue.*

Curiosity came through the link. *Who do you need to rescue now?*

Charlie grimaced. *Can we change the subject?*

You need a nap. Stop torturing yourself. Rex's input grew more distant through the link.

But Charlie couldn't settle. "RAMoD, assist me." Maybe another bathroom run was in order. It had been a while, and anyway it was *something to do*, besides dither in his damned bed. No cast for the robotic arms to lock onto, now, but they'd managed this trip a few times already. He grasped the handhold.

A mundane errand like this couldn't derail his thoughts, though. *No such luck.* They went straight back to Hildie. If the past few years had taught him anything, it was that Hildie had been the real deal. Getting things wrong with her was his single most devastating regret. And now—lucky man—he had an opportunity to screw things up *twice.*

Oh, God. Not if he could help it.

Better listen and adapt. Better not get ahead of himself. Way better and smarter to let *her* lead the dance.

If she came back. His gut twisted and his breath came short.

Oh, please let her come back.

CHAPTER 10

TESTING HYPOTHESES

C hief Klein's office on the twenty-fifth floor of the Civic Center had floor-to-ceiling windows and a panoramic view to spinward. Rex figured the location and view from this aerie likely had been designed to keep its occupants cognizant of the Borough they served. And, especially for vision-oriented creatures such as humans, it probably was damned impressive.

But the Chief wasn't looking at his view, just now. Instead, he gave Rex the kind of long, grim stare that probably made police captains sweat.

Rex sat at "parade sit" with his forepaws together on the floor in front of him, ears up, and tail straight back. He'd had a lifetime of practice masking his reactions under critical scrutiny. The secure knowledge that there'd be no beating at Klein's hands reassured him. That, and the man's scent factors. Contrary to his body language, Klein smelled conflicted.

Ah. This is about the auto-nav. Rex did not loll his tongue, but the urge teased him.

Klein sighed. "Whose idea was the Citron Flash?"

Now Rex couldn't resist a tongue-loll. "I take it you agree with Mimi and Shady that it is too conspicuous."

Klein hesitated. "Mimi?"

"Charlie's mother. I believe his father got me the car pass in part so he could borrow it."

"I see. The picture comes into focus at last." Klein nodded slowly. "Well, Shady and Mimi are correct. I fear Charlie's father will have to find some other excuse for leasing a Citron Flash. I'm issuing you a Police Department auto-nav, which you are to use until further notice."

"I understand, sir. What shall I do about the Citron Flash?"

"I'll deal with it. When you finish work for today, check in with the Garage Supervisor's office. The staff will have orders for you."

"Thank you, sir."

Klein gave him a rueful look. "I'm sorry to take away your pretty toy."

Rex wagged his tail. He actually *had* expected to feel more disappointed, but he still had access to an auto-nav. Things could be worse! "It was a very smooth vehicle, but you, Mimi, and Shady are correct. Perhaps after this business with the Trans-mondians is over, I can try it again."

Klein nodded. "Here's hoping."

REX PADDED QUIETLY into the war room a little before the humans normally began returning from lunch breaks.

Elaine looked up. "Oh, good! You're back. We need to talk."

He pulled his thoughts away from unhappy impressions coming through the link from Charlie and refocused his attention. He couldn't help Charlie, but he definitely had ideas about changing some of the Pack's assignments. He approached her and sat, ears up.

"We're not finding anything new in the explosives layers." Elaine glanced at the case pad she held, then met his gaze. "SCISCO wants to bring in another consultant from Station Polytechnic, but I'd like to have our experts discuss it with nem first. Of course, that means Joe, and I'd like to have Tux and Georgia go with him. Do you think Crystal and Cinnamon can cover the work in the evidence cavern?"

Rex went breathless. She'd included Tux among "our experts." As if the Pack's nerdiest XK9 was *of course* one of the experts to be consulted. Competent to evaluate AI professor SCISCO's request, in collaboration with Joe, a human Tech Specialist with a doctor's degree in the field, and Georgia, an experienced field technician with several years' work on the STAT Team's Bomb Squad. That acceptance was so very far from the way the Pack had been treated all their lives—until last week —that for a moment he hung frozen.

"Rex?" She frowned. "You okay?"

"Apologies! Yes. Certainly. That rearrangement should work well."

"Good. Nobody can bring quite the same perspective and insight as an XK9, and Tux slings the lingo with the best of them. Now walk with me."

She led him to the ready-room, helped him gown up, then put on her own containment gear. They moved from there into the evidence cavern. There weren't as many pallets as there had been last week, but hundreds remained. If they had to sort through all of the shattered remains of the *Izgubil*, retrieved from the spacelanes by SDF recovery crews, they'd be working here for many more months.

Rex didn't plan to spend that much time. His nose and the noses of his Packmates had made short work of several hundred irrelevant pallets of debris already.

Elaine stopped well away from the first rows of pallets. "Shady and Pam have led an effort to locate remains of people crushed between bulkheads by shockwaves from the explosion. We figured there'd be some, just from the smell alone, but we've already found more than two dozen, and the survey has barely started. I want to give Shady and Pam two or three XK9 teams to help to find the rest."

Rex kept his ears up. He stifled an impatient growl, out of respect for Elaine. "Is that a priority?"

"You should ask those whose loved ones are missing."

Rex dipped his head to acknowledge this. "Granted, everyone is someone's kinfolk. But many of them probably worked for the Whisper Syndicate. They were not exactly 'good guys.' And we may find that identifications and notifications might never be possible for some. Meanwhile, we are no closer to catching the perpetrators."

"How very Transmondian of you, Rex." Her dark eyes teased him over her mask.

He snapped his ears flat. "We need to find and interview more of Elmo's group." He kept coming back to them. He'd found a scent-trail made by exactly the right-size group of people to have sabotaged the *Izgubil*, if they'd used the likeliest method. Their trail led in and out of the *Izgubil*. It had been deposited in time layers that placed their access to the ship in the right window of time to have sabotaged it. He had identified the scent profile, based on an earlier encounter, of a small-time mugger named Elmo Smart among the group's members. Surely that was enough to make his group persons of interest!

Rex's hackles prickled with impatience to *get on with* what smelled to him like the most important task at hand. "The installation team is our most concrete link to the people who masterminded the destruction of the *Izgubil*. Whoever they were."

Elaine frowned. "That's the hypothesis, anyway. But we've based it purely on our own speculations and a single drop of adhesive. It's a circumstantial argument at best."

"Shady said Elmo Smart clearly knew what he and the crew were doing on the ship, but he was terrified to admit anything when they tried to interview him," Rex countered. "And I know what I smelled!"

"But you didn't smell anything to link the crew directly to the adhesives or the explosives. Where's our probable cause to move forward with warrants? One drop of adhesive isn't enough to convince most judges, even with the circumstantial case."

She had him there, dammit. *Rex* might think they had enough, but the humans apparently needed more. "I wonder what we could find inside that access hatch."

Her brows slanted in a frown. "That *is* the question, isn't it? But it won't be easy to answer."

He stared across the evidence cavern. "Have they found any trace of that hatch?"

She grimaced. "Oh, we know where it is. I just don't know how to get you there in a way that will allow you to use your nose on it. You see, it's still in space."

THERE WAS a message from Grandma Hestia, a little red dot blinking at the bottom of her HUD interface, when Hildie woke from her nap. It said, "We should chat. I'll be at Spinward 32 or vicinity till about 17:00."

Hildie let out a long breath. Normally she looked forward to going out to the paddies for a chat with Grandma Hestia. She'd loved the rhythm of Grandma's work since she was a little girl, and Grandma always had sound wisdom to share. But today she hesitated. Grandma was not *only* the Master Gardener for Feliz Family's agricultural operations, which explained her presence at Spinward 32. She also was the official Head of Feliz Family. Hildie's change-of-relationship-status notification would have gone to her first. *Gee. Guess why Grandma wants to chat.*

Hildie brushed the tangles out of her hair, then tied it up.

"Mr-r-r-ow. Mr-r-r-ow. Mr-r-r-ow." Kali twined her furry little orange, black, and white body around Hildie's legs.

"No, it's *not* time to eat." Thank goodness Abi and Smita always made sure Kali was fed on time, brushed, and played with when Hildie wasn't home to do so. The litterbox was all

Hildie's, but she didn't mind. She stroked the cat under her chin and along her cheek but had the gall to stop too soon. Instead, she lay back down on her rumpled bed with a groan.

An hour and a half wasn't enough sleep, but she'd kept drifting into that damned nightmare about pulling Charlie out of T-1. In the dreams, he was always hideously dead from some grisly fatal wound. Each time it was a new horror. All of his gory fates were wounds she'd actually witnessed, which redoubled the horror. The space docks were dangerous. In her decade on the ERT, she'd seen a *lot* of disfiguring fatal wounds. She woke from each nightmare with a shout—or sometimes with a scream.

Compared to another round of that, even an uncomfortable conversation with Grandma held a lot of appeal. A second little red blip pulsed at the bottom of her interface, too. She grimaced. *Better open that one while I'm at it. Get it over with.*

Yes, it was from LaRock—Captain LaRochelle. "How did this Boyfriend materialize out of thin air, and when do you plan to report for duty again, Sergeant?" was all it said.

She scowled, her gut in a sudden knot. She hadn't expected him to be pleased, but this was unusually surly, even for him. She almost deleted it, then thought again and copied it to her file titled "Documentation."

After that she heaved up from the tousled bed sheets, threw on skudgy farm clothes, and headed for Spinward 32.

Number 32 was the experimental plot where Grandma tested new varietals. Hildie navigated switchbacks between the paddies, climbed a final set of steps, then stopped in surprise. *Woah.* From the look of the grain heads, this plot was ready to harvest as soon as they could drain the water. That seemed *fast.*

She spotted her wiry little grandmother on a narrow path near the back of the paddy. Grandma frowned at something in her palm. She poked at it, then picked up a small object between finger and thumb and bit it. *Ah. Testing for ripeness.*

"Is it ready?" Hildie headed down the path.

Grandma looked up. "Seems so, but it's only been 96 days."

"Isn't this this the batch that's *supposed* to mature early?"

"Mm." Grandma poured the rest of the grains from her hand into a small bag, then tucked that into a pouch at her waist. "We'll see." Hildie knew that tonight Grandma would spend hours running tests to ensure the genetic soundness and nutritional completeness of the grain. She never stinted on the testing process. "If you don't test it, you'll never know," she always said.

Feliz Family's primary crop was the nutrient-enriched rice they grew in their three hectares of paddies. Most Family properties were limited to one or two hectares and offered a truck-farm-style variety, but rice was a staple. That made it a matter of national security. It earned Feliz Family and other designated rice farmers special status. Civil Defense hadn't needed to commandeer rice in a generation. Not since Hildie was small, and there'd been a brief food crisis at the end of the final immigration wave of Norchellic refugees.

But everyone knew it *could* still happen.

Grandma continually had a new, genetically-engineered varietal growing. Plant scientists at Station Polytechnic always sought new, better approaches. Grandma and growers like her strove to differentiate, evaluate, and grow the most desirable of these. If the grain samples passed her tests, they'd harvest the plot. The Family regarded their work as a sacred trust.

But Hildie was here on a different matter. "You wanted to talk?"

"Got the status-change notice." Grandma moved to the next row's marker in the test plot for her next sample, then pierced Hildie with a direct look. "How is Charlie?"

"They took his arm."

"Ah." Grandma already knew most of his history, including the part Felicia had played, now that Hildie had learned about it. "He asked you to be there when he woke up."

She sighed. "Yeah."

"And you were."

"Yeah."

"Damn straight. As you should've been." Grandma's gaze didn't waver. "So. Is he just an ordinary man to you now? Or is there still magic?"

Hildie's breath came short. "Charlie *was* never, and never *will be* 'ordinary.'" She grimaced. "And yeah. There's still magic."

Grandma's mouth made a wry twist. "You gonna chickenshit out, or reach for your heart's desire?"

"Is magic *really* possible? To sustain, I mean."

Grandma stripped another grain head. She examined it. Tested one grain's texture between her teeth. Carefully filled another bag with this sample. Tucked it into her pouch, then finally looked up. "Anything that's tortured you for this long is *real*. And sustainable. That's actually not your question." Grandma frowned. "He's got what you want—or at least, you're still convinced he does. You gonna try to kill it *again*, just when you finally have the chance to try something different?"

Hildie grimaced. "Nothing I've done or thought or decided has killed it so far."

"Uh-huh."

Instead of running away, I should run toward him? "I'm scared."

Grandma shrugged. "So what?"

"There's only one way out of this dilemma? Is that what you're saying?"

"I'm saying if you don't test it, you'll never know."

CHAPTER 11

DEBRIS IN THE AFTERMATH, OR STARTING ANEW

S hady stopped on her way to the ready-room at the end of her watch. She turned to look back. They'd found the remains of thirty-seven individuals today, pancaked between sections of debris. Even in space the compacted layers had stuck together, bound by human—or occasionally ozzirikkian—"glue." Like infernal plyboard.

Pam took a few steps farther toward the exit, then returned to her side. *What?*

That is a LOT of debris. And we found a LOT of squashed people today. She stared across the evidence cavern. Techs and field agents carefully wrapped pallets piled high with debris. Wrapping them seemed to keep the scents fresher for longer. Some of the pallets they'd wrapped last week had been removed to a different dry, cool storage area. The rest stood like mummified monoliths in the half-light of the cavern.

Yeah. Pam nodded. *Kinda daunting. And imagine how it would be for the folks we've found today: you're doing whatever it is that you do, and suddenly the walls collapse in, and you're crushed in a final smush of agony. Horrifying.*

Somebody DID this. She and Pam stood far enough away from the evidence for Shady to growl with her own voice and not worry about DNA cross-contamination. She laid back her ears, sickened. *Somebody planned it. Worked it all out. And then they made it happen. All those people got squashed in a big, horrific crunch, because someone made elaborate plans, and went to great lengths to carry them out. Why?*

If we could answer that, we'd be a lot closer to "who." Pam stroked her ears.

Was it hatred or profit motive or … Shady gazed at the silent piles. *Who had reason to hate the* Izgubil, *or what it represented, or someone who was on it? Who stood to profit by its destruction?*

Pam yawned behind her mask. *Those are not new questions.*

No. They're not. Shady's hackles prickled under the stifling containment gown. The investigation had been asking those questions since the day it happened. The problem wasn't that there couldn't be anyone in the "hate" or "profit from" categories. The *Izgubil* had been the very definition of a den of iniquity, run by the feared criminal organization known as the Whisper Syndicate. It was more that there was potentially an overwhelming number of people who could have hated the ship and everyone on it. Or stood to profit from a body-blow like this to the Syndicate. The problem was that the investigation knew about too few of them.

Too few, but not *none.* One in particular kept rising to the forefront and ringing alarm bells for Shady: Emer Bellamy.

Got that right.

Shady looked up to see Pam's suspicious, narrow-eyed glare toward the pallets. They'd processed the body of Emer's father during morgue duty last week. Hideki Bellamy Moran had been a child-rapist, his body smeared with the tortured, terrified scent of the little girl he'd been abusing when the ship blew up.

Shady shouldn't be glad someone was dead, but she'd make an exception for Hideki. *Did he treat his own daughters that way? Did young Emer experience that same torture, that same terror? What kind of family dynamic existed in that household?*

Pam scowled. *And I thought MY childhood was lousy. At least that never happened to me.*

From what Shady had been able to gather, Pam's father had perpetrated a different type of abuse. He'd abandoned the family while Pam was still very small. Pam had been left behind with her emotionally-distant mother. Shady suspected his irresponsible departure had planted the seeds of her own frustrations about living with Rex.

But Pam stayed focused on Emer. *Now that Hideki is dead, what part of his enormous fortune does Emer inherit? I mean, when you're rich already, you'd think more money wouldn't be that much of an incentive, but history says you'd be wrong.*

It did seem counter-intuitive, but humans could be peculiar about the made-up social construct they called "money." Maybe for rich people it was like mass in space. The bigger the gravity well, the stronger the money-suck? *Huh.* She could make the same analogy about poor people and small gravity wells.

Shady turned toward the ready-room once more. *The thing about Emer is that Hideki isn't her only connection to the case.*

Pam followed her. *I know Elaine's got Iruka and SA Hunter working on Fredericks, but I don't think they've made any progress.* Emer's one-time Amare was Dr. SCISCO's vanished advisee Rory Fredericks. His dissertation project closely resembled the nanotimers used with the *Izgubil* explosives.

Fredericks had disappeared a year and a half ago, just a few months short of finishing his doctorate. SCISCO said the improvements on his earlier methods made it extremely likely he was still alive, and still refining his methods. If only they knew *where.* Balchu's friend Iruka Jones had caught the case when the man first turned up missing, but even with SA Hunter's fresh insights, they'd made no progress on the case.

This tired loop of questions about Emer put Shady in mind of a short, narrow pen with a locked gate. They needed to find the key or break the lock or dig under a back corner of it. *I know*

Elaine doesn't want to alert Emer that we're watching her—but I'd really love to ask her some pointed questions.

Pam chuckled, then opened the door to the ready-room. *I know what you mean, but she wouldn't answer any of them. Her lawyers wouldn't let her. And then where would we be? No, we need to "dig under the back corner" by finding new evidence. We just have to keep looking.* She closed the door behind them, then allowed herself a massive yawn. *But not tonight. I need a brain break!*

Shady pulled her feet from the containment booties while Pam undid the gown fasteners along her back. *I know you don't want to talk about it, but I'm staying with Rex tonight.*

You're right. I don't want to talk about it. Pam frowned. She removed Shady's head covering and slipped the straps of her mask off of her ears. *There's nothing left to talk about.* The smoky low tones of melancholy in her scent factors echoed the emotions coming from her through the link. An acidic hint of resentment tinged them, but the muddy dullness of resignation dominated.

Shady hadn't thought her muscles were tense until they relaxed. *Thank you for not fighting me*

There'd be no point. Pam removed her own mask. Her mouth made a rueful twist. *You're right. He's your Amare, and you should live with him.* She let out a long breath. *I'm sorry. I realized I've been acting like Mother. Way, way too much like Mother.*

Forgiven! Thank you! Shady reared up, wrapped her forelegs around Pam, and pulled her in close. She hooked her chin over Pam's shoulder to draw her nearer and breathed in Pam's wonderful personal scent-bouquet. *I'm sorry I can't live in two places at once. I'll miss you—and I'll even miss Balchu. I love you so much!*

I love you too. Always. Pam hugged back, just as hard.

Then she stepped away and Shady went back to all-fours.

I'd better go find Rex.

Pam smiled. *Have fun riding home in the Citron Flash.*

CHARLIE'D HAD BETTER MORNINGS, and that was before Internal Affairs called to summon him for an interview. They'd been ready to schedule him that very afternoon, until he informed them he was in the hospital, just post-amputation.

The clerk didn't make any effort to hide her dislike of being told "no" for valid reasons, but she'd agreed to reschedule "later."

So, um, *yay?*

What did they want to interview him about? The clerk wouldn't say. *Shit, do they think I did something wrong?* Had he done anything they might think was questionable? He wracked his memory but came up empty and bewildered.

He hadn't been in a very good mood, even before that. The tiny portion of his breakfast that he could worry down lay like a lump.

He did his first round of post-op physical therapy. Replied to a smattering of "good morning" well-wishes from various Family members and friends. And he had a conversation through the link with an extremely happy Rex, whose new Amare had taken up permanent residence at Corona Tower last night.

At least someone's love life is working out well. An old, familiar emptiness seeped back into his sinews and pervaded his heart once more. Maybe he should just curl up in the fetal position under his covers for a while?

He took a long cleansing breath. *I need perspective. A good bit of that reaction is depression and exhaustion speaking.*

Hell, yes, he was depressed. The thing he'd feared most had happened faster than he'd thought possible, and now Hildie was gone. Probably for always, this time.

He'd fully earned the exhaustion, too. Kept pushing during PT. *Harder. Faster. Increase the reps.* His therapist had ended the session early, with a warning about overdoing it. Now that he'd stopped, his body made it clear that she was right. In the moment, rising pain had blocked out thought, had centered him in the *now*.

In the aftermath, he ached *everywhere*.

He grimaced. *Congratulations, Idiot. Screwed up again.* He closed his eyes. Genuinely exhausted, he slid into an uncomfortable doze. His muscles relaxed under the influence of pain meds. The all-over ache didn't disappear, but it receded. His sense of time slid away. He might have slept for a while.

Nanda stepped into his doorway. "Finally resting," the nurse said. "He had a really rough night and morning."

Whoever he was talking to released a long breath. "Mmm. Me too."

That was —Charlie opened his eyes, astonished.

This morning Hildie wore a light lime-colored cotton kurta and churidar. A duffel rested at her feet, but the worry in her expression made her thoughts hard to read. "Sorry! I can come back later."

He struggled upright. "Wait! Don't go!"

"I didn't mean to wake you."

"Don't go. Please." He reached out to her, as if he could somehow grasp and hold onto her from across the room. "Please know that you are *always* welcome. Did you get your bhaate-bhaat?"

Her uncertain posture relaxed. "Yes. And I got some rest, and I fed my cat." She lifted the duffel. "I'm prepared to encamp, if necessary."

This was more than he'd dared to imagine. "Please come in. Encamp at will, and welcome."

"Thanks." She dropped the duffel in the family alcove, then folded out the temp-bed.

He watched, lightheaded with lingering disbelief. "It is really good to see you. I'm pleased—*more* than pleased. But—may I ask? I could've sworn you were saying goodbye, yesterday afternoon."

She sat on the temp-bed's edge with a grimace. "I kinda

thought I was." She looked away. "Sorry. Emotionally, I'm all over the place. I'm not as brave as you are."

"You came back. That's—I'm good with that. I've been kinda all over the place too. I—" He stopped himself. *It's about HER. Shut up.*

She stared at the floor. "I can only begin to imagine what you must be going through. I hope I'm less of a drag on you than I am a help."

"Oh, you *definitely* class in the 'help' category." He let out a cautious breath. "It's really good to see you. And to know you don't—I *hope* you don't—despise me."

She frowned. "Seriously, Morgan! If you're still worried about that—"

"No. Not anymore." He lifted his hand, then lowered it and offered a rueful smile. "Well, maybe some. And *you* seem to keep worrying that you won't be welcome. So maybe we both have things to work through."

"You think?" She walked over to sit in the chair by his bed.

He took her hand.

She didn't pull back. Instead, she offered a rueful smile. "I haven't given you—me—us—a very good chance. All those years, I felt like you didn't—" She flinched from his gaze and fell silent.

"Tell me? Please?" Charlie wasn't sure he wanted to learn how much he'd actually hurt her, but he needed to know. "I'll admit up front that I was an idiot. I had no idea how rare it was —the friendship we had. Not until it was gone."

She looked down. "Friendship, yes. And friendship is valuable. It's important. It *is*. But you felt no ... no physical attraction."

"What are you talking about?" He gaped at her. "Do you have any idea how hard I worked to keep myself from—"

She scowled. "From what?"

"I had an *Amare*. I made *promises*." Despair ached in his throat and filled his chest with cold stone heaviness. *There's no changing past blunders.* "I didn't *dare* let myself think about you that way. I did everything in my power *not* to see how breathtaking you are."

She went very still. Stared at him.

"Please try to understand. People who cheat on their Amares are despicable. I couldn't do that. I couldn't. I *wouldn't*." Loyalty *mattered*, damn it. Promises *mattered*. Even when they were inconvenient. Even when keeping them hurt. If his word couldn't be trusted, what kind of slimebag did that make him?

Hildie bit her lip. Her hand clenched his.

Charlie couldn't meet her eyes. He bowed his head. "I promised I'd help Felicia launch her acting career. She warned me sometimes that takes a long time, and I swore I'd be there for her. Swore she could count on me." Pain like shards of glass tore his chest. "I promised I'd—I'd always—" His voice broke. He swallowed hard, sick with despair. "Always be there for her. No matter what."

CHAPTER 12

ETHICAL CONSIDERATIONS

H ildie sat breathless, frozen on the chair by Charlie's bed. His hand clasped hers as if it was a lifeline.

Of course, Felicia made him promise. She knew what he was made of. Hildie fought the urge to scream *how could you let her use you like that?* Strove for calm. She breathed through waves of rage and regret and reverberating anguish until at last she found her calmer, more timeless center.

Charlie, bless his wise soul, waited for her.

"Felicia was so beautiful." Hildie met his gaze. "I never thought I could compete."

His face hardened. "Felicia was *glamorous*. There's a difference. Glamour is an *illusion*. It's a lie. In typical fashion, I learned that way too late for anybody's good."

"So … you *didn't* think I was ugly next to her? Because she always made me feel so gawky. Awkward. Plain." That smug, supercilious way Felicia always looked at her—the memory still burned.

"No, no, no." He shook his head like an animal in pain. "The day I met you, I smacked headlong into a terrible realization. I had thought I'd found perfection, but I was *so desperately wrong*."

"Wait. *What?*"

"I was wrong. I made a horrible mistake. I'd fallen for a shadow. An illusion. It all came blazingly clear when I met the real thing. But by then I'd bound myself to her with *so many* promises! And at the time, I thought she'd been true to me. So how could I honorably pull away?"

"'At the time?'" Hildie frowned. She'd always thought Charlie and Felicia at least had that. Because who would even look twice at someone else, when she had Charlie?

"After she left, people spoke up. Not to me. To Uncle Dolph."

Charlie's uncle Dolph was an actor of System-wide repute. Charlie'd once told Hildie that he'd first met Felicia at a cast party after one of Dolph's productions wrapped.

She scowled. "They couldn't even face you *then*?"

"Well, at the time I was in re-gen."

Eww. "How, um, courageous of them."

"Yeah." His expression puckered with distress. "Turns out, while I was working all that overtime, she wasn't doing auditions, as she claimed. Instead, she was doing producers and directors."

Hildie swallowed, nauseated. *Could a betrayal be any more complete?* "I sincerely hope that didn't help her career."

"Once Dolph knew the score, he quietly put out the word that he wouldn't be associated with any production that included her. He only had to enforce that decision once, but it sent the needed message. I don't think she's worked in the industry again. At least, no role bigger than spokesmodel."

Hildie'd never seen a vindictive expression on Charlie's face before. Its strangeness and fury chilled her. She eased out a breath. "Well, that's fitting, I guess."

He scowled. "I guess. More effective than violence, which was all I could think of, for a while." He gave her a pain-filled look. "Violence is a wrong and stupid answer, and at the time I learned all of this I was only about two days out of a month-long re-gen."

A month-long re-gen would have left him too weak to feed

himself without help, much less act out violent urges. "That must have been frustrating."

"Just as well. Saved me from doing something stupid. I've split a punching bag or two since then, thinking about it. But that's all."

Who could blame you? She nodded. "Better the bag than a person."

"Definitely. My police career had enough challenges already. Better not add more."

"Your career?" She couldn't imagine how a man of Charlie's intelligence and integrity—

"I'm glad you've had success with *your* career, anyway." He smiled. "You so completely deserve it."

LaRock and his attitudes taunted from the back of her mind. "Thanks. I try to take it one duty-watch at a time and focus on the important things." *But none are more important to me right now than you.* She bit her lip, afraid to say that aloud. But Grandma had asked, *you gonna chickenshit out?* She took a breath. "Important things … like you."

The dawning joy in his face filled her heart. "I can't even express how much that means to me. Can we *please* try again? And give it a *real* try, this time?"

"I'd like that. Yes. But also this time—if you don't mind— don't hold back?"

"You've got it. I won't, if you don't." His smile took on a hungry eagerness. He slid his hand up her arm, sat forward, tugged her gently closer. The few centimeters between them closed. His one-armed embrace pulled her into a passionate kiss.

Her heart rate doubled. *So totally NOT my imagination.* She returned his kiss for all she was worth. Desire ached through her. Breathless, she slipped her hand under his bed sheet and found exactly what she wanted.

He gasped. Pulled back with an astonished expression.

She kept her hand where it was, heart pounding hard. *Did I misread him?* "You did agree I shouldn't hold back."

"Caught—" He said in a strangled voice, then cleared his throat. "Um, you caught me by surprise."

"I'll go slower, if you prefer." She lowered her chin and regarded him through her eyelashes. *God, he's gorgeous. Have I just messed it all up?* "But now my cards are on the table."

He gulped. Gave her a worried look. "Your cards are amazing. I love your cards. But I'm afraid in my current condition I'd fold way too early."

"I'm willing to stop here. For *now*." She gave him a gentle squeeze, then ran her hand languorously down his inner thigh. "To be continued later?"

"Yes, please." His words came out in a breathless whisper. "As soon as ever I can!"

"You're on, then, Morgan. No take-backs."

"Wouldn't dream of it." He pulled her close for another kiss.

Oh, yeah. The old magic *was* still there. Still there, and stronger than ever.

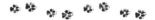

REX'S HUD blinked with a new message. From Klein. *Oh.* Queasy foreboding had him stress-yawning before he knew it.

Klein kept it short: "An interviewer from the SDF is here."

Rex snapped his ears flat. "Charlie is asleep. This is not a good time." His partner'd had a startling but intense and ultimately reassuring morning. No surprise he was deep asleep now, able to relax at last with Hildie there. "He needs that rest. I won't interrupt it if I can help it."

"Come up and meet her, at least. Cornwell wasn't much inclined to wait, as you might recall."

"All too well. That does not mean I am willing to be constrained to his time frame, but I shall alert Elaine and come upstairs. Where should I go?"

"Interview A. I'll meet you there."

Interview Suite A was the one with all the bells and whistles.

The one where they did the highest-security interviews. Nice enough furnishings to place the richest citizen-witnesses at ease, but secure in ways no layperson would suspect. Even a top-level spook from SDF Intelligence might begrudgingly accept it. And apparently *had*.

Rex arrived to find Klein chatting with a slender woman outside Observation A, the surveillance center built next to the interview room. The Chief turned to him. "Rex, I'd like you to meet Ayaana Chaten. She's here to conduct an interview for Commodore Cornwell."

She stood with a smile that bared no teeth, politely averted her gaze, and extended her hand sideways, fingers relaxed, to adapt for either a sniff or a shake. "Thank you for agreeing to speak with me, Pack Leader Dieter-Nell."

Rex wagged his tail and extended a paw to shake. "Someone coached her well," he texted to Klein.

"I first wish to apologize on behalf of Commodore Cornwell. The Service regrets the bad first impression."

She explained the protocol Klein had arranged for the proposed interview: a thorough debrief, but not to exceed three hours per session. Rex would be allowed drinks and rest breaks as needed. It was agreed there would be no yelling, no touching unless Rex invited it, no intimidation, and no threats of any sort. Rex was there on a voluntary basis and could call an end to any session at need. If he became uncomfortable with what was happening, he could reach out to Chief Klein via text for help. Otherwise, his coms were to remain offline.

In return, he would describe his experiences with Col. Wisniewski and any other Transmondian Intelligence Service contacts in as much detail as possible. And if he could supply visuals, maps, or other supplementary materials, they were requested.

Rex nodded at the end of this explanation. "That arrangement seems fair. I agree to it in principle, but we have an issue of timing. First, I must warn you that it may require several sessions, and we shall wade into some deep weeds, so to speak."

She gave him a tight-lipped smile, again careful not to show her teeth. "Thank you. That is what we want. Shall we begin?"

"Not yet. Do you understand the nature of my brain link with my partner?"

"I understand that you have a verbal interface with your human partner through an implanted chip. We expect you to turn that off."

Rex exchanged a look with Klein. "That is a potential problem, because unless one of us is under anesthesia or unconscious in a deeper way than sleep, Charlie and I are always at least slightly connected."

Her eyes widened. "Are you saying you *can't* turn it off?"

"That is correct. I can attempt to minimize what Charlie is able to receive—but emotions often come through, even if words do not. Whether we want them to or not. He is sleeping now, but when I go through some of the emotions I know I shall feel if I talk about Jackson Wisniewski and my interactions with him, it is likely that I shall awaken and seriously distress Charlie."

"His partner Charlie is hospitalized," Klein added.

Agent Chaten sat for a moment, frowning. "How—how likely is it that you might interfere with your partner's healing?"

Rex snapped his ears flat. Every hackle rose. "Col. Wisniewski tortured and abused me for weeks on end. I detest him with every particle of my being, and I have a highly superior autobiographical memory. Speaking of our interactions to you will in effect be re-living that period in intense detail. I shall not impose that on my partner while he is in the hospital fighting for his life."

Chaten let out a soft breath. "Not the ideal thing to inflict upon a hospitalized patient, even vicariously."

"No."

Agent Chaten's face puckered, troubled, and her scent soured. "This is an ethical dilemma we had not anticipated. Your information is important, but we haven't been able to interview the captured Transmondian agent yet." She frowned. "Nor will we get to, for another week. So, this is technically not an emergency—*yet*." She turned to Klein. "In light of the health issue for his partner, is it fair to say that our interview with XK9 Rex must be postponed?"

"As I have stipulated, it is XK9 Rex's decision. The OPD supports his refusal, especially in light of the threat to Detective Morgan's health."

Chaten sat silent and frowning for a few moments. Consulting with her boss via text? Possibly. She bit her lip, then looked to Klein again. "Would it be possible for me to interview XK9 Tuxedo?"

The Chief quirked an eyebrow at Rex. "Pack Leader?"

Rex sat, to keep himself from pacing. "I know neither Tux nor I would prefer to relive that period. But Tux's partner is healthy. I think you should ask him if he is willing to submit to questions. Treat him as fairly as you were prepared to treat me, and he may make himself available. I will back a refusal, but I will not stand in your way if he agrees."

"I COULD SEE HIM RELAX, the moment I showed up with my duffel." Hildie scrunched a bit deeper into the waiting room privacy pod she'd commandeered after Charlie fell asleep. It wasn't much past lunchtime, but he'd had a rough night. She'd had a rough night too, but she needed perspective from a trusted friend more than sleep at the moment.

"Well, *sure* he relaxed." Theresa's voice through her com carried the hint of a laugh. "I bet you relaxed, too, now that you've made a decision. This is one of those 'meant to be' situations."

Hildie was by no means finished with Charlie or their plans for future mutual relaxation therapy. *Meant to be* remained a bit of a stretch, though. "I have a sense that none of this surprises you."

Theresa laughed. She was working "up top" at the Hub today, but on break at the moment. "I remember the old days, so no. I'm not the least bit surprised you reconnected when the opportunity arose. I'm a little surprised you might actually get to pull off a happy ending after all these years. But you two were the best-matched pair I ever met. I never did figure out what Charlie saw in Felicia. How'd he get shed of her?"

Hildie hesitated. "I want to actually see your face when I explain about that. It deserves a girls' night out for full coverage."

"Ooh, you're on. Now you've got me curious."

Time to change the subject. "Would you believe LaRock texted me to ask where this 'Boyfriend out of thin air' came from?"

"Of course he did." Theresa made a rude noise. "You should know he came by and grilled us this morning. Wanted to know if you've been keeping your boyfriend secret from him. We told him you and your old friend just reconnected recently."

"Thanks." LaRock didn't need to know she'd become romantically involved with a recent patient.

"He's too nosey and suspicious, which of course I never said."

"No, never." Hildie grimaced. "And, of course, I never agreed with you. I did save a copy of his message in my documentation file." *Speaking of which, Theresa's just given me more material for it.*

"Good for you. It's none of his business that you just reconnected with the love of your life. So. You say they took Charlie's arm? What's he gonna do now?"

"That's the big question of the moment. I didn't realize how limited the prosthetic options are for police officers. I can just imagine what Mac and Yo-yo would think." She grinned. "Actually, listening to them riff on it might be hilarious. But it wouldn't help Charlie."

"Mmm, the 'cyborg cop' laws, right? Well, that bites. So, will he try re-gen again? Or go with plain-vanilla prosthetics?"

"We're waiting to hear from a guy who's had a special kind of re-gen. Zuni had to get it authorized by the government before he could even suggest it. It's supposed to make Charlie harder to injure."

"Special *kind*? Or special *ops*?"

Hildie frowned. "That's what I'm worried about. Rex is excited because he thinks it would make Charlie 'XK9 tough.'"

"Oh, right. Rex." Theresa hesitated. "I can't believe I didn't even remember he could *talk*. Sheesh!" Last week she'd been charged with decontaminating Rex after the crew pulled him and Charlie out of their emergency bunker. She'd treated him like any other dog until he started critiquing her bedside manner. She was still working through her embarrassment about it.

"I'm sure you worry a lot more about it than Rex. He's command staff now. Working the *Izgubil* case."

"How's that going, do you know?"

"Rex doesn't talk to me about the case."

"Sorry, I guess he wouldn't." An all-too-familiar klaxon went off in the background on Theresa's end.

"Uh-oh! Stay safe!"

But her friend was already gone.

CHAPTER 13

SHIVA AND THE MEDICINE GODDESS

H ildie's HUD beeped with a text from Charlie. Apparently, Rex did know the augmented guy, and they would arrive soon.

"I'm on my way," she texted Charlie. But she left the privacy pod frowning. Worry slithered within her. She wasn't completely sold on the genetic-augmentation idea, even though Rex seemed all-in. *Now we may learn more. Will Rex's friend offer clarity?*

She returned to the room, then stopped in the doorway, startled.

Charlie had mustered the strength to move to the chair by his bed. He lit up with visible delight the moment he spotted her.

Warm pleasure cut through her incipient concern that he'd pushed himself too far, too fast. It had been a long time since anybody reacted with such obvious joy to the mere sight of her. *Hot damn, I could get used to that.* She leaned in for a kiss. *Oh, yeah.* She could get used to those kisses, too.

"You left your duffel, so I figured you hadn't disappeared on me."

"Oh, you'll not get rid of me that easily. I called no take-backs." She pulled another chair over, so she could sit next to him. He clasped her hand in his.

Rex bounded in scant seconds after she arrived—ears up, tail wagging, and *huge*. Each time she encountered him she had a surreal moment of *no dog is this big*. The human-like intelligence in his eyes and face just added to the *oh, this is different* reaction— kind of like the way she'd felt meeting her first ozzirikkian.

"Come in, Shiv! Sit down." Rex pranced with evident excitement. "This is my partner Charlie, and his girlfriend Sgt. Gallagher. Charlie and Hildie, please meet Lead Special Agent Shiva Shimon."

Hildie pulled her gaze from Rex to his companion, a tall, muscular, pale-blond man with an almost unnaturally handsome face. She recognized him from the news vids. He was one of the SBI people.

Charlie pushed up from his chair but wavered and abruptly sat back down when he tried to extend his hand. "Hello, LSA Shimon. It's good to meet you in person. Please come in."

"Call me Shiv. And the pleasure is mine. I've been eager to meet Rex's partner." Shimon kept his expression pleasant and his gaze on Charlie's face when he shook hands. *Interesting*. Most people would've looked at least briefly toward the bandaged stump, especially after Charlie's attempt to stand. The next moment, Shimon's intense gray-blue eyes shifted to focus on her. "Sgt. Gallagher, hello."

"Hildie. Pleased to meet you." She stood to greet him, then wondered if Charlie minded that she could, when he couldn't.

Shiv's firm, dry grip and calm nod put her somewhat at ease. "Dr. Zuni asked me to answer any questions you might want to ask." He smiled at Rex, then at Charlie and Hildie. "So fire away."

"Please have a seat." Hildie sat again, too. "How long since your procedure?"

"Nine years."

She nodded. "Enough time to experience both good and bad. If you had it to do over again, would you?"

"Yes, I would. Definitely! But there are things to consider."

Shiv leaned back in the chair and crossed muscular arms over his burly chest. His focus flicked from her to Charlie, then back. "How long have you been in a relationship?"

How should they answer? She looked at Charlie. His uncertain expression said he wasn't sure what to say, either.

"We were friends and co-workers a few years ago." She offered a tentative smile and kept Charlie at the edge of her vision. "We've recently reconnected on new terms."

Shiv nodded. "It's good that you were friends first. It's also fortunate you're at the beginning of a new phase of your relationship. Fewer habits and assumptions to change, if you accept the augmentations, Charlie."

That sounded like the voice of experience. Hildie frowned. "What should we watch out for?"

Shiv sighed. "Well, understand that a physical mismatch is inevitable. These augmentations increase endurance and reduce the rate of muscle fatigue."

So, um ... stock up on personal lubricant? She glanced at Charlie and caught him glancing at her. *There goes the "might fold too early" concern.*

"No normal human physiology works the way these augmentations do." Shiv hesitated, frowned. "Unfortunately for me, my former Amare was extremely competitive. He and I had plenty of other problems, but that one definitely became a big issue."

Ouch. "I appreciate your willingness to speak about it."

"It was a while back." Shiv's dismissive shrug didn't quite convince. "I thought a warning might help you avoid some pain."

"Thank you," Charlie said.

"On a related cautionary note, I should mention some other practical realities you'll want to consider. Charlie, if you go this route, you'll always get the difficult jobs. Just plan on it. If it's dangerous or requires maximum strength or endurance, you'll get all of those calls." He grimaced. "Command always knows about the augmentations."

Charlie frowned, but nodded.

Shiv hesitated, then sighed. "They'd rather I not talk about this next fact. Ranan Intelligence may never ask you to do anything—but they *could*."

Hildie caught her breath. *Special ops was a good guess, Theresa.*

"And they'll definitely *know* about you," Shiv continued. "Seems to me it's only fair that you should know, too. I don't remember if anyone clued me in, before I got my treatment. It was probably buried in the fine print." His broad shoulders slumped. "I didn't think to look. But then, I was about as green as they come."

Hard to imagine the man across from them as a wide-eyed rookie, but everyone started that way. And apparently he'd had a rough rookie tour. "How old were you?"

"Twenty-one—well, twenty-two, by the time I got out of re-gen." Shiv frowned in the general direction of the floor, then looked up at Charlie. "I wasn't conscious, for long stretches of twenty-two."

"Mm, I can relate." Charlie's rueful tone sent a pang through her. "I also lost a big chunk of twenty-two."

Hildie grimaced. *It probably did seem like that to him.* But her curiosity burned. *What kind of injuries put Shiv into re-gen for that long?*

"Anyway." Shiv straightened. "Other things to watch for. I had persistent problems with muscle cramps, early on. Here's hoping you don't. Your appetite changes, too. You'll be voracious, especially for the first month or so."

Hildie frowned. "I imagine that's from the metabolic changes."

"Your metabolism definitely *does* change." Shiv looked from Hildie to Charlie. "Stay in close touch with Zuni and your favorite Listener, because you'll need to deal with some things. You'll also probably have to adjust your meds at least once.

Some days, everything will make you angry. Especially as your physical strength grows, that can be terrifying."

Charlie gave Hildie a worried look.

Unless he'd gone through a major personality change since she'd known him, excessive anger seemed unlikely. She squeezed his hand. "I've seen you in a lot of moods, but by the time you'd get angry, the rest of us would've already blown our top long before. You may be kind of a gloomy Gus, but you've got a long fuse."

From Shiv's expression, the blond agent was less sure. "These treatments don't change your basic nature. You'll still be you."

Charlie released a breath. "That's a relief."

"But you already know there are lots of things about rehab that can make a person lose it." Shiv met his eyes. "Stay alert for this, because the metabolic changes add fuel to every fire, and the augmentations put unfamiliar power behind every punch. I guarantee you'll break things you didn't mean to break."

"But it can be managed, right?" Rex asked.

Shiv nodded. "Certainly. Yes. Takes thinking ahead and being open to talking about it. And likely a change in your meds." He gave Charlie a rueful look. "Yeah, sorry. You get more meds. On top of all the ones to keep the re-gen stable."

Hildie hadn't yet thought about what sorts of drugs a re-gen patient needed to keep his system stable. She took a moment to exercise her rights as Girlfriend-of-Record and access his medical records. She checked the scripts. *Oh, my. That's a list, all right.*

"You'll sleep a lot at first." Shiv had focused on Charlie once more. "Don't fight it. It's what your body needs. It'll eventually normalize, except when you over-exert yourself." He grinned. "That takes some doing, but it's possible. It's easier to do while you're still healing. And don't fool yourself. Healing doesn't happen overnight. You'll seem to recover really fast in a lot of ways, but *full* healing takes at least a year."

"But you said you'd choose the augmentations again anyway?" Charlie frowned. "Why?"

Shiv leaned forward in his chair with a smile. "Because once you heal, you get to be a genuine badass."

Hildie frowned. Didn't Shiv know Charlie's history? He was *already* a badass!

"There are limits, don't get me wrong," the blond agent continued, "But seriously. Ever dream about being a superhero when you were a kid? These augmentations put you partway there for real."

Charlie's expression turned sheepish. "I, um, always wanted to be SuperCop."

Hildie gave a startled laugh. "I never knew that!" Watching that show as a kid, she'd had her earliest inklings of wanting to be a first responder. She'd pictured herself as SuperCop's trusty friend Dr. Divya, who was always there to patch up both the victims and the captured bad guys.

"You too?" Shiv's grin widened. "I loved that show." Then he shook his head. "This is nothing like that."

Charlie mock-groaned. "Aw, damn. You mean we can't really fly?"

"Sorry, no flying." Shiv's eyes glinted with humor. "I know. It sucks. No seeing through walls with laser-vision, either. Gotta do it the normal way, with your HUD."

Charlie chuckled. "So. Only *semi*-SuperCop. Well, that's underwhelming. What *can* we do?"

Hildie drew in a breath, not sure what to anticipate. *Here it comes.*

"What you *can* do comes down to three basic but important things." Shiv raised his index finger. "Strength. Build up to it, and you can lift four or five times your own weight. Maybe more."

"Like that shed," Rex said.

Shiv glanced at him. "Comes in handy sometimes."

"Shed?" Hildie hadn't heard that story. From the look that passed between Charlie and Rex, however, it promised to be interesting. She fought to shove aside hurt, left-out feelings. *Listen, and maybe you'll learn.*

But Shiv had already refocused on Charlie. A second finger joined the first. "Reflexes. You'll find yourself catching things you or others drop—don't even have to think about it. Study a martial art, nobody gets past your blocking." His look went rueful again. "If you can find sparring partners."

Rex wagged his tail. "If he does this, you two should stay in touch. Charlie is proficient in karate."

"Oh, really?" Shiv quirked a pale eyebrow. "We could spar in the police gym. Once you're healed, of course. *If* you do this." His smile turned wistful. "A real sparring partner. That would be nice."

Those two? In peak condition? In a gym setting, where most everyone's naked? Hildie chuckled, picturing it. *That wouldn't just be 'nice,' it would be epic.* "I know women who'd pay good money to watch."

Charlie gasped. He met Shiv's eyes. "*Private* session. *Closed* workout."

"You're on." The blond man's grin flashed fierce.

What a pair of killjoys. But maybe she'd have special status and would get to watch anyway. She smiled, warm with anticipation.

"Third thing." Shiv firmly pulled the conversation back on track. "Endurance. Are you a runner? You won't hit your limit in the time a normal officer has to train."

Charlie frowned. "That brings up a new question. How much do you have to train each day?"

Hildie gave him a worried look. *Will this make it harder for him to work?* Charlie was a detective. No beat to walk, like a patrol cop. Plenty of formwork, though. *Of course, Shiv's a kind of detective, too.*

"Oh, there's never enough time." Shiv shook his head. "That's a given. You have to get creative, because there's a minimum level to how sedentary you can stand to be—and investigations involve a *lot* of sedentary work. If you're like me, after a while you'll get too jittery to sit any longer."

"Shiv has been known to jog around the evidence cavern, keeping an eye on multiple work groups." Rex wagged his tail. "He can do it for hours, but I am faster."

"True." Shiv grinned. "Even with our quicker-firing muscles, he'll leave us in the dust. The laws of physics do still apply to us." He gave Rex a long look. "If I'm not mistaken, you have parallel augmentations." His face relaxed into a fond smile. *Remembering what? Something about a shed, perhaps?* Oh, she *definitely* needed to hear that story someday. *Soon.*

Charlie gave a slow nod. Hildie noted that he'd slumped back against his chair. "So, maybe 'XK9 tough,' but not XK9-fast."

"Exactly. Neither one of us'll win a foot-race with Rex." Shiv's brow furrowed. "But that brings up another thing. All's fair in charity events. When the money goes for a good cause, you'll get to be the ringer. That can be fun, especially if they let you show off a little. But otherwise, if you get these augmentations, you'll be barred from competitions. No matter how hard you kick the champion's ass in practice, *he'll* be the competitor. Never you."

"I guess that figures." Charlie sighed. "Martial-arts tournaments?"

"Exhibition only."

Charlie nodded. "Anything else?"

Coupla last things. EStees are almost as effective on us as anyone else. And we can still be killed, although that generally takes *considerably* more effort."

He drew in a breath to say more, but Hildie lifted her hand. "Paramedic question, here. Are there any special considerations a medical crew would need to know? Do you guys get a health beacon?"

People with severe allergies, a range of health conditions, and those who were on certain medications typically had a little chip implanted with information for emergency staffs and medical personnel. These medical beacons had been standardized across much of the Alliance. They had saved countless lives when patients were unable to speak for themselves.

Shiv nodded. "As you might imagine, there's been occasional pushback from intelligence organizations. A few, most notably the Transmondians, don't chip their agents. But it's wiser to do so, and it's mandatory on Rana."

Hildie gave Charlie a worried look. "I'd like to know the cautions those beacons list."

"We can ask Dr. Zuni." Charlie stifled a yawn, then turned back to Shiv. "What else?"

"We have a higher pain tolerance, but injuries still hurt like hell when they're bad enough," the man replied. "And we probably get more of them, because we get more dangerous jobs."

Charlie gave him a wry look. "Semi-SuperCop doesn't get a break, eh?"

"Not even a little."

"I definitely don't love that part." Hildie also didn't love the way Charlie'd begun to sag in his chair, eyelids half-down. *We need to let him rest. He shouldn't be out of bed. Better wrap this up.* "Any other last things?"

Shiv grinned at Rex. "If I had a memory like our XK9 friend, here, I'd know for sure. But I don't *think* I've left anything out."

A new message-light popped up on her HUD.

"That's my personal contact," Shiv said. "If you have any other questions, please ask. I'll get back to you as soon as possible." He stood. "I can tell you're getting tired, Charlie, and I know you, Hildie, and Rex may want to talk. I'm afraid I've told you more drawbacks than advantages, but I wanted to be honest about the realities."

Charlie frowned. "Do you honestly think it's worth it?"

"Yes. When you need the power or the endurance, and it's *there*?" A wide grin crossed Shiv's face. His eyes glinted with pleasure. "Oh, yeah. It's worth it. No more broken bones? Fewer aches and pains? It's worth it. A feeling of being generally 'on top of things,' and you're routinely more aware? *Definitely worth it.*"

His enthusiasm brought an answering smile to Charlie's face. "It's been a while since I felt 'on top of things,'" he admitted in a rueful tone.

He's gonna do it. Hildie bit her lip. *Is this genuinely the best solution?*

"Look, I have selfish reasons for hoping you'll accept." Shiv spread his hands wide. "It gets lonely being the only one. There aren't many of us on Rana, and most of the others are retired military guys in a little enclave of expat Primerans on Wheel Four. That's where Zuni's from, so it's pretty easy to see how he came to specialize in re-gen. One of his grandfathers is—or was —a Takhiachono Marine."

Woah. Hildie didn't know much about military history, but everyone had heard of the Takhiachono Marines of Primero. They were the most celebrated military cadre in the Human Diaspora, reputed to be the toughest human fighting unit in history. *Oh. Duh!* "Augmentations are their secret weapon."

"Yes. They've been perfecting these techniques for more than 200 years."

"Which means it hasn't been experimental for a long time."

Shiv nodded. "Exactly. These are proven techniques."

"That makes me feel better." All the same, Hildie frowned. *At least, better in some ways.* "I assume they've figured out remedies for all kinds of issues, and Zuni knows them."

"Yes. Those are added reasons why I genuinely think it's a good option to take," Shiv said. "It has to be your choice, Charlie. But I can't really imagine how police-legal prosthetics could possibly be anything but disappointing by comparison."

CHAPTER 14

POSSIBILITIES

R ex and Shiv stepped through the S-3-9 entrance, then
Shiv laughed. "Well, look who's back! Hello, Mike!"
I should have alerted him to Santiago's return. They'd
aligned with the man's scent-trail at the elevator. The SSA's
departure for wherever-he'd-gone hadn't lasted long.

Elaine looked up from her case pad with a smile. "How'd it
go, guys? Did you convince him?"

Shiv grinned. "Maybe."

"Probably." Rex lolled his tongue.

Santiago's brows rose. "Really? That could certainly ... He's
already pre-cleared as a Reserve Agent, isn't he?"

"Yes, but let's not start harvesting till after the crop's planted." Elaine frowned at him. "I'm gonna need him for another
purpose entirely—and mine's tailor-made for an officer on light
duty. Don't you dare break him before he's healed!"

Santiago sighed. "No, dear. Of course not."

Rex observed their exchange with concern. Did their
comments bode ill for Charlie? Maybe not. He trusted Elaine, at
least.

"May I change the subject?" Shiv asked. "I need input to
schedule my afternoon."

Elaine nodded. "You have the floor."

Shiv turned to Santiago. "What did Montreaux learn? What did she tell you?"

"She told me to take it up with Rooq."

Rex didn't miss Santiago's side-eye toward him. He laid back his ears. "Cornwell placed conditions upon your request? I can guess what he asked, but what did you want from him?"

Santiago blinked, then turned to Elaine.

"Sapient," she said. "And a fast learner. Explain it to him."

"Elaine tells me you need access to the forward section of the *Izgubil*. I realized that SDF Intelligence might have a prototype fully-enough developed to give it to you."

Rex put his ears back up. "How? As I understand it, the thing is in space, and far too large to bring into the Station so we could examine it in an atmosphere."

Santiago shot a questioning look at Elaine.

"Pod Three. Activate the sound-dampening equipment, if you feel it's necessary. Shiv, set it up and stay to listen."

Shiv led the way to Pod Three, a conference room adjacent to the war room. Rex and Santiago stepped inside, then Shiv closed the door and activated a security device designed to scramble any attempts to eavesdrop. Unlike Chief Klein's counter-surveillance shielding that deactivated , among other things, journalists' and political opponents' miniature drone-cams, this device created a high-pitched screech.

Rex's hackles prickled. He gave a soft growl. "Is that truly necessary? It hurts my ears."

Shiv's eyebrows rose. "I don't hear anything."

"Humans hear only slightly better than they smell." Rex lolled his tongue.

Shiv laughed. "And we smell terrible?"

"Exactly."

Santiago looked from Rex to Shiv, then shook his head. "I think we're safe enough with the door closed and the standard measures in place."

"As you wish." Shiv deactivated the screech.

Rex flicked his ears several times, until his head stopped hurting. "Thank you!"

"Sorry." Shiv eyed him with chagrin.

Santiago gave Rex a long, rueful look. "You are gonna drive Rooq nuts."

"Oh, excellent!" Rex lifted his head and wagged his tail. "I look forward to it. But meanwhile you were going to tell me how I might examine an important potential treasure-trove of evidence, without blowing out my lungs."

A slow smile spread across Santiago's face. "I was, yes." His scent factors took on the tangy fragrance of a human with his curiosity aroused. "In space, anyplace you can securely enclose can contain an atmosphere. Picture an enormous bubble, with the craft's forward section inside."

Shiv whistled. "That'd have to be a hell of a bubble. How could they keep it stable long enough to fill it with sufficient atmosphere?"

"The SDF has been working on this technology for years. Decades, really. I was still on the Force, and working much more closely with Rooq, well after they started it. It's been a top secret project, because it's a real game-changer. Apparently, they're willing to risk revealing it now, because this would be a great way to field-test the late-stage prototype with a real-world application."

Rex would ask him about when he'd worked with Cornwell later. The more enticing scent-trail was the one that could lead him to his much-desired evidence. He cocked his head. "Why is a great big bubble in space hard to make?"

"Not so hard to make, but very hard to maintain," Santiago said.

"Too many micrometeoroids." Shiv's brows puckered in a frown. "Also, too much human-made debris."

Santiago scowled in agreement. "It seems to be a price of humans doing business in space. No matter how careful we are, debris happens—and then occasionally people blow up space-ships, breach docks, or crash their craft into things."

"That definitely does not help," Shiv said.

"Earlier bubbles have always been prone to piercing," Santiago continued. "*Especially* in the Chayko System."

Rex had learned last week that their home system was infamous for naturally-occurring meteors of all sizes. Frequent large meteor-strikes had prevented any native sapient species from developing on Chayko. That was the only reason the Alliance of the Peoples had allowed humans, who'd developed an effective way to shield the planet, to settle there. "Out of all the other species in the Alliance, are you telling me no one has ever solved this problem?"

Santiago frowned. "We know of at least three other species who have something like what the SDF has developed, but they're not sharing. The best efforts in the Human Diaspora till now have been temporary, relatively small bubbles. They normally start to lose integrity within a few hours."

Hmm. Rex flicked his ears. "A collapsible—therefore portable—structure? One big enough to engulf the broken-off front third of a space barque? Something that could remain stable for several days?"

"Weeks," Santiago said. "Potentially a month or more."

Shiv gave him a startled look. "That long?"

"The goal is a year."

Rex nodded, human-style. "That sounds useful, especially if nothing like it has been available previously." He didn't know much about space, because Dr. Ordovich hadn't thought dogs needed to. But he'd learned all he could once he realized it might be important. Clearly, there was lots more to know. "Why won't micrometeoroids and human-made microparticles be a problem for this thing?"

Santiago smiled. "They've worked out a really clever deflector system. I'm told it creates a 'flow pattern.' Got some kind of synthetic cilia that make the bubble's surface look like an undulating field of grasses, but charged. The way they dumbed it down for non-genius types like me is that the charged cilia make high-velocity particles skip across the surface. That's how they don't punch holes, even though they travel at hypersonic speeds. And no, don't ask. I haven't the faintest idea how or why it works. It involves some crazy-complex kind of math I can't even begin to follow."

"Okay, that is interesting. I wonder what Tuxedo and Crystal would think about it. I wonder if Crystal and Connie could do the math."

Santiago gave him a puzzled look.

"Crystal and her human partner Connie are the Pack's math wizards," Shiv explained.

"Oh. No idea." Santiago shook his head. "But it's interesting that you think Tuxedo might want to know about this prototype."

Rex snorted. "Cornwell wants to trade access to his bubble for our interviews, does he not?"

Santiago gave him a slow, pensive nod. "Tuxedo did not agree to an interview." His rueful frown made it clear he found this both frustrating and inexplicable.

Rex snapped his ears flat. "Consider what Cornwell is asking of us. We both have highly superior autobiographical memories. Remembering and describing our interactions with Col. Wisniewski will be for us a concentration of several weeks' physical and mental abuse." He explained again about the brain link, and his reluctance to inflict vicarious pain on Charlie while he was hospitalized or recovering.

"However, if he accepts the augmentation . . ." Shiv quirked an eyebrow.

Rex nodded. "That is my thought, as well. He will be in regen. It would provide a window of opportunity. I would vastly prefer that he never be burdened by all the things I suffered at Wisniewski's hands."

"Even though he's your partner?" Shiv asked.

"There are some things it is not necessary to share." Rex's hackles prickled.

Santiago frowned, but nodded. "Elaine would agree with you on that point. Some things are simply too painful to call back into memory—at least, not until one is fully ready. I respect that."

Last week Rex had learned that Elaine was in the first group of immigrant-refugees from the war along the Norchellic Frontier's Rift Valley. Her dog-phobia came from a physically-scarring encounter with military dogs when she was five, not long after the start of the war. How many other horrors must have happened to her, as a child-refugee fleeing ethnic cleansing? Clearly, her Significant understood about the lingering pain of trauma. Santiago notched up a little higher in Rex's estimation. "Then you understand Tuxedo's reluctance."

Santiago sighed. "Yeah. And yours. I'm sorry. I hadn't grasped all the dimensions of it."

"Neither has Cornwell." Rex laid back his ears. "He seemed less interested than you in understanding our perspective."

"Or in considering the XK9s to be full-fledged persons," Shiv added.

Rex gave a soft growl. "He is far from alone in that regard."

Santiago's frown deepened. "But in this case, pivotal. I'll see what I can do to close that gap."

"Thank you."

Shiv ran his hand down Rex's back in a smooth caress. "Now we just have to hope Charlie chooses what we'd prefer."

THIS WAS IT. Decision time. Charlie sat propped up in his hospital bed. Hildie sat in her customary bedside chair and held his hand. Rex had arrived soon after the end of his Tuesday day-watch, and now lay at Hildie's feet. Gran Annie sat between Mama and Aunt Hannah, facing them.

Mama finished her report. She'd summarized some important realities of living with a prosthetic and outlined the most relevant of the biological studies done on the augmentation treatments Zuni had proposed. Aunt Hannah's review of case law in regard to each choice had come earlier.

Now Mama set her case pad aside. "So, that's it. Do *you* have questions?"

Charlie focused on his elders. *Here we go, then.* "Is either option something you would *not* recommend?"

Gran Annie looked at Mimi and Hannah. Both shook their heads. "Well, that's it," his grandmother said. "I'll encourage the Family to endorse whatever you choose. *Including* the augmentations, if that's your choice."

Go-lights for both. Corona wouldn't vote against the recommendations of these three, especially not Head-of-Household Annie. He let out a careful breath, nodded. "Thank you." *It's good to have a choice.*

You know my advice. Rex stood and rubbed his head along Charlie's side. *I'll leave you to talk with Hildie, because she needs to weigh in, too.*

Gran Annie pushed up from her chair. "You have a lot to consider. We'll let you be, now. Rex, are you riding home with us?"

Rex lifted his head and wagged his tail. "I sent Shady home earlier in my auto-nav. Do you have room for me?"

Hannah smiled. "We can order a car that'll take us all."

Gran Annie, Hannah, and Rex said their goodbyes, then departed to get the car.

Mama kissed Charlie's cheek, but hung back, brow furrowed. "Remember when we thought the GR Unit would be a nice, safe place for you to work?"

"Ha!" He huffed out a surprised half-laugh, then frowned. Sour memories flooded back. "That was a lovely illusion while it lasted."

"We never get to know how things will turn out, until after

the decision's made," Mama said. "Whatever you decide, I know you're happiest when you do the thing your heart calls you to do, not what your mama thinks is safe. So do what makes you happy."

He sighed. "Working on it."

"I know." She glanced at Hildie. "Thank you. And now I'd better get moving, or they might leave me to walk home." She grinned, waved, and left. The room seemed lots emptier, all of a sudden.

The earlier warmth he'd felt had fled. Now in his mind he stood on the precipice of a primary terrace, alone in the wind. *Do or die time.* He caught his breath. *Or would it be, 'do and become harder to kill'?* "I guess this is it." He met Hildie's worried gaze and let out a shaky breath. "Everybody else has weighed in, except the opinion I care about most. What does the Medicine Goddess advise? Should the driver go for Semi-SuperCop?"

She bit her lip. "What do *you* want?"

"I don't want to hold Rex back. I want to be a worthy partner." He searched her face. *What does she truly think?* His throat constricted. "But oh, Hils, that 'worthy partner' wish goes for you, too. There's barely been time for an 'us,' yet. We know what we'd get with the prosthetics, but I have to be honest. I'm not excited about the police restrictions. On the other hand, the augmentations throw in *a lot* of random variables. I don't want to do *anything* that might mess 'us' up."

"'Us.'" She took a shaky breath. "I don't want to mess 'us' up, either." She paused, eyes huge in a worried face. "But you know challenges come, no matter what. Random variables happen, even without augmentations."

Is she really going to sign off on this? "Does that mean yes to augmentations?"

She looked terrified but nodded. "You won't get this opportunity again. If you want to do this, do it. I'm inclined to say random variables be damned. I'll be right there by your side, no matter what."

His skin tingled. In that moment, there was no one else but him and Hildie. "No matter what?" He met her gaze, eyebrows up and throat so tight he could barely speak. "You really mean that? Because—because I do."

She gave him a wobbly grin. "We called no take-backs, right? Well, yeah. I do, too."

CHAPTER 15

JACKSON WISNIEWSKI

Shady saw and smelled the change in Rex on Tuesday night. The dip of his head. The pinned-back ears. The sudden burst of dark, sharp anguish in his scent. They'd been resting in the evening shadows on the inner balcony lounges outside Charlie's bedroom suite. Now Rex leaped off and paced toward the far end of the balcony.

She caught up, half-trotting alongside him. "They have put Charlie under, have they not?"

Rex stress-yawned but kept moving. "Yes. His re-gen and augmentation treatments have begun. I cannot sense him, and he cannot sense me or my thoughts now. I am free to speak with Agent Chaten. I should alert Chief Klein."

"Tomorrow." Shady nuzzled his cheek and kept pace with him. "Tomorrow is time enough. You have worked all day. Commodore Clueless might want you interviewed tonight."

"I just want to get it over with."

"Not in this state. You will be a mess for days."

They reached the elevator doors on the far side of Rex and Charlie's living room, but Rex turned right. He headed past the empty unit where Charlie had set up a home gym. "I am likely to be a mess for days, anyway."

He could pace an entire circuit around the inner balcony—and in this mood he would keep at it, circling and circling until he was completely exhausted. She pushed herself in front of him, forced him to stop. "Rex. Please. Do not go into this interview already tired. It will be hard enough after you have rested."

He growled. "What makes you think I shall be able to rest?"

"Perhaps you will fret all night. But your body will be resting."

He looked away. "The dread is a form of pre-torture. I shall remember in spite of myself, and that will be extra torture."

"Then use this time to prepare yourself." Her idea formed as she spoke. "Were there not codes you had to learn? Puzzles to solve? Mazes to run?"

His ears clamped so tightly to his head she could barely discern them in his black fur. His hackles spiked straight out. "Yes. Many of them."

"Focus on those. Note them all down in a blank form. Collect all you can beforehand, so you have them ready to transmit when you see Agent Chaten."

He growled again. "I suppose that might waste less of her time. She will need to provide them to her boss."

"Push the bad memories aside as much as you can. Just create the report. Make it as detailed as possible. Focus on that. Can you quiet your mind enough to do that?"

He stress-yawned again. Licked his lips and panted hard. "I suppose I can try." His scent was crazy-wild with stress and fear and pain. He did one of the breathing patterns he'd learned from Charlie, and his scent moderated slightly. He allowed her to nudge him back toward the lounges.

He did not stop at the lounges, however. One of Charlie's french doors stood half-open for ventilation. He nudged it wider and went in. Less than a stride beyond it, he nosed open the door to Charlie's walk-in closet.

Ah. Understanding dawned. She followed him inside. Charlie didn't have too many things hanging in there. A few uniforms, including his dress blues. Other clothing: some casual slacks and shirts, as well as a couple of things that looked like formal wear. Lined up under them on a rack lay several pairs of Charlie's shoes.

Rex pawed one out of line, off its rack. Rolled it toward himself. He lay down on his belly, wrapped his forepaws around the toe, then thrust his nose deep inside.

Oh, good thought. She let her tongue loll. Humans' shoes and stockings smelled more strongly of them than most of their other garments, except maybe their underpants. Rex needed a good hit of Charlie-scent to help calm himself. He licked the inside of the shoe to release more of Charlie's scent. He breathed and licked and breathed and licked. The stress in his scent factors scaled back.

Remind him not to chew it up, Pam suggested through the link.

Shady wagged her tail. *I'll offer a caution if he seems to forget himself.*

Good thing it may have time to dry out before Charlie gets home and sticks his foot into a clammy wet shoe. That is NO fun. Her partner's amusement echoed through the link. *Until I learned how much scent means to you guys, I never understood this behavior.*

Shady's tongue lolled long. *Oh, there is nothing like a good shoe-chew, to release the scent. But Rex knows better.*

All the same, keep an eye on him. He's under a lot of stress. She hesitated. *If he just can't resist, make sure he chews them in pairs and carefully disposes of the evidence afterward.*

Plausible deniability. Got it. Shady wagged her tail harder, tongue lolling and heart filled with conspiratorial pleasure. *Thanks for the tip.*

EARLY ON WEDNESDAY MORNING, Rex sat in the corner of Interview A with his head bowed. He took deep, even, slow breaths and strove to center himself. He let Agent Chaten take as long as she liked to look through all the materials he'd just transferred to her HUD. Shady's idea had been a good one. If he could save himself even a few minutes of recalling his time with Col. Wisniewski while under examination by a spook—even if she was a Ranan spook—well, that worked for him just fine.

He'd curled up in the walk-in, with Shady dozing warm against his side, surrounded by Charlie's scent from his clothes and with a sacrificial pair of Charlie's shoes between his jaws. There, it had been a little easier to face his memories than it would be if he were doing it now. He'd exhaustively compiled codes, mapped out obstacle courses, and diagrammed sequences of actions he'd been expected to perform.

Now Chaten read and read. He watched her eyes twitch back and forth, focused in a middle-distance HUD stare.

His gut slowly relaxed. Maybe this would be enough. Maybe she wouldn't need to ask about the rest.

There was another spook in Observation A. He'd summarily evicted the OPD's sound tech, Samuels. Banished him from the premises and taken measures to make sure no one from OPD could record any aspect of the proceedings.

Once he'd heard Samuels' brusque dismissal, Rex had swallowed a growl and quietly taken steps to set up his own personal recording. *Screw them!* If he was going to be forced to relive all that abuse, he damn well meant to share the information with his colleague Lt. Patel without having to go through it all yet a *third* time. Patel was preparing the OPD's case against the Transmondian government. She would no doubt find it useful. The SDF could go suck lemons if they didn't like it.

All too soon, Chaten exhaled, sat back, blinked, and then refocused on Rex. "That was … quite exhaustive."

"I do not wish to spend any unnecessary time reliving the abuse I suffered at Col. Wisniewski's hands. It seemed reasonable to relay the information in a more organized form. I tried to be complete, and of course all of it is scrupulously accurate."

"'Of course'?" She quirked an eyebrow.

He laid his ears back with a soft growl. "For well or ill, XK9s cannot forget anything. It is how we were made."

"I want you to know that we honor the sacrifice you are making to impart this information."

Rex snorted, not really concerned that it might seem rude. "This is purely transactional, Agent Chaten. Commodore Cornwell controls classified technology that will allow XK9s to examine the forward section of the *Izgubil* by scent. He will allow us to utilize this technology if I give you all the information you require about Col. Wisniewski. Therefore, I shall tell you anything you ask on that subject. That is the deal. As for honor, I do not care how you or Cornwell feel about the sacrifice I make. I do it to obtain access to an otherwise-inaccessible crime scene. But let us be clear. I expect no less than for him to fully honor his end of the bargain."

She nodded. "Understood, Pack Leader. Understood, and I am authorized to say your offer is accepted. I do still have questions, though not as many as before."

Crap. He stress-yawned, and hoped his sudden queasiness would subside. "In that case, let us proceed." He activated his private recording.

"Tell me about your first encounter with Col. Wisniewski."

As if from a distance, he heard his vocalizer-voice describing the big indoor training arena where Ordovich delivered him. But his bred-for-perfection memory returned him to that first day with all the clarity of living through it.

As it had that day, a chill mist of dread pervaded his heart. Cringing horror curdled his stomach and sent icy prickles through his pelt. He smelled again the sour sawdust underfoot and the sharp, harsh reek of steely anticipation in Wisniewski's scent. Saw once again the cruel glint in those cold gray eyes, the light lancing down from skylights, and the grotesque mannequin wrapped in putrefying raw meat set up in the center.

"I did not yet realize that I would receive no sustenance except for the meat on that thing while I was working with

Wisniewski," Rex said. "If I wanted to eat, I would have to tear it off of the mannequin."

"Why did he do that? Did he ever say?" Chaten asked.

Rex laid back his ears. "I think he wanted to break down my inhibitions about actually harming a human. Not that any XK9 would ever confuse that abomination for a real human. Our inhibition against attacking humans had been carefully ingrained in all of us from birth, so it did not affect that, although Wisniewski's later actions inspired me to make one exception." He shook his head with a growl. "But by the end of that first week I was confused, bruised, and ravenous."

"'Bruised'?"

"Whenever Dr. Ordovich left us alone together, I would quietly explain to Col. Wisniewski that I hated him with all my being and would love to shred his body in a variety of violent, painful ways. I would describe these attacks in detail to him and keep making up more details until Dr. Ordovich came back."

"Why did you do that?"

"Wisniewski had pulled me out of the group that included my mate Shady. Commodore Cornwell might remember having met her." The deep, visceral hatred he'd felt against Wisniewski renewed in a hot rush. Rex's hackles prickled, but he swallowed a growl. "I did not wish to be separated from Shady."

"When you said those things to him, how did he respond?"

Rex showed all his teeth. "He responded in a highly satisfactory manner: he was terrified, although he tried not to show it. The first two times I did it, he complained to Dr. Ordovich. Ordovich gave me a beating each time, and after that I would have to recover for a day. The third time I did it, Wisniewski did not complain. Ordovich assumed I had learned my lesson."

"Why did he stop complaining?"

"I believe it was because the beatings delayed our progress by a day, each time. Perhaps he also perceived that the beatings would not deter me. Instead, he started bringing a firearm to our sessions."

"Did that make you stop threatening him?"

Rex shook his head, even though he now understood how much closer he might have been to death than he'd thought then. "No. In my state of mind at the time, I did not care if he shot me. But after that, we kept it between the two of us. When Ordovich was there, Wisniewski would make me run obstacle courses and attack the mannequin, but nothing more. After Ordovich stopped attending any part of my classes, Wisniewski began to teach me simple codes to solve and sequences of actions to perform."

"The earliest entries on your lists?"

"Yes."

"Tell me how things progressed from there."

"You see the lists. He added more sophisticated codes and demanded more and more speed each time I went through an obstacle course. I only had the meat on the mannequin to eat. Sometimes he'd give me all the water I needed, other times not."

"How long did this go on?"

"He, or sometimes his assistant, worked with me for five weeks, three days, four hours, and twenty-six minutes." Exhaustion sapped Rex, just remembering. Sensory memories gripped him anew: parched throat, aching legs, empty belly, or that revolting meat. And through it all, a soul-ache of despair that the demands would ever end.

"Two questions: what can you tell me about the assistant? And why did they stop working with you after that period of time?"

"The assistant was younger than Wisniewski, but just as relentless and demanding. He also carried a gun whenever he was around me. I overheard Wisniewski call him "Clint" one time, but I never learned a last name."

"Why do you think he carried a gun?"

Rex snarled with sour satisfaction and wagged his tail. "I believe Wisniewski had warned him to be careful, and of course I also threatened him."

"The same way you did with Wisniewski?"

"Yes. It scared him the same way, too." He pictured himself as he must have seemed to the men: huge, black, half-starved and snarling. Anyone would be frightened.

She nodded. "Do you think these were actual firearms, or trank pistols?"

"There is no confusing the two. They look and smell quite different. Both men carried firearms. I think they hoped it would deter me more effectively."

"Were they right?"

"Yes. I would have attacked them with little compunction, if they only had a trank pistol."

"So, you did care."

He growled. "Some, I suppose."

"What brought these interactions to an end?"

Rex was on his feet before he could think about it. He didn't *want* to think about it. Not *any* of it. Icy prickles lanced across his skin, turned his gut leaden. He paced three circuits around the room, panting.

Chaten sat quietly, her case pad in her lap.

At the end of the third circuit, Rex licked his lips, stress-yawned, stretched, and then sat. His throat ached and his stomach clenched, but maybe this would satisfy her. "It ended because I tried to kill Wisniewski."

"I'm surprised he didn't kill *you* at that point."

"I feel certain he would have liked to." Rex snarled. Disgust filled his mouth with sour bile and roiled his gut with nausea. "But I was worth a lot of money. I am certain he did not wish to pay millions of novi or risk his organization's relationship with the XK9 project for the joy of killing one insubordinate dog."

"Why did you try to kill him? You had gone all those weeks. What changed?"

Rex rose to his feet again, then stopped. Sat. Looked away from her. His heart labored for each beat. His lungs struggled for each breath. His whole being shrank away from this telling. "Everything."

She waited.

Just get this finished. "Each night after the first week, they kept me in a bare concrete cell. By the third week they'd rigged a kind of chain-link corridor between my cell and that day's training area. They used robots with prods to force me out of my cell and down the corridor." Chain link fencing and bare concrete, or even the smells of such a combination, had made his hackles twitch and his skin crawl ever since. "I thought of them as torture arenas."

She consulted her case pad. "In your notes you described the place with the sawdust floor and the meat-mannequin, the modular obstacle course area, and the data-board with the lights and switches and buttons. Are those the places you mean?"

"Yes. Those were the three places they always took me. But on that last day, they took me someplace much worse."

"Tell me about that."

Rex couldn't get comfortable. He stood. He sat. He stood again and paced another circuit around the room, heart pounding. His tongue hung long and dry. Part of the agreed-upon room setup included a large bowl of water. He drank it dry. *Bad move, probably.* Now his gut hung heavy. But he backed away from it again and sat. "It was another concrete cell. Bigger this time, with a drain hole in the center. No windows. It reeked of terror and blood and human waste, although it appeared to have recently been hosed down. And in the corner stood a naked man in shackles."

Chaten drew in a breath. "Okay, I need some clarification. When you say the place 'reeked of terror,' are you—"

"I am speaking of scent factor residue. Humans exude different scents when they experience strong emotions. This tendency appears to be universal. No matter what the person's background, the same scents reflect the same emotions. This room was saturated with the human scent factor that reflects terror. As in, great and overwhelming fear. There were other stress-related scents, too, and there were a variety of associated scent profiles—that is, more than one human had been terrified in that place. But the dominant scent factor was that of terror."

"Oh." She swallowed, her own scent factors by now shot through with a fair level of dark, sharp horror and pungent disgust. "Not a metaphor. Good to know."

"No, not a metaphor. I make it a point to be forensically accurate."

"Tell me about the man in the new room."

"Pale skin. Covered with bruises and scrapes. He appeared to have suffered several beatings, because the scabs were in various states of healing, and the bruises were different colors. Some were purple or blue, but others were that grayish-brown color a human might see as some variation on either green or red. His lack of clothing made it easy to see them."

"Describe him."

"He was tall, possibly 1.8 or 1.9 meters, but somewhat emaciated. It looked as if they had not been feeding him any better than they had been feeding me, but maybe he had been their captive longer. I would hazard a guess that his hair was what humans call 'red,' although it looks kind of grayish brown to dogs. It had a fuzzy, curly appearance, but what you might call a fine texture. His eyes were blue. High cheekbones. Pale eyebrows. Bushy beard."

"That is a lot of detail." Nose-itching dread seeped into her scent.

"Highly superior autobiographical memory."

"Our forensic artists would love working with you." She shook her head, frowning. "And he was in shackles?"

"Wrists and ankles, although the two sets of shackles were not connected by a chain as I have sometimes seen done to prisoners. He also was not chained to anything in the room, such as a wall or a loop in the floor. When the door opened to let me in, he said nothing, but his fear-scent ballooned immediately. He shuffled as fast as he could to the farthest reach of the back corner and tried to wedge himself into it, as far away from me as he could get. I did not blame him. I probably looked terrifying. Even though I was a puppy, I was bigger than a normal dog by then."

Her frown deepened. She turned her regard to the case pad, and scrolled through his documents. "How long ago was this, again? How old were you?"

"I was Col. Wisniewski's unwilling captive last January and early February. I had turned six in November."

"And you're now seven."

"Yes."

She scowled at the case pad, then looked up, but carefully avoided meeting his gaze. "So, the human prisoner retreated to the back corner. What happened then?"

"Col. Wisniewski's voice came out of a speaker in the ceiling. He said, 'There! You see, Stubbs? I was—'"

"*Stubbs?*" Chaten stared at him, for once forgetting protocol. Her sharp anguish overwhelmed other odors in the room. "Wisniewski addressed him as *Stubbs?*"

Rex stress-yawned. "You knew him."

"I—" She bowed her head. Bitter certainty filled her scent. "Yes. I think I may have."

"I am sorry for your loss."

A new burst of dark, sharp anguish suffused her personal bouquet. She drew herself upright, bit her lip. "What happened?"

Rex stress-yawned again. "As I said, Wisniewski's voice came through the speaker in the ceiling. He said, 'You see, Stubbs? I was not bluffing. Rex, rip his throat out!'"

"So … You did?"

Rex snorted. "Of course not. I told the bastard to come in there and make me. That was the last straw. I was done with Wisniewski. I did indeed wish to rip out a throat, but I had no incentive to kill my fellow sufferer."

"Did he come down?"

"Yes. Unfortunately, he anticipated or saw on surveillance that I had set myself up at the door to attack him. He and his assistant Clint came in together like trained STAT officers. Clint tranked me, but before I passed out, I saw Wisniewski shoot Stubbs twice, in the head and the heart. Even after the trank wore off, my nose was still full of the smell of his death."

CHAPTER 16

TAKING CARE OF BUSINESS

Shady stepped into the Morgue Annex on Wednesday morning with Pam at her side. They confronted a scene odd enough to distract her momentarily from worrying about the ordeal Rex was probably enduring.

Dr. Chinbat the Medical Examiner stood with two of her techs on one side of an autopsy table. On the other side stood three strangers, similarly garbed in lab coats and face masks. Between them on the table lay a tray covered with a layer of what looked like fine-grained gray gravel.

A range of scent profiles and emotion-driven scent factors hit Shady all at once. She sorted through them. Dr. Chinbat and her techs had presented a tray of what Shady recognized as bone fragments to the newcomers. From their sour mid-range smells, the newcomers felt daunted, but determined.

"We believe this is most of the cranium," Chinbat said. "DNA-matched. Every fragment is from the same individual. Can you help us?"

The stranger in the middle rubbed the back of his neck and stared at the bone fragments. "This will certainly test the limits of our aggregation-analysis equipment. Not to mention my graduate students. How much of a reconstruction do you need?"

"If you could give us a minimum-40% reconstruction of the facial area, we can extrapolate a fairly accurate phenotype, based on the DNA," Chinbat said. "More is better, of course. We're still seeking resources and an artist or two for the portrait reconstructions, to finish the job."

"Mm, good luck with that. We're acquainted with your GR Unit's reputation." The lead stranger shook his head. "Need C.O.D. on any?"

"We're reasonably certain we know when and how they died." Chinbat's tone was dry as the bone dust on the tray. "Of course, if you notice anything unusual, please flag it."

He nodded. "So. Are they all like this?"

"We have ten like this. Thirteen others have some larger fragments."

Shady curled her lip. *And about twenty-seven more are still being processed. With no end to the 'infernal plyboard' in sight.*

Lucky for us, bone doesn't rot like soft tissue. Pam quirked an eyebrow. *I'm guessing these are the forensic anthropologists from Green Mountain U.*

Shady lolled her tongue. *Naw, she shows her bone fragments to all the strangers who walk in.*

Smartass. Pam huffed a little laugh. *C'mon. Chinbat looks busy. Let's see where Adeyeme wants us today.*

Turned out she wanted them back in the evidence cavern, sniffing away at the as-yet-uninspected pallets in additional rows they'd identified as the probable remains of belowdecks areas. No surprise there. Shady took her time with a long, full-body avoidance-stretch and a jaw-cracking stress-yawn, before she trailed Pam into the ready-room. *This feels like busywork.*

Pam shook her head and began helping Shady into her gear. *It's not busywork. We have to find them and retrieve their remains. That'll make it possible for Chinbat to autopsy or at least analyze what's left of them and extract the cranial bones. The Green Mountain people can then do their part. And if our team can find a good portrait-reconstruction artist, we probably can make recognizable likenesses.*

Maybe at the end of all this, some of them can be identified and returned to their families.

That sounded like busywork to Shady. More important, it wasn't likely to solve the case. She lifted one forepaw after the other so Pam could slide on containment booties, but growled. *They're mostly bad guys. Why do they even need to be identified? This is a waste of time. We should be working on the case!*

We ARE working on the case, just not the part you want. Pam blew out an exasperated breath. *Yeah, it probably does seem like a waste of time to someone reared and trained in Transmondia.* She pulled on Shady's third bootie.

What's that supposed to mean?

Pam finished the fourth bootie, then straightened. *Transmondians don't value and respect individuals' lives the way Ranans do.*

Shady cocked one ear toward her but swept the other ear back. *That sounds like propaganda to me.*

Believe it. Pam scowled. *The dead people here—nobody deserves to die without warning in the middle of living their life. Not even if they were doing bad things. Alive, they could have changed. Could've done something better. Could perhaps have told us things. Now that they're dead, they can't do anything. Their chances were all taken away from them.*

Shady resisted this logic. Deep dubiousness tightened her gut and curled her lip. *That's pretty idealistic, coming from a cop.*

And you don't value idealism? Pam gave her a hard look. *You, a newly-recognized sapient being? Your sapient nature was denied by the Transmondians, because they were being expedient and making money. If Ranans weren't idealists, where would you be?*

Shady looked away.

Exactly. Just remember, even Ranan cops are idealistic, compared to most of the human and ozzirikkian universe. We actually do believe—well, most of us want to believe—that all the aspirational stuff in our Constitution about empowering everyone to realize their full potential is not only a good idea, but it actually might be possible.

Ranans are very strange people. You know that, don't you? Shady flicked her ears.

Pam laughed. *Yes.*

Okay. As long as we're clear on that, I guess we'd better go finish with as many of the belowdecks pallets as we can, so we can get back to fighting crime. Shady stress-yawned again. *I really want to nail the bastards who did this.*

No argument there. Pam followed her toward the pallets.

"FOUR OR FIVE DAYS, I'm afraid." Hildie pulled on the reflective coverall over her Safety Services jumpsuit, then snugged the hook-and-loop fasteners tight. "I'm back on the roster till then." It was Wednesday morning. Charlie's re-gen would end Saturday or Sunday.

Theresa floated beside her in the ERT Base's locker compartment. "That's a long re-gen."

"Well, they have a whole arm to propagate from the bicep down. It's a complex limb structure. And after the muscle sheath breakdown from the last procedure, they added another treatment to stabilize it better." She frowned. The queasiness in her gut didn't only stem from normal body-fluid rebalancing in micrograv.

"That special-ops thing you mentioned?"

Hildie sighed. "We probably shouldn't talk about it like that, but yeah."

"You seem worried." Theresa gave her a sharp look.

"Any medical procedure carries risks." Hildie didn't say *and so does any new relationship* out loud. But concerns over all of the choices she and Charlie had made in the past few days tightened her chest and put her nerves on edge.

"We've barely talked about Charlie himself. Is he still the same guy?"

"No. Well, I mean, he's still Charlie." *Still gorgeous, despite the scars. Still melts me into a puddle of goo with those eyes. And if I'd known about those kisses back then* — maybe her self-control would've cracked years ago. *But now I have a second chance!* Little bubbles of pleasure lightened her heart. She smiled, but then sobered. "He's had a rough time of it, these last few years. They've left their marks on him. He's not quite as quick to laugh as you probably remember him."

The locker compartment's hatch dilated. Captain LaRochelle poked his head and shoulders through, scowling. "I need a word with you, Sergeant."

Theresa's back was toward the hatch. She wrinkled her nose with disgust, then gave Hildie a look of rueful sympathy.

Hildie turned a practiced expression of bland neutrality toward the Captain. "I'll be right out, sir." The last thing she wanted was to be trapped in this narrow space with LaRock. Thank goodness Theresa was here.

She grabbed her med-pack and strapped it to her waist above her utility belt. Then she and her friend pushed off from hand-holds to float themselves out. Theresa's exit through the hatch blocked their supervisor long enough for Hildie to escape into the common area.

LaRochelle's frown deepened. "My office, Sergeant."

She activated microjets located on the epaulettes of her coveralls and the sides of her utility belt to follow him.

His office didn't offer much more elbow room than the lockers, but two walls consisted mostly of windows that overlooked the ERT Base he commanded. They'd be in full view. The other two walls held racks of monitors and gauges from which he could oversee telemetry, life-support readouts, activities within the rescue runners, and varied other functions. The only place with similar monitoring capacity was Topside Dispatch.

He pulled himself to a screen with the scheduling display opened on it. Harsh light accented his scowl and the scraggly texture of his goatee. "Setting aside questions about the legitimacy of this Boyfriend of Record, what makes you think you're gonna need that much time off, after he gets out of re-gen?"

She swallowed her anger and met his eyes with what she hoped he'd read as firm boundary-setting. "I'm following the guidelines the head physician gave us."

He eyed her balefully from beneath a furrowed brow. "Corona Family has no resources to help?"

It was a ridiculous question, and seriously out of line. She and Charlie had every right to use the time Dr. Zuni'd prescribed. Especially after such a long truncation of their relationship, they needed that time to see if they were still as good a fit as they hoped. Hildie met LaRock's gaze without flinching. Surely her frosty silence would speak for itself.

"Well, Sergeant?"

She grimaced. *Then again, maybe it won't.* "Do I truly need to spell out for you how inappropriate that question is?" Her pulse pounded in her ears.

His mouth twisted with disgust. "Seriously, Sergeant? Perhaps I ought to ask how inappropriate it is for you to take up with such a recent patient? Or how inappropriate it is for you to rush headlong into such a serious commitment?"

She clenched her hands on the anchor-points she'd used to stabilize her position, and breathed through blinding fury. "The Emergency Family Leave I have requested is fully within my rights. You have my required notification." She pulsed jets to turn and leave.

"Sergeant." His hand on her arm stopped her.

Her pulse hammered in her ears. "Release me, sir."

His grip didn't slacken. "If you would just listen to *reason*—"

"Let *go* of me." Alarmed now, she tried to pull away.

"Stop that!" His grip tightened. "Hear me out!"

"No! No! Let go!" She raised her voice and struggled with more force.

He scowled. "Stop making a scene."

"*I'm* making a scene? *Let go of me!*" She planted a boot against his ribs and pushed off. This time she broke free, fired jets, and catapulted out into the commons. She burned retros to halt herself by the opposite bulkhead, then turned and scowled back at him.

He glared at her through his office's hatch. "You're making a mistake."

"Maybe. But it's *my right* to make it."

He blew out a hard, irritated breath. "Here's hoping you don't pay too dearly."

She clenched her fists, then pushed away from the wall. Aimed her trajectory for the *Triumph*'s open hatch, fuming. *Oh, I'll pay. You'll make sure of it, you slimy bastard.* She ground her teeth.

"Hils, you okay?" her partner Eli wisely didn't try to touch her, but his pinched face and angry eyes gave ample clues to his mood.

She grimaced. "Let's get to work."

REX TOOK ONLY one step into the war room on Thursday morning before his com dinged. *Chief Klein.* He halted, uneasy. He'd finished with Agent Chaten yesterday—at least he hoped so. He'd been looking forward to *finally* getting a chance to do his important *regular* work today. "Rex here."

"Rest easy. Agent Chaten hasn't come back with a dozen more long-form questions." Even without scent factors, Rex didn't miss the amusement in the Chief's voice.

The Chief couldn't see him, so he put his ears down and curled a lip. "I am glad to hear it. But in that case, to what do I owe this call?"

"Did you wonder how you and the rest of the Pack were going to maneuver in microgravity when they open up your new crime scene?"

"Actually, yes." Each time he thought about the new access

he'd so painfully won for them, cold apprehension swept through him. The last time he'd been in micrograv, he'd almost killed Charlie.

"I hope you'll agree that untrained XK9s in micrograv don't mix with nearby humans—much less evidence-handling protocols."

Rex's gut relaxed. "As I have too many reasons to remember. I am glad you also see it that way."

"Starting at 10:00 today a group of engineer-designers from Station Polytechnic will arrive to measure each of you for micrograv harnesses. This means you'll need to send us two Pack members at a time this morning, starting then. I hope you can rotate them off of other duties and spare them for about half an hour each."

"I can arrange that." Klein couldn't see it, but Rex cocked his head anyway. Hope warmed him. His pulse kicked up to a faster tempo. "I did not know anyone made micrograv harnesses for dogs."

"No one does. Not yet, anyway. Dr. Emily Rashidi and her team from Station Polytechnic plan to collaborate with The Learned Shik'ki-dok'tuum of Wheel Five's Institutes of Ascended Contemplation. It's a parallel institution to S-Poly. We humans have been creating steerable micrograv suits, packs, and sleds for centuries. Ozzirikkians have been doing the same for fur-clad beings, for at least that long. Between all the geniuses and the Learned Minds, I bet they'll come up with something that works for you."

Electric excitement tingled through him. Rex wagged his tail. *A whole new dimension to conquer! And we'll be the first space dogs who can actually maneuver there!* "I shall look forward to seeing how this project unfolds."

CHAPTER 17

NEW HORIZONS AND CHALLENGES

Shady's HUD dinged, just before lunch break on Friday. She lifted her mask-shrouded nose from the pallet she'd been searching and discovered a new deposit record. She blinked. Deposit? Well, the Department *had* set every XK9 up with a Borough Bank account for the food stipend. She looked more thoroughly. That seemed like … a lot of money. But really, what did she know about money, and how much was "a lot"?

Money? Pam straightened, gave her a curious look from over her own mask.

Shady studied the form. "Detective Level One," it said in the "rank" box under her name. *I think I just got paid a salary for the first time.*

Seriously? That's awesome! Pam's scent factors suffused with sweet delight. *You realize what this means?*

Shady met her gaze. *It means I am a person.*

This means you're officially considered a real, genuinely sapient, Ranan citizen. A citizen! Rising excitement bubbled up. *Oh, Shady! No more of that 'forensic equipment' nonsense! This is so totally smooth! This is huge!*

All over the evidence cavern, scent factors shifted and brightened, although no one spoke. Suddenly a great many bootie-muffled feet turned toward the ready-room.

It's lunchtime. Let's go. Pam turned that direction too.

Shady hung back. *It'll be wild in the ready-room for the next ten minutes. Meanwhile, I have a question.*

Okay. Pam hesitated, looked back.

What is 'back pay'?

Pam's eyes widened. *That's what they owe you from previous pay periods.*

Oh. That explains it, I suppose. The 'back pay' doesn't give dates. There's a smaller amount in the 'current period' section.

Pam's brows puckered in a frown. *Pay periods run roughly two weeks. You've been here on Rana more than two months. Um ... May I ask?*

Shady wagged her tail. *Thank you for asking, and not demanding.*

Her scent factors took on a musky, rueful tinge. *I'm trying to adjust my attitude.*

I appreciate the effort. She shared the file.

Pam went still. She stared into the middle distance. Her eyes twitched. It was a typical reading-on-one's-HUD motion, but her gaze seemed to be tracking back and forth over the same area, not moving on.

Pam?

Shady couldn't read much clarity in her partner's clashing scent factors, beyond the icy muddle that bespoke astonishment and confusion.

Pam?

Pam drew in a soft breath.

Pam? Are you okay?

Your back pay added up to a lot. She blinked, stared some more, then made eye contact with Shady. *If they paid all the others that much, too ... Where did that money come from?*

Shady flicked her ears. *They did stop paying the Transmondians for our purchase.*

Okay, that would help explain it. Pam nodded slowly. *I'm not sure how your numbers compare to whatever the purchase payments were, but the Borough did commit fifteen million novi to purchasing the whole Pack.*

Which they now are not *paying, because: sapient trafficking.* Shady cocked her head at Pam. *How much is your monthly rent?*

What? Wait. Shady, if you're —

I owe you and Balchu back rent, don't I?

Pam set a fist on each hip and scowled at her. *No. You don't owe us rent. Not for that damned hard floor you always complained about.*

I know you don't have much money.

Pam shook her head. *Let's discuss this later, after you've gotten some good, solid financial advice. However, I would accept it if you wanted to buy me lunch.*

Lunch? I could have lunch? Always before, everyone had always said dogs didn't need lunch. It had been a source of many complaints among the Pack.

Pam chuckled. *You're a citizen with your own, independent means, now. You can have five lunches a day, if you want to pay for them — and risk getting fat.*

Lunch! She could have lunch! Like a real person! Shady couldn't resist doing a little dance.

Oh, Shady. Sharp sadness filled Pam's scent. Her eyes brimmed with sudden tears. *I never realized it was so important to you. And of course you're a real person! You've always been a real person! And you've always deserved lunch. I just —*

It's okay. Shady's tail fanned faster, though she wished her mouth was free to lick away Pam's tears. *It's all right. Will you please allow this real person to buy you and Balchu a real lunch at LEO's?*

NEAR CHARLIE, a voice counted in a low, steady tone. "Twenty-seven. Twenty-eight. Twenty-nine ...." A beloved voice. A voice he'd know anywhere. The all-over agony of re-gen-emergence syndrome wracked his body, but he clung to the sound of her voice.

Rex's excited greeting burst into his mind. The brain link delivered a strong surge of love, delight, and eager anticipation.

Throat still like burning sandpaper, Charlie struggled to meet the flood of input.

"Thirty-four. Thirty-five. Thirty-six," Hildie counted, steady as a metronome.

"Uh-oh. I have anomalous readings." Zuni's voice went tense. "This looks like ... Charlie, can you raise a finger if your dog is distracting you?" They both knew Charlie couldn't talk yet.

Charlie's finger ached from the effort to move it.

"Good. Saw that!" The smile in Zuni's voice came through clear and heartening.

Softly, he wished into the link.

Sorry! Rex muted his reaction, although it still came across as thunderous. *I really missed you. I mean, really a lot, this time. I just suddenly was so overjoyed—Did I hurt you?*

Charlie labored to create mental words. *Worry Zuni.*

Rex's presence within the link receded more. *It's hard to be patient. I'm so, SO very pleased you're back!*

He couldn't smile. Still couldn't speak, much less ask *okay, what's happened?* But he could radiate love in Rex's general direction. It must have been enough. Rex backed off a little more, then bathed him in tender delight.

"Okay that's better," Zuni said, somewhere far away.

"Forty-two. Forty-three. Forty-four . . ." Hildie kept up her steady count.

He still couldn't talk. But now his eyes opened.

Hildie sat by his bed, robed and gowned like the others. He could only see her hazel eyes and small glimpses of her beautiful brown face. But she held his hand, and he'd swear he saw love in her eyes. "Forty-eight. Forty-nine. Fifty. Welcome back."

He gazed up at her, amazed. *How is she here?* It was only ever Zuni and the nurses when he woke up from re-gen all the other times.

A new nurse arrived to apply the minty gel that would soothe his burning throat. He relaxed as best he could while they removed the ventilator.

He kept his gaze on Hildie. "Thank you," he whispered. It was the best voice he could manage.

She leaned in, smiling, to bestow a gentle kiss through her surgical mask. "You don't have to thank me."

"I do," he whispered back. "You're here. Like … a miracle."

She'd bent close to kiss him, stayed close to hear. Now she whispered back, "I have special pull with your doctor. And there's no place I'd rather be."

"It's Saturday," Dr. Zuni said. "Your procedure looks to be all go-lights and open spacelanes, so far. I'm very pleased. We're going to give you a few hours' normal sleep, now. We'll start physical therapy once you're rested."

"Can hardly … wait," he whispered. New drugs filtered in. Neural pain-blockers lulled his aches. Hildie's hand still clasped his. He held onto it until he faded completely out.

EVERYTHING HURT TOO much to stay asleep. Charlie yawned. He arched his aching back in a stretch. His right arm twitched, swung out harder and faster than he expected.

Crash!

The tray table next to his bed careened into a row of monitors. Shrill *beep-beep- beep-beeps* erupted in chorus.

He made a reflexive grab with his left—*Oh, damfuckinshit-shit-SHIT!* Sharp new pain lanced his left arm like a drill to the marrow. It echoed through him, so harsh that for a moment he couldn't see. Somehow, he'd flipped onto his right side, and slammed his chest and face into the raised bed rail. His left arm ached like a mofo. His chest and face stung.

Charlie froze. No more reactions, no more disasters. Holy crap, what just happened?

Woah! Are you all right? Rex demanded through the link. *What happened?*

Not sure. Charlie stayed rigid, not daring to move.

"Charlie!" Hildie's worried face swam into view. "What happened?" behind her, monitors beeped and shrieked and blinked. "Are you all right?"

Is there an echo in there? Rex asked.

I don't know. "I don't know," he answered aloud through clenched teeth. His voice rasped, hoarse with tension. *Mm, I guess there is.*

Hildie reached out, touched his IV, then gave a little gasp when her fingers brushed his skin. "You're absolutely rigid."

"Scared to move." Hard to talk or breathe, lodged against the rail like this.

"Try just relaxing your muscles where you are," Hildie suggested. "Don't try to move yet."

At the edge of his vision, he caught a glimpse of Nanda. His nurse spared a quick glance at him, then darted out of view. One by one, the damned beeping monitors stilled, until blessed silence reigned.

"Thank you," Charlie rasped.

"RAMoD, roll him onto his back," Nanda directed. "Careful —be gentle."

Soft whine of treads. Hydraulics whirred. Grippers on the Robotic Assisted Mobility Device's hinged metal arms clasped his torso cast—*aw, damn, I have a torso cast again*— then rolled him slowly onto his back. Pain wracked his muscles from long disuse and new movement, a lingering effect from multiple days of re-gen. But his breath came easier.

"Thank you." Charlie's jaws ached from clenching them. "What happened?"

"You're my first augmented patient, so I wasn't sure what to expect," Nanda said. "I apologize. It appears that your new reflexes need some fine-tuning."

"You think?" He still didn't dare try to move.

"I know it's got to be unnerving. The physical therapist is on her way. She's going to help you learn how to control those fast new reflexes. Meanwhile, please concentrate on your breathing. We're gonna go over your body, part by part, and try to get you unlocked."

He'd clenched every muscle. Now he wasn't sure which parts were safe to relax.

"Can you feel your toes?" Nanda asked. His voice lapsed into the calm, tranquil tones of a negotiator trying to calm an irrational subject. "I'd like you to take a deep, slow breath and relax your toes."

Charlie grimaced. *Is that what I'm reduced to? An irrational subject?*

Not you, but possibly your body, for the moment, Rex replied. *It feels as if your new reflexes are faster than your ability to control them, but you've done controlled breathing for a long time. Start there. Focus on Nanda's voice. You'll be okay.*

Hildie held his right hand, the one with the IV, in hers. With her other hand, she gently stroked his arm, in time with Nanda's words. Just looking at her calmed and centered him.

Maybe it would be safe to relax his toes ....

CHAPTER 18

SEMI-SUPERCOPS

C harlie's right shoulder ached. He scowled, jaws clenched, and intensified his focus. His hand made another sketchy circle in the air. "Twenty." *Last of this set. And last set for now.* He sighed, rolled the shoulder to loosen it, then shook out his arm and hand. *Ugh!* Not only were they hard to do, they were boring. Thank goodness they'd removed the IV before his session with the physical therapist.

Irritation snarled in his mind and heart, dammed up for now by determined control. But the fear that he'd made a horrible mistake seeped in like mist to chill him.

"I think you're doing better," Hildie said. That looked smoother."

Charlie sagged back against the elevated head of his hospital bed. A knot of misgivings tightened in his chest. "If you say so."

She chuckled. "Yes. I do say so. You always were a pessimist. But the Medicine Goddess has hereby proclaimed that you're doing better, so get with the program."

"Well, then, it's settled." He offered her a rueful smile. It had been a rough re-entry from his re-gen this time. He'd started working on retraining his reflexes last night. Today might be going a *little* better. But it was almost time for Sunday supper and he was still working on the damned arm-circles and dice drills.

"Remember when we worried that this treatment might make you short-tempered?" Hildie's grin grew wider. "Well, I guess you've proved *that* didn't happen. You'd have been all bent out of shape already, if you weren't your usual, patient self."

"Didn't happen *yet*, anyway." His irritation persisted like an itch he couldn't reach, and that knot of worry in his chest tightened. Dr. Zuni had said the metabolic changes from his augmentation procedure might continue for months. And Rex's friend Shiv hadn't said anything about uncontrollable reflexes. Had that been a problem for him? Or was Charlie just an extra-klutzy patient?

You can ask him yourself, Rex said through the link. *He and I are headed your way.*

"Oh. Rex just told me he and Shiv are on their way over here."

Alarm widened her eyes. "Here? *Now?* I'm a mess!" She leaped up, then rushed over to the "family member" corner of his room.

She grabbed up a hairbrush, ripped the elastic tie from her long black ponytail, then bent to the task of teasing out the tangles. "My hair is a haystack, and my scrubs—" She paused to sniff an armpit, then grimaced. "How long do I have?"

He eyed her curvaceous, intent form, angled toward the mirror, and suppressed the urge to suggest she could stand there and display her magnificent ass for as long as she liked. "I'll check." *Rex? ETA? Hildie tells me she looks a mess.*

How long does she need?

Can I tell her twenty minutes?

Seems reasonable.

Thanks. "Twenty minutes," he called to Hildie.

She huffed out a breath. "I can take a shower!" She darted

into the bathroom, shedding scrubs as she went. This offered a brief but exhilarating glimpse before the door thumped shut.

What just happened? Rex asked. *All of a sudden, you're happy.*

Charlie's frustration flowed away. His tight gut relaxed some. *An absolutely amazing Medicine Goddess loves me.*

Who, Hildie? Yes. I told you that already.

Charlie eyed the closed bathroom door. *I've started to think you might be right.* Beyond the door, the shower hissed.

Scent factors do not lie.

So I'm told. Deep, joyous contentment filled him. *And I believe.*

By the time Rex updated him that he and Shiv were entering the hospital, Hildie had showered, dressed in fresh clothing, shoved a clip into her hair, and proclaimed herself "fit to be seen."

"I've been seeing you all along," Charlie said. "And you do look fine."

She laughed. "I kinda got smelly and scraggly, though. I know you understand, and you'll cut me some slack. For which I thank you."

"Hils." He managed to catch her slender brown hand without throwing himself on the floor or crushing her bones. *Maybe the stupid arm circles are working?* "Look, I get it. Shiv's almost a stranger, and he's certainly 'company coming.' But what you've done for me—all of this—I don't want to minimize it."

She bit her lip, then leaned forward. Slid her hand underneath his shoulder. He wrapped his free arm around her and gave himself fully to a deep, lingering kiss.

Is it safe to come in? Rex apparently hadn't had much trouble interpreting emotions through the link.

One more minute? Charlie stole just a little more time, then ended the kiss with a sigh. "They're here."

She pulled back. "Guys, it's safe to come in now."

Perhaps it was Charlie's low perspective from the bed, but Lead Special Agent Shiva Shimon was damned tall. Even on a late Sunday afternoon, he arrived dressed in impeccable SBI dark blue. Hildie probably felt much more at ease for having cleaned up some. But Shiv's pale, rectangular face relaxed into a delighted smile as soon as he entered. "So! You went and did it —you got the augmentations. How do you feel?"

Charlie grimaced. "Like I just came out of re-gen. Still working on reflex control."

"Shove over, Shiv." Rex pushed through like an enormous black arrow with a one-track mind. Hildie wisely pulled back, too. Rex made it to the bed in a single stride, then thrust his snout under Charlie's covers.

Charlie flinched at the first freezing contact. "Oh! Yikes! Your nose hasn't gotten any warmer since last time!"

As he had when Charlie'd come out of re-gen two weeks ago, and again when they'd amputated his arm last week, Rex proceeded to give him a complete, relentless, forensic-level sniff-over.

Hildie and Shiv greeted each other and settled into chairs. They watched without comment as Charlie twitched, jumped, and gasped through Rex's examination. At last, the big dog stepped back.

"So. What's the verdict?" Charlie spoke aloud for the other humans' benefit. Had Rex left a single square centimeter of him un-sniffed?

Rex eyed him, head cocked. "Well, that is interesting."

"What? Do I still smell like myself?"

"Yes … And no." Rex's furry black triangular ears canted backward and forward, a signal that he was making compar-isons of some sort. He licked his lips, then whirled to shove his nose under Shiv's jacket.

"Woah!" The SBI agent flinched but stayed put. He moved his arm so Rex's head could push farther under his jacket.

"He has no sense of personal space, does he?" Hildie asked.

Charlie sighed. "Oh, he's aware of the concept. Just doesn't let it get in his way when he wants to study a scent." He grinned at Shiv. "I see you've been working with him long enough to speak 'dog.'"

"Working with the Pack, you get used to new paradigms."

Rex withdrew his nose from Shiv's ribs, then sat where he could make eye contact with all three humans. "I just learned something. The augmentations have their own scent signature, and I can now detect it. I suspected it before. Charlie, you have allowed me to be certain."

"You're welcome."

"You can tell from a scent signature variable that someone's been augmented?" Shiv asked. "That could be helpful."

Hildie nodded. "It makes sense. There's a metabolic change."

"It is a subtle variation, so I was not sure until now." Rex flicked his ears. "Comparing Charlie's original scent profile with the one he has now—checking the variable with you, Shiv, and remembering the agent last week—I need to have the whole Pack come here and smell this."

Charlie caught Rex's gaze. *Oh, the hospital staff will love that. A parade of nine other XK9s in and out? But it'll be nice to see them.*

Rex wagged his tail. "Hypothetically, we could predict it. But until now I have not had a large enough pool of augmented individuals to compare and isolate the common variables. This could be very useful."

"Especially if you encounter more Transmondian agents." Shiv frowned. "Add a report about this to the case book, but you might want to hold off on the comparisons until Charlie's well enough to come to work."

Charlie gave Rex a worried look. "I fear it'll be *when* you encounter more. Chief Klein definitely needs that report, too."

"Agreed." Rex yawned, then rested his chin on Charlie's bed near the end of the bed rail. This placed his nose right next to Charlie's leg. *Even with the new element, your scent makes me happy.*

It's good to see you, too. Warm joy buoyed Charlie's heart.

Shiv sat forward in his chair to make eye contact with Charlie. "Now that you're out of re-gen, I thought you might have more questions."

"Mm. Mostly about controlling my erratic reflexes."

"I apologize—I forgot about that." Shiv shook his head. "Should've warned you."

"My physical therapist has me doing arm circles and breathing exercises."

Shiv's wry expression summed up Charlie's opinion well. "Yeah, those are supposed to help, and I guess they do. Eventually, you'll figure it out." He hesitated. Gave Charlie a considering look, then stood and approached the bed. "You said your martial art is karate, right?"

"Yes." *Though by now I may have to start over with the basics.* Every Police Academy cadet on Rana Station chose a martial art. Karate had seemed the most intuitive for Charlie. Except when hospitalized, he'd practiced it ever since. It had helped keep him sane, especiallly during his months with the GR Unit.

"Okay. Remember when I asked you if you'd ever dreamed about being a superhero when you were a kid, and we realized we both wanted to be SuperCop when we grew up?"

Charlie laughed, but with an inward squirm. "I was embarrassed to admit that at first."

"Yeah, me too. But now … " Shiv grinned, then took a knee to place himself on Charlie's level. "Humor me for a minute. I know you've only got one arm free, but I'm gonna throw a few gentle punches. I want you to block me."

Hildie frowned. "*Punches?*"

Charlie pushed himself as far upright in the bed as he could, then raised his arm into as close to a classic opening block position as he was able. "Open-hand?"

Shiv nodded. "Whatever is comfortable. Here we go." He started with a rather slow, gentle downward chop. Charlie blocked him without even thinking. *Woah!*

Shiv aimed another strike, faster this time.

Charlie blocked him again. *Yes!* Another, faster. Charlie blocked him. *Oh, yeah!*

Faster still, Shiv chopped. Block. Strike. Block. Strike-block-strike-block-strikeblockstrikeblockstrikeblock till their arms were a blur and their breath came hard and it took all their concentration. Rising delight lifted Charlie up, strengthened and empowered him.

But then he faltered, pulse thundering. Barely managed to block.

Shiv slowed down but kept coming.

A few strikes and blocks later, Charlie faltered again but again rallied. Fatigue built in his arm and ached in his shoulder muscles, but it couldn't dent his euphoria.

A little slower strike from Shiv.

Charlie blocked. *Yes!* Another. Charlie blocked again, but less forcefully. His heart pounded, his breath came in gasps, his arm throbbed, and he felt *amazing*.

Shiv straightened, still panting. Offered a wide grin. *"Now* how do you feel?"

Charlie laughed, still breathing hard. "Oh, that was fun. That was—I never thought I could move that fast."

"You'll move faster yet, with conditioning." Shiv grinned at him, still puffing himself. "You're gonna be—an awesome sparring partner—when you come into your own." He leaned back, then shook out the arm that had delivered most of the strikes. *"Damn,* that felt good!"

"To you, too?" Charlie's arm pulsed with pain from the unaccustomed exertion, but it was a righteous pain.

Hildie groaned. "Trust *guys.* You're both gonna be bruised as heck."

"Good bruises, though. The right kind." Shiv chuckled. "You just got your first taste, Charlie. And *I* may finally have discovered somebody who might actually give me a run for my money someday in the sparring ring." He angled himself back into his chair. "This was a taste of that 'Semi-SuperCop' stuff we laughed about last week. I hope now it's a little more real."

"I—" Charlie smiled. "Yeah. I'd kinda started to wonder if it really was worth it."

"Still wondering?"

The last of that worry-knot in his chest eased. "Not anymore. I'm beginning to see the potential. This could be good."

CHAPTER 19

A STEP CLOSER TO
SPACE DOGS

E arly Monday afternoon, Rex stood next to a row of mesh-webbing seats along one wall of the main Central Plaza Police Express elevator to the Hub. It carried him, the Pack, and their partners upward. This afternoon they would begin the first of five half-days' training to gain their Class B micrograv certifications. Next Monday, they'd take their certification tests. By then he hoped that the SDF would get their giant space-bubble stabilized.

Rex had been startled to learn that none of his Packmates' human partners had anything beyond Class-A, or super-basic, micrograv certifications. That was the kind all Ranans first earned around age 12 in Intermediate School. They'd be learning almost as much as the dogs.

Was *that* why the watch officer had sent him and Charlie to the Hub on that fateful night, now three weeks ago? Charlie *did* already know how to handle himself in microgravity. Going there triggered debilitating stress reactions, but he possessed the knowledge and he'd once had all the skills. When he was on the ERT, he'd held a Class-C, the highest certification. Even though he wasn't certified anymore, he had lots more Hub experience than any other XK9 partner.

On your way, eh? Charlie's input through the link echoed with regret. *I should be there with you.*

Rex laid back his ears. *Not for another six weeks.* Charlie was grounded from micrograv exposure of more than eight hours a week while his arm healed. Recertification would take more than twice that long, assuming he could function once he got "up-top." *And I have to ask. Do you really WANT to go back into micrograv?*

You'll need to go there from time to time. He sensed Charlie's scowl through the link. *That means once I'm well, I'll also need to. Maybe I'll do better than you think. I actually didn't do too horribly, once we got there three weeks ago. I was holding it together.*

Until everything went to hell.

Charlie's disgruntlement came through loud and clear. *Yeah, well, until then. And after that, everybody had trouble, not only me. It's just that I wanted to be with you when you earned your qualification. I need to requalify as soon as possible for sure, so I won't hold you back.*

Rex gave a soft growl. Not holding him back seemed to be Charlie's new motto. *Not happening today, so let's not argue about it. I want to look forward to why we're doing this now. I have a crime scene to investigate! A pristine crime scene! I can hardly wait!*

Charlie's rueful chuckle echoed through the link. *You're right. I'll shut up and go back to the damned coordination drills. Have fun, and good luck!*

Just to Rex's left, Pam settled Shady's new micrograv harness onto his Amare's back.

Shiv pulled the new harness on over Rex's head, then made sure it was seated properly. "Tell me if something feels off." Shiv apparently had once held a Class-B, but he'd let it lapse. Now he would once again act as Rex's stand-in partner. He adjusted harness fasteners one by one.

"That last one's too tight."

Shiv let the strap out a little, but then it wouldn't latch.

Rex craned his neck to look. "Is the latch centered?"

"No." Shiv re-threaded it, but it still wouldn't latch. "It's catching on something."

Devin, one of the harness designers, hurried over to them. "That's the trickiest one. Try this." He adjusted the strap and snapped it down. His fingers lingered on Shiv's just a bit longer than necessary. "You see now?"

"Got it." Shiv gave him a curt nod.

"If you need anything else, just let me know." Devin moved his hand away with languid reluctance.

From his scent factors, Shiv felt more exasperated than intrigued by the man's attention.

"Not your type?" Rex texted.

Shiv scowled. "This is neither the time nor the place." He glanced to his left, bit his lip, then focused with great intensity on the balky buckle.

Curious, Rex glanced that way too. There was Berwyn, bent away from them across Cinnamon's back to scrutinize Scout's harness and discuss something with Nicole. *Oh, excellent.* Rex allowed himself an approving tongue-loll. Devin might as well pack it up. According to Shady, Berwyn had been smitten with Shiv since the first Task Force meeting. While they worked in the same command hierarchy it would be unprofessional to pursue a relationship, but Rex meant to make sure the *Izgubil* case didn't last forever.

Emily, the team leader, walked to an open area at one end of the car, where a screen and podium had been set up. "May I have your attention, please?" She launched into a description of the new harness design, and how it had been developed.

Rex followed the presentation with keen interest. He'd discussed the creation of these harnesses with Hector the other day. Emily's team hadn't used all the same ideas he and Hector had spitballed, but Charlie's inventor-uncle would want to hear about both the parallels and the differences in approach. Rex looked forward to their discussion tonight. The design itself was pretty smooth. Tiny retros had been strategically placed along the bands of the harnesses, controllable via the brain implant.

"We owe a lot to Dr. Santos of Station Polytechnic, who crafted the interface," Emily said.

Rex wagged his tail. He remembered Dr. Dave. He was a friend and colleague of Dr. SCISCO, the AI professor. He'd helped the OPD prove that the XK9s' implants contained no flaws, even though the Transmondians claimed they did.

The Transmondians had never wanted to know the extent of what XK9s could do. They'd been too invested in denying that XK9s were sapient. But there were no such restrictions of imagination on Rana Station. Warm gratitude filled him, along with a feeling something like Pack-love, only broader. It embraced the whole Station, and all the beings who shared it with him.

What you're feeling is patriotism. Charlie's emotional echoes told Rex his partner was feeling it too. *You get more Ranan every day.*

By the time Emily finished, they'd climbed near enough to the Hub that gravity pulled on them noticeably less than normal. "Test your jets," the chief designer urged. "We're in light enough gravity to feel their effect."

Rex triggered brief, tiny bursts from them with only a thought. They pushed him ever-so-slightly this way or that, until he halted his momentum with an outstretched paw.

"Remember, the jets can both start you and stop you," Emily said. "Don't forget to use them as retros."

Oh. Good point. This time Rex stopped himself with his jets.

Victor drifted into Cinnamon, which pushed her against Scout.

"Watch it!" Cinnamon showed teeth.

But Scout was already pushing back. Now she bumped into Victor.

Cinnamon powered the thrusters on her chestband to push herself out from between the two half-brothers. Berwyn scrambled to follow her. She halted herself next to Rex with a snort, a burst of aft retros, and braced hind legs.

"Wow, Cinnie, you've discovered how to tail-park," Berwyn said. "Nice job."

Rex texted Shiv, "Should I bump into her?"

I don't think she's in the mood, Charlie said.

Shiv smiled but shook his head. "Tempting, but no," he whispered.

"I heard that," Cinnamon said.

"You'll help us test the harness rigs this week while you're training," Emily said. "This should give us needed feedback and reveal more things about them that need adjustments. Don't hesitate to bring any concerns to our attention. Our objective is to give you as much control and flexibility in micrograv as humans or ozzirikkians have."

"In that case, you will need to design grapples that mimic hands with thumbs," Shady said. A swell of human and vocalizer-voiced approval greeted this idea.

"Believe me, we're already working on it," Emily said. "It's a more complex thing to design than your harnesses, but there's already a lot of robotic tech we can draw from."

An overwhelming rush of excitement filled Rex. He exchanged an amazed look with Shady. Scent factors all around them said the rest of the Pack and partners felt similar amazement. "How long do you think that will take?" Rex wagged so hard he had to fire his chestband thrusters to stay in place.

Emily grinned. "We hope to have practical prototypes later this year."

Talk about a game-changer! Charlie's reaction echoed Rex's, but in a minor key. *Once you XK9s can manipulate objects with your own "hands," we're in a whole new world of possibilities.* His emotions through the link shifted toward morose. *You'll need me even less than you already do.*

You're unduly pessimistic today. Have you taken your meds?

He sensed Charlie's groan. *You sound like Hildie.*

She's a smart woman. Rex laid his ears back. *Have you?*

Okay, okay. I'll do it now. Charlie muted most of the rest of that thought, but Rex caught a faint sense of *it's not like I have all that much else to do.*

And after that, take a nap, Rex added. He'd swear Charlie replied with a growl.

Rex's com beeped with the particular tone that signaled an incoming call on the Command Channel. He and Shiv shared a startled look.

"This is Rex."

"Shiv here."

"I just received this notice from SCISCO," Elaine said. "It appears that once again our AI friend knows things before the rest of us do."

Rex flashed on the call he'd gotten from SCISCO through his brain implant a few weeks ago, warning of a planned predawn attempt by the XK9 Project and SDF Admiral Virendra to kidnap the Pack. It was an attempt the AI professor's warning had enabled them to foil.

Now Elaine's transmission made a soft *click*, and they heard SCISCO's vocalizer. "We appear to have a troubling development," nir voice said. "This just hit the first Ranan feeds. Still processing. The *Ministo Lulak* was a mining vessel. On approach to Mahusay Station today, it was explosively micro-deconstructed less than ten minutes before docking. There is some damage to the docks, and the vessel was completely destroyed. Initial vids and telemetry are coming in now … And they look remarkably similar to the destruction of the *Izgubil*."

"Should we return?" Shiv asked.

"No. Continue with your training mission." Rex could hear the troubled frown in Elaine's voice. "As ne said, there's still a lot of information coming in. I intend to monitor it for a while. See if I can establish communications with their investigators. Meanwhile, there's not much you can do that's more valuable than what you're doing already. Getting you and the Pack certified and fit for micrograv work may ultimately prove to be the most essential task you can perform right now."

Shiv frowned. "Have you talked with Mike? Is the *Ministo Lulak* connected in any way to the Whisper Syndicate?"

"That's definitely on the list of questions I mean to ask. At any rate, you've had your 'breaking news' update. I wanted to catch you while you were still on your way up, before you got into the thick of the training. I hope to know considerably more by the time you return."

Once she'd disconnected, Shiv frowned. "Well. This case just got a whole lot more complicated."

"SCISCO does not seem to have any doubt that the two ships were destroyed the same way." Rex's itchy hackles paralleled the uneasy flutter in his gut. "The perpetrators have gone international, and perhaps they are not finished. Who else might be next?"

"The more we learn about the *Ministo Lulak*, the better we may be able to answer those questions." Shiv's brow furrowed. "The more we know, the better we can narrow down the suspect pool."

Rex nodded, but he couldn't help feeling that they'd just added a whole new Station full of suspects instead.

CHAPTER 20

A MAHUSAYAN CONNECTION

H ackles up, Rex crossed the Global Reconstruction Unit's threshold late on Tuesday afternoon. What day or time was it on Mahusay Station and its associated asteroids? Whenever, they had a meeting to get to.

So, what was the holdup?

A few steps down the narrow main corridor, Elaine confronted a tall, rail-thin woman with angry scent factors and sparse, steel-gray hair scraped back into a tight knot.

"You can't just waltz in here and expect us to drop everything," the woman said. "We don't work for you!" That was true, although not relevant. Technically, this conference was an SBI operation. But even if it had been an OPD conference, the Global Reconstruction Unit wasn't an OPD unit. It was a separate part of the Safety Services Department, not directly supervised by the Police Department, Fire Department, Prosecutor's Office, Borough Court, or Family Services Department. At times it worked with all of them, which was why it had its own separate status.

But Rex knew for certain that they'd reserved the GR Conference Suite, and requested one composite GR. Even if this woman didn't work for Elaine or Klein directly, she was supposed to *cooperate* with them.

Tux stepped up next to Rex. He seconded his Pack Leader's growl. Behind them, Shiv, Georgia, and SBI explosives expert Joe Raach crowded close in the narrow space. Their scent factors smoldered with angry impatience. Last in line, SCISCO's focal-object android didn't emit scent factors, but a glance showed even its pigment-pixel expression frowned.

Elaine shook her head at the woman. "The Chief—"

"Has no idea what it takes to do this work," the woman cut in. She crossed her arms and leaned forward with a glare, so she loomed over the diminutive SSA. "It'll be ready when it's ready."

Hot frustration surged in Elaine's scent. "I only asked for simple, slo-mo rotation based on available surveillance—"

"Which isn't as simple as you think." The woman's bony chin jutted.

Elaine drew in a slow breath, held her ground. "Coordinating with the Mahu—"

"Not my problem." The woman turned away, then stopped at the sight of the others. She glared at Rex and Tux. "Oh, *hell*, no. You get those enormous brutes *out of my unit!*"

Rex's hackles rose. He felt Tux's taut, bristling body shoulder-to-shoulder with his. The corridor was so narrow they touched.

"Reserve Agents Dieter-Nell and Moondog-Carrie are valued members of my liaison team," Elaine said. "I require that my entire team be accommodated."

The woman glared at Rex and Tux. "Agents? Liaison team? Good God, what next?"

"Next would be our pre-arranged and *confirmed* access to the Conference Suite," Elaine said. "*Preferably* with the rendering we ordered."

The woman gave her a venomous look but pointed farther down the hallway. "There. Go."

"Thank you," Elaine said.

Rex pushed past the woman with a low growl and a quick flash of teeth. The others followed. The woman stayed where she was, arms crossed, an obstacle to the bitter end.

They stepped inside a round room with a curved table and several benches. Most of the room was taken up by a large cylindrical structure made of a clear, thin substance. It smelled of synthetics and electricity. Although it nearly filled the room, it looked oddly insubstantial.

Elaine walked to the control console. She studied it for a few seconds, then gave the rest of her group a rueful look. "Of course, she hasn't provided a technician."

Shiv grimaced. "This is more like the cooperation we *usually* get from locals."

Elaine frowned at the controls. "Any of you know how to run this rig?"

Joe, Georgia, and Shiv also moved to the console, but SCISCO's android stayed back. The humans stared at the controls with wary expressions.

Rex stepped closer. He could make no more sense of all the buttons, dials and sliders than it seemed the others did, but Charlie probably could. His partner had qualified as a Global Reconstruction artist after he couldn't return to the Emergency Rescue Team. Rex had a sense that Charlie hadn't stayed with GR work for very long, but he undoubtedly remembered how to turn the thing on.

Rex reached out to his partner though their link.

CHARLIE DOZED in his hospital bed, tired from a morning of physical therapy, loggy from lunch, and bored.

He missed Hildie. She certainly hadn't been able to utilize a very long Emergency Family Leave. Her captain had called her multiple times yesterday to describe desperately short-handed conditions and pressure her to return. Unfortunately, when she'd called Theresa and Oz to check the story, they'd confirmed it. They'd urged her to take as much leave as she needed, but she'd gone back to work. Charlie hated to admit it, but he probably would've done the same in her place.

He came alert with glad recognition at Rex's contact. *Good afternoon! I figured you'd be tied up in your meeting.*

We had hoped to be, but we're in the Conference Suite of the GR Unit, and we have no one to operate the equipment for us.

The GR Unit? Charlie grimaced. Memories of his brief, inglorious GR career put him in mind of taking a big bite of something rotten.

Rex explained the situation.

Oh, man, that's Missy on a tear, for sure. Sorry you have to deal with her. She's just — Charlie scowled. Even one thought about his former boss could sour his whole day if he let it. Typical Cranston move, giving them access but no tech.

Can you at least tell us where the 'on' switch is?

Charlie grimaced. *Unfortunately it's not that simple.* He hesitated, tempted by a sudden impulse. Oh, Missy would be SO pissed … he smiled. *Open the link as wide as you can. Show me the console.*

Rex opened his perceptions to Charlie and faced the console. A color-shifted look at the familiar controls showed Charlie Rex's view. The big dog could see yellow, blue, and violet, as well as shades of dark and light, but not red or green. Unaccustomed colors notwithstanding, they hadn't changed the equipment in the past year. *Wow, that brings back memories!*

How do we turn it on?

Charlie focused on the power button. *It'll be a little clumsy, but I can walk you through it, if you want. Start by punching that.*

I'll have someone with fingers do it. Rex passed along his first instruction. A man's hand appeared in Rex's view, then the dog looked up at a tall fellow Charlie hadn't met. *This is Joe. He will provide fingers. May I put you on the com?*

Please do. It only took a thought to activate his CAP and

HUD, but thinking into the com as Rex did when he made words come out of his vocalizer wasn't a thing Charlie's side of the apparatus could do. "RAMoD," Charlie called. "Bring me my case pad." Through the link with Rex, he heard the rising hum of the GR tank powering up.

The robot stirred to life in the corner of his hospital room, rolled to his personal-belongings cabinet, then brought the requested item to him.

He activated it. *Ready to patch through.*

"Hello. Detective Morgan?" Sounded like SSA Adeyeme's voice. Her name popped up on the HUD channel a second later.

"At your service, ma'am. Good afternoon."

"I apologize for disturbing you, but the Director of the GR Unit has left us without technical help."

Charlie made a disgusted noise in his throat. "You got the Full Cranston. I know it all too well. I probably should warn you that Director Cranston and I are not on good terms. It's just as well I'm not there in person."

"I have no right to activate a Reserve Agent while he's hospitalized, but some guidance would be appreciated."

"This is lots more fun than what I was doing. Will you be running the controls?"

The man he'd originally seen through Rex's eyes opened a vid. "No, that'd be me. Specialist Joe Raach, here. Just call me 'Fingers.'"

Charlie laughed. He'd been Rex's 'Fingers' often in their partnership. "Okay, Fingers, let's run through the basics."

Another channel opened: Georgia Volkov. "Tux and I are here, too, Charlie. I'd like to learn this as well. Joe may have other things to do once the interview starts."

"Do you have coordinates for the Mahusayans' tightbeam access?" Charlie asked. Once he'd explained how, Georgia input them with a few quick keystrokes.

"Now we wait," Charlie said. "Are they relaying from Mahusay Station?"

"No, from the asteroid 1226437 Ministobrila Base Four, which was the origination-point for the *Ministo Lulak's* last flight," Joe said. "It's a little closer than Mahusay Station itself. We're anticipating a two-minute transmission lag."

"Oh, that'll get old," Charlie said.

I also should tell you that Dr. SCISCO is here. Rex provided a view of the AI's android focal object.

"Charlie, I wonder if we can link you to this console through your CAP and HUD," Joe said.

He and Joe shifted to another channel, so Joe could coach him through the connection process.

Odd sensation: through the link, Charlie still received impressions from Rex, who continued to watch the control board. But now there also was a set of virtual controls on his case pad. Lights flickered and blipped on both control-panel views, in response to Charlie's touch. A slider adjusted, seemingly on its own from Rex's point of view, when Charlie adjusted it virtually through his case pad.

"That is so smooth," Charlie said. "I've got it."

They lapsed into brief silence, but Charlie was able to observe through Rex's eyes. *Thank you for looping me in like this.*

My pleasure. It's nice to work with you again.

Joe glanced at Georgia. "I've never met a Mahusayan. Is it true they all have the same name? How would that even *work*?"

Georgia shook her head. "Everyone in a *collective* has the same *last* name."

"These Inspectors—their word for detective—are from the Kiuvidas Security Collective," Shiv said. "Check your HUD. Should be in the briefing."

Rex had of course already read it, but Charlie could feel his lingering confusion. "Are they private eyes, or police?" Rex asked.

"Sort of both," Georgia said. "Mahusayan collectives contract with other collectives for all services. The Ministobrila Collective owned the *Ministo Lulak*. Looks as if they've hired

Kiuvidas and two other security collectives to investigate its destruction."

Charlie's virtual connection flashed a warning. "We have an incoming burst," he said. "See the flashing? It counts down. In three—two—one."

Through the speakers, a woman's voice spoke. Charlie recognized the language, but he didn't follow all that she said. He'd never been fluent, and his Mahusayan was now six-years-rusty. He sensed Rex's disgruntlement. *You're still ahead of me. I wish Shady was here.* Rex's mate, the Pack's only linguist, spoke many languages, apparently including Mahusayan. But in the Conference Suite, as throughout the GR Unit, space was at a premium. It seemed Adeyeme had chosen technical expertise over linguistic.

Georgia replied to the woman in vastly-more-fluent Mahusayan than Charlie could've managed, then turned to the others. "Incoming transmission in four minutes."

The door of the teleconferencing room banged open.

Rex and Tux wheeled toward it, hackles up and teeth bared.

"Who authorized you to mess with my equipment?" The near-year since he'd last seen her clearly hadn't improved Missy Cranston's disposition. Ol' Pissy Missy looked even less agreeable through Rex's eyes. "You're not certified to *touch* it!"

SSA Adeyeme crossed her arms. "On the contrary, Reserve Agent Morgan is fully certified. He is working via remote connection. Therefore, if you have indeed failed to complete the rendering we ordered, we have no further need of you. You have not been cleared to observe this teleconference."

If Charlie'd had a tail to wag, it would be fanning right along with Rex and Tux's. He grinned.

Cranston's face went stony. "*Charles* Morgan? That miserable son of a bitch is permanently banned from this unit!"

"Apparently not, since he has access," Adeyeme said. "You, however, must leave now."

Shiv, Rex, and Tux closed in on Cranston.

Charlie shouldn't be enjoying this as much as he was.

Missy's eyes narrowed to slits, an all-too-familiar expression. But, faced with two enormous dogs and a tall, very fit man, she retreated. Shiv closed and locked the door behind her.

Charlie laughed out loud, alone in his hospital room, but still connected through the com. *Oh, that was fun to watch!* Soon the telltale on his case-pad-based virtual control panel blinked. "Here they are. See the blink? Three—two—one."

The Mahusayan woman's voice spoke again.

Inside the GR cylinder, a life-size image of three humans sitting at a table gradually appeared. It looked like dust swirling into shapes that grew more and more clearly defined. Charlie'd seen the effect dozens of times, but it always seemed like magic.

One man and two women wore their straight black hair in similar short haircuts. All wore dark brown coverall uniforms. All had medium golden-tan skin and dark brown eyes. On first impression they resembled triplets, but a second look revealed individual differences. One of the women had a larger bone structure than the other, and the man was taller.

The image blipped. For an instant, Charlie feared that Missy Cranston had pulled the plug on them out of spite. But then the smaller-boned woman was on her feet.

Charlie felt Rex's distress through the link. *This image is so realistic I feel I should smell them. It's as if my nose quit working.*

The three Mahusayans smiled. "Is pleasure of the greatest to speaking vith you," the smaller woman said in Commercial Standard. "I am Inspector Anne Kiuvidas, and these are being my fellow Kiuvidas members, Super-Inspector Kabira Kiuvidas —" The larger woman stood; "—and Inspector Clovis Kiuvidas." The tall man stood. "Ve all most grateful for you are calling viss information about *Izgubil*." Their images froze.

"Time to record our burst," Charlie said. "When the red light goes on."

Georgia eyed it. When it blinked on, she faced the GR imaging tank, which the transmission recorders would relay so it looked as if she was facing her Mahusayan listeners. She greeted the Inspectors Kiuvidas and asked them to pass on Rana Station's condolences to Ministobrila Collective, for the loss of its senior member Kalan Ministo, and to Taios Collective for the loss of their crewmembers. She spoke first in Mahusayan, then repeated herself in Standard. Initial greetings finished, she moved on, speaking Standard for her introductions of herself and the rest of the group. Each person stood when she spoke their name, as the Mahusayans had. Georgia even introduced Charlie, explaining that he was using remote access.

What will the Mahusayans think about dogs being introduced as officers? Rex worried.

I guess we'll find out.

Adeyeme nodded when the introductions ended. "We, too, deeply appreciate your willingness to cooperate. I hope you have received the files we sent and have had a chance to look them over. We are convinced there are important similarities between the blast pattern that destroyed the *Izgubil*, and the one we saw with the *Ministo Lulak*." Georgia translated as she spoke, then stepped back from the imaging area.

"You can sit down now, if you wish," Charlie said on the com. "I've sent our burst."

"Show me how you sent it," Joe said. He and Charlie once again shifted to a different channel.

Charlie demonstrated the procedure for him, then explained how to watch for, and respond to, the return burst. "That's really about all there is to do for a teleconference. You want to try it when their burst comes in? I'll stand by to observe, but I bet you've got this."

"Sure. Thanks."

Charlie was interested in the teleconference. It certainly was relevant to the case he hoped at some point to be working on. But his strength had started to flag. So much for a proto-Semi-SuperCop's vaunted endurance. He yawned but dared not fade out until he knew Joe was all right working solo. He kept himself awake by poking around in the files to see what he could access.

The first thing he found was a short composite GR marked 'for SBI.' Curious, he ran it. Turned out to be a slo-mo rotation of a ship exploding. No need to ask what ship it was. Not only did it jog vague, disjointed memories, but it had the remains of a berthing cone still locked in its docking grapples. The short file had been built from all the many surveillance devices that had captured some or all of the incident.

From the sign-in, Charlie saw his former co-worker Ernest Porringer had created and filed it late last night. The timestamp told Charlie he'd worked well past the time he was supposed to have logged out for the day. Charlie smiled. Ol' Ernie P. had gone well above the call of duty and made an excellent GR.

What did you find? Rex asked. *Is that our missing file? The one Cranston said would 'be ready when it's ready'?*

How typical, that she'd try to hide excellent work from another agency. If anyone dared challenge her for withholding it, she'd probably say it was so the SBI wouldn't hire Porringer away from her. She'd pulled that one out of her drawer in the past, and maybe she really feared it. Or maybe it was just more spite. Someday maybe she'd finally pay for all of the abuse she'd heaped on her staff. *It's a short compilation of the* Izgubil *exploding. If that's what you're looking for, here it is,* he replied.

Yes! Outstanding! Let's show it to Elaine.

CHAPTER 21

DEADLY PUZZLES

By the time Rex, Elaine, and the others emerged from the GR Conference Suite, it appeared that Director Cranston and any other GR artists who might have been there had left for the day. The unit lay silent and dark except for baseboard-level navigational lights that blipped on when they approached.

"I wonder if she locked us in." Tux's vocalizer sounded loud in the stillness.

"Civic Center doors open outward as a safety measure, at least for everyone with the security clearance to be here in the first place," Georgia said. "Getting back *in* can be a different matter."

The doors did, indeed, open outward. Shiv waited for them to close with a *click*, then tested to make sure they had locked.

They headed back toward Elaine's war room. "I like your partner, Rex," she said. "Operating our equipment from his hospital bed is truly above and beyond the call of duty. I hope he knows how grateful I am."

Rex wriggled with pleasure at this. "I shall make sure he does." Charlie had faded out before the end of the conference, but he'd roused enough to walk Joe and Georgia through the equipment's shutdown sequence.

"And I'll plead an emergency with our union," Georgia added. "They're sure to balk at setting *this* precedent."

"With good reason. I don't intend to abuse the privilege, but I'm grateful for Charlie's help." Elaine's brows furrowed, then lifted. "Also, *I* want to be a 'Super-Inspector.' What a great title!"

Georgia laughed. "The Mahusayan word actually means '*lead* inspector.' Anne's grasp of Standard is a little sketchy."

Rex lolled his tongue. *That* was clear. She'd been hard to follow in Standard.

Elaine grinned, but shook her head. "Don't spoil it with reality!"

Joe gave Georgia a quizzical look. "You seem well-acquainted with Mahusayan culture, and you speak the language very well."

"My apodeddi—one of my grandfathers—is Mahusayan. He taught all of us kids to speak it by telling us bedtime stories. For a while, I thought the only language you could *tell* bedtime stories in was Mahusayan." She grinned. "He would say, 'Come, Ve telling stories so you sleep now, yes?' Of course, his stories usually made us more excited than sleepy. He grew up in a wildcat mining collective, then joined an engineering collective before he came here. He had plenty of tales to tell."

"How'd he end up on Rana Station?" Joe asked.

She chuckled. "Is story long, personal, colorful. I telling you someday, perhaps."

The investigative center's main door opened with its characteristic high squeal in response to Elaine's palmprint and retinal scan. She took her favorite chair by the coffee maker with a grimace. "Well, that gave us a lot of new information. Impressions? First thoughts?"

Shiv took the chair next to her. "For me, the big news is the steganographic pulse." Kiuvidas Collective's signals intel specialist had discovered a secret transmission to the ship, cloaked in normal automated chatter after the vessel hit turnover and began its approach to port.

"Yes, that is huge." Tux's ears and tail stood straight up with excitement. "I want to know how they found it. And we must compare the telemetry with all the transmissions to and from the *Izgubil*."

"Tech specs are in the signals information they sent," Georgia reminded, with a glance toward Dr. SCISCO's android. "My Mahusayan may not be good enough, but Doc's probably is."

Scowling, Joe threw himself into a chair facing Elaine and Shiv. "Hiding the pulse in the transmission data is brilliant, but sick."

"It's almost *got* to be an inside job, doesn't it?" Georgia took a seat next to him. "But assuming these incidents are connected, how does Ministobrila Mining or Taios Collective line up with the Whisper Syndicate? Or perhaps the connection's within the collective that runs the asteroid's traffic control? Or ... something or someone else entirely."

"I think we can assume they're connected somehow," SCISCO's voice might be quiet, but everyone turned to face nir focal object. "Each step of the sequence needs review, including that mysterious, vaguely-worded threat they received after the launch. It concerns me that they couldn't dig out the source."

"We'll probably never know if the Syndicate got one." Shiv shook his head.

"But what's the source of the message for the Mahusayan craft?" Rex asked. "Who sent it?"

"Also, the timing," SCISCO said. "The remote triggering just after turnover—that seems deliberate."

"Some of that might be simple practicality—a greater volume of transmissions then?" Elaine asked.

"Possibly. Or the length of the timers' setting," SCISCO replied. "The craft was destroyed when it was just barely out of reach by their Emergency Rescue Teams. Perhaps the intent was not only mass murder, but also to inflict mental anguish."

"On the people from Ministobrila and Taios, certainly. They lost people." Georgia frowned. "But folks at the port must have wanted to save the people onboard."

"That is another difference from the *Izgubil*." Rex lowered his head, ears back. "Why destroy the *Ministo Lulak* when it was just out of reach of rescue, but explode the *Izgubil* well within range of the ERTs? Not many survived, but we did rescue some." His mind leaped to the two little girls Shady had helped calm and interview the day after that explosion.

"Unfortunately, those interviews have not been terribly helpful." From Elaine's frown and murky scent factors, she also must be thinking about the girls.

"I wonder if the dock breach factored into the timing, for the *Izgubil*. The *Ministo Lulak* was right on schedule." Shiv's pale eyes had a faraway focus. He chewed his lower lip with a pensive frown.

"Until we know why they breached, that's hard to say." Elaine grimaced. "We keep coming back to the same problem: we don't know enough."

"We need to review it all." Joe ran a hand over his face. "The technical report on *Ministo Lulak*. The telemetry from the *Izgubil*. The GR." He shook his head. "Man. That GR! What a find!"

"It really was illuminating, the way the artist put the surveillance views all together." Georgia glanced at Rex. "How did Charlie find it? Director Cranston made us think it hadn't been made."

"Not sure how he found it, but I could not see half as much from the bunker's window during the actual event." Rex's eyewitness view hadn't been that clear. And he'd completely missed the barrage of escape pods from the ship's belly. He looked forward to reviewing it several more times by memory, for additional insights.

"We need to be careful how we talk about that GR." Elaine's sober tone startled Rex. "Charlie texted me privately to say Director Cranston has her own, paranoid reasons for undermining her people. She didn't want us to see it. The artist who compiled and rendered it on his own time after-hours will be in trouble if we openly praise him. Charlie suggested I speak confidentially to Chief Klein about how to convey thanks without making the man a target."

Georgia's brow made a troubled pucker. "I knew Charlie worked there briefly, but he never said much about it. Looks like he left for good reason."

"Charlie generally has good reasons, although sometimes you have to ask persistently." Rex planned to persist in asking about the GR Unit until he knew a great deal more.

EARLY WEDNESDAY AFTERNOON, for the last time during this hospitalization, Charlie watched Nanda run a test-check on RAMoD. Zuni'd said he needed to pass one more blood panel, and he'd be cleared to go home!

He'd taken quite a few spins around the Re-Gen Unit with RAMoD for therapy, but his current outing wasn't for exercise. Internal Affairs meant to interview him without further delay. His appearance today was the work of many hands. His aunt Hannah had provided him with legal counsel. The Med Center's barber had ensured that he would go to the interview clean-shaven and presentable.

His cousin Manny had brought Charlie's dress blues early this morning on the way to his job as a sous chef in one of Central District's trending restaurants. It even looked as if someone had bought him a brand-new pair of shoes to go with his uniform. They weren't as comfortable as his old, well-worn pair, but they did look better.

Nanda helped Charlie into the parts of the uniform that he could wear. At least he'd left the torso cast behind. But to accommodate today's arm cast they'd had to substitute a modified scrubs top for the regulation shirt, then add a sling for the cast and drape his jacket over his left arm.

Nanda adjusted Charlie's jacket across his shoulders, then re-fastened the top button and made sure his OPD badge was on straight. He also reverently pinned Charlie's Station Medal of Valor into place. An officer wore his formal uniform to an interview with I.A., but the interviewer, Lt. Harrison Broaddus, hadn't wanted to wait until Charlie could wear a lighter arm shield that would fit through a normal sleeve.

"You look good," the nurse said. "I bet a jury would love you."

Charlie blew out a long, nervous breath. "Let's hope it doesn't come to that. Thanks for all your help." He and RAMoD moved out of the room and down the hall.

Nanda smiled and waved. "Good luck!"

Good luck! Rex echoed through their brain link. *If you don't mind, I intend to monitor this interview.*

Maybe not a bad idea. Broaddus probably wouldn't like it, but he didn't have to know. And whatever this was about, if it affected Charlie, it affected Rex.

He'd received a stern warning that he'd better let Hildie know how things were going. Charlie entered the hallway, took a calming breath, then texted her and his Family: "Headed to my meeting now."

Her answer came swiftly. "Good luck! Don't let them pull any shit!" In a chorus of *dings* on his HUD, his Family wished him strength and success.

His counsel, Shomari Hondo, intercepted him outside the meeting room. A slender young man in an expensive suit, he came from the well-respected law firm of Harris and Odi. They'd spoken on the com, but Charlie hadn't met him till now. Hondo flashed a smile. "Detective Morgan? How are you today?"

The walk had left Charlie winded, but not as sweaty as he'd feared. "I'll do, thanks."

"Good to meet you." Hondo pushed the door open.

Rangy, olive-skinned Alphonse Rami and Lt. Broaddus, a tall man with skin the color of burnt umber, sat across the table from each other. Arms crossed and eyes half-closed, they'd looked as if each meant to stare the other down, but then turned toward the new arrivals.

Charlie already knew and trusted the Union rep, Rami. They'd first met when his problems with Missy Cranston, the Global Reconstruction Unit Director, came to an impasse.

He hadn't previously met Broaddus, but the man wasted no time once Charlie took a seat. He recorded everyone's self-introductions, stated date and start-time, then turned to Charlie. "I assume you knew it was only a matter of time before we contacted you."

Charlie glanced at Rami, but the rep maintained a neutral expression. "I'm sorry, sir, but no." Charlie met Broaddus's gaze across the table. "Ever since your office made contact, I've been trying to guess what you wanted to ask about."

Broaddus frowned back, unflinching. "Detective Morgan, do you know how or why your microgravity rating was changed?"

It was? What the hell? Charlie shot an eyebrow-up toward Hondo. The attorney nodded. He turned back to the lieutenant. "Glitch? Data-entry error?"

Broaddus simply continued to look at him.

Okay, then. Not accidental. A chill swept over him. *How could ... Who did I piss off?* "When I received the order, I thought maybe somebody ... assumed I must be better, by now?" It honestly had been what he'd thought on that almost-fatal night. But saying it aloud, it sounded stupid. "My partner wondered if it was because I was the only XK9 partner who had micrograv experience."

"Did you arrange to get it changed?"

"No." Humiliation closed Charlie's throat. "Are you ... " His voice tried to cut out. He cleared his throat and tried again. "Are you aware of my diagnosis?" Post-traumatic stress reactions and panic attacks weren't normally behaviors he cared to highlight, but they did give him a solid reason not to have wanted his micrograv rating reinstated.

"Yet when you were ordered to the Hub, you went."

Frustration filled him with hot, tight rage. "They needed an XK9 team. I *do have* the skills."

Broaddus said nothing, just looked at him.

Charlie deflated with a sigh. "It needed to be done. I—I found a way." Ashamed of his panic reactions, cringing inside, he closed his eyes. *Am I already screwed?*

You shouldn't be. He felt Rex's rumble of a growl. *What is his game?*

"Detective Morgan has now expressed, in moving terms, that he not only did *not* direct that his rating be fraudulently changed, but that he struggled against rather large impediments, in order to do his job," Hondo said. "Are we finished, here?"

Broaddus shook his head. "Not at all." He fixed Charlie with a hard stare. "So, then, Morgan. Who wants you dead?"

A cold spike of apprehension shot through him, robbed him of breath. But it was the next logical question. He had no recourse but the truth. "I—I don't think ... wouldn't have thought anyone does. Except maybe on general principles because I'm a police officer?"

Or an XK9 partner? Rex's growl resonated through the link.

Broaddus looked at him. Said nothing. The silence dragged.

What had he overlooked? Failed to realize? Charlie drew in a breath. "It couldn't be about the *Izgubil.* That happened after we went to the Hub." By the same logic, it couldn't relate to Rex's case against the Transmondians. Could it?

"If your rating was willfully changed without your consent, the OPD would consider that to be the reckless endangerment of an officer," Broaddus's voice remained flat, emotionless.

Reckless endangerment?

Oh, yes. Definitely. Rex's suppressed fury chilled him all over again.

But I managed okay in the Hub. He'd focused on his performance, more than how-could-they-send-me. He'd been so *grateful* not to lose his shit this time. He'd stayed on task. He'd fought back his fear. He'd *worked the scene*.

Yes, you did. But if someone set you up, they wouldn't expect you to succeed.

Broaddus let the silence continue until it was clear Charlie had no answer. "Let me put it this way. Who dislikes you? Who regards you with malice?"

Charlie froze. "*Malice* only describes one person I can think of. But even so, how she could possibly …? It makes no sense."

"Let me be the judge of that. Who?"

Charlie grimaced. "A former supervisor, Melissa Cranston. But that was in the GR Unit. We had nothing to do with microgravity. She barely let us out on break, much less to view a crime scene. Certainly, never a crime scene at the Hub. She wanted all of us right there in the unit. Always."

Having met her, I believe that. Charlie sensed a prickle in Rex's hackles.

Broaddus regarded him from beneath half-closed eyelids. "Did she say why?"

Pure cussedness? Charlie shook his head. "We always figured it was to keep us under her thumb."

"'We'?"

"My co-workers Ernest Porringer and Jenny Evans. Might say 'fellow prisoners.'"

Broaddus frowned. "Anyone else dislike you?"

Charlie chewed his lower lip. Considered this. "Dr. Ordovich wasn't happy when Rex Chose me." In the flickering bonfire-light that night, Charlie'd caught an expression of … dismay? Fury? There, but then gone in a flash. "I think he wished Rex had Chosen someone else."

Got that right, Rex said. *Ordovich never liked you, from the moment you arrived.*

Charlie met Broaddus's gaze. "But he's a Transmondian. I

doubt he could change my micrograv rating. And why would he?"

"Mmm." Once again, the silence stretched.

Through the link, Charlie felt Rex catch his breath. New suspicion dawned in his partner's emotions. *Ordovich might not, but Wisniewski has greater reach. And possibly a mole inside the OPD.*

Charlie went cold. He swallowed, then spoke carefully. "Perhaps I *could* be a target, simply because I'm Rex's partner. If someone wanted to sabotage the XK9s, striking at their partners would harm them. It could be a separate issue from trouble with the Transmondians, or the *Izgubil* investigation."

"Someone inside the OPD?" Broaddus's eyes narrowed.

Hondo and Rami both went alert.

Uh, that's not good. "Well, I do remember a lot of grumbling in the ranks about changes to the budget."

Hondo shot a glance at Rami. The Union rep frowned but nodded, his face grim.

"Do you remember any *particular* grumblers?" Broaddus kept his expression deadpan. "Anyone who knows you went into the XK9 program?"

Charlie sat back in his chair. *Any number of people, at one time or another.*

This is not the time to hold back, Rex said.

He wants a suspect. I'm reluctant to throw anyone under the bus when I don't know it's them. Charlie bit his lip. *But there was that one guy ....* "It's just ... It's pure speculation."

"You got a name to go with that speculation?" The steady pressure of Broaddus's gaze bored into him like a laser. "What does your gut tell you, Detective?"

His gut was a big, cold stone. "There was a guy who got dropped from the STAT Team about the time I learned I was headed for Solara City. He always beefed about the 'XK9 boon-*dog*-gle,' as he called it." Charlie pinched the bridge of his nose. He could *almost* dredge up a name, but it had been more than a year, and he'd detested that guy. "He knew I'd applied, and that

I was testing for the program. Used to rag on me about it pretty hard."

"You were never on the STAT Team." Broaddus gave him a dubious frown. "What's the connection?"

"My friends Eddie Chism and his cousin Brock Rivers are on STAT Blue. We've enjoyed working out together since back when the ERT and STAT shared gym time. Sometimes other team members were there, too."

"Think they'd remember his name?"

Oh, Eddie and Brock are so gonna love getting a call from I.A. Charlie groaned inwardly. "Probably."

"Anybody else fall into that category?" Broaddus asked.

"Nobody else leaps to mind." *It's all guesses. I don't know anything solid. That's the worst part of all this.* "That's the lot of them, I think: some nameless guy, Ordovich, or Cranston."

Wisniewski, Rex said. *Don't forget him.*

Charlie blew out a breath. "Or maybe Jackson Wisniewski. He hates Rex."

CHAPTER 22

HILDIE'S HARD DAY

Hildie bit her lip. One member of the transfer team locked in the med-bed. The other checked the monitors and grimaced. The doors of the hyperbarically equalizing Emergency Services Express elevator closed, and they were on their way down.

Hildie lingered a moment longer, heartsick.

Eli gave her shoulder a squeeze. "We did all we could, Hils."

She shook her head, throat tight. Her gut might literally be in freefall, but her stomach felt like a stone in the lowest sublevels. "He's gonna bleed out on the way down. We all know it, but we have no choice. Topside Trauma needs more surgical capability *here*. He needed surgical help *before* they went down."

Eli's grim expression echoed her mood. "Yeah, right. Dream on."

There were maybe a handful of doctors on all of Rana who could do that procedure in micrograv, and none of them worked for anything close to Emergency Services pay. Most who could do such work had been snapped up by competing mining or manufacturing concerns. Either that, or they were paid like admirals and pampered like royalty on long-range SDF craft.

Hildie blew out a long breath. "I *hate* losing a patient." He'd be en route to the hospital's morgue before she even finished his formwork. Had to do the formwork anyway, though. *Best get to it.* She turned back toward base.

Then she stopped again. "Chief Zhang. Good afternoon."

Emergency Medical Services Chief Lexie Zhang rarely came up-top. After all, she had the whole Orangeboro EMS Department to run. But there she floated, a lean older woman with high cheekbones, deep bronze-colored skin and penetrating black eyes.

EMS personnel didn't salute superiors the way police or firefighters did, but Hildie always kind of felt as if she should make an exception in Dr. Zhang's case. She offered a quick micrograv-adapted bow, instead. "Namaste."

"Good afternoon, Sergeant Gallagher, Paramedic Isaiah." Zhang nodded to both. "Unless I'm mistaken, it looks as if you just had a bad call."

"I'm sorry to say that yes, we did." Hildie hesitated. How much of their conversation had she overheard? "May we help you with something, Chief?"

Zhang smiled. "A moment of your time, please, Sergeant?"

My time? Hildie tried to keep her face impassive. "Of course, Chief."

"I'll let the crew know where you are." Eli headed back toward the base.

Zhang held her position with a hand on a navigation rail. She gazed at the narrow, bare-bones Topside Trauma facility for a long moment.

Hildie waited, respectful but curious. Apprehension nibbled at her.

"I understand congratulations are in order, Sergeant." Zhang's eyebrow arched. "On your renewed relationship?"

Hildie couldn't stop her smile, despite the circumstances. Zhang had good reason to remember Charlie. Her official Girlfriend status made the relationship a personnel issue. "Thanks. It's been … kind of amazing."

Zhang's expression went rueful. "Unfortunately, poor Charlie appears to have had a rough time after the *Asalatu*."

Hildie nodded. She stared across the Topside Trauma facility, but all she saw were her anxieties about Charlie, his prognosis, and their relationship. "The new injuries on top of the old ... complicate things."

"How are you doing, Sergeant? Have you been adequately supported by Safety Services and our department?"

Eww. Should I say what I really think? "Adequately?"

"Yes. Have you felt supported and affirmed, in this problematical period when your boyfriend is gravely injured, and particularly in light of his stressful interview today?"

Hildie gulped. *How does she know about Charlie's interview? And how should I answer her question?* She bit her lip, then let out a long exhale. "Staffing has been a problem while I was away, I'm afraid."

"When you are on Emergency Family Leave, staffing should not be your concern."

She bowed her head. "I care about my team a lot."

"Your loyalty to your team is admirable."

"Thank you, Chief."

"But I think you should go home now. As soon as we finish talking."

Hildie gasped. She lifted her head to give Zhang a worried look.

Dr. Zhang's alert, dark eyes met Hildie's firmly. "I suspect that your loyalty and your selfless impulses have been abused. I also imagine that Charlie needs you more direly than we do today."

Hildie'd worried all through this shift so far about the Internal Affairs meeting. She hadn't yet heard from Charlie. Was it still going on? What were they talking about? She drew in a breath, then cleared her throat a couple of times, to make sure she could speak. "Then Eli will have no partner."

"We can take care of personnel coverage." She gave Hildie

long, considering look, then her brows drew together. "Now tell me about the incident with Captain LaRochelle last week."

Hildie flinched away from eye contact. "He probably would say that he only had my best interests in mind."

"To the numerous individuals who reported the incident, it appeared that he attempted to physically restrain you. And that you felt it necessary to forcibly pull free, while shouting, 'Let go of me.' Would you please tell me about that? Is that what happened?"

Her face heated with humiliation, even though she'd done nothing wrong. "He said I was making a mistake by moving too quickly into a relationship with someone who'd too recently been my patient. It made me uncomfortable, but when I tried to leave, he grabbed my arm, and—well—you know the rest."

"I saw the security vid, so yes, I do. You seemed rather upset."

"He's never made it physical before."

"Never made it physical *before*, you say. That's interesting. Does that mean it was all verbal and psychological pressure prior to this incident?"

Hildie lifted her chin and met Zhang's gaze. "I'd have to say yes."

"We have a clear pattern of behaviors?"

Hildie nodded. "I looked back through some of the other incidents I'd documented." She grimaced. "After I wrote about the one last week, that is. I was kind of surprised there were so many."

Zhang's expression showed a flash of dismay, then returned to cool, masklike neutrality. "Perhaps you would be so kind as to forward a copy of that file to me?"

"If you wish, Chief." *In that case, better send a copy to the union, too.* She'd been in no rush to send that file anywhere, uncertain if the things she'd documented truly built a compelling case.

"How widespread is this pattern?" A small furrow formed between Zhang's brows. "Does he treat everyone this way? Or would you say that he treats you differently from other personnel?"

Hildie hesitated. "From my perspective it's difficult to generalize, but he seems to have an uncomfortable level of interest in my personal life. I mean—I'm quite certain he's never critiqued any of *Eli's* relationships."

Zhang nodded.

"I honestly—" Hildie scowled. "I really sometimes worry that I'm blowing trifles out of proportion, but then there's an incident like last week."

"If it was glaringly obvious all the time, we could take action sooner. Thank you for speaking with me candidly."

"You're welcome." *Oh, crap. How's he gonna make me pay for this conversation?*

"I know you originally scheduled your leave through tomorrow night, but then amended the request."

"My crew—"

"*Not* your problem. That leave is now reinstated, and you'll be compensated for the unplanned extra time you've worked, at a double-overtime rate. For now, though, go home."

"Thank you." Hildie offered another "micrograv bow" and turned toward the lockers. Her breath came a little easier, knowing that now she could personally see how Charlie's interview had gone. But foreboding rode her, too. *LaRock will utterly hate that double-overtime. How will he extract payback?*

HILDIE FOUND Nanda at his station outside Charlie's door, wrapping up for the end of his shift. The nurse looked up with surprise. "Welcome!"

"How is he?" Hildie shot a worried glance toward the closed door.

"The interview seems to have gone okay." Nanda also cast a worried look toward the door. "Rex is with him, but I'm sure he'll be happy to see you." He focused on her. "Are you here early?"

Hildie nodded, her throat suddenly tight. "I needed to be *here*, not *there*." She knocked on the door, then poked her head in.

Charlie sat in the bedside chair, still in his dress blues. Rex had been standing in front of him, head down, face pressed against Charlie's chest in a way she'd seen him do several times. Charlie's hands—*both of them mobile! With only an arm cast on the left, now*—stroked Rex's neck. At her knock, they both looked up.

Rex's ears lifted. He stepped back from Charlie. His tail wagged like a big, furry black fan.

Charlie gave her a heart-filling look of startled delight that left her breathless. He rose from the chair, and, *oh, wow,* did he ever look handsome in that uniform.

He took a stride toward her. She met him halfway and let his arms enfold her. Let his kiss send all other thoughts completely elsewhere for a long, sweet, blissful moment. The tension melted out of her body. She clung to his strong, comforting warmth. *I could just stay here for a long time and not think. That would be so, so good.*

Too soon, however, he pulled back and gave her a curious look. "You're here earlier than I expected. Is everything okay?"

She grimaced. "Dr Zhang had some questions about an incident last week, then she let me off early."

Charlie frowned. "What happened last week?"

"A small issue with Captain LaRochelle." She shrugged. "I think it's been dealt with now, but it was vexing for a moment."

Charlie's frown deepened. "Is he treating you all right?"

"We ...." She grimaced. "We appear to have a few issues to iron out. But not till *after* I finish the Family Leave I requested and was granted. Meanwhile, I'm getting double-overtime for the unplanned work."

"What *issues* do you need to work out with your captain?" She recognized that hard edge in Charlie's voice, the set of his jaw, and the angry spark in his eye. The man could get stubborn. And protective.

"I'm—" she hesitated. Avoided his gaze. "I'm not entirely sure I'm ready to talk about it. To *anyone*. I think I need more perspective, and that can only come with time and distance."

He expelled a breath. "Okay."

"Lucky for me, I now can have both some time, *and* some distance." She glanced up at him. His expression had shifted to worry. She offered a rueful smile. "Thank you for not pushing it."

"Sometimes a boss can drive you wild." His mouth made a wry twist. "If you ever *do* want to talk, just know that I've been there, too."

She nodded, then leaned in and wrapped her arms around his torso again for another hug. He cradled her against his chest. *Can we please just do this, for a while?* But he'd had a stressful day, too. "I want to hear about *your* day. I've been thinking about you a lot. What did Internal Affairs want?"

He grimaced. "They asked about the night we were sent to the Hub. The night of the dock breach. It appears that someone falsified my personnel record to make it look as if I still had my Class-C."

The hell? "Falsified your record? Why?"

"That *is* the question." His arms tightened around her. "They had to check, of course, to see if I changed it myself."

Hildie shook her head. "How could you manage to do that? And why *would* you?"

"Exactly. I had no access, need, or desire to do so."

"Did they believe you?"

"I think so."

Rex growled. "I was not allowed in, so I could not check their scent factors, but they did appear to believe him."

Hildie gave him an askance look. "You were not allowed in, so you attended through the link?"

"Certainly."

"Did they know that?"

Charlie cleared his throat. "I, um, failed to point it out to them, but it didn't matter. I would have told Rex all about it afterward, anyway. I value his perspective."

What would the Internal Affairs investigator have thought if he or she had known? "You must realize that raises an ethical question."

Rex and Charlie exchanged a look. Charlie nodded. "It's become more of an issue, now that XK9s are recognized as sapient."

"Next Pack meeting, we shall talk." Rex's ears flicked. "And we need to have another one soon."

Hildie frowned. "Back to the personnel record. That false record put you in mortal danger."

Rex growled again. "The OPD has taken the position that changing it constitutes the reckless endangerment of an officer. I completely agree. It endangered both of us."

"I assume they're looking at ways other XK9s' partners might have been endangered or somehow sabotaged." Charlie's grim expression matched his tone. "But if it's a one-off, then somewhere I have an enemy who wants me dead or badly injured."

Hildie's chest tightened. "And who already succeeded with the 'badly injured' part." What if she'd had to pull his mangled *dead body* out of that bunker? What if that had been *for real*, instead of one of her many nightmares? Or what if he'd been injured the way her patient this afternoon had been? What if she'd had to send him down that elevator knowing he would surely die before help could reach him?

Abrupt horror swamped her, dizzied her. Her heart thundered in triple-time. She shuddered, wrapped her arms around him more tightly, and pressed her face hard against his chest, in spite of all his lumpy buttons and pins. A hard shudder ran through her body.

"Hils?" Charlie's voice held a sharp note of alarm. "Hils? Are you all right?"

She shook her head, unable to speak.

"Her scent is full of fear," Rex said. "I would go so far as to label it 'terror,' or 'horror.'" He nuzzled the side of her face. "Hildie, what happened just now?"

"Give her a minute." Charlie held her close. He kissed the parts of her that he could reach. "It's all right. I'm here, I'm alive, I'm okay, and you're all right."

Might-have-been images pulsed through her mind in horrifying waves, part flashback, part imagined terrors based on real ones. She struggled to draw in a breath, held it, then slowly let it out, too shaky to count as she'd been taught. *Again! In, hold, out.* The nightmare-flashback receded. *In. Hold. Out.*

"You're safe. I'm here. It's all right." Charlie's arms held her, steady and warm. His voice murmured close to her ear. "You're all right. I've got you. I love you. I won't let anything hurt you. "You're all right. Everything's okay . . ."

She sniffled. Her face was wet, and ... what *was* all that hardware on his chest? Whatever, it hurt. She pulled away from it, tilted her chin upward, and gave him a chagrined look through wet eyelashes. "You do?"

His eyes widened, then he smiled. "Caught that, did you? Well, it kinda slipped out, but yeah. I do. I think on some level I always have."

She nodded, relieved to have it out in the air and spoken. "Me too."

"Really?"

"Really."

"So, what just happened to you?"

She blew out a long breath. "Flashback. At least, sort of." She bowed her head. "I have these nightmares, sometimes. Where I —" She gulped. "Where I pull you out of T-1, but instead of being like it was, which was bad enough, you're really, horribly, very clearly dead. Dead like some of my real patients have been." She shuddered. "Or, more recently, I pull you out of that b-bunker—" Her voice shut down on her. A sob wracked her. For a while after that, all she could do was cry.

Charlie held her till she'd cried herself out. He handed her tissues once the worst was over, and murmured comfort, and kissed her again and again.

Hildie pulled herself back together with effort. Her pulse hammered hard and fast. Her breath came ragged. She hiccupped, sniffled, then blew her nose. "Sorry. I know men just love it when women blubber all over them."

"Oh, yeah. Like I'm gonna be put off that you had a flash-back. Me, the king of panic attacks." He kissed her forehead, let her finish wiping her nose, then homed in on her lips.

By the time that kiss ended, they both were breathless. Hildie giggled, giddy from emotional gyrations. "We're kind of a mess, aren't we?"

"Kind of," Charlie agreed. "But I think—I hope—we can sort it out."

CHAPTER 23

RETURN TO CORONA TOWER

"Rex wants to bring me home in *his* auto-nav," Charlie explained to Mama on the com. As he'd hoped, she quickly adapted. All of his many trips home after procedures in the wake of the *Asalatu* had been multigenerational Family affairs, but on this fine Thursday afternoon it was just him, Hildie, and Rex.

Is this my new personal family unit? I'd like that. He smiled. Although he probably should include Shady in that count, shouldn't he?

Nanda earnestly tried to get him to ride down in a wheelchair. "After all, it's hospital policy!"

Charlie shook the faithful nurse's hand, but politely declined. "I'm 'XK9 tough' now. You and the rest of the team did your job so well, I'd feel ridiculous."

So, no wheelchair.

No RAMoD.

Just Hildie's hand in his, and Rex prancing—yes, literally prancing, with head and tail held high—on their short trek down to Orangeboro Medical Center's Police Access Garage.

Hildie carried her duffel. Charlie'd offered to carry it for her, but she insisted. His only burdens consisted of a drawstring bag

202 | A BONE TO PICK

of his own clothes in need of cleaning and his dress blues in a travel sleeve slung over his left shoulder. And the lightest arm shield Zuni had. *This* one would've fit through his uniform sleeve. *What a difference a day makes.*

For any of his earlier trips home from Orangeboro Med, he would've gratefully accepted the wheelchair and piled his burdens in his lap. This time, the extra clothing and the arm shield barely felt like any load at all.

Colors glowed brighter. He'd always striven for situational awareness, but now it took less effort. His body's strength pleased and reassured him. The vibrant joy of being alive hummed through him. He hadn't felt this good in a long, long time. Maybe ever.

Rex badged Charlie and Hildie into the secured garage as his guests. A boxy, beige auto-nav halted before them. *Mm-hmm. Plain-vanilla police vehicle. Perfect.*

Rex wagged his tail. "This is not as aerodynamic as the auto-nav your father tried to get for me, but it has more room inside." The doors and baggage compartment all popped open at once.

Charlie deposited his and then Hildie's bags in the storage compartment.

"Chief Klein was displeased with the vehicle your father provided." Rex's tongue lolled. "He said this would attract less attention than the Citron Flash."

Hildie sputtered a laugh. "A *Citron Flash?*"

"That is what Balchu called it. It was yellow."

"Yes, they tend to be." She quirked an eyebrow at Charlie. "A Citron Flash?"

"My father's got a thing for them." He grinned. "Papa would never indulge in one for himself, but he'd happily borrow Rex's on a regular basis."

"That makes no sense at all, and it reminds me of something my uncle Liam would do." She shook her head and got into the car.

All the way home, Rex chattered about a range of topics,

especially his experiences in micrograv training each morning. The Pack's micrograv harnesses made it easy to maneuver, he reported. "We have become flying dogs!"

Charlie still regretted being unable to train with him, but many of Rex's observations about operating in microgravity paralleled his own experiences. Sharing thoughts with Rex and Hildie helped assuage some of his worry about returning to the Hub.

More than once, Rex also mentioned his wish to ride with his head stuck out of the auto-nav's window, but to Charlie's relief, he refrained from actually doing so. Charlie and Hildie held hands and leaned against each other. Charlie glanced sidelong at her from time to time when she and Rex traded comments. He loved the play of emotions on her face.

My new personal family unit. If I can keep it. A warm rush of pleasure made his belly relax. His breathing slowed and deepened. Sparkling joy welled up within him. *This. This is my heart's desire.*

The car pulled into Corona's basement garage. The last time he'd come home from the hospital, the stairs had looked high and steep as a primary terrace. This time he beat Hildie to the auto-nav's storage compartment and snatched up her duffel along with his bags, its added weight negligible. "We can drop all of this at the cleaning station."

Hildie gave him a concerned look. "I can carry that."

He grinned. "I'm good." He resisted an impulse to bound up the stairs two at a time. Instead, he matched his pace to Hildie's. They climbed side-by-side.

The Family waited in the Courtyard. *All of them,* or at least most of them. From 128-year-old Great-Grandma Loretta to two-year-old cousins Hakan and Kristen, they grinned and called out greetings. Mama stepped forward to give him a hug, then she gave Hildie one, too. Papa grasped his hand and patted his shoulder. Next it was Caro's turn for hugs, and after that his little nieces Sophie and Lacey closed in. He handed off the laundry to Papa so he could scoop them up in his arms. Their squeals and sweet baby-kisses filled his heart.

Hot damn, it was good to be home!

Rex lifted his ears and tried to sort through the babble of sounds from the Family's welcome-home greetings to Charlie. He'd caught that odd *bzzz-zzzz* sound again. It was a new sound. He didn't remember it from any time before he and Shady heard it on the inner courtyard steps this morning. He and his Amare couldn't pursue it then, unless they wanted to be late to work. But now ….

There weren't many insects on Rana, only carefully-controlled populations of pollinators, scavengers and some farmed for protein or other products. It hadn't been a matter of conscious thought for him to memorize their characteristic whirs, buzzes, and chirps, but he knew them by now. This? This was different. Freshly suspicious after recent events, he refused to let a strange buzz go uninvestigated.

There it was again. Just for an instant, he glimpsed a tiny, hurtling speck. It darted between tables, zipped through dappled shadows, zoomed under a chair seat. Rex waited till it zinged away from beneath the far side of the table. He followed, thankful his eyes had evolved to catch just this sort of movement.

Ears up, he followed it toward Corona Tower's Memory Garden. He placed his paws with deliberate care to silence each step. *Over here somewhere.* He stopped. Cocked his head. Strained to filter out the soft splash of the Memory Garden's water feature and the babble of human voices in the background. Tried to listen past the *legitimate* bugs' sounds among the planters, Gloria's wind-chimes up on Level Four, and the rustle of air movement through thousands and thousands of leaves. These sounds echoed down from the five above-ground residence levels that loomed over him, along with the ambient creaks of a large, 90-some-year-old structure.

But he lost the buzzing intruder among the roses' leaves near the water feature. He settled in to detail the rose leaves, aware at the back of his mind that Charlie and Hildie had now started up the steps. *Ah!* Here came that *bzzz-zzzz* again. A flash of motion zoomed upward.

He watched to see where it landed, then ran for the stairwell. Soon he sorted through the intricate depths of the inverted tomatoes that vined downward from their roots on the level above. Their strong blanket of odor mingled with peppery, companion-planted marigolds in baskets suspended from nearby columns. No scent of something electronic penetrated any of that—assuming it was a surveillance device, and not some newly-introduced species of bee.

Lots of more-familiar bees zoomed about. Not only were the marigolds in bloom, but clusters of tiny yellow blossoms accented the tomato vines. On the next section over, cucumbers vined on a trellis and opened their golden trumpets to welcome apian visitors. Equal-opportunity pollinators visited them all.

Rex pulled back, wary lest he disturb them. Was the source of the mystery-buzz here somewhere, or had it eluded him while he was in the stairwell? He growled and continued his search.

HILDIE CLIMBED the stairs side-by-side with Charlie. The grin on his face and the spring in his steps told her he was flying high on enthusiasm and Semi-SuperCop energy. Her heart soared in parallel with his mood, but she'd seen his strength suddenly cut out on him more than once since he'd emerged from his final re-gen. No harm in keeping an eye on him.

Otherwise, being here gave her a sensation of having somehow stepped into a time warp. The people were older and there were new little kids, but Corona Tower itself didn't seem to have changed in the last five years. She even remembered most of the New Year's holiday lights and streamers from before.

Back when she and Charlie worked together, she'd joined the crew many times at his and Felicia's place. They had a massive 3D wall-screen in their living room that made viewers feel as if they were *right there* at every quiddo match. The year before the *Asalatu* accident, the Comets had enjoyed a winning season. Every match had been a must-see, from the season opener right through the team's ultimate victory in the Station Championship. And unless they were on duty, the *Triumph* crew had watched every single one at Charlie's.

But lots of things had happened since then. Charlie had refused to see any of the old *Triumph* crew at the hospital after the wreck. She hadn't seen him again until his three heart-breaking attempts to requalify in a MERS-V, each attempt thwarted by a crippling panic attack. He hadn't wanted visitors after those, either.

New people came and went from the *Triumph* crew. She'd made Sergeant. Abi and Smita had moved from dating casually to being Amares, and last year to being Domestic Partners—all while wedged into the apartment she and Abi had shared since they'd first come home from the University. Then the dock breach happened, like one of her nightmares brought to life.

But that seeming nightmare had opened the road to today. If things worked out this time with Charlie ... She bit her lip and squeezed his hand. *One step at a time.* What would she find at the top of the stairs? Would Charlie's home remain as unchanged as the rest of this place?

By the time they started up the last flight to the fifth level, his steps had slowed and he was breathing more heavily. So was she, but she wasn't the one who'd just come home from the hospital.

Woah. She halted at the top. This was different. The lounges outside his bedroom french doors had changed little, but beyond that lay a large open space. She remembered a dinner table and chairs out here. The widened inner balcony area where she and the crew had eaten so many pre- and post-match dinners lay empty, except for a few fallen leaves. No table. A few chairs stacked by the dining-room louvers. But the dusty louvers were closed. Cobwebs and dead leaves tangled among the chairs' arms and legs.

Next moment, the door to the living room swung wide.

"Welcome home, Charlie!" The security system greeted them in Uncle Hector's voice. "Welcome back, Hildie!"

She laughed. "Wow. It remembers me, from way back—" She stepped forward to go inside, then gasped.

CHAPTER 24

THE GHOST OF THE PURPLE PALACE

C harlie looked at Hildie. She'd halted in the doorway to his living room.

She simply stared for a second, mouth open. "You, um, certainly opened up the place."

A rush of old memories, still sharp with the heart-stab of betrayal, ambushed him. He visualized the way it used to be, the way Hildie would remember it. The ruffles, the gold-leaf, the curlicues. Shades and tints of purple, lilac, lavender, pink. Silk and velvet, ribbons and lace. Not his style at all, but Felicia had loved it. And when Felicia was happy, she'd gone out of her way to make Charlie happy. At least, in the beginning.

He stared into his living room as it was now, actually looking at it for the first time in ages. Plain white walls. A brown, threadbare sofa. An end-table supported an unlit lamp and a small collection of used coffee mugs, drinking glasses, and empty beer bottles. They huddled like refugees in the shadowy far corner. The only remnants of Felicia's reign were a big wall screen he'd never bothered to remove after it shorted out, and the light lilac, cut-pile carpeting. By now the carpet was mud-stained and worn, especially since a certain enormous dog had moved in.

"What—?" Hildie asked. "Um, where did it all go? With *her*?"

His throat ached and his breath came short. "No. She left everything here." Like him. Abandoned.

"Mm. I bet that was no fun to deal with."

He ran a hand over his face and drew in a breath. "I'll owe the Family a massive debt forever. They handled it. Once I was awake again, they asked me what I wanted to do." He shook his head. "I-I didn't want to think about it. But I also didn't want to come home to it. Andy, Quinn, and Aunt Serafina packed it all up. They took it to be auctioned on consignment. I told them to divide the money between them. They put it in the Family Trust account. Before I came home, it was all gone and sold."

"I can't even begin to imagine how you must have felt."

Old heartache throbbed like a bone-deep bruise. He'd felt as if wind could echo through him, he was so hollow. Caro and Andy had dragged the current pieces of furniture up from Corona's storeroom, while his cousins hastily painted over the mauve-and-pink walls. There'd still been a tang of fresh paint in the air when they brought him home from the hospital.

The paint-smell might be long gone by now, but almost nothing else had changed since then. Except for the clutter on the side table and the stained carpet, it almost looked as if he hadn't been home since. He stared at the large, muddy paw prints. Evidence of life had begun to accumulate again, once Rex arrived.

Hildie's fingers tightened gently on his hand. "I remember so *much* overtime to support this place. All the luxuries." She glanced significantly toward the now-dead screen.

"I never could make enough money." The exhaustion of that period, the deepening despair, descended upon him again. He shook his head. "At the end, I'd go days away from home. Work, rent a sleep box, then back on. I picked up patrol work, too."

"*How* many hours up-top?" She gave him a worried look. There were caps on how many hours a person was allowed to work in micrograv without returning to 1-G.

He sighed and avoided her gaze. "Not over the limits. I pushed 'em, sure. But I rotated down when I needed to."

"I'm glad you had that much sense."

"Frankly, there was less and less reason to go home." He frowned. "I never figured out how to rekindle what we'd had." He'd given it his all. Not that it had helped.

"Normally, that takes mutual effort."

The old pain drove its claws deep. *Damn it,* hadn't he worked through this, already? "Please promise you'll at least talk to me, before you walk out?"

Silence. He looked over to see anger in her face.

"What makes you think I'll walk out?" Her voice was higher, tight.

Heartsick dread washed over him. "Well, my track record's not real great. Felicia left. Pam left. She and I *did* talk before she went, but it didn't help. I didn't get her jokes, and I kept waking her up with my nightmares. Have to face the chance that maybe someday you'll get bored, or I'll exhibit some quirk you can't live with."

"I forgot about Pam." Hildie let out a breath. "I guess I can understand, after you've been burned twice. But trust me. I'm not like that faithless Felicia, and I'm no damned Pam, either. I already know you get my jokes, and any time *I'm* not pleased with you, you'll know it!"

He gave a rueful grunt. "Like now? Sorry. I'm a little skittish on my blind side."

"Uh-huh." She walked ahead of him across the worn lilac carpet, then turned toward the central hallway. He followed, still holding her hand. "I can tell you're starting to sag. You need a nap, if you want to be ready for the welcome-home dinner tonight."

"Yes, Nurse." Their footsteps sounded on hard bamboo flooring, where deep-purple carpet once had been laid. He glimpsed his kitchen when they passed it, with the dishwasher door open and large dog food pans dropped in at haphazard angles. "Ah. XK9 housekeeping at its best."

Hildie stopped. "What?"

"In the kitchen."

She backed up a few steps, then laughed. "They haven't quite got the dishwasher figured out yet, have they?"

"I suspect the lack of thumbs doesn't help their accuracy."

She stepped into the kitchen, then bent to rearrange the chaotic collection of dog food dishes that cluttered the bottom rack. "These prongs weren't spaced for pans like this." She moved some to the top rack. "You have a *lot* of dog dishes."

"Two XK9s in residence."

She laughed. "That's right. They're now Amares."

He nodded.

"How did Pam take that?"

Hildie'd been back at work and he'd been back in re-gen while Shady and her partner had worked that out, but Rex had recapped some of it for him. "Oddly enough, Rex and Shady found an ally in Balchu. Well, Balchu, their apartment's size, and the food bill. Apparently, Rex stayed over at Shady's for at least one night, that first week after the dock breach. And that dog can *eat*."

She frowned. "Balchu?"

Charlie looked away with a grimace. "Pam's Amare. The one she left me to go back to."

Hildie closed the dishwasher, punched it on, then walked back over to him and took both of his hands. *So nice to have both available.* She looked him in the eye. "My gain, and I don't care about her."

He smiled. "So. You're not bored yet?"

"Not yet. Let's get you to bed."

"Wow, *that's* direct."

Her grin flashed. "Not how I meant it, Morgan, and you know it. Not right now, anyway." She hesitated. "Unless you're less tired than I think you are?"

Oh, that sounds promising. Too bad she's right. "The results will probably be better if I nap first."

Her grin tantalized him. "You should know that I intend to test your hypothesis. After all, if you don't test it, you'll never know."

"True." Breathless but suddenly less tired, he followed her toward his bedroom. With *that* hypothesis set to be tested, would he be able to sleep after all?

She pushed open the door, then laughed. "What? You didn't keep the bed?"

Back in the days when the *Triumph* crew had nicknamed his apartment "The Purple Palace," the main bedroom had been draped in purple damask and golden lace. It had featured a large, heart-shaped bed with purple silk sheets and an elaborate, tiara-like canopy affixed to the ceiling.

He half-groaned and shook his head. "The bed was the first thing to go." He hadn't dared show his crewmates Felicia's *sanctum sanctorum.* She often retreated there for privacy whenever they came to visit. If the *Triumph* crew ever *had* seen it, he'd feared the teasing would be merciless. "How do you know about the bed?"

She gave him a rueful look. "I snooped. Sorry. I just—my resolve wore down over time, and I couldn't resist. I apologize."

"Forgiven." He smiled at her. "Water long under the bridge, by now."

"Oh, I paid for my trespassing. I used to daydream about getting you between those heart-shaped silk sheets. Made the jealousy even worse."

He grimaced. "If it's any consolation, the worst fight we ever had was over that bed. She bought it on a whim, and had it installed while I was away on a twelve-hour. Never even asked me."

"Mm. I bet it wasn't cheap, either."

"Cost more than a month's pay. And I was *already* working overtime to cover the bills."

Hildie blew out a breath. "Eww. The sheets alone probably cost a fortune."

"It was ridiculous." Indignation burned his gut. He took a moment to center himself. No need to get angry about it now. He glanced up at the ceiling. If one knew where to look, there was still a divot where the "tiara" had been harder to dislodge than expected. Quinn told him they'd hired the same crew who'd installed it a year earlier. Charlie had considered filling in that divot, but ultimately decided to leave it as a reminder of glamour's unexpected hazards.

His current, rectangular bed worked just as well, and fit the room better. Speaking of which, Hildie was right. He probably—okay, he *did* need a nap. "This plain, ordinary bed will work just fine. I'm sorry I can't be a better host and test your hypothesis sooner."

"That's all right. I could do with a nap on a real bed, myself." She pulled her arm half out of one sleeve, then stopped. "You okay with that?"

"Yes! Definitely." The likelihood of his actually being able to sleep faded once more.

"Nap *first*, mind you. But there's no reason we can't spoon." Off came the kurta.

He shed his clothing as fast as he could without looking away from her. All thoughts of napping disappeared. He'd caught tantalizing glimpses of her in his hospital room—and it wasn't as if they'd never shared a locker room, back in the day. But back then he'd been assiduously struggling not to notice. Now she riveted every particle of his attention.

Unlike him, she took her time and made a little show of the unveiling, although any coyness in her sultry poses was belied by the huge grin on her face. Charlie's pulse doubled and redoubled. She reached out to draw him closer.

He caught his breath at her touch, then pulled her into a skin-on-skin embrace. It took a couple of tries to make his voice work. "You know, it occurs to me that we can't actually test whether it's *better* after a nap, until we have a 'before' sample."

Her brows rose. "Oh, that's an excellent point. We shouldn't skimp on our scientific method, should we?" Her lips captured his before he could answer.

CHARLIE'S UNCLE Ralph turned away from his irrigation readouts to quirk a grizzled eyebrow at Rex. "New species of bee?" He shook his head. "Not that I've heard of."

Rex had found him in a corner of the ground-floor farm-equipment storage area, after the greeting party disbanded. "Just to be thorough, do you know of any insect that makes this sound?" Rex played back the mystery *bzzz-zzzz*, as picked up via his OPD-issued wearable audio recorder.

Ralph's eyebrows puckered into a frown. His hazel eyes narrowed. "Play it again."

Bzzz-zzzz rattled Rex's vocalizer.

"Again."

Bzzz-zzzz.

Ralph shook his head. "Nope. Can't say that sounds familiar."

"If you should happen to hear it while you're working, please see if you can catch a glimpse of whatever made it." Rex laid his ears back. "I am worried it could be some kind of surveillance device."

Ralph's frown deepened into a scowl. "From the same lowlifes who sent that agent to go ruin Reihan's quinoa?"

"Yes." Reihan Khan Al-Masri was next-door Bonita Tower's master gardener. She'd already plowed the ruined stalks under and re-planted, but Bonita Family had taken the loss of that crop pretty hard.

"If I find one and it's electronic, can I smash it?" His fierce grin and angry scent said he'd enjoy doing that.

Rex flicked his ears. "If you can't capture it intact, go right ahead. Even the wreckage should offer our techs some clues. But be sure to save all the pieces you can."

"Will do." His grin left Rex in some doubt that he'd 'be able to' capture one intact.

Rex padded back up the stairs to the first level, then a short distance down the balcony to the workshop of Charlie's other blood-related uncle, Hector. The Family's foremost inventor had an office in the downtown corporate headquarters of his Hectorvault Security business, but he spent at least half his time here, tinkering with new ideas. He and Grant, the eight-year-old younger son of Charlie's cousin Gloria and her husband Quinn, looked up from a worktable covered with robotic parts.

Rex lolled his tongue. "Is this a school project, or do you have a new co-inventor?"

Both faces, one dark with graying eyebrows, the other smaller and medium-tan, split with near-identical grins of delight.

"Yes!" Hector patted Grant's slender shoulder. "At least, he's *also* getting school credit."

"It's a new manipulator for one of Great-Uncle Ralph's planters." Grant gave a little wriggle of delight. "I thought up an improvement all by myself! If it works, I can apply for a patent!"

"Here is hoping it works." Rex wagged his tail—but carefully. He never knew which objects in Hector's workshop were just stuff sitting around, and which were delicate prototypes he might destroy with a single wag. "Hector, may I ask you a security-related question?"

"Certainly." Hector stood. "Grant, d'you think you can take it from here for a few minutes?"

Grant's eyes widened, but he squared his shoulders and replied with a sharp nod.

Hector smiled and headed for the door. "Come walk with me, Rex."

Rex followed him to the stairwell. "It involves potential Transmondian surveillance devices," he texted to Hector's HUD.

Charlie's uncle nodded but said nothing. They retraced Rex's earlier path to Ralph's lair, then out through the rear double doors. Hector led him to the edge of the almond grove, just beyond the vineyard. Then he turned to stare off across the Sirius Valley. "Think this'll do it?"

The almond trees were no longer in bloom. Fuzzy oblong proto-fruits had begun to form. The grape plants on the nearby vineyard rows had progressed past blooming, too. There, the someday-grapes resembled tiny, hard knots in clusters among the wide leaves. Both crops could poison a dog who ate them, but he didn't think Hector had meant to imply anything. More likely he'd wanted to go someplace outside the residence tower. Interesting that he'd chosen a place where few pollinators would come.

Rex listened for the mystery-buzz somewhere nearby. Nothing but the wind through the leaves, and his and Hector's heartbeats and breathing. The distant thunder-and-shriek of the Rim-Runner maglev echoed from the far side of the torus. Other ordinary noises ebbed and flowed. But no buzz. "Have you heard this sound?" He played his *bzzz-zzzz* recording.

Hector's mouth tightened. "That's not a bee, is it?"

"Ralph and I do not think so."

"Neither do I." Hector frowned. "Just heard that for the first time this morning. I've been running scans on several frequencies ever since, but I haven't picked up anything yet. Covert tech usually transmits in micro-bursts. Gotta monitor 24-7 on exactly the right frequency to catch it." He quirked an eyebrow. "Your SBI pals have any tips to offer?"

"I intend to ask them about it as soon as I return to work. This is better discussed in person, in the secured environment of the investigation center."

CHAPTER 25

CHARLIE WORKS OUT ...
SEVERAL THINGS

C harlie stopped in the entrance to his home gym, sighed, then stepped inside. Might as well jump-start his Saturday morning with something positive, despite Hildie's having had to go back to work at the crack of dawn. Melancholy dragged his mood into bleak, gray depths.

Their "hypothesis-testing" on Thursday had led to spectacular outcomes, but, they both agreed, inconclusive results. Re-testing had been necessary after his "Welcome Home" supper. They'd both slept extremely well that night. This led him to one conclusive result, anyway: he never wanted to sleep any way but spooning with Hildie after this.

Hypothesis-testing had resumed the following day. Hildie declared that she wanted enough data-points for a statistically valid sample. He smiled. *Fine with me.* The day also had provided a pretty good test of his growing Semi-SuperCop stamina. That was coming along nicely, but there *were* limits.

All too quickly, Hildie's leave ran out. As she predicted, her captain booked her for back-to-back 12-hour shifts. *Rat bastard.* She still hadn't told Charlie about the "incident" Dr. Zhang had wanted to discuss with her last week. Maybe so Charlie wouldn't find it necessary to hunt that lowlife down and make a few things very clear? Charlie scowled. *What did LaRock do that was bad enough to concern Zhang?*

Hildie's absence ached like a day-old wound. But Charlie's physical therapist had come out to do an eval yesterday. This had created an inconvenient-but-necessary pause in the hypothesis-testing. The PT prescribed an assortment of stretching and strengthening routines, most of them familiar from the last time Charlie'd gotten out of re-gen, but the ramp-up this time was quicker, the routines more strenuous, in recognition of his augmentations. Even if it *wasn't* as pleasant as *yesterday* morning's wake-up exercises, maybe starting the day with these routines would give him an endorphin boost.

Maybe it would help clear his head.

Damn, he missed Hildie.

He yawned. Restlessness had goaded him up and out early. With Hildie gone, the bed was a desolate place.

He walked to the mats on one side of a space that originally had been built to be a living room. He'd created his gym inside the empty shell of an unoccupied residence unit at right angles to his apartment. He and Rex currently had all of Level Five to themselves, other Family members having chosen units on lower levels. Corona, like most Ranan residence towers, was built on stronger-than-needed foundations, sturdy enough to support eight above-ground levels. An expanding Family might someday need them.

Level Five had gone up the year Charlie turned seven. The Family had looked at his generation, done some simple math, and decided they needed more room, unless they wanted some of the kids forced to move out when they grew up. The place had been a construction zone for several months. He, his sister, and their cousins had played on piles of building materials and chased each other through the framed-in parts, once the floor was solid. They were *supposed* to stay out. And they did, while construction workers were actively building there. But once the workers went home, he and the other kids delighted in sneaking up here. It was a wonder nobody got hurt, but they'd had a blast. And now here he was, "pioneering" on this level in his own 158-square-meter living space. Rex and Shady might eventually move into an adjacent unit to rear their puppies. Would Hildie someday live with him here at Corona? He smiled. *I can hope.*

He began his first set of stretches. With part of his attention he listened for the *"bzzz-zzzz"* sound Rex had recorded and shared with him just before supper on Thursday. Were the Transmondians electronically spying on Corona Family now? Hector's counter-surveillance efforts continued, bolstered by aid and input from the SBI. Rex had found help from SSA Mike Santiago and a member of Santiago's team. Signals intel tech specialist SA Pat Cornwell's uncle might be Rex's least-favorite Ranan, but Rex said Pat was nice enough. So far their efforts had turned up nothing, but that didn't mean there was nothing to find.

Uncle Ralph, for one, was on the hunt with a vengeance. And a hammer on his tool belt.

Aunt Hannah had hoped to meet this weekend with Bonita Family representatives, the legal team she'd assembled, and the entire Pack with their partners, here at Corona. She'd first brought the team together to oppose Transmondian efforts to "recall" the Pack as "defective." Now she also meant to join forces with Bonita Family and sue the Transmondian Government over the damaged crop, as well as breach of privacy. But if the Transmondians were listening in, this was hardly the place to discuss legal strategies against them. Her plans had to be scrapped. It was another irritation on top of the worrying prospect of court battles and legal fees.

He moved on to the warm-up sets with hand-weights. Tried to smooth out his mood, focus on counting reps, and forgo his worries. The Semi-SuperCop augmentations should allow him to surpass the extent of his former natural strength, even in his regenerated arm. A goal worth working for!

He'd heard nothing more from the investigation into his

altered personnel records. *Of course not.* Until Wednesday, he'd been a suspect. Might still be, for all he knew. He ground his teeth. Keeping him in the dark was sound investigative practice but irritating as hell.

Damn. He'd lost count of his reps. He started the set over again. Soon enough, a sub-level ache in his muscles told him he was pushing into hypertrophy, breaking down tissue so it would self-repair stronger.

Anger at the unknown record-saboteur was less easy to dismiss than irritation with Broaddus's investigation. Charlie scowled. Was Wisniewski's hypothetical mole behind that falsification? He couldn't know for sure. Rex's attempt to use his Admin status to poke around in Charlie's personnel record had been frustrated by a firewall. And they had no other good places to seek concrete clues. He clenched his jaws and kept lifting. Faster. Harder. *Dammit.* For now, anyway, he and Rex would have to let Broaddus handle the investigation.

Okay, better not get carried away with the weights and over-train. He'd finished that set and then some. He racked his hand-weights, shook out his arms, then moved back to the mats for the second series of stretches.

Sure would be nice if he could talk with Hildie about all of this. She might have a better perspective. *Not happening, damn it.*

She'd go home to Feliz Tower tomorrow for a mandatory 24 downside. If she was as dead-tired as they both knew she would be, she should sleep for as much of that time as possible. Much as they might yearn for more hypothesis-testing, they had agreed it was smarter to remove temptation. Then she'd go back for another damned twelve-hour. *What does LaRochelle have against giving her a few straight-eights with normal breaks?*

Enough stretching. Time to move to the more serious weights. He fiddled with his cable machine's calibrations a little, to follow his PT's prescription, then started with pull-ups.

Hildie's work schedule was also problematical for another important reason. On Monday, while she was trying to sleep for

twelve hours during the day—the hardest time to get any sleep
—Rex and the Pack would test for their Class-Bs. Charlie had no
doubt all would easily pass.

Back when Charlie'd earned *his* original Class-B, the test at
the end of the 5-day certification course had happened the
following Monday, just as the Pack's test would. Charlie's Class-
B "graduation" had been a simple gathering of the class after the
test. There'd been handshakes, congratulations, and a distribu-
tion of certificates. Done. But no such luck for the Pack.

He moved on to crossover pulldowns without derailing his
train of thought.

Members of the Orangeboro Pack were arguably the most
famous dogs in all the Systems of the Alliance right now, thanks
to Rana Station's claim that they were sapient. According to the
news feeds, the Universe was fascinated with a possible new
uplifted species.

Once the press got wind of this upcoming Pack achievement,
their graduation had morphed in the planning from a quiet
recognition held in Police HQ Meeting Room Two, into a glitzy,
sold-out event in the Civic Center. The Civic Center event
required considerable elaborate planning and was now scheduled for Thursday night.

Gaaah. Enough crossover pulldowns. He shifted to bench
presses.

Charlie might not be able to graduate with the Pack, but he'd
missed enough of their milestones already. He'd reserved front-
row seats for himself and Hildie. Of course, there'd be media
coverage. Lots of it. From all over the Universe. And the color
commentators were guaranteed to mention him. They'd taken
note when he *hadn't* been there, so his return was bound to spark
comment. No question they'd also spotlight his companion.
Poised, beautiful Hildie would become a new media sensation,
at least until the next sparkly object caught their attention.

And once those buzzing vid cams zeroed in on him and
Hildie, every single friend, acquaintance, associate, or distant

connection of *both* their Families would sit up and take extremely interested notice.

He sighed and started the last set. *Let the gossip-games begin.* Probably well before the end of the live broadcast on Thursday night, dozens of extended family and friends would start hitting both Corona and Feliz with about a million questions. Personal, probing, Family-matter-type questions. Questions Feliz Family couldn't answer unless they'd had a chance to meet him beforehand.

One last sequence of curls and reverse curls. He fell into a steady rhythm that let his mind go straight back to Feliz Family. He didn't know them very well. He'd been to Feliz Tower a few times long ago, but that didn't really count. A new Boyfriend- or Girlfriend-of-Record who wasn't already well known to the Family must be formally introduced. Yes, and questioned on important matters of Family interest once the relationship became official. It could get pretty intense. He remembered when Caro had brought Andy home with her one New Year's from Green Mountain University.

Normally, the love interest was more familiar to the Family than Andy had been. Or even than Hildie had become to his Family in the last few weeks. Corona Family had long since vetted Hildie. Every encounter they had with her told Charlie they'd found her more than acceptable. She fit in easily. Got along with everyone. The Family could trust her to be a compat- ible neighbor and a reliable person who knew how to pitch in and help, as Felicia never had.

But it was a different story with Charlie and Feliz Family. They probably had only faint memories of a young MERS-V driver who'd stopped by a handful of times as part of Hildie's crew of co-workers. Charlie needed to be re-introduced. Properly and formally, this time. The full treatment.

Charlie wouldn't get any opportunities to see Hildie again before Tuesday night. *Damn you, LaRochelle!* And thanks to her crazy schedule, they couldn't have his formal introduction dinner with Feliz Family before Tuesday night. It was a problem for other Family scheduling to have the dinner Wednesday. So the date for the big event was set for Tuesday.

And that dinner was a *big* event.

He shook out his arms and moved back to the mats for a last round of stretches. What if Feliz Family didn't approve of him? Charlie grimaced. The old Ranan saying "love is personal, but children are Family business" applied here. What if they balked at the "Semi-SuperCop" augmentations? Hildie said it wouldn't be a big deal, but would they agree with her?

He deepened his stretch. Tight arm muscles slowly eased and lengthened under his gentle pressure, but his gut stayed tied in knots at the thought of that dinner. If Feliz Family didn't conclude he was acceptable as a potential Family member and progenitor of possible future generations, then he and Hildie would never be able to take their relationship beyond being each other's Amares. Well, not without stepping outside of her Family's good graces.

That's what had happened with Felicia. Corona had tolerated her, but they hadn't liked her, even though Charlie was head-over-heels in love with her. Once Felicia realized she'd never be approved beyond Amare status, her demands for more luxuries and pretty, shiny things had escalated. Overtime started eating him alive. *How did I not see that for what it was?*

He shook his head and stretched his other side. No need to wallow in those self-recriminations. Right now he had a more important concern. Because if Feliz didn't approve of him, Corona might have difficulty accepting Hildie without losing some of their own social standing.

Hildie had scoffed at this idea. "I love you, and they will, too. Don't worry." Rex and Shady also had dismissed it with snorts and tongue-lolls, as if XK9s reared in Transmondia understood all about Ranan social politics. But would it really be as easy as they thought?

He'd better make sure his dinner jacket still fit, but it went way beyond needing to make sure he looked okay. Because, along with the Semi-SuperCop thing and the abrupt plunge into a serious relationship after five years of estrangement, there also was a cultural question.

About a generation ago, Rana Station had gone through a period when seemingly everyone was exploring their ethnic backgrounds. The Human Diaspora had drawn people into space from all over Heritage Earth. During the early decades of space expansion, many cultural practices had been lost. But a few generations after its founding, family-oriented Rana Station had collectively decided they must "reclaim their roots," in an effort to "fully embrace the nature of their being." Or something like that.

People all over the Station suddenly yearned for knowledge of the cultures they'd descended from. Religious and cultural festivals, ethnic foods, and traditional clothing all became important preoccupations.

Charlie finished his last stretch, then grabbed a handful of wipes to clean the exercise equipment. Many people still observed aspects of their heritage cultures. Far as he could tell, a lot of people had cherry-picked the clothing, foods, festivals, rituals, and other practices they liked best, and ditched the rest. But did it really make a difference how they'd settled on something, if they found it fulfilling?

Corona had done its back-to-our-origins research, too. His parents had been young adults back then, about the age he was now. After the Family's flirtation with Chinese, central African, north European, and North American cultures, Corona's way of operating hadn't ultimately changed much.

But Feliz had taken its cultural heritage far more seriously than Corona had. They'd enthusiastically embraced their ethnicities from Ireland in the British Isles, the eastern Mediterranean, north Africa, and especially the Bengal region of northeast India. They'd embraced several traditions, many of the foods, and an assortment of clothing types suited to Rana's climate.

What if Charlie said something insensitive, or unwittingly violated a cultural norm that offended them?

"You worry too much," Hildie had said. "Just follow my lead." Later she'd relented enough to send him a couple of articles about cultural customs. "They'll appreciate any sincere attempt. Just relax."

Relax. Sure. Piece of cake. He blew out a long, worried breath and tossed the last of the wipes into the recycler. Then he caught himself. *Aw, dammit.*

For a man who'd just done stretches to loosen up, he sure was tense.

CHAPTER 26

THE DINNER AND THE BUG HUNT

C harlie fended Rex's wet nose-pokes away from his hand, then re-straightened his dark blue dinner jacket. It was early Tuesday evening. In one short hour, he was due at Feliz Tower.

"Are you really going to wear that jacket?" Shady had enthroned herself on his bed to observe from a distance. "It is too small."

He scowled at his reflection in the triple mirror across from the walk-in. She might be right. Damned thing constricted every movement, not only where the arm shield made his left sleeve tight. But he didn't have another that would serve for tonight. And he'd had this one specially re-tailored to fit, just last Saturday. What the hell? He ran a breathing pattern, wiped sweaty palms across his thighs. This evening *had* to go well.

"You will feel better once you see Hildie again." Shady stood up in the middle of his bed.

He missed her so much his throat hurt and his breath came short. "If she's not too exhausted."

Shady stretched, then hopped down from his bed and shook vigorously. "Working in micrograv is hard. That is true."

"She was smart to go straight home to sleep between

watches. She needed it." Charlie hoped she'd actually gotten some sleep. "Squeezing in a dinner party during a mandatory 24 downside would be bad enough. Squeezing in one as important as this?" He grimaced. The day Caro'd brought Andy to Corona Tower for the first time had been … intense. To his shame, he hadn't helped things any, with his stupid-little-brother practical joke.

He released a shaky exhale, then turned for a side view in the mirror. He was as ready as he was going to get. He unbuttoned the restrictive jacket, straightened his bow tie, then turned to face the XK9s. "How do I look?"

"Nervous." Rex lolled his tongue.

That's it, laugh it up. "I don't have toilet paper stuck to my shoe, my fly's not open, stuff like that, right?"

"No, those things are fine. You look nice." Shady flicked her ears. "Try not to hyperventilate. Or overstress that jacket."

"You always look nice to me," Rex said. "Let us go see what Mimi and Caro say."

His mother and sister waited in the courtyard, along with Papa and practically everybody else in Corona Family. They all looked up when he and his furry escort came down the stairs.

Mama went over him with her lint-lifter. It came back black and gray with dog hairs and festooned with a tuft of tan undercoat.

Caro frowned, buttoned his jacket, frowned harder, then unbuttoned it again. "I *thought* you'd started bulking up in the shoulders already. This proves I'm not seeing things." She eyed him critically. "I don't think anybody else in the Family is the right size to lend you something, though. You're just gonna have to go with the stuffed-sausage look tonight."

"Thanks for that." Charlie grimaced. "You're a real confidence-builder."

Caro laughed. "You could have it much worse, little bro. You think I don't remember what you did the night Andy came over for The Big Dinner?"

Fu-u-uck. His stomach dropped. Was she planning payback? "God. I am so sorry. I really didn't understand—"

Rex's ears went straight up. *What did you do?*

Later. Please. He rubbed his face, still queasy. *I was a really bratty little brother.* Full understanding of how she must've felt hadn't dawned until this moment.

"Water under the bridge. All is forgiven." Her eyes glinted. She leaned in, whispered, "Or is it?"

"Cut it out, both of you!" Mama frowned, sized him up. "I'd better call the tailor tonight while you're out. It won't do for your dress blues to fit that way Thursday."

Too true. "You're a lifesaver." Charlie gave her a quick kiss on the cheek, then squared his shoulders. Carefully.

Aunt Serafina elbowed Caro aside, to pin a boutonniere on his lapel. He stood still for it but endured a humiliating flashback to his first neighborhood dance at age fourteen.

"Blue delphiniums, dear." Aunt Serafina patted his cheek. "For an open heart and an ardent attachment. Goes with your jacket."

His ears burned, but she meant well. And the boutonniere did add a nice grace note. "Thank you. Namaste." He placed his hands together and gave her a little bow. He'd been practicing the unaccustomed gesture, hoping not to make a fool of himself tonight.

"That looked *almost* natural. Keep practicing." Caro patted his shoulder, then laughed. "Damn, you could bounce a metal novum off that! Breathe shallow!"

"Here you go, son." Papa handed him a wrapped box of Cousin Manny's signature chocolate truffles, and—*woah.* A bottle of the Year 51 Corona Tower Merlot? The weather supposedly never changed on Rana Station, but somehow that didn't mean the wine always came out the same. The 51 merlot from all along Starboard Hill was legendary to wine lovers on-Station. Corona Tower's had been judged in the top tier.

Charlie gazed at the bottle reverently. This was one of Corona's last few from that 43-year-old stock. Hildie's relatives might have adopted many north Indian practices, but abstention from alcohol was not one of them. They would appreciate this gift and read the meaning: *Corona has sent you our very best. We strongly approve of this relationship. We hope you do too.* Warmed, he could only babble his thanks.

"Now relax!" Papa patted the drumhead-tight jacket fabric stretched across Charlie's shoulders. "Everything will go fine, tonight. You'll see. Have fun!"

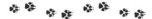

"Mama, where did Uncle Charlie go?" Sophie asked. "Why's he all dressed up?"

Rex lifted his ears.

Caro smiled. "Come on over here, and let's talk a little. Uncle Charlie's going over to Hildie's home tower for a very special dinner." She led Sophie to a bench near the trunk of the courtyard oak. The bench faced the Memory Garden, a shell-like rock structure hung with sparkling crystals and little golden tags. A small waterfall tumbled down the rocks into a small pool. Rosebushes grew on either side of it, seemingly always in bloom.

Rex followed them, curious to hear what Charlie's sister would say.

Shady joined him. Corona kids Owen, Grant, Leeli, and Jalani drew closer, too. The youngest cousins looked up briefly from their play, but only Lacey moved away from the sandbox to join them. Shady lay down by Caro's feet. Lacey curled up with her like a puppy, to rest her head against Shady's furry side.

Rex parked himself at the edge of the group.

"Is Charlie going to marry Hildie?" Sophie asked.

"Maybe." Caro smiled. "This is a first step in that direction. Do you remember when … " She stopped, gave a little laugh. "Wow. I guess the last time we thought maybe there'd be a new adult coming into the Family was quite a while ago. We're all a bunch of old married folk with kids, now, except for Charlie."

"What's so special about tonight?" Owen asked. "Doesn't Charlie already know Hildie's Family?"

"He knew them years ago, just as she knew us. But when it begins to look like there might be a Family-addition negotiation in our future, things get a whole lot more formal and businesslike."

Shady's ears went up. "Even though she has only just started to be his girlfriend, Charlie has said he might like to go beyond being Amares with Hildie. Maybe much farther, was what he said."

Caro's eyebrows rose. "Oh, *did* he?" A glad smile spread across her face. "Good!"

"Aunt Caro, does Charlie … " Leeli hesitated. Her hands clenched and unclenched. "Do Charlie and Hildie wrestle in bed like Mommy and Daddy?"

Caro froze for a moment, mouth open. "Um, that's kind of a private thing between grownups, honey. Have you, um, talked with your mommy or daddy about it?"

Leeli hunched her shoulders. "I wasn't supposed to open the door. But I wanted a cookie, and Grandpa said no."

"I see." Caro nodded slowly. "How did you feel about what you saw?"

"I dunno. Kinda weird." Leeli's eyes were wide and dark.

Caro sighed. "You need to know that it's an okay thing for mommies and daddies to do together. They're not hurting each other. It means they love each other."

"Oh. Okay." Leeli seemed happier.

Caro made earnest eye contact with each child in the group. "Anytime you have questions, it's okay to ask. You understand? Talk to one of us. Talk to a Listener. Talk to somebody you trust. Okay? We want to help you grow up safe and happy."

Bzzz-zzzz. A blur of something tiny darted into a gap between the leaves of a nearby climbing rose.

Rex went instantly alert. He swiveled his ears toward it, studied the roses to spot it. After a brief burst of its near-inaudible sound, it silenced. Drowned, even to his ears, in the splash of the waterfall. But after days of listening in vain, he at last had a new lead on it!

Behind him, Caro continued her conversation with the children.

He sifted through scents in the odd sound's vicinity. The rose in question had been trained up the rocky side of the Memory Garden's central water feature. The smell of the plant, its blossoms, the dampness, the soil, the rocks, the .... *Aha!* Just the tiniest whiff of carbon fiber! A touch of silicone!

He stilled a growl. Activated his CAP and HUD, then switched to thermal-imaging.

There: a tiny spark of heat, about the size of a bee. Bees didn't generate that kind of heat, though. This was artificial.

Yes! He silently triggered an alert-ping to the Precinct Nine communications hub, then added Hector and Mike Santiago to his follow-up text. "I have eyes and nose on a confirmed bogey."

"Roger that," the dispatcher replied. "Keep the kids well back."

"On my way," Santiago answered.

"I see where you are," Hector texted. "Scanning the water feature now, with everything I've got."

"Maybe this time we'll bag it," Rex texted back.

"I don't want Charlie to move away! He'll take Rex and Shady! We won't get doggie-back rides anymore!" Jalani's cry startled Rex, but he kept his focus on his quarry.

A pinpoint of light blinked on. Rex could make out small details now. Roughly beetle-shaped, but neither bees nor beetles had a row of optics all around their perimeter. Whatever had activated, it swiveled toward Jalani's voice.

"Charlie's not going anywhere. Certainly not for a while yet, anyway," Caro said. "He and Hildie might live here. Maybe you should be really nice to Hildie, so she has good reasons to stay."

The light was too low for his own optics to send more than the murkiest image, and a laser burst to aim them would alert the operators, if they weren't already aware that their device had been spotted. He texted a written description to his assorted backups.

Through the link he sensed Charlie's attention. *Everything okay?*

Focus on your dinner. I'm on the trail of a bug, and don't need distractions.

Good hunting! Charlie's curiosity blazed through the link, but he pulled his attention back and focused elsewhere.

"I take it you've found one," Shady texted to him. "How can I help?"

"We need to move the Family away from it, but I don't want to alarm them or alert the operators of the device. How should we do that?" Rex texted back.

"Give me a minute to think."

Caro was saying terse, unfriendly things about Felicia's never having been a suitable candidate for inclusion in the Family. Rex wished he could pay more attention to that. He kept his focus on the bug, but it wasn't going anywhere.

"Hah! Caught a signal!" Hector texted.

"Don't respond! Just monitor," Santiago advised. "Pat and I are on our way. Unless it moves, leave it alone. It might be armed."

Rex stiffened. *Crap.* "Understood." He sent a new text to Shady. "We need to get the Family out of here. This thing might blow up."

Did you say something might blow up? Charlie's mental voice through the link radiated alarm.

Rex gave a soft growl. *It's covered. Relax. Don't distract me.*

Yeah, that's not comforting. Charlie pulled back from the link again.

Shady had been lying by Caro's feet while Lacey used her as

a pillow. Now she dipped her nose to give the child a gentle poke. "Excuse me, honey." Lacey sat up. Shady stood.

"You okay?" Caro turned toward Shady.

"I apologize, but would you mind coming over here with me?" Shady asked. "I need to show you something. Bring the kids."

Caro gave her a startled look. "Um. Okay."

A new sound came into range: the *whump-whump-whump* of a fast-moving flitter.

"I hear a flitter. Is that you and Pat?" Rex texted Mike.

"Probably."

Shady's tail was up and waving. "Come see."

The flitter drew nearer.

The humans got up one by one and trailed after Shady toward the front gate.

Caro caught up with Shady. Rex stayed put, watching them.

Shady's nose went up. Rex couldn't hear her vocalizer, but Caro stiffened.

By now the flitter sounded less than half-a-klick out, closing rapidly. Its thunder echoed across the valley.

Grant looked up. "I hear a flitter! Let's go outside. Maybe we can see it!"

"Better hurry! I hear it too," Caro said. "Sounds like it's really moving fast!"

The children ran the rest of the way across the courtyard toward the gate. Caro shooed them on outside, and snagged a couple of the nearest adults, too. Shady circled back around to alert more Family members.

Rex stilled the growl in his throat. He stood, stretched languorously. It might seem suspicious to the device's operators —assuming they were operating it in real time, since Hector had caught a transmission signal—if he didn't go "investigate" the flitter, as well. He curled his lip, then trotted toward the gate.

A couple of meters away, he darted between tables and circled back around. Hoping he was out of the device's line of sight now, he approached the Memory Garden's water feature from the walkway that ran behind it, under the balconies. He stopped with his nose just a few centimeters away from where the device had previously landed. He couldn't see it, but he could smell it was still there. "It has not moved," he texted to Mike and Pat.

CHAPTER 27

A DINNER TO REMEMBER

C harlie'd been reluctant to take Rex's auto-nav. It was meant for Rex and Shady's security. It was a self-indulgence.

It was butt-ugly.

Rex had insisted, however. And every Family member he asked agreed. It was getting late. The car was the fastest way across the valley, short of the tram. With the tram station located half a kilometer's walk from Feliz Tower, Charlie gave in. Neither he nor Cousin Manny's truffles would survive that trek unmelted in the late-afternoon heat.

The boxy police-issued auto-nav was by far the least-elegant car Charlie'd ever seen. Riding in an auto-nav might be an indulgence in one way, but riding in this one was also an exercise in humility. Forget practical jokes from Caro. This thing *was* the practical joke. What would Hildie's Family think?

Anxiety prickled his skin. But his mental course-of-action range-finder for once shone a strong, bright green TL, *Target Locked*. He knew what he wanted. He knew what he had to do. Just wished he was sure he could pull it off.

He tried to rub his sweaty palms dry, and worried about Hildie's state of exhaustion. He messaged her, but she didn't answer. Probably too busy. He wished she could be sleeping, or at least resting. Micrograv work took an extra toll. After the schedule she'd just worked, she'd be a sleep zombie for most of her mandatory 24 downside. Good thing she had tomorrow and Thursday off. She'd need the time. Hell, *he* needed the time. Every moment away from her echoed with lonely desolation.

The car pulled onto the siding. "You have reached your destination: Feliz Tower on Port Hill Rim Eight Road," the car's voice announced. "I hope you had a nice ride, Charlie. You may now disembark or ask for a new destination." Ironic that he and Hildie had grown up on opposite hills, but both on Terrace Eight of Precinct Nine. Both in multi-generational Chartered Families. Both on intensive-farming plots, though hers was larger and located on the warmer, Port side of the valley.

He emerged from the car. Juggled truffles and wine.

Feliz Tower rose six stories above ground-level, a fantasy in turquoise, pink, yellow, green, and terra-cotta. It stood well back from the road, elevated to mid-level with rice terraces all around it. An avalanche of memories, tinged now with regret, descended on him at the sight of it. He'd been so *young* back then, so full of illusions. So blind.

A gaggle of children charged across the grassy strip by the road.

"Mom! Hildie's boyfriend is here!" a girl about Owen's age hollered down the entrance corridor. Could that possibly be Cormac's daughter Jeliza? She'd grown so tall! The other kids jostled each other just beyond arm's reach. They stared at him.

He searched their faces for a hint of any Feliz Family members he'd known from before. There'd been three toddlers and one or two babies in residence then. They probably were seven or eight now, and likely among this group, but where had all the others … Maybe some were neighbors?

He traversed the white gravel path that laced back and forth up the rice terraces to the house. By the time he'd topped the path edging the last sparkling, water-flooded paddy, Hildie's five male cousins had emerged from the gate. Four of them eyed him in stony silence, arms crossed. Fahim, however, stared with a horrified expression at the police auto-nav, as if he didn't quite believe his eyes. Tall, stocky Babu, the eldest, beckoned Charlie forward and inside.

Oh, yeah, he was clearly on probation. Still breathing hard from nerves and the climb up the terraces, he squared his shoulders, careful of his overly-tight jacket. He tried to appear calm.

In the entrance corridor's cool darkness, he shed his shoes near a line of other footwear. Prepared, he'd worn slip-ons. One look at the cousins' stern stares—and Fahim's askance regard—warned him off idle chatter.

Hildie's father, Pari Gallagher Bannerjee, stood at the end of the entrance corridor. Her mother, Dara Bannerjee Gallagher, stood a little back and to Pari's left. Hildie's not-so-little brother Abhik Bannerjee stood back and to his right.

Charlie approached them respectfully, then bowed once he'd reached them. "Namaste. Good evening. Corona Family hopes these will please you." He offered the wine and truffles.

Pari's expression remained as stern as Babu's. He held Charlie's gaze for several extremely long seconds, then relaxed with a smile and a nod. "Good. Very good. Come in and be welcome."

Charlie gasped in a quiet breath. *Okay, then. First test passed?*

Pari and Dara led him into the central courtyard. Like Corona's, it was festooned for the coming New Year holidays and filled with tables ready for a feast. Family members stood in small clusters near the perimeter to observe. Even more people lived in Feliz Tower than in Corona, thanks to the extra residence level—and it looked to Charlie as if *everyone* was here.

Everyone except Hildie. And Grandma Hestia. Head-of-Household Hestia Saha Gallagher was small, fierce, and probably a good preview of Hildie in another fifty or sixty years, although Hildie was taller. He caught his breath, seized by unexpected longing. Would Hildie still want him? Would the Family have accepted him? Would they still be together in another fifty or sixty years? In his mental age-progression, she'd still be adorable. It made tonight all that much more important. He couldn't afford to screw up.

As custom demanded, Pari and Dara opened the host and hostess gifts right away. Dara exclaimed over Manny's justifiably-famous chocolate truffles. "I have heard about these, but never tasted one."

"I've never known him to fail. I hope you'll enjoy them."

Pari's eyebrows rose when he saw the merlot was a Year 51 vintage. "A magnificent gift." His smile spread wide. "We shall have this tonight."

"Now come," Dara said. "Someone has been waiting for you." She took his hand, led him to one side of the courtyard, then pushed open a door.

He froze, breathless. At first glimpse Hildie looked resplendent, arrayed almost as elaborately as a bride. Her ruby-and-gold saree glistened in the warm light. Golden necklaces draped her shoulders, and her thick black hair had been swept up in an elegant, intricate style. But he knew her too well to miss the subtle marks of exhaustion beneath the gorgeous presentation.

He looked her in the eye. "You all right?"

"Been more alert." She offered a small, tired smile.

"You look fabulous."

The tight little smile relaxed into a grin. "You clean up pretty well, yourself." She half-turned, her movement slightly stiff as if her joints ached. "You remember Grandma Hestia?"

Hildie's grandmother didn't appear to have changed at all in the years since he'd last seen her. Same steel-gray hair pulled back in a knot, same alert black eyes, same small, wiry frame. She and her famously rigorous standards scared him more than ever, tonight. She would have the final say over whether or not he was acceptable.

Charlie offered her a polite bow. "Namaste."

"Huh." She studied him, eyes sparkling, then gave a single, sharp nod. "Namaste. You'd better be good to her!"

"That is my earnest intention."

"I guess we'll see, won't we?" She waved a bony brown hand. "Go. Eat."

"Good night, Grandma." Hildie kissed her cheek, then hesitated to hear something quiet that her grandmother said. Then she smiled and turned to Charlie.

He took her bangle-bedecked arm. She leaned on him rather heavily, although his new strength allowed him to bear the weight with ease. Nice to be the one offering support for once. But her fatigue sent a cold lance of worry through him. She must feel terrible.

Through the link, he sensed Rex suddenly go alert. Charlie redoubled his focus on Hildie.

She guided him to a small, screened area in the courtyard with an elaborately-set table and six chairs inside. Together they got her seated, along with all the seeming kilometers of mysteriously-wound and draped silken fabric.

No stumbles, no rips, no untucking anything.

So far, so good. He pulled out the chair next to her, intent on staying close at hand to lend support.

"Charlie, you'll sit over here." Pari indicated a seat across the table from Hildie.

Charlie froze. He shot her a worried look.

She bit her lip, but nodded. Gave his hand a squeeze, then released it.

With his concerned gaze still on Hildie, he took the seat between Pari at one end of the table, and a woman whom Abhik introduced as Smita Rostov, his Significant. Abhik took the place at the other end of the table, facing his father.

Smita gave Charlie a cool-eyed nod but said nothing. He replied with a smile and a nod back, then spotted the small, neatly printed place card with his name on it, just at the far edge of his plate. *Oh, man.* It had been a long time since he'd attended a dinner this formal in a private home. He'd forgotten about place cards.

Through the link, he felt Rex's troublement. *Everything okay? Focus on your dinner. I'm on the trail of a bug and don't need distractions.*

Good hunting! Charlie's curiosity flamed up, but he determinedly focused on Hildie's Family.

MOM TOOK the chair Charlie'd half-pulled out. Hildie bit her lip, certain he'd already be obsessing over the trivial mistake he'd made. He certainly looked handsome tonight. Kinda tightly-packed into that jacket and nervous as hell, but so *earnest!* How could Mom and Dad help but be charmed?

Mom pinned him with a penetrating stare straight out of Grandma Hestia's playbook.

Guys, please give him a break! Unfortunately, they hadn't appreciated all the years of her angst and Charlie's obliviousness.

"It's been several years since we've heard from you," Mom said. "What have you been doing with yourself?"

Charlie swallowed hard. "Well, first of all, there was re-gen. Then rehab, and lots of physical therapy. I trained for a bunch of months to go back to the ERT. Which, um, didn't go so well." A somewhat haunted expression flitted across his face. He squared his shoulders with care. "I wrapped up my Bachelor's, after that my M.S. in Criminal Justice from S-Poly. Got certified in Forensic Global Reconstruction."

Her Family members looked at him with polite, expectant expressions. "And then?" Mom asked.

He gulped a breath. "Then I worked in the GR Unit for about a year. Did some patrol duty. After that the XK9 opportunity came up, and—well, you know how that turned out."

"Hildie said you live with … with Rex. And his mate, too?" Mom frowned. "They are enormous dogs. Is there still room for you?"

"I have my own apartment. Right now, I'm in one bedroom. Rex and Shady have the other. We share the kitchen, dining, living room, and balconies. We're currently alone on the top level, with three expansion units."

Abhik's brows rose. "So, then. You have a unit—a whole *level* —all to yourself?"

Charlie drew in a sharp breath. He got that distracted look on his face that she'd learned meant Rex was talking to him through the link. Mom, Dad, and Abi frowned at his slow response.

Time to step in. "To clarify, he has one-quarter of the residence level, and access to the rest, if he needs it." Hildie lifted her chin. "He has *plenty* of room."

Her Family members nodded.

"And your intentions?" Mom gave Charlie a challenging look. "What do you envision for your relationship with Hildie?"

Yikes, Mom, way to be subtle about it! Hildie's face heated, but she held her tongue. It was necessary to ask the question *somehow*, although she'd expected more finesse from her mother.

Charlie met Hildie's eyes across the table. Electric connection sizzled between them. "I envision whatever Hildie wants. I feel lucky we reconnected."

Mom nodded, still frowning. Still challenging and pushing. "You're willing to make this a Family matter, then?"

Hildie hunched her shoulders. *Smooth, Mom. Sheesh!*

"I don't want to make assumptions." Charlie kept his gaze on her. "Don't ever want to take you for granted, Hils. I'll go fast or slow, as long as you're okay with it. But if it turns into a Family matter, I'm good with that."

Warmth flooded her. *You had me at 'don't ever want to take you for granted,' my love.* Her heart might burst if this went on too much longer.

Dad's turn. "You have remained single for several years." He frowned. "Are you willing to give up that freedom?"

Charlie blew out a breath. "Loneliness doesn't feel like freedom to me. I don't enjoy dating around, or having people try to 'fix me up' with women who have nothing in common with me. I've had more than enough of that."

"You have a past in common with Hildie. What will carry you forward?"

Oh, please. Hildie scowled at him. "We *talked* about this, Dad!"

"Yes, and now it's his turn to answer. I want to know how his thoughts align with yours."

Charlie refocused on Hildie, spoke directly to her. The open earnestness in his face tightened her throat and sent her pulse into a wild gallop. "Getting to know you again—it's been like coming home. I love you. I trust you. I don't ever want to hurt you. And I miss you like he—" He grimaced. "A *lot*, when you're gone. What will carry us forward? Sharing the adventure, I hope."

Her heart filled so full she could scarcely breathe. *Oh, man, GOOD answer.*

"So, you have a home to share with her, and you don't mean to play around on her." Abi *almost* managed to stifle his smile. "This is good. Do we need to discuss anything else, or can we eat now?"

"One more thing, or he'll have to answer directly to Grandma." Mom pinned Charlie with a dead-serious gaze. "This treatment they gave you. This 'Semi-SuperCop' systemic makeover. What'll it do to your children?"

His face went slightly gray. She wished for a brain link of her own. *Chin up, Charlie. It's okay.*

"My Family's delegation did thorough independent research." He gave her mom a level, open look. "That includes a legal background-check and a survey of the peer-reviewed medical and psychological journals. When they called a Family vote, the approval was unanimous."

Then his eyes widened. Was Rex interrupting *again?* What was *wrong* with that dog? He *must* know how important this was!

Hildie turned to Mom, as much to divert attention away from

Charlie's distraction as to clarify. "I was able to look the documentation over in detail since I'm his Girlfriend-of-Record. It shows no ill effects have been found among children, grandchildren, or later generations with an augmented parent." She tried to sound crisp and academic, but the longer she spoke the harder it became to breathe. *My kids. I'm talking about potentially MY kids.* "In fact, the only effect seemed to be a higher percentage of athletically-talented offspring."

Mom frowned but nodded. "Well, that doesn't seem so bad."

A military-grade flitter *whump-whump-whumped* into earshot. Sounded like it was headed to leeward down the valley, approaching fast. Everyone glanced upward. Soon its thunderous presence seemed directly overhead. Foreboding slithered in Hildie's gut. *Does that have anything to do with all of Rex's interruptions? What the heck is going on at Corona?*

Aunt Keya arrived with a large platter of kebabs, the first of many planned courses. They smelled wonderful. She set the platter carefully in the middle of their table.

"At last!" Abi sat forward with a grin

CHAPTER 28

TRANSMONDIAN FIRECRACKERS

R ex swiveled his ears toward the device in the roses. *Eat. Relax,* he told Charlie. *We've got this.*

Fewer distractions would be better, just now. This damned thing must be dealt with carefully. He caught snatches of the children's excited shouts over the flitter's thunderous descent toward Corona's driveway. Thanks to Shady and Caro, most of the humans in the household had moved out the front gate.

Bzzz-zzzz. The distinctive buzz came from above and to his right this time.

Shit. Another one? Nose focused on the original bug, Rex moved only his eyes to glimpse a blur of movement. He studied the support column to his right. *Ah.* Now that he knew what to look for, it was easier to spot. There it was, nestled into a carved detail of the column's capital. He choked back rising fury. "Found another," he texted.

"There could be dozens," A new, younger-sounding voice spoke in his ear: Santiago's tech Pat. "Hi. We've landed. Mike's talking with your Head of Household. Come on out. We're setting up for a sweep of the Tower."

"Roger that." Rex withdrew his nose from the roses near the

Memory Garden, then trotted along the walkway toward the entrance gate. The uncharacteristic stillness of the place made his hackles prickle. Corona Tower normally pulsed with life, but now it lay empty. Dozens? Yikes. That wasn't being bugged—more like being infested.

Dozens? Charlie demanded through the link. *You said 'infested'? What's going on over there?*

Sorry. Didn't mean to disturb you. Don't worry. We're on it. Rex reached the entrance corridor. Trotted toward the early-evening light outside beyond the front steps.

Dozens of surveillance devices? Infested with them? Rex pictured his partner's frown. When Charlie was in this mood, he'd persist till he got an answer.

We're working on it. Mike and his tech specialist are here to remove them.

The hell you say! Charlie's anger blazed through the link, as well as a feeling of being torn between urgencies for his attention. *Keep me posted!*

Roger that. He shared Charlie's rage that Wisniewski's damned spooks had dared to fly surveillance devices into their home, but he throttled it down to a slow burn.

Outside, he saw that Shady had herded the rest of the Family several meters away from the house. Even Loretta was out there on the driveway in her wheelchair, not far from the flitter. Pepe edged her closer to Annie and Hector, who were talking with Mike. The older Corona children, still supervised by Caro, stared at the flitter and the equipment Mike's companion had unloaded.

Rex joined the younger man. "Hello. Pat?"

He straightened with a grin. "Hello! Yes!"

"Thanks for coming so quickly."

"My uncle's given me a deactivation code, but he says these things usually self-destruct before they can neutralize them." Pat gave the house a squint-eyed look. "I'm hoping we can get 'em using an alternate frequency. We want to secure some intact."

Rex's gut went slippery-queasy. "Self-destruct?"

Self-destruct? Charlie had focused fully on Rex by now. *What does he mean, self-destruct? What do they do when they self-destruct?*

Pat punched a button on his console.

Rex lifted his ears at a salvo of distant bangs, like the fireworks Transmondians loved to set off on every conceivable holiday. "How much damage are they doing in there?"

Pat gave him an uneasy look. "What do you hear?"

"It sounded like Transmondian firecrackers." Rex underscored his words with a soft growl.

"Dammit." Pat scowled at the house. "Has it stopped yet?"

Rex laid his ears back. Now he whiffed a tang of gunpowder in the air, but the popping noises had stopped. "I believe so."

Pat sighed. "Keep the Family back. Our sweep team should be here shortly."

CHARLIE FOCUSED FULLY ON REX, horrified. *What does he mean, self-destruct? What do they do when they self-destruct?* he demanded through the link.

At the edge of his attention, Hildie spoke rapidly in an urgent tone to her Family members. "Something's going on with Rex. He can get very distracted, sometimes. They can't entirely turn off their brain link."

Oh, crap. Charlie grimaced, torn between explosions inside Corona Tower and the realization that he must look demented to Hildie's Family. With effort, he pulled back from the link. "Sorry." He focused on their worried expressions. "I apologize. That was unexpected."

"What happened?" Abhik asked.

Our home was filled with Transmondian surveillance devices, and they exploded? That seemed an awfully alarming thing to admit to a Family who was vetting his suitability to become one of them.

He grimaced. "The Transmondians don't want to admit the XK9s are sapient."

"What did they do?" Hildie caught and held his gaze.

On the other hand, he'd better not lie to Hildie. He drew in a breath. "Did you tell your Family about the agent in the quinoa, and the mysterious buzz?"

Pari turned a startled look on Hildie. "*What* agent in the quinoa? What does he mean by 'mysterious buzz'?"

"Agent?" Dara sounded alarmed.

Hildie scowled, focused on her Family members. "Transmondian Intelligence sent an agent to spy on our XK9s, but Shady noticed him right away. She and Rex captured him almost immediately. That was on the night of the presentation, when the whole Universe learned about the Pack."

"It's hard to sneak up on an XK9." Charlie couldn't guess what Hildie's Family members must think.

Hildie's chin rose. "They haven't tried that again." Her voice carried both satisfaction and a fierce challenge.

"Apparently they've been sending in tiny surveillance devices, instead," Charlie said.

Hildie's eyes narrowed. "Just as we feared. Damn!"

Charlie sifted through the impressions he'd gotten from Rex. "Rex spotted one and managed to see where it landed. The SBI was hoping to capture it intact, so they hurried a signals expert out to Corona."

"That flitter we heard." Understanding dawned in Smita's expression. "That was the SBI? Going to *Corona Tower*?"

"I think so." He'd also caught impressions about something to do with SDF Military Intelligence, but that wasn't something to discuss with civilians.

"So? What happened?" Hildie asked. "Did they get one?"

Charlie frowned. "It appears the devices self-destructed when the signals expert attempted to neutralize them. They're doing a sweep of Corona right now."

Hildie stiffened. "They self-destructed? Inside the *house*? How much damage did that do?"

"Let me check." Charlie widened his connection through the link. *How much damage?*

Seething fury greeted him. *Enough. There are little round, burnt divots blasted out of many surfaces. All over the house, but mostly in our quarters.* Rex growled. *This is Wisniewski's doing. I'd like to rip his throat out.*

Be careful who you say that to. All the same, Charlie wouldn't intervene, if it ever came up. He tried to imagine how his apartment must look. It hadn't exactly been an interior designer's showplace, but still!

I've never seen your uncle Hector this furious. He's grilling Pat right now, about frequencies and how to neutralize the damned things.

Charlie nodded. *He's not waiting for the SBI or the SDF to protect us, is he?*

"What's he saying?" Hildie asked.

Charlie gave her an unhappy look. "My place got hit pretty bad. Rex says little round, burnt divots all over."

Her lips thinned to a grim line. "Those bastards!"

He met her gaze with a fierce nod. "Well, they're finished getting access to Corona. Rex says Hector's already gathering information to set up counter-measures."

"Your uncle, isn't he?" Pari asked. "Founder of Hectorvault?"

"Yes. And he is furious." Charlie scowled. "But no angrier than I am."

"We need to get over there." Jaw set, color high, Hildie's eyes held a dangerous glint. "I want to see for myself!"

Pari's brow wrinkled. "Sweetheart, is that safe?"

"Safer now that the bugs blew up." Her jaw jutted with determination, eyes narrowed to angry slits. Bad idea to argue with her in this mood. "This is way past being *safe*, Dad. This is war."

"But we only just now got the kebabs," Abhik said.

"I'm not hungry anymore." Hildie stood. "We need to get over there."

Charlie rose to his feet as well. "You probably should change."

She spared a glance for the elegant saree, the half-dozen golden necklaces. "Roger that. This getup weighs a tonne."

Smita jumped up. "I'll help you." She and Hildie hurried away.

Charlie turned to Pari, Dara, and Abhik. "I, uh—this didn't turn out—"

Pari chuckled. "As ever, Hildie will what she will. Our daughter has chosen. We'd best get into line."

"That girl!" Dara's gaze followed Hildie and Smita. She bit her lip.

Abhik laughed. "Damn, man. You sure you're up for *her*?"

Charlie watched her stride away, vibrant with fury, back like a ramrod. She truly was magnificent. "Second chances like this don't come too often." He drew in a breath. "I hope you didn't open the wine yet."

By the time they reached Charlie's living room, Hildie's strength had flagged, but not her indignation. He half-supported her with an arm around her waist. The shorted-out wall-screen that had covered the spinward wall of his living room lay shattered. And that crown moulding would never be the same.

She surveyed the room with a scowl, then sighed. "We need to redecorate."

We? His heart lifted. "Not in purple or pink, I hope."

"Good God, no." She made a rude noise. "And this time you *do* get a say."

"You may have noticed I'm not picky."

"Understatement." She shot him an amused look. "We'll

come up with something. And you *will* get to weigh in, whether you think you have an opinion or not. I insist."

He didn't care about decorating. Just having her here brightened the room. Just knowing she was in his life for an indeterminate future span comforted and settled him. "Whatever you think would be good."

She squeezed his hand. They moved on. The hallway had taken a few hits. So had the kitchen. He didn't want to think about the bathrooms. Worst by far was Rex and Shady's bedroom, but both of them stared, incensed, at the strategically-placed scars on the walls and ceiling of Charlie's bedroom. A bunch of Transmondian assholes had listened to their intimate conversations. Had seen them kiss, disrobe, sleep. Had watched them, um, test their hypotheses, over and over again.

"I want to eviscerate those bastards." He'd never heard such cold hatred in her voice.

"I'm right there with you, and so are Rex and Shady."

"Just don't try to stop me from piling on, and we're good."

"You may have *carte blanche*, as far as I'm concerned. I think we both have a great big bone to pick with Col. Wisniewski."

CHAPTER 29

MOUNTING AN OPPOSITION

It was still dark the next morning when Hildie's warm body startled in the bed next to Charlie. She pushed herself up to sit. "Gallagher." Her voice was so heavy with sleep she sounded drunk.

Charlie sat up too, scowling. He activated his CAP and HUD.

Hildie's shoulders slumped. "But I'm not on call." She rubbed her forehead, a weary gesture. "I reserved today and tomorrow off."

Charlie couldn't hear what the person on the other end of the conversation said, but Hildie shook her head. "No, that's wrong. No." Then once again, more hopelessly, "No."

She leaned against Charlie, apparently still listening to the caller.

Charlie accessed a file via his HUD, thankful now that he'd thought to prepare himself. "Patch me in."

She gave him a confused look. "It's my supervisor."

"I know. Patch me in."

She hesitated.

"There's an ordinance for this situation. Patch me in."

"Um, 'scuse me. My boyfriend wants a word with you." She

patched him in without waiting for permission, then slumped back against the pillows with a groan.

"—can't say anything that will—"

"Safety Services Employment Code Section 5-C," Charlie cut in.

Yikes. This guy sounded like a male version of Ol' Pissy Missy on a tear. He didn't even hesitate, just kept haranguing.

"Safety Services Employment Code Section 5-C," Charlie repeated, louder. "You're in violation. My next call is to the Union."

That stopped him. "*What?*"

"I said, you're in violation of Safety Services Employment Code Section 5-C." Charlie kept his voice cold and even, though his pulse thumped with fury. "Actually, you're in violation of several important ordinances, but that's the most egregious. Ordering a Safety Services employee into hazardous duty when the employee is physically unable to perform the tasks required is a Level-Three violation, actionable through a Union complaint."

"What are you talking about, physically unable?"

"By the standards of Section 2-A, she hasn't yet completed her mandatory 24 downside."

"Only by a few hours," the man said. "By the time she gets here, the mandatory 24 will almost be over."

"That's not even close to being within tolerances. The ordinance specifies full one-G for the entire 24. It doesn't count 'almost,' it doesn't count 'only by a few hours,' and it also doesn't count elevator time, because elevator time isn't full one-G."

"We have a staffing emergency. She's young and resilient. I'd like to see you make any of your objections stick in a hearing."

"You might succeed in bullying someone else to back down. However, as a recent former member of the Emergency Rescue Team myself, I know how to judge when a fellow team member is unfit for duty as a result of excessive fatigue. And believe me, you do not want this woman making split-second, potentially life-or-death decisions in a hazardous environment, in her current state of exhaustion. Shall I spell out the objectively observable criteria for you, as established in Section 5-H?"

"Who is this? How do I know any of this is true?"

"Detective Charles Morgan, OPD, Shield 4822." He gave the man a moment to look him up. Heard a muffled curse and smiled.

"This exhaustion she's suffering—that wouldn't be your fault, would it, Lover Boy?"

"In my professional opinion, it would be the fault of whoever scheduled her for multiple, back-to-back twelve-hours, after she'd just returned from an emotionally draining—and illegally interrupted—Emergency Family Leave, then tried to short her mandatory 24 and void a pre-arranged day off." He scrolled to another section of the ordinance. "Failure to allow for a duly reported Family situation is covered under Section 7, right after the article about refusal of pre-arranged time off without notice. Shall I quote them, or can you find those on your own?"

The man on the other end—Capt. LaRochelle, Charlie presumed—cursed without bothering to muffle it this time. Then he clicked off.

Charlie met Hildie's gaze. "I guess he found them on his own."

"I will pay for that." Her sigh turned into a yawn. "But not today, thank goodness."

"Retaliation for a lawful employment action is a violation of Section 9." Charlie scowled. "So is the creation of, or the failure to ameliorate, a hostile work environment. I kinda know all of Nine by heart, thanks to Missy Cranston of the GR Unit."

"Oh, is that how you came to sound like a Union rep?"

He grinned. "Alphonse Rami is my guru on all things Safety Services Employment Code-related."

"Well, hallelujah for Alphonse Rami. Can we sleep some more?"

"Please, let's."

He was afraid they both might be too angry, but Hildie almost immediately slipped back into the deep, regular breathing of exhausted sleep. It took him considerably longer.

CHARLIE SPENT much of the rest of Wednesday waiting for Hildie to wake up.

He did his exercises. Talked with Hector about the Transmondian bugs and the counter-measures he and Pat Cornwell had set up. Got re-measured by the tailor, who kept staring with disbelief from the new readouts to Charlie and back again. Her reaction might make a person think he'd sprouted horns, not increased his biceps and chest by three centimeters in less than a week. Granted, that was ... well, unusual. But still.

He also placed a call to Alphonse Rami.

"Nice save." But Charlie could picture the Union rep's scowl, after he'd described the situation between LaRock and Hildie. "You say this is a pattern? Have you documented it?"

Charlie grunted. "After Missy? Of course I have, and so has she. I've been documenting as much as I've personally seen, since the time I became aware of it. I was still in the hospital. Hildie says it got lots worse about the time she went on record as my girlfriend."

"Mm." Rami's voice hardened. "I need to do some poking around, ask a few questions. Keep me on your 'updates' list."

"List?"

"While you've got Hondo on retainer, you might shoot him a heads-up. Ditto Klein—or ask Rex to. We may be able to shake LaRochelle off his pattern just by poking around and asking questions, but if not, there are intra-departmental issues Klein should have a chance to see coming."

"Got it. What about Pandra? Or Zhang?"

Rami shook his head. "Ask Hildie to update Zhang but leave

Pandra to me. After your tangle with Missy, you're the wrong messenger." Oma Pandra, Orangeboro's Secretary of Public Safety, oversaw the entire Safety Services Department. He was both Klein's boss, and LaRochelle's boss's boss. He also was Missy Cranston's brother.

"True." Charlie grimaced. "Thanks. I'll stay in touch."

Late in the morning, Abhik and Smita came over with Hildie's clothing for the graduation. Everyone who was home came out to say hello and welcome. The couple toured some of the ground level and stared at blasted-out divots where Transmondian bugs had been hidden, then stayed for lunch. But they agreed it would be better timing to see Charlie's apartment later, when Hildie was awake.

He lingered in the courtyard after they left. Got into a conversation with his cousin Germaine and her wife Beryl, who was seven months pregnant. Charlie might be on sick-leave, but Beryl and Germaine were home for Family Rotation today. Six kids with reading devices sprawled on the grass nearby. Corona's crop included Owen, Jalani, and Leeli. The others came from next-door Bonita Tower, plus neighboring Fairleigh and Trondheim Towers. Ostensibly they were being supervised by Germaine and Beryl, but they posed few challenges. Owen and his three classmates combined forces on a research project, sharing ideas and factoids in quiet voices. Charlie couldn't say what Jalani and Leeli were reading, but they seemed engrossed.

Bang! The explosion had come from outside, but it echoed off the courtyard walls.

Charlie leaped up. He crossed the courtyard to Ralph's equipment-storage center in a few long strides.

Hector burst onto the First Level balcony from his workshop and sprinted for the stairs with Grant at his heels. "Got one!"

Charlie bolted through Ralph's area and out the back exit. A puff of smoke thinned in the light breeze by the road near the vineyard. He activated his CAP's emergency ping to Precinct

Nine. "Got a small explosion at Corona, port-leeward perimeter, near the road. Suspect another Transmondian device."

"Keep the kids well back." The Dispatcher gave the standard reply. No matter what tower called, about what issue, at what time of day or night, there were *always* kids on-site.

"Roger that!" Charlie sprinted ahead of the others, then stopped at the edge of the vineyard, puffing only a little. Hector, Grant, the other kids, and Germaine arrived soon afterward, breathless adults to the rear.

Charlie raised an admonitory hand to halt them. "You kids know the drill! Stay behind that trellis row."

"But we gotta find it!" Grant cried, but he stayed where he'd halted.

Charlie frowned. "Don't you remember yesterday?"

"Yeah, but Rex an' Shady aren't here today!"

"All the more reason not to mess up a potential crime scene."

Nura, Ric, and Jimmy, the kids on Owen's school team, all gasped.

"Crime scene?" Jimmy asked.

"Really?" Ric's face lit with excitement.

"Transmondians tried to in-filter us." Nura's chin went up. "They trashed our crop, but we're gonna make 'em pay!"

Charlie wished for his duty rig with its pouch full of laser-markers, but not badly enough to send a kid upstairs to rummage through his walk-in. *Maybe* Hildie had been able to sleep through the bug's destruction. If so, he wanted to minimize noise. Meanwhile, he kept everyone behind that vineyard trellis. He squinted in search of any tiny glint that might be part of a wrecked bug but saw nothing in the grass.

A couple of radio units from Precinct Nine arrived within minutes, sirens blaring. A quarter of an hour after that, Pat Cornwell's flitter thundered in for its second landing on their driveway in less than 24 hours.

Oh, yeah. Great job keeping the noise to a minimum.

Charlie reported where he'd seen the puff of smoke, then left the scene to the UPOs. He and Germaine shooed the kids back up to the house.

Hildie waited for him just inside Ralph's lair. His heart leaped at the first glimpse, then quailed with guilt. Her sleep-mussed hair hung loose, and dark circles lingered under her eyes. She wore his thick blue bathrobe, the one he'd acquired a few months ago in Transmondia. It could get so cold there that sometimes frozen water fell out of the sky. The robe was too heavy for a warm Ranan afternoon, but easy to pull on. And it preserved her modesty in front of the neighbor kids, the officers from Precinct Nine, and the signals tech team from the SBI.

She offered a weary smile. "This place is hell on naps."

He reached out with a pang of regret and wrapped her in a tender embrace. "A bug tried to cross Hector's perimeter."

She yawned and snuggled against him. "I bet that's what woke me. I couldn't tell if something fell or what. Then the sirens, and after that the flitter—figured I'd better come see what's going on."

Her palpable exhaustion pained him and roused fierce protective urges. "Let's hope the invasion's over for today. Leave mop-up to the professionals."

She gave his chest a soft nuzzle and chuckled. "Aren't *you* normally one of the professionals?"

He kissed the top of her head, still aching with regret that he couldn't shield her rest better. "Not today. Today I'm the victim of a would-be privacy intrusion, whose true love was rudely awakened."

"It *was* very rude of them." She yawned again and relaxed inside the circle of his embrace.

On impulse, he swept her up into his arms.

She clasped his neck with a little squawk. "Is that wise?"

He considered how he felt. "I'm good for a few minutes. Bet I can make the elevator."

"Very gallant." She smiled. "If we hurry?"

His left arm twinged. "Yeah, better go now."

They did make it to the nearest elevator. Barely. He set her down *almost* gently, then shook out his arms. Maybe that hadn't been his best idea.

The doors slid back. They stepped inside and started upward.

"Morgan, you are *such* a goofball!" She wrapped her arms around his torso and hugged him hard.

He smiled and hugged her back. "Gotta push the envelope."

"Well, *that* hasn't changed." She shook her head in mock dismay but held on.

"Would you want it to? Really?"

She didn't answer for a moment. Had he said something wrong? Then she released a soft breath and shook her head. "I might not recognize you if you ever wised up about *that*."

They rode the rest of the way up embracing. He reveled in her soft, curved shape against his body, the full-length contact, the warm strength of her arms around him. "Don't ever leave," he whispered into her hair, soft as a sigh.

"I heard that," she whispered back. "Did you mean for me to?"

The car stopped. The door opened on Level Five.

Despite the implications of what he'd told her Family last night, total honesty scared him. Hell, the power of his feelings scared him. Everything was moving *so fast*. He let his kiss linger before answering. "No, I didn't think you'd hear."

"Did you mean what you said?"

He bit his lip. But it was time for full honesty. "Saturday, after you left … it felt wrong. And it didn't stop feeling wrong, all the way till last night. Even with all the damage and the Transmondian intrusion—when you're here, it feels better."

The door gave another soft *ding*. *Get out or go back down*, was what that meant. They stepped out onto the balcony near the unit Charlie'd begun to think of as Rex and Shady's future home. The closest elevator to Ralph's lair lay crosswise from the one he usually took.

Hildie's lovely hazel eyes held his for a long moment. "You already knew I've had an enormous crush on you since forever. But especially after the dinner last night—that rosy daydream of mine just got freaking damn *real*."

Worry tightened his chest. "Are you okay with that?"

"A little terrified, but okay." She shivered, then snuggled against him.

"A little terrified is a pretty good description from my side, too. Can we actually make this work?" They walked together toward his unit.

"I don't know. But this is a scary moment, just naturally. This is where we start to figure out if we *can* actually pull it off."

"I think we're doing okay so far. Aren't we?"

She gave a soft laugh. "Oh, man, *so far*, I feel like I've stumbled into some kind of heaven."

Her words made chest go tight. *Heaven? Really?*

The balcony made a right angle turn at the stairwell next to his bedroom. The french doors to his master suite opened at their approach. "Welcome home, Charlie. Welcome back, Hildie," the security system said in Hector's voice. How soon might it welcome *her* home, too?

She turned to him. Her eyes searched his face. "I know this kind of heaven isn't long-term. This is lust and limerence, and maybe something longer-lasting. But we don't know that yet. We've developed habits from living on our own all this time. We *will* get on each others' nerves eventually."

Twenty-seven months of Felicia and four months of Pam had taught him the practical reality of that. "Yeah, that's when my lovers tend to get restless." He grimaced, his throat tight with helpless anxiety. "No matter what I do."

She shook her head. "I don't want to do *that*, either. I want to find a way *past* that. My fantasy crush happened because I saw what a good and decent man you are. I saw how hard you worked to honor your commitment to Felicia, even though she wasn't worthy of you. I want to do better. I want to be worthy!"

Charlie cradled her in his arms. Each word filled his heart with greater gratitude. Maybe they could somehow make it work this time. "You *are* worthy. I just hope I am, too. Nothing's ever felt as right to me as being with you. But you have a point. A good relationship needs time. Let's give ours time to grow."

She relaxed in his arms with a sigh. "Yes, let's. Thank you."

CHAPTER 30

EXORCIZING FELICIA

W hat a wonderful thing, to sleep as long as she wanted! Thanks to her guardian defender and his command of the Safety Services Employment Code, Hildie had slept till well past noon again today. Better yet, there'd been no exploding bugs. No sirens, no thunderous flitter-arrivals. Just the wind in the branches and the music of distant wind chimes. Occasionally, the far-off chatter of children who were *not* her responsibility. *Heaven, indeed!*

Now she stood before Charlie's triple mirror in her short-sleeved red and gold blouse and red petticoat. She tucked the first section of the silky saree fabric under the drawstring waist of her petticoat, across her abdomen from hip to hip below her navel. Then she wound the initial length of cloth around herself. Thank goodness Abi and Smita had brought everything she needed yesterday, so she hadn't been obligated to go back across the valley for it.

Charlie strolled over to join her at the mirror, his tie draped over his broad shoulders and collar open. *Mm-mmm, that man looks fine.*

The appreciative way he smiled back at her in the mirror tempted her to consider more hypothesis-testing, but that would make them late. And she had to admit all the unaccustomed exercise after several years of celibacy had led to considerable chafing and sore muscles. Semi-SuperCop's lover needed to rest and heal up some. It was just as well they didn't have time right now.

She pleated the embroidered end of the pallu fabric back and forth between her thumb and index finger, then smoothed the pleats to make them lie as they should. "Incoming! Left shoulder!"

Charlie gave her a puzzled look, but then dodged when she slung the embroidered fabric over her shoulder. The mirror let her see his bemused look, watching as she put on finishing touches.

She adjusted the length of the pallu behind herself, positioned a section to drape over her hip, then worked on the front pleats. A final positioning and tuck for those, then she gently pulled the pallu wider, to drape its fabric over her left arm. *There. That works. I don't look half bad.*

Charlie's reflected face regarded the results with a combination of bewildered awe and delight.

Warm, bubbly pleasure lightened her heart. "I think I'll hold it down to one necklace tonight." She studied her image in the mirror. "Don't you think? All that extra gold is just—"

"Gilding the lily?"

"Overdoing it, was what I was going to say." She turned to give him a rueful look. "More like gilding the stinkweed."

He gathered her into his arms with utmost gentleness. "You're the most marvelous flower in the Universe. Don't speak to me of stinkweed."

She melted into his embrace. "Oh, my, you're good for my ego." She gave him an extra squeeze, then stepped back, and turned once again to the mirror. She examined her reflection, struck by sudden doubt. "It's not too old-fashioned, is it? Too stodgy?"

"Are you kidding? A saree is timeless. It's *always* in fashion."

She frowned, uneasy. "I can't help thinking Felicia would wear some fabulous, avant-garde creation from the hottest new designer. She *did* have a flair for fashion. I always figured that's what first caught your eye."

"Felicia was sexy as hell. *That's* what caught my eye." His reflected expression pinched with regret. "I was nineteen, and already dazzled to be surrounded by glamorous theatrical types at My Uncle Dolph's cast party. Very heady stuff. Then suddenly there was this absolutely gorgeous woman who seemed to think I was the hottest stud at the party." He grimaced. "I had no defences. Heck, I was still a virgin. Well, I was till later that night. I don't think my feet touched the ground for at least a week afterward."

"Oh, my." A heavy, dull ache filled her chest. She could picture it all too well. Felicia wasn't much older than Charlie chronologically, but she, um, had not led a sheltered life. "You were just a baby. And probably very sweet meat, indeed."

"Uncle Dolph didn't realize what had happened till way too late in the evening. By then I was totally besotted." Charlie shook his head. "He and other Family members warned me that she was just using me, but I didn't want to hear it."

"You can be stubborn."

Charlie sighed. "I'd *like* to think she stayed as long as she did because she also enjoyed being with *me*. But that's pretty much of a stretch at this point."

Old rage flared back to life in Hildie's heart. It pounded in her ears and shortened her breath. "Or maybe because you worked toxic levels of overtime to keep her stocked in trinkets, jewelry and clothes."

He looked down. "Yeah, or maybe that."

Hildie clenched her fists. "Oh, how I'd love to give her a piece of my mind! Now more than ever."

"Why now?"

"I always did think she was using you." She narrowed her eyes, her vision clouded by rage. "Now I know it was calculated from the very start. She was always *so* damned smug! Always *so* quick with a put-down. And she treated you like dirt. I hated her. Now I realize I was way too nice to her!"

"Well, there's not a lot we can do at this point. Try to learn and move on."

The rueful sadness in his voice and face sent a pang through Hildie. *Maybe I shouldn't be so quick to trash his past judgment and the genuine love he gave her. That is what I just did, isn't it?*

Charlie released a slow, cautious breath. "She never liked you, either. Probably because she realized you were a credible threat. She always nagged me to end our friendship, but she never pushed it to the point of asking me to choose. *You* were where I drew the line."

"Thank you for that." Hilde bowed her head. "I'm sorry. Felicia can't be an easy topic for you. Maybe I should call Caro for help with my hair, now?"

After all, it *was* getting late.

CHARLIE'S SISTER arrived in record time, armed with an array of hair-implements. She exclaimed over the saree, then the two women got down to business.

While they combed and braided and smoothed and pinned, Charlie tied his tie, and pulled on the jacket of his dress blues. A *way* less complicated garment than that saree. The tailor had targeted his size better this time. The uniform fit like a comfortable glove. From what he could see in the over-the-sink bathroom mirror, he looked okay.

The full-length triple mirror might be monopolized for a while yet, but he didn't mind. Contentment loosened his belly and warmed his core. When Hildie was here, this place felt *right*. Like a real home, not just a place to sleep or make a sandwich. In a lot of ways, it felt more right than it had the whole time Felicia'd been here. Even Rex hadn't made it quite complete. But with Hildie here, it was perfect.

"So. How do I look?"

He turned to see, and froze. Breathless. Speechless.

Caro hooted with glee. "Oh, man, the look on your face! Hils, I think we nailed it."

Hildie dimpled, eyes sparkling. "Damn, you're good for my ego, Morgan. I take it you approve."

Charlie gasped in a breath. "Good. You look good!"

Both women laughed. Hildie stepped in for a hug.

"I'm gone! You kids have fun!" Caro hurried out, still chortling.

Time ticked ever shorter, but he held her for a moment. Wished it never had to end.

She pulled back. Eyed him. "You haven't put on your medal. May I?"

The anticipation in her face didn't ease his flash of discomfort. "Mm. Just as soon leave that in the drawer, but people would talk."

Her eager gaze morphed into a puzzled look. "What's wrong with the medal?"

Icy fingers of dread wrapped around his heart, sent an ache up the back of his throat. "I think ... timing, if you want the truth. As in, worst ever." Heartsick, he looked away. *Maybe better come clean now.* "Did you, um, did you know I spent a week in the psych unit? After I ... washed out that third time?" He remembered only fragments of that week. Mostly pure, utter, black despair.

"Charlie! No."

His gut twisted into a chilled knot. He couldn't meet her eyes. *All the way clean. She should know.* "Yeah. Um. Suicide watch. Not my best moment."

"Oh, my God!" She wrapped her arms tighter around him, hugged him harder than ever. "After you were so incredibly brave!"

"So stubborn and stupid, you mean." He forced the words out from a throat thick with self-loathing.

"*Not* stupid!"

He shook his head, and avoided eye contact. "Stubborn, anyway. I failed again and again. Couldn't get past the panic. I felt like the biggest coward in the Universe." Grinding nausea gripped him.

"That's just it! You were terrified, but you tried again anyway. That's the very *definition* of bravery."

"Didn't help, did it?" He blew out a breath, his mouth sour with the bitterness of regret. "Anyway, *that's* when they decided to give me the damned thing. Exactly the moment when I knew for sure I was the worst coward ever." The Ranan Medal of Valor was the Station's highest honor for courage. "It felt like a mockery. Still does."

"You saved all those people, lost your arm, and almost died!"

"It was my job. On a really hard day, but my *job*."

She frowned. "Then there are no heroes."

"There are. They just … to my mind, they don't include me."

"Makes *one* with that opinion. The rest of us beg to differ. And anyway, it's part of your official uniform now, so let's have it."

He dragged the heavy little wooden box out from the back of his sock drawer and handed it to her.

She accepted it with a reverent look on her face. Opened it, then sighed. "It *is* beautiful." She lifted it from its black velvet lining. Held it up. Its thick golden disk hung on a flat, silken braid of green, violet, black, and white, suspended from a golden bar bearing Rana's double stars. The admiration that shone in her eyes as she pinned it on his chest almost *did* make him feel like a hero.

Briefly.

Then it was time to brush off the eternal dog hairs and go.

The Civic Center was already aglow with lights and alive with activity, building up to the Pack's graduation. Charlie helped Hildie wrangle the silky folds out of the car. *Not* Rex's auto-nav. He'd rented his own for tonight.

They turned straight into a buzzing cloud of cameras. He grimaced and batted them away, shielding Hildie. *Yikes. Already?*

Are you out front? Rex asked through the link.

Would another entrance have been better?

No, they're all wild. You were doomed whichever way you came. Ah, there's the picture. You and Hildie look nice. We've been watching what Shiv calls the "pre-game show" on our HUDs. Shady says your jacket fits much better tonight than that thing you wore Tuesday. He paused. *There's a lot of chatter from the commentators about your "beautiful date."*

His throat tightened. *Yes, she is, isn't she?* He turned with a smile to admire her. The cameras swooped closer.

Oh, that set them off. Amusement rolled through the link. *The hunt is on, among the announcers, to find out more about her.*

Charlie and Hildie made it inside. Here came a new press of bodies, along with fresh swarms of cameras. Then the bodies parted.

An artful vision of voluptuous womanhood thrust herself into his path. She wore a slinky, silk-and-sequined purple gown. A cloying cloud of all-too-familiar, sweet perfume closed his throat and made his eyes itch. The bodice plunged to her navel. The side slits reached her hipbones.

Charlie's gut twisted into a queasy knot. Few features of her perfect body remained for the imagination, but it didn't matter. He knew them all. Intimately. Like the dread-laced details of a recurring nightmare.

Felicia tossed her glittering golden mane and gave him her million-watt smile. "Hello, Amare."

Charlie recoiled with horror. *Holy crap. Speak of the devil!*

Hildie stiffened, then took a step forward. "You have a hell of a nerve to come here."

Forced back, Felicia's chin went up. "Oh, now who is this?"

her voice dripped with disdain. "It's that little medic Hildie, isn't it?"

"You know perfectly well who I am." Hildie's flat, cold voice could slice steel. "You've no business here, so step off."

"Oh, don't rush away. I was hoping to renew an old acquaintance." She sidestepped toward Charlie. Reached a languid hand toward the medal.

Hildie moved to interpose herself, but Charlie'd whipped up a martial-arts side block faster than thought. Felicia's hand bounced off his sleeve-encased arm shield, which hardened on contact.

She pouted at him. "So cold! You used to be more gracious."

"I used to be an idiot." He turned toward Hildie, but Felicia followed, grabbed for him again.

"No! Wait! Charlie! Don't be rude."

Hildie surged forward. "Oh, you do *not* start in on 'rude,' bitch." Her cheeks flushed dusky-rose. Her eyes glittered with fury.

"*Enough!*" Charlie's voice boomed louder than he'd intended. The entire room went silent. Everyone turned to look at him.

"That's *enough*, Felicia," he continued at a lower volume, but just as firmly. "You gave up any claim for my time or attention the day you decided you couldn't be 'hitched to a cripple,' and left me to wake up alone in the hospital."

"I'm sorry, Charlie. I was wrong."

"Yes, you were. You burned that bridge very thoroughly. I have no interest in rebuilding it, nor have I anything more to say to you, except: Go away. *Now*."

"But—but *Charlie!*"

Charlie focused on Hildie and turned his back very pointedly to Felicia. *Here's hoping she doesn't have a knife.* "Come, my love. Let's see if we can find our seats without meeting any more apparitions from my past."

Aw damn, Rex said through the link. *We were all ready for a fight. So that's the infamous Felicia. Hildie looked like she was ready to throw down, right there. You should hear the commentators now! Are you okay?*

Charlie smiled. *I'm good. That actually felt amazing.* His gut eased. He bent to kiss Hildie's cheek. The cameras buzzed closer. "To answer your question from earlier, Hils, no, I actually think that saree is *much* more elegant."

CHAPTER 31

ONE STEP FORWARD AND
TWO STEPS BACK

R ex arrived at work early Friday morning. Shady nuzzled his ear, wished him luck, then went back to the outer corridor to greet Pam and await their assignments for the day. The Pack *finally* had their Class-Bs. Maybe—*maybe*—they could at last begin to move this case forward again!

He allowed himself a quiet growl, then lifted his nose to seek out Shiv and Elaine. Lately it seemed to Rex that the investigation had spent far too long chasing its own tail. Elaine had tried to console him earlier this week when he vented his frustration. "It's a pain in the butt, but it's endemic to this kind of investigative work," she'd explained. "When the leads stop turning up, it's time for old-fashioned police work."

The humans had followed up on a rash of what turned out to be dead-end leads and inconclusive trails through shell companies. One task group had focused on the people behind the *Izgubil*. Another had been sorting through the Mahusayans' information, seeking connections between the *Ministo Lulak* and the *Izgubil*. They'd discovered that Ministobrila Collective had a reputation as an unscrupulous, exploitative organization. Though widely disliked, it wielded a lot of power among the asteroids controlled by Mahusay Station. So far, however, they'd found no direct links to the Whisper Syndicate.

Meanwhile, the Pack had rotated between miscellaneous patrol duties for the OPD and locating yet more "infernal plyboard" in the evidence cavern. Dr. Chinbat and her team had worked with one of Shawnee Kramer's joint OPD-SBI sub-groups, attempting to establish the identities of squashed bad guys, casino workers, and sex slaves, even though that wouldn't help them solve the case. The humans said it was necessary. Rex couldn't see the point.

The whole maddening process was like *knowing* there was a scent-trail out there, but the wind was blowing in the wrong direction and he couldn't circle around far enough to find it. Even worse, although he knew where a great scent trail probably was, he couldn't reach it. Not yet, anyway.

Commodore Montreaux and the SDF had been trying to set up their giant space bubble since last week. Their goal had been to get it stabilized by last Monday. Then it was by Thursday. Now it was supposedly today. He was beyond ready to form up teams so they could go to the Hub take a crack at that forward section of the *Izgubil*.

As usual, he found Shiv and Elaine sharing coffee with Shawnee on the far end of the war room. "Okay, Rex, how are we dividing our teams?" Shiv asked.

Rex laid out who he wanted in which team, how he meant to deploy them, and what tasks he thought each should tackle.

"Sounds good. Let's get the Pack up to speed."

They briefed everyone on their roles. They were ready. Things looked promising at last! They headed for the elevator.

Then Shiv halted as if frozen in the middle of the hallway. "Shimon here." He frowned into a middle-distance HUD stare. The rising stress in his scent factors roused Rex's misgivings.

Rex stifled a growl, and poked Shiv's hand with his nose. "What?"

Shiv's hand absently slid across Rex's neck. "Damn it. We

should have expected this, but damn, damn, *damn*! Montreaux has another delay." His fingers made a second pass through Rex's fur. He'd never done that before. Surprising, but it felt kinda nice.

Rex snapped his ears flat. "Why should we have expected that? Did they not say 'Friday for sure'?"

"It's a massive experiment. We're the smoke test." Shiv continued to scowl into his HUD. He stroked Rex's neck some more. "There were sure to be more glitches than we want to imagine."

Glitches. Great. That meant more delays.

"Sorry. False alarm," Shiv announced to the rest of the team. "We need to regroup. Go back to your previous assignments. We'll keep you posted."

Dogs and humans alike let out a collective groan.

Shiv's hand kept up its rhythm of calming strokes. Charlie would be jealous if he could see this, but the more the LSA stroked his neck the more the man's stress-scent moderated. The unexpected caresses calmed Rex's impatience some, too. "I have heard Hector use that term 'smoke test.' I was never sure what it meant."

Shiv's hand hesitated. Rex looked up to see that he was smiling at him. Then the smooth strokes began again. "The smoke test is the first practical trial of a new design. You build a device you think will work, then power it up and see if anything smokes."

"As in, it burns up?"

Shiv shook his head. "Not literally. At least, not most of the time. But yeah, that's the metaphor." They returned to the war room. Shiv found an empty workstation, logged on, then opened a realtime report from Montreaux and put it up on a screen.

Unease slithered in Rex's gut. "Are you telling me that the integrity of our crime scene depends on a glitchy, half-baked space experiment? I thought it was better-developed than that."

"Well, no." Shiv's left hand resumed stroking Rex's ruff. "To be fair, this technology *is* pretty well developed. It's been Top Secret because it's a real game-changer. They're willing to risk revealing it now because this is a great way to field-test the final prototype on a real-world application. But the first time they try to use something like this at scale, the process can be full of surprises. I guess 'smoke test' is the wrong term. More like a first shakedown cruise."

Elaine approached them. "Did you get the word from Montreaux?"

"Yes," Shiv and Rex replied simultaneously.

She eyed them for a moment, one eyebrow up.

By this time Rex had his chin on Shiv's knee, and Shiv's hand was buried in the fur of his ruff.

"Um, am I interrupting something?" she asked.

Shiv shared a look with Rex, then crossed his arms. "Why, no. Whatever could you mean?"

"Right. Well, if we're on indefinite 'hold,' I have a request from Chief Klein to temporarily detach an XK9 partner-pair for a murder investigation."

"I shall need more details. I shall call him." Rex stepped away from Shiv and placed a call to Klein. "Tell me about this murder, please."

"Lew Penny's the lead, over in Homicide. You should talk with him. I want you to meet him in any case, for reasons that have to do with a new XK9 Special Investigations Unit I've been contemplating."

Rex's tail was already at full-fan before the reverberations from that idea finished ringing through him. "A new unit? For the Pack?"

"I know you're bound for the Hub today—"

"Unfortunately, that is on hold for the moment." Rising excitement pulsed through him. *A new XK9 Special Investigations Unit?*

"Oh. Could you come up for a quick conference?"

"Most definitely. I would much rather talk with you about a new unit than do formwork."

The Chief chuckled. "Call Penny first, then come on up. We have plans to make."

Rex called DPO Penny. He learned that Penny suspected a drug-abuse angle to his case, and that Chief Klein had strongly advised working with an XK9 team. "I'm not sure how one of your teams can help, but I'm open to any angle I can find on this one. We have a dead woman in a neat, orderly room, without a mark on her."

"Is she still at the scene?"

"Yes. I just got here myself."

"You need Victor and Eduardo." Rex wagged his tail. "Victor specializes in all manner of controlled substances and their effects on human body chemistry. No one in the Pack can evaluate those variables more precisely."

"XK9s have specialties?"

Clearly this benighted soul needed to be brought up to speed. "XK9s can differentiate and analyze smells with at least as much acuity as a human with excellent vision can discern subtle variations in color and texture. Forensic olfaction is such an enormous discipline, no individual could master all of its aspects."

"Oh … kay. Well, that could probably be helpful."

"Please allow CSU to finish their imaging work, but tell them to observe scent evidence protocols."

"Scent evidence protocols." He repeated the words as if he'd never heard the phrase before. "They'll know what that means?"

Didn't Homicide get training on this? "Certainly. We work with them often. Send me your location, and I shall direct Victor and Eduardo to join you."

The pair looked and smelled delighted to leave the search for infernal plyboard and go to a brand-new crime scene. Rex called Petunia and Walter in to replace them, then headed for the Chief's office suite on the twenty-fifth floor.

A new XK9 Special Investigations Unit? *Yes!*

❖❖ ❖ ❖ ❖❖ ❖ ❖

THE FRONT GATE ANNOUNCED HILDIE.

Charlie halted his late-Friday-afternoon workout, startled by a sudden uprush of delight. She'd come back here! When she left early this morning for work, she hadn't been sure if she'd return to Corona or Feliz after her twelve-hour up-top.

"Welcome back! I'm in the gym," he commed to her.

"Nice. On my way up." The hint of a purr in her voice made him chuckle.

He saved the metrics his CAP had recorded from his workout. He'd hear from his physical therapist about the truncated exercise session. *Too bad. Some things are more important.*

He toweled off sweat and listened for her. In the Station's hothouse climate, nearly all Ranans worked out naked, a custom Charlie followed. Anything else was just too hot and restrictive. Still warm from his workout, he bent to wipe down his exercise equipment.

In a few minutes the elevator rumbled up to halt on Fifth with a *ding*. He smiled.

Footsteps on the inner balcony. He kept wiping.

The footsteps stopped. She chuckled. "I do like the way the bruises have faded." Her purr had gone sultry. It sent a tingling thrill through him.

He looked over his shoulder. There'd be no hiding his reaction when he straightened and turned around. *As if she couldn't guess.*

She leaned against his door frame with a teasing smile on her face and a hand on one hip. "Oh, yeah. This day just got lots more scenic."

"You seem lively for someone who just got off a twelve-hour." He faced her.

"I started it well-rested, for once. And it was a fun watch." She looked him up and down with a broadening grin. "Now I'm having even more fun watching."

"You plan to do something besides watch?"

"Why don't you come over here and find out? Maybe we can test a new hypothesis." Her gaze darted toward the mats by the wall, then back to him.

He closed the distance between them. "I should warn you I'm all hot and sweaty."

Her grin widened further. "Yes. You. Are." She moved forward to meet him. Wrapped her arms—

Bang! echoed up from the road by the vineyard. *Pop!* Something exploded above roof-level.

Charlie and Hildie froze.

A babble of voices erupted from almost every residence level.

Charlie ground his teeth. "*Damn* you, Wisniewski!" He spun, bolted down the inner balcony, then charged up the steps to Corona's rooftop garden. *That bastard!*

What happened? Rex asked through the link.

Another bug! Unaccustomed fury pulsed through him. He halted on the top step, raging. Searched for any trace of smoke in the air, or a half-blasted device on the decking. Had he taken too long to get up here? His hands clenched and unclenched. But blind fury would mess with his judgment. He took a long, deep breath.

Have you pinged Precinct Nine? Rex asked. *Because I just did.*

Thanks. I hadn't gotten that far yet. Rage seethed within him. *That bastard won't leave us alone! But one sounded like it didn't completely blow up—more of a 'pop' than a 'bang.'*

Maybe we'll get a better look at one of his gadgets this time! I'm on my way home.

Charlie tested the breeze for a trace of gunpowder, but he couldn't detect anything. *We've got to find that damned thing. This CANNOT continue!* Rage thundered in his pulse, irresistible as rising magma. *Damn it! Where is it?* He glared across the deck and the raised beds overflowing with root and leaf crops. They couldn't lose it this time! *Where, damn it?* He slammed his fist against the railing.

It splintered under his blow.

Hildie's footsteps mounted the stairs, then she faltered to a halt. "Woah. Did it hit the railing?"

"No. Um, actually ... I did." Not quite believing, he stared at the splintered bamboo, formerly a stout, 6-cm width. Then he looked at his right hand. Yeah, that was gonna leave a bruise. He hadn't felt much when he struck, but now it stung. All at once he felt kinda flash-fried, like maybe he was still smoking.

"Are you sure you're all right?" He hated the worry in her voice, the touch of fear in her face.

He massaged his bruised hand and offered her a rueful look. "Frustrated. I ... really didn't think I'd hit it that hard."

"Your hand okay?"

"A little tender, but I'm not supposed to be able to break bones anymore."

"Just bruise the hell out of your hand?" She frowned, then seemed to remember what she'd carried upstairs with her. "I thought you might need this." She handed him a sarong.

"Probably. Thanks." He wrapped it around his waist. His right hand twinged with the movement.

"I take it you didn't find the bug?"

"Still looking. At least one professional nose is on his way home, so I'm gonna confine myself to a visual scan from here. "Sounded like it was on this side."

"What are we looking for? It didn't sound like the usual bang."

"I'm hoping it didn't completely explode. Maybe we can find parts of it."

"How big, compared to the divots?"

"Lots smaller than those. A whole one is about the size of a bee, according to Rex. Of course, there could be a million little pieces all over, now." He grimaced. "I'm not entirely sure it didn't land in the tree."

"Sure. Why make things easy?"

"I need to laser off this rooftop. Could you please stand right here and warn anybody else who comes up that we haven't found it, and we're preserving the scene for XK9 backup? I have laser markers in the closet."

"Of course, you do." She kissed his cheek. "I'll hold the fort."

Sirens approached. He leaped back down the steps, grabbed his bag of laser-markers from the walk-in, then bounded back up to Hildie. He lasered off that stairway access point, then spun to dash back down and along the inner balcony. He lasered off the elevator entrance on the leeward corner, made another dash to the far stairwell-corner, then sprinted onward to the final elevator entrance. He rode down, still breathing hard, his anger now a smoldering ember.

Hildie intercepted him outside the elevator and led him over toward the lounges by his bedroom's French doors. "How's your hand?"

"It's okay." He walked with her, still breathless. His head spun.

She took his half-empty bag of markers, then placed it on the table between the lounges. Looked him over, frowning. "You need to cool down."

He bent over and braced hands on knees, lightheaded. "Catch my—breath in—a minute."

"Are you dizzy?" She tugged him to one of the lounges.

He sat like a sack of rocks. "I'll be all right." A thudding knot of pressure built behind his forehead.

She checked his pulse. "Uh-huh. You will be, if you cool it right now. Sit there for a minute."

Damn you, Wisniewski! He didn't want a spinning, achey head, a solicitous nurse, and an impending invasion of investigators. He wanted his "Plan A" back!

CHAPTER 32

BUG BUSTED

Hildie bit her lip and kept her fingers on Charlie's wrist. His naturally bronze-colored skin had gone a bit gray. He let her push him against the back of the lounge, eyes closed. "Just sit there for a moment."

His elevated pulse and lightheadedness suggested he'd become dehydrated. Maybe overextended himself, between his exercise session and all that racing around to laser off the rooftop garden. She rose to go for a glass of water. The elevator by the living room arrived with a *ding*. Two UPOs emerged. Looked like the same pair who'd responded on Wednesday afternoon.

Charlie sat up, attempted to stand, then abruptly sat back down. "Hello!" he called to them. "Welcome back to Corona Tower!"

"Where should we set up the perimeter?" the female UPO asked.

"Already done. On the roof." Charlie gripped the arms of the lounge. He still looked a little gray. "We have at least one forensic olfaction specialist on the way, plus the SBI team."

"Thanks for the breather, then. I take it you mean Rex." The woman grinned, then glanced at Hildie.

Charlie performed quick introductions: Marya Seaton with

her silent partner Bob Wells, out of Precinct Nine Station. They'd barely gotten past "Hello," before the thunderous *whump-whump-whump* of Pat Cornwell's flitter descended toward them.

Seaton shook her head. "Has this become routine to you guys, yet?"

"I'd like for it *not* to." Charlie leaned back against the lounge with a frown. Hildie didn't miss it when he ran a quiet breathing pattern. "I'll be right back." She hurried into the kitchen, then returned with a full cup of water.

Seaton went into a brief HUD stare. "They're calling us downstairs again." She and Wells hurried back to the elevator.

Hildie focused on him. "Are you thirsty?"

He squinted at her. "That's a good thought. Maybe it explains the headache." He drained the first cup. She refilled it. He downed that one, too, a little more slowly. She brought a third but set it on the table between lounges. "That's probably enough for now," she warned. Gave him a rueful look. "How are you?"

"Still dizzy, dammit. Head hurts."

She kissed him. "Building up to Semi-SuperCop is a process. But that splintered railing was—um, startling. How's your hand now?" She lifted it, unsettled, to examine the contusion he'd given himself. He'd shattered that stout railing with one blow, in a highly uncharacteristic fit of pique. *Fuel to every fire*, Shiv had warned. *Unfamiliar power behind every punch.* She gulped, but the cold lump in the pit of her stomach remained.

"It'll mend." He closed his eyes with a grimace. "I was angry. Frustrated. Needed to hit something. But I never ...."

She blew out a long breath. "Shiv *did* say you'd break things you didn't mean to."

"It was weird. I was suddenly just absolutely furious. I guess he predicted that, too." Charlie ran another breathing pattern and grimaced again. How bad *was* his headache? "I've been through re-gen before. I'm way ahead of last time, in strength-building. I know it's a process, but—gotta push that envelope."

"Even when it bites you in the butt?"

"Yeah." He let out a long, frustrated breath. "Yeah, even then. This is *not* how I wanted things to go. Especially not, based on when you arrived. What happened on your watch today? They hand out aphrodisiacs at break-time?"

She chuckled but kept a wary eye on him. His color was returning to nearer-normal. "Not exactly. But it *was* a fun watch."

He raised an eyebrow. "No death and dismemberment, just parties?"

She shook her head and couldn't resist a smile. "Neither death nor dismemberment. If only we could always say that! No, we had a dislocated knee, a compound fracture, a heart attack, and an allergy attack, but otherwise it was quiet. And in between calls I heard from a lot of topsiders who watched the XK9s' graduation. They ran a broadcast at the base."

He gave her a wary look. "Mm. Not sure I want to know what topsiders think of me, these days. They saw your confrontation with Felicia?"

"I got a few questions from people in other departments wondering who she was, but the *Triumph* crew congratulated me."

"I thought most of them were new. How'd they know about Felicia?" He sat a little straighter.

"The drivers are all new since your time, but Eli, Theresa, Oz, and Veda are still there. They remember the old 'Purple Palace,' and they had no trouble recognizing Felicia." She grinned. Theresa had greeted her with a whoop and a laugh. "Lotta high-fives from *them*, today."

His eyebrows took on a rueful angle. "Let me guess. They didn't like her, either."

She grinned, shook her head. "She didn't have any fans on the crew." A touch of last night's triumph and elation lightened her heart. "What most people wanted to talk about, however, was you."

His rueful look turned to worried. "What *about* me?"

Her smile widened. Amusement bubbled through her. "The

women and the gay guys who didn't know you from before were all, 'Girl, where did you find *him*, and does he have any brothers?'"

He grimaced.

"If it's any consolation, a lot of people remembered you from before. Most have been following your public career, ever since the *Asalatu*."

"Didn't think I *had* much of a 'public career.'" He looked away. "No cop wants to be famous. Interferes too much with the work. Puts the Family in danger."

"They remember when we pulled you out of the wreckage alive, after you saved all those people. You probably don't remember, because you were in re-gen, but that got a lot of media time. It was almost the only bright spot in that horrific disaster."

He grimaced. "Mama kept a vid-file. I've never asked to see it."

Sadness ached in the back of her throat. *Of course not.* "They paid attention again later, when you got the medal. And all of that was recent enough, they recognized your name in the news items about the XK9 project. Who made the final candidate-cadre was news, and of course when you came back with a dog. And then there's *Rex's* public career."

"Yeah, well, I guess there's that."

"Just sayin', Morgan." She gave him a half-teasing, half-challenging look. "If you ever decide to hang up your badge and go into politics, you had a certain level of positive name recognition built up, even *before* your partner turned into an Alliance-wide sensation."

"Politics?" He scowled and shook his head. "I'm not the one with all the charm and charisma. That's Rex's wheelhouse. I suppose I might be his sidekick." He grimaced. "Actually, so far I'm only a semi-part-time sidekick."

"Time'll mend that. And meanwhile, the folks from up-top were pleased to see you looking well after your latest misadventure. The ones who remember you from 'back when' wanted to know if you've been working out."

"What did you tell them?"

"Nothing about the Semi-SuperCop stuff. I said you're careful to do what your physical therapist tells you to."

"Except when a sexy Medicine Goddess shows up and seduces me."

"*Almost* seduces. Exception noted and appreciated, *despite* Col. Wisniewski's worst efforts." She moved over to share his lounge and leaned in with a smile.

He gave himself fully to a lingering kiss.

She sat back, eventually, and checked his pulse again. *Ha. Nicely elevated, but not in a bad way this time.* "What were we talking about? Oh, right, my co-workers. Their main reaction was 'that must be one hardcore PT regimen.'"

"It's rigorous, that's for sure." He sighed. "Seems like every time my muscles ease up aching, she piles on more reps or new routines."

"Mm-hmm. It makes you all hot." He definitely looked as if he'd recovered from his over-exertion. It probably wouldn't be difficult to get rid of that sarong.

He frowned. "I bet I can think of one person who failed to be impressed."

Oh, man, way to spoil a mood. "Well, after this week, he can't complain that I conjured you out of thin air."

"He's a lot like Missy, I think. Controlling tyrant bully. I called his bluff, so now he hates my guts."

"Hates your guts more than ever, you mean." She gave him an unhappy look. "He's been dead-set against you from the moment I registered a boyfriend."

Charlie gave her a speculative look. "Hils, has he ever come on to you?"

"LaRock?" *Eww.* She grimaced, revolted. "Not … not overtly, no."

"What about that *incident,* a couple of weeks ago? The one you wouldn't tell me about?"

"That was—" Hildie stopped. *That* was *about my relationship with Charlie, wasn't it? Crap. Have I been reading this all wrong?* She shook her head. "What happened two weeks ago was definitely *not* a come-on. He grabbed my arm when I tried to end a conversation that made me uncomfortable. He wouldn't let go, so I kicked him in the ribs and broke free."

"The hell you say!" Charlie stared at her. "That's not an *incident,* it's an assault!"

"I ended it. Dr. Zhang talked to him. Nothing like that has happened again." She grimaced. "Now you know why I didn't talk about it before."

"Nothing so obvious has happened since then, maybe." Charlie's voice had a steely quality she'd rarely heard him use. "No, instead he tried to short your mandatory twenty-four and drag you back on-duty when you were too exhausted for safety. Are you gonna tell me that's not personalized spite?"

She looked away from his glower. "No. Not after Dr. Zhang already told him to respect my time off."

"Are you gonna report it?" The challenge in his voice allowed only one answer.

She nodded. "I have a documentation file I've been compiling."

"Have you shared *that* with Zhang?"

She nodded again. "Everything that was in it, up through last week when we talked. I'll need to add this." She looked up. "You already reported it, didn't you?"

"Same day." His mouth made a thin, humorless line. "Spoke to Rami, as well."

She sighed. "I guess that means he'll be expecting my file, too?"

"If you would, please."

There's no walking this back, is there? Her gut did a queasy twist. "LaRochelle will see this as 'war.'"

Charlie scowled. "He started it."

"Oh, yeah, Morgan. That's real mature." She sighed. "Look, I appreciate your indignation on my behalf, but meanwhile I still have to keep working with the man."

"I get it." Charlie pulled her into a warm, gentle embrace. "I do understand where you're coming from. But you can't let this type think they can get away with pulling this kind of shit. You've got to call 'em on it, or it'll just keep getting worse."

She bit her lip. "Did reporting it help you with Missy?"

He gave a little groan and rubbed his forehead. "Missy is Secretary Pandra's sister, so no. Not in that case. But LaRochelle isn't as well-connected."

"Maybe not, but he's a longtime careerist with a good enough record to make Captain." She blew out a troubled breath. "I just want to do my work and be left alone. Work topside, like I have for the last ten years, and where I know how to handle the micrograv issues. Just do the work and save all the lives I can. Is that so much to ask?"

His arms tightened around her. "One would hope not."

The elevator rumbled to a halt on their level with a *ding*. The moment the doors opened, Seaton, Wells, Rex, a black and white XK9, a blond woman, and a slender young man burst out. They laughed and exclaimed about the tight fit to get all of them in there at once.

"Hi, Charlie!" the blonde called out. "Take us to your bug pieces!"

Charlie let go of Hildie and stood to face them. "Georgia, Tux, Pat, I want you to meet Hildie."

REX AND TUX both stepped away from the humans and shook vigorously. Rex lolled his tongue. "We really should have taken the stairs."

Tux's tail wagged high and happy. "Probably. But this was

kind of fun." He surveyed his surroundings. "This level is all yours?"

"Mine, Shady's, Charlie's, and pretty much Hildie's, too, lately. I think we plan to keep her."

The humans already had trooped over to talk with Charlie and Hildie by the French doors to Charlie's bedroom. They were smiling, but Rex could sense through the link that Charlie was not as happy to see everyone as he tried to act. Rex didn't have to wonder why.

Respecting Charlie's wish to be left alone suited Rex's purposes, too. They had a bug to find! "Let us bypass the introductions for now." He swung his nose toward the stairwell just beyond the clustered humans. "Stairs are over there. They are closest to where Charlie thinks the bug landed."

They made the rooftop in two bounds. Perimeter lasers blinked at their badges, then let them in.

Tux elevated his nose, nostrils working. Tux always preferred to air-scent, while his currently-absent mate, Elle, always went for details on the ground. Together, the two missed next to nothing, but their contrasting preferences never failed to amuse Rex.

He did his own air-scenting, too. Hard to ground-track something that had exploded in the air and then landed … *hmm.* Through the link, he'd gathered that Charlie thought the sound had come from over this way. He and Tux walked between rows of raised planter beds. Along the outer rail, Ralph had removed the last remnants of his recently-harvested sweet potatoes. The tubers now lay curing in a controlled-atmosphere section of the Corona Tower cellars. Little sprouts, new since Rex's last trip to the roof, poked up through the finely-worked soil in these planters—but pieces of a Transmondian listening device among them? Nope. He had nothing.

Tux worked the planters on the other side. There, beet-tops and lettuce had leafed out more than enough to make it hard to glimpse any fragments. Tux moved slowly, his body tense, ears up and nose busy.

Rex moved on to the section of planters nearer to the leeward elevator. These, too, had been cleared and replanted after the sweet potato harvest, but they offered no faintest fragment, nor hint of any explosives, foreign metallics, or synthetics. He couldn't see the color "green," but there was plenty of the plant-scent he associated with that word. The planter soil smelled the precise way Rex had come to recognize that Ralph liked it for these beds. Until he'd met Charlie's uncle, he hadn't realized you could condition soil to smell *just so*, like a well-tuned chord.

Tux's personal scent abruptly transformed. From itchy harsh frustration, it modulated to excitement's bright, sharp heat. "Found it."

"Pat!" Rex called on the com. No need to alert Georgia—she'd already know. "Tux has it. Do you mind if I call Hector?"

CHAPTER 33

MONDAY MORNING CHALLENGES

Shady lifted her head in the Monday morning predawn darkness, ears up.

Beside her Rex lay inert, snoring softly. She lolled her tongue, warm with satisfaction. He'd had a busy weekend. Analysis sessions with Tux, Georgia, Pat, and Hector had taken part of it. They'd finally secured a Transmondian listening device, mostly intact, after its self-destruct didn't work properly. Rex checked in regularly, while the experts dissected it with delicate care, and then discussed their findings in High Geek. Shady's tail thumped the bed. She spoke a lot of languages, but not that one.

Rex had also monitored updates on Commodore Montreaux's space-based "bubble cordon." The SDF commodore had predicted that it wouldn't be ready till later today. Well, they *hoped* it would be ready today. All weekend Rex had vacillated between dithering over the bubble cordon and enthusing about the new XK9 Special Investigations Unit Chief Klein wanted to create at Central HQ. Finally, last night, he'd collapsed from nervous exhaustion. Now he could relax, because he trusted her to remain in "guard-dog mode."

And she'd awakened for some reason. Better check into it.

Someone walked barefoot across the bamboo flooring to Charlie's bathroom in the larger suite. Wrong gait, not heavy enough to be Charlie. He was scheduled to start light duty half-days later this morning, but this was way too early for him to get up.

Shady waited. Listened. Couldn't smell much, two rooms away. Couldn't hear as much as she normally should, either. Hildie seemed to be taking pains not to wake her lover. That did not bode well.

The woman stayed inside the bathroom for a while. Quiet splashes and gurgles suggested toileting, and maybe hand- or face-washing. Her footsteps moved to the walk-in closet. A zipper opened, ever-so-quietly.

Shady gave a soft growl. She extricated herself from Rex and the bedding. Time she and Hildie had a little talk. She padded out into the hallway, then pushed open the larger suite's door.

On the bed by the French doors to the outer balcony, Charlie lay in the deep sleep that had characterized his post-augmentation rest cycles. Judging from his breathing and general level of torpor, Hildie could drive a PTV through here, and he'd only roll over with a snort. Shady wagged her tail. It was kind of cute that she was trying to stay so quiet.

But now Shady needed to present herself without giving Hildie heart failure. She relaxed her feet so her nails clicked on the bamboo flooring.

The furtive movements inside the closet halted.

"Good morning, Hildie," Shady texted to her. "We need to talk. I'm coming in."

"O-Okay," Hildie whispered, tense.

Shady claw-clicked through the bathroom. Nosed the connecting closet door wider.

Hildie had activated dim ambient lighting inside the walk-in and donned some under-things. Her long hair had been twisted into a knot and pinned down tight. She sat on the dressing bench as if frozen, one sock half-on.

"Early call-in?" Shady asked.

"Um, yeah." Hildie finished pulling on her sock, then reached for the second one. "LaRock is still pushing it. He just called me in for another 12-hour, but this morning it's legit. I didn't take today off."

Shady laid back her ears. Hildie had worked the day after the Pack's graduation and also for part of the weekend. "That will be three 12-hours in five days, after an exhausting previous cycle and major personal stress. Is that legal?"

"Yes, but only just." Hildie grimaced. "This is payback for last week when Charlie crossed him." She yawned, rubbed her face. "At least after this, I have to stay downside for a minimum of 36 hours, or both Charlie *and* the Union will have a case to bring."

"So, that means you will go back to work on … Wednesday night?"

Hildie groaned. "Probably."

"I am sorry your boss appears to be so unreasonable."

"Me, too." She shook her head. "It's not so much the *length* of the shifts, although that can be rough. It's micrograv, plus the different wake-ups and sleep times. My body's usually too keyed up to relax right away, so I just lie there. About the time I finally go to sleep, it's time to wake up again."

"When prison guards do that to inmates, it is called torture," Shady said. "How can you perform your work?"

She drew in a long breath, frowning, then blew it out hard. "That's my biggest worry. People's lives are riding on my ability to make good judgments." She reached into her duffel, still frowning, and retrieved a Safety Services jumpsuit.

"A mistake in those circumstances would not be good. However, I should warn you about something else that would not be good."

Hildie stood to pull up her jumpsuit, but at that comment she paused, one eyebrow quirked.

"Judging from your heroic efforts to dress quietly, may I take it you do not plan to wake Charlie before you leave?"

"He's sleeping so deeply." She sounded envious. "How could I do that to him?"

"Let me tell you a short, sad story." Shady sat. "I fear I must bring up history that you may find unpleasant."

Hildie thrust an arm into a sleeve. "This story involves Pam?"

"Yes. She and I lived with Charlie and Rex during part of our training in Transmondia. We had been assigned to different teams for one of the drills. One morning Pam and I had an early rotation. We made the same assumption you appear to be making: that it was kinder to let Charlie sleep, while we slipped out quietly."

Hildie frowned. "It wasn't?"

"Rex called me in a panic. Charlie … he did not exactly have an anxiety attack, from what I can tell. More like a waking nightmare. Rex said his reaction seemed to blindside even him."

"Blind side," Hildie echoed. "Oh, crap."

"We had been with our partners only a few weeks. We still knew little about them. It terrified Rex." Shady's memories rushed back. Her hackles rippled. "Only later, when I learned about Felicia, did his reaction begin to make sense."

Hildie let out a soft sigh. "'Thank you for not being gone.'" Sadness filled her scent.

Shady cocked her head.

"It's what he said to me when he came out of that second regen, and I was in his room. 'Thank you for not being gone.' As if he expected to be left, to be hurt again. As if he was astonished that didn't happen. Even though I'd promised I'd be there." She blinked hard, then wiped her face. "Oh, man, I almost blew it, didn't I?"

New memories flooded in, of the night Pam told Charlie she was going back to Balchu. What a horrible night! She and Rex had been distraught, but Charlie seemed oddly resigned. As if, for him, being left was an inevitable outcome.

Hildie slipped on her shoes, straightened. "Thank you!" Gratitude surged strong in her scent. "You really saved my bacon this morning!"

There's bacon? Shady flicked her ears. She knew better: it was just another inscrutable human figure of speech. "You are welcome."

She left the necessary follow-up to Hildie. Headed for the kitchen. There *might* be bacon.

Behind her, Hildie strode from the walk-in to Charlie's side of the bed. Shady heard a kiss, a soft groan from Charlie, then, "Sweetheart, I'm so sorry to do this ...."

CHARLIE DREW in a breath and kept his face impassive.

Adeyeme gave him a rueful look.

He tried not to wince. *It's going to be boring, isn't it?*

You're on desk-duty. What did you expect? Happy Monday! Rex's amused response included no sympathy, as far as Charlie could sense.

"This'll be a less-than-exciting first day on the team, I fear." Rex's favorite SSA shook her head. "We're still figuring out how the *Ministo Lulak* fits into this picture. My Special Agents Emshwiller and Finlay are working through the kind of records it's hard to run a data search on, looking for correlations. There's got to be a non-random reason why the *Ministo Lulak* and the *Izgubil* both were targeted. If we can establish that, maybe we can figure out the most salient aspects of the victimology."

Charlie released a soft breath. *Good old-fashioned police work. Yippee.* "Got it. I'll do what I can."

Soon he sat at a workstation, while Special Agent Gillie Finlay pulled up screen after screen of records, manifests, and reports. This kind of data quickly induced headaches if you tried to switch between too many screens on a neural HUD, so they did it the ancient, workstation-and physical-scrim-based way.

Finlay straightened. "That should be enough for now. I know this is a lot to throw at you, but we keep hoping we'll see a pattern in there somewhere."

"That's always the hope." His stomach plunged. This was the kind of tedious work he'd envisioned *avoiding* by going into police work, back when he was a kid in upper-levels. He scanned through each for a sense of what they were, first. Then he sat back to stare at them.

Finlay clearly had not chosen random lists. She appeared to think there might be a pattern in the manifests of certain types of shipments by certain companies. Charlie frowned at them, arms crossed, although that action hardened his arm shield. This collection suggested she thought there might be a commercial reason for the ship's destruction.

That was possible. But was it likely? Commercial competition might lend itself to cheating, records-falsification, smuggling, sure. That happened all the time. Especially among pirates, commercial competition could lead to violence. But *spacers*, blowing up other *spacers* in the middle of the Black Void? He scowled. His gut said that spoke to deeper motives.

He glared at the screens, not really seeing them. Death by explosive decompression was a spacer's worst nightmare. In his years on the ERT, he'd rescued dozens who awakened frankly disbelieving they'd survived. Once you went into the Black Void unprotected, you knew you'd never come back.

Setting up a ship to shatter in space? Even a psychopath didn't do that purely for commercial reasons. *Not* if he or she was a spacer. And to have known all the details necessary, at least *some* of the conspirators must be spacers.

Charlie chewed his lip, scowling. This was a distinctive MO. Unique, though damned hard to spot beforehand. The murderer had sent that cryptic message to *Ministo Lulak's* owners. As if he was taunting them. As if he wanted them to look back after it

294 | A BONE TO PICK

was too late, and think, *Oh my God.* Had he sent a message to the
Izgubil, too? Maybe. But Whisper wasn't talking to the SBI.

He pulled up the text of the cryptic message sent to Ministobrila. The original was in Mahusayan, but the case book
included a literal translation into Standard. The message read:

SHAME *to the Pilot for a reckless course.*
Overreaching ambition makes fools.
How many lives destroyed? Now payment comes.

HE PUZZLED over it for a while and compared it to his own inept
translation. Who or what was "the Pilot"? He checked the crew
roster. No one on board had the title of "pilot," though the navi-
gator might be considered one. There was one Ministobrila
Collective member among the dead, but Kalan Ministo's title
had been Executive Administrator, not Pilot. If there was a secret
meaning in the Mahusayan, he wasn't fluent enough to know it.

Whose "overreaching" ambition did the writer mean? The
Pilot's? Ambition for what? Who had been made a fool? What
lives had been destroyed? He cross-checked with the manifests
and other guesses in the case book, but nothing seemed to fit.

Charlie glared slit-eyed into the middle-distance. *History.* He
wanted histories. Human history was full of overreaching ambition that destroyed lives, but what specific instance or pattern
did the message-writer mean? The kind of calculated cruelty
embodied in the ship's destruction felt *personal* to Charlie.

Personal history. It came down to personal history. He
frowned. Ministobrila first: their record should be pretty easy to
trace. How long had they been around? He accessed the information portals the Mahusayans had granted. Not amazingly, the
records were in Mahusayan. That other investigators had
already traveled this thought-path was clear from the presence
of a translation already in the case book. Most of it was beyond

his proficiency. Where he could, however, he preferred to read the original.

It made for dry reading, whichever language he chose. The official Collective History droned on like all those damned annual reports Gran Annie expected the Family's entire adult population to review, each time they re-evaluated Corona Charter Fund's portfolio. If there were skeletons in Ministobrila's closet—and from other sources, the investigation knew there were—they weren't going to show up in that material. But the history did say this was by now a generational Collective that had endured for nearly seventy-two years. It had already started to pass its assets to a third generation of leaders.

Charlie needed to find somebody who knew more. Somebody who knew the Mahusayan-controlled asteroids.

Hmm. He texted Georgia. "Would your *apodeddi* be willing to talk with me about old times in the Mahusayan Asteroids?"

There was a brief pause, then the channel blinked with her reply: "Better to ask, would he be willing to stop before you fall over in a dead faint from exhaustion?"

Charlie chuckled, then texted back: "I need to ask him if he knows about any atrocities, massacres, purges, revolts, or other violence that relates to Ministobrila Collective. Probably something that happened at least a decade ago."

His com beeped. He picked up. "Ministobrila," Georgia said. "Case-related, then?"

"I just can't buy a profit motive for these killings. Ask any spacer. The worst possible death is being dumped naked into the Black Void."

"Ergo, it's personal." Her sigh gusted in her mic. "I'm not sure Apodeddi Mamoor can help, but I'll happily set up the introduction. He may be able to point you to other resources, whether he knows he's doing so or not."

Charlie smiled. "Roger that." he glanced at the time. His four hours weren't over yet, but the time had gone by faster than he'd expected, despite the dryness of the reports and other materials he'd been wading through. "How far away is your Family tower?"

"Monteverde, but only Second Precinct. Getting there takes about an hour. I can guide you. Do you have a game plan? I can call him now, if you like."

"You'll bring Tux?"

He could almost feel her grimace. "Tux and Joe are pretty far down the wormhole, and will be for a while."

Charlie frowned. "Understood. But I want an XK9 on hand."

She laughed. "It's a brave new world, my friend. Ask your Pack Leader to detail one. Let me know, and I'll set it up with the Family."

"Um, sure. Okay." Charlie clicked off. Clearly, Rex did, indeed, now outrank him. *Rex?* he asked through the link.

You need Shady, Rex said, once Charlie explained. *We really should have had her there when we talked with the Mahusayans in the GR teleconference. I missed both her insights and her command of Mahusayan. I first must speak with Elaine, to let her know what you wish to do. Gillie is good, but she is strictly a records analyst. She will not see your point. I believe Elaine will.*

That jibed with Charlie's private analysis of SA Finlay—but another concern nagged. *Bringing Shady along means bringing Pam. Right?*

Ah. Possibly.

He scowled. *That ought to be fun. How should I proceed?*

I shall alert Elaine that you wish to explore an alternative investigative focus. Meanwhile, I suppose it cannot hurt for you to continue looking over those records.

He sighed. *Yeah, Sure. Back to the scutwork. Hurrah.*

Amusement came through the link. He could picture the tongue-loll. *Meanwhile, we finally get to go check out the wreckage!*

Don't rub it in.

Almost at the end of his four hours, Charlie stretched, yawned, and rose in quest of his fourth—or was it his fifth?—cup of coffee. He might be vibrating at a low hum already, but it was an excuse to get up and walk around a little. *Anything,* for a break from all those rows of irrelevant numbers. He'd flagged a couple of wonky-looking manifests for further scrutiny. They almost certainly represented coverups of illegal activity, but he doubted they held keys to *Ministo Lulak's* demise.

"Morgan!" SA Finlay inclined her head toward Elaine's office. "Boss wants you."

At last! Charlie logged off.

Adeyeme's door stood ajar; inside, he glimpsed her massaging her temples, head bowed. He rapped a knuckle on the doorframe. She looked up with a smile. "Rex tells me you've developed a hypothesis that has nothing to do with shipping manifests."

"Due diligence demands that they be checked. I get that. But I can't believe a spacer would send dozens of people naked into the Black Void to die because of an accounting irregularity. I think this relates to personal history."

She gave him a speculative look. "'Naked into the Black Void,' you say? Tell me more."

CHAPTER 34

THE MURDER BROTHERS

Rex's group took their by-now-usual Police Express up from HQ. His nasal passages swelled on the trek upward, but he'd proved to himself last week that it couldn't keep him from working.

He rode with Shiv and the group he'd organized into Team One. The LSA once again would be his sort-of-partner for the day. Scout, working with partner Nicole, was the tracking specialist. Cinnamon, with partner Berwyn, would take the lead on explosives and other substances of interest. Rex would act as Team One's leader, making independent observations, but he must rely on the others' partners to do scent-sample collection.

Shiv meant to get an overview alongside Rex. Mike had joined them to liaise with the SDF. After all the connections he'd noted since meeting the man, Rex wasn't surprised to learn that Mike's career had started in the Station Defense Force. Only after a career-crippling dispute with Admiral Virendra had SBI Director Perri been able to recruit him to her agency.

A crew from the OPD Crime Lab rounded out their expedition. They'd be needed for every step in the process of opening a brand-new crime scene.

The group took a couple of Safety Services shuttles to the

Port Authority Base, where their equipment was kept. Multi-Passenger Transit Shuttles—acronym MUPATS—resembled small, wheelless auto-nav bus frames with seats and a cargo area that could carry up to twelve humans plus their equipment. Between the XK9s and all the CSU equipment, they needed both vehicles.

First goal: get into their micrograv harnesses. The property supervisor, an older civilian clerk named Lorena, scowled at the dogs as usual. Rex had the impression she continually expected one of them to misbehave. But their equipment was ready when they arrived.

Shiv helped Rex into his harness. The humans wore similar equipment, adjustable for each of their body shapes. The humans' harnesses were not custom built, but in training last week they'd each claimed one, then fiddled with the straps for a while to make it fit right. They were stored alongside the XK9s' rigs, reserved for their users till the end of the investigation.

Rex lolled his tongue, which always felt strange in micrograv. He did a lazy loop-the-loop in midair, just because he could, while he waited for the humans. Cinnamon slow-rolled past him, then Scout made a slightly faster swoop around both. Not fast enough to be reckless, but enough to make his ears flap. Lorena made a disgusted face and shook her head.

Rex made a swoop like Scout's, then imitated Cinnamon's roll.

Shiv ducked—quite needlessly. Rex hadn't gotten that close.

Berwyn laughed. "Get over here, Cinnie! You'll flop into someone."

"I shall not." Cinnamon swooped around him. "I have excellent control."

Her partner grabbed for her. They tumbled into Shiv at low velocity. Cinnamon quickly jetted free, then halted to regard the two upended humans with self-satisfied scent factors and a wicked tongue-loll.

"Oh!"

"Yikes!"

"Sorry!"

Mike scowled at them. "Enough! Form up!"

Shiv and Berwyn scrambled to stabilize and right themselves. Their reactions smelled of strong embarrassment, with odd little notes of startled arousal. Rex sorted through their scent factors, then texted Cinnamon. "You did that on purpose."

"Sometimes humans need to be thrown off-balance. Gives them new perspectives."

"Are you attempting to provoke them be unprofessional?"

Scout joined Nicole. Berwyn and Shiv, uninjured but flustered, disentangled themselves and joined the others.

"No, just a little ad hoc wish-fulfillment," Cinnamon texted to Rex. "They've been wondering for weeks how it would feel to touch each other."

An irritable prickle made Rex's hackles itch. "You now have a brain-link with Shiv, too?"

"I've been paying close attention to his scent factors. He's very good at hiding his emotions from humans, but—"

"Our next stop is the SDF's Wheel Two Hub Base." Mike's voice cut across all else. He still smelled and sounded aggravated. He gave the little group a drill-sergeant-style glare. "They do *not* look kindly upon frivolity. Don't embarrass yourselves. Back to the shuttles!"

"We would never act silly at a crime scene," Rex texted Shiv. "We were simply testing our jets while waiting."

"He still doesn't know you that well." Shiv used a quiet voice. "The Commander at the post is a former colleague, so he wants you to make a good impression."

"We shall not fail him."

Commodore Clarimonde Alvaro Montreaux turned out to be a petite, slender woman with black hair and pale skin. She met the SBI-OPD group at the entrance to the base, flanked by two muscular male MPs. All three eyed the XK9s with dubious expressions. "Are you sure about these dogs?" Montreaux asked. "Won't they contaminate any evidence they might find?"

Mike shook his head. "We have containment gear for them to put on in the shuttle. The Pack has by now processed many of the recovered victims, and committed their scents to memory, along with scents of other individuals of interest. They'll be able to identify any of them who may have been in contact with surfaces on the bridge. We hope they may be able to help us unravel at least a few clues about why the ship breached."

Montreaux nodded but didn't lose the frown. "The entire command module broke away from the main body of the ship during the explosions. It embedded itself into Docks 23 and 24. We removed the entire section, ruined dock and all, but until you and SSA Adeyeme indicated you wanted to examine the inside we hadn't tried to separate it from the debris wrapped around it. We have removed only as much of the dock material as necessary to clear access to the entry hatch. It's now inside the secured bubble-cordon, but we've been waiting to open the hatch until you and the CSU crew were here to observe and document it."

Rex's pulse sped up. "Pristine scents—not disturbed at all?" He used his jets to keep himself in place, but he couldn't help wagging his tail with delight at this.

Montreaux stared at him. "Talking dogs are going to require some getting used to."

"You'll be surprised how quickly the weirdness wears off." Mike glanced toward Rex. "But your decision not to break into the bridge is much appreciated."

"It does not get better than a sealed-since-it-happened crime scene," Scout said. "How soon can we access the inside?"

Montreaux's frown deepened. "My techs are running checks now, to see if it's safe to power the hatch. It looks as if it may not be jammed too badly."

Rex quivered with eagerness to *go!* To *hunt!* He held himself in place. If only he could do a few more loops or rolls! But no. He must behave himself according to Mike's standards. By the time they got the all-clear to move, he left a cloud of stress-shed behind. His group proceeded in an orderly fashion to enter a closed shuttle lined with small portholes.

Then came the tedious process of removing their harnesses, putting on containment gear, then putting the harnesses back on. The shuttle was a good place to use as a ready-room, to minimize cross-contamination. If they'd put on their containment equipment earlier, it could've picked up random substances on their journey here.

Montreaux suited up, too. She probably was curious about the evidence her people had preserved for so long. Probably also wanted to keep an eye on Rex and his Packmates.

Finally ready! Now came a short ride through hard vacuum. Rex peered out one of the portholes. The gigantic, cilia-textured bubble's surface rippled with endless movement. He'd known it was big but hadn't imagined it would be this huge. Presumably, it more-than-adequately encased what was left of the fore section. Their shuttle approached slowly, then docked with it. Four by four, XK9s, partners, agents and CSU techs cleared the airlock.

Before them lay an eerily familiar form. The wreck's features stirred unpleasant memories. A growl vibrated Rex's throat. His chest went tight, hackles a-prickle. Most of this had been encased in a berthing cone the last time he'd gotten this close. The left end was a jagged mass of twisted metal. It gave silent physical testament to the power of a million simultaneous micro-deconstructions meeting the momentum of the ship's spin. Parts of it looked melted.

The combination of forces had sealed the broken end of the former corridor. They were lucky to have a hatch available. Otherwise access to the bridge would've required slicing through the hull and bulkhead.

The round hatch the SDF techs were trying to open was marked "Service Entrance," with the words aligned around it in four different orientations. Memories hit Rex like a board to the head. *Wow. That brings it back.*

Charlie didn't answer. From the feel of it, his partner was asleep. By now he'd been home for a couple of hours. Just as well he was sleeping. Anything Charlie remembered of this view would be colored with agony.

Rex's gut squirmed. In his mind, lights pulsed on, then circled that hatch in a repeating cycle. The display panel next to it lay dark now, but a vision of it, lighted, with *"Izgubil"* and *"vacuum locks engaged"* in blinking letters, blazed in his memory. He licked his lips and shuddered.

"Are you all right?" Shiv asked.

Rex growled. "Bad memory. I saw and heard that hatch lock, just before the dock breach."

Shiv stroked his shoulder. "I know how bad memories can feel. Take a moment. Breathe. Try to relax."

Rex used one of Charlie's breathing patterns and bowed his head. The memories receded to a less unsettling level. "Thanks. I shall be all right. I am curious to learn what was happening on the other side of that hatch while I was clinging to the gantry."

"Let's hope they get it open soon."

Montreaux's people monkeyed around for a long time with the wires they needed to connect.

Rex floated closer. "One moment. Move back."

Montreaux turned a scowl on him, but she and her techs moved back.

Rex sniffed over the hatch opening in detail. He used his jets so he wouldn't have to touch it with his paws. He closed his eyes in hope the bad memories would stay at bay. Growled when they didn't and pushed through them. He focused on his scent impressions.

Oh. Here! Yes! His pulse kicked up again. Traces of a big, sweaty handprint from Thud, the elder of the two Murder Brothers, was smeared on the framework. A few layers of microscopic emissions trace overlaid it—but not as many as if it had been left uncovered in space for the past five weeks. Leaving the dock material wrapped around it until they needed access had been a very good idea. "Scout, Nicole, confirm and document." He angled his jets to move out of their way.

"What did you find?" Shiv asked.

Rex quietly explained about the handprint. "I think Thud swung inside, to propel himself forward. There ought to be some sign of Blunder, too. We know they came back, because I tracked them here. I still do not understand why they returned. They had just killed a valuable slave. Their employer would want to punish them."

Shiv frowned. "Here's hoping we'll soon have some answers."

Once Scout and Nicole were finished, CSU imaged it. Then the tech who'd first connected the power fiddled with a new-looking keypad that floated, anchored by a few wires, next to the hatch's framework.

Metal scraped metal, audible in the pressurized atmosphere of the bubble. Something went *snap*. The hatch rotated half-open, then halted. Its motor whined, but although the tech cycled it several times, it opened no wider. Montreaux might be able to get through there; Elaine could, if she were here. But none of the XK9s was small enough to squeeze through, even without any gear. Neither were Shiv or the partners.

One of the tech crew brought up a spreader-tool. It widened the opening, ratchet by difficult ratchet. Once it was open, the tech peered inside. "There's another closed hatch."

"Move aside." Rex could get through now, but first the CSU team must image it in painstaking detail. He fidgeted but let them finish. Then at last he floated into a cylindrical passageway, maybe three meters long. About one-and-a-half meters in diameter. Cramped quarters, but a lot to go over in detail. Small lights from his harness glimmered across its varied access panels, grab bars, and other surfaces. He worked his way in slowly.

Here was Blunder's scent, along with more from Thud. They smelled almost fresh, on a handhold and a strap.

"We have a couple of places you shall need to confirm and document, in here." Scout, Nicole, Cinnamon, and Berwyn waited outside with Shiv.

Rex retreated. Scout and Nicole took scent samples and documented them. Then Montreaux's techs moved in to work on the second hatch. Once it was opened, Rex saw the short entrance tube opened at a 90-degree angle into another cylindrical passageway that was about three meters wide.

Sealed by that mass of mangled metal a short distance to the left, a third closed hatch blocked the cross-passage on his right. Once again, he found Thud's handprint on the upper framework. "Thud went inside. It is possible he locked it behind himself, to block others' access." *What must he have been thinking, at that moment? What was his plan?* Did Thud's body await them, beyond that third hatch?

Scout and Nicole entered next. They confirmed and documented the strap, handhold, and handprint, then retreated. Cinnamon and Berwyn found where Blunder had grabbed another handhold just outside the third hatch. Had he gone through it, too? Rex checked the schematics on his HUD. This third hatch led through an escape pod evacuation area, directly behind the cockpit-like bridge.

As he'd guessed, this third hatch was locked from inside. It took two techs almost an hour to override it. After an eternity of panting hard inside his mask but *not* doing loops and barrels, the pesky thing slid open.

The techs looked inside. Their headlamps lanced through the darkness. "Uh-oh. We've got a body." They carefully backed out.

Rex entered, followed by Shiv. The first section was an extension of the corridor. About three meters long, its walls on all sides held a veritable honeycomb of escape pod access panels. This area smelled more clearly of Blunder than Thud. Rex and

Shiv stared past it, through a dilated hatch into the cockpit beyond.

A woman's body floated in the middle of the cockpit's wider area, tethered at the waist to the control console. Her head, partially severed from her neck by a deep throat-slash, was cocked at an unnatural angle. The distinctive, metallic scent of blood, as well as what looked at first like dark red marbles, filled the air.

Time to retreat for CSU's imaging.

Once they were done, Rex pulsed his jets. Floated into the cockpit. The roughly ripe-apricot size of the dried blood spheres could tell the CSU team how long it had taken for the blood to clump, clot, and dry enough that the liquid spheres no longer continued to agglomerate.

He looked around at the interior surface. It was coated with a layer of rust-colored dried blood, drawn there by ventilator action until the craft lost power. He smelled remnants of Thud's urgent, fearful scent, residual throughout the cabin and pressed across the dead woman's back. "We shall need an analysis in normal gravity when we process her, but contact scents suggest Thud attacked her from behind."

Cinnamon moved inside carefully. She hovered near the controls, nostrils working, eyes alert. "He cut her throat after the breach. No fingerprints in the blood layer."

"Put a knife to her throat and forced her to breach, then killed her anyway." Berwyn's disgusted tone matched Rex's revulsion.

Scout had stayed in the passageway near the escape pods. "Blunder is all over these access panels. I have residuals for fear, urgency, impatience."

"The ones you're calling Thud and Blunder must've locked the hatch." Montreaux had ventured into the now-open third hatchway. "They denied other passengers access to several dozen escape pods when the ship blew."

"I find the same pattern of touch marks on each of these pads," Scout said. "What was he doing?"

One of the techs looked his way. "Show me the pattern."

"There are finger-touches here, here, here, and on these number pads." Scout pointed with his nose. "The scent is Blunder's. Almost no trace of Thud here."

"Timed releases." The tech scowled. "That's a delayed-launch code. They set the pods to launch empty?"

Rex rotated slowly, to face Scout. "Thud's body is not here, and neither is Blunder's. Which pod did they take?"

"Here," Scout indicated an access panel near the edge of the cockpit. "They took this one."

"They didn't know the ship was about to explode," Berwyn said. "I bet the empty launches were to cover their own escape. On the vids afterwards, the delayed releases looked like a normal release of pods upon breakup."

"We recovered all the pods," Montreaux said. "None were manned."

Mike frowned. "Check the telemetry again, and inventory any left here unlaunched. I'll bet there was one with no beacon, manually overridden, hiding among the others." He met Rex's eyes with a grim look. "You called it."

Montreaux looked from Mike to Rex, eyebrows up. "The *dog* called it?"

Rex snapped his ears flat. "It was the only reason I could imagine why we did not find the smallest shred of their bodies. Either they were inside here, or they managed to get into a pod. If we can find that pod, we can narrow our search. I shall not be satisfied until we find and capture the Murder Brothers."

CHAPTER 35

THE HOLY GRAIL

The elevator floor under Shady's paws vibrated. She yawned. It had already been a full and busy watch. Unfortunately, it wasn't over. XK9 Field Team Two—Shady, Elle, Crystal, and their humans—had been tapped to relieve Rex's group. Scentwork in micrograv could wear a dog down fast. Teams needed to cycle downside every four hours. *So, of course it makes sense to send up a "fresh" team who's already worked a full watch.*

Pam rubbed her lower back but shook her head. *Now that they've opened it, the clock's ticking on those scents. Team One barely got started, after all the delays.*

Shady originally had envied Rex his first-on-scene status ... until he and the others were forced to wait around while the techs did their whatever-it-was, time after time, to open each hatch. Field reports from Rex, Scout, and Cinnamon had been tantalizing. And Pam was right about the fragility of the scents. But *damn.* She yawned.

She also stopped panting and pacing. Instead, she lay on the floor to conserve strength and mulled over the data her Packmates had collected. Perhaps naturally, Rex's thoughts and nose had been full of the Murder Brothers, the homicidal siblings he'd originally scent-trailed on the night of the dock breach.

Shady had a different group on her mind. That hatch also had been the entrance and exit point for Elmo Smart's group, whom they suspected of rigging the explosives. Surely, she must find some trace of them in there!

A pair of morgue techs rode with Shady's team. They brought equipment to transport the *Izgubil* pilot's body. Downside, Razor and Liz stood ready to conduct a pre-autopsy once the techs returned to S-3-9 with their partially-mummified new morgue client. They, too, were working an extended shift. It was vital to conduct a full 1-G analysis as soon as possible, to either confirm or amend Team One's findings.

Their elevator ride ended. Their MUPATS shuttle crawled from the elevator's upper terminal to equipment storage, and then to the SDF base.

Rex must have been watching for her. He jetted straight over.

As ever, her heart warmed and her pulse kicked higher at the sight and smell of her mate. They exchanged a quick nose touch and nuzzle, but his ears and tail drooped with fatigue. She sniffed him all over, noted the points of inflammation, and the place on his side where the harness had rubbed him half-raw. *Uh-oh.* Her ears snapped flat. "This buckle still chafes."

He growled. "I am tired of trying to fix it. Easier to live with it."

She growled back, tense with annoyance. "Until you start bleeding on the evidence! Report it to Lorena, and at least request a pad."

He gusted out a sigh. "Yes, dear." They ran through her briefing.

Scout and Cinnamon briefed Elle and Crystal, respectively, on their assorted findings: tracking specialists looked for different things than explosives-chemicals-and-weapons specialists. Their partners exchanged questions and answers.

Rex wished Shady success in her search for Elmo's team, then nodded goodbye to Pam and Shiv, and followed his teammates to the airlock.

Since he was the LSA on-site, Shiv planned to stay through Team Two's watch, then cycle downside with them. Shady eyed the man. Was he as tired as she already felt? He'd been working since seven this morning, just as she had. Working this watch made Team Two's Monday a 12-hour. Doing her last four in micrograv gave Shady a new appreciation for Hildie's grueling schedule, but that was not a thought to share with Pam.

Her partner frowned. Sickly, acidic jealousy spiked in her scent. *Keeping secrets?*

Dammit, no. Shady hated that smell in her partner's blend. *Hildie has been working frequent 12-hours in micrograv. I was comparing how I feel to how that must be.*

Oh. Pam's frown deepened, but the jealousy leached away. *Oh, yikes. I always came home slammed after four. She must be loads of fun in bed after twelve.*

Several replies occurred to Shady, but none seemed likely to go in constructive directions. She and Pam let Elle, Misha, Crystal, and Connie go in through the hatch before them. Those teams would take up where Scout, Cinnamon, and their partners had left off. They must scent-check every square centimeter of the cockpit and escape pod bay, while their partners gathered scent-card samples.

Shady stayed in the entrance corridor. Elmo's group wouldn't have ventured as far forward as the cockpit area. But they would have come through here, on both the inbound and outbound trips. *Somebody must've touched something.*

You would think. But by now it's several scent layers deep.

Shady and Pam spent several minutes just looking and, in Shady's case, sniffing at the various surfaces. One portion of the frame on the second hatch seemed shinier to Shady. Perhaps people entering or exiting tended to brush against that part. It should mean rub-created scent-spatter would gather by the edge of the frame. *Here.* She moved in, and found a nice sampling.

Hmm. I have every single member of Team One coming out. Also Col. Montreaux, and a couple of others I'll assume are her techs, since they're in her layer. Team One going in. Here are Thud and Blunder, below them. Hmm. Who else?

She worked her way deeper, puzzling through unknown scent profiles. She did find three of her morgue clients from that first group of *Izgubil* victims they'd processed weeks ago. *I guess this proves twenty-five, thirty-two, and thirty-nine were crew, as we thought.*

I'm making a note. You're right. Guests wouldn't come in here.

Deeper .... *Mmm. Okay, here.* Her breath came a little shorter. She stilled her rising excitement, relaxed her gut, and took another sniff. *Yes. That's Stinky.*

Excitement surged through the link and lit up Pam's scent factors. *You found them? Is there enough for a sample?*

No, the court is gonna have to take my word for it on that spot. But if there's one, there should be more. Let's see .....

In the next couple of hours, Shady located places where their subjects Dopey, Sweaty, Elmo, and Kieran had bumped an elbow or a knee, or pressed a hand to a wall. In Kieran's case, she found where he'd lingered for several full minutes in one corner by the second hatch. He'd laid in a nice, sample-ready layer of scent-trace there.

Why stay put for so long? Not that I'm complaining. Pam took eight of the strongest samples, following Shady's guidance.

Why, indeed? Shady rotated cautiously, careful to touch nothing. She strove for detached objectivity, but hope quickened her pulse and squeezed her chest. Must focus! *He lingered here. There are no instruments he could have been operating. Was he looking at something?*

The opposite wall featured several access panels. Some were unmarked, but a large one just inside the hatch was marked "BRUSCAR." Shady drew in a sharp breath. A frisson of excitement prickled her hackles.

What? Pam frowned at her. *What does "bruscar" mean?*

It's Ullach Gaelic for "trash." I think Kieran was watching the trash bin.

Now she felt it in Pam, too. *Or watching people put things into the trash bin.* She gulped and gave the access panel a wide-eyed look. Her scent factors leaped up, bright with excitement and hope. *Ready for a dumpster-dive?*

You're the one with the fingers. Shady repressed an eager wriggle. Her breath came in faster panting gasps.

Pam stripped off her old gloves, then pulled on a fresh pair. She grinned. *Don't want to risk contaminating the trash.*

It could be nothing. Just trash.

It could. That's true.

Shady went through Rex's favorite breathing pattern a couple of times to center herself and slow her hyperactive panting. *Don't get ahead of the evidence,* she cautioned both herself and Pam. But elation bubbled in her chest and electrified every nerve.

Pam opened the access panel.

Shady leaned forward on an inhale—then pulled back instantly. Blazing delight radiated through her. Her pulse thundered. Her throat closed. *Seal it up! Seal it up! Don't let a single molecule escape!*

What did you find? What is it? I couldn't see.

Shady turned. Met and held Pam's gaze, dizzy with awe. *We just found the Holy Grail.*

EARS UP, body tense, Shady focused her full attention on each move the CSU techs made. Fierce protectiveness sparked through her with an adrenaline-sharpened edge.

They unbolted the wall panel in front of the trash bin. This left it freestanding, but intact and unbreached. Then they carefully unbolted the bin itself from its mounts. It remained attached to a couple of meters of ductwork that led to some sort of closed segment-hatch. The rest of the ductwork beyond the hatch appeared to be empty.

"What is that?" Shady asked. "That closed hatch?"

"When the bin reaches a certain level, it automatically evacuates into the decomposer," one of the techs said.

Shady turned to share a haunted look with Pam.

"It was full, right?" Pam asked. "When you stuck your nose in there, it was full?"

"Yes." Shady's gut went all slippery-queasy to think they could've lost the whole load. It was full to near-brimming. If just a little more trash had gone into that bin, their evidence could all have gone to the decomposer part of the recycler. She checked the schematic. *Oh, crap.* The decomposer in question *might* still have contained some evidence. If it hadn't been centrally located and blasted to bits more than a month ago. She let out a shaky breath. "We lucked out."

CSU sealed the bin-access, the hatch, and the bulky, packed-full section of ductwork between them. Then they removed the entire, awkwardly-long assembly, angled it down the entrance tunnel, and hauled it out into the bubble-cordon.

Shady stayed with them, on alert the whole time. Pam and Shiv flanked her, equally watchful.

Three techs crated it. They security-sealed every edge of the crate, and at last lifted it out of the bubble cordon through the airlock—a tricky maneuver in itself.

Shady, Pam, and Shiv followed on the next airlock-cycle.

The closed shuttle ferried the bin and its vigilant escort through hard vacuum to the Hub. Shady, Pam, Shiv, and the three CSU techs stayed with it through every step, railing-grab, and retro-pulse of the way.

There would be an unbroken chain of custody, *or else.*

Adeyeme herself awaited them in a shuttle just outside the SDF Base entrance, with Rex by her side. Santiago and SCISCO backed them. A surprisingly strong force of uniformed OPD officers in two additional shuttles drew up on either side of Adeyeme's MUPATS.

Shady eyed the beefed-up component of uniformed Military Police officers who flanked Commander Montreaux. They clustered around the outer access of the SDF's Hub Base like a security detail.

MPs and UPOs stared at each other with cold, narrowed eyes, hard faces, and suspicion in their scents.

"What's up with all the MPs and UPOS?" she texted Rex.

Commodore Montreaux nodded to Adeyeme and Santiago. "May this turn out to be all that you hope it is."

In the next moment a new shuttle came into sight from down-Hub. Admiral Virendra emerged. He stiffened when he spotted Adeyeme's group.

"Admiral Virendra has offered to 'secure' our evidence for us." Rex kept his even outward demeanor, but his hackles twitched. The rage in his scent was clear to smell. "Elaine thanked him, but declined the offer on the com. I do not know why he is here."

Shady snapped her ears flat, then lifted them again with effort. Suspicion coiled cold in her gut and prickled through her hackles. Virendra had done everything in his power to cast Adeyeme, her investigation, and the OPD into a bad light since the first week of the investigation. And that was *before* Shady and the Pack had chased him away from the evidence chamber. That incident, caught on surveillance, had made him a secret laughing stock among his enemies in the SDF, according to SSA Santiago. It also had put Shady and the rest of the Pack permanently on his shit list.

The Admiral approached Adeyeme. His retros did a slow burn to propel him forward at a stately pace.

His retros had nothing on Shady's temper. She pulsed her own jets, to arrive first at Virendra's probable intersection point.

"Somehow, it all stems from an old and bitter conflict with Mike," Rex texted. "I wish I understood more."

"Let's just make sure he and his MPs get no closer to our crime scene," Shady texted back.

"Agreed." By now she was close enough to hear his soft growl.

Adeyeme gave Rex a brief, startled look. But his focus stayed on Virendra.

Shady moved closer with another burst of retros. "Good evening, SSA Adeyeme." She made a point of not greeting the rapidly-approaching Admiral. Instead, she blocked his path.

"Get this animal out of my way." Virendra made a shooing-away motion aimed at Shady's snout.

A quick snap of her jaws caught his arm before it could smack her. *Oh, give me a reason, Admiral!* She jaws ached to clamp down but kept her grasp soft.

The Admiral froze. He stared at Shady's teeth on his arm.

She put her ears up, wagged her tail, but met his eyes with a steely challenge. "It would not be good if you struck an OPD officer, even if it was only by accident. I shall release your arm, but you should control it in a nonviolent manner." She opened her mouth.

He snatched his arm back, cradled it to his chest. Gave her a scandalized look.

Behind her, she felt Pam's worry through the link. But she also noted with approval that her partner, Shiv, and the techs had wasted no time loading their evidence crate into Elaine's shuttle while she distracted Virendra.

"I trust you shall find I left no bruises." Shady lolled her tongue at Virendra. Her tongue didn't loll as well in micrograv as it would have in 1-G, but she made her point.

"Admiral, I'd like to take this opportunity to thank Commodore Montreaux and SDF Intelligence for the use of the bubble cordon. It is proving to be most helpful to our investigation." Adeyeme's scent factors held an odd mix of dark, hot anger, fragrant pleasure, and peppery frustration. "I shall make a

316 | A BONE TO PICK

point of praising Wheel Two Hub Base in the strongest terms during my press conference in the morning."

Virendra scowled. "How nice." His scent and his eyes smoldered, but he pulled back.

"Will Elle, Misha, Crystal, and Connie be all right?" Shady texted Rex.

"We're leaving a contingent of UPOs and half the CSU team to ensure that," Rex replied. "But our first priority is to get this evidence downside. Now."

Shady climbed aboard.

Adeyeme's shuttle retreated toward the elevators. The two others, full of UPOs, remained in place.

Shady took the spot next to Rex. She used her vocalizer this time, so the humans could hear. "I am eager to see what is inside that trash bin."

"As are we all." Adeyeme gave her a thoughtful look, then frowned. "Shady, Pam—how many hours have you been on-duty?"

Shady checked the time. "Oh." She'd been on the clock for nearly eleven hours. No wonder she felt achey.

"Since seven this morning." Pam stifled a yawn.

"Exactly." Adeyeme grimaced. "This evidence has been securely sealed. It should be stable for a few more hours. But none of us will be at the top of our game till we've gotten some solid sleep. And we must—*we must*—make no mistakes with this."

Shady bowed her head. "I guess if it has waited this long ..."

CHAPTER 36

TEAM ONE EMPTIES THE TRASH

C harlie's heart lifted at the excited chatter in the prep room early Tuesday morning. The electric sense of being right on the edge of a breakthrough sang in his veins. The investigation had hypothesized how the explosives could've been distributed throughout the ship's service corridors. Unfortunately, they hadn't been able to prove it.

Not yet, anyway.

According to Shady, the evidence was in the trash bin recovered from outside the bridge. She'd called it the "Holy Grail" when she came home a few hours ago, so excited she could scarcely breathe.

It had taken a bit of digging on his HUD to decipher "Holy Grail." A story from the Middle Ages on Old Earth. "How do you even know about that?" he'd asked her.

She'd rolled her eyes at him. "You call yourself an educated being? It is a Terran cultural reference!" Turned out she'd encountered it when she studied Anglofrankish and took a literature course.

It was kind of gratifying to hear other teammates confused and speculating, too, this morning.

After he'd deciphered the implications, he'd realized even more clearly that she thought this was big. This could break the case. If he could trust his thrilling inward sizzle of anticipation, maybe they'd make that big find.

But a different sharp, almost painful pleasure settled and filled him. He found it even more satisfying: today, he'd work with Rex again. *At least for a while this morning, I can be a real partner.*

Rex growled, glanced over his shoulder at him. *You already have acted as my partner several times since you came out of that first re-gen coma. Remember the onstage presentation, when we showed the Universe what we could do? I would've been a wreck without you. Remember the conference with the Mahusayans? We needed you then, too. And you came through brilliantly.*

Charlie bowed his head. *But not for the certification.*

Rex's growl rolled louder, so forceful that Shiv and Cinnamon gave him a puzzled look. He turned to face Charlie with ears laid back. *We discussed this.*

I know. Charlie looked away.

It's over.

I know. You're right.

Get your head in the Now.

Charlie met his eyes, frowned. *I'm ready. Do we have to—*

You started it.

Yeah, yeah. He blew out a breath and tried to center himself.

Good thing the whole Pack wasn't trying to cram in here at once. Team Three had pulled the overnight shift on the *Izgubil's* bridge, and pretty thoroughly wrapped up the last of the micro-grav work. Like Shady's Team Two, they had orders to sleep this morning, and clock in later. That left Shady's "Grail" for Rex's team to open.

Charlie accepted containment garb from a field agent, then turned to Rex. *It's been a while since I worked scents with you.*

Rex pranced around with delight. *I am excited to work together again.*

That's lovely. Hold still. Four legs and a tail on Rex's containment garment. First, however, he must catch the big dog. It took a while to contain Rex, both figuratively and literally.

While Charlie worked on that, he reviewed what was known or hypothesized. Based on debris evidence, the conspirators had sprayed a layer of adhesive onto support joints inside the ship, accessed through utility tunnels. The adhesive mixture contained a conductive element and Rory Fredericks's unique nanotimers. While the adhesive was still wet, they'd then broadcast explosive pellets onto it. Those were designed to detonate when the nanotimers sent current through the conductive material.

How could they manage to do all of that, right under the Whisper Syndicate's nose? The investigators speculated they'd posed as exterminators, or perhaps as a work-group applying paint or sealant. They'd need respirators for any kind of spraying job. Wearing respirators to cover their faces, along with matching coveralls that looked official, they'd be impossible to recognize or distinguish from one another. Joe Raach, Connie, and Crystal had calculated that eight or ten, working in two-person teams, could cover the *Izgubil* in one long workday.

Thanks to Rex, the investigators even had a group of eight prime suspects. The Pack had documented the fact that a group that included their suspects Elmo Smart and Kieran O'Boyle had gone to and from the *Izgubil*'s service entrance. The scent-layers they'd documented indicated they'd done this eight days before the ship blew up. But inside the access corridor that led from the main dock to the *Izgubil*, the Pack had found only one drop of incriminating adhesive mixture. It was in the same scent layer as these men's scents, but it wasn't enough to prove a link.

It certainly inflamed speculation, though. And with luck, today Team One would confirm that connection, or put it permanently to rest.

Garbed, masked, and gloved, Team One assembled. One by one, they stepped inside the first of a line of three linked hazmat tents at the edge of the evidence cavern. Everyone looked to Rex.

He and the other XK9s would do the talking, when needed. Their vocalizers didn't risk DNA cross-contamination the way human speech did.

Rex wagged his contamination-garment-sheathed tail. "Optics on, everyone. Charlie, please open the access panel."

Charlie tried to set aside speculations. Where would the evidence lead?

First, it led to ... candy wrappers. *Yikes.* Loads and loads of candy wrappers. He pulled them out one by one and handed them off to Nicole.

"Somebody really loved their Starry Bars." Berwyn kept his voice low. In his defense, the risk of contaminating this "evidence" seemed pretty low.

Rex sniffed at them. "These all have the pilot's trace on them, imbued with scent factors for stress and fear. I am rather surprised she was not fat, considering all this candy-consumption. Even if she ate them over eight days, that is still a lot of candy."

"Well, it is a trash bin. I guess there is no accounting for people's tastes," Scout said. Throughout this speech, his partner Nicole silently accepted each item, imaged it, then placed it on a nearby exam table. "In eight days you could build up .... Wow. Really a lot of candy wrappers."

He hesitated.

"Nicole just suggested that perhaps the pilot was a 'stress eater.' Well, I suppose working for a criminal organization like the Whisper Syndicate could be stressful."

Charlie kept digging, edging deeper and deeper into the bin. She *had* built up a lot. He also found a drink bottle with a hole in it. Several clean-up towels. Somebody's toothbrush? And some other things he hesitated to identify, but which he handed up to Nicole. Plus lots more Starry Bar wrappers. At last, he found the final layer of wrappers. They were stuck to something. He pulled on it.

It took determined tugging, but he managed to peel up a work glove, with the bottom layer of wrappers stuck to the top of it. *Got a really sticky work glove.*

"Work glove coming." Weird, to need Rex to speak for him! "Careful, it's sticky."

Charlie handed the glove up to Nicole.

There was a moment of charged silence. "Yes," Scout said. "Your guesses are correct. It is sticky with the adhesive we hoped for."

Cinnamon made an excited squeak. "With the nanotimer mixture!"

It's Kieran's glove, Rex exulted through the link. *It's the adhesive with the nanotimers! We've got them! Oh, Charlie! We've got them!*

Charlie kept his head, shoulders, and by now torso inside the bin. He focused on the evidence at his fingertips. Here was the second glove, stuck to something bigger. Something fluorescent green, flexible, there was a lot of it, and it was wedged into the bin really tight. He tugged harder. Drew it upward with difficulty. Another yank, and a piece of it pulled away with a gooey, sucking noise. But it tore only so far up from the amalgamated ball of the rest of it. Looked like a coverall pantleg. Sticky. *Really* sticky. What a mess!

He levered himself backwards out of the bin, dragging the second glove.

His colleagues kept quiet, wary of the cross-contamination risk. But Nicole and Berwyn mimed hands in the air and did a bouncy little dance-in-place. Above their masks, the skin by their eyes crinkled from their huge smiles. Rex, Scout and Cinnamon pranced and leaped as much as the confined space allowed. All three containment-wrapped dog tails wagged at full-fan. The whole crew probably was laying down a new scent layer that Rex would say smelled happy. It was good to celebrate for a moment, even if they couldn't whoop, holler and bark.

But soon it was time to get professional again.

Big, sticky ball of coverall in here, Charlie reported through the link. Rex relayed his words like a vocalizer-voiced echo.

He studied the problem by the light of his headlamp, pulling at the gooey bundle, but it appeared to have bonded pretty tightly. *I think our best bet is to open the bin and the duct along the side and remove the contents very carefully that way,* he told Rex. *Dragging them out through the access panel isn't going to work. We're gonna need industrial-strength adhesive-release to unfold them. Maybe even just to get them out.*

CHARLIE SAID good day to Rex and the others, then retreated to the prep room alone at the end of his half-shift. He yawned. Stripped off his gloves, mask, and cap, grateful he didn't have to put in a full watch. He'd dug through trash and helped cut the trash bin open, but that was the easy part. Muscling two sets of glued-together coveralls out of their balled-up wads after that had been plenty of work for one day.

He rolled his aching shoulders, then fumbled with the containment garment's fasteners. Despite judicious applications of adhesive release, the saboteurs' stickum had proved to be powerful stuff. He, Shiv, Berwyn, and Nicole had engaged in an epic tug-o-war with the stubborn material. Even Shiv had broken a sweat.

All Charlie wanted by this time was three Pana-Cees and a long nap. He might be a nascent Semi-SuperCop, and his home workout routine might already be bulking up his shoulders, but enough was enough. Good thing Rex's car knew the way home.

The ready room's outer hatch swung open. SSA Adeyeme poked her head inside. She smiled. "Ah, excellent. Right on time. I need to talk with you before you leave." She inclined her head toward the evidence cavern. "I've been watching the preliminary reports come in. How's it going?"

Charlie stifled another yawn. "It's not the most powerful

adhesive in the Universe, but no explosive pellet was ever going to fall off, not in a million years. Did a jim-dandy job of plugging the trash evacuation chute, too. Those coveralls were never in any danger of making it all the way to the decomposer." He rolled his shoulders again, but it barely eased their achey stiffness. "We found a back-mounted tank sprayer stuck to the bottom of the pile, but I have a feeling the rest of those did go on down."

Her satisfied smile matched her low chuckle. "One ought to be enough. SCISCO's already agitating to examine everything." Then her expression sobered. "I don't know if you've had time to think that far, but I'm afraid I'm going to have to postpone your field trip to Monteverde."

He hadn't, but it made sense. "You can't spare an XK9 team."

"I can't spare *any* of you. Now that we've opened the bin, the clock is ticking."

"That's scent-work, all right. So far today, we managed to pry open the coveralls that Kieran and Dopey wore. Found their gloves, respirators, and boots, too. We got very good, ID-worthy DNA samples, once we could get inside the various pieces—and the adhesive mixture on the outsides is the unique mix that was used to kill the ship."

She drew in a sharp breath. "That alone should be enough to convict them." Until then, he wouldn't have said she'd seemed oppressed. But the palpable easing of her posture and her face spoke volumes. Like the team when they'd first realized what they'd found, she basked for a moment in visible joy. Then she let out a long exhalation and met his gaze. "Now we must deal with the rest of it. What've we got?"

"Evidence doesn't *get* better than this." He grinned, pleased by her reaction. "There are six more rolled-up coveralls to go. We dug through eight days' worth of trash to get to them, but if our crew doesn't manage to pry open at least two more and process them before the end of the day-watch, I'll be surprised."

"I'm going to call both night-watches in at three, so they can

get started. We can make room for all of them to work at once."
She looked up at him. "Now that we've started connecting our
suspects to individual coveralls, we'll have grounds for
warrants. Rex wants to mount a hunt in the Five-Ten. He talked
about it weeks ago."

"Oh, yeah." Charlie gave a weary chuckle. "He's told me all
about it. A bunch of times."

She met his eye. "What do you think of the plan?"

"It's a sound strategy, if that's what you're asking. The Pack
will pick up the scent of any suspect whose profile they've
memorized. If any of that crew are in the Five-Ten, and left a
walking trail, the Pack will find them."

"They're amazing at autopsies and static evidence, but I was
less sure about a live hunt."

"Remember how dogs evolved." Tracking, trailing, and
hunting in varied terrains had formed a large part of their
training in Transmondia. "XK9s, like their wolf and dog ancestors, were literally born to hunt. You've never really seen them in
their element till you've seen and heard them on a Hunt." He
blew out a fervent breath. "It's … powerful."

She bit her lip, shot him a rueful look. "And you're on
restricted duty."

Again. Still. His shoulders drooped. "Yeah, I know."

"You also know there'll be other hunts."

"True. I hate to miss this one, but you're right. There will be."
He squared his shoulders. "What'll you have me doing,
instead?"

"After we finish with the evidence from the bin, I need a GR
made."

Unexpected pleasure filled him. *A GR?* He'd thought that
career was behind him, but he'd loved the work itself. "Okay."

"First, of course, I'd like to observe a sample of your previous
work, to see if you can handle the level of detail I need."

"That's fair." By law, his old casework should still be on file.
Even Missy wouldn't dare delete archived evidence just because

he'd been the artist who developed the rendering. She was legally required to hold it until fifty years after the death of the person who'd been either convicted or exonerated by it. There was one in particular .... He grinned. "If it's detail you want, I know just the GR to show you."

CHAPTER 37

OLD ENEMIES AND FRIENDS

C harlie wished Rex and Shady success in their practice runs with the STAT Team on Wednesday morning. Tuesday had yielded more than enough probable cause to secure arrest warrants for what must be some of the strangest suspect-identifiers the Borough Court had ever considered. Apparently, however, language such as "the suspect identified via scent-profile as Unknown One, AKA Stinky" was deemed an acceptable level of identification. Once it was processed, they had sealed up the rest of the evidence to the best of their ability and moved to the Hunt-planning stage.

Charlie bade them farewell but took a different path. Away from the SBI's investigative center.

Warm contentment eased his chest and put a little bounce in his step. He had no complaints about his life right now. Hildie had stayed at Corona Tower ever since her Monday twelve-hour ended. She didn't have to go back up-top till tomorrow. The new crime scene had yielded a flood of great clues. Rex's Hunt-with-a-capital-H promised to bring in more. On a different front, yesterday evening Uncle Hector had reported new success from Pat Cornwell and his team. They'd quickly found definitive evidence to source the half-exploded listening device from Corona's rooftop. No doubt lingered now: it was from Transmondian Intelligence. By last night, they'd found a way to neutralize and even possibly take control of the devices.

It did seem that the Transmondians had stopped deploying them in Orangeboro, at least for now. There'd been the two on Friday at Corona, plus one the following day at Glorioso Tower, where Tux now lived with Elle. The OPD, the SBI, and Hector-vault Security had equipped all of the Pack's homes with Uncle Hector's perimeter-tech, after a thorough sweep of each premises. Tellingly, only Corona and Glorioso had "infestations," but it seemed even those were finished for now.

Charlie's smile widened. To cap it all, he'd had two encouraging conversations at the end of his half-watch yesterday. The first, with SSA Adeyeme, had unexpectedly revived his hope of ever doing another Global Reconstruction. The second, with Chief Klein, confirmed Rex's elated reports, and opened a glimpse of the Chief's plans for a new XK9 Special Investigations Unit at Central HQ.

Rex would direct it, as Pack Leader. Each XK9 would get an office adjacent to their partner's. Two veteran detectives, DPO Lew Penny from Homicide and the still-recuperating DPO Helmer Fujimoto, would serve as advisors and coordinators. Charlie looked forward to working with Fujimoto again. The heroic DPO had saved both his and Rex's lives during the dock breach.

Best of all, Charlie's space would include his old GR Chamber Three, directly accessible via a relocated entrance. It would become his domain once again, on the logic that rendering scent evidence visible for judges and juries might become essential for prosecuting cases. He smiled. Best of both worlds, to his mind. He'd get to work with Rex, and also do the global-reconstruction work that fascinated him.

How had Klein prevailed on Secretary Pandra to take Chamber Three away from Missy? That could not have been easy. However he'd managed it, Charlie stood in awe. He hoped he could employ GR visualizations to help numb-nosed humans understand all that scent evidence could reveal. Tomorrow, a construction crew would arrive. They'd work for several weeks to reconfigure a full block of offices—plus GR Chamber Three—into the new unit's headquarters.

All the same, his steps slowed as he neared the GR Unit. His earlier ease vanished. His chest tightened and his stomach soured, especially on that last turn of the corridor. He halted. Ran a breathing pattern. It had been a year since he'd last walked down this hallway, but his first glimpse triggered a headache.

He scowled, squared his shoulders. *Back then has no bearing on right now.* He didn't need Missy Cranston's approval, and certainly not her permission, to be here. He was pre-authorized in his capacity as an SBI Reserve Agent, with clearance from Mayor Idris herself, to use GR Chamber Three. He activated his wearable optics and audio pickups to make sure what happened next was recorded.

The instant he pushed open the door to the GR Unit, Missy burst out of her office. "You bastard, Morgan! Get the hell out! *Now!*" She leaped into his path to block him. Her cadaverous face, perennially bloodshot eyes, and frizzy, graying hair always put Charlie in mind of something aggrieved and undead.

Sudden, fierce anger sped his pulse. He no longer had to make nice. "Stuff a sock in it, Missy. You know I don't have to listen to that anymore."

"You're barred for life! How dare you darken this door! And if you think you can just up and *steal* Chamber Three, let me tell *you* a thing or two! Nobody pulls that shit on me!"

"Excuse me, Missy." He tried to step around her.

She moved with him. Her eyes bulged with bloodshot rage. Her indignant bony finger jabbed at him with accusatory vigor. "Oh, no, you *do not*, you slimy back-stabber!"

"Shut the hell up and move aside." He placed his hands on her bony upper arms, then gently but firmly lifted her out of his way. Almost as tall as he, her angular frame massed only about half his weight.

"Police brutality! How dare you assault me in my own unit!" She leaped back into his path.

He carefully moved her aside as he had before and struggled to put a lid on his own flare of fury. Easier if he didn't listen to her words, but the shrieking created its own type of physical assault. He ran a careful breathing pattern and managed half a meter of ingress toward Chamber Three. She once again bounced with outrage, cursing and lecturing right under his nose. This was unusual persistence, even for her. What was she screaming? Something about siccing IA on her? She certainly seemed to have a multitude of grievances.

He sighed and swallowed all the hot retorts that sprang to mind. Better not to talk. *Don't engage.* He removed her from his path once again. Tried not to hear her words. Meter by meter, they made it to Chamber Three's door.

Missy stayed in full-out harangue mode the whole distance.

Charlie put his head down and kept moving. Firm. Deliberate. Careful not to leave bruises, although that took increasing effort. The urge to smash her into the side wall grew, but he remembered that shattered railing from last Friday, and recoiled with an inner shudder. At long last he grasped the latch. Strode past her into Chamber Three and closed the door with a firm *click.*

Whew! He leaned against the door, then ran breathing pattern after breathing pattern. Molten anger coursed through him. It pounded in his throat and soured his gut. He almost thought he could still hear muffled shrieking outside, but the soundproofing in these walls could render even a gunshot blast silent to outside listeners. This guarded against anyone gaining unauthorized intelligence about what evidence an artist was handling. It also eliminated all sounds from outside. Maybe it was just that his ears were still ringing.

He gave a final shudder, straightened, and looked around the dimly-lit, circular room. Adrenaline burn-off made his hands shake. He breathed through that, too, and focused on his surroundings. The GR tank filled most of Chamber Three. Its soft blue glow offered just enough illumination to make dim details visible. Walls, floor, and ceiling were all a uniform, matte-finish charcoal color. The place smelled of warm, stagnant air, old sweat, and dust. Lots of dust.

Charlie flicked on the ventilation. He selected a combination of patchouli and mint to help calm, ground, and keep him alert. He also activated the housekeeping functions, then stepped aside for the floor-vac. In the low light, scuttling, efficient brush-, polish-, and mini-vac units busied themselves on other surfaces. He moved out of the way again for the vac's return pass and imagined dozens of spiders bolting for the nearest crevices.

Next on his list: a message to Adeyeme. "I'm inside GR Chamber Three. Gonna need about half an hour to warm up the unit and eradicate all the dust and cobwebs. Be aware that the guardian door-dragon is in a particularly foul mood today." He forwarded the vid his optics and audio had captured.

He considered for a moment, then also sent a copy of the vid to Alphonse Rami, with a short note to explain his authorization to use Chamber Three. "Just FYI," he added.

He made his way past the charcoal-colored observers' chairs to the charcoal-colored console, with its charcoal-colored operator's rig. As soon as the mini-vac was done with it, he slid into the rig to initiate the start-up sequence.

His fingers flew over the keys with the satisfying familiarity of muscle memory. He sat back, then his spirit warmed and a grin spread across his face. The lumbar support was still calibrated for him. Had anyone used this chamber since he'd left? The unit hadn't added an artist since then, so maybe not. Nice. Chamber Three was *still his*. The tank's glow brightened. A midtone hum filled the air. It would take several minutes for it to fully come online.

Memories rose thick around him. So weird to be back. He

adjusted his HUD's settings for the interface, then accessed his old case files.

REX LIFTED his ears with a surge of pleased recognition. "Anthony! Sevencrows! Hello!" He trotted across the STAT Team's sub-level practice area to greet them, tail wagging. He'd met the UPO partners five weeks ago, during his original foray into the infamous Five-Ten neighborhood with Shiv. The pair later had testified to Lt. Patel's investigation and a Council committee in support of his probable sapience.

A grin split UPO Lynn Anthony's normally-stern face. "Hey, Rex! Figured we'd see you here today. How's it going, Pack Leader?" The muscular, middle-aged woman reached out to deliver a friendly head-rub.

"It is going well, thank you."

Her tall, younger partner Henry Sevencrows offered Rex a smile and a pat when Anthony stepped aside.

He gave each a thorough sniff-over. "Are you here to give your lecture about blowpipes?"

Anthony laughed. "How'd you guess?"

"It seemed likely that you would not wish to rescue our broken asses and mop up after us in the Five-Ten this time, any more than you wanted to do that for Shiv and me a month ago."

Sevencrows gave a shout of laugher. "He's got your patter down cold, Lynn."

"He's right, though." Anthony's grizzled brows pinched with mock ferocity. "I hate doing that." From what Rex had gathered, she'd patrolled her subterranean beat for most of her professional life. No one in the OPD knew the place better.

People weren't supposed to live in the Five-Ten, but they did. It had become a haven for criminals, unregistered persons, and hard telling who or what else, ten levels below Orangeboro's urban center. A literal underworld.

"We're also here to provide some practical examples," Seven-crows added. "It isn't every day you get to shoot pea gravel at the STAT Team."

"Not and live to tell the tale." One of the STAT Blue Team members, Charlie's friend Eddie Chism, walked over to join them. "Ho, Lynn, Henry. How's life Down Under?"

"Been quiet, but kinda tense." Anthony reverted to her default semi-scowl. "Something's about to break loose, from the feel of it. And now it looks like you're gonna stir the pot."

Rex cocked his head. "Any idea why things have been tense?"

Anthony and Sevencrows exchanged a look.

"Been building up since about the time you bagged Elmo Smart." Sevencrows grimaced. "We've heard rumors about murders, but no one saw anything, they only heard. Plus, we've found no bodies."

"Have you seen Kieran O'Boyle recently?" Rex asked.

Anthony's grizzled brows rose. "Is he one of your hush-hush warrants? 'Cause he's one of the alleged murder vics whose body we haven't found. We also haven't seen him in at least a month."

"What about Turlach?" Rex and Shiv had briefly encountered Kieran's surly father during their pursuit of Elmo Smart last month. He ran a shop in the Five-Ten called Ostra Import-Export Emporium. There weren't supposed to be shops there, either, but that hadn't stopped anyone. "Have you seen him?"

"Turlach dropped out of sight about the same time as Kier-an." Anthony's scowl darkened. "We didn't hear his name as one of the murdered, but we'd begun to wonder. Then he showed up at Ostra last week, all covered in half-healed cuts and greenish-purple bruises, like he'd taken one helluva beating coupla weeks before. Said he took a bad fall and didn't want to talk about it."

"And hell no, he wasn't pressing charges." Sevencrows

grunted a mirthless laugh. "I'll admit I asked him, just to poke the beast."

"What do you think really happened?" Rex asked.

"Well, the main questions are who beat him up, and why." Sevencrows gave Rex a puzzled look. "People say he's worked for Whisper since—" he glanced at his partner.

Anthony shook her head. "Since before you took your Mid-Levels."

Rex had no idea how long that might have been, but "a long time" seemed a safe interpretation. According to Anthony last month, the Whisper Syndicate ran things in the Five-Ten. At least in Toro Enclave, the part where Ostra was located. But if Turlach worked for Whisper, wouldn't he be untouchable?

"Whisper's not gentle with screw-ups, but what did he do?" Anthony asked. "What did he *fail* to do? Was it someone else who delivered the beatdown, not Whisper's people? Until now, we had no idea. But if you guys are looking for Kieran, that puts a different light on it. What did *Kieran* do?"

How should Rex answer? If their interpretation of the evidence was right, Kieran had played a role—possibly a *coordinating* role—in the destruction of one of the Syndicate's most valuable assets.

"Time for the briefing!" Shiv called from the far side of the practice area. He stood near the briefing screens and several long tables with chairs, where he'd been talking with the STAT Team's Captain Hariri.

"Red and Blue Teams, get over here!" Hariri bellowed. Eddie pivoted instantly. He jogged across the room without a parting remark. Rex, Anthony, and Sevencrows followed.

CHAPTER 38

ARTISTS, AND THE XK9 EDGE

C harlie used Chamber Three's security camera to tell him the exact moment to unlock the door. Adeyeme made a fast hop inside, then Charlie slammed it in Missy's face. He swallowed a sudden upsurge of savage glee. *Damn, that felt good.* The temptation to slam it several more times, just for the joy of doing it, dizzied him for an instant. He sucked in a strong breath and restrained himself.

"Whew!" Adeyeme stood blinking by the doorway for several seconds, then made her way through the semidarkness to a chair near his bench at the control console. "I suppose you know that Rex and the Pack are at the STAT Team's practice ground with Shiv."

"He's been keeping me updated."

"How're you doing?"

Charlie blew out a breath. "I'm jealous of Shimon, but mostly glad I have something to take my mind off of it, besides SA Finlay's spreadsheets. Thank you."

"You're welcome." She gave him a long, penetrating look. In the low light, he could barely see the pucker between her brows. "Morgan, forgive me, but I have to ask. Your whole career has been physically active. Patrol, the ERT, working with Rex. What made you think you'd like GR work?"

This choice had bewildered a lot of people. "You're right. It seems at odds with most of the other things I've done. Same when I was in school. I was always kind of a jock, and I had my heart set on a police career since I was six. But I was also good at art. I think my upper-school art teacher took it pretty hard when I turned down an honors admission to art school and went into the Police Academy. Even though I warned her I would."

In the dim light he barely caught Adeyeme's quizzical look. "Art school? Which one?"

"Green Mountain, in Monteverde. Why?"

She chuckled. "I thought it might be. It's a very good school. Mike's mother taught there. He has several artists in his Family."

Charlie nodded, not sure how to respond. Then it clicked. *Santiago. Monteverde. Taught at—Holy crap.* He stared at her. "Providence Atelier?"

"Mmm. You *do* know your Ranan art. They welcomed me into the Family by telling me that Mike might be a jackbooted government thug, but he's *their* jackbooted government thug, and they love him anyway."

"Is he an artist, too?"

"Depends on who you ask." She grinned. "But we're not here to see Mike's art. We're here to see yours. Now that I know your backstory, I'm more curious than ever."

"Well, let's not keep you in suspense." He hit a key.

The GR chamber seemed to melt away to black. Inside the tank, an office took shape. The original had belonged to a robotics research lab's director. It was jammed with robot-parts, circuitry panels, and testing devices. Stacks of case pads, components, readers, and analyzers crowded every flat surface. Several large wall screens took up the vertical spaces. Little information flags sprang up throughout the scene, displaying evidence-catalog numbers.

"Nice. Excellent detail!" Warm approval filled Adeyeme's voice.

This reconstruction had marked the bitter end of Charlie's short, miserable career in the Safety Services GR Unit. Missy'd once again caught him sneaking out for coffee breaks by a sunny window down the hall and pronounced him a chronic "attitude problem." She'd given him this crime scene reconstruction as a punishment for one too many requests to go out and view the actual site of a crime scene he'd been assigned to reconstruct. She never wanted any of her minions out of her control during work hours.

She herself wouldn't have had the patience for the painstaking detail this scene required. That's why she'd assigned it as a punishment.

Honestly? Yeah, he'd rendered it with over-the-top, nit-picky, exacting care partly to aggravate Missy. He'd logged massive overtime hours in the process, for which he was harangued at length, and never paid.

But ultimately it wasn't about bugging Missy, it was about the case. This whole case had been all about what investigators could derive from seemingly-small details in the complex crime scene.

The prosecutor's office requested a GR because otherwise they feared the overwhelming mass of data would stun and confuse the jury. Charlie had made it possible for them to *show* what the data added up to, not rely only on *telling* in exhaustive detail. It had turned his already-good reputation to solid gold in the Borough Attorney's Office, and thereby sealed his fate with Missy.

Inside the tank, an image of the complainant walked into the office. He carried a small collection of parts in one hand, a case pad in the other. He was an older gentleman in a lab coat, with wispy steel-gray hair and a magnifying visor pushed up on his forehead. He walked with a slight limp.

"You rendered that portrait well, and the motion looks true to life." Adeyeme kept her tone cool, but Charlie thought he detected respect in there, too.

Mingled pride and a heartsick swell of memory tightened his throat. He paused the reconstruction. "A little *too* true to life, I'm afraid. We showed this in open court, and the man's daughter broke down at the first glimpse of her father." Regret tasted sour on his tongue. "I was so focused on making a perfect re-creation, I forgot how upsetting it'd be for the Family."

"I don't think it's unusual for a murder victim's Family to find a GR disturbing."

He grimaced. "You walk a fine line, with GRs. Juries have failed to convict, if the portrayal is too far off. The question becomes, 'if that's wrong, what else is?' But GR artists also have been sued for libel over a recognizable depiction of a suspect who turned out to be innocent. Also, extreme realism can make it as traumatic to watch as witnessing the original crime."

"Noted, and I'm bracing myself. Please continue."

In the GR, the old man set the case pad down on one counter. An information flag appeared with the evidence catalog number, then flashed an image from the original crime scene that showed it placed exactly where Charlie's reconstruction depicted the complainant placing it. The old man pulled his visor down over his eyes with his freed-up hand. Behind him, his assistant slipped through the doorway and raised a kitchen knife in his right hand.

The image froze. Another information flag appeared. It gave the evidence catalog number for the murder weapon, showed an image of the actual knife used, itemized the fingerprints, and listed everyone whose DNA was found on the knife. Next came a short animation of the rationale for identifying it as having been held in the right hand, raised to this precise angle, and how it all correlated to the defendant's height and muscle strength.

"I should mention that I extrapolated most of these actions." Charlie glimpsed Adeyeme's interested expression and body language. "The first UPOs on-scene found the complainant with his visor down, which would have obstructed his peripheral vision. And his hearing had been declining for several years, so it's likely he never knew his attacker was approaching him. With scent evidence, we would know exactly where the defendant placed his feet when moving forward, and of course we'd have his scent profile. I had some floor-scuffs to work from, but that's all."

Adeyeme's nod was a shadow-movement in the darkness. "Understood."

Motion resumed in the GR. The assistant slashed downward. The knife penetrated the complainant's back. Another information flag appeared. It noted the ME's identification of this as the site of the probable first strike, with a brief cutaway to show the depth of the stab and identify the anatomical structures affected by it.

"Stop," Adeyeme said. "I've seen enough. This is exactly what I need."

Charlie stopped the playback with a pang of dismay. Missy had never submitted it—no surprise there—but a GR-program classmate from Pueblo PD's GR Unit had told him his blood spatter recreations in this GR were better than that year's All-Station award-winner. "If we stop now, you'll miss the blood spatter."

"Perhaps another time." She gave him a bemused look.

Charlie stifled a sigh and terminated the playback. She probably didn't have the sixty-four minutes and thirty-five seconds it would take to watch all seventeen stabs in slo-mo with annotations. And it did seem kind of a macabre objection, now that he'd voiced it. "So, if I've passed your test, what do you want me to reconstruct?"

"Oh, you passed with flying colors." She smiled. "The GR I need is a reconstruction of the Murder Brothers' actions on the *Izgubil* bridge. When we bring them in, I'll need to show a judge and jury what we've extrapolated from the scent evidence."

Yes! Exactly! His chest expanded with zest for the challenge.

"That will be my pleasure! Ever since I first began to learn how the dogs interpret actions based on scent evidence, I've thought we needed GR visualizations to really make it clear."

She nodded. "Excellent. Let's get you started on the bridge data."

"All I need is an order from you. I can download all of the CSU material directly to this unit." A new thought occurred. "Once I've reviewed all the data, would it be possible for me to visit the crime scene itself?"

She elevated an eyebrow, gave him a questioning look. "It's in micrograv."

"I know." His mouth went dry and his pulse sped up, but he needed to face this issue if he meant to keep up with Rex. He must find a way to function in micrograv. The sooner the better. "My Class-C has been canceled, but I still have a Class-A."

"How'll it affect your arm?"

"Long as I'm up there less than eight hours, I'm good. I probably can see what I need for the GR in less than two."

She nodded. Her little half-smile suggested that she'd guessed his secondary agenda, and approved. "Works for me. I'll make the arrangements."

Rex caught a brief flash of satisfaction from Charlie through their brain link. But then Brock stepped through the doorway before Scout, caught a *ping* of pea gravel to his helmet, and Rex called, "Stop!"

"Oh, damn," Brock said. "Double damn. Sorry." He retreated to the starting mark.

Rex walked over to him. Brock, like his cousin Eddie, was one of Charlie's friends on the STAT Team. "I understand that normally you are the one who enters first."

Brock sighed. "Years of drills, man."

"If you could see around corners as easily as we can hear and smell what's in the next room, there would be no problem. But what if someone is lurking just inside?"

"Whoever has that quarter would clear it."

Scout's partner Nicole frowned. "If the bad guy didn't drop him first, as UPO Sevencrows just demonstrated. Scout could've told you he was there. You wouldn't have to rely solely on reflexes."

Brock gave her a rueful look. "I know—in my head. It's a hard habit to break."

Rex snapped his ears flat. Brock had nailed the problem. "Break for a conference," he texted Shiv.

"Captain Hariri," Shiv said, "could we call a break and have a short conference?" Chief Klein had insisted that STAT be involved in the warrant sweep. It was a precaution Rex appreciated. But so far, their practice runs had not made much progress before one or more of the STAT Team forgot to wait for the dogs.

"Okay, let's take five," Hariri agreed.

Rex joined Shiv and Hariri. This time he used his vocalizer, so Hariri could hear, too. "I want to run Blue Team against Red Team. Have them set up ambushes for each other. Go a round without the Pack, just Anthony, Sevencrows, and their wicked gravel-shooters. Then do another round with the assigned Pack members leading one of the teams, but not the other."

Hariri nodded, then smiled. "I have an idea to add to that."

Rex, the rest of the Pack, and their partners withdrew to the perimeter. Hariri directed his teams in the new exercise. "Let's make this interesting," the captain added. "We'll count points like in the Wheel Challenge—which, I might remind you, is coming up in two short months. Blue ambushes Red first, then Red ambushes Blue. Whichever team loses, buys a round for the others at LEO's—and admits *why*, to everyone there!"

Nicole laughed. "Side bet: I say Red takes Blue."

"You're on." Misha grinned. "I'm backing Blue."

Once the humans had made their wagers and the teams had taken their places, Rex focused closely. The scoring system was pretty simple, but both teams proved they could prepare crafty ambushes. Their opponents demonstrated they could clear a room with admirable efficiency. And squads managed fairly well, despite the ever-present threat of fiendishly-accurate blowgun pellets from Anthony and Sevencrows.

At the end of the two rounds, Blue edged Red by a single point. With laughs and groans, everyone settled up the side bets. It looked to be a raucous night at LEO's—*later. After* the operation. It was still an open question whether they were "go" for tomorrow, or needed another day to prepare.

"All right," Shiv said. "Now let's see how things change when Blue ambushes and Red clears—but Red works with XK9s."

Once the ensuing round of additional wagers had been agreed upon, they went to work. Rex had to give credit to the ambushing teams, as well as to Anthony and Sevencrows. They were sneaky. Not sneaky enough, of course, but they gave it a good try. One Blue Team squad almost managed to fool Victor when they climbed to the top of a wall.

Blue and Red swapped roles after the first round, while Red's XK9s sat out and Blue's went into action. After that, Red and Blue were dead even. Then both sets of XK9s pitched in and battled it out to a draw. By the end of the afternoon, however, even Anthony and Sevencrows had stopped scoring hits, and no one from either Red or Blue Team forgot to let the dogs go first.

All in all, a satisfactory outcome. Rex lolled his tongue and indulged in a leisurely stretch. Little groups of humans gathered equipment or headed for the showers.

Shiv and Hariri stood nearby. They didn't smell quite as gamey as the others, but they'd done their share of running, jumping, and climbing. The STAT captain watched Rex approach. "All right, Rex. I'm a believer. And I don't ever want to serve another high-risk warrant without at least one of your Pack along with us!"

CHAPTER 39

SCENT IDENTIFICATIONS

Rex ached from nose-tip to tail-tip, but Elaine's message stressed it was important. "I shall call the car back later," he told Shady. "Go on home."

She nuzzled his muzzle and licked his face. "I love you, but I cannot guarantee I shall be awake when you get home."

"Rest, so you are strong for tomorrow."

He padded toward S-3-9, head down. Was it possible to limp on all four feet?

It's possible to limp on two, Charlie said through the link. *I imagine the biology extends to however many feet one has.*

Rex lolled his tongue and projected love through the link. *How are you? How did your GR demo go?*

I'm now the designated GR artist for the bridge reconstruction. Rex received a strong sense of pleasure. *I spent most of my half-watch reviewing CSU's scans and the other reports from the bridge.* Rex had a sense there was something more, but Charlie changed the subject. *How did your practices with the STAT Team go?*

He yawned. *We're a coordinated team, now. Hariri and Shiv were initially convinced we'd need another day to practice together, but at this point we have a go-light for tomorrow.*

Will you be home soon?

Depends on what Elaine wants to discuss.
Mind if I look over your shoulder via the link?
If it's classified, I'll have to block you.
Understood. And, of course.

Rex took the elevator, then forced his stiffening legs to move down the corridor.

Elaine greeted him at the hatch. "Oh, you look all-in. I'm sorry to delay your bedtime, but I figured you'd want to see this right away, and it's not very long."

He followed her into the war room, to a screen that had been parked in dormant mode. "This message came through an anonymized private account, flagged Urgent Personal, from Ensolay, a small village on the outskirts of Solara City. Yet it was sent to the investigation, using official routing."

Rex cocked his head. "Who sent it?"

"A woman who identified herself as Dr. Frederika Cho, of the XK9 Scent Reference Lab. Do you know her?"

Rex's ears went straight up with an astonishment he could feel echoed in Charlie. "Certainly I do. She is my mother's partner."

"Oh? She didn't mention that."

Sadness rose in him. "Outside of the Breeding Operations Department, the Project does not consider kinship relationships between dogs to be relevant." Rex lowered his head. "I am one of the very few in my generation who actually knows what has become of my mother. Dr. Cho is among the older generation of humans at the Project."

"Shady mentioned there was a division." Elaine gave a thoughtful nod. "Was Cho on good terms with Ordovich?"

Rex snapped his ears flat. "She and Dr. Ordovich disagreed about many things, but she and Dr. Imre, the head of Breeding Operations, have an even more contentious relationship. I have heard them shout at each other several times." Rex half-raised his ears, struck for the first time by something he'd simply taken as a *given* for most of his life. "Yet Dr. Cho still commanded the

Scent Reference Lab, last I knew. I do not know what influence she has, to remain in that position."

Elaine shook her head. "Can't help you there, but she said in her message that the Scent Reference Lab has a clear duty, which overrides other administrative directives, to deliver investigation-related information."

"Other" administrative directives? Charlie asked. *Such as what, exactly?*

"What 'other administrative directives'?" Rex asked, relieved that Charlie seemed wide enough awake to think of the question.

She frowned. "Suggestive, isn't it? She sent IDs for the Murder Brothers, based on the transferred scent samples Liz and Razor sent from their murder vic. Scent, trace, and touch-DNA Pam and Shady recovered from the Hub corridor you flagged corroborated it." She smiled at him. "Just as you said, the two men are brothers. The elder, Rufus Dolan, is the one we've been calling Thud, while Blunder is his younger brother Neil Dolan. They are natives of Uladh Nua, and members of a violent nationalist group that calls itself the Saoirse Front."

Rex's hackles prickled. "What were they doing on a Whisper ship?"

"Mike says he's identified many strong links between Whisper and the Saoirse Front, so it's not surprising." Elaine gave him a wry look. "I think we should assume they're still alive, based on what we learned on the bridge, and the report Mike just got from Commander Montreaux. There *was* a pod with its emergency beacon disabled. It appeared to be one of the type it's possible to guide, but without its beacon, among the multitude that launched, it's nearly impossible to trace."

"Should we put out an APB on them?"

She pursed her lips. "I've considered it. But they were trying to hide from Whisper, for urgent survival reasons. Whisper has surveillance and analysis capabilities of its own, but Mike's convinced they also have moles in many Ranan civilian entities and law enforcement agencies. So far, it's possible Whisper thinks the brothers are dead, but an APB would make it clear we think they aren't. I *want* those men, and I want them alive. They're not only murderers within our jurisdiction, but they also know valuable things about Whisper's operations."

"And Whisper wants them dead for parallel reasons." Rex's ears had by now gone from drooping to straight up. The call of the hunt sang within him. He sensed Charlie's amused affection like a low laugh at the back of his mind. *What?*

You're a detective who'd make your hunting dog ancestors proud. You're exhausted and set for a predawn hunt tomorrow—but you're already eager to go after the Dolans.

Rex lolled his tongue. *Of course, I am. I mean to get them, too.* He cocked his head at Elaine. "Did Commander Montreaux develop any clues about where that beaconless pod might have gone?"

"She's still working on it. From what she and her analysts have pieced together, the Dolans may be headed toward Wheel Three." Elaine frowned. "There's an Ullach community in Howardsboro on Wheel Three that harbors Saoirse Front sympathizers, as well as a few active members. Mike's team has been wrapping up a Whisper-related case after a couple of months there. Part of his team is still in Howardsboro. He's been shuttling between here and there for the past month. If the brothers are alive, it's likely that's "home" to them. They'd be stupid to go back there, but people do stupid things all the time."

"Especially if they are frightened. And these men were terrified." A soft growl slipped out. "We should go to Howardsboro."

"One hunt at a time, big guy." Her small hand stroked his neck. Her chuckle sounded remarkably like Charlie's. Best of all, his growl hadn't sparked even a small upsurge of fear scent.

He dared to lean his head against her, then wriggled with pleasure at her tentative ear-scratch and the smell of her burst of pleasure when he did.

She laughed. "We'd better watch ourselves—we'll make both

Charlie *and* Mike jealous. Anyway, there's Dr. Cho's recording still to watch." She turned toward the dormant screen, but one hand remained on his withers.

The screen glowed to life. Rex opened the link wider, so Charlie could receive visual impressions. Dr. Cho's normally friendly, smiling face seemed to peer directly at them, her expression pinched. She sat in a darkened room, in a straight chair drawn up to a table. His mother Nell stood close by her shoulder. Larger than most female XK9s, Nell's black sable fur had a charcoal-gray undercoat beneath the black guard-hairs, unlike Shady's lighter tan undercoat. But the chilling detail for Rex was his mother's face. It had paled to white across her muzzle, nose, and eyebrows.

Woah. Charlie's concern came clearly through their link.

Yeah. "Please pause the playback."

The image froze, though it had barely begun to move. "What?" Elaine asked.

"Was all of it recorded in this location?"

"Yes. Is something wrong?"

Rex laid back his ears. "Everything is wrong. Nell and Dr. Cho look as if they have aged years in the three months since Charlie and I last saw them. The place where they are looks like a residential dining room at dusk, with no lights on. Recorded at Dr. Cho's home, perhaps? At night? I am concerned for their safety."

"I also am concerned." Elaine gave a short nod. "Shall we continue?"

Rex yawned a wide stress-yawn. "Yes, please."

The playback resumed. "We thank you for entrusting us with your samples, despite the current difficulties between your agency and the XK9 Project," Dr. Cho said. "We are delighted to report that we've found two matching profiles. Their complete dossiers are attached. I do not know how they may be connected to your investigation, but please be careful if you must approach them. As you'll see in their files, they are not our planet's most peaceful denizens."

Beside her, Nell alerted to something beyond the recording's frame. Dr. Cho glanced that way with a fearful start, then returned her focus to the recorder. "The Scent Reference Lab has a clear duty to deliver this information, despite any administrative directives that—well." Her expression hardened. "Investigations *matter*. The transfer of information between agencies is more important than—than other imperatives. That is ... perhaps a dying perspective, around here."

Still focused on something outside the frame, Nell's hackles rose. She growled softly. Rex's own hackles rose in response. What did she see? Who was coming?

Dr. Cho drew in a sharp breath. "I hope I can work with you again." She reached forward. The playback cut off.

Every hair on Rex's body went erect. "Is that all there is?"

"I'm sorry, but yes, that's all." Elaine gave him a worried look. "Mike and I have a friend who is the Sheriff of Bordemer Canton. It encompasses Solara City's northern outskirts, including Ensolay. I'm considering calling him, to ask for a confidential welfare-check on Dr. Cho, but I'm worried that if there's a TIS source embedded in his department, this might tip off Wisniewski."

Rex laid his ears back. "Your friend is the sheriff. He is in charge of his department. If he is half the leader you are, he will have the measure of his deputies and staff."

Elaine let out a soft breath. "Bruce is pretty sharp. I trust him. But it *is* your mother."

Rex nodded. "Then please alert him to the situation and ask him for that welfare-check."

"Thank you." Her scent turned hunt-fierce. "I'll do that next. Meanwhile, you must go home and try to rest."

REX, Shiv, the other XK9 teams, and STAT Red and Blue disembarked from their Personnel Transport Vehicles into the 03:00 darkness of the Five-Ten's Toro Enclave. They'd pulled to a halt outside a night-shuttered Ostra Import-Export Emporium.

Rex had caught muted whiffs of the neighborhood's unique cachet during their progress to the disembarkation point. But it burst upon him full-force when the doors opened, familiar and pungent. A gritty blanket of dust and machine oil overlay everything. Scents of damp rock, mildew, and old urine, mixed with moldy basketry and unwashed humans added to the, um, bouquet. Every surface seemed imbued with residual scent factors that spoke of defensive fear.

Claws scrabbled on regolith gravel. Human boots made soft thuds and scrunches. The Pack assembled near the motorbike racked on the PTV's front grille, with their partners close behind. Dogs and humans alike wore body armor. His Packmates' bright eyes, wagging tails, and fierce scents told Rex they were ready.

His pulse thumped double-time. Hunt-joy surged through him. He glanced at Shiv, caught the man's fierce smile, then felt a pang of intense jealousy through the link from Charlie. *I'm sorry you can't sleep through this.*

I don't want to. If I can't be there with you, I can at least follow the action in realtime.

Is Hildie awake?

Loving amusement came through the link. *She tried to stay awake, but she just came off another 12-hour, and she's exhausted. I'm sitting up in bed. She has her arm around my hips, and .... Yeah, she's out.*

Elaine had stayed in the command cockpit of the PTV, with Lynn Anthony by her side for guidance on local issues. Elaine, Shiv, STAT Captain Hariri, and Rex all had access to the Command Channel, but Elaine would run this Hunt. "Link-checks and com-checks, everyone."

"Comlink still good?" Rex asked Shiv.

"You bet," Shiv said.

"Back at you."

"Rex and I are good."

A side channel switched into Rex's main HUD-view. Each time Elaine pinged a badge, a tiny yellow human-shape or little tan dog popped up on a detailed, multi-level chart for this section of the Five-Ten. In his current view, they all clustered near the blue box that marked the command PTV's location.

Rex let his tongue slide out in a silent dog-smile. "Circle up, Pack. Time to get in tune." He loved this part.

Elaine had worried at first, until Rex explained why it didn't matter whether the suspects tried to flee or not. In Transmondia, where criminals knew the sound of a Hunting Pack, it was hoped they *would* run, but the smart ones hunkered down. Anyone who ran left a fresh scent trail. Those were the easiest to find. The OPD had the Enclave's elevator and two egress-ingress hatches covered, so no one could leave the Enclave unseen.

His Packmates gathered around him. Rex lifted his nose and uttered a long, piercing howl. One by one, the other XK9s joined in. Each Pack member had a distinctive howl, from Tux's deep bass to Crystal's soaring soprano. Rex himself howled a ringing baritone. On the hunt, their howls would keep them in touch with each other, oriented from Rex's voice. They held a long major chord, then fell silent and stood. The Hunt had begun.

"That was amazing," Shiv said. "Seriously, Rex. Goosebumps."

"Wait till you see us hunt." Rex lowered his nose and began to quarter the area. Almost immediately he struck a familiar scent—but one he was astonished to find. This man was supposedly dead. "I have . . ." Could Whisper somehow listen in? Rex changed his answer halfway through. "Never mind," he said aloud. "Sorry." But to Shiv and Elaine he texted, "I have Kieran O'Boyle."

CHAPTER 40

REX'S HUNT IN THE FIVE-TEN

S hiv's pale eyebrows shot upward. He stared at Rex, then gulped. "Man, I thought you had something for a minute, there. Well, keep looking."

"Yeah, sorry," Rex said aloud. "I shall keep looking."

That's a smart call, not saying Kieran's name. Charlie's approval resonated through the link. *Whisper undoubtedly has surveillance devices planted all around Ostra.*

"Thanks for not saying his name aloud," Elaine texted.

Rex soon lost Kieran's trace beneath more recent traffic, but it was likely he could find another fragment if he kept searching. To Shiv and Elaine only, he texted, "The track is a few days old. Partly overtrodden. This is a pretty busy area. Following this track will be difficult, but I may be able to move from fragment to fragment and get a line of travel. Guidance?"

"Lynn's been hearing rumors he was dead for more than three weeks. You just found proof of life, well within that time-window," Elaine texted back. Rex knew her well enough by now to imagine her hunter's smile, her rising scent factors. "We want him alive, so the sooner we capture him, the more likely Whisper won't. See what you can do with that scent trace." Over the com, she said, "Maybe fan out more."

"Copy that. Rex out." He exchanged another look with Shiv, then returned to the fragmentary scent trace. It wasn't hard to make it look as if he was quartering the area. The trace soon disappeared again, obliterated by traffic in the street outside Ostra. This time, Rex couldn't pick it back up. Charlie would have sensed this immediately through the brain link, but Shiv and Elaine needed to be texted. "Lost it. For real, this time."

Now Rex must start again. "Stay where you are," He instructed Shiv aloud, then moved outward in careful, widening sweeps. This time he ran into overtracks from the Pack and partners exiting the PTV. "Damn. We had to get out of the truck somewhere, but—damn."

"Hard to put crime scene booties on a PTV," Shiv said.

Charlie's amusement rolled through the link, along with a ludicrous mental image.

Rex lolled his tongue, then resumed his search.

Elle's bell-like howl sounded near an alley opening on the street-side of the storage building next to Ostra. "Found Dopey's trace. Maybe nine hours old."

"Good hunting!" Elaine replied. "Now tracking your badge-pings."

Rex cast about in circles beyond the PTV, but with no luck, one ear canted toward Elle's progress. On his HUD, the little tan dog with her name on it left a yellow-dotted trail.

He stopped to evaluate his terrain. If Kieran had realized he might be tracked by XK9s, he might've walked straight down the middle of the street to optimize his chances of obliterating the scent trace.

He didn't think about XK9s. Too busy worrying about Whisper, Charlie said.

Rex laid back his ears. *Agreed. He'd go for visual cover as soon as possible.* That meant he'd left the main drag and gone into the alleys. Rex knew about Five-Ten alleys, after his previous foray here. *There are two alley-openings I want to check.* Oops. He'd told the wrong partner. Shiv still waited by Ostra's porch, watching him but not moving. "I'm checking alley-openings," he texted. Shiv nodded.

The first opening, the one that led to the box-alley behind Ostra, yielded nothing.

"Aroo-o-o!" Shady howled, from approximately a block away. "Found Greasy's trail. Maybe twelve hours old."

"Good work!" Elaine replied. "Tracking your badge, too."

The second alley opening, across the road from Ostra near the place where Rex and Elmo had nearly come to grief under an illegal shed's collapse, yielded better results. Rex looked up, met Shiv's eye. "Found it again," he texted.

Shiv grinned. Followed.

"Aroo-o-o!" Scout howled. "I'm on Stinky's trail."

"Excellent! Tracking you," Elaine replied.

Rex shifted his focus back to his HUD. Shady's track looked like a yellow dashed line. Scout's looked like a line of yellow asterisks.

Other XK9s who hadn't yet locked onto a suspect's trail moved outward from Ostra in a systematic quartering maneuver that everyone in the Pack had practiced since early puppyhood. If Poopy, Sweaty, or Clumsy were in the Five-Ten tonight, XK9s should find their trails.

Elle's howl shifted to a lower, baying sound. She'd found Dopey's hole-up. Other XK9 voices converged on Elle and Misha's location. Pack members who had not yet picked up a suspect's trail circled around, to cover possible escape routes.

Rex stopped to watch them converge in miniature on his HUD-view. Now STAT Blue piled out of their PTV to join them. The HUD-image showed them as blue humans.

Shiv halted beside him. "Nice. That happened faster than I expected."

"If all goes well, we should bring in at least the three whose trails Elle, Shady, and Scout have so far crossed." Rex opened the feed from Misha's optics into his main view.

He saw an outer door on a boxlike storage building. Misha's

hand raised to knock. *Bang-bang-bang.* Rex was only a block away. He didn't need the mic to hear that. "Police! We have a warrant! Open the door!" *Bang-bang-bang.* "Open the door! We have you surrounded!"

The right side shared a wall with another storage building. Packmates closed in on the exposed "Bravo" and "Delta" sides. Their baying confirmed the "surrounded" part.

"Four humans went in, ten to eleven hours ago," Elle said. "Two of those are in the front room. No weapons. They were asleep until a moment ago, but now they are holding still. I hear movement farther back in the building."

Misha bellowed, "Police! Open the door!" He banged on it again.

"The people in the front room are having a whispered argument over what to do," Elle reported. "One wants to open. The other wants to run."

Misha banged again. "We're not going away! Open the door!"

"One of them is now standing just inside the door." Elle amped up the volume on her vocalizer. "Please open the door. We do not wish to harm you."

"Don't break the door!" the person inside cried. "I have to undo all the locks." *Snap. Click. Rattle. Pop.* One by one, they unlatched. The door opened. She peeked out, her eyes wide with terror. "Wh-who are you looking for?"

"Ma'am, I seek a slash user, whose scent profile I have memorized," Elle said. "You are not the person I seek. Neither is the man behind you."

The woman gasped. "A slash-user!" She whirled on her companion. "There, now! You *see?* I *told* you Betty Jean's boyfriend was nothing but—"

"Runner!" Georgia cried. "We have a runner, Delta side!" Then, "Ha! Tux got him. Nice takedown, Tuxie!" Heavy breathing, a scrabble of zip-cuffs. "Suspect is in custody," Georgia reported. "Repeat, suspect Dopey is in custody."

Rex left the details of prisoner transport to others. He returned to Kieran's faint, appearing-then-disappearing scent trail. With Shiv, he moved down an alley behind a block of storage buildings-converted-to-tenements, interspersed with light-industrial storage blocks that still served their original purpose.

The days-old trace disappeared at the edge of another, more traveled path.

Rex resumed his careful quartering. Elle's success heartened him. His prediction to Elaine that the Pack would find at least some of their suspects in the Five-Ten was proving true. He searched the mouth of the nearest alley. No Kieran. He lifted his nose, snorted to clear it, then moved to the alley that was next-nearest to where he'd lost the scent.

Shady's howls shifted into her trademark, full-throated bay. Joy filled him. *Yes!*

"Suspect Greasy is in custody," Shady reported on the com, a few moments later. "He bolted even quicker than Dopey but gave up without a fight." Rex pictured her triumphant prance, tail high and waving.

"Confirming, Suspect Greasy is in cuffs. Need pickup," Pam added.

"Nice work," Rex texted to them. *Now, if I can just ...* He went back to seeking Kieran's fading trail, but then he crossed a fresh new scent. "Oh!" He pulled back, snorted to clear his nose, then checked it again. "I have a trail for Sweaty that is perhaps five hours old."

"We can come back for your first target. Follow the new trail," Elaine texted.

"Aroo-o-o!" Rex howled, then used his vocalizer on the com for all to hear. "I have Sweaty's track!" He leaped forward, pulse pounding. With luck, the man had passed through here on his way home. Maybe right now he lay fast asleep, waiting to be cuffed. His path led through a maze of the sort of empty, shad-owed alleys that Rex had come believe were typical of the Five-

Ten. He encountered no blowgun hazards, but it was ten till four. Even blowgun sharpshooters had to sleep sometime.

They passed a row of shops, then came to another makeshift tenement, this one so tall it almost touched the ceiling, twenty meters above them.

"Aha!" Rex followed Sweaty's scent up a flight of steps to the back of the building. Older Sweaty-scent marked this as a place he frequented. "Probably lives here."

He called for reinforcements, then pressed his nose to the crack under the door. He found scents of dust, grime, mildew, rust, and wet rot in the wall-plaster somewhere nearby. The fairly recent scent-trails of six other people in addition to Sweaty suggested a main hallway or foyer on the other side of the door. Nothing stirred.

"What do you think?" Shiv asked.

"Empty public space beyond the door. We need to go through and farther in."

Shiv tested the door: locked. He scowled. "Mmm. Pretty flimsy door." He bent, then bumped it near the lock with a sudden, hard shoulder-thrust. The door popped open, with only a little noise. "As I thought—just a bit warped. It was open after all."

Trail-calls from his Packmates Cinnamon and Victor confirmed their movement on Rex's Command diagram. It showed them drawing closer, with Berwyn, Eduardo, and a STAT element of three trailing them.

Rex led Shiv through what could be called either a narrow, empty foyer or a wide, empty hallway. Sweaty's trail went upstairs. Rex made the first floor in two bounds, then followed the scent down a dark, narrow hallway with creaky floorboards. No way to pass through silently, damn it.

The trail stopped at the last door. Rex sniffed around it. Sweaty had definitely gone in. He also had not come out this way. Rex put his ear against the door. Tried to listen past the floor-creaks and subvocalized curses that marked Shiv's approach. The apartment lay utterly quiet. No movement. No breathing, even.

His ears and HUD display confirmed that Victor and Cinnamon had stopped outside the tenement. Eduardo and Berwyn jogged the final few meters to join them. Rex texted them all: "Check the back and sides. First floor, far end. Take the alley on the left."

Shiv fetched up next to Rex, breathing hard. He smelled irritated. "Is he in there?"

"I do not think so."

"Of course not."

"Aroo-o-o!" Tux's deep howl came from several blocks away. "I have Clumsy's trail!"

"Tracking you!" Elaine made no effort to keep the delight out of her voice.

Rex wagged his tail. *Vindicated! Or at least sort of. I still need to catch Sweaty.*

You'll get him. Charlie's warm tone boosted his spirits.

"Oh, yes!" Victor texted. "Strong scent out back, very recent. I can smell him in general, but I don't see him. I haven't crossed a trail yet."

"Up!" Cinnamon texted. "Up the fire escape!"

"Got him on night-vision," Berwyn said. "Hanging off the roof's edge. Looks as if he climbed up from a window on the Baker side. It's out of range for my Estee—anyway, the drop would kill him. I'm going up the fire escape."

"On our way to the roof," Shiv said. "Meet you there!"

No elevator, of course. The stairs grew steeper and more rickety the higher they went, but Rex and Shiv climbed as fast as they could. The Five-Ten's slightly heavier gravity made Rex's body armor feel heavier than it normally would, but if Cinnamon, also in body armor, was climbing the fire escape with Berwyn, she'd be having a much worse time of it.

Rex and Shiv burst onto the roof, gasping. Somewhere nearby, metal clanged on metal. Sweaty's scent still hung in the air, mingled with the pervasive smell of fungi. They rode a burst of stronger-than-expected breeze. First actual breeze Rex remembered since they'd come to the Five-Ten this trip. *Ventilator fan nearby?*

Uh-oh, Charlie said. *That's not good.*

Why is that bad? Tall stacks of planter boxes with spaces between the boxes, like multiple bunk-beds filled with odd, lumpy-looking bags, rose on either side of the door they'd just come through. Three similar stacks stood a little farther on. Yeah, this perpetually-murky place probably was perfect for growing mushrooms.

I should withhold my speculations about inter-levels and let you search, Charlie answered.

Inter-levels? Rex stalked forward, hackles up, senses alert. Folding stepladders stood by several of the planter stacks. One was canted funny. Pushed by Sweaty's foot?

He darted over to it. Sweaty's scent hung thick and recent all around it. He looked up. The top stack was too high for him to jump up there. He grasped one leg of the stepladder in his teeth and tugged at it.

Shiv arrived a few steps behind him, helped him right and steady the ladder. Rex bounded up. Sweaty's scent hung strong and heavy. Their subject had shoved and crushed his way across a loamy carpet of mushrooms in this uppermost planter. His muddy swath of destruction went halfway across, then ended under a hole in the ceiling, which was within easy reach from there. This was the source of the breeze Rex had felt earlier.

Oh. Inter-levels. "Damn." Rex stared upward. "He has gone into the inter-level. What surfaces are available for walking?" Rex craned his neck, but the inner recesses lay in inky shadow.

From somewhere off to his right, he heard Berwyn's voice, calling encouragement to Cinnamon.

Shiv activated a hand-beam. It didn't help much but left an after-image that hampered Rex's night vision. "There are catwalks." The LSA glanced toward Berwyn's voice, then refocused on Rex. "That's what I've heard, anyway. Never been in one."

Hariri spoke on the com. "Don't risk it. Too easy to get ambushed, or step wrong and fall through."

Rex had been so hunt-focused he'd actually forgotten that Hariri and Elaine could hear everything they said.

"Agreed!" Elaine practically shouted into the com, her urgency clear. "Rex! Shiv! Don't do it! Voice of experience, here. It's too damned risky. Don't worry—now that we know he's here, we'll stay vigilant. We'll get him."

Rex growled. "I can almost taste him." The scent rafts falling from the hole in the ceiling were still warm. Sweaty was up there. Probably watching them and laughing.

"Stand down!" Elaine's voice went steely. "That's an order."

Rex sighed. "Yes, ma'am."

Shiv stepped back so Rex could come down. Then he sprinted to the fire escape, to help Berwyn and Cinnamon onto the roof.

CHAPTER 41

SHADY'S HUNT

Shady's elation over Greasy's capture didn't last long. The tall, round-shouldered fellow seemed confused at first, but he allowed Pam to cuff him and came along peaceably.

The human officers hustled him into the prisoner-transport vehicle to join scrawny, naked Dopey, whom they'd wrapped in a blanket pending the issuing of coveralls "upstairs" in Detention.

Greasy wore no more clothing than Dopey. No Ranan ever wore clothing to bed, as far as Shady could tell. Greasy dwarfed his fellow prisoner. He also appeared to know him. "Feek-man! Dey get you, too?"

"Ho, Till." Dopey sounded as mournful as he looked. "Keep it down, willya? Gotta hell of a head on me, s'morning."

"Sorry! Sorry," Greasy lowered it to a whisper. "Get worse, too. Cops ain't got no drops."

Dopey drooped a bit more. "Mebbe this time kill me, get it over with."

"Man, don' talk like 'at." Greasy also received a blanket from Doug, the UPO in charge of prisoner transport. Doug wrapped it around him, then strapped him in so he could ride safely.

Shady cocked her head. *What are 'drops'?*

Street slang for the smallest amount of slash the dealers will sell. Only the most destitute addicts buy it in that small a quantity. Pam directed a sidelong look at their prisoners. *These two sure don't seem like my mental image of mass-murderers.*

Shady agreed. *Greasy smells as if he's more worried about Dopey than he is about being arrested.*

The com abruptly went lively with Scout's news that he and Crystal had captured Stinky, only a few blocks away. Perhaps this new suspect would be more the desperado type. Shady almost hoped so, although she'd feel uneasy to put a truly dangerous man into prisoner holding with "Feek-man" and "Till." Everyone climbed aboard the transport and rode to the next pick-up.

She needn't have worried. Stinky turned out to be almost as tall as Greasy, almost as scrawny as Dopey, and almost as menacing as both combined. He gave his fellow prisoners a startled look when he stepped up into the prisoner compartment.

"Sh-h-h-h-h!" Greasy warned. "Feek-man got a bad head."

"Ho, sorry t' hear." Stinky gingerly settled his bare haunches onto what must surely be a cold metal bench. He smiled gap-toothed when he got his blanket-wrap, then leaned back to make it easier for Doug to secure him. "Ain't seen you guys since the bug-spray job. You hangin' okay?"

"*Was* hangin' decent good, me," Greasy said. "Gettin' arrested's a suck."

"Whadda they think we do?" Stinky asked.

Greasy shook his head. "Bin tryin' t'figure."

"Thought it's drugs," Dopey said. "Don't figure what else, me."

Doug closed the door to their section, but of course this was all on the system's recordings.

The 'bug-spray' job? Pam shared an incredulous look with Shady. *Can they truly be that clueless?*

I guess it confirms our hypothesis about their cover story, Shady said.

Pam grimaced. *Easier to sell the story to the marks, if part of the crew actually buys it?*

Nicole stared at the closed door of the prisoner-transport compartment. "I doubt we've just captured the masterminds of this operation." They climbed aboard for the ride back to Ostra.

Shady, Pam, Scout, Nicole, Crystal and Connie disembarked near the command PTV.

"Take 'em upstairs." Adeyeme's voice on the com sounded pleased. "Nice work."

It was a bad idea to park a prisoner-transport in the Five-Ten for too long, especially not once there were subjects inside. Shady had heard of units being rolled or attacked if they didn't leave quickly. This trio didn't seem likely to run with the types who would do that, but they *had* been part of that crew that rigged the *Izgubil*.

The transport pulled away with a whirr and the soft crunch of tires on gravel.

Shady resisted melancholy, watching it go. It was never wise to leap to conclusions about a subject, but she worried how "Feek-Man," especially, would fare in Detention.

Cold nose, soft heart? Pam chuckled. *They'll be okay.*

None of these guys look to be the sharpest tack in the box, but he's small and scrawny. And he's in withdrawal.

They'll take care of him. It's not as if our Detention officers are monsters. Pam frowned. *We have addiction specialists on staff. All rehab and detention centers do. I suspect he's going to be our guest for a while, so they'll probably help him get clean.*

Shady cocked her head at Pam, dubious. She'd heard that the Ranan corrections system was different from Transmondian prisons, but all the same …

What? You thought they'd just let him puke his guts out, or maybe go into a seizure? Pam grimaced. *Our Department of Corrections and Rehabilitation takes its mission seriously. Ranans don't throw people away.*

Shady flicked her ears. *And yet, there's the Five-Ten.*

I don't know why anybody would live here, but they didn't ask me. Pam shook her head. *Time to re-focus.*

Tux was on Clumsy's trail, but the Pack still hadn't turned up trails for one of their subjects. Rex had encountered him here a month ago, but where was Poopy now? He and Sweaty both had been part of a menacing crowd. They probably weren't nearly as ignorant as "Feek-man" and his friends seemed to be. Had Elmo's capture tipped them off that they, too, might become targets of the police?

Rex had said he'd encountered the men in the alley behind Ostra when he and Shiv came after Elmo. Did they come to Ostra regularly? She eyed the terrain around her, then put her nose to the ground, moving to portside through the branching alleys. She put several turns behind her.

Foop.

Something struck her neck, then fell with a *clack* to the gravel.

Shady halted, flash-chilled by surprise at the unforeseen attack. She ... did not seem to be hurt, however. She and Pam scrambled for cover.

Woah! I did not see that coming! Are you okay? Pam's shock and fear resonated through the link.

Now fury boiled through Shady. She spotted a homemade dart on the ground. She moved forward, got a good whiff of the blower's scent profile, and looked up, all in one, smooth head-swing. *They're small. And sneaky.* She locked her gaze on the perp and unsheathed her teeth. Then uttered a low, loud, angry growl.

The dart-blower, a boy of perhaps eight, froze on a shadowed ledge. His scent flashed from triumph to terror. Two other kids of about the same age crouched behind him, equally terrified.

Shady laid back her ears and fluffed up all hackles not crushed by her armor. Tail stiff and head low, she uttered another menacing growl. *Stay there. I'll deal with this,* she instructed Pam. "Come down here. All three of you."

No one moved. Likely paralyzed with fear.

Shady? Pam's uncertainty echoed through the link. *What are you doing?*

Making an impression, I hope. Please request Lynn Anthony to come here. Shady growled again and focused on children who cowered on the ledge. "Do not make me come get you."

Slowly, hesitating, the girl climbed down from the ledge and walked forward. "I ain't d-do it." Her whole body shook. "J-jus' watchin', m-me."

"Keep coming. I do not bite—*as long as* you follow my instructions. Are your friends too afraid to come forward? Do they need to be fetched?"

The dart-blower slowly climbed down.

"Good," Shady said. "I hate dragging people out of hiding. So much needless screaming and bleeding. Must I retrieve your cowardly friend with my teeth?"

The other boy, slightly taller and maybe a year older than the dart-blower, hastily scrambled down. The three of them shuffled sheepishly to a point about halfway between their erstwhile shelter and Shady. The hum of a police motorbike drew gradually closer.

Shady closed the gap, circled them, then looked the dart-blower in the eye from a few centimeters' distance. At this range, she was clearly taller. "What were you thinking?"

The dart-blower lowered his trembling gaze. Mumbled, "T-t-toop d-dared me." He still held his blow-pipe, a homemade bamboo object. Pam stepped forward, plucked it from his limp, sweaty fingers with one gloved hand, then dropped it into an evidence bag.

He stiffened. Stared at her with renewed horror in his scent.

"What's your name?" Pam sealed the bag, frowning.

"K-kee." From his scent and belated gasp, he hadn't thought to lie till too late.

Pam's mouth tightened. "From now on, Kee, tell Toop to pull his own stupid stunts."

The motorbike halted half-a-meter behind Shady.

Shady shifted her attention to the taller boy, who stood almost eye-to-eye with her. "I take it you are Toop."

He nodded, wide-eyed, then cast a worried look past her, toward the sound of stern, advancing footsteps.

"Conspiracy to assault an officer is a bad thing to have on your record." Shady turned to the girl. "That goes for you, too."

She threw up her hands. "Wait! I ain't—"

"Did you tell your younger friend to ignore Toop?"

"I—" She shot a glance beyond Shady, toward Lynn Anthony's unamused scent-presence, and her own apprehension grew. "No." Her voice shifted to half-whisper, half-squeak.

"Silence is a way of agreeing with something." Shady held the gaze of each, then cocked her head at Anthony. "Do you know these children?"

"Mm. Meet Sair, Kee, and Toop. Thought they were smarter than this." Anthony scowled at them. "I see you secured some evidence." She accepted the bagged blowpipe from Pam.

"You're the community relations advisor. How do you advise we proceed?" Pam asked.

Anthony eyed the children. "Do I need to cuff you?"

They shook their heads, eyes huge.

"All right, then." Anthony gave one sharp nod. "I'll take 'em back to base. Call in their folks from there. This operation's no place for kids *or* civilians."

Pam stared after Anthony and the kids, her scent factors and emotions through the link unsettled. Shady caught a hint of a memory before her partner closed it off. Pam drew in a breath, turned to Shady. *I'll keep better watch. I'm sorry.*

I know. It was a good wake-up for both of us. Shady went back to work. She quartered the space in widening circles.

This is pretty well-trodden ground. What do you expect to find?

Shady answered both with her vocalizer and through the com. "I think if I find any trace from our remaining fugitives, even an older fragment, it might lead me to someplace where a fresher track could be found." She also opened her perceptions more fully to Pam via the link.

"Oh, good thought," Crystal answered on the com. "I can help."

"Agreed," Connie chimed in. "We'll join you."

"Good hunting. Keep me advised," Adeyeme said on the com.

Shady resumed her search. Crystal soon caught up to her. Elle, Razor, and Scout joined them after that.

"Rex and his group have lost Sweaty into the inter-level," Adeyeme announced on the com. "They're resuming Rex's earlier search. Walter and Petunia are joining them. No luck to leeward."

Shady moved systematically down the block. Her neck still prickled with the remembered sensation of Kee's homemade dart striking her. *I did not sense them.*

I should've kept my focus on the upper levels. Regret echoed through the link. *I got distracted. That won't happen again.*

Shady wished she could shake, but the armor made it difficult. She firmly refocused. *Greasy, Dopey, and Stinky are in custody, along with Elmo, of course. Kieran's in the wind or dead. Sweaty's out of reach in the inter-level, at least for now. Tux is after Clumsy. That leaves only Poopy to find.*

I think we're all doing that same countdown. Any sign of him?

Not yet, but it helps to keep his profile top-of-mind. She moved along a narrow passage, then found a wider place, where five women often sat in a circle. With baskets? *Hmm.*

Baskets of what? The echoes of Pam's mystification matched Shady's.

Not sure. Each seemed to have her own spot, because the newer scent layers overmarked earlier trace laid down by the same individuals, sitting in the same positions day after day. The companionable harmony in their scent factors made an unusual contrast with the other smells in this neighborhood.

Why are they in a circle?

Shady puzzled over it, sniffed around, then shook her head. *It'll have to wait. Not relevant to the Hunt.* She took a couple more steps. *Oh, but here's something that is.* "Found Poopy's trace, about two days old," she reported on the com.

"Good! Stay on it," Adeyeme said.

Several blocks away, Tux's triumphant baying said he'd caught up with Clumsy.

"All XK9s who can help, Tux needs assistance," Adeyeme urged.

Crystal, Elle, Razor, and Scout wheeled toward Tux's voice. They lifted their voices to let him know they were coming. Shady heard Petunia's voice from a different block, also closing on Tux's position.

Shady hoped her Packmates could cover the need without her. Here was the women's departing trail from yesterday evening. Next layer down was their arrival-track, from several hours before. Below that, little fragments of Poopy's scent teased her. She traced the broken trail bit by bit. At the next alley, the women's paths joined in the lower level and parted in the upper.

Her Packmates' voices shifted from the *tracking* song to the *surrounded* cry, several blocks away.

"Squads, stay with your assigned XK9s!" Captain Hariri cried on the com.

A flurry of yelled warnings, commands, and other exclamations flooded Shady's com. Next came the *bang* of a long-barreled EStee.

Shady and Pam paused. They stared toward the sounds.

"Suspect Clumsy is in cuffs!" Georgia's voice rang with triumph.

Clumsy didn't go down peacefully, from the sound of it. Pam's frown pinched her brows. *I hope everyone's okay.*

"Ambulance called for prisoner-transport," Adeyeme said. "Everyone else all right?"

A chorus of reassurances came in. Shady released a sigh. *All good. They're unhurt.* She and Pam paused a moment in salute to their friends' efforts, then Shady bent to her task once more. A while later, she found a spot where Poopy's track crossed under that of one of the women. His two-day-old trail led her piece-by-piece down a narrow street, where it had been cut and overlain by more recent scents—unfortunately none of them his. Following it was more like jumping from stone to stone across a flowing stream than following a clear path.

She lost and reacquired it several times. The street ended in a ninety-degree turn to her right, plus two tight passageways between buildings. One led slightly to starboard. Another led hard to port. Poopy'd taken the starboard-trending passage, so Shady did too. She whiffed him on the walls of the tall storage structures that flanked it, as well as on the footpath beaten into the regolith gravel.

Her Packmates rejoined her, having remanded Clumsy into custody. Crystal first, then Elle, Scout, Razor, and Petunia. A few minutes later, here came Tux. Their human partners stayed back but shadowed them.

The passageway opened onto a small plaza. Shady lost Poopy's trail again in a jumble of smells. Odors of people, spices, foodstuffs, basketry, newly-dyed fabrics and more brought to mind a small marketplace. "He came into this plaza, but I have lost him again."

"Let us spread out," Crystal said. "The market-stalls' setup and takedown have made this harder."

"Wait!" Pam warned. "Remember there may be more danger in the upper levels than just a few kids. Give us humans a moment to see how much access we can gain to them."

Boots scrunched on gravel. Footsteps made muffled thumps on steps and furtive rattles on fire escapes. The XK9s held their positions at the mouth of the passageway.

"We're in place," Hariri reported after several minutes.

"XK9s, deploy," Adeyeme said.

Shady, Crystal, Tux, Elle, Razor, Petunia, and Scout spread

out to search the edges of the area, where scent might have been deposited in places sheltered from the market's traffic.

"Here is Clumsy's scent." Elle had worked her way along the port side of the plaza. She stood at the mouth of another narrow passageway between buildings.

Tux joined her, dipped his head. "This trace is approximately the same age as Poopy's." Tux moved a few paces up the narrow passageway, then retreated, placing his feet with care. "He came into this plaza two days ago, through here. He did not leave by the same route." He gazed across churned-up dirt and gravel.

No scent trail could survive that much activity. They continued their search of the perimeter, moving carefully, sniffing each centimeter in detail.

"Poopy! Found Poopy again," Scout called from a passgeway on the starboard side.

"Here is Clumsy again." Razor had gone to the plaza's far end, just down from where a road entered it. He lifted his head to look down an alley between buildings, sniffed around some more, then stopped, tail up. "Oh! Here are both Poopy and Clumsy! They went down this passage together, two days ago."

This gave them a new thing to ask Clumsy about, assuming he would talk to them. Finding the scents of both men together in the same layer suggested they knew each other better than men who'd met for the first time on the *Izgubil* job. What else had they been up to?

"Great find!" Adeyeme said. "Go carefully."

"Hold till my squads shift position," Captain Hariri said.

Razor waited, tail wagging, tongue lolling.

Shady and the other XK9s headed straight across the plaza toward him.

Razor swung his head around to look back at them.

Swift blur: something tiny.

"Yipe!" Razor ran a couple of paces back into the plaza. His legs buckled, then he collapsed.

CHAPTER 42

CHALLENGES

"Officer down! XK9 Officer down!" panic edged Liz's voice through Rex's com.

Pulse-pounding, blind, raging fury seized him. *My Pack! They attacked my Pack!* He halted, hackles at full bristle, then checked the map diagram. His heart thudded hot and hard. He located Shady's little tan dog icon first. Like the others, she'd retreated to the edge of the plaza. Most of his Packmates crouched in entrances to passageways, or behind architectural features such as steps and porches. Tiny yellow human shapes also crouched in concealment.

Except for Liz. She'd stayed with Razor.

Rex shook with fury. His growl reverberated through him. He leaped away from Shiv, Cinnamon and the others.

Careful, Rex. Alarm rang in Charlie's mental voice.

I am in no mood for 'careful!' He lengthened his stride with a snarl.

"Paramedics are en route to your location," Elaine's voice reported. "What happened?"

"I pulled a damn trank dart out of his neck!" Liz's angry voice half-sobbed, half-screamed. "Don't know what's in it, but he's trembling and drooling and he can't get up!"

Rex bared his teeth, running. *Must bite — tear — slash — !*

Woah, Rex! Calm down! Charlie cried through the link. *Don't go homicidal on us! Think!*

"Blowpipe?" Anthony's voice rapped out the word, hard and cold.

"The dart has kind of a puffball on the end of it." Liz's voice shook.

"Blowpipe." Disgust filled Anthony's tone. "Can't hear the good ones, especially not if you're any distance away. Five-Tenners grow up shooting rats with 'em, so folks here are wicked-accurate."

"Shelter in place, everyone," Adeyeme ordered. "Assume poison. Liz, can you estimate direction?"

"Shooter is farther down the passageway Razor had just come to. Spinward from us."

By now Rex had the location in sight.

"Rex! Stand down!" Elaine cried. "You and Tux get to the PTV!"

Stand down? No! Rex snapped his ears flat. He ducked right with a snarl, down an alley just short of the little plaza where Shady and the others hand been. If he could approach from the rear ....

"I am still pinned down, ma'am," Tux reported. "I am not far from where Razor fell. If I move, I may draw fire."

"Stay put, then," Elaine said. "Rex?"

"On my way." Rex lifted his nose. He caught the live scents of several humans he knew, plus one he didn't.

The stranger exuded cold satisfaction.

Not for long, you bastard.

"On your way to *where*, Rex? That's not the route to the PTV." Elaine sounded angry.

"One moment, please. Something I smelled." Rex leaped up a half-flight of steps to a small porch, then crept along the length of it. The stranger's scent grew stronger.

Rex! You're out of line! Charlie cried through the link.

He closed off as much of the link as he could, then focused forward. One building, only about a meter away, was a hodge-podge of walkways, spans of flat roof, and pocket balconies at various levels. He cleared a staircase in one bound. Ignored a muffled sense of Charlie frantically trying to break through to him and stalked across one of its porches.

There! Movement in the dim light: a man knelt on the end of the walkway across from him, turned three-quarters away toward the plaza. He held what looked like a long rod in one hand; a dark-colored bag lay open on the deck by his knee.

Rage thundered in Rex's ears. "Building 581 on the diagram," Rex texted, too close to risk vocalizing. "Leeward corner, on the second-level walkway. I can take him."

"*No!*" Elaine's voice had a hard, cold tone Rex had never heard before. "You will *stand down right now*, or you are *off this team.*"

Rex halted. Rage still drove him, but Elaine's voice sent a chill to his heart. His breath came sharp and painful, sharp-edged with guilt. *What am I doing?* He'd exposed his throat and sworn to do whatever Elaine said, just five short, eventful weeks ago. She'd given him her support and belief. Would he now betray it all? *No!* He was a professional. Under orders. He licked his lips. Ran a breathing pattern. Gave in with one last snarl, then bowed his head. "Yes, ma'am."

Thank you. Mingled relief and anger burst through the link from Charlie. *Damn it!*

I'm sorry. Guilt-stricken, Rex retreated backward along the porch. His heart pounded so hard he shook. He ran straight to the PTV.

"Target acquired," someone on the STAT Team reported. "Took night-vision, but I have him."

"Bring him in. Alive, please." Elaine's voice still sounded tight, angry, and oh, so cold.

Rex cringed inwardly. He no longer feared he would receive beatings from his Ranan friends and colleagues. But losing

Charlie and Elaine's respect would be infinitely worse. He flinched at the hard *bang* of a long-barreled EStee.

Shiv waited by the PTV. He opened the door without a word.

Rex scrambled inside, tail tucked. He ran all the way to the back, then curled into a tight, miserable ball under the ledge of the fold-out rear seat. He hid his face behind the brush of his tail.

MORE ANGRY THAN frightened for her own safety, Shady nonetheless squeezed her body into the scant shelter behind a stoop near the plaza's edge. A shot echoed across the plaza from one of the STAT Team's long-barreled EStees.

"Subject is down," Hariri said on the com.

Shady leaped away from her cramped shelter, stretched, then lifted her nose. A couple meters from her, Razor's terror filled his scent, edged with the taint of the poison.

Liz knelt by him. She smelled near-distraught. Her shaking hands slid across his armored side again and again. "It'll be all right. It'll be all right. It'll be all right," she whispered, like a mantra. Or a prayer.

"Shady, you're Pack Leader for the rest of this operation," Adeyeme said on the com. New inputs blossomed in her HUD-view, including a side-channel with a 3D map-diagram populated with little tan dog-images and yellow Human-images.

She opened the Command Channel. "What about Rex?"

"Rex and Tux are on security stand-down. Razor may have been the one hit, but I fear they're the preferred targets. I'm sending them to HQ in the first available patrol unit, to help with interviews."

Shady drew in a sharp breath. "Wisniewski?"

"Likely." Adeyeme's voice had a hard edge.

Shady appreciated the SSA's caution. Of course, Rex would utterly hate this. "Thank you for securing them, ma'am."

"My honor and duty," Adeyeme replied. "Command Staff calls me Elaine."

Emergency lights flashed through the road entrance near Razor's end of the plaza. An ambulance pulled up next to his fallen, twitching form. Paramedics leaped out, bent over him. Liz stumbled up and back.

"There's only the one shooter?" Elaine's voice sounded tense on the com.

"Yes," Rex said. "Begging your pardon. I only smelled one."

"Hariri?" Elaine asked.

"We've only found one. Subject is secured. He has a kit with a dozen more of these darts, and several vials of something."

"To the ambulance! Right now!" a new voice cried. Paramedic? "Seconds count. Knowing *what poison* is key!"

"On the double," Hariri promised.

"Tux, report to the Command PTV," Elaine said.

Shady approached the ambulance. She glimpsed a flash of movement beyond it. Brock Rivers swung down from the second-level balcony with a bag slung across his back. He volleyed off the neighboring building's wall, grabbed a column to slingshot around it toward the ambulance, then sprinted the last five meters. She lolled her tongue. For all their vaunted sophistication, humans were indeed still primates. "Nice moves, Brock."

He slid to a halt, ripped the bag from his back, then handed it off. He gave her a tense nod. "Hope it helps!"

"Has the elevator been called? Is it down?" Elaine demanded. "Emergency override!"

The paramedics lifted Razor into the ambulance. Liz leaped inside with them. Wheels kicked up gouts of dust. It tore out of sight.

Shady stared after it, heart pounding, tongue long. Then she pulled in her tongue, gave herself a whole-body shake. "We still have a trail to follow."

"That you do." Elaine's voice held a note of satisfaction.

Shady dipped her head. They would get along.

REX CURLED into the smallest ball he could. Bitter shame, worse than any beating, ached through him. *Disappear. Just sink down into the dust and melt.* No decking, floor covering, or dirt had ever granted that wish. Nor did the metal surface beneath him now.

He shuddered, snarled, cringed. *Razor! My Pack!* He cowered under the PTV's back bench, squeezed in an airless clench of dread.

He sensed Charlie's worried attention through the link.

Go away.

Sorry, I'm fresh out of general anesthesia. All the same, Charlie closed the link as much as anyone could.

New remorse seared him. *Charlie didn't deserve that.*

And Elaine! He moaned but tried to do it quietly. *What must Elaine think?* He'd failed her. She must hate him.

At the front end of the passenger transport section, Tux and Georgia boarded. Then they hesitated. Stayed silent. Stayed at the front end. Their scent factors reached him, full of caution and embarrassment. Tux could smell his anguish. Georgia could see his cringe. The thought of their gaze directed toward him made his gut squirm and his fur twitch.

Unworthy. Untrue. Forsworn. How could he ever face the Pack? How could he ever face Elaine? He'd offered her his throat and his belly. The most binding oath a dog could give. He'd submitted to her. Promised to obey her. *I'm faithless. Contemptible.* A soft whimper leaked out.

I dunno, but that sounds more like Ordovich than Rex, to me. Charlie didn't direct his thoughts *to* Rex, but he allowed Rex to sense them. *I bet ol' "Odious" talked to Rex that way all the time.*

Rex winced. Cringed into a tighter ball. Memories crashed down on him. All the hateful words his creator had ever said. Turned out, he deserved them *all.*

Oh, I'm not so sure about that. Rex had a sense of Charlie shaking his head. *No, Ordovich blew hot air all the time. He was full of that bombastic bullshit. Anyway, he's a criminal. Bad idea to take your cues from a lowlife, scummy sapient-trafficker.* Charlie paused. *Just saying.* He paused again. *Personally, I wouldn't.*

Rex growled. *Are you trying to cheer me up?*

Me? What? There was that Charlie-shaking-his-head impression again. *No! Perish the thought! Wouldn't dream of it! The link's hard to shut down, but a man's entitled to his own thoughts, isn't he? You know? 'Think, and let think'?*

Yeah, right. Rex growled again. *Think softer.*

Aww. Am I ruining your self-pity party?

Hot fury flared in Rex's heart. He half-rose from beneath the bench. Unsheathed his teeth in a snarl. *It's not self-pity, damn it! Can't you tell? I'm being penitent!*

Charlie let the silence echo.

Rex flopped back down onto the floor with a *humph. Penitent! I am!* Yeah, well ... maybe it did seem like a pretty inwardly-focused 'penitence.' *Damn it.* He growled again.

She'll forgive you.

Rex bowed his head. *I don't deserve her forgiveness.*

She'll forgive you anyway.

Why should she?

Ah, Rex. Charlie's sad smile vibrated through the link. *Because she loves you. And because she knows why you disobeyed.*

She was furious with me!

She was terrified for you. So was I. We—neither one of us—want to lose you.

Rex's chest torqued tight. Such a strange thought. *Ranans.* Who could understand them? No human but Charlie had ever ... had ever ... *loved* him, before. A sharp stab of pain knifed his throat. Lodged in his chest.

He loved *Elaine.* But to think that she ... loved him *back? Even after this?*

He focused on Charlie. *We really aren't alone. We XK9s. Are we?*

Charlie's smile warmed him, calmed him. *No. Not alone. Loved.*

Rex pulled himself out from under the bench, his head and ears still down. *I'd better grovel to her on my belly.*

Mmm, possibly. Charlie released a long breath. Rex caught a feeling of relief as if he'd laid a burden down. *I suppose it couldn't hurt. But do it AFTER she's done running the Hunt.*

"Rex?" Georgia called. "Did you check your HUD? New orders! We're headed to HQ!"

SHADY STEPPED past the spot where Razor had fallen, then sniffed around. Here was the place where Clumsy and Poopy had met, then walked down this alley together, two days ago. *Time to see where our subjects were going.*

"We'll flank you. We command all the surrounding upper levels, now," Hariri said.

"Let us see what we can find." Shady followed her nose by stages, halting twice for STAT to reposition. The old trail down yet another alley to round, empty area next to the spinward wall of Toro Enclave. Elle, Crystal, and Scout followed. Clumsy and Poopy had turned right, two days ago—and had met Kieran O'Boyle by a stack of bamboo stalks set to dry at the alley's dead-end. Then all three apparently had disappeared. "Clumsy and Poopy met . . ." *Isn't Kieran O'Boyle rumored to be dead?*

Yes, that's what I'd gathered. Pam shared a worried look with her.

I don't think I should say his name on the open com.

I don't think so, either.

"Shady?" Elaine asked.

"Clumsy and Poopy met a third individual," Shady continued. "Then all three trails just stop, right here. They got into some kind of vehicle."

Elle, Crystal, and Scout quartered right, left, and center.

Scout brushed past Shady. He explored a patch of gravel near the bamboo pile. "Muddle of older scents. Can't separate." Scout carefully stepped around it, then poked his nose farther under the bamboo. "Hullo, there is a small building under here. I have several layers of old scent from . . ." Scout glanced at questioningly at Shady. "A third individual," he finished.

"What kind of building?" Elaine asked.

Shady could see its rough outlines, now that Scout mentioned it. "Storage shed, maybe?"

"Sit on it and keep it secure, my friends." Shady could hear Elaine's smile. "Hidden that way, it could be important. Our current warrants don't cover a search of it—but I want no taint on any evidence it may contain!"

"YES, I'M SURE," Charlie reassured Adeyeme on the com. "I'm up anyway, and wide awake. I'm happy to come in and assist Rex with interviews."

"We certainly could use your help. But keep an eye on the time."

"Will do." *I have the okay to work interviews with you.*

Rex's glum, guilty mood lightened some. *That will be good. I like working with you.*

Charlie kissed Hildie into semi-consciousness, promised to come home before lunch, then slipped out to take the car down the switchbacks in darkness. He leaned back in his seat and accessed the case book. Information on the captured subjects ... Yeesh. Calling it "thin" would be exaggerating.

Shady and Pam had captured Greasy, who said his name was Attila Usher. He would be Charlie and Rex's interviewee. He hadn't yet met their supervisor, Special Agent Melynn Hunter. She'd be waiting in the Detention area.

Charlie refocused on the file. Like most of the sabotage team, Usher was unregistered. Authorities hadn't known he was on Rana until this morning. It was a side-issue for the *Izgubil* investigation, but not for Immigration. Their agents had already scheduled their interview with Usher for later today. His teammate Dopey, also unregistered, was deep in the throes of slash detox. He was now under continual medical supervision at Orangeboro Medical Center. He might be able to give an interview several days from now.

Walter and Petunia had returned to HQ to help SA Reza Gerritsen cover the interview with Stinky, who'd identified himself as Wayne Purdy. Yet another unregistered man. Just as there weren't supposed to be people living in the Five-Ten, there also weren't supposed to be ways to bypass registration. He scowled. Would the *Izgubil* case give these issues a high enough profile for them to be addressed at last? Earlier experiences cast long shadows of doubt in his mind.

Georgia, Tux, and Shiv had already entered Detention M to interview Clumsy, but Charlie entertained doubts about any progress happening there. Clumsy hadn't submitted quietly. Once he'd recovered from the EStee drug, they'd had to physically restrain him, even with Tux snarling in his face. His tattoos declared him to be a Saoirse Front member, but so far that was their only ID on him.

Yeah, good luck to them with that one. Charlie reviewed the recordings from Usher's capture for the rest of the journey. He found a dejected, subdued Rex and SA Hunter, a generously-proportioned young woman with long, flaming red curly hair, outside Detention Suite E.

Rex lifted his head at Charlie's arrival. A flood of relief poured in through the link. The enormous dog leaped forward into Charlie's arms. He buried his face under Charlie's left armpit with a whimper. Wrapped one foreleg around his waist and pulled him close. His whole body trembled.

Charlie held him for a long moment, his cheek pressed against Rex's neck. *It'll be okay.*

Rex's ribs expanded, then he released a huge sigh. *Having you here helps me believe that.*

Believe it. Charlie grinned, straightened, gave the dog's side a loving thump. "Ready to work?"

Rex stepped back, ears and tail up. He even managed a tongue-loll. "Ready."

Hunter offered Charlie a smile and a nod. "Welcome. Your file says you and Rex are an effective interview team, so I'll let you work this one while I observe. I'll feed you questions if I decide to follow a line you're not pursuing."

Charlie nodded. "As you prefer." They did a quick com-check. Then he ran a breathing pattern to center himself, shared a look with Rex, and stepped inside Interview E.

CHAPTER 43

"THE BUG JOB" AND THE MYSTERY SHED

A tall, stoop-shouldered man with a gloomy expression awaited Charlie and Rex in the Detention Center's Interview Room E. He sat in one of the chairs beside the metal table. No one had manacled him, although he appeared large and muscular enough that he might pose a threat. Even to Charlie, if so inclined.

But he barely glanced up.

"Good morning." Charlie placed his case pad on the table and took the remaining chair. "I am Reserve Agent Charles Morgan. My colleague is XK9 Rex Dieter-Nell."

The man stared at Rex. "That ain't t' one catch me."

Rex shook his head. "No, that was XK9 Shady."

The subject's eyes widened. "Damn! Dog *did* talk."

"We XK9s can talk through our vocalizers," Rex said.

The man shook his head. "Hoo-ee." He stared at Rex, as if entranced.

I fear if I ask him questions, he'll be distracted. Rex's ears canted back, then lifted again. *Better let you do the talking, at least for now.*

Fair enough. Charlie offered their subject a smile. "We introduced ourselves. Would you mind telling us who you are, for the record?"

"Oh!" He pulled his attention away from Rex to give Charlie an apologetic look. "Sorry. Attila Usher, me. Call me Till. How'ya, okay?"

"Okay. Thank you. And you? Would you like something to eat or drink?"

Usher answered with a tentative, worried half-smile. "No, m'good."

"Till, I need to advise you that we're recording this interview," Charlie said. "You've been detained for questioning. It is your right to say nothing, but it may harm your defense if you do not mention, when questioned, something you later rely on in court. Anything you do say may be used against you in a court of law. It is your right to have an attorney with you while you are questioned. If you can't afford an attorney, we will provide one to you at no charge. Do you understand these rights I've explained to you?"

Usher hesitated, his expression uncertain. "I'm arrested, but you can get me a lawyer?"

"If you ask for one. Definitely. And you don't have to pay, if you don't have money."

He gave his head a rueful shake. "Don't never got money, me."

"Will you talk with us this morning? Or should I call a lawyer for you?"

The rounded shoulders rose and fell. Confused brown eyes searched him. "Sure. Talk with you. Guess why not?"

"Thank you."

Through the link he sensed Rex's empathy for the man. *His scent factors are completely without guile. He has no idea why he's here. I know you went through the warning, but ... should we get him a lawyer?*

No. A lawyer will close him down, and we need his information. "Could we talk about a job you worked a few weeks ago? With Kieran O'Boyle, Elmo Smart, and your friend Wayne Purdy?" Charlie asked.

The puzzled look lingered for several seconds, but then the man's eyebrows rose. "Oh! It's *that* ship blowed up later, wa'n't it? Oh! Well, sure. What d'you wanna know?"

Rex's ears went up. *He's not worried. Doesn't seem to think he did anything wrong.*

Charlie stifled his disbelief, even though the arrest vid had alerted him to this. *Hard to believe.* He took a breath. "How'd you get involved?"

"Allus askin' roun' buncha of places, me. Damn hard get legal work. Ain't worked reg'lar, not since t' ship ditch me. Take jobs as-can."

Charlie frowned. "Your ship left you?"

The man's eyebrows knotted in a frown of outrage. "I *know.* Right? Put me real bad. Ain't complain though, not me. That'll get'cha spaced, lotta places."

Well, that explains some things. Charlie drew in a breath and struggled to find a good reply. "For the record, Till, please know this. On Rana Station, we don't space people. Not for that reason, and not for any other reason."

The man's brows rose. "No? Well, hot damn. Already kinda liked it here."

"May I ask what ship left you?" Charlie made an effort to keep his expression neutral. Abandoning crewmembers was a felony-level breach of interstellar regs, but it happened. As Fee would say, the devil was in catching them.

"*Ronin Guerrero.*" Usher scowled. "No pay, neither, jus' ditch-n-go."

Trust Rex to run a search on the fly. *The* Ronin Guerrero *last docked at Rana Station more than two and a half years ago.* The big dog flagged the ship's file for investigation on the abandonment charge and linked the information as a sidebar to the interview recording. *Usher must've lived here, unregistered, ever since. What sort of existence would that be?*

Likely hand-to-mouth. Charlie focused on his subject. "How did you end up in the Five-Ten?"

Usher smiled. "Ol' Feek-man, he hear cargo crate goin' south. Takin' rats, even as couldn't pay."

Rats? Rex cocked his head at Usher.

Warehouse 'rats.' Charlie resisted frowning. *Disrespectful slang for vagrants in the Hub. It's a persistent problem.*

"Jump on t'chance, us. Good break. Head-hit on ship, me. Bad, awful no-good in Hub."

Not only abandoned, but abandoned after an injury? Rex ducked his nose below the edge of the table, but Charlie saw and felt the snarl. *If he had a head injury, that would be dangerous in the Hub, wouldn't it?*

Untreated brain trauma in micrograv can kill you if it's bad enough. We always put head trauma patients high on the list for early evac to 1-G. Charlie kept his focus on Usher. "You rode in a crate? Whose crate was it? What kind?"

The man's whole demeanor drooped. "Dunno. Purt bad off, me."

Charlie nodded. *I suspect he's suffered some brain damage.* "You were going to tell us about the job on the *Izgubil*. Why did you take it?"

Usher grimaced. "You got any clue how hard's t'find decent-pay work ain't illegal? Jump right on it, me."

"How'd you find out about it?"

"O'Boyle call. Good man." Usher smiled. "Call special. Feck an' Wayne, too. Owe him a big'un, all us."

"Which O'Boyle?"

"Kieran. Don' truss' ol' snakey Turlach, not me."

Charlie lifted his brows. "Why not?"

"Mean one, him. Nobody ship-dump ever any good, he say." Usher scowled. "Nary givva chance. His boy better'n him."

Charlie nodded. "So Kieran gave you a chance?"

"Good'un, yeah." Usher's face relaxed into a smile. "Give us chanct' learnin' trade, mebbe. Newstyle bug-spray."

The hope in the man's face made Charlie's stomach go sour, but he must remain objective. He cleared his throat, and strove for a cool, neutral tone. "Could you tell me about that? What did Kieran teach you?"

Usher shook his head. "Kieran, no. Diff'rent guy. Not know 'em, me."

Rex's ears went up. *Another man?*

"Can you describe him? What's his name?"

Usher chewed on his lip, thought for a while. "Shorter'n me. Fancy talkin'."

"Dark? Fair? Fat? Skinny? Anything unusual about him?"

"Little lighter'n me. Not fat, not skinny. Like I say, fancy talker."

Great. Medium height, medium skin, medium build. That ought to narrow it down. Charlie kept his expression neutral, but Rex lolled his tongue.

"Name?" Charlie prompted again, but with fading hope.

"Kieran say call 'em 'Sir,' us."

How helpful. "What did Sir teach you?"

"Come in nex' mornin', real early. Go t'shed, us. Dem show how do spray."

"Where is this shed?"

Usher's face went pensive. "Weird thing. Stack'a bamboo poles front'a door."

"Bamboo poles?"

"Yeah. Had t' move'um, me." He scowled. "Heavy. Tattoo guys jus' watch, dem. Nary lift a finger."

"Tattoo guys?"

"Tree dem." Usher held up three fingers. "No-good 'uns. Mean. Laugh ugly, dem."

"Did you hear any of their names?" Charlie didn't have high hopes, but he must ask.

Usher's eyelids lowered. His mouth pursed. He sat very still like that for several seconds, then looked up. "Rad, one dem. Rad Nall Wall. Crazy name, um."

"Sounds Ullach," SA Hunter said on the com. "Fits, if they're Saoirse Front."

Charlie nodded to Usher. "His name is Rag Nall Wall? That *is* an odd name."

"Rad Nall got orange hair. Other two Bry, an' Ferg. Dunno last names, dem."

"It's a start. Thank you." He hoped the names were puzzle pieces that might corroborate other facts learned later. "Now, about this shed. If I showed you a map, could you point out where the shed is?"

Usher's face scrunched with regret. "Not s' good on maps, me. Sorry. 'Caus'a head-hit. Some stuff scramble, now. Cain't see 'em right. Maps not s' good."

"That's okay. Let's try this. Is it near Ostra?"

Usher shook his head. "Over by boun'dry." He chewed his lip. "Leeward? No, spinward. No ... aw, hell. Sorry. Not sure. Feek know. Find by follow Feek, me."

Rex flicked his ears. *Feek's the one in detox, of course.*

"Never mind. Please tell us about the spraying. "How did you do that?"

"Got suits, helmet, gloves, boots—lot t'put on. Hot in there."

"I bet. What sort of tools did you use?"

"Tank, hose, trigger-nozzle. Feek small, do spray, shoot way high up. Twirl dem pellets, me. Hafta hold up high." He raised his arm, then circled his wrist as if twirling something above his head. But then he lowered his arm and rubbed his right bicep. "Arm hurt fer days."

Charlie could imagine. "So, then, walk me through this. How'd you get up to the Hub and back?"

"'Nother crate, up an' back." Usher frowned. "Hate damn crate. Too small. Stand whole trip, us. Head hurt worser an' worser all day, plus whole week after. Purt bad pain. But pay good."

"Whose crate did he travel in, this second time?" SA Hunter prompted.

"Till, I know you hated the crate, but where'd it come from? Do you know whose it was?"

"Dem new guy. Sir."

"To clarify, the crate belonged to Sir, correct?"

He nodded. "Some kinda special linin', but no seats. Purt damn doosh, y'ask me."

Charlie nodded. "Passenger comfort wasn't a priority, eh?" *What kind of contraband was it intended for?* He'd let the Port Authority and Immigration follow up on the nature of that 'special lining.' "When you got out of the crate, where were you?"

"Warehouse. Suit up in warehouse, us." He sighed, shook his head. "Don' ask. No idee which 'un, me."

Charlie offered a wry grin. "It's okay. You're doing really well, Till. Truly, you are."

"Yer okay fer a cop." Usher smiled back at him. "You ain't hit me once't."

"That's another thing we don't do on Rana Station—we don't hit subjects during interviews."

Usher shot him a dubious look. "True?"

Charlie met his eyes, held his gaze. "Any Ranan cop ever hit you?"

"Mostly try t' stay clear, me." His doubt lingered in his expression and body language, however. And in his scent factors, according to Rex's interview notes.

Time for a redirect. "From the warehouse to the ship, did you have far to go?"

"Seem far enough. Damn gear hot." He frowned, eyes downcast, hands in his lap. "Go down two-tree halls, then on tether t' service hatch. Jus' follow Feek, me."

Under the table, Rex put his chin on Charlie's knee. *That little drug addict seems to always be Till's guide. Let's hope he survives his detox. Maybe he'll know more.*

SHADY LIFTED HER NOSE. The perpetual murk of the Five-Ten slowly lightened with the onset of "dawn." Normal Thursday-morning activity began to stir in the Enclave, but not near the Mystery Shed. This out-of-the-way back corner didn't have any scent trace fresher than a week old, except for a few rat tracks.

Soon after they'd first arrived, Elle and Scout had noticed a new, unknown profile in addition to "third individual" Kieran.

But the unknown's scent was so elderly and faint Shady wouldn't have noticed it at all if they hadn't pointed it out. She could gain a basic sense of it, now that she knew where to sniff, but she still couldn't develop a full profile from it. Stung, she tried not to show it. "Good catch, Elle and Scout. Let us call this new profile Individual Four."

"Need some suggestions, interim Pack leader," Elaine said on the com. "How should I redeploy the Pack for best use of skills?"

"Send Elle, Scout, Victor and their partners out to parts of the Enclave the Pack hasn't yet searched. They may find a fresher track for Poopy." Rex, Tux, and Petunia, along with partners Georgia and Walter, already had returned to the investigative center to do interviews. "I'll stay here at the Mystery Shed with Crystal and Cinnamon. If we find any explosives residue here, I want our experts available."

"Thanks," Elaine said, then followed her advice.

Woah. No argument. No second-guessing. No *I'm-the-human-so-we'll-do-it-my-way.* Shady wagged her tail. *I could get used to this!*

Pam settled into a spot opposite the Mystery Shed, with her back against a nearby storage building's blank wall. She chuckled. *Rex has trained her well.*

Shady lolled her tongue. *Rex has delivered results.* Pride in her mate filled her, but also concern. He would *hate* being pulled off the Hunt, no matter how valid the security concern. She hoped working with Charlie would help.

Before long, Joe arrived with a search warrant and a team of blue-garbed CSU techs. They removed the bamboo poles, broke a rusty-looking lock, and after some exploration found a hidden latch. At last the door swung open to reveal cobwebby shelves in a surprisingly shallow space. The air here smelled rich with promise—but nothing on the shelves proved relevant.

"Something is wrong," Shady said. "Our Third Individual's scent should be here. It was on the lock, but not here."

"None of this stuff has been touched in months, except this corner." Cinnamon pointed with her nose.

The CSU team imaged it, then one of the techs used his gloved fingers to explore the area Cinnamon had indicated. "Ah!" His eyebrows rose.

Shady heard a soft *click*, then the entire wall swung open.

"This is more like it!" Cinnamon's tail went up, waving. She waited again for CSU's all-clear, then trotted straight into the newly-revealed space. Crystal followed half a pace behind her. Both reared onto hind legs, squeaking and wagging their tails, but not bracing paws on *these* shelves. "Top shelf! We need a ladder!"

"Hold on a minute." Berwyn unfolded a small, portable ladder from the CSU cart.

Cinnamon scrambled up, careful not to touch the shelf itself. "Bingo! Got a spot up here that smells of adhesive and nanotimer-carbon. Good scent profiles for Individuals Three and Four. The adhesive kind of 'fixed' their scents. This probably will give us DNA. Maybe fingerprints, too."

"Back off and gown up, before you go any farther," said the tech who'd opened the second latch.

Once properly garbed, Cinnamon and Crystal leaped into their work eagerly. Shady stayed back. It was their expertise the investigation needed most, not hers.

"I smell characteristic explosives here, but the box is empty," Crystal said. "K—um, Individual Three's scent is here as well, and also Four."

Cinnamon examined the scent residues in careful detail. "Four is not a profile we have encountered before, but he is all over the top shelf, and his scent is layered into the explosives residue on the empty box. His is not the only profile in the explosives, however. I have a sense there is at least one other. We can certainly link the one we are calling Four to the materials that destroyed the ship. He may well be our fabricator. Could this be Rory Fredericks?"

"Let's not get ahead of the data," Elaine said. "So let me get this straight. You now have strong samples for Four, but there's also a Five, and perhaps others?"

"That is my impression. Yes."

Shady took a turn. "I agree this disposition of scents probably means Four made or helped make the devices this box once held. I also agree there is a Five, and possibly a Six, but we almost certainly cannot lift an identifying sample for either of them. And we cannot assume any named identity yet."

"Agreed," Elaine said on the com. "Just follow the evidence."

Shady left the teams to collect, bag and catalog their finds. Instead she gave the rest of the place a good sniff-over.

Looking for something in particular? Pam asked privately.

Shady sniffed along the lower edge of the false wall. It had the same thickness as a real wall of shelves. Oh, here was something interesting. *Our warrant specifies the shed's entire contents, doesn't it?*

I think so. Pam relayed the question to Joe.

"With an emphasis on explosives-related materials, but yes." Joe craned his neck to see. "Did you find something?"

"I simply wish to make certain no explosives-related—" Shady stopped, sniffed again, then lowered her forequarters. She thrust her nose into the toe kick under the pseudo-bottom shelf. "Ah!"

Pam knelt beside her, then went down on her belly to shine a light under there. *Is that a box?* She reached in with a gloved hand to gently dislodge a flat box, made just the height to fit a narrow compartment built in below the toe-kick. "Looks like a cash box," she said into the com.

Shady sniffed it over in detail. A tingling rush of excitement washed through her. "The predominant scent is Three's, with traces of slash and hard currency. There are small smears of adhesive, plus explosives residue here on the side."

"That's 'explosives-related.'" The energy in Elaine's voice on the com lifted Shady's heart even more. "Good find!"

CHAPTER 44

TURNING THE PAGE

R ex thanked Charlie and saw him off with a nuzzle and a tail-wag, once his half-watch ended. Then he reported to Elaine's tiny office, as ordered.

She did not rise from her chair at the workstation or look up from her case pad. "Close the door."

Rex nudged the door till it clicked, then parked himself at parade-sit. Wonder of wonders, vanishingly little of her old phobia rose up in her scent, even with the door shut. Cautious hope filled him: her scent also contained little anger, although a degree of sadness resonated.

"I need to be able to count on you." She kept her focus on the case pad.

Rex ducked his head, fluttered his tail. "I have no excuse, ma'am. I failed you. After I had earnestly promised to do anything you asked, I failed to keep my word in that moment. I cannot deny it. I also do not ever intend to transgress in that way again."

Her gaze flicked up from the pad to meet his. "I know."

Rex held his submissive crouch but lifted his ears. "You do?"

"If I am not mistaken, it was an error in judgment, born of habits you developed when you worked under less-than-trustworthy human leadership." She met his eyes coolly, steadily. "Neither Dr. Ordovich nor Col. Wisniewski ever had your best interests at heart. They never understood the importance of the Pack, nor your covenant with them." She put the case pad down, stood. "I think it is important to make sure you know that I do."

Rex straightened. "You, out of all the humans, were the first besides Charlie who truly listened to me. You sent me after Elmo with Shiv, when you could have ordered me to go away. You were the one who invited me into the elevator that first week, and thereby into Command ranks. You gave me the chance to speak with credibility on the Civic Center stage. I do trust you."

"Don't forget, you helped me out of a jam, too." A wry smile flickered on her lips. "Imagine where this case would be without the Pack."

"Imagine where the Pack would be without this case. We continue to need each other."

Elaine nodded. "Then let us move forward together." She frowned. "As of fifteen minutes ago, the medical staff was still trying to stabilize Razor's symptoms."

Rex's hackles prickled with a sudden chill. "Still? Even though they could identify the poison? It has been hours."

"It is a customized neurotoxin that they could only imperfectly counteract. Razor continues to have seizures and partial organ failure, but they tell me they still hope to save him."

Rex shuddered, every hackle up. "A customized neurotoxin? From Wisniewski?"

Elaine's grim scent and expression did not calm his fear. "We've sent samples to several experts, including to Mike's friend Rooq for a more complete analysis."

"What about the shooter?" Rex asked. "Who is he? Where did he get that stuff?"

She frowned. "He remains in detention. He has already demanded a lawyer, so we cannot question him at this time. He is unregistered and refuses even to give us a name."

Rex growled, then shot a worried look at her.

"Oh, I quite agree." Her fear-scent remained low, especially compared with the new, surging anger in her scent-mix, and the cold purpose in her face.

"I should like to question him, myself," Rex said.

She smiled without merriment. "I'll pass that along. You may get your chance."

FRIDAY MORNING'S plan called for Charlie, Rex, and Hildie to ride to the Hub together. Hildie and Rex could see how he reacted to microgravity. Just as important, Charlie could see for himself whether there might be a chance for him to function in microgravity after all.

If all went as they hoped, Hildie then would report for what was *supposed* to be an 8-hour watch. If LaRock didn't change it on her without warning. Meanwhile, Rex and Charlie would traverse the SDF Wheel Two Base, to examine the bridge crime scene he'd been assigned to recreate. This was a now or never opportunity, because the bubble cordon was due to come down today. It had begun to develop new issues after its two-week test run.

Charlie's little primary family unit rode in Rex's closed car from Corona's underground garage to Glen Haven Station for the 06:10 commuter to the Hub. Dr. Sandler and her team were still trying to stabilize Razor's condition. No one cared to expose Rex to any chance of such a hazard today. "Park," Rex told the car, then they waited inside it. Only after the elevator had actually opened did they emerge, to scuttle directly across the waiting area and in through its doors.

No blowguns. No rifles. No ambush.

All three breathed a quiet sigh when the doors closed. There were only a few other commuters at this hour. Neighbors greeted them, but left one of the large, multi-passenger commuter car's side-chambers open for them. Charlie strapped

Rex in before he secured himself. This wasn't a Safety Services Express, because they weren't on an emergency call. It took the full 54 minutes of normal transit time to elevate to the Hub. They activated news feeds on the way. Checked in with their Watch Officers. Rex described for Hildie how the XK9s' micrograv harnesses were designed.

But they fell silent in the final minutes of the climb. By then the floaty, nausea-inducing sensations of low-G had fully set in. Through the link, Charlie sensed when Rex's nasal passages swelled. It bothered him less that his did, too. The St. Michael's medal around his neck floated away from his chest, to bump his chin.

He ran a breathing pattern but felt steadier than he had in years.

He flashed on the last time he and Rex had ridden to the Hub, the night of the dock breach. The lower the gravity had gotten, the more intense his self-loathing had grown. The more excruciating his skin-crawling shame. But that horrible, humiliating burden at last was gone. He had ... as it turned out, he had no reason for shame.

Hildie rode beside him, her hand warm in his. She met his gaze and offered a smile, then squeezed his hand. She didn't despise him. He *hadn't* disgraced himself beyond redemption in her eyes, as he'd believed for years. According to her, quite the opposite. She'd reassured him she thought he was brave to try again and again.

Rex rode on his other side, ears up. He nudged Charlie's arm shield, which hardened on contact, then wagged his tail. *No, I don't despise you, either. Never have and never will. I know you can do this.*

He squared his shoulders, let out a long breath. *Yes. I know I can, too.* After all, he had operated for years in this environment. In an earlier time, micrograv had been his second element. Weirdly, their ascent today seemed like coming home after a long, weary war.

"How do you feel?" Hildie's hazel eyes tracked him closely.

"Better than in a long, long time." No tremor in the hand that clasped hers. Well, almost none. Last time, he hadn't been able to hold off the shakes. Now he felt mostly calm. He felt ... good. Could his reactions truly hinge so massively on Hildie's regard?

Rex lolled his tongue. It floated straight outward from his mouth. "Of the few times we have come to the Hub together, I have not known him to remain this calm. You are a good influence, Hildie!"

She offered a wary half-smile. "I'd love to think that."

"Believe it." Charlie leaned toward her. She met him halfway for a kiss. "Your being here, your belief in me—it makes more difference than you imagine."

They disembarked at the apex into a world of muted lighting, polished metal, and almost-cold air. The Hub never changed, but this time, painful memories didn't overwhelm him as they had so many times in recent years. Hildie and Rex believed in him. And at last, *he* believed in himself, too. The darkness stayed back, though it still lurked at the edges of his mind.

"Time for a few exercises." Hildie guided him to one of the utility zones, away from the commuter corridors. "Show me the Class-A drill."

Charlie almost scoffed. Every Ranan learned the Class-A drill in primary levels. But then he wobbled on one of the rolls, and completely missed a grip on an overhead reach.

He halted, scandalized by his own ineptitude.

"Give yourself a chance to get warmed up." Hildie's voice held no mockery. Her gaze remained direct, open, and calm, but with a hint of a concerned brow-pucker.

He remembered an evening years ago. He, Hildie, and the crew had gone to a hangout near here to play Clamps, a complicated micrograv game requiring speed, accuracy, and coordination. He and Hildie had joined forces that day. As a team, they'd ruled all comers. "I'm not quite ready for another game of Clamps, am I?"

She gave him a startled look, then a rueful laugh. "Some stuff has happened since then. Pretty soon you'll be ready for Semi-Super-Clamps. C'mon, let's see that roll again."

He nailed it on the second try. Made the overhead reach, too. Got through the rest with no do-overs, but kind of a shaky finish. More winded than he'd expected, he steadied gradually from gasps to normal breaths.

Hildie took his pulse, checked him with an expert's evaluating gaze. "That's enough for now. You're not conditioned yet. I've got to get moving, but promise me you won't overdo it this morning?"

"I promise." Damn it, she was right. Fatigue sapped him already. "Stay safe, yourself."

"Roger that." She grinned, kissed him, then turned to Rex. "Keep it under two hours. I mean it."

CHAPTER 45

WISDOM, FOOLISHNESS, AND CONSEQUENCES

S hady emerged from Interview B's observation booth with a stretch and a yawn. Stiff muscles all along her back ached in chorus.

Rex trotted over to her from where he'd been waiting in the corridor. He greeted her with a nuzzle and a nose-touch. "Am I correct that you and the others have mostly been monitoring interviews so far today?"

"Yes." She gave herself a vigorous shake. "How did Charlie do up-top?"

His scent went fragrant with sweet relief and bright joy. "Much better than before! We toured the *Izgubil*'s bridge for slightly more than an hour, and he took lots of images and notes. He talked some nonsense about taking the rest of his half-shift in the GR Unit, but you know how micrograv can take it out of you."

She yawned before she could stop herself. "Um, yes." Just thinking about working in micrograv weighted her limbs and made her ears droop.

Rex lolled his tongue. "He did not even realize we took the Ninth Precinct elevator until I woke him when we arrived at Glen Haven Station. I am not sure he even got his clothes off before he fell asleep again on his bed at home, but I could not help him. That is Hildie's job now."

Pam had approached and caught the last of that. "I suppose she's working another twelve-hour?"

Rex laid back his ears. "It is supposed to be an eight-hour, but I will only believe that when I see her arrive before dark."

Pam frowned. "She must work for the Boss from Hell. I had a Field Training Officer who was that demanding, but only for a few days. I was lucky our captain caught on quickly." Shady sensed little jealousy remaining in her partner's scent, but greater levels of plummy, upper-mid-tone empathy. Maybe Shady's own growing fondness for Hildie had started to rub off on Pam.

"I cannot disagree about the Boss from Hell characterization." Rex couldn't quite keep the growl from his voice. "Unfortunately, Captain LaRochelle *is* the captain. I would like to have words with him, but I think Charlie has found more effective ones."

Pam's eyes widened. "Oh, you do *not* want to cross Charlie when he's in a protective mood!"

Shady wagged her tail at an upwelling memory of Charlie in action, defending Pam from a criticism during their XK9 training days. She sensed parallel memories in Pam. Her partner got *that* right.

"Agreed. But this conversation does not support the *Izgubil* investigation very much." Rex flicked his ears and refocused on Shady. "You were explaining how the Pack is deployed."

Back to business. Got it. "Yes. Victor and Eduardo are working their OPD homicide again with DPO Penny. They say he is a good investigator, and they are looking forward to when he joins our XK9 Unit. I think they have been having fun showing him some of the things XK9s can do."

Rex nodded. "That bodes well. And I know Fujimoto is a solid man." DPO Helmer Fujimoto was the other veteran detective Klein had selected to advise the new XK9 Unit.

"I'm looking forward to working with him," Pam put in. "Balchu really respects him."

"Scout and Petunia are doing onsite interviews with dock workers topside this morning," Shady continued her report. "Working with Reza, Nicole, and Walter. I am envious." She yawned again, this time from remembered tedium. "Elle, Misha, Pam, and I have been working with Iruka and Melynn. Our humans have been interviewing a bunch of mid-level bankers and law clerks in the OPD's interview suites here at HQ."

Rex snorted. "Let me guess. They all swear they know nothing about anything nefarious going on, and they are scandalized that any such thing might be alleged."

"How did you guess?" Shady let her tongue slide out. "Both Elle and I have been pushing for a chance to wander around their workplaces and see what we can sniff out, but so far, the humans refuse. They have a different method." She snapped her ears flat. "As far as I can tell, their method is not working very well."

Rex eyed the row of interview- and observation-room doors along the corridor. "Ranans do not always take as straightforward an approach as Transmondians. I am still getting used to their methods."

Oh, my, was that ever an understatement. "Talk with Elaine, please." Shady let a soft whimper slip out. "You and she need to discuss all the XK9 deployments, but I would appreciate a word in favor of letting us out of those cramped interview boxes. I know we can sniff something out, if we can go on-site. So far, nothing is breaking in regard to Emer Bellamy. I want her butt in an interview chair!" She rubbed her face against his ruff.

"Innocent until proven, my love."

Shady growled. "You sound like Pam."

He arched his neck over her shoulders, pulled her close to him, then released her. "I shall see what I can do about the interview boxes." He departed for S-3-9.

Shady wheeled toward her partner. They were due for a break.

They'd finished with their captured installation-team subjects yesterday. Dopey, AKA Feek, was still undergoing detox in the Addiction Behavioral Unit at Orangeboro Medical Center. He hadn't yet been interviewed. His friend Attila Usher also was now hospitalized, undergoing re-gen therapy for brain trauma. Both had security details, but neither was in any condition to escape. Instead, Security was there to protect them from The Whisper Syndicate's revenge.

Their friend Wayne Purdy, the one the Pack had nicknamed Stinky, remained in an underground section of the Detention area designed for suspects awaiting trial who couldn't be released with implanted location monitors. He seemed an unlikely flight or violence risk, but, like his friends Feek and Till, he was in mortal danger from the Syndicate. Shady'd been startled to learn that Purdy's quarters resembled a nice furnished studio apartment.

Presumed-innocent, Pam said, when Shady questioned the accommodations. *You are certain he did it. Because of that, I am certain, too. But humans can't smell who's guilty and who's not. And anyway, his current quarters aren't that much different from prison.*

Shady flicked her ears, dubious about all of it, especially that last statement. *This is nothing like what I was taught.*

Taught in Transmondia. Pam's frown and the reaction echoing through the link made her disapproval clear. *That's a different legal code.*

You can say that again.

Trust me, it's much better to extend qualified trust, while making sure they're actually not moving out of reach or threatening anyone before a judge or jury has decided their case. Pam gave her a rueful look. *Didn't you say that according to his scent factors, he genuinely thought he was applying bug spray? So, what, exactly, is he guilty of, again?*

You are making this complicated. A hint of a growl lingered in Shady's throat.

Actual justice, as opposed to the politically-convenient kind, is often complicated.

But not so much, when we talk about Clumsy. The aggressively uncooperative Clumsy had continued to defy interrogation. He had a right to refuse, but *sheesh.* He wouldn't even tell investigators his name. They suspected he was a Saoirse Front member named Raghnall Wall, because of his Saoirse Front-style tattoos and Attila Usher's report that "Rad Nall Wall" had "orange hair." According to Pam, Clumsy's hair was "a shrieking-bright carrot-top." Looked dull, grayish-tan to Shady, but of course she couldn't see "orange."

Yeah, that Clumsy's a real piece of work. Pam shook her head. He'd been formally charged, so the OPD and the SBI were under no obligation to release an obvious violence and flight risk. Especially not since he *also* was in mortal danger from the Syndicate.

They'd put him in living quarters like Purdy's, but he'd immediately started smashing and throwing things. Now he remained under what Pam had called a "behavioral curb." The Listeners managing his case had decreed a methodical, inexorable, but nonviolent approach. Unless one could call the implanted behavioral curb "violent." Like an EStee, it delivered a painful shock if a subject made a sudden, violent movement. If this didn't halt the unwanted behaviors, it then administered a dose of EStee-like tranquilizer.

Detention staff monitored, fed him, made sure he had exercise and proper medical care ... and waited. Pam alleged that they only spoke to him kindly. Shady had her doubts, but this *was* Rana, and Ranans got weird when it came to incarceration and civil rights. She cocked her head at Pam. *Do you think the Listeners are right about how to handle him?*

They have an excellent success record. It's not quick, but it's usually effective. I guess we'll find out. Pam's smile turned pensive. *The Pack has been taught how to motivate an uncooperative witness.* Shady didn't especially enjoy scaring people—well, she *would* happily make exceptions. But she didn't like scaring *most* people, even though the Transmondians had prized an XK9's large size for "making an impression" on detained suspects.

You know Ranans don't use dogs for that. Anyway, witness intimidation is against the law. Her partner straightened, stretched, then walked over to a hydration station on the corridor wall to fill her water bottle and Shady's bowl.

It might speed things up.

The legal code and protocols were established for good reason. Pam set the filled bowl down for Shady with a frown. *Shortcuts aren't always as useful as they appear in advance. All too often, they backfire.*

Shady didn't reply. She drank her water and hoped the Ranans knew what they were doing.

A LOW-LEVEL HEADACHE brought Charlie to a groggy, half-waking state, overheated and restricted. He realized, chagrined, that he was still wearing his rumpled, sweaty clothing from this morning. His successful return to micrograv, on top of residual fatigue from yesterday's early call and short night, had taken more of a toll than he'd expected. What the heck time was it, anyway? His HUD said ... *16:00? Seriously?*

Well! The dead do arise. Charlie could picture the tongue-loll and the teasing glint in Rex's amber eyes, even though presumably his partner was still at HQ. *How do you feel?*

A bit like I was run over by a cargo transport. It took people's bodies a while to acclimatize when they first started working up-top. Only after some of his little cousins entered primary-levels had he noticed that teachers always timed kids' earliest field trips into micrograv just before naptime. Canny tactics he'd never noticed when he himself was a kid, but he knew better now. He should've expected this. *I clearly have lost all my micrograv tolerance.*

I feel you. Remember, too, that you're still healing.

The gate announced Hildie's return.

Wow. She worked an actual *eight-hour?* Charlie pushed up to sitting.

Seems miraculous, Rex agreed through the link. *I'll let you focus undistracted.*

Charlie peeled out of the gummy, scrunched-up jumpsuit's top, but he was still sitting on the bed half-dressed and rubbing his temples when Hildie arrived.

She grinned. "Looks like you've had a productive day."

"I *did* get some good notes for the GR while Rex and I were up-top." He labored up from the bed and onto his feet with a yawn. Every joint ached.

"Actually, I meant it looks as if you've caught up on some sleep. That's good. How do you feel?"

Claustrophobic anger spiked hot in his gut. "Just wonderful. How do I look?"

"Mm. So, will that be two, or shall I make it three Pana-cees?"

He swallowed a hot retort, not quite sure why he was irritated. She certainly didn't deserve to be the brunt of his pique. "Better make it three."

"Coming right up." How could she act so *perky?*

He sat back down on the bed. *Yeesh,* he hadn't even taken off his shoes? It was a wonder he'd made it to the bed at all. His head pounded. Was it stifling in here, or did he just have on too many clothes? He fumbled off a shoe. Was still struggling with the second one, when Hildie returned and sat next to him.

"Stop a minute and take these." She tipped three Pana-cees into his palm, then handed over a glass of water.

He knew the drill. She'd insist that he drink *all* the water. No sense in arguing. He downed it with slow swallows. Kept his gaze on her.

She stood again. Unpinned her hair, then shook it out. It fell long and shining, soft by her face, spilling over her shoulders. Next she peeled out of the top half of her coverall. The bra came off after that, then she moved into a luxuriant stretch. Arms swept up, back arched, eyes closed, with a small, relieved smile.

She is so beautiful. Each time she came here after work, he rejoiced in this gradual unveiling of his Medicine Goddess.

She bent to pull off her shoes, then dropped the rest of the coverall and kicked free of it. At last she turned to him with a smile. "Oh, that's better."

He grinned at her. "I know *I* feel better." The Pana-cees hadn't had time to work yet, but that little ritual always filled him with joy. Even when the rest of him felt crappy.

She slid him a come-hither look. "How *much* better?"

He released a soft breath. "Better enough to appreciate you." All the same, his head pounded like a hammer on one of Uncle Hector's anvils. "I'm glad it was only an eight-hour."

Her expression betrayed a brief flash of worry, but then she yawned. "Yeah. Me, too."

He frowned. Little tongues of irritation flared into smoky anger. "All right, Gallagher, spill it. What happened?"

She avoided his gaze. "Nothing."

"Don't do that." His anger roared hotter and his frown deepened into a scowl. The headache doubled down on head-splitting agony. "What did LaRock pull this time?"

She sighed, still avoiding eye contact. "Nothing. Really! *Nothing.* He didn't get a chance. Oz caught him coming across the commons at the end of my eight-hour and hit him with a bunch of questions about an equipment requisition. I got away clean."

"Oz is solid. Always was." Oz Meredith was the MERS-V drivers' Squad Commander. Charlie had considered it a privilege to work under his command, in part because the team could always, always count on him to have their backs. It seemed that had not changed.

"Yeah. I owe him one."

"Doesn't change the fact that he had to run interference." Charlie ground his teeth. A blaze of fury kicked his pulse faster.

The damned headache blurred his vision. "I doubt it's the first time he's had to do that. *Is it?*"

She bowed her head. "Can we please not talk about this?"

He clenched his fists. "I want to know about it, whenever LaRock pulls something!"

"So you can do *what*, exactly?" She gave him an exasperated look. "So you can run to Alphonse Rami, and get me into even deeper shit?"

Heat flashed through him. His head might explode. He rolled out of bed on the opposite side. Glared at her. "Is that what you think I do?"

She glared back. "It's what happened the last time. I got caught in the middle!"

"We can't just let him get by with it! He's putting your patients—your crew—most of all, he's putting *you* in danger." He gasped short, tight breaths, too angry to see. Too sick with terror to pull away. "If he gets you hurt—if he gets you—gets you—" He couldn't finish. Couldn't say the word *killed.* A tiny voice at the back of his mind warned he was overreacting. But the raging inferno in his heart drowned it out.

"He won't. He's not." Now her face pinched with fear. "Charlie, please—"

"You're *defending* him?" This was too much. He couldn't stay here anymore. He flung himself through the French doors onto the outer balcony, then slammed them with all the force of his rage.

The doors and every pane in them shattered like a small explosion.

He froze.

No sound from Hildie. She stood on the far side of his bed, as if paralyzed in place.

So, Rex said through the link in a careful tone. *What just happened?*

I, um. Charlie rubbed the back of his neck. His mind reeled. He stared at the shattered doors. *I just kinda went ... apeshit.*

Do you feel better now?

The queasy horror in his stomach made it hard to choke in a breath. *No. I yelled at Hildie. I broke a door. Er, two doors.* Rex probably was getting a visual impression of the destruction through the link.

Do I need to come home? Do you need help?

I. Um. I'm not sure why I ....

I'm coming home. Don't yell at Hildie anymore. Let the house-keeping vacs get all the glass shards. You're barefoot, right?

At least he hadn't shed the whole jumpsuit yet, or he'd be mooning the entire Sirius River Valley. *You don't have to come home.*

He pictured Rex's ears clamp flat, the steely look in those amber eyes. *I'm coming home. Stay calm.*

Charlie sighed. *Yeah. I think I can do that.* He hoped he could do that. Like the time he'd shattered the bamboo railing, he felt kinda flash-fried. What was *wrong* with him?

One of the doors from Rex's bedroom opened. Hildie stepped halfway out. Gave him a wary look. "Did you cut yourself?"

"I don't think so. Hils, I'm sorry! That was—"

"Careful. I think most of the glass is inside, but I see pieces out here too." Little cuboid bits of tempered glass lay scattered everywhere.

The room vacs were already at work, but no single unit had a very high storage capacity. Designed to deal with a single shattered tumbler, they had to make multiple trips to empty and return for this job.

He skirted the glass bits, joined her by Rex's door. "I'm *so* sorry!"

She let out a long breath. "Forgiven. I'm sorry for my part in that. I could see you were upset, but ... I guess now we know what Shiv was trying to warn us about. The sudden bouts of anger."

"That was ...."

"Terrifying."

"I never, *ever* want to scare you like that again." He searched her face. Her earlier pinched, fearful look haunted him. "Scare *me* like that, either."

"I touched a nerve I didn't intend to touch. I really regret that."

"And I never let you finish a thought." Lightheaded nausea overtook him on a wave of self-disgust.

She gave him a wry look. "I was only thinking of myself. I can imagine how hard it must be for you to watch my problems with LaRock, and not be able to fix them." She reached up to touch his cheek. Was it his imagination, or did a trace of fear still linger in her body language? "He'll never change without consequences. I know that."

"But I have no call to make your work harder." He slipped his arm lightly around her waist, then waited to gauge her response.

"No, you just want to protect me." She pulled him close. Hugged him hard. "I love that you do. I just wish it was easier to balance."

"Yeah. Me too." He hugged her back, misgivings on high alert and heart too full for further words.

CHAPTER 46

A MEDICAL EMERGENCY

Hildie steered Charlie through Rex and Shady's room, then out to the lounges on the inner balcony. His skin had taken on a grayish cast, like the day he'd shattered the bannister and overextended himself setting out lasers. That time, he'd been breathless and dizzy.

This time, he seemed almost dazed. He didn't fight her guidance. When they reached the lounges he sat down like someone had flipped the "off" switch to his legs. His forehead puckered in a frown that her instincts and experience told her probably came from the mother of all headaches. Those three Pana-cees clearly weren't up to *this* job.

She didn't like the little sheen of sweat on skin that was noticeably hotter to the touch than it should be. Didn't like the gray skin tone, the elevated pulse, the faint tremor in his muscles. "Lean back for a minute. Rest. How do you feel?"

"M'okay," he mumbled.

Sure you are. "Can you say more about that? What feels okay?"

The confusion in his beautiful brown eyes made her throat ache.

Stay professional. Emotions later. "Let's try this. What *doesn't* feel okay?"

"Head hurts," he conceded. "I feel kinda flash-fried, like I did the other day."

She gulped. Her heart rate shot up. "When you shattered the railing?"

"Like I'm a charred cinder, still smoking." He grimaced.

This was definitely beyond her scope. She bit her lip. "I think we need to talk to Dr. Zuni. This might be one of the odd reactions he said could happen."

"Jus' lemme rest a minute. I'll be okay" His color did seem to be improving.

She nodded. "I think you will, actually ... until the next time it happens. And I'm afraid the next time it happens will be a little bit worse. Just sit there for a while. Can you do a breathing pattern?"

He closed his eyes and started a simple but ragged slow-inhale-hold-slow-exhale pattern.

She triggered her com for Dr. Zuni's office. It was by now after hours, but the answering service sent her call to Zuni himself. She sketched the sequence of events and her assessment of Charlie's condition immediately afterward.

"Yes, I definitely want to see him. Orangeboro Med, stat. You're in Ninth Precinct? I'll order transport and specify details. I want measured vitals at specific intervals, and a sequence of blood draws. Keep him on that lounge till they get there and let the ambulance crew move him."

"Oh, he'll love that." She gave Charlie a rueful look. Then she relayed Zuni's orders, and texted Rex and the Family.

She rode in the back of the ambulance with Charlie and held his hand. Weird to be a "civilian" this time, to see the other side of the experience. Her downsider colleagues quite properly kept their focus on Charlie, once they'd assured themselves that she was unhurt. Zuni had given them detailed instructions. And there was that sequence of blood draws via an IV line, timed and documented down to the tenth of a second. She didn't envy them the exacting routine.

No longer required to do anything but hold Charlie's hand and stay out of the way, emotions emerged. Her sickly terror at the rage in his face when he'd lost control and she could do nothing to help. The unreal memory of the shattered French doors squeezed all her breath out. The stomach-plunge of horror at his physical crash afterwards. That, and her helplessness against its onset. She clung to his hand and rode out a case of the shakes.

"Hils? You okay?" Charlie's voice sounded hoarse.

"Lie still," one of the EMTs admonished. But she also pulled a blanket out of the warmer and offered it to Hildie.

"Th-thanks." Crap, her teeth were chattering. How often had she made this same offer to *her* patients? Countless times, but the comfort it gave surprised her. She snuggled into its warmth, kept her grip on Charlie's hand, and fought tears.

FASTER. *Faster!* Rex growled. *Faster, dammit!* "Carma" the police auto-nav proceeded toward Corona Tower at a safe and reasonable speed. It moved in sync with all the other auto-navs on the road. "Faster" was not in its programming.

Rex groaned and flopped down onto his bench seat. The impressions he received through the link from Charlie worried and confused him. *What is happening to you?*

Don't know. Feel like crap. Hildie's worried.

The car had barely cleared the Sixth-to-Seventh Precinct border when Hildie's text pinged his HUD. *Holy shit.* This really *was* as serious as it had seemed to him through the link. "Carma," he ordered, "Delete the destination: Corona Tower."

"Deleting the destination: Corona Tower." The car pulled

over to halt on the siding. "I hope you had a nice ride, Rex. You may now disembark or ask for a new destination."

Like I want to disembark here! Stupid car. He huffed out an impatient breath, but cursing at it would only make it tell him again that it hoped he'd had a nice ride. By now, he understood the importance of giving it clear directives. "Carma, go to new destination: Orangeboro Medical Center Secured Access Garage."

"Departing now for new destination: Orangeboro Medical Center Secured Access Garage." The car smoothly rolled out into a gap in the evening traffic, proceeded to a roundabout and used it to reverse course toward the new objective. At a safe and reasonable speed.

Just before the car reached the Med Center, it pulled over onto the siding without warning.

Alarm spiked like a knife through his chest. Rex crouched, defensive, hackles straight up. What happened? Was he trapped? Had the Transmondians hacked—*No. Get a grip. Observe.* He ran a shaky breathing pattern so he wouldn't hyperventilate. Looked at what was happening outside the car.

All the auto-navs he could see on this street had also just pulled over.

Next moment an ambulance rolled past, running lights but no sirens. It moved faster than "Carma" ever had. Without hesitation, it swung smartly into the Secured Access Garage entrance down the block.

Did your ambulance just arrive? Was that you?

We just stopped. EMT says we're here. Charlie's mental voice had a worrisome slur to it, as if he were drugged or exhausted.

I'm on a siding down the block. Yep, Carma's pulling back onto the road, he added, as the auto-nav resumed its route. Relief flooded through him. He gaped a wide stress-yawn, then shook himself. *I'll see you soon.*

Now that XK9s were people, they were allowed in the ER. But where was Charlie?

Rex's nemesis of five weeks ago, the chubby, blue-scrubs-clad fellow who'd thrown him out into the night, didn't seem to be working today. But Rex recognized the woman at the intake desk. "Hello, Shirley. My partner Charlie Morgan of the OPD just arrived by ambulance. Do you happen to know where they took him?"

She gave him a perplexed look. "Rex, right? I'm sorry your partner's hurt again. Lemme check." She didn't spend much time in her HUD stare. "He's not here—went straight to the Re-Gen Clinic. It's down that hall."

"As it happens, I know the way. Thank you!"

He found Hildie in the waiting room, wrapped in a thin hospital blanket and parked on a chair in the back corner. Head down, eyes closed, she'd drawn her knees up to her chest and clasped them in her arms. Her scent factors filled the almost-empty waiting room with the aching mid-tones of worry.

Rex went straight to her. "Hils, it is me." He nuzzled her, rubbed up against her. Discovered she was trembling. "Can you talk to me?"

Her answer came as a gasp and a lurch forward to wrap her arms around him. She pulled herself tight against his body and buried her face in his ruff. "What have we done to him, Rex?" she whispered into his fur. "What have we done to Charlie?"

CHARLIE LAY silent and alone under Zuni's scanner. He forced himself to breathe, to stay put. How long had he been here? Where was Hildie? Blood-draw after blood-draw in the ambulance and a long battery of scans and metabolic tests told him something must have gone badly wrong. Moments ago, this room had been full of techs and movement. Now Zuni'd gone off somewhere to burn serious com-time on spacelink calls to Primero.

Part of him quailed at the things he was feeling. *Run away!* But where?

Another part of him wanted to *smash something!* The urgency, the desire grew. But no. No! Definitely not that. *No smashing! No more smashing.* He'd done all too much of that. Would this push Hildie away? Would even *Rex* want to rethink having Chosen him?

No, I don't. I Chose you for life. He sensed the strong hint of a growl in his partner's mental voice. *It'll take something a lot worse than this to drive me away. Don't get all wound up. Hildie and I are in a waiting area. We will still be here when all of your tests are done, but we had to get out of the medical staff's way.*

Sorry. Thanks. Charlie closed his eyes. He ran through several breathing patterns, one after another. Each breath deliberate. Each one timed. He struggled to focus on that. Nothing more. No speculation. Worry gnawed at him. *No. Breathe.* Maybe Zuni would find a way to stop the rage attacks.

He dozed fitfully. Then startled awake from a dream about being crushed under Zuni's scanner.

Where was Hildie now? Had she already made her escape? His mental targeting readout pulsed a heart-sinking blood-red TLL, *Target Lock Lost.*

No, it's not. Rex's love pushed through to wrap him in tender warmth. *Your target's not lost. Hildie's sitting right here with me, waiting for you.*

Charlie sighed. *How's she holding up?*

Rex hesitated.

Alarm pulsed through Charlie. *Rex? How is Hildie holding up?*

He felt his partner's reluctance. *Don't take this wrong. She's crying, just at the moment. This has been pretty stressful. But Shady always says that crying is a stress-releaser for humans.*

I made her cry? This was terrible. What had he *become*? How had he allowed himself to accept this treatment that made him violent and angry, and took away his control? Shiv had tried to warn him, but—

His exam room door opened. Dr. Zuni stepped inside. "Okay, we're gaining some clarity on this thing. We believe you're having a rare, atypical drug reaction. I need to do another blood draw, to get a better idea of what's happening in your body chemistry."

Charlie scowled at him. "You … you *think*? You're still *not sure*?"

"Gaining clarity." Zuni's firm, forceful voice cut across Charlie's frantic, rising irritation. He reached for the IV line the EMTs had inserted into Charlie's elbow. The scanner extended a phlebotomy device.

"Haven't you sucked me dry *yet*?" Anger surged through Charlie's body. Spurred his pounding pulse. *This better do it, dammit.* He was tired of this!

Careful. Rex's worry through the link sparked new anger.

Charlie's fury erupted in a roar of rage. He kicked the scanner with all his might. Zuni yelped and leaped back. The massive scanner head smashed backward into the cabinets. It exploded into a rain of shards on impact.

Charlie flung up his arm-shield-encased left arm. It protected his face, but a rain of stinging shards swept across his body. He lurched up, enraged.

Something huge and heavy and furry and black slammed him down. Held him still. Poured love and hope and firm confidence and control into his brain link. *It's okay. You're all right. We're here. It's all right. You're good. Relax. Breathe.*

Cool, steady fingers finished taking the blood sample. Charlie's vision cleared enough to see Hildie hand it off to a distraught-looking Dr. Zuni. Several members of Zuni's staff peeked timidly around the edge of the door, their eyes wide and fearful.

Hildie offered a somewhat-watery-but-triumphant smile. "*That* ought to give us a definitive sample!"

"Yes." Zuni gulped, straightened, then passed the sample to a tech who'd been brave enough to approach.

Rex slipped sideways off Charlie's chest. "He is better, now. The fit has passed."

They helped him sit up.

It took a moment to get his breath back. Now he was flash-fried all over again, but also stabbed in dozens of places by tiny, sharp fragments. *Just great. I made shrapnel, and Rex dug it in.* Plus, his headache was back with a vengeance. That head-spinning, queasy aftermath had begun to feel way too familiar.

"Perhaps you two should stay with him this time," Zuni's PA said to Rex and Hildie. She moved them across the hall to a new exam room, then commenced gently tweezing out the several-dozen bits of broken scanner that were still embedded in his skin.

Charlie closed his eyes and lay back. "I think my trigger's getting touchier." He sweated and shook through the ordeal, as the rest of his spell or reaction or whatever-it-was gradually passed. *What have I become?* The question pounded through him to the rhythm of his pulse. *What have I become? What have I let myself turn into?*

The PA's ministrations barely registered. She finished plucking sharp pieces out of his skin at last. "I think I got them all, but let me know if you find any more. Unfortunately, I can't give you anything for the pain until we know what's happening in your body chemistry."

Of course not. "Thank you for getting the sharp stuff out."

"Just lie quiet and try to stay calm. I think Dr. Zuni is closing in on a solution."

He grimaced and opened his eyes. One of the staff had closed the door on the wrecked room across the hall and sealed it with an "OUT OF ORDER" notice. *All that expensive equipment.* Fragments of memory showed him more than enough to make him squirm.

"I keep thinking this is partly my fault," Hildie's face puckered with worry. "I'm the one who said, 'random variables be damned.' Should've *realized* I was tempting fate!"

"Me, too," Rex added. "I am the one who could not imagine why you would ever refuse to take this treatment."

Charlie shook his head. "If it's anyone's fault, it's mine."

"No, it most certainly is *not.*" Hildie scowled. "It's a bad reaction, like hives. Would you say it's all your fault if you got a bad rash?"

Charlie flashed on the shattered railing, the destroyed French doors. That scanner, for pity's sake. The appalling disarray he'd wrought. "Hives don't smash things."

"Neither does anaphylactic shock." Hildie hadn't lost her frown. "Doesn't mean it's harmless *or* voluntary."

Rex lolled his tongue, then nuzzled Charlie's side. "You are not going to win this one. She knows too much."

"That's true," Hildie agreed. "I do."

Rex walked over to poke his head out into the hall, then widened the brain link so Charlie could gain a sense of what he saw. Zuni was back on another spacelink to Primero in an open cubicle down the hall. He conducted an animated conversation in Chonoan, then pulled up Charlie's latest blood panel on his case pad, and visibly shifted to excited relief.

Once off the com, he came to the new exam room and explained his conclusions in medical-ese. Hildie listened and nodded. She apparently followed all the hormones, chemical reactions, and drug names. Charlie and Rex sat well within earshot, listening to every word. But through the brain link they admitted to each other that neither quite followed what Dr. Zuni said.

All I know is that your personal scent undergoes a shift when you get angry, Rex said. *It's pretty distinctive.*

I wonder if a safe word at such a moment would help you warn me?

I suppose we won't know till we try. What safe word should we use?

Charlie's mind blanked. What safe word could possibly get through to him in the heat of such a moment? *What do the changes smell like?*

Rex laid back his ears. *I get notes of coffee grounds, burnt rope, and rat poop.*

Well, that's pretty humiliating. Really? I smell like rat poop?

Rex lowered his head and fluttered his tail. *Kind of rat-poop-ish. Along with the others.*

Pretty distinctive safe word, though. Charlie sighed. *"Rat poop" it is.*

Rex fluttered his tail again, then his tongue flicked the underside of Charlie's chin. *If you're okay with it.*

Hildie turned to Charlie. "Did you follow all that?"

"I'm sorry, no. Rex and I were discussing how I smell when I have an episode."

Dr. Zuni froze and stared at him. "The metabolic shift is discernible to him?"

"Oh, yes," Rex said. "We worked out a safe word for when I detect it. We thought there is a chance it might help."

"Like a medical-alert dog?" Zuni asked.

"Forensic olfaction specialist," Rex said. "Scent discernment is my thing."

Zuni nodded. "Of course. That's brilliant. But with any luck, I now know enough to shift your drug regimen so you won't be so vulnerable to these reactions. Give me a minute to do that." He picked up a case pad, then scrolled through its readout with a scowl.

"Meanwhile, let me translate his diagnosis," Hildie said. "We think you've hit a tipping point for an unusual drug reaction. It's been building up, all through your recovery. Sometimes this kind of issue doesn't manifest right away." She gave Charlie a rueful look. "And as if that wasn't bad enough, the chemical change triggers an adrenal overreaction. That's what—to use layman's terms—makes you go berserk."

He frowned. "So … It's all in my chemistry? Not in my head?"

"Oh, it's in your head, too." Zuni looked up from his case pad. "The latent psychological issues that come with post-traumatic stress can't be minimized. But the hormonal shift from the drug reaction is what removed your control. That's the piece I'm working on now."

He can give me a sanity pill? Charlie ran another breathing pattern, while that idea rolled through him. He shared a look with Rex and Hildie.

We can only hope, Rex said.

CHAPTER 47

A STRATEGIC RETREAT

Charlie lay on a recliner in Zuni's infusion suite and tried not to feel daunted. Turned out his doctor didn't exactly have a sanity *pill.*

"You'll need a series of IV infusions." Dr. Zuni looked up from his case pad. "I've decided to start with one now, then another tomorrow, and the third Sunday. Come by for the last one on Monday after work. I'll review a blood sample before and after each one. See if your chemistry is normalizing properly."

Just what I wanted to do. Charlie glanced toward Rex, but he would've caught the tongue-loll and the tail-wag through the link even if he hadn't seen it. "Here's hoping it works."

"Roger that." Hildie straightened in her chair by the door, but Charlie read stress and fatigue in her expression and body language.

"Hils, there's no point in your sitting around in the waiting room for another hour-plus." He might long to snuggle with his Medicine Goddess once this was over. But it took a while for Zuni to craft a treatment plan for him. During the wait she sagged deeper and deeper into an uncomfortable-looking slump in her chair, dark-circled eyes closed.

He hated the thought of sending her away, but she'd come to Corona in search of mutual relaxation and walked straight into a nightmare. "You probably should go home to Feliz and get a good night's sleep."

"Yeah, I think you're right." She dragged herself to her feet.

Mindful of Goddess-care, he added, "Let me call a car for you."

But then Zuni's nurse arrived to start the infusion, while another drew more blood from his arm. Next thing he knew, Hildie had gone.

I need to pop over to Elaine's for a few minutes. Rex retreated to the door. *I'll be back before you're done here.*

Charlie closed his eyes and tried to rest. They darkened the exam room and gave him a light blanket. There was only so much one could do to make any room restful during an infusion, but he was tired enough to doze. An indeterminate length of time later, he blinked, yawned, and checked his HUD readout.

He'd been here ... nearly two hours. The IV pump registered 2% to go. Maybe he should check if Rex was back?

His HUD beeped: a message from Hildie. His chest tightened.

HI, CHARLIE,

WE NEED TO TALK. DO YOU MIND COMING BY FELIZ SOMETIME THIS WEEKEND? PLEASE LET ME KNOW. I REALLY NEED TO SEE YOU IN PERSON.

LOVE,

HILDIE.

P.S. DON'T WORRY ABOUT INTERRUPTIONS FROM LAROCK. THERE'S A LISTENER-MANDATED 36-HOUR CONTACT-BLOCK ON HIM.

P.P.S. PLEASE COME.

. . .

SEVERAL SECONDS TICKED BY. He stared at the words, chilled with foreboding, until they swam in his vision. *Breathe, stupid!* He gasped in a ragged breath, then ran a careful breathing pattern. It did nothing to still his misgivings.

She'd signed it, "Love, Hildie."

She "needed" to see him.

Those were good signs … Right?

This breathing pattern was a mess. He swallowed, gasped, then tried again.

Oh, God, what could he say to her, after this disaster of an evening?

How should he—

The IV pump started beeping. It was empty. The beeping made him frantic. Part of him rose up with fury and wanted to rip out the IV line—! No, that part probably smelled way too much like rat poop, and he was already exhausted. He scowled and squashed the impulse. This time it subsided after a brief struggle and left him only *semi*-flash-fried. *Ugh.* He should always be so lucky.

One of Zuni's nurses arrived to turn off the beep and remove the IV, then take a follow-up blood sample. "That's all for today. I can release you now." The nurse helped Charlie sit up, then made him stay there until he was certain Charlie didn't feel dizzy. "Take it real easy this weekend. Get all the sleep you can. We'll see you tomorrow."

"Sure. Yeah." Charlie trudged out the clinic's exit. He met Rex in the hallway outside. *We need to go to Feliz Tower.*

HILDIE PUSHED past Abi at the Feliz gate. Her brother caught her arm, frowned. "He should come to you. Make him come to you."

She scowled back at him. "He *did* come to me. Straight from the hospital. After more than an hour on an IV, and a *hellish* evening. He already felt horrible. I'm *not* making him walk up all those switchbacks!"

Abi's mouth set in a humorless line. "Then I'm going down with you."

"No. Please!" She pulled away and headed for the switchbacks.

Abi didn't follow, but she knew him. He'd be watching. She figured a lot of her relatives were. She hurried down the white gravel way. Charlie toiled upward considerably more slowly.

She reached out to him as they closed the last meter. The pain and exhaustion on his face appalled her. She pulled him straight into a hard, full-body embrace. His arms tightened, warm and strong and wonderful, around her.

"I am so, *so* sorry," he said. "Oh, Hils, I *never* wanted to scare you like that."

"I know." If only she could abide in this sweet moment! But a tremor deep in his body told her he'd pushed himself well past exhaustion. He was probably only on his feet by force of will. She soaked up as much of his embrace as she could take in good conscience, then pulled back. "Let's get you to the car. You need to sit, and I want to talk in private."

He glanced uphill over her shoulder, then nodded. They made their way back to the car and Rex.

"Transmondians probably will not expect me to be here," Rex said. "Should I take a hike?"

"No." Hildie grimaced. Even sitting here inside this car raised his risk, didn't it? *Crap.* "No, stay. You need to hear this, too."

Charlie's eyes widened. He went a little grayer than he already looked. Unfortunately, he wasn't wrong.

They sat in the car. The doors closed and the cooling system kicked on. She looked up, startled.

"Safety feature," Rex said. "Leave it powered down, and it rapidly turns into an oven, especially during daylight." He squeezed into the far side of the passenger cabin. "I shall shut up now. Pretend that I am a rug."

Hildie gulped. *I can do this. I have to do this.* She and a Listener had talked about it, after she'd tried to nap but kept startling awake from dreams, flashbacks, or whatever one wanted to call them. Now she just needed to say the words to *Charlie.* "A kiss, for courage?"

He gave her one of his patented knee-melting, panty-moistening, *Oh, my God, how can I possibly say these words* kisses. She gave as good as she got, for this one, last time. When they pulled back, his eyes had brightened and his color was better.

Her pulse pounded like thunder. She was *so* gonna miss those kisses. She blew out a breath, shaken. "I need to stop seeing you."

He stared at her.

The stricken anguish on his face made her want to flinch away, but she held his gaze. "While you're dealing with this anger thing, it's not safe for me to be around."

He shook his head. "Hils, no! I—"

She raised her hand. "It's not safe for our *relationship.* I know you'd never willingly hurt me. You've never yet been directly violent toward me."

His shoulders drooped. "Then, what? Why?"

"It's the sheer violent *force* of your reactions. I keep flashing back to you shattering those doors. To the wreckage of that scanner. To the fury on your face."

He went ashy-gray. "You're having *flashbacks?*"

"Sorry, but ... yeah." She hunched her shoulders and gave him a rueful look, her stomach like a stone. "That's not good for our relationship."

The horror in his expression deepened.

"I think maybe I need some distance." The need to admit this cut sharp as a knife through her heart. "We can't predict how many more times you'll have a 'rage attack.' And ... well, maybe it's better if I don't see them. I've only experienced a few incidents, so far. I think—I *believe* I can work through those."

Charlie grimaced. "But there's a limit."

"If I'm going to stop being afraid, I can't live in fear." She shook her head, her gut an icy chasm. "And right now... a part of me is afraid of you."

Charlie's body slumped. "The rage incidents came too rapidly. You never had time to recover."

Her throat ached. She'd been determined not to cry, but tears spilled down. "I l-love you so m-m-much! And yet I'm s-s-scared we'll go back to C-Corona, and it'll ... it'll h-happen again!"

He gathered her into his arms. They clung to each other. Why did this have to hurt so much?

She frowned into his shoulder. "I believe—I *know* that you and Zuni will work it out. I feel like such a *weakling*, to pull away now! I'm letting you down, after I said 'no matter what.' Washing out, just when you need me!"

Charlie shook his head. "No. No, that's not a helpful way to frame it. Sometimes a strategic retreat is simply the thing you have to do."

"So ... you understand?" She was having a hard enough time understanding it *herself*. She gazed at him, heavy with regret.

He tucked her in closer against his chest, but he moved gently and *so very* carefully. His ribs expanded, then a gust of air moved across her arm from his sigh. "Maybe I wouldn't have, before the *Asalatu.*"

Before everything changed. She bit her lip.

"Maybe not even till after I washed out of the ERT that third time." He gave her a rueful look. "But we can't always be as impervious as we think we should be."

He really does understand. The tightness in her chest eased a little.

"We call it 'being strong,' but it's a false and brittle imitation of strength." Charlie bowed his head. "Sometimes, all we can do is recognize a bad situation and withdraw from it while we still have other options."

She grimaced but nodded. "This sucks *so much.*"

"Let's just say we're taking a break. Give Zuni time to get me balanced. Then … when I think I can trust myself again … may I call you?"

Oh, God, please call! "Yes. Call me. You'll know when it's time. And I'll *always* take your call."

CHAPTER 48

RECOVERING

The sharp smell of sawdust and the racket of power tools greeted Charlie before he reached the doorway of what would someday be the XK9 Special Investigations Unit. It was early Monday morning after an endless weekend without Hildie. Charlie yearned for something positive to focus on, and this looked promising.

Only two weeks out from a time when this place was no more than a twinkle in Chief Klein's eye, they'd made great progress. Already he could get a sense of what it would become.

The bones of it were there, sketched in by the rough framing. There'd be a central common room, with office spaces around the perimeter. Not just little cubbyhole spaces the size of a sleep box, either. These had room for XK9-sized dog beds and full, double-sided workstations for partners and dogs, plus places for Penny and Fujimoto. And GR Chamber Three. He smiled. *Looks promising.* He widened the link for Rex.

Charlie received a surge of pleasure, an impression of a tail wagging at full-fan. *I haven't looked in since last week. They must've worked all weekend.*

A sawdusty woman in a hardhat and coveralls approached him. She retracted her eye protection. "Help you?"

"Can I access GR Chamber Three from this side yet?"
She shook her head. "'Nother week."

"Thanks."

She gave him a vague wave, reactivated her eye protection,
and returned to work.

He sighed. *Well, it was worth a shot. Damn. Basilisk Passage,
ho.*

Better you than me. Good luck.

Some faithful dog you are. Charlie marched down the hall,
rounded the corner. Activated his wearable audio and optics and
steeled himself.

Just as she had last time, Missy Cranston leaped into his path
with an infuriated shriek. "Out! Out! Get out of my unit!"

Charlie pushed past her as gently as he could. *Calm. Professional. Just get through this.* "You know I'm authorized for
Chamber Three." Irritation clawed at him. He avoided making
eye contact, but his patience shredded and his pulse kicked
higher.

"I don't care what high muckety-muck told you that, you're
still not welcome here! You're nothing but trouble! You've never
been anything but trouble! You're a loser, and you always will
be! Get out!" She scrambled alongside, then thrust herself into
his path a second time.

Irritation roared into fury. He clenched his jaws. Struggled to
maintain control, but red rage clouded his vision. The urgent
need to smack her away—*hard!*—surged through him.

Rat poop! Rat poop! Rex cried through the link.

Charlie stopped, head down. Fists clenched. *You can't smell
me from there.*

*I can feel you! Don't listen to her! She's trying to get a rise out of
you, but she has no idea how dangerous you are. Charlie! Listen! You
could kill her, if you don't get a grip.*

Charlie dragged in a desperate, labored breath. He clenched
his jaws and clung to the last shreds of his control. Counted to
five. He was on new meds. He could resist this. He held himself

still. Breathed through the desperate need to smash her into silence.

He pushed her from his path again as gently as he could make himself be.

She shoved herself in front of him again. "Bully! Big bully! You've got some nerve!"

Next time he came here, he must wear ear protection. He ground his teeth. Took long, careful breaths. Focused on the door to Chamber Three. He could do this. Just get past her.

"And if you think you can get me jammed up on some kinda stupid-ass, trumped-up charges, you better think again! You have no idea what you're messing with!" She quivered with fury.

He shook his head. Kept his gaze locked on Chamber Three. Dragged in another breath and prayed for calm. "Just let me do my work. You're making no sense."

"Like hell I'm not!" She launched herself at him, hands like claws, aiming for his eyes.

He caught her wrists, spun her, pinned her arms behind her. It was a move he'd practiced regularly while patrolling the Entertainment District on the graveyard watch. A crappy patrol, but she'd made his life so miserable he'd have taken *any* assignment, just to get out of the GR Unit.

The practiced movements came easier with his new strength and quicker reflexes. It felt good to *do something*. His fury ebbed. A new protocol kicked in from months of training and practice.

She struggled in vain to break free. "How dare you lay hands on me!"

"You're the one who assaulted me, remember?" He held her in a firm grip, but he also now had a better grip on himself. He blew out a long breath in relief. Adrenaline reaction made his hands shake, but he held her just firmly enough. Mustn't break those sticklike bones.

She assaulted you? For real? Rex asked.

Charlie forwarded the recordings from his wearables. Missy

yelled and twisted, but she wasn't going anywhere. An old proverb about having a tiger by the tail leaped to mind.

Oh, yeah. That's clearly assault, Rex agreed. *And now she's resisting arrest.*

Rex ... was right, actually. If it was anyone else, they'd already be in cuffs. *Okay, then.* He retrieved zip-cuffs from his belt. Cinched them tight on her wrists, but not too tight. Relief washed over him. Yes! Back in control!

Missy froze. Blessed silence ensued. Possibly she was too astonished to speak, or maybe she realized she'd stepped too far across a line.

"Melissa Cranston, you are under arrest for assault on an officer of the law." Mind reeling a little, ears still ringing in the abrupt silence, Charlie rattled off the warning about her rights and gratefully fell back on his training. There was a protocol for this, thank God, and he knew it by heart. "Morgan to Dispatch. I have an incident in the GR Unit. Assault on a law enforcement officer. Subject is in cuffs. Request transport."

Uniformed Police Officers arrived within a minute. He explained the situation and the assault charge, then forwarded his sensors' recordings. "I'm on a tight time frame to get some data downloaded in GR-Three, so she was also interfering with the discharge of my duties."

"We'll take her, Detective Morgan," one of the UPOs said. "Please upload your incident report ASAP."

Like I needed more formwork. But they had to receive it, to press charges formally. "Will do. Thanks for the backup."

They nodded, then took her away.

Charlie let out a long, shaky breath. *That was unexpected.* He shuddered, but the flash-fried sensation packed only a shadow of its former punch. He kept his feet, not even dizzy, and stared after her. *After all those months of her abuse, this seems unreal.*

But you controlled yourself. You did exactly what you needed to do. Rex's relief poured through the link to match his own.

That was way closer than it should've been. Maybe he should sit down pretty soon.

The important thing is—this time you regained control. You didn't go into a rage. You can do this!

I owe you for the safe word. He smiled. Turned toward Chamber Three, then stopped again.

Ernie and Jenny, his erstwhile fellow sufferers, had emerged from chambers One and Two at some point during Missy's arrest. They gaped at Charlie.

"You actually ... *arrested* her." Jenny sounded as if she didn't quite believe that was possible.

Charlie grimaced. "She assaulted me. It's all on my optics."

Jenny peered at him, face pinched with sudden worry. "Are you injured?"

"Don't think so." She'd been going for his eyes. His quick reflexes had saved him.

"There's a scratch by your eye." Ernie looked him over, then glanced toward the exit. "How long d'you think she'll be gone?"

"Not sure." Charlie sighed. It really was hard to guess that answer. So far, she'd used her connection with her brother to get away with outrageous things. But had she ever been caught by wearable sensors assaulting an officer before?

"You should go to the Med Station." Jenny's worried look hadn't eased. "Have them certify you fit."

"But my downloads—clock's ticking, and they're waiting on my After-Incident, over in Detention."

"Don't worry." Ernie smiled at him. "Go ahead and initialize the downloads. Use a blind case number, so it stays confidential. I can tend 'em for you. I owe you, after that bonus from the SBI."

Charlie smiled. "So you did get one? Smooth."

"Better yet, Missy was none the wiser."

"Excellent. Now, if you'll excuse me?" Charlie opened the door, made his way to the controls, then sat heavily and powered up the unit. He leaned back against the ergonomic support with a sigh. That scratch by his left eye stung. Jenny was right. He'd alleged assault. He *should* go to the Med Station, even though he knew he wasn't seriously hurt. Maybe he could work on his After-Incident while they had him under their scanner. His console blinked "ready." He set the controls to blind the case number and initiated his downloads.

His mind replayed the arrest like a repeating loop. It still didn't seem real. In all the time he'd known her, Missy'd never made such a blunder. She'd always stopped just short of an arrestable offense. Her record with Human Resources was atrocious, but Secretary Pandra had always shielded her from facing consequences. Nothing she'd done had violated a criminal statute, until today. Why slip up now? What had changed? And how would her brother react?

Charlie blew out a worried breath. He might be getting a handle on his unbalanced meds—but had he just destroyed his career?

It took Razor a couple of tries, but he got to his feet by himself when Rex arrived at lunchtime on Monday. Liz hovered nearby, just in case. Razor seemed happy to see him, but Liz looked and smelled exhausted. She sagged back onto a recliner, once it was clear Razor would be steady on his feet.

"We have been worried about you." Rex sniffed him over in detail; Razor returned the gesture.

"I have improved a lot since I came out of re-gen," Razor said. "I can smell you!" His ears drooped. "Some, anyway. My nose is still not working well, but I improve a little each day. I am 'exercising' my nose, along with my legs. Come! Let me show you the obstacle course."

Liz sat up, bleary-eyed. "Give me a minute to find my shoes."

"Stay there," Rex said. "You need to rest. I can take care of Razor."

Liz hesitated. "I probably shouldn't—"

"You worry too much." Razor's ears went down. "Sleep! It is painful to see you like this!"

She lay back down with a groan. "If you insist," she mumbled.

"Room, darken," Razor said. The window opaqued, until the formerly sunny room was shrouded like twilight. He turned to Rex, dialed his vocalizer to its lowest setting. "Maybe she will sleep."

It pleased Rex that Charlie had finally managed a nap, too. After his adventures in the GR Unit, he'd shuttled from the HQ Med Station to Dr. Zuni's suite at Orangeboro Med for his second infusion, then home in Carma. He was sound asleep at Corona Tower now, and Rex hoped he'd stay that way for a good long while.

Razor led Rex through an outer door to a courtyard that had been the source of the light in his room. "Welcome to Dr. Sandler's new rehab wonderland."

Rex stared. He hadn't been out here since well before the yard's transformation. The exercise area once had consisted bare dirt interspersed with listless clumps of grass. Now an undulating series of grassy hummocks rolled along the left-hand wall, all the way to the hydrotherapy pool. A level area full of new equipment lay just outside the door. He looked up to check the upper levels, then blinked. A clear security dome now capped the entire courtyard. Dr. Sandler—or was it the OPD?—certainly had spared no expense on security.

"Pretty amazing, is it not?" Razor stared upward also, then met Rex's gaze. "It seems elaborate, but ... I hate to say that before they put the dome on, I was afraid to come out here. I am gradually growing more brave again, but I am grateful for the dome."

Worry nipped at Rex. How could Razor work, if he feared to come out under the open sky—or even what passed for sky on Rana? His Packmate's motor coordination might slowly be coming back, along with his sense of smell. Maybe his courage would, too. "Show me your obstacle course."

"It is short and simple now. It will become more complex as I improve." Razor approached a pair of low poles held in place by a frame. He walked across them, stepping between the poles, then looked back at them. "Until yesterday, I could not do that with all four feet. Not without stopping, or touching a pole, anyway. Now it is becoming easier."

Rex stepped over the poles with barely a thought about how to place his feet.

But Razor had focused on his next objective. He moved on to a ramp that created a small incline up. It stood backed against another ramp that led down. He rocked forward to get himself started up the first ramp. He staggered at the top but did not tumble off. Very carefully, he made his way down the other side. At the bottom of the second ramp, he sighed, panting. "That one is still a challenge. I need to stop for a moment."

Rex walked around the ramps. They would have posed no difficulty for him, but perhaps Razor didn't need to see that. He smelled his Packmate's fatigue, his frustration. Suddenly the Chief's elaborate security precautions looked more reasonable. One blow-dart out of nowhere had done this to Razor. He was coming back from it, but his recovery clearly would take many more weeks.

"Chief Klein has come to check on Liz and me every day, even before I could have visitors. Pam and several other friends have come to see Liz, too." Razor's tongue hung long, but he lifted his head. "I showed the Chief my scent wall." He swung his nose toward a head-high wall at the right-hand edge of the yard. It was perhaps half a meter thick and five meters long, with all sorts of cups, tubes and boxes recessed into it.

Rex approached it. A variety of scents quickly wafted past his nose: different ones emanated from each cup, tube, or hole. It looked like the scent-discrimination training boards his puppy group had used when they were babies. These scents were kind of basic and obvious, but if that was where Razor needed to start, to regain his earlier, fine-tuned olfactory skills, Rex was glad it was here. "It is helping?"

"Yes. Both the practice, and the variety. I am greatly relieved that each day my nose works better." Razor hesitated. "Chief Klein told me the man who shot me still will not talk, but they are now certain the poison is from the Transmondian Intelligence Service."

Rex returned to Razor's side. "Yes, we heard that too. It is not a surprise."

"I hope he will talk." Razor showed his teeth, ears laid back. "I would like to ask him several things, myself. Truth be told, I also would like to bite his throat out, but that would inhibit his ability to answer questions."

"True." Rex lolled his tongue, pleased his Packmate could make a joke about his situation. "I think the whole Pack shares your wish. The throat I crave the most, however, is that of Col. Wisniewski."

"Too bad he is in Transmondia." Razor emphasized his words with a growl.

Rex growled his agreement. "Or so we believe."

"What?" Razor's ears snapped erect. "Where else would he be?"

Rex hesitated. He hadn't even shared this with Shady yet, but no one had a better right to know than Razor. "Do you recall having met Col. Wisniewski?"

"I am happy to say that the poison did not affect my memory as badly as my nose and legs. I only met him once, but I do remember."

Rex nodded. Once would be enough. "Do you know if Petunia met him?"

"She was in my group, so yes, she met him once for sure." Razor cocked his head. "Why?"

"On Friday, she and Scout patrolled in the Hub. They assisted SA Gerritsen's onsite interviews with dock workers. They hoped to scare up leads about anything unusual that the workers might have remembered from the time the *Izgubil* was docked there, so she was primed to notice anything odd."

"What did she notice?"

Itchy prickles ran down Rex's spine. The hunter within him lifted its ears. "She said there was one brief moment when she thought she smelled Col. Wisniewski. She and Walter investigated, of course. She never managed to reacquire the scent. Our people at the Port have been on the lookout since then, but no one has been able to scare up any other sign of him."

"You think there is a chance he is on-Station?"

"I think it is possible. Elaine refuses to let me go up there and sniff around. 'Too dangerous,' she says. She is adamant. Will not even discuss it."

"She is right. Wisniewski is clearly after you. Why else send an agent to spy on you, then bug Corona Tower after you caught the spy?"

Rex growled. "I keep thinking someone should sniff around up there and see if they can find him."

"I think that would be an excellent way for a dog to get himself shot with a poison dart." Razor laid his ears back. "You do not want to feel what that is like. Listen to SSA Adeyeme."

Rex sighed. "Now you sound like Charlie."

"You should definitely listen to him, too. Let us change the subject. Did they ever find your mother and Dr. Cho?"

"That actually may not be changing the subject much." He underscored his words with another growl. "Mike Santiago's friend Sheriff Ibsen went to Dr. Cho's home, after Elaine and I requested a welfare-check. No one was there, but he said little things did not seem right. As if they had left in a hurry. He ordered two of his deputies stake the place out. A pair of armed men came to the house, looked all around, then broke in. At that point the deputies arrested them, but within an hour Transmondian State Police came and took them away. They basically ordered everyone to forget that anything had happened there.

Sheriff Ibsen is not happy. He is quietly continuing to look for Dr. Cho and my mother, but that is all I know."

"I always liked Nell and Dr. Cho. I hope they are all right." Razor yawned. His tongue was not hanging quite so long now, but he probably should return to his room soon.

"Me too." Rex cocked his head. "Pardon, but is there a place to get a drink?"

"Over here." A small water feature by the wall provided a basin of fresh, always-running water. Both Rex and Razor took a long drink. When they'd finished Razor yawned again, then glanced toward his room. "I wonder if Liz is sleeping."

"We probably should—" Rex's com rang. Startled, he saw it was Elaine's line. "Rex here. What has happened?"

"Sorry to interrupt your visit. They've spotted Neil Dolan on Wheel Three. I've asked Howardsboro PD to pick him up."

"Are you in the war room? I can be there in five minutes." He sent the call-signal for his car.

CHAPTER 49

HOWARDSBORO

Rex bounded into the war room, fresh from the Sandler Clinic and his visit to Razor. "Is Dolan in custody yet?"

"Not yet." Elaine looked up from the screen she'd been studying with Mike, Shiv, and a man in SBI blue-black whom Rex had not yet met. "Howardsboro PD lost him."

Rex's ears clamped flat at this news, but then bounced erect. The new man had a gun case slung from a strap over his shoulder. It smelled as if it had a real rifle in it. "Elaine, who is our sharpshooter?"

Ranan citizens were barred from using what Rex thought of as "real" firearms, but he'd learned that the Station's law enforcement agencies maintained a small cadre of sharpshooters for unusual situations.

Mike and the new man gave him startled looks, but Elaine and Shiv smiled.

"Rex, this is my senior Lead Special Agent, Dominic Wei," Mike said. "He and the rest of SIT Alpha were about to transition out of Howardsboro and come here, but this latest turn of events has put that on pause. Dom, this is XK9 Pack Leader Rex Dieter-Nell."

"So this is the leader of the famous talking dogs," the new man, Wei, said. "Hello. What makes you think I'm a sharpshooter?"

Rex snorted. "Aside from the gun case? Real guns are easy to smell. How long have you been in the cadre?"

Wei's smile crinkled the skin by his eyes. His scent blossomed with fragrant appreciation. "Reserve cadre now, but still qualified. About eight years."

Elaine grinned, too. "I was surprised to discover that Rex is something of a firearms enthusiast—but he *is* Transmondian born and trained."

"An enthusiast as long as they are not aimed at me," Rex said. "A nine-mil is far superior to an EStee for stopping power."

"True, but I *also* appreciate not having them pointed at me." Wei tipped his head toward the diminutive Senior Special Agent. "Cadre's an interesting career. E. recruited me."

Rex wagged his tail. He'd discovered a few weeks ago that although Elaine no longer had time to maintain first-line proficiency, she was still in the reserve cadre herself. "At any rate, I welcome it today, if we intend to assist Howardsboro with their apprehension efforts. I am pleased you seem to be taking Dr. Cho's warning about the Dolans seriously."

Elaine frowned. "I'm putting together a group for Howardsboro, but I hesitate to add you to it."

Rex laid back his ears but did not argue directly. He knew why she hesitated. "Perhaps you could get me up to date on what has happened."

"Biosensors picked up Neil Dolan's face, gait, and even some touch-DNA, near a subterranean plaza in Howardsboro, on Wheel Three," Elaine said. "Unfortunately, Howardsboro PD lost him."

"I can sniff him out." Rex's tail waved high and fierce. "A trail that fresh? It will be easy."

Reluctance surged In Elaine's scent factors. She frowned. "I know it *would* be."

"We must find Dolan as quickly as possible." Rex curbed an impulse to bolt out the door, bound for Wheel Three. He growled under his breath, couldn't hold his feet still. "If Howardsboro PD knows this, Whisper may know it, too."

Elaine shared a look with Mike. "I told you that's what he'd say."

"Send me." Rex's pulse pounded harder. This could be his chance to get back into a Hunt in person! "Time is of the essence. I am here now. I can leave immediately."

She scowled. "We've been through this. I know you're going stir-crazy, but I don't want you exposed to any TIS agents."

Rex clamped his jaws tight on a snarl and bowed his head. *Elaine will respond best to reason.* "Will any TIS agents be looking for an XK9 in Howardsboro?"

Her expression and her scent bespoke resistance, but she hesitated.

"He's right, you know," Shiv said. "The only people who will know an XK9 is coming to Howardsboro are Bridget, her team, and our Borough Office chief. Plus, he *is* already here."

She gave him a long, hard stare. Deep affection and terrified reluctance blossomed in her scent.

Her affection warmed Rex, even though it complicated his goal. *She cares for me. It would grieve her to see me harmed.* But the call of the hunt pulsed through him. *How can I convince her?* He widened his eyes, lowered his head, and fluttered his tail. "I will not defy you. But I will plead."

She frowned. The reluctance in her scent swirled cold and fearful, but gradually a steely new scent of decisiveness pushed it aside. She groaned but nodded. "All right, damn it. You're right. *Damn* your puppy-eyes and your logic!"

Rex kept himself from bounding about with great volleys of delighted barking, but he straightened, ears up and tail fanning his delight.

She grimaced. "This is against my better judgment, but I can't think of a counter-argument that holds water. I do want at least one more XK9 to go with you, though. Which one should I send?"

"Elle or Scout are our best trackers, but they are both far away." He clamped his ears flat. Elle was in court today, testifying about her part in tracking down a burglary ring two months ago, and Scout had gone to Green Mountain University with Petunia to speak to a Forensics class. Tux and Crystal were almost as far away, consulting with Dr. SCISCO at Station Polytechnic. Victor was working his murder case. Shady and Cinnamon were due back from lunch soon. They'd been working in the Evidence Cavern. "I would prefer that if I am gone, Shady stay here to manage the Pack, although I will admit they are scattered elsewhere today."

"That leaves Cinnamon," Shiv said. "I, um, was in the middle of lunch with Berwyn, Cinnamon, and his sister Rowan when you called, E."

Wei shot a curious look at Shiv. "Lunch?"

"We bumped into each other in Central Plaza." Shiv's scent went hot and sharp with embarrassment, despite his airy tone. "Pure chance. I thought, 'Sure, why not?'"

Rex kept his mouth closed. He looked away. *Oh, yeah. That was a pure-chance meeting, for sure.*

From their expressions, Elaine and Mike were not buying this, either, but not willing to challenge him on it, any more than Rex was.

Elaine bit her lip and keyed her com. "Hi. Adeyeme here. Please convey my apologies to your sister, but I need you and Cinnamon in the war room, stat." She grinned at his reply. "See you in five, then. Thanks!"

She clicked off, laughed, then shot a look at Shiv. "He's on his way. Said if he had to look at one more cute outfit for Cousin Willow's baby, he was going to run screaming through Central Plaza."

Shiv sighed. "We did hear a lot about Cousin Willow's baby at lunch. Rowan's in the city to do a little pre-Solstice shopping."

"Solstice?" Wei asked. "On a space station?"

Shiv shrugged. "The Family is Wiccan. They're observant. The date is traditional."

Wei gave him a long look. "Traditional. Ri-i-i-ight."

Shiv scowled at him. "You questioning people's religions, now, Dom?"

Wei shook his head. "Far be it from me, to hoot and point at superstitious claptrap."

"Your forbearance is effing damn breathtaking." Shiv's frown deepened into a scowl.

Wei held up his hands. "Solstice. Got it." He sighed, then muttered, "Criminy!"

THE EMERGENCY SERVICES Express elevator landed inside Howardsboro's Grand Central Terminal. Rex, Shiv, Cinnamon, Berwyn, Mike, and Wei emerged, having changed into personal armor on the way down. Mike and Shiv handed their gear bags, now stuffed with the humans' regular on-duty clothing, to a pair of young men in SBI blue-black who'd been waiting next to the elevator. "See you back at HQ," Mike told them.

They nodded. "Good luck, sir," one of them answered.

Next a slender young woman strode forward to greet Rex's Orangeboro group. Her gray-tan gear and her burly, similarly-garbed companions made her and her crew stand out rather starkly from the crowd. She'd taken off her helmet to reveal all of her face. Her curly, shoulder-length hair was the same tone as Cinnamon's. Humans probably would see it as "red."

She grinned at Mike and Wei. "Welcome back t' Howardsboro. I see ye've brought some o' th' wondrous hounds."

Mike smiled. "Good to see you again, Bridget. Please meet LSA Shiva Shimon, and Reserve Agents Berwyn Yael, Rex Dieter-Nell, and Cinnamon Lightfoot-Floss." He turned to his own party. "This is DPO Bridget Riordan Ryan of the Howardsboro PD. She's been helping us unravel some of the connections between the Saoirse Front and the Whisper Syndicate."

Ryan and her crew led them through the terminal crowd, into a Central Plaza ringed by birches and Japanese maples. No oranges in bloom. Rex hadn't expected to miss them so much.

"Neil was spotted on the Sionainn's Sub-Level Six." Ryan pronounced the neighborhood's name "Shon-*inn*." Having seen it spelled in the report, Rex had wondered. There also had been a surveillance vid-clip attached to the report. In it, Neil Dolan walked into the corner of the surveillance-cam's view carrying a pizza box. He stopped, looked up, made a horrified expression, then darted out of frame.

Rex wanted to see Neil run like that in real life. He'd give him the kind of takedown he loved best. "Where are the elevators to the Sionainn? I am eager to start our hunt."

"Sure an' *that'll* take some gettin' used to." Ryan smiled at Rex. "Tis one thing t' know ye talk, another to hear ye."

He cocked his head. "What sort of place is it?"

"Oh, we'll be guidin' ye into one o' the real beauty-spots o' Howardsboro, today." Rex already had imagined that Neil Dolan was holed up in the Howardsboro version of the Five-Ten. Her ironic tone confirmed it.

He nodded. "What weapons might we face there?"

"There's th' usual run of illegal EStees, knives, clubs, an' th' like."

"What about *real* guns?" Rex glanced toward Wei's rifle case.

"'Tis *possible*, but I hope not likely." Ryan frowned. "The sightin' location's not far from the elevator—about three blocks. But I'll warn ye, it sees some foot traffic. Our K9s couldn't follow the scent. 'Course, we didn't have much of an exemplar."

"I have memorized the scent profile, and so has Cinnamon," Rex said. "Our noses have cleared, and the trail is fresh. Foot traffic overlay should not be an issue."

Ryan put on her helmet. Rex and the others followed her into the Safety Services Express. Even though the elevator car was larger than a normal civilian one, she and her six-person squad, plus two XK9s and the four humans from Orangeboro, filled it. They rode to Sub-Level Six. The doors opened on a place that looked and smelled almost as much like the Five-Ten as Rex had expected. With a maybe touch more boiled cabbage and machine lubricant in the mix.

The HPD detective led them a few blocks to a crossroads near a line of food-vendor carts and a few quick-serve eateries in shop spaces. She pointed to a walkway Rex recognized from the vid-clip. "That's where we spotted Neil Dolan."

Rex and Cinnamon trotted forward. The scent was clear. Neil hadn't bathed in a while, so his scent was not only fresh but strong. Rex took a deep breath, pointed his nose toward the ceiling, and bayed, "Aroo-o-o-o-o!"

Cinnamon's resonant alto quickly joined his. "Aroo-o-o-o-o!" Their voices harmonized, then both fell silent and moved forward as one.

Nearby civilians stared. So did the HPD team, Wei, and Mike.

Shiv and Berwyn grinned at them. "You should hear the whole Pack tune up," Shiv said.

"Yeah." Berwyn nodded. "It's pretty amazing. Good luck keeping pace, once they get moving!"

Rex and Cinnamon shared an amused look and a tongue-loll, then got down to business. Neil Dolan had run for a short distance, then doubled back and forth through a maze of alleys. Rough or cluttered decking and narrow passages hampered them. Civilians seemed perversely oblivious when human cops tried to pass, but their faces drained of color and they scrambled aside for Rex and Cinnamon.

The two XK9s took turns trailing and keeping situational watch around and above. The humans soon lagged behind, but urgent foreboding filled Rex. Cinnamon seemed to pick up on the same urgency. Neither XK9 moved as slowly as they had on their Hunt for the installation crew in the Five-Ten. There, they'd had all night. Here, a nagging sense that they must get to Neil

Dolan as quickly as possible grew within Rex. If Whisper had a mole in the HPD ... Well, better not waste any time.

"Keep going," Mike said on the com. "We've got your badge-pings on our map." Maybe Mike had that creeping sense of racing unseen competition, too.

Rex and Cinnamon pushed on. Neil had made a circuitous hike with his pizza. Rex admired his skill at dodging surveillance points.

He smelled a group of unmodified mongrels approaching on his left. The little pack ranged from a bench-legged terrier to a lanky shepherd mix who seemed to be the leader. They formed a ragged, barking line across the mouth of an alley. Their stiff-legged stances and bristling hackles warned Rex they meant to defend their turf.

Rex growled. He didn't have time for this. "Neil did not go that way. Let us ignore them."

Cinnamon laid back her ears. "They will follow and keep barking."

Rex tried to focus on Neil Dolan's scent trail, but the mongrel pack did follow. He heard triumph in their yapping, smelled their glee. The leader darted in to nip at Rex's flank.

Rex spun. He caught the leader by the throat, then pinned him to the grimy decking until he hoped he'd made his point.

Tail tucked, the dog ran away yelping. The rest of his pack followed.

Rex stared after them, hackles up. Cinnamon stood next to him, seconding him. He snorted, smoothed his hackles, then returned to the hunt.

Cinnamon fell in alongside. "That was weird."

"You said it. We probably should warn the humans about them."

"No worries," Shiv said on the com. "We heard you end it and watched on your optics. I don't see any sign of them now."

Rex stopped by a gap in a corrugated-metal fence that

surrounded a small, dismal playground. It pained him to compare this with the play area at Corona Tower.

Cinnamon stopped beside him. "They grant parents' licenses to people here?"

"Some of 'em immigrate with minors in tow," Bridget Ryan said on the com. "An' poverty won't stop a Family from lovin' their kids."

"Sorry." Cinnamon ducked her head. "Of course, it won't."

"O'course, we also have unregistered folk in the Sionainn," Ryan added.

Rex flicked his ears. Unregistered people in the Sionainn. Unregistered people in the Five-Ten ... did every Borough have an unregistered population? How many people were unregistered on all of Rana? He shook his head: not the time to ask.

He refocused on the trail. Bleak ranks of gritty-gray residence towers stood beyond the playground. Neil Dolan's scent trail led toward them. He snorted. "I do not like those tenements. Too many potential ambush positions."

The residence towers rose four stories to the ceiling of Sub-Level Six. Oxidized metal stairways with faded, flaking paint connected each of the floors at the near corners of the towers. The gaps between buildings made narrow, shadowed canyons, with balcony-walkways along each level.

They made every street a potential Funnel of Death.

Rex and Cinnamon sampled the air currents, redolent with cooking odors, unwashed humans, dust, and poorly-composted garbage. Threaded faintly through them, Rex whiffed the faraway, itchy scent of gunshot residue. And it was *not* coming from Wei. His hackles rose. "Did you catch that?

Cinnamon's ears clamped flat. "Only for an instant. Maybe something else?"

Rex growled softly. "Nothing else smells like *that*." He accessed his com. "I am glad LSA Wei brought his rifle. We have scented a stranger's firearm down the block."

CHAPTER 50

BLOOD, JUSTICE, AND BETRAYAL

"They have a *what?*" Rex was too far away to smell Bridget Ryan's scent factors, but from her tone they would be full of outrage. He and Cinnamon crouched by the edge of the shabby playground fence, hackles prickling.

Good luck, and be careful! There was a sleepy residue to Charlie's mental voice, but *firearm!?* echoed in his thoughts.

Love and gratitude surged through Rex. *Sorry I woke you.*

He received a sense of Charlie's worry and love, but no resentment. *Partnership isn't always convenient.*

"A firearm? Are you *sure?*" Mike's dubious voice came through the com.

Rex refocused. "Nothing else smells like that." *But considering the Ranan attitude toward them, how could someone smuggle one in?*

How did all the unregistered people get here? Charlie asked through the link. *There must be a way.*

Rex crept along a gravel path by the playground fence, Cinnamon at his shoulder. *But what made it worth the risk?*

It seems beyond credence that they brought a gun here—now—by sheer coincidence. He could feel Charlie's grimace.

Many of the Dolans' strategies were counter-measures to fool Whisper. Rex stopped at the end of the fence.

Cinnamon halted beside him. "I wonder if HPD harbors a Whisper mole." She'd dialed her vocalizer low.

And if they do, is the mole listening? Charlie asked.

The expedition's humans didn't respond—probably didn't hear Cinnamon's words. But Charlie'd made a good point. Rex sent her a private text: "Maybe keep such questions off-com?"

She growled softly but nodded.

They remained hunched at the end of the fence. An empty transport driveway lay between them and the blocks of tenements. People occasionally came or went along the walkways and rickety balconies, including a few children. Everyone appeared to be focused on errands.

Good luck. You'll need all your focus now. Charlie closed the link as much as either of them could.

"The residents do not act vigilant." Cinnamon made her vocalizer loud enough for the others to hear, this time.

Rex caught their humans' scents. Soft footsteps approached on the gravel path behind them.

"You and Cinnamon move more silently than we can." Mike kept his voice low. "We'll hold here till you have a better picture, then proceed as you advise."

"Copy that. Stand by." Rex turned to Cinnamon. "Wait here until I cross. If all seems clear, come to me. We shall take turns on point, block-to-block."

She nodded.

At a moment when no one seemed to be looking, Rex darted across, into a patch of shadows.

No reaction came from anywhere that he could detect.

Cinnamon fetched up beside him in the shadows a moment later, then moved past him. Head down for a clearer scent in the slightly heavier gravity of the sub-level, she led the way to the far end of the building at a smooth, quick trot. Rex followed, watchful above and all around. They stopped at the break between buildings.

Rex looked back. A block behind them, their humans hurried

across the driveway in twos and threes. No one from the neighborhood seemed to react. *Good.* For the next block Rex followed the scent trail, nose down, while Cinnamon kept watch.

At the end of the second building, he found three extremely fresh profiles. Two men and a woman had passed here within minutes. He bristled at the stealthy, menacing tang of their scent factors, and the unmistakable odor of gunshot residue. "Hold! New scents." Rex kept his vocalizer low but com-audible. "They smell unfriendly, and one of them has a firearm."

Cinnamon stopped beside him. She growled softly.

"The gun you smelled earlier?" Shiv whispered into his com. "Or can you tell?"

"Hard to say. I certainly hope there is only one."

"They are on the hunt, exactly as we are." Cinnamon kept her volume low, too. "Went down the block in the same direction as Neil."

"Hurry!" Mike whispered urgently into the com. "Stop them! Ryan, call for backup! Rex! Cinnamon! *Run!*"

Rex and Cinnamon darted forward. The three new scents followed Neil's trail: a right turn along another block, across another gap between buildings, then onto a set of rusty steps at the corner.

Rifle fire roared.

Rex dived for the dubious shelter beneath the metal steps.

Cinnamon yelped. Collapsed.

Rex's world slowed down.

His Packmate lurched in weird, desperate, elongated side-lunges across the pale regolith dust.

Rex's pulse reverberated through him like a ponderous drum. He leaped as if through viscous fluid to reach her. Clamped his jaws on her harness. Dragged her away—like pulling her through heavy mud. Each step took forever. Under the balcony. Out of range. Out of the shooter's probable view. A long, dark smear in the dust marked their movement.

His muscles strained. His back ached. *Out of sight! Farther back! Out of danger!* His heart might explode in his chest. The gunman could shoot downward, but how could he know exactly where to shoot, if the balcony's decking hid them? *Must get farther back!*

Cinnamon gasped, glassy-eyed, jaws wide. All Rex could smell was her blood. He stopped once he'd dragged her halfway down the block. He released her harness, hung his head, and the world sped up to normal again.

"Officer down!" Berwyn shouted on the com. "Need an ambulance! And a veterinarian! *STAT!*"

"Rex!" Shiv cried. "How bad is she?"

Rex didn't want to give the gunman any location clues. "Alive," he texted. "Shot. Probably several times."

"Where should Dom set up? We're a block to leeward."

"Shooter's on the first balcony by the steps. Above the blood smear."

"Roger that!" Shiv's breath rattled in his mic. Running.

Far away, sirens wailed. Then a new sound blotted them out. It was a scream, but unlike anything Rex had ever heard. Unspeakable, animal agony—but from a human throat.

Rex's hackles went straight up. The scream lasted almost a full, horrible minute, then subsided into wracking groans and sobs.

Cinnamon lay at Rex's feet, panting hard. Her tongue and gums looked pale. Blood flowed from wounds on her foreleg and right shoulder.

He pressed his forepaws against the worst of them, chilled. *Does this really help her?* Without human hands and equipment, what else could he do?

Are you in a safe spot? Charlie asked. *Can the shooter hit you?*

I don't think so.

Can you stop the bleeding?

Another scream tore the air. The same man? *No!* Beneath it, the first man's moans continued. *Both* Dolans?

He'd wonder about it later. Now he bent over Cinnamon.

Indecision choked him, blinded him. Made him pant like a bellows, his tongue long but dry. *This isn't enough. I can't do what she needs. I'm pressing hard but she's still bleeding.*

Berwyn slid to a halt beside Rex, having come from behind him. Must've run the long way around the tenement, to stay under cover. He crawled forward, gasping. Threw his jacket across Cinnamon's body. Repositioned her over the edge of the walkway so her head hung down a little. Retrieved the first-aid kit from her pannier. He yanked out a wad of clot-accelerating gauze and pressed it against her shoulder wound.

Oh, thank goodness! Rex moved back from Cinnamon to give Berwyn room but stayed under the balcony. Frantic fear drove him back and forth, back and forth, pacing and yawning with stress.

He could feel Charlie trying to calm him through the link, but it didn't help.

One of Wei's high-powered rounds punched through the balcony decking and smacked into the dust a couple centimeters from Berwyn's knee. Its report blasted an instant later. Its echoes reverberated along the artificial canyon of the tenements' walls.

"Crap!" Berwyn looked up, face horrified, his scent sharp with fear.

A burst of automatic fire answered Wei from above them on the first floor.

Get them farther back! Charlie cried through the link.

Rex had already grabbed Cinnamon's harness again. He and Berwyn didn't stop dragging her till they'd reached the far end of the building and rounded the corner. Berwyn fell to his knees beside her once more, resumed pressure on her shoulder wound. Her shot leg hung at a sickening angle now. Her head lolled over the walkway's edge; her tongue dangled long and slack. Her armored side heaved for each breath.

Wei fired a single shot.

The enemy returned another barrage of fire, for what seemed like forever. Rex cowered away, tongue long but breaths short and shallow. The noise blotted out sirens, screams, moans, and any other sound. Echoes rattled down tenement-tower canyons after it finally stopped. Only after they stilled could Rex again hear nearing sirens, sobbing moans from the first floor, Berwyn's shuddering breaths, and Cinnamon's gasps.

Wei fired a single shot.

Rex braced himself, but no barrage answered this time.

"Target neutralized," Wei reported.

Rex leaped over Cinnamon's legs, propelled by fury. "Moving in!"

Careful! Charlie cried through the link.

"Careful, Rex!" Shiv said. "I'll have your six."

Careful did not fit Rex's mood, but *rash* wasn't his plan, either. The block flew past him in a blur. He took the bottom half of the steps in one snarling bound but slowed near the top. Here the pungent scents of death intensified.

The gunman lay in the half-opened doorway, his military-style rifle now silent near his hand. Wei's bullet had blown out the side of his skull.

"Very effective headshot, Wei." Rex craned to peer through the doorway, snout wrinkled and teeth bared.

So. Much. Blood.

Two gutted bodies hung twitching, groaning, suspended by their arms from the walls. Blood still flowed from slit throats. "Got two desperately wounded in here: Neil and Rufus," he texted. "Need help, stat! Their attackers are gone, but they left within the last minute." He whirled toward Shiv's footsteps and scent on the top step behind him. "Quickly! Where would they go?"

"Back doors lead out the other side," Bridget Ryan said on the com.

Rex left the crime scene intact. Instead, he sprang along the end-balcony with a growl and a scramble of claws on metal decking. He rounded the far corner.

Strong scent. Movement toward the far end. "Aroo-o-o-o-o-o!"

"The far stairs! Head them off!" Shiv cried into his com.

Rex plunged flat-out down the balcony. Screw the stairs—he leaped down in one bound. Off to his left by the corner, Berwyn still crouched over Cinnamon. Rex couldn't see the suspects, but the scents of his quarry burned in his nose. He rounded the next tenement. *There!*

They fled headlong, their scents sharp with terror.

Yes! "Aroo-o-o-o-o!" *Oh, yes!* He closed fast—bunched his haunches, then struck with forepaws to their backs. Drove them to the ground. "You are under arrest!"

They writhed beneath his paws.

Rex flung his body across the man's back, clamped jaws onto the woman's knife-hand wrist.

The woman's free hand snatched up the knife. She slashed at Rex.

The man bucked beneath him.

Rex twisted away from the knife, jaws still clamped on the woman's arm. He roared a growl, closed down just enough to draw blood. "Stop! I shall bite!"

She shrieked wordless fury—slashed again. Pain seared across his face.

"Stop! I shall bite!"

The man squirmed and rolled under Rex's body. One hand dragged at Rex's armor.

The woman's blade tore through Rex's cheek again.

Rex jerked and dodged. "I shall hurt you! Stop!"

Her blade flashed back for another strike. Rex clenched his jaws. Bones crunched. His mouth filled with blood.

The woman screamed. Her body arched with pain. Her blow fell wide.

Running feet, approaching fast. "SBI! You're under arrest!" Shiv's EStee popped, popped again. An electric tingle buzzed Rex's teeth. Both suspects went limp.

He released the woman's broken and bleeding arm, then lurched up and back from the suspects' bodies, to stand with his head down, panting.

"Officer needs assistance!" Shiv called into his mic. "*Veterinary* assistance, *stat*! Two suspects in custody. One of them also needs medical assistance." Still breathing hard from his run, Shiv bent to secure the suspects' weapons and stared at the woman's mangled arm. "Remind me never to piss you off, Rex!"

Rex lifted his head. "Do not stab me, and we shall have no problem."

"Deal. Don't you have a first-aid kit in those panniers?"

"Top left." Rex shifted position so he could more easily reach it.

Shiv fumbled through it, yanked out clot accelerating gauze. He wrapped Knife Woman's arm first. "Don't want her to bleed out before we can question her!"

"Agreed." Rex underlined his word with a growl. "Hobble their legs and wrists as soon as you can, please. I do not want her free when she wakes."

"In a minute." Shiv squinted at Rex. "She really got you good. Your cheek may need re-gen." He reached for another pack of gauze.

A Uniformed Peace Officer jogged up to join them, EStee in hand. Anguish filled his scent factors. "Oh, God. You got them!"

Rex whirled. What was wrong with him?

Shiv looked up with a grin. "*Rex* got—"

The UPO shot Shiv with his EStee.

Rex lunged at him with a roar.

The man pumped two bolts into his bleeding face.

Searing pain sizzled through his head. Rex's legs went nerveless. He fell over Shiv's limp form.

Heartsick despair filled the UPO's scent. "I am *so sorry*!" He shot Rex's bloody face again.

Hissing blackness filled Rex's vision.

He thought he smelled someone new. Heard, "Get 'em up!

Move!" But like his vision, the sounds and scents ... faded ... out
....

REX AWOKE with a roar and a snarl of rage, then froze.

A young woman in scrubs leaped backwards with a yelp, her gloved hands up, eyes wide above her surgical mask. Behind her, Rex glimpsed white walls, an IV pole, a sink. The place smelled of disinfectant and blood.

Not the Sionainn.

He focused on the young woman, a stranger he'd never seen before. "I am sorry." His voice came from a countertop in the corner across the room.

"No, I understand." The young woman sounded breathless. "Caught me by surprise."

Rex lay his head back down on the hard exam table. "Makes two of us," his voice said from the corner.

She glanced toward it, then looked at him again. "That is a really strange effect. We took your collar off so I could get to all of the slashes on your cheek and neck."

"She kept stabbing me."

The young woman frowned. "So I see. I am attempting to help with that. Please lie still now."

Rex sighed. He lay as still as he could. Odd sensation in his face. Inert, fuzzy. As if it halfway wasn't part of him. She appeared to be gluing it back together.

Good to know you're awake again. Charlie's voice through the link seemed shaken, but relieved.

Chagrin stabbed him. *Are you all right?*

More amusement than irritation came back to him. *I'm not napping anymore, that's for sure. Not since you had your run-in with "Knife Woman" and the UPO.* Charlie's ruefulness sharpened. *I'm almost to the Hub, headed your way with several Packmates and some SBI people. I should arrive at your end in another hour or so.*

It will be good have you here. Do you know anything about Shiv or Cinnamon? How are they?

Physically, Shiv's okay. I'm told he woke up swearing like a dockhand.

Kind of the way I did, except I was growling and snarling. I apologized, once I realized where I was. The vet is working on my face now.

Cinnamon's still in surgery, but so far still alive, Charlie continued. *They took her to a human-designed hospital, Howardsboro General. They have a surgeon there who emigrated from Uladh Nua. She's had experience with gunshot wounds. There's also a vet assisting, and Dr. Sandler is remote-consulting from Wheel Two. Berwyn and Shiv are waiting at Howardsboro General. Berwyn's understandably devastated but not injured. Listeners are with them. Once Cinnamon's been stabilized, they plan to bring her home as soon as possible.*

Tension eased in his gut. *I'm grateful she's still alive.*

So are we all. Uh-oh. We're slowing. I need to go. I'll be with you as soon as I can. Try to rest in the meantime.

Good luck in the Hub. Rex yawned. Resting was probably a good idea.

CHAPTER 51

"DON'T MAKE ANY MESSES"

Microgravity in the Hub had done its usual number on Charlie. His stress reactions had muted, but not disappeared. Now post-micrograv lassitude sapped him. He stared out the left rear window of the SBI auto-nav and attempted to stay vigilant. But his heavy eyes and sluggish body dragged him down toward sleep.

Their auto-nav descended from the Terrace Four transit terminal into a quiet, outer-suburb business district. It was late enough that the businesses lay silent and dark, accented by the low, misty glow of security lights.

From what Charlie could make out in the shadows, palm trees and ornamental grasses ringed the clinic building. A half-level and a series of dog runs topped what looked like ground-floor exam facilities and a storefront. More grass, edged by a safety railing, covered the roof. Probably a boarding operation up on Level One. Was that where they'd put Rex? Charlie could sense he was somewhere nearby.

Their car made a slow circuit around the clinic. Gil, one of Mike's field agents, called in to put them on-scene at the Heart-O-Howardsboro Veterinary Clinic. The other field agent, Zane, sat on the other side of the car to keep watch in that direction.

Their auto-nav halted by the dark front door. A light came on. The door opened, and a stout, middle-aged woman stepped into the doorway. Charlie blinked at her, confused. Rex had said the vet was young. *They assigned an XK9 to … an assistant?*

Gil popped the storage compartment.

"We'll keep you covered, Morgan." Zane flashed a grin. "Sleep tight."

"Yeah, thanks." Charlie consciously relaxed his jaws and shoulders. Breathed in through his nose and blew it out, willing all the stress to go with it. *Don't jump to conclusions.* He pulled a large duffel from the storage compartment, slapped the "close" panel, then turned to the woman with what he hoped was a pleasant expression. "Dr. Hart?"

"Reserve Agent Morgan?" She frowned. "I'll need some ID."

Like you could stop me if I don't have any. Charlie unclenched his fists, then slung the duffel's strap over his left shoulder. He stepped forward, flipped open his badge wallet with his right hand, and extended it to her. "How is Rex?"

She scrutinized the SBI certificate alongside his OPD badge, then looked him up and down. "They grow 'em big in Orange-boro, I guess."

Charlie feared his Hub-lag would make any response to that come off as ill-tempered. "I take it my partner's in Healing Sleep?" Rex had relaxed with a sigh of relief and fallen asleep once Charlie reassured him he was on his way and doing okay in micrograv. But what would Hart say?

Dr. Hart's frown still hadn't eased up. She also continued to block the door. "Yes. All is well. He should sleep till morning with no problem."

Oh, if only I could count on that. Misgivings slithered in his gut. Howardsboro PD's Chief Garrett had long since made it clear he didn't like Mike's SIT Alpha on his turf. HPD's officer Danesh, the man who'd shot Rex and Shiv, had been a Whisper asset. Were Wisniewski's agents *also* embedded at HPD? Maybe not, but Charlie wouldn't count on it.

Hart met his eyes, still frowning. "So, why are you here?"

Because I'm afraid he'll be killed by Transmondians or Whisper agents. Also, I promised Shady. "Security precaution." Standing here spotlighted in the doorway made his skin crawl. "Let's talk about it inside."

Her frown deepened. "Security? This isn't exactly a high-crime area. The police here are highly competent."

Yeah, right. Urgency spurred him. "Call me paranoid." *Why doesn't she want me here? What's her game?* He edged closer to her. "Can we go in now?"

She glanced toward where the car had been. "Your friends left."

"Yes, because I'm supposed to be *inside* now." He crowded her until she backed into some kind of waiting or reception area, then thumped the door closed and stepped out of line with it. Stout though it might be, that simple wooden door wouldn't stop a slug from a firearm like the ones they'd used in the Sion-ainn. Of course, neither would the walls. Nowhere in this waiting area would be safe.

"Well, excuse *you*." She scowled at him. "Just exactly what kind of danger have you law enforcement types gotten my clinic into?"

He met her angry gaze with one of his own. "It seems likely you know how Rex was injured."

"I took him in because I treat HPD K-9s. Once their on-scene action is over, it's *over*. We don't tolerate trouble around here."

"And we have every hope that's how it'll be with Rex, too. But XK9s aren't ordinary K-9s."

"Huh. Got that right." Her furrowed brow smoothed some, and her tight mouth relented a fraction. "Your Rex made quite an impression on my daughter."

"He can be a charmer." He offered a cautious smile.

Her brows pinched again. "*After* he almost took her hand off."

"Almost. But you'll note he didn't. And he apologized afterward. He'd had a stressful day."

She lowered her chin, gave him a grudging look. "It's never fun to get stabbed in the face and shot with an EStee. That's true."

"So, then, where is he?" *Somewhere on this floor.* He could sense that much.

"We put him in an exam room. He wouldn't fit in any of the kennels. Had to pull a cot out of storage."

Oh, there's a thought. A cot might be more comfortable than the inflatable mattress in his duffel. He quirked an eyebrow and smiled at her in what he hoped was a charming way. "You wouldn't have a second one, would you?"

She crossed her arms. Her frown descended again. "No. Just how long do you do you imagine you're staying?"

"Till I can take him home."

"You can't sleep here! I'm not zoned for it."

Charlie ground his teeth and met her gaze, unblinking.

She narrowed her eyes. "Don't you glare at me. I'm *not.*"

"Do you mean to tell me neither you nor any staff member has ever stayed overnight to tend an ailing patient?"

"We don't let strangers sleep over."

"Noted." He turned. Pushed through a doorway in the back wall of the waiting room that felt right.

"Wait!" She followed him. "Where do you think you're going?"

"I need to see Rex." He'd entered a corridor with open doors on each side. *Down this way.*

He found Rex in the third exam room on the left. They'd set up the cot along the back wall. The big dog lay inert, stretched out on it full-length, with his feet and part of his tail hanging over the edges. In the light from the corridor, Charlie saw his ribs rise and fall in slow, deep-sleep breaths.

Charlie's whole body relaxed. He sagged a little, every muscle gone slack. "Ah, Rex. There you are." He bit his lip and walked over to the cot. The duffel's strap slipped off his shoulder and down his arm shield, until the bag landed on the floor. He took a knee by the cot and reached out to stroke his partner's tousled black fur. Teased out a few tangles.

He let his fingers sink into the warm, soft pelt, and his eyes adapt till he could see the already-healing places where the knife had left its mark. He leaned his forehead against Rex's chest and blinked back excess moisture. Wrapped his right arm around the big dog's ribs.

Dr. Hart gave him a moment, then let out a soft sigh. *"Told you he was okay."*

"It's one thing to know he's okay." Charlie looked up, his throat tight. "Something else to *know* it."

"Mm." Her mouth made an irritable twist, but then she relented with a sigh. "Well, sorry. I really *don't* have a second cot. I'm locking you in, and the SBI will get my complaint. First kennel staff arrives at five. Restroom's down the hall to the left, if you need it."

"Thank you."

"Don't make any messes."

That might be a hard promise to keep. "I'll do my best."

DR. HART WENT HOME *at last.* She left the lights on in Charlie and Rex's hallway.

Charlie dragged himself to his feet. *Time to make tactical adjustments.* He used his CAP to dial the hall lights down, and some of his tension eased. Dr. Hart's lights would've made this corridor a glaring target.

If Whisper sent someone this soon, he'd be surprised—but probably also outgunned, unless the dead rifleman from the execution team was a one-off. *We can hope!* If a Transmondian agent came, Charlie had to assume he'd be augmented and armed with Wisniewski's damned neurotoxin.

In either case, it wouldn't do to leave Rex neatly framed on the back wall of a small, windowless chamber with only one door.

An assassin would expect Rex to be in the kennels or maybe an exam room. That made moving Rex somewhere else Charlie's first priority. *But where?* He needed a sense of this place's layout, and *quickly. Before* an attacker could arrive.

He stepped out into the hall and pulled out a small hand-light. Flicked it on, but kept it pointed low. *I still think onboard lighting would be awesome.* He shook his head, then moved to the nearest open door.

There were plenty to choose from. Doors stood open on both sides, all along the corridor. This clinic looked big enough to keep several vets busy.

Charlie moved as quickly as he could. Eyed the silent, shadowy equipment in each room, then closed its door with a firm *click.* Why make anything easy for the enemy? Force him to open each one.

Clear. Clear. Clear. Clear. His pulse raced. *Faster. Faster!* Dr. Hart had implied that he and Rex had this floor all to themselves, but Charlie couldn't rely on careless assumptions.

Farther in, a cross-hallway transected the building. Beyond it? *Hmm.* He strode to the crossing. Exits to the outside lay on each end of the cross-hallway. Looked as if his corridor jogged left at this throughway, then continued to the back of the building. He ventured partway down: two offices lay on his right, and a larger ... looked like an operating room on the left. A plan took gradual shape. He continued his explorations.

Storage at the back. Another exit at the end of the hall. He returned to the cross-hallway. A corridor parallel to Rex's led to a receptionist's office and the lobby where he'd entered. Exam rooms backed up to Rex's on his left, with another office and a small breakroom on the right. He didn't see an upstairs access. Must be outside. *Good. One less point of potential attack in here.* He had enough holes to plug, as it was.

"Fifteen-minute check." Gil's voice spoke through the com. "Mark 20:30."

Charlie smiled. "Copy. All clear so far."

"Copy," Zane said. "Clear."

"Copy," came a voice from SIT Alpha HQ Base. "Stay vigilant."

Roger that. Charlie did a couple of shoulder rolls. First priority: move Rex.

That took some doing. Shiv might have been able to dead-lift Rex's limp 130 kilos, but the dog was considerably heavier than Hildie. Charlie's attempt to scoop him up sent instant, shooting pain through his left arm.

Well, damn.

The cot was old and not too sturdy, especially not when being dragged. Charlie had to stop frequently to smack wobbly joint-connections back together. He tried not to leave any tell-tale scrape marks on the floor to betray which office he'd chosen.

Oh joy. Carpeting. Heart pounding with urgency, he wrestled his partner, cot and all, behind a desk in the second office back from the cross-corridor. He smoothed the scuffed-up carpet nap and tried to ignore a chill of foreboding. If any enemy got close enough to see scuffs in this carpet, both he and Rex were in trouble.

One thing done. Dozens to go. And however far he got with his countermeasures, he'd need eyes on the situation. He opened his duffel and pulled out a box. The tiny mobile cameras inside had been Klein's idea, with Mike and Elaine's hearty endorsement.

No time to waste! Deploying the cameras was only the first step.

Dr. Hart had said, "Don't make any messes."

But was it really a mess, if he planned to put it all back, afterward?

❖ ❖ ❖ ❖ ❖ ❖ ❖ ❖

ALL AT ONCE, Charlie was awake.

By the 24:00 check-in with Zane and Gil, Charlie'd had to admit he needed rest. He'd staged his air mattress half-under Rex's relocated cot behind the desk. It was just about as comfortable as he'd anticipated, but he was so exhausted that didn't matter. "I've got to sack out for a while," he explained. "I'm still healing, and the micrograv did wore me out." Not to mention moving all that stuff tonight.

"No worries, man," Gil replied. "We've got this."

"Sleep well," Zane said. "Let us know when you're back online."

"Thanks, guys. Morgan out." Charlie yawned. He'd fallen asleep before he'd fully stretched out on the air mattress.

Now The HUD said 03:14. He opened his channel to Zane and Gil, but waited for their 03:15 check-in. No sense in jumping the gun. Those guys had been like clockwork all night.

Behind him, Rex snored on the cot. He seemed fine. *Okay, so, why am I suddenly awake?*

Charlie pushed to his feet and stretched. Checked his EStee. full charge, full 10-shot magazine. His fingers found the duty belt he'd staged on the desktop, then strapped it on, checked it. Everything on it was where it was supposed to be.

Zane and Gil hadn't checked in yet. What time—? 03:16.

Shit. Charlie moved around the desk, then stepped silently into the corridor and closed the door. He halted at a faint sound. *What was that?*

He held his breath. Listened hard. Wished for XK9-level hearing. He checked the surveillance cams he'd positioned along the tops of the corridor walls. Similar to journalists' cams, they were designed for field use when there was no building-system surveillance to tap into. He switched to night vision. Too dark for optical feeds.

Still nothing from Zane or Gil. Now it was 03:18. Something was definitely wrong. Charlie's mouth went dry. *Oh, crap. This is it.*

Quiet rasp of a latch: in the cam-view, the leeward side door on the cross-hallway edged open, and immediately thumped into a tall shelf.

Charlie silently pinged SIT Alpha HQ: INTRUDER ALERT! with location. Then he slipped down the corridor and stopped at the cross-hallway.

A collection of exam tables, chairs, desks, workstations, lamps, and other objects made up the barricade pile he'd placed to block each outer door. Well, they'd block it for a while, anyway.

He crouched around the corner out of sight. Focused on taking slow, even breaths. All of his senses went hyper-alert.

Bang! Thump! Crash! So much for stealth. Now that the intruder knew he was expected, they'd both lost the advantage of surprise.

Charlie edged around the corner just far enough to see. His cameras showed a large, angry man.

The furniture-barricade rattled and vibrated.

Charlie lifted his EStee.

Crash! Crunch! Stamping sounds. Oh, yeah. That guy was pissed off.

A gap opened. Charlie drew a bead on movement beyond the barricade. If he could halt things *right now* .... Took a steadying breath. *Wait for it.* He needed to be sure of what he was shooting.

On the cams' view, the heavily-muscled man moved with the quick precision of a machine to dismantle the furniture-pile. Augmented, for sure. That probably meant he was Transmondian, not Whisper. He'd be fast, and once Charlie fired, the agent could pinpoint his location.

Didn't help Charlie's confidence to realize he hadn't thought to requalify with his weapon since he'd been out of the hospital. *Here's hoping I've still got it.* He lined up his shot, released a controlled breath, and squeezed one off.

"Damn you!" the agent heaved a chair toward Charlie. It slammed into the wall just short of Charlie's corner, crashed to

the floor, then skidded past. The man kicked a cabinet aside, picked up an exam table to use as a shield, and charged toward Charlie.

Great. Charlie fired another bolt at the man's legs, then retreated down the cross-hallway. He didn't expect to hit the intruder—and didn't. But if he could lure the man down this way ...

The agent reached the mouth of Charlie's original corridor, shoved the exam table toward Charlie, then ducked out of view.

Oh, no, you don't! Charlie's cams showed he'd turned down the corridor between the operating room and the offices. Way too close to Rex! Charlie squeezed past the upended exam table, rounded the corner, then fired at the man's retreating back. His bolt *should've* penetrated—but it bounced off the guy's jacket.

The hell? Charlie shifted his aim to the back of the man's shaved head.

That bolt connected. The agent flinched, staggered. A normal human would go down.

Damn you! Charlie sprinted after him, closing fast.

The man whirled. All in one flash of movement, he leveled a trank pistol at Charlie and fired.

Charlie threw up his left arm, more by reflex than thought. The trank dart bounced off his arm shield and shattered against the wall, but sharp pain from the impact radiated through Charlie's arm. The pain redoubled when Charlie hurtled into the man.

They went down together. Charlie only half-evaded a punishing blow from the other's upthrust fist, but slammed his right elbow into the guy's face. He straddled him to pin his legs. Grabbed for the trank pistol with his semi-numb left hand.

The agent bucked desperately under his weight. His left hand grabbed for Charlie's right wrist.

Charlie slugged the guy with the butt of his EStee. That stunned him long enough to jam the weapon's muzzle against his neck and deliver a point-blank EStee bolt.

The man's back arched, then he went limp.

Charlie pushed up, lurched to his feet with a gasp. He kicked the trank pistol away from the agent's hand. Kept a wary eye on his captive. Still breathing hard, he unclipped several zip-cuffs, then rolled the man to triple-bind his wrists and ankles.

That done, he positioned the man on his side and tilted his head to maintain his airway. Charlie wanted him alive to interrogate, but unable to harm anyone once revived. He activated his com to Alpha HQ. "Subject subdued and cuffed." He struggled to catch his breath. Through the link he could tell that his partner slept on, oblivious. *That's one good thing, at least.*

"HPD's been alerted." Santiago's voice on the com sounded angry. "Not sure if we'll get there first. Do you have eyes on Zane or Gil?"

"Negative. Can't raise them on the com, either." Charlie hesitated. "When you get here, use the leeward side door. I've barricaded the others."

"Roger that."

Sirens came into earshot. Charlie bent to check the intruder's vitals. The man's pulse thumped steady and strong. His breathing seemed normal. Most people tolerated the EStee's tranquilizer drug with no long-term harm, but a double dose could cause problems.

He hazarded a short jog to the place where he'd secured his and Rex's badges—no need to plant locators on themselves, when he hadn't been sure if intruders could ping them. But if Howardsboro PD arrived first, he wanted his badge with him. The intruder was still there when he returned. Still out, still lying on his side. Still breathing normally but drooling some.

The first siren drew closer. Another chimed in from farther away.

Charlie half-collapsed onto the floor beside his captive. Shaky with adrenaline burn-off, he leaned his back against the corridor wall. His right cheekbone ached and his left arm throbbed.

After a while, someone banged on the front door. "Police! Open up!

Charlie didn't move. He used his CAP to turn on the lights in in the cross-hallway.

Eventually, the geniuses at the front door came around the corner to investigate the light shining out onto the pavement on Bravo side. Two sets of booted feet clumped inside, then stopped, silhouetted at the mouth of Charlie's corridor.

UPOs. *Great.* Howardsboro had won the race to get here. They leveled their EStees at him, although Charlie'd be astonished if he was actually within their range.

"Police! Hands where we can see them!"

Charlie lifted his hands so they could see both were empty. Too risky to go for his badge at this point—getting EStee-bolted wouldn't help things.

The younger UPO stepped forward. He scowled at Charlie. "Who are you? What happened here? Who is *that?*"

"I'm Reserve Agent—" More sirens arrived. Charlie couldn't even hear *himself* over them. Once they'd cut off, he finished his self-introduction.

Young Howardsboro frowned in what he may have thought was an intimidating manner and strode closer. "Need to see a *badge*, mister!"

Charlie kept his hands up. "It's inside my jacket. Shall I—"

"Don't move!" The young officer gave the trussed and inert subject a long, hard stare. "Who's that?"

"Best guess? Transmondian Intelligence agent. He didn't introduce himself."

The UPO stared at the man. "You ... killed him?"

Sure. That's why he's triple-cuffed. "EStee. Took a couple bolts to keep him down, but he'll wake up sooner or later."

"And that mess at the door?"

"Counter-measures. I kinda expected him."

The probable Transmondian twitched, then uttered a soft groan.

Young Howardsboro flinched back a couple of steps, then scowled at Charlie some more. "Is he—"

"Waking up? Maybe." Fatigue dragged at Charlie's arms. He lowered them slightly, but kept his hands in sight.

"Hold it right there!" Charlie couldn't see who spoke.

"I have a couple of Reserve Agents in here." That was Mike Santiago's voice. Charlie glimpsed him beyond Young Howardsboro. It was barely 04:00, but Santiago wore his full SBI uniform.

"Wait!" The other UPO followed on his heels. "Let us secure the—"

"Looks as if Reserve Agent Morgan has already done that." Santiago strode forward. "Excellent work, Morgan!"

"Thank you, sir." Charlie climbed to his feet.

Young Howardsboro stiffened but seemed unsure where to point his EStee.

"Stand down, Officer. We've got this." Mike edged past the UPO, then halted beside Charlie and the Transmondian. "How's Rex?"

"Still in Healing Sleep."

"We need to take him back to HQ. That's the only place we can be sure he's safe."

Charlie blew out a breath and sagged back against the wall. "Thank you! I couldn't agree more!"

CHAPTER 52

HOMEWARD

The Howardsboro cops argued, but Mike had brought nearly everyone in SIT Alpha to the vet clinic. HPD grudgingly stepped back.

Mike sent most of his agents to search outside. They'd barely started before they found Gil in the shadows of the ditch by the road. Zane lay behind a pile of boxes at the back of the clinic. Both were still breathing, but they bore clearly visible head injuries. It didn't look as if they'd been shot with the trank pistol. Paramedics arrived quickly to collect them.

The SBI Wheel Three CSU team arrived only minutes before Dr. Hart's kennel staff. Since the kennel workers' business didn't affect the crime scene, they were allowed to go up an outdoor stairway to do their work.

Charlie made it a point to be on hand when the team collected the trank pistol. "Orangeboro PD on Wheel Two needs to know the test results from the formula it was armed with." Stomach like a stone, he added, "We already have two XK9s in the hospital, one poisoned by a Transmondian neurotoxin that nearly killed him. We need a complete analysis of what was in that pistol."

The evidence officer made a special note. "We'll let them know, as soon as possible."

The prisoner transport finally pulled in. Four field agents came with it.

"He has received augmentation treatments." Charlie worried what they'd think to see an unconscious man in restraints. "His reflexes are twice as fast as yours, and he's half again as strong. He didn't go down without a fight, and I doubt he'll wake a changed man. Keep him restrained, and do *not* relax your vigilance."

Mike dispatched a couple of burly young field agents named Beck Crombie and Jack Evanovich to help Charlie. The three of them muscled the enormous, limp mass of Rex into a separate section of the prisoner transport. At SIT Alpha's HQ, they lugged him to hurriedly-prepared temporary quarters.

"Thank you!" Charlie gasped. He, Jack, and Beck didn't *exactly* drop Rex onto the air mattress Mike's team had provided for him. The dog roused long enough to snuggle in, then commenced snoring.

Charlie straightened painfully, more relieved than he could say. "I never would've gotten him here by myself. Thank you!"

"Piece of cake." Jack laughed. He stretched his arms upward, then shook them out.

"Yeah, no problem." Beck rolled his shoulders a couple of times. "Especially since he's *your* problem now, eh?"

"He's worth the effort." Charlie grinned at his somnolent partner, then sobered. "Listen, I hope Gil and Zane recover all right."

Beck's expression clouded. "Yeah, me, too."

Jack gave a sober nod.

Once they'd left, Charlie fell onto the cot they'd set up for him. It had nothing on his bed at home, and deplorably lacked a Medicine Goddess. But it was better than the air mattress on the floor at the Heart-O-Howardsboro Veterinary Clinic, so he'd take it. He'd been determinedly staving off his own incipient exhaustion ever since he'd awakened in the vet clinic. Hauling Rex in here had wiped out his last reserves of energy.

He woke an hour or so later, groggy, irritable, and still dressed. *Damn.* He needed to stop pushing himself till he literally fell over. *Yeah, like I planned that.* Every morsel of him ached. His heavy limbs and throbbing head argued for more sleep, but a persistent wakefulness dogged him.

Damned cot was half-bed, half-torture device. He sat up. Rex didn't appear to have moved. What time was it? He checked, then groaned softly. 06:40 wasn't *that* early, but he didn't hear any movement in the building. If SIT Alpha kept hours like Delta, they'd be stirring about in their base closer to 07:00. Even after the early call-out to the clinic.

With Rex still in Healing Sleep, Charlie was stuck here, at least till his partner woke up. Alone with this thoughts. And his thoughts gravitated straight to his lack of Hildie.

When had reaching out to touch her in bed become like breathing?

When had he fallen into the habit of thinking about her whenever he had a second of downtime? The tone of her voice when she teased him, her sparkling eyes, her vibrant spirit?

He missed her so much his skin hurt.

Would she mind if he called her?

Well, she'd *said* to call. But when? Was this too soon?

She probably was working, or up and preparing to leave for work. He hated that he didn't know her schedule today. Maybe she was off. Maybe she was sleeping.

If she was sleeping and he woke her he'd feel horrible.

But he kept thinking about it.

He just wanted, just *needed* the sound of her voice.

The line buzzed. *Wait!* Had the program read his yearning as a command to place the call?

"Charlie?" She sounded startled, but not annoyed. And not asleep.

"I'm sorry to interrupt. I—"

"Is everything all right?"

Good question. "I'm—actually, I'm in Howardsboro."

Silence for a beat. "On *Wheel Three?*"

"SBI operation. Rex got stabbed."

"*Stabbed?*" Her voice ended the word on a squeak.

"He'll be okay. He's in Healing Sleep. We'll probably come home today." He hesitated. "They, um, they shot Cinnamon."

"Oh, my God! *Charlie!* Is she—"

"Still alive, but critical."

"*None* of this is on the news feeds!"

He sighed. "Oh, give it time."

"Are *you* okay?"

"I wasn't there for the exciting part." He'd tell her about the Transmondian later. "I'm fine. I just—I thought—maybe you'd want to know."

"Definitely! Yes! Is there anything I can do?"

Come. Hold me. He ran a hand over his face, then winced when it hit his puffy right eye. "Well, anyway. I guess I should …
"

"Charlie?"

"Yes?"

"When you bring him home—"

"Later today, I hope." He glanced at Rex, inert on the air mattress. "*Sometime* today, probably. When we come back depends on when Rex wakes up."

"Whenever it is, I'm at the ERT Base. Please stop by?"

"I—depending on how Rex feels, yeah. Maybe we could do that."

"I hope you can."

His heart clenched. "Yeah. Me, too."

Rex startled him with a toothy yawn. "I shall be ready soon. Just need to rest a little more." He shifted position and immediately started snoring again.

On the com, Hildie laughed. "I heard that. You both must've

had a bizarre night. Let me know when you're headed for my part of the Hub. I'll finagle a break."

"That would be—" *wonderful. Amazing. More than I imagined.* "I'd like that. I'd like to see you." *I need you,* he wanted to say. *It's awful without you.*

"I'd like to see you, too." She hesitated. "I missed my morning kiss."

You did? "Well, *that's* motivation." Charlie bit his lip. "Now I *really* want to stop by. I'll let you know. When we're on our way, I mean."

"I—I miss you."

So very, very much. His voice didn't work on the first try. "Miss you, too."

"Hope you can come."

"I love you," he blurted out before he thought.

"Me, too." Her voice didn't sound quite steady.

Rex rolled over. He stopped snoring, but there was nothing wakeful about his deep, regular breathing.

Call ended, Charlie paced around the room a few times. He struggled to get his emotions latched down under better control.

He reviewed his notes from last night, filled out an After-Action Report ... But, where to file it? *Aw, hell.* Rather than bother Mike with questions, he just went ahead and filed it with SIT Alpha, SIT Delta, *and* the OPD. Let *them* sort it out.

From the sounds of movement downstairs, Mike's people had begun to arrive. Formwork done, he went in search of breakfast. The SIT Alpha agents seemed friendly. They shared the good news that Zane and Gil were expected to make full recoveries.

But they all had jobs to do. Charlie tried to stay out of their way.

His HUD dinged: a new report. *Ah.* From the SBI Wheel Three Crime Lab. Charlie read it with a growing chill. After consultation with the OPD, they'd concluded the agent's trank pistol was armed with the same neurotoxin as the blowgun dart that had dealt such a hard blow to Razor.

No surprise—but Charlie sat down abruptly. Took a moment to get his breath back. Realization hit him like a full-speed bus. If he hadn't blocked that dart with his arm shield ... If he hadn't overcome the agent ... *if* and *if* and *if* tortured him for a long, heart-shaking moment.

Charlie drew in a breath, then blew it out hard. *Enough of Howardsboro! Time to go home!*

CHARLIE AND REX left Mike's Howardsboro base late in the morning, after Rex staggered to his feet and pronounced himself ready to go. He'd roused a couple of earlier times, then subsided into sleep. His latest nap had been a spontaneous event on the floor by Charlie's borrowed workstation.

Mike gave the big dog a dubious look, then quirked an eyebrow at Charlie.

"We do need to get back." By now, all their enemies knew they were in Howardsboro. Even though the SBI shielded him and Rex, urgency to get home tightened Charlie's chest. "I probably can handle him."

"You're still in an arm shield. *No.* That's an order." Mike summoned Jack and Beck again. After yesterday and last night, no one harbored any illusions that HPD should be trusted, even briefly, with Rex's security. Jack and Beck arrived well-armed.

Rex roused, stretched, yawned, then climbed into the closed car Mike provided. On the trip around the corner and a few blocks down to the Express, Rex went back to sleep.

The elevator arrived. Rex made a visible, and partially successful, effort to wake up. Jack and Beck helped Charlie haul his still-mostly-asleep form into a private side compartment on the elevator car to the Hub. Once inside, Charlie and the two field agents left Rex slumped against one wall long enough to retract and fold away a full section of eight seats.

Beck surveyed the results with a smile. "That ought to give him room to stretch out."

"Too bad we couldn't bring the air mattress." Jack eyed the grooves and hinges on the floor.

"We're leaving full gravity soon." Charlie guided Rex into the newly-cleared area. "He probably won't get too many bruises. He tells me XK9s are tough."

Beck laughed. "Tough to wake up, that's for sure!"

Rex didn't even circle three times. He just collapsed with a grunt and went back to sleep.

The elevator began its ascent. Charlie was still makeshifting a strap-down for Rex when the first sensations of lightness began. Once he'd secured his partner, he strapped himself in. That was much easier to do with elbow room in near-normal gravity than it had been on a crowded car in microgravity yesterday.

He reclined his seat and dozed, but didn't realize that he too had fallen asleep until he woke himself with a snore. His mucous membranes had definitely started to swell. He checked the compartment's altimeter. Yeah, fifteen minutes from the top felt about right. He wasn't floating yet, but the gravity felt much lower.

He called Hildie again, more bold after their earlier contact. "Getting close to the Wheel Three Hub, but I also wanted to ask you something. Have you seen anything on the news yet?"

"Oh, my goodness yes. The newsies have gotten hold of it now, for sure. They're calling it the 'Shoot-Out in the Sionainn.' It's mostly the talking heads freaking out over the firearms, though. They mentioned that one XK9 was shot and seriously injured."

"Was there anything on the news feeds about a disturbance at a vet clinic in Howardsboro?"

"No. What happened?"

"Transmondian agent. I took him into custody, but we kinda trashed part of the clinic."

She gasped. "Are you all right?"

"I'm good. Got a black eye, but you should see the other guy."

"Mor*gan!*" There was no mistaking the warning in her tone.

"Seriously. I'm okay. I got him with my EStee."

Silence. She blew out a breath. "I bet you're both exhausted."

"Rex has been sleeping most of the morning, and we both dozed off on the elevator. We have a small compartment all to ourselves. Just Rex and me, plus Jack and Beck, from SIT Alpha." He felt a surge of wakefulness from his partner, looked over to see his eyes were open. "Ah. Rex just woke up. Looks as if we may not have to float an enormous, sleeping dog through the Hub after all."

"That would have been an interesting spectacle."

"The last thing we need is an interesting spectacle. He'll be interesting enough, awake."

"Still think it's safe for the two of you to come by and say 'hi'?"

Charlie hesitated. He wanted that morning kiss, and he couldn't imagine how the Transmondians might pull off an ambush in the Hub. But was it really a good idea to take extra chances? He gave a soft groan. "Probably not, unfortunately. Too risky."

She sighed. "Let's be clear. I *do* still want my morning kiss. But not if it puts you and Rex in danger. I love you."

Warmth filled him. Maybe she'd missed him as much as he missed her. His throat tightened with yearning. "Love you, too." He hoped she'd never, *ever* stop wanting her morning kiss.

CHAPTER 53

THE SCENT OF AN ENEMY

C harlie blinked HUD-dazzle out of his eyes, then realized Jack and Beck were both grinning at him.
"What?"
Their grins widened.
Jack quirked a brow at him. "She makes you say the L-word a lot?"
"She *inspires* me to say it. May you be so lucky, someday." Charlie laughed. The warmth that Hildie's words had inspired buoyed his heart and spirits.
"Oh, man, she's *good.*" Beck shook his head and made *tsk* sounds. "She's got you convinced!"
There'd been a time when Charlie would've squirmed on the receiving end of such teasing. Back when he'd been at increasing odds with Felicia—and a lot younger. Weird, how it merely amused him now. Jack and Beck … Had he been that callow and superficial when he was younger? He gave them a long, level look. "Let me guess: you're both 'free men,' and that's how you like it."
Their smiles flashed smug and white.
"No strings attached. I like to play it wide and loose." Beck spread his arms wide. "Let *all* the ladies have a piece of me!"

"Yeah," Jack agreed. "No woman dictates *my* moves!"

Uh-huh. Charlie remembered delivering lines like that. Not even that long ago. But with him—he suspected also with them—it had been bravado, a way to frame a period of overall low satisfaction so he didn't feel so bad. He hadn't been lying when he'd told Hildie's father that loneliness didn't feel like freedom. "Well, then, good for you. Enjoy it."

Beck laughed. "Look at you, all ready to settle down and be domesticated. You've got it *bad*, you know that?"

Charlie just smiled and shook his head. Things with Hildie might currently be unsettled, but *she'd* said "the L-word" *first,* this time.

Fifteen minutes later the chill air, lighting, and noises of the Hub greeted them. Charlie tried not to give mental space to the flutter of deeper-than-normal nausea, or the hints of tremor in his hands. This was no time to be distracted!

They emerged from the car into the hubbub of midday lunch-rush. Beck and Jack flanked them. Rex had roused again. He could operate on his own, and he gave Charlie an interested look. *You are doing much better in micrograv!*

Charlie focused on keeping his breathing steady. *Getting there.* He was still a long way from 'Semi-Super-Clamps' readiness, but staying alert for ambushes kept other worries at bay.

Their little group got startled looks and a wide berth on the Trans-Hub Train. Charlie helped Rex into a transit hammock. It irised to its max to make room for a great deal of dog. After that, Charlie managed his own. Not gracefully—not with the arm shield. But he managed with a little help from Beck.

The train slid out of Terminal Three. *Heading home.* He would *not* miss Howardsboro.

How is Cinnamon? Have you heard? Rex's ears canted back, a sign of troubled thoughts confirmed by emotions through the link.

She survived several hours of surgery. Last I heard she was resting and has a pretty good prognosis—but she'll be recovering for weeks.

Berwyn hopes to bring her home as soon as she's stabilized. That may not be till tomorrow. Charlie grimaced. He didn't want to imagine what Berwyn must be going through, but it was scary-easy to do.

How's Shiv? Something resonated below the surface of this odd question.

Charlie gave him a quizzical look. *I have the impression he's more upset than I would have expected.*

You'd be less surprised if you could detect scent factors. Rex lolled his tongue. *Shiv and Berwyn don't seem to have crossed any professional lines, but if Berwyn weren't in Shiv's chain of command, they'd be a couple.*

Charlie blinked. Took a moment to wrap his mind around that.

Rex cocked his head at him. It made the transit hammock bulge oddly. *Cinnamon's off the duty roster now, the same way you were. The same way Razor is. That'll change Berwyn's status, too, won't it?*

Charlie rubbed the back of his neck. *Um, yeah. Berwyn's on Emergency Family Leave until further notice. He's off the duty lineup, just like Liz.*

I guess we'll see what happens next.

Huh. I guess so. Charlie shook his head. First Razor, now Cinnamon … Not to mention Rex's own injuries. *Man, this hasn't been a good month for the Pack, has it?*

Rex sobered. *No. Between Whisper and Wisniewski, we've got some serious payback to serve.* He growled. *I hate it that Knife Woman got away.*

For now. Elle and Petunia have established scent profiles for her, her partner, UPO Danesh, and two other men who helped them escape. Last night they tracked them to a place where they must've gotten into a vehicle. They couldn't follow from there, but Nicole and Walter pulled excellent scent samples. They're in our system now.

Rex snapped his ears flat. *Too bad the Scent Reference Lab is closed. Maybe they could make better IDs. Damn Wisniewski!* He growled. *Last time I visited Razor we discussed how much we'd like to rip his throat out.* He flicked his ears and curled his lip to show a flash of teeth. *But I want answers, far more than blood. And why let him off easy by killing him? What Jackson Wisniewski wants is power. Take that away, and it's a meaningful punishment.*

You'd rather incarcerate? I wonder what restorative justice principles would dictate.

I'd prefer to lock him up where he can't influence anything. Preferably for the rest of his life. He'll hate that lots worse than death.

Well, okay, then. At least we have a plan.

Rex snorted.

Exactly. It was a great plan, if one didn't consider the improbability of catching the man, then somehow extraditing him to Rana Station where they could make the charges stick. But they could dream.

The Wheel Two Hub Terminal hadn't changed since last night. Assortments of colored lights had been strung everywhere in the terminal. Charlie figured they could stand equally well for New Year's, Hanukkah, Solstice, Christmas, Zhixizzixi, and Bodhi Day, though by now that last one was over. The place had never looked more beautiful to Charlie, but not because of the lights. *Almost home!*

He, Rex, Jack, and Beck joined the flow of people pulling themselves off the train—well, joined it as much as they could with a meter-wide bubble of open air all around their little group. At the other end of the car, a flood of riders pulled themselves inside and claimed newly-vacated transit hammocks.

Charlie struggled to maintain his situational awareness, but it was impossible to look everywhere at once. He, Jack, and Beck made three points of a protective triangle around Rex, everyone's head on a swivel. But cold realization remained: it still was possible they all could miss an ambush till too late.

Midday rush remained near its peak. People moved everywhere, in all directions, positioned in all orientations, an undulating, living river. Miraculously, no one collided, and many even managed to score some lunch.

Work crews of ozzirikkians glided past on their trademark purple jet-canoes. Humans in corporate jumpsuits of various colors, travelers, dockhands, and myriad others moved along the Hub. They scuttled down pipe-like ladder-poles with protruding rungs, swung from handholds, navigated half-pipe corridors, or piloted personal sleds through the multitude. Most people were either human or ozzirikkian, but he spotted a fair number of Galactics, individuals of several other species, too. Rana was, after all, located near an interstellar jump-point, and many species of oxygen-breathers lived in this arm of the galaxy.

Charlie, Rex, and their escort had come at a busy time, partly in hope that the crowd would give them cover. Malevolent entities might not care to risk a move among a literal great cloud of witnesses. Their little group moved through the long, 360-degree vendors' sector. Colorful pocket booths offered a dizzying array of souvenirs, emergency supplies, sundries, toiletries, clothing, jewelry, and food. Edible options ranged from the genuinely nutritious to the authentically ridiculous—Real-Cultured-Bacon-Wrapped Fried Cheese on a Stick, anyone? Well, *some* people thought it was a good idea. There was a longer line for that booth than for the espresso bulbs down the way.

Rex's nose swung in the direction of the bacon-and-cheese booth. *Oh! That smells wonderful!*

Charlie laughed. *Of course, you'd think so.*

I've barely eaten anything today.

You've barely been awake.

Cleaner-vacs clustered and circled. They remained especially vigilant near the booths that created the most crumbs.

Charlie'd indulged in several varieties of the Bubble Tea Bulbs himself, in the past. But no Bubble Tea Bulb or Bacon-Wrapped Cheese Stick could garner a second look from him today. He needed to get Rex home. They stuck to the express lanes.

All the same, it took a while to reach the first major trunks that led to docks and warehouses in Wheel Two's jurisdiction. Many of the commuters flowed into them. Others moved farther on, bound for more distant docks or manufacturing facilities. *Stay alert! Look everywhere!* This was exhausting.

Beyond the nearest trunks, in somewhat wider-open lanes, lay other areas important for the Hub's smooth functioning. Over on Charlie's left and above his head in his current orientation, arched the Port Authority Base and Customs Post, from which his cousin-in-law Fee and her Port Authority colleagues embarked to conduct inspections, spot-checks, or enforcement actions. Any cargo headed downside to Wheel Two must be scanned at Customs there.

On his right glinted the steely teeth of the Station Defense Force Beta Base's main gate, a segregated complex of docks, warehouses, and repair facilities that served about a third of the Fleet. He and the *Triumph* crew had aided a rescue on a Base dock once, but that and his excursion with Rex to view the bridge crime scene were the only times he'd ever gone inside.

Farther on, next to Customs, lay the ERT Base, and Hildie. If only ....

Wait! What? Rex went hyper-alert.

Charlie slowed with a reluctant frown and a frisson of concern. *We need to keep moving.*

Rex darted across the flow of oncoming commuters by launching himself from ladder-pole to ladder-pole. People scowled and dodged him.

"Stop!" Jack cried.

"Rex! Where are you going?" Beck demanded.

Rising hunt-joy and focused intent flooded the brain link. Rex had smelled something he considered important. Or at least, he *thought* he'd smelled something important. Charlie recognized this phase of the Hunt. Rex was establishing if the target actually existed, and if so where it was. "Hold on, guys." Charlie redoubled his efforts to stay aware of everything around him—all the more so with Rex so hyper-focused on the scent he'd picked up. "He's got something."

But what was the target? Charlie made his way in Rex's wake to the side of the main corridor. He hoped he managed to do it with more diplomacy. The two field agents struggled to follow. He and Rex moved nearer to the SDF Base, with Beck and Jack behind them. Charlie parked himself at a handhold, then watched Rex work.

The big dog slow-bounced between the triangle-points of three handholds. He centered his focus on a particular area of airflow.

Charlie could only follow Rex's analysis in general, during this first phase when the XK9 evaluated the scent-spectrum. It was clear he sought a specific scent-profile, but no subject's name or nickname resonated through the link. That was professionalism at work. Dwelling on what he *wanted* to smell could bias his reading of the *actual* scents before his nose.

Rex pushed off, floated forward, then braked on one rung of a ladder-pole. He opened his mouth, tasting the air. His nose sampled short puffs.

Then he lunged forward, hackles bristling. Clarity blazed through the brain link. *He's here, Charlie! He's here! Right now! He's inside the SDF Base! Colonel Wisniewski is here!*

Wait! Are you — Charlie stopped the question. When an XK9 reacted this way, he was sure. *Hold up! There's a protocol for pursuit of a subject onto an SDF base. Stop!*

Rex snarled, bristled, but stopped. *I don't want him to get away!*

Then let's do it with cooperation from base personnel. You call Elaine. I'll contact Chief Klein. As I recall, we have multiple open warrants on the man.

Elaine will forbid me to go in. I shall lose the scoundrel!

Charlie scowled. *You'll lose him anyway if you try to go in without authorization.*

You call Elaine. Maybe you can convince her. Rex's hackles puffed out. A small nimbus of stress-shed surrounded him.

Charlie whirled to Beck and Jack. "Rex has scented Col. Wisniewski, of the Transmondian Intelligence Agency. He's here, right now, on the SDF Base! Call Mike!"

Next up: Elaine. "Good morning!" He could hear the smile in her voice. "Homeward bound?"

"We're in the Wheel Two Hub, and Rex has a lock on the clear, present scent of Jackson Wisniewski."

"Oh, does he, now? That's interesting. We had another reported scenting a few days ago, but then they lost the scent."

"I'm surprised he'd be here, with warrants out for him."

She made an irritated sound in her throat. "He's the Transmondian Intelligence Service's chief of Rana Station operations. He periodically comes here, then leaves again. We've tried to figure out how, without success to date. And he's been eluding warrants for years."

"You never had XK9s to work with before. Perhaps we'll learn more this time."

"Where did Rex catch his scent?"

"Just outside the SDF base."

She hesitated. "Have you called Klein?"

"He's next on my list, but we're assigned to you."

She let out a tense breath. "Run this one through Klein. OPD has recent, active warrants out on the man, and I have a feeling the less SBI involvement, the less resistance you'll receive on an SDF base. Meanwhile, I have some other calls to make. Good luck!"

"You, too." He looked up to meet Rex's eyes. *She said we should call Klein and make the request through the OPD.*

Rex nodded. *There is little love lost between the SBI and Admiral Virendra. Dr. SCISCO warned us about this. If Wisniewski's on the base, it's likely Virendra has something to do with it.*

How—what in—never mind. Charlie planned to ask many questions. Later. He patched Rex in, then called Chief Klein.

To his astonishment, Klein himself answered. "What has Rex found?"

How did the Chief—never mind. "Clear, present scent trace. Jackson Wisniewski is inside the Wheel Two SDF base."

"Right *now?*"

"Yes," Rex answered. "What is the protocol to get inside the base, so that we may serve an active warrant?"

"Pretty simple. I call Commander Montreaux. Hold, please."

Rex eyed the gate. *I really want my micrograv harness. It's not far. Just over at the Port Authority.*

Let's hurry. They crossed the diminishing tide of midday-rush commuters to the other side. Jack and Beck trailed them.

Charlie helped Rex into his micrograv harness, then adjusted it to accommodate his armor. After that, Charlie hastily donned Shiv's. It fit … Rather well, actually. *Smooth.* His authorization code synced the harness controls to his Cybernetically-Assisted Perception and provided a readout on his HUD. The interface followed a universal standard found on all micrograv equipment, from a quiddo-player's sled to Charlie's old MERS-V. Memories thickened around him, not all of them bad. His micrograv-jitters backed off another notch.

While he adjusted the fittings, Charlie switched to a different channel and called Hildie. "Rex has caught the scent of a subject for whom we have several open warrants. We're arranging access to pursue right now."

Hildie sighed. "Good hunting to you, then. Let's hope this one doesn't have a knife! Please stop by afterward?"

"I promise to *try.* Not sure how things will go, or how long we'll be."

"I get that. But I want to know everything you can tell me, after it's over. Don't wear yourself out, okay? You keeping track of your hours in micrograv?"

Charlie called up the time readout he'd set to calculate it. "Three hours, thirteen minutes' realtime exposure so far, for the week. Not close to my eight hours yet."

"Remember, that's eight hours *max*. You don't *want* to run them all out."

"Not if I can help it!"

Klein's incoming reply blinked. "And I've got to go. Love you!" He shifted channels, but Rex beat him to it. His ears went hot. Had Klein caught his parting words to Hildie? "Yes, sir?"

"Report to the gate. Commander Montreaux will meet you. She is interested to observe this hunt, and deeply displeased that Wisniewski might be there!"

"Will she go against Virendra?" Rex asked.

"She answers to a different admiral, one who's a rival of Virendra's, but she must respect Virendra's rank."

Rex growled. "In other words, hard to say."

By the time Charlie and Rex arrived at the Base gate, Charlie'd mastered the harness jets to the point of almost not having to think about them. His breath came more naturally. His hands barely shook.

Jack and Beck trailed them, now at a disadvantage with no micrograv harnesses. "What should we do?" Beck asked.

"I'm really not sure." Charlie bit his lip. "Stand by to relay information? Might want to see what Mike prefers."

"Sounds like a plan. Thanks."

The two MPs stationed at the gate to the base smiled when Rex and Charlie approached. "Hey, it's Rex," one said. "What brings you here today?"

Rex wagged his tail and accepted an ear-scratch, even though his urgency to hunt blazed hot through the link. "We are awaiting Commander Montreaux. I believe you have met my partner."

"Let them in." Montreaux jetted toward them in her own micrograv harness. "Show us the way, Rex."

CHAPTER 54

REX'S HUNT

"The scent is several minutes old, and it has drifted." Rex watched Commander Montreaux for her reactions. She seemed much more willing to listen to him, much more willing to believe what he said, than she had been on the day they'd first met. "The air currents here have moved the scent molecules from their original position. Please allow me a few moments to evaluate the speed of the breeze and establish a more accurate path."

She triggered her jets to move back. "You're the expert. Lead on!"

The Call of the Hunt surged within him. He followed his nose, confident the humans could find their own way. A gentle pulse of jets let him glide in Wisniewski's invisible-but-clear-to-smell wake for several meters, until he moved into a burst of sharp, peppery astonishment, quickly eclipsed by pungent alarm-scent. Next instant, the scent was gone.

Rex had strayed. Or, more likely, Wisniewski had abruptly changed course here. Rex circled, reacquired the scent-drift, then searched for where it might've originated. Perhaps that ladder-pole?

He glided over to it. *Yes! I have handprints and body-contact. There should be ample touch-DNA, and a fresh scent sample.*

Hold on a moment, we've run into a snag.

Rex looked around to see Charlie, Montreaux, and several of her people in a cluster, still far back by the gate. They weren't moving in Rex's direction. They weren't moving at all. From their body language, the people who'd just pulled up on a micrograv sled were arguing with Charlie and Montreaux. Echoes through the link from Charlie confirmed an argument.

Rex laid back his ears with a snarl. Clearly, an SDF uniform was no trustworthy guide to tell allies from obstacles. He used his harness-optics to image the area where Wisniewski had been, with brackets around the places where he'd scented the handprints. He forwarded his images to Charlie, Elaine, and the head of the OPD's Crime Scene Unit, along with annotations and embedded location coordinates.

Then he moved on.

From the shift in his scent factors and direction, Wisniewski had discerned a threat. He was searching for an escape … No, there wasn't enough anxiety in this profile. He wasn't searching. He knew where he needed to go, or thought he did. After his initial burst of alarm, the scent cooled, darkened, steadied.

Rex followed it from the ladder-pole to a side corridor like those that typically led to docks or warehouses. It wasn't the route to Warehouse 226, where he and Charlie had been dispatched on their ill-fated errand a month and a half ago, but it looked eerily similar.

He imaged the entrance, again with embedded location coordinates as well as a helpful number painted on the hatchway frame. Again he forwarded it to his humans, then glided inside with a subtle pulse of jets.

A chill washed over him. Rex shuddered. This looked extraordinarily like the tunnel down which he'd trailed Neil and Rufus Dolan six weeks ago. Guilty realization stabbed him. Both Charlie and Fujimoto had warned him he was going too fast that night. He'd discounted their warnings, but they'd been right. Urgency to reach Wisniewski burned within him now, but he moderated his pace. *This chase had better not result in another damned dock breach!*

Where are you? Charlie asked. *I can't see you at all.*

Irritation prickled his hackles. *Check your Inbox. I'm sending coordinates.*

Admiral Virendra just arrived. He's blocking us.

Montreaux, too? A growl burned in Rex's throat.

He outranks her. They're arguing.

Of course he does. And of course they are. Because he's been played and now he realizes he's in trouble. The trail entered another branching corridor. Rex paused to image the entrance to this one, embed coordinates, and send. *Wisniewski's scent factors are growing more confident the farther I follow them. I fear he is planning an escape.*

Maybe. Rex felt the frown behind Charlie's words. *Or maybe he's planning an ambush.*

ANXIETY PUNCHED Charlie's pulse into overdrive. He must follow Rex! But a pair of armed MPs on a micrograv sled blocked the way. Six more in micrograv harnesses backed them up. Not to mention Admiral Virendra himself.

Charlie'd never met Virendra in person, but he recognized the tall man with the stiff brush of white hair. Between replays of Shady's infamous corridor-chase and a history-making vid in Central Plaza that he'd watched from his hospital bed six weeks ago, it would be hard to mistake the man.

Virendra wasn't any more accommodating for Charlie and Montreaux now than he had been for Rex six weeks ago in Central Plaza. Even in microgravity, he was doing his best to loom over Montreaux with a commanding glare. "Stand down, Commander! You're not authorized for access to that dock."

Montreaux pulsed jets to meet him at eye-level. "The hell I'm not! This is my base!"

His face took on a peevish squint. His jaw and lower lip jutted. "You're not on a need-to-know status." His haughty tone made Charlie want to punch him—and the refusal wasn't even directed at Charlie.

Montreaux stiffened. "Not on need-to-know? Since *when?* I repeat—It's *my base!*"

He lifted his chin. "Special operation."

Montreaux returned a smoldering glare. "I'd be more likely to believe that, if a known Transmondian agent hadn't been verified as present *on my base* in that precise area. I want him in custody! *Now!*"

His brows bounced, then he reassumed his haughty stance. "What verification?"

"Positive ID by a witness to whom he is known."

He folded his arms. "Where is this 'witness'? I see no witness."

"Positive scent ID, by XK9 Rex—" She scowled, looked around. "He was here a minute ago."

"See? You have no verification. Stand down."

Montreaux turned to Charlie. "Where's Rex?"

"Chasing Wisniewski."

"Alone?" Montreaux asked.

"What?" Virendra demanded. "Call off that dog! Neither one of you is authorized!"

"You're keeping me from following him." Charlie clenched his fists. But even a full-strength Semi-SuperCop *without* an arm shield would be wise not to tackle eight armed MPs and a furious admiral all at once.

"You have a com! Call him!"

Charlie keyed his com, then activated his speaker. "Rex, Admiral Virendra just ordered me to order you to stand down." *You're on speaker,* he added through the link.

"Tell the Admiral to stuff a sock in it," Rex's vocalizer-voice replied. "I am busy."

Virendra's face purpled. "Are you going to let him talk to you like that?"

"With respect, Admiral, he outranks me." Time was passing, and Rex was alone. Charlie'd sent a silent call-for-backup once already, but so far he'd gotten no—he caught movement at the edge of his view, and turned.

More SDF uniforms. Charlie'd rarely felt so outnumbered. A Commodore in the lead, but his insignia marked him as assigned to yet *another* branch of the service.

"Why, Nolan," the new man said. "I wouldn't have thought you'd personally insert yourself into something like this."

Virendra gave him a cold look. "You're wasting your time, Cornwell. Nothing to see, here. Go away."

"On the contrary, I have a tip from a highly trusted source that you're harboring a wanted fugitive."

"If you mean that dog, forget it."

Commodore-apparently-Cornwell turned to Charlie. "Morgan, please confirm. Positive scent ID? Wisniewski?"

"Yes. Rex is currently in pursuit on Dock—" Charlie glanced at the latest image from Rex. "Dock 68-Q. Without backup, thanks to Virendra." *How does this Commodore Cornwell know who I am?*

Long story, Rex replied. *Are you coming soon?*

I hope. But don't hold your breath.

"Obstructing an investigation?" Cornwell raised his eyebrows at Virendra. "Interfering with the execution of an active warrant?"

Virendra shook his head. "Nothing of the sort. Wisniewski isn't here."

"Yes, he is," Charlie said.

"I concur," Montreaux agreed. "Admiral, if he isn't there, you have no need to block us. Let us go see for ourselves."

Through the link Charlie sensed a surge of alarm from Rex.

He eyed the ladder-pole where he'd last seen the big dog. "I need to get to my partner. Something's happening!"

REX LET his tongue slide out in a silent dog-laugh at the echo of Virendra's reaction that came through the link.

But he'd better not let it distract him too much. And he'd better not make any needless noises while floating through these seemingly-deserted passageways. Scent rafts didn't fall in micro-gravity, but they did cool and decay at about the same rate as they did in similar air-temps elsewhere. From the warmth of the ones hanging in midair here, Rex had almost caught up to his quarry. And Charlie'd made a good point earlier, about ambushes.

He closed his mouth. Brought himself to all-stop as quietly as he could. Even the near-soundless hiss of his retros seemed loud to him. He halted about half a meter back from the nearest branching corridor. It opened into the "ceiling" from his orientation.

How does Cornwell know who I am? Charlie asked.

Long story. Mm. Cornwell was there? That was … *possibly* a good thing. *Are you coming soon?*

I hope. But don't hold your breath.

Great. He didn't exactly hold his breath, but breathed carefully through his nose, floated quiet as death, and listened. The faintest sigh of an air current emanated from the branching corridor. It carried Wisniewski's cooling scent, but also a growing load of a new and unexpected one.

Flowing stronger.

A soft *thump-thump-thump* of grips on handholds grew louder. Knife Woman's partner. Coming this way.

Alarm stabbed through Rex, but this was not a moment for panic. Cold with purpose, Rex timed a pulse of his jets so one of the man's quiet, rhythmic *thumps* would mask it. He glided forward, used another *thump* to position himself by the far side of the opening. The man was taking pains to move near-silently. He would expect not to be heard. And he'd expect Rex to be coming from the same direction Wisniewski had. Rex imaged the opening and sent coordinates. *Knife Woman's partner is approaching.*

Astonishment echoed through the link. *Holy crap. Is that how they do it? Wisniewski's teamed up with Whisper? And both with Virendra?*

Rex laid back his ears. *Speculate privately. I must focus.*

Sorry. Charlie conveyed wordless good wishes, then muted his input as fully as he could.

Thump. Thump. Directly overhead. The man stopped.

Click. Rex knew that sound. That was a trank-pistol cocking.

Long moment. What was he waiting for?

A quiet but elevated heartbeat, just centimeters away. Scent drifted lazily into Rex's range. He swallowed a growl. *Afraid of me, are you? Good.*

Trank-pistol first, Knife Woman's partner slid partway through the opening. With his back to Rex.

Rex struck before the man could look around. Clamped jaws around his neck and bit down hard.

He'd expected another steel girder—yet *more* augmented bones.

But *no.*

Knife Woman's partner barely made a quiet gasp. His cervical bones splintered in an instant. Blood filled Rex's mouth. Filled his eyes. Filled everything. Sudden death reeked in his nostrils.

Revolted, he spat it out.

He recoiled down the corridor. Shuddering. Aghast.

Couldn't get that taste—so much blood!—*Horrible* blood!—out of his mouth.

He retched. Full-body revulsion rolled through him.

Rex! It was an accident! Get a grip! Charlie cried through the link. *Wisniewski's still after you! FOCUS!*

Rex gave another whole-body shudder. *Focus. Right.*

Yes. Focus, Charlie affirmed. *Job's not over. Deal with the dead man later.*

Rex growled. Deep and ferocious, it came out from the depths of his old life. The years of abuse. The terrible weeks in Wisniewski's house of horrors. All the stuffed anger. All the despair. *Job's. Not. Over.*

Deal with the dead man.

Deal with Wisniewski.

Deal with him NOW.

CHARLIE GASPED, swallowed, looked up, breathless.

He was clinging to the micrograv sled with trembling hands. Head still filled with death and blood, he tried to pull out, to pull back, to get a grip.

Commodore Cornwell and his two aides, Commodore Montreaux, Admiral Virendra, and eight MPs all stared at him with wide eyes and expressions that teetered between fascination and horror.

He drew in a deep breath. Held it. Let it out slowly. "I need to get in there."

"Good God, Charlie," Montreaux cried. "Are you all right?"

"Brain link," Charlie gasped. "It can get intense. I need to go to Rex."

"What happened?" Cornwell demanded.

Charlie looked him in the eye. "Wisniewski has been working with Whisper. I imagine that's how he's gotten in and out so many times undetected. A known Whisper operative just tried to kill Rex, but Rex killed him first. We need to get in there!"

Cornwell stared at him. "Then it's true! *Whisper! Fuck!*"

Virendra shook his head. "That's ... That's insane." But he sounded as if even *he* didn't believe his own words.

Montreaux wheeled on him. "*WHISPER? You allowed a FOREIGN AGENT! And THE WHISPER SYNDICATE! Onto MY BASE? They're here RIGHT NOW, and you're STOPPING US?*" She drew back. Her fury steamed from every centimeter of her. "*Arrest* this man—or be traitors along *with* him!"

"Seriously, Clarimonde," Virendra began.

One of his own MPs pulled his arms behind him. Another slapped on cuffs.

Charlie didn't wait to see the end of that. He powered toward the ladder-pole.

CHAPTER 55

THE ANSWER TO A CRYPTIC CLUE

All around Rex, ventilator fans kicked on.

Oh, crap! Biohazard! Of course! The sensors would trigger containment.

Screw the risks. He had to get out of here *now.* He kicked the corpse out of the way and darted through the opening Knife Woman's partner had just used. It was already closing. He flashed on a surveillance vid-image of Neil and Rufus Dolan, escaping from Warehouse 226 and the body they'd left behind. Sensed a parallel memory in Charlie.

No ambush awaited in the new corridor. He let out a gusty breath, coughed more blood from his mouth, strove to clear his nose. He sneezed, then froze when the sound echoed.

Once again, fans kicked on all around him. *What the hell?*

How bloody are you? Charlie asked.

Oh. I am, um, kinda covered in blood. A floating, snarling, stress-shedding biohazard, all wrapped up in one big, armored dog. *If there was gravity, I'd be dripping.* As it was, he emanated a mist of blood.

Better move faster than the containment measures.

Roger that! Rex pulsed his jets, glided faster. Wisniewski wasn't captured yet. The Hunt continued.

The hatch behind him snapped shut. *The farther I go, the more sections will seal. You can't follow me now, Charlie. I think I'm on my own.* A hollow opened in the pit of his stomach, but determination overrode it. *Forward. Deal with Wisneiwski!*

He hoped at least *some* of his optics weren't covered in blood, but it was hard to tell. Ears alert for the smallest noise, cold with purpose, he pulsed his jets harder.

I'm still getting partial views, so not everything's covered. Sure would like to take a washcloth to your forward-facing lenses, though. When Charlie got that rueful tone in his mental voice, his expression was usually a grimace.

Rex opened the link more widely to him.

That helps. Thanks.

Rex continued down the corridor, his nose full of Knife Woman's partner and Wisniewski. He stayed just ahead of the containment closures. Were they making too much noise? Probably. His hackles prickled, but the ones not itching under his armor felt matted and sticky. Where was he going? *Wisniewski must have a ship.*

You're approaching the docks, so that's a pretty good bet. He needs a way to get from Rana to Chayko and back.

A Whisper- or Transmondian Intelligence-affiliated ship? At an SDF dock? Rex laid back his ears, and glimpsed droplets fly at the edges of his vision. *How do you know I'm approaching the docks?*

Montreaux has pulled up a schematic of the base. It shows us which areas have sealed, what ships are docked, which docks are being serviced or repaired, and it even pings your badge.

Smooth. Is there another way for you to reach me?

She's figuring that out right now. There should be.

Where am I?

Corridor 68-Q345, approaching Docking Bay 68-Q-7. It's marked as closed for repairs.

I'm gonna guess it's not really under repair. Rex approached another cross-corridor. No heartbeat, no breathing, no scent of someone waiting to attack. *The scent trail turns at this corridor.* The section behind him snapped closed. A couple meters down the new corridor he saw a gantry with its gangway still attached.

As we thought. You're headed into Docking Bay 68-Q-7. You followed Wisniewski through a back way where there's not much traffic. We're headed there now, on a much more direct route.

I'm going in. I'd like to surprise them if I can. Also, not be contained in the corridor.

Be careful!

Rex pulsed his jets. The gangway was like a large, clear, collapsible tube, latched to the berthing cone. The entry hatch and both sides of the airlock at the end lay open. *Oh. It's open for Partner. They don't know he's … not coming.*

Rex slowed. The gangway couldn't seal on him. It was just a clear-sided foldup. He owed it to himself to make sure no ambush lurked ahead.

Lights started blinking. "Intruder!" a deep, mechanical-sounding voice intoned. "Intruder! Intruder!"

Rex blasted his jets, dove through the closing outer hatch. The inner hatch ripped hairs from his tail-tip when it snapped shut behind him. Rex rebounded off a bulkhead, then spun toward Wisniewski's scent.

"What the hell, Fowler!" Wisniewski yelled. "Didn't you—"

Rex barreled through. Clamped jaws on his wrist. Pinned both Wisniewski and his trank pistol to the back of the small compartment.

"No, he did not kill me," Rex said. "You are under arrest."

"Launch!" Wisniewski yelled, from underneath Rex. "Brenny! Launch! Launch! Launch NOW! Before they lock us down!"

CHARLIE GASPED. "They're launching! Can you lock them down?"

"Command override!" Montreaux shouted into her com.

"Protocol Romeo-Niner-Alpha! Lock down Docking Bay 68-Q-7! Stat!"

"Did it lock in time?" Charlie and the three MPs in micrograv harnesses who'd come with them hit their sirens and accelerated. Dock workers lunged for the margins or the bulkheads.

Commander Montreaux oscillated between scowling into the middle distance and glaring toward their goal. "Command override! Protocol Romeo-Niner-Alpha! Lock down Docking Bay 68-Q—*Dammit! I don't have time for this! Why is this even on my readout?*"

"What is it?" A chill coiled in the pit of Charlie's stomach. *Surely not.*

"Never mind. Let's get to the dock!" Montreaux's jaw jutted. Her glare could cut a diamond.

We're almost to the dock, Charlie told Rex. *What's happening?*

Kinda busy now! He sensed pain and tumbling movement. His partner focused elsewhere.

Okay. Rex needed no distractions.

"Commander Montreaux, I apologize, but—what was on your readout?"

She grimaced, shook her head. "Some kind of idiotic, nonsense poetry. Maybe a glitch. Not important."

"Three lines?" Charlie hoped his hunch was wrong, but it *was* a Whisper ship. "Starts 'Shame to,' stuff about recklessness and ambition?"

She burned braking jets. He slowed with her, having expected it. She stared at him, dumbfounded. "How did you know? What is this?"

The MPs braked and looped back around to them.

"Go! Go!" She told them, then turned to Charlie. "Give."

"Read me the message, and I'll tell you."

She frowned into her HUD. "Shame to the Colonel for a reckless course. Overreaching ambition makes fools. How many lives destroyed? Now payment comes." She looked up at him, bewildered.

The pit of Charlie's stomach dropped into an abyss. "That ship is going to explode. Like the *Izgubil*. Like the *Ministo Lulak*. If you've received that message, it means the nanotimers are already burning."

CHARLIE BURNED jets for the ERT Base. Wisniewski's—Whisper's —covert Dart-Class craft had managed to launch before lockdown, despite Montreaux's best efforts. And it was fiendishly maneuverable.

The SDF had gone after it with everything available, from fighters built like racing yachts to the massive starship *Fairboro*. But they could only kill it, not stop it. Montreaux had provided him channel access. On one side of his HUD, Charlie followed their pursuit.

Anyone inside the little Dart who wasn't strapped down would be helplessly tossed around. Just as it seemed, from link-impressions, Rex was. His partner wouldn't make it to an escape pod at this rate.

"Rex chased Wisniewski onto a Whisper ship," Charlie blurted to Klein, Elaine, and Hildie simultaneously on the com. "Montreaux got a message—just like *Ministo Lulak*. That ship is going to blow!"

"They're tracking his badge, right?" Klein asked. "Can you help them?"

"I can track him through the link while he's conscious," Charlie said. "That's more accurate than a badge-ping. Put me in a MERS-V!"

Dead silence all around.

"I'm serious! It's *Rex! Put me in a MERS-V!* I can get him!"

"Your call, Klein," Elaine said.

"Can you really do it?" Klein asked.

"I *have* to. It's *Rex!*"

Klein drew in a breath. "Watch-Sergeant? You have the final say."

"Get over here, Morgan." Hildie's voice was all-business. "Get over here *stat!*"

THE SHIP SPUN. Rex and Wisniewski tumbled into walls, or the ceiling, or the floor. Whatever. All were made of the same gray metal. All hurt like hell to smack into. Rex had been in a bunker with thin wall-pads during the dock breach. He'd thought that was bad, and it had nearly killed Charlie. But now he and Wisniewski tumbled longer distances, with nothing at all to pad them when they crashed into each other and the bulkheads.

Wisniewski's wrist bones grated between Rex's teeth, but did not break. The old man made a guttural pain-noise. His trank pistol bounced away.

Rex hadn't meant to bite down, but their collisions with the walls made it impossible not to. *Well, damn.* He'd feared Wisniewski might have augmentations like so many of his agents. Now he knew he did. How strong did augmented humans remain in their senior years?

They went airborne briefly, then crunched against yet another hard metal surface. This time Rex lost his grip on Wisniewski's wrist.

The trank pistol bounced toward them.

Wisniewski fumbled for it. The ship made another dive. They piled up across the room. That hard thing poking his leg was probably the trank pistol.

The ship made a rolling maneuver, then leveled out. Now Rex was upside down on top of Wisniewski. His head spun. G-force dragged harder than in the Five-Ten. He must be crushing Wisniewski. He struggled to move off the man. Didn't want to suffocate him. Plan was take him prisoner.

Rex! Rex! Get to an escape pod! Charlie shouted through the link. Rex groggily realized he'd been shouting this for a while already. *Do you read me? Get into an escape pod NOW!*

"Get into escape pod," Rex said.

"Like I'd tell you where one is." Wisniewski's voice sounded as thick and slow as Rex's thoughts.

Your ship is rigged like the Izgubil. *It's gonna blow up!* Charlie yelled.

Rolling terror tumbled through Rex. "Ship rigged. Like *Izgubil*. Going to blow!"

"Yeah, tell me another!" Wisniewski squeezed out a derisive laugh.

Rex dragged himself toward the airlock. Most ships had their pods stowed near exits.

The ship spun, threw him into the far corner. Wisniewski slammed against him.

CHARLIE CLAMBERED out of Shiv's micrograv harness. *Just go. Don't think.*

Oz Meredith frowned at him. Hesitated. Grimaced. "Take T-7." Cold eyes, grudging tone. He'd given Hildie hell about this already, no doubt. Probably would again.

Before the *Asalatu*, Charlie'd driven T-1. As Squad Commander, Oz always designated the oldest in the lineup, the reserve unit, as T-7. Charlie nodded. "Roger that." He was damned lucky Oz would give him a MERS-V at all.

The entire *Triumph* crew watched him, their faces uneasy. The new drivers, Martin, Sally, and Ramón, scowled. They didn't know him or trust him. Charlie didn't blame them. Vilma, Theresa, Frank, and Eli all looked worried. Hildie met his eyes with a defiant lift of her chin, as if to say *you've got this, dammit. Now show them!*

He kept his focus on her. Managed a nod and an almost-smile in return. The last time he'd tried this ... *didn't matter.*

He dragged in a strangled breath. Focused on his task. He could put the control suit on in his sleep. Just step in backward. Pull it closed. Activate seals. Keep his mind on routine, on mechanics, on step-by-step.

He climbed into T-7, and settled into the familiar embrace of the couch, half-numb. Strapped down. His hands shook. *Don't think. Just do.* "Suit's coming online." His voice sounded almost steady. His cockpit lit up. "Running checks." All gauges blinked *go.*

"He didn't get this far, before." From Theresa's soft tone, she hadn't meant for him to hear.

No, he hadn't. Charlie's chest constricted. *No, don't think.* He kept his breathing even by force of will. His pulse thudded in his neck, his wrists, his gut. Through the link he felt Rex land on Wisniewski. *Gotta do this. Can't fail this time.*

He ran the systems-check. It was hard to breathe. He frowned at the readout: O_2 mix normal. Were his gauges off? *No. Not the gauges at fault.* He dragged in another breath. Answered the com check in order: first Ramón, then Sally, then Martin, then Charlie. The fourth driver, the spare.

Triumph vibrated. Launch sequence started.

He closed his eyes. Breathed in, held it, then out. Panic clawed him, roiled his gut.

Bang! Docking grapples unclamped. His breath accelerated. Turned to choking gasps. *No, dammit!* He held a gasp, fought for control.

Gentle push. Inside the launch tube now.

Charlie let air out *slow-slow-slow*, then dragged in another breath. *I'm coming, Rex.*

REX DRAGGED his body toward the airlock.

I'm coming, Rex, Charlie seemed kinda shaky through the link.

I'll be here. You okay?

In a MERS-V. Coming to catch you.

Rex's heart constricted. *Seriously?*

Get into a pod. We'll talk later.

Behind him, Wisniewski grunted, gasped. He, too, struggled against the G-force, but Rex knew he wasn't trying for an escape pod. The trank pistol had tumbled that direction. If he got it before Rex could jump inside a pod ....

With effort, Rex swung his head around.

The fingers on Wisniewski's still-functional hand trembled, strained, reached toward the pistol's grip. Just a centimeter away.

How long since the nanotimers ignited? What should he do? Try to stop Wisniewski? Get to a pod?

The ship made a dive.

Rex flew through the air.

Everything around him went bright.

CHAPTER 56

BRINGING THINGS HOME

B right burst.
Flying bits.
Charlie's mind flashed on another such moment, but bigger. Nausea, vertigo, the mother of all headaches clutched him. Blinded him to the present. Seized him in a crushing grip.

Rex emanated terror, disbelief, freezing chill.

Charlie fought the flashback. Rex needed him clear-headed. Centered on *now. Breathe out! Relax your muscles!* he cried through the link.

"Deploy T-1," Oz's voice cut like steel across his com.

Bang! T-1 was away. "Deployment nominal," Ramón said.

Charlie's stomach clenched. His head throbbed. He desperately swallowed bile.

"Deploy T-2."

Bang! "Deployment nominal," Sally said.

"Deploy T-3."

Bang! "Deployment nominal," Martin said.

"Deploy T-7."

Charlie pressed thumbs on triggers.

Bang! Deployment felt like a kick in the kidneys, but it was his call to action. T-7 jetted forward. "Deployment nominal." Charlie hoped he sounded steady.

He could sense that Rex was over somewhere in *that* direction. Made a local sweep with his targeting lidar. Amber SMA, *Search Mode Activated*, blinked on his screen. He tried to trigger a badge-ping.

Badge-ping returned. Amber AT flickered on his screen: *Acquiring Target.* Another badge-ping, then a glowing green TL. *Target Locked.*

Go! Go! Go! T-7 punched through the darkness. "Target acquired and locked." He dragged in a shuddering breath. *Go! Just go!*

"Roger target acquired and locked, T-7. *That* was fast!"

"Have an unfair advantage." Charlie smiled, or at least he bared his teeth. *I'm coming, Rex!* A counter pulsed at the edge of his HUD. Rex's 90-second margin of life was closing fast.

Holding you … to that. Rex's consciousness faltered.

Lidar swept. How far, now? Badge-ping, good and strong. Target Lock glowed green.

Then his cockpit lights went amber.

Onk-onk-onk-onk—the klaxon warned of approaching debris, then shifted to the rising *bwee-e-e-e, bwee-e-e-e* of Collision Avoidance Activated. T-7 jerked him. Jinked. Hitched. Dropped.

Shrapnel everywhere.

Bwee-e-e-e, bwee-e-e-e.

Smaller bits rattled, barely audible. Bigger ones banged. Their impacts on T-7's hull sent vibrations through Charlie's atmosphere.

Bwee-e-e-e, bwee-e-e-e.

He cut the klaxons. *Yeah, yeah, I know. Shut up.*

T-7 dodged the biggest ones. Charlie didn't ever want to hear *that* kind of warning klaxon or contact-sound again.

Badge-ping in the Black Void centered on Rex's fading consciousness. Target Lock glowed strong.

I'm coming! I'm coming!

The first ten seconds ticked away. Rex passed out. Dropped off the link. Black dog in the Black Void. Gone, except for the badge-ping and the Target Lock.

"Locked on T-7's heading," Ramón said. "He's nailed it."

Charlie's heart lifted some. Finding the vics' exact heading was always the first challenge. Just a second or two could separate life from death. He focused on Rex's badge-ping.

"Roger that. Locking," Sally replied.

"Locking," Martin echoed.

They rode out collision avoidance. Closed on the wreck. Proximity alert flickered. Lidar focused. T-7 hinked and jinked. Still dodging shrapnel. Still closing in. Charlie switched on lamps. Light flashed across rolling, floating objects. Spatters of small pieces rattled across T-7's hull. Collision avoidance sensors zigged and zagged him.

Badge-pings resumed after each hop and bounce. Target Lock glowed bright. A point enlarged. Became a black lump. Legs and tail splayed. It drifted, lazily rotating toward him. Other objects tumbled near Rex, many hard-edged, angular. Some trailed wires or pipes. But one was longer, with arms and legs. *Wisniewski?*

He targeted secondary lidar. Amber SMA shifted to the flicker of AT, then resolved into bright green TL.

"Base, I've got a lock on Rex. Also one human."

Distantly, he heard Martin. "Locked on what looks like a sealed med-bed and a human."

Then Sally. "Locked on three humans. Closing."

Finally Ramón. "Got two more humans. Locked on."

Charlie's focus narrowed. T-7's Arms of Life could hold up to a dozen people, but the trick was to catch them. He checked the timer, still clicking. Rex's 90 seconds weren't gone yet. He extended the Arms from Traveling Empty Lock. They snap-tele-scoped to make long, inward-curving fan-shapes like massive bats' wings with membranes between the ribs.

Time spun by, but you couldn't rush this part. People had

been decapitated or dismembered by Arms too quickly snapped shut. Long-practiced habit kicked in. Charlie's hands were steady on the controls now. Taut with concentration, Arms at their widest, he centered on Rex and one human who tumbled within a couple meters of each other.

Smooth, sweeping motion. *Steady on. Steady on. Steady on.* Charlie closed the Arms around them. Locked Arms together. Inflated with the O$_2$ mix. He'd beaten the 90-second margin. Rex and his fellow passenger still had a chance to live.

Charlie sucked in a harsh breath. "T-7 is loaded and locked. Two in Arms. Returning to Base."

"Roger, T-7. Come on home."

Tears filled his eyes. "T-7 coming home, out." He sat back with a gasp. His body trembled, slick with sweat. His head spun.

Coming home, yes.

At long last.

Coming home.

IF CHARLIE'D had any illusions about falling into Hildie's arms after climbing down from T-7, he'd ditched them well before final storage shutdown.

Med-bay overflowed. They'd retrieved seven besides Rex. They'd reached them quickly. It was possible all might live, but not without swift medical intervention. All hands in the med-bay were more than busy right now.

Com chatter said SDF debris mop-up had already started. Safe commercial and military navigation required clear space-lanes. They had to get every particle they could gather. More-over, the remains of the Dart constituted a crime scene—one with Adeyeme's name on the "deliver to," no doubt.

Charlie maneuvered T-7 into its stall, then ran standard systems-checks before shut-down. He was no longer certified or licensed, so a *Triumph* crewmember would have to do those all over again, but he might as well show them he was competent. It mattered to *him*, whether it did to them or not.

He'd gotten them into enough trouble already. Hildie and Oz were probably looking at administrative leave pending investigations, even though they'd had Klein's blessing. This was a small way to say thank-you.

Next came muck-out, the process of cleaning the unit, removing and replacing the gamey control suit liner, switching out depleted gas tanks for full ones, and doing assorted other little routine maintenance and resupply tasks. He fell back into the rhythm pretty smoothly, but being able to access the checklist on his HUD saved him from screwing up several steps he would've forgotten.

He connected the final replacement cylinder and locked it down, then withdrew backwards from the guts of the vehicle.

"You know I have to re-check all of that," Oz said.

Charlie straightened, turned to face him. "Yeah. Wanted to help if I could, though."

"Mucking out's a help." He nodded, stared at T-7. "'Preciate that."

"I owe you."

Oz grimaced, then looked at him. Charlie met his scrutiny straight-on.

"I'll take it out of your hide someday, maybe." Oz shook his head. "Eight living rescued. Probably couldn't have gotten 'em all in time, without you. What price for a life, eh?"

"Even if most of them are Whisper?"

"Nobody deserves to asphyxiate in the Black Void." He hesitated. "Well, maybe the guy who blew them up."

Charlie released a breath. "We're on his trail."

"Yeah, I know." Oz nodded. "And you'll hunt better with your partner. That's one major reason I let you go out. Can't lose Rex. You two need to end this."

"That we do. Thank you."

"Come on with me now. You need a shower!"

In the worst way. Rank with flop-sweat, he urgently craved a shower, but he hesitated. "Can't take the arm and arm shield into a sonic unit."

"Definitely not." Oz shook his head. "Planned on rigging up the de-con unit for a light wash. I'll run the controls for you."

Charlie laughed. "That ought to do it. Thanks." He pulled himself into the shower room.

Whoops, cheers, whistles and claps erupted the moment he appeared. The echoes rattled and multiplied in the small space. Ramón, Sally and Martin grinned like crazy people. Of *course*, they'd finished their muck-outs faster—they did it every day. They also looked post-shower clean. *Dang. I'm even slower than I thought.* But he grinned back at them and pulled himself inside.

Ramón, the lead driver, kicked away from the opposite wall to join Charlie and Oz. He pumped Charlie's hand, his face lively with excitement. "You did it, old man! What an honor to drive with a living legend! That was amazing!"

Everyone renewed their clapping and cheering. Charlie accepted it with as pleasant an expression and attitude as he could. They clearly meant it well. But *"old man?"* Even "living legend" made him feel antique. He was only twenty-seven! Of course, Ramón couldn't be more than … Maybe eighteen? The drivers all looked like they were still in upper-levels.

Oz clapped him on the shoulder, leaned in to speak in a low tone. "Never mind them. They're all just cocky babies."

Charlie sighed. "Exactly like I was."

"Here's hoping they're never tested as you were." He squeezed Charlie's shoulder, then released it. "Now let's get you into that shower."

By the time Charlie had showered and put on a fresh jumpsuit, the young driver trio had gone silent, round-eyed, and almost painfully respectful. They'd gotten a look at his scars.

Their reactions did nothing to make him feel less ancient. Melancholy and adrenaline let-down sapped him. He gathered the rumpled clothing he'd worn earlier, plus the two micrograv harnesses. Donned Shiv's, then bit his lip and bagged Rex's with the clothing.

Rex wouldn't be needing his for a while.

But those concerns fled when he and his little band neared the commons. He recognized the haranguing voice that echoed down the corridor's metal walls to greet them.

"... had the incredible *unprofessionalism* to allow an uncertified, unlicensed, *civilian* on deck, much less *into a MERS-V and out loose in space!* Of all the lame-assed, idiot moves! I can't believe you!"

Charlie scowled. Burned jets. He burst into the commons.

Hildie floated motionless in a corner, eyes averted, her body language tight and closed. Not for any amount of money would Charlie have crossed her when her mouth made that kind of grim line.

"Actually, Captain, that last part was my call." Oz's voice carried across the commons from behind Charlie. "Eight living retrieved as a direct result. Far as we can tell that's all hands. A 100% retrieval from a catastrophic event like this won't hurt your stats at all."

The man who spun to confront them—then kept spinning till he found something to grab onto—was probably a few years older than Charlie. He had pasty-pale skin, the beginnings of a pot belly, and a scraggly brown goatee. He scowled at Oz. "I'll deal with *you* in a minute."

"Care to deal with *me*, first?" Charlie fired braking jets at half a meter.

Captain LaRochelle's body flinched backward. Then he stiffened and drew in a sharp breath. "*You* get off my deck. *Now!*"

He *did* have the right to order him out. Charlie clenched his fists and gave him a long, hard stare.

LaRochelle paled a little more, but he held his ground. Lifted his chin and glared back.

Charlie looked toward Hildie.

She met his eyes with an unhappy expression. Bit her lip and gave a little nod.

He replied with the best "namaste-style" bow he could manage in micrograv and pulsed jets to turn. Bile rose in his throat, to be forced to leave her there at the captain's mercy. He ground his teeth and made for the exit.

Oz and the three drivers pulled closer to their transit pole to give him room.

He paused. "Thanks again," he said quietly to Oz. He saluted the three drivers.

They directed defiant looks toward their captain, then crisply saluted back.

Charlie burned jets for the exit.

He stopped at the Port Authority to check the harnesses back in. Two messages hit his HUD almost simultaneously. He opened Dr. Zuni's first. His doctor wanted him back at Orangeboro Med, *stat*, for an exam after his longer-than-expected stint in micrograv. He checked his timer, startled to see he'd been up here more than six hours all told. *Yikes.*

The other was from Hildie: "Meet me at Topside Trauma. I have a ride for you."

His tight gut eased. Topside Trauma wasn't technically on LaRochelle's "deck," and the Emergency Express there offered a fast, direct route to Orangeboro Med. "Thanks. On my way."

Without the harness he had to pull himself along via handholds and transit poles, but he'd definitely gotten his "micrograv moves" back today. He made good time, even as exhaustion set in more fully.

The forlorn slump of Hildie's body uncurled and brightened

the moment she caught sight of him. No hesitation, no fear, just intense relief in her face.

His throat tightened. Here was his harbor. *Here* was his home. Certainty blazed strong, a bright green "Target Locked" that thundered through his body and filled all his senses. He pulled her straight into his arms with a little sob of joy.

CHAPTER 57

TURNING POINTS

H ildie folded out seats from the walls of the Emergency Express and gave Charlie a worried look. He should be exhausted from the day he'd had. The patients from the Dart would already have arrived at Orangeboro Med by now. In the quiet after the rush, she felt no hesitation about transporting someone whose doctor had told him to get to the med center as soon as possible. And focusing on immediate needs staved off the hovering devastation of things she didn't want to think about. "Sit here."

Charlie sat. "Thanks." He fumbled with the straps.

She untangled the jumble and secured the latches, but didn't bother with her own for the moment. "We may still be in micrograv, but I have a sense that your day just landed on you like a load of bricks."

"Heh." He gave her a rueful look. "How'd you guess?"

"Too much adrenaline, too much micrograv, too much drama." She grasped his hand to check his vitals, but the warmth of that sorely-missed hand, now clasped with hers ... his vitals were probably okay. His lips were all she wanted.

He enfolded her in another knee-melting hug, held her once

again in those beloved, strong arms. Warmth and life surged through her.

Could she please just float there in his arms for a while? His touch soothed her. The amazing fact of his love warmed her in all of her starved and frozen recesses. And the control he'd displayed with LaRock in the commons eased any last fears of uncontained violence. She buried her face in his shoulder and hung on tight.

"If you don't want to talk, I won't." The warmth in his voice filled her heart.

She pulled back enough for a long, self-indulgent moment to study his beautiful face. "Is there something you'd like to talk about?"

His mouth twisted with regret. "I'm gonna hazard a guess that you're on administrative leave because of me. You, and probably Oz, too."

She blew out a long breath, looked away. *Damn. I guess we do need to talk.* "Supposedly, LaRock fired me."

"*Fired?*"

She offered him a rueful look. "I called Alphonse Rami, of course. He told me he can't actually do that, so, you're right. I'm on administrative leave." She sternly stifled the gibbering panic that clawed at her. Ran a quiet *in-hold-slowly-out* breathing pattern.

"Oh, Hils." He drew her closer. "I owe you *everything*, after today."

She shook her head. "It seemed pretty simple to me. You had to save Rex. All you needed were the tools. We placed those tools in your hands, and you did the rest." Warm, upwelling amazement thickened her throat. "You were amazing. You showed everyone how it's done."

"The brain link and the badge-pings made me look good. The rest was luck, long-established habits, and not letting myself think too hard about what I was doing." He bowed his head, grimaced. "Hils, am I *old*?"

She sputtered a startled laugh, but understanding unfolded along with her amusement. "Those drivers *do* look more like babies every year. Hard to imagine we were ever like that, but I'm pretty sure we were."

He sighed. "I guess you have to be a certain kind of really young and seriously crazy to do that work. *And* to make some of the other stupid decisions I made back then."

"Those old, bad decisions helped grow you into who you are today. And the guy I see right now looks pretty amazing."

"At least I haven't gotten out-of-control furious and broken anything since Dr. Zuni adjusted my meds the last time."

"You did show a lot of control, facing LaRock." That look of smoldering fury, those clenched fists—she'd seen the captain blanch. But Charlie'd held himself in check. He'd withstood what must've been a massive temptation. "If you were going to lose it, you would have, then."

Charlie grimaced. "I hope I'm done with that. But you're right. It was a pretty good test. Better yet, I don't feel even a *little* bit flash-fried."

"Thank goodness!" It seemed Zuni really had found the right balance this time.

He licked his lips, bowed his head. "I was, um, wondering if you'd like to ... it's okay if you want to go slower. Truly. But I ... oh, God, I *really* miss you!"

Yes! Euphoria sent rising bubbles of joy through her, till her skin tingled and her heart sang. *Oh, yes! Thank you!* She hugged him with all her heart. "Me, too. I miss you so much it physically *hurts*. If it's okay with you, I'd like go back to the 'us' we were starting to build before. Could we try again?"

"How about let's go forward into the new 'us'?" He looked up with a soft smile. "If there's one thing I've learned, it's that the past may ride us, but we can't go back there once it's over."

"To the future, then," she agreed. "To *our* future."

❖ ❖ ❖ ❖ ❖ ❖ ❖ ❖

"B<small>RING</small> me clothing or other porous objects that have been in close contact with each unidentified subject," Shady directed. The people "up top" had managed to ID only Rex, Wisniewski, and UPO Danesh.

Shawnee, Frankie, and Pam saw to the erection of a new line of hazmat tents in the evidence cavern. Elle, Misha, Petunia, and Walter reported to the evidence cavern for additional duty. CSU techs arrived on their heels with sealed, coded evidence bags containing samples for Elle and Petunia to sniff.

Shady watched their little procession pass by, then glanced at Elaine, who stood next to her in the war room. Hunt-joy filled her chest. It pushed aside all other worries. "Soon we shall know more."

Elle and Petunia were sniffing out what Shady hoped would be new clues in the hazmat tents right now. Scout had been scheduled for the evening watch.

Dr. Sandler called. Rex had arrived at her clinic. She told Shady that initial scans looked as if Rex would need to stay there several days. He'd be in re-gen till tomorrow evening. She also warned he'd be short of breath for weeks. Shady thanked her, grateful to the point of shaky legs and a moment without breath. But there was work to do. She lifted her head and updated Elaine.

"You sure you don't want to go over there?" Elaine quirked a questioning eyebrow.

Shady lowered her ears. "What good would that do? Rex is in re-gen. He would not know if I am there or not. Someone has to be in charge of the Pack."

"Couldn't Tuxedo cover for you?"

Shady snorted. "Tux is a brilliant dog, but he is not an administrator, and he's obligated elsewhere. Elle would be better for the job, but she has evidence to analyze. Razor is nowhere near being ready for duty. Between the efforts of Whisper, Col. Wisniewski, and the perps who keep blowing up ships, we are running low on XK9 leaders."

Elaine frowned. "On XK9s, period."

"True." Shady laid back her ears with a little snarl and a tinge of heartburn. Of the ten Pack members, Rex, Cinnamon, and Razor were now off-duty and seriously injured.

Tuxedo and Crystal were deep into some kind of in-depth analysis of the first new explosives evidence. It already had begun to come in, and they'd been eager to start work on it. They and their humans had gone to S-Poly, to maintain chain-of-custody and examine it with Dr. SCISCO and nir colleagues in their specialized lab.

Elaine turned toward the ready room. "Walk with me. Normally I have these councils with Rex. I need an XK9 perspective."

Better get used to this. Shady would be the Pack Leader until further notice—and it would be a while. Rex had a lot of healing still ahead of him. Not to mention an investigation into his use of deadly force.

Military police were handling the body of the man presumably named Fowler, whom Rex had killed in the tunnels of the SDF base. Accidental or not, there must be a death inquiry. MPs had preserved Fowler's trank pistol. They were testing the trank formula now. CSU's military counterparts had conducted a forensic analysis of the scene. OPD couldn't investigate an OPD-officer-involved death, so Monteverde PD would receive all of that evidence and conduct the probe.

Shady and Elaine gowned up. Shady marveled once again at how little of her former phobia remained in Elaine's scent and body language after six weeks of daily contact with XK9s. Once inside the evidence cavern, the diminutive SSA moved away from the line of illuminated hazmat tents. Through the link, Shady sensed Pam over there on the com, liaising for the analysis team with one of Santiago's people.

Shady and Elaine passed the remaining pallets of *Izgubil* debris, then moved into the shadows beyond. If any place in

Orangeboro was secure without using one of the sonic barricades that XK9s found so annoying, this probably was it.

"Danesh was in handcuffs." Elaine strode steadily forward. "His *own* handcuffs."

Shady flicked her ears. "That lines up with Rex's report that he did not appear to be a willing accomplice."

"Mike's team has uncovered evidence in the past that Whisper operatives will sometimes kidnap hostages to coerce individuals whom they cannot bribe or blackmail. There is some speculation among the SIT Alpha crew that Danesh's wife and child may have suffered that fate."

"Surely he must have reported the kidnapping, if such a thing happened. Why was it not on record?"

"Howardsboro PD is unlikely to provide any answers." Elaine frowned. A stink of old resentment smoldered in her scent. "But I also have another question. Whisper had no more apparent use for him. He blew his cover when he helped Knife Woman and her partner escape from Rex and Shiv in the Sionainn. It is normal for Whisper operatives to kill an asset once he's ceased to be useful."

"You think they were not done with Everett Danesh." Shady growled. "I wonder if he could tell us what they meant to do next."

"Probably not. Why tell their pawn beforehand?"

"Do you know how soon we can question Wisniewski and Danesh?"

Elaine frowned. "Danesh is younger than Wisniewski, but he appears to have received a beating on board the ship. He may have been unconscious when it was destroyed. Between those injuries and the lung trauma, he likely will be hospitalized for at least a week before we can talk with him. Wisniewski is older, but he's had augmentations. He'll probably be out of re-gen in a few days. The SBI has been given access to question him once he wakes up."

"May I assist that interrogation?"

Elaine grimaced. "I'd welcome your input, but you have a conflict of interest that any competent defense lawyer would use to disqualify the interview."

Crap. Shady couldn't argue with that. *Dammit.*

"I'm guessing the two men who joined Danesh to help Knife Woman and Fowler escape are among the other subjects the ERT rescued," Elaine continued.

Shady wagged her tail. "I agree." Identifying those two in particular was the job Elle and Petunia were tackling right now. Hard telling who they might turn out to be, but all four of the unknown men's tattoos marked them as Saoirse Front members. Too bad the Scent Reference Lab was closed!

"I'd bet a big pile of money that the woman inside the medbed with the mauled arm is Knife Woman." Elaine's lips curved into a hunter's smile. "We're keeping her here in Orangeboro, where neither Rooq Cornwell nor Howardsboro PD's Chief Garrett can claim priority access. Mike's been after her for years. He wants first crack at her."

"Cornwell can't take Wisniewski away from us, can he?"

"Over Klein's dead body, maybe." Elaine gave her a wry look. "Orangeboro has a lot of recent, very serious criminal warrants out on him, and there's one hell of a civil suit active from Corona and Bonita Families, too, as you probably know."

"However, espionage is possibly even more serious." Shady laid back her ears. "Cornwell can't barter him away as leverage, can he?"

"I fear that's yet to be determined. Ambassador Nunzio really wants him back, and Premier Iskander's already putting on pressure."

Shady's hackles prickled. "Of course, they are." The Transmondian Ambassador and Rana's Premier too often seemed unsettlingly well in sync with each other's political desires. "Are they also arguing on Admiral Virendra's behalf?"

"No, actually. Not at all." Elaine chuckled. "No one mentions his name or acts as if he even exists. He was clumsy enough to get caught openly consorting with foreign agents *and* the Whisper Syndicate. It's really hard to make a political comeback after something like that. People tend to treat you like poison. Iskander wants his story to die and be forgotten as quickly as possible."

Shady snapped her ears flat, then lifted them again. "Is the Admiral really gone, then?"

"He'd already made a lot of enemies in the SDF, even before he embarrassed all of his allies." Elaine frowned. "I suppose that as long as he draws breath, he'll be some level of threat. But he's blasted himself down to the bottom of a very, very deep hole."

Oh, Shady! Pam's startled amusement burst through the link. *You and Elaine need to get over here. You'll never guess who two of the Saoirse-tattooed guys are! We've found Poopy and Sweaty!*

Shady halted, hackles prickling. *On a Whisper ship? After they helped rig the* Izgubil? *Are you serious?*

Kind of appropriate for them to get blown up just like their victims on the Izgubil. *But those guys seem to have been playing a seriously twisted game of double-cross.* She visualized Pam shaking her head. *I guess they found out that payback's a b—"* She caught herself before she used Shady's least-favorite derogatory term. *"It's, um, a bad thing."*

So it is. Shady lolled her tongue, then turned to Elaine. "They have made a startling discovery in the hazmat tents. Let us go over there."

SHADY STOOD by Rex's bed in the Sandler Clinic on Sunday evening, and sniffed her sleeping mate from nose-tip to tail-tip in exhaustive detail. The more she sniffed, the more her gut relaxed and the less her pulse pounded. There was still healing to be done, but now it could be done in Healing Sleep. Re-gen was over.

"When will he wake?" Shady cocked her head.

Dr. Sandler studied her case pad. "Probably not till tomorrow morning." Her gaze lingered on the latest scan's results, then she met Shady's eyes. "His metabolism is equalizing. We administered an IV nutrient bolus about thirty minutes ago, and we believe he has already gone into the desired Healing Sleep state. We'll monitor for a while longer, before we stop fluids and discontinue the IV. Probably another hour or so. Don't want him to become dehydrated, but we also don't want him tangled in his IV."

Shady nodded, human-style. A new tracery of white hairs marked her mate's beloved black face. Her heart clenched in a short, sharp spasm. *Knife Woman left her mark.* Most XK9s developed white on their faces with age, but this was different. "How long will he have white marks where his scars are?"

"It's possible they'll persist, especially since they're on that thin skin-and-muscle part of his face," Dr. Sandler said. "But it's just as likely they'll revert to black during one of his Healing Sleeps. They may re-emerge in the future, during the natural aging and graying process."

Shady tried to imagine Rex growing old, but dogs were not particularly visual creatures. She remembered seeing elders' whitened faces but imagining how that would look on Rex was harder than imagining the changes that might occur in his personal scent.

Would Rex even *live* to get old? A chill swept through her. His latest adventures worried her, especially if there'd truly been a kill-order put out on him. That seemed all too likely. Would Wisniewski's presumed order be rescinded now, or would the Transmondians continue trying to kill him and Tux? And after what he'd done to Knife Woman and Fowler, would Whisper put a price on his head?

She shuddered, chilled anew. Then she flicked her ears and refocused her thoughts toward the more immediate future. "May I sleep here with him tonight? He often sleeps better when we are curled together. For that matter, so do I."

"You're his Amare. Of course, you may stay. I've adopted the standard human Family Leave and Family access protocols for all XK9s. That includes Amares, of course. I've also added 'Immediate Family' designations for human partners. It'll be just like humans or ozzirikkians in a hospital. I figure the law will soon mandate it anyway. Once the IV is removed, we can put the two of you into a bed that is big enough for both of you."

"Thank you." She passed along this news to Pam. *I guess I won't have to endure your living room floor to be close to Rex, after all.*

I kinda hate to admit it, but we were a little worried about fitting you back into the apartment. Pam made no effort to mask her rueful tone, and for some reason her thoughts briefly touched on Balchu's father, Feyodor. *I finally have been able to come around to Balchu's point of view. This place really is too small.*

I hope that means you are feeling less abandoned. Shady restrained the surge of victory within her heart, but a warm, joyous glow filled her body.

Pam sighed. *I still miss living with you, but ... I'm not feeling as forlorn or hopeless as I did.*

Again, Shady received an impression of Feyodor and a secret project he might be working on. Could it connect to whatever he'd had brewing at lunch all those weeks ago? Never mind. Questions about that could wait. Instead, Shady allowed her delight at Pam's acceptance to spill over into the link and focused all her energy there. *I love you. I wish we could live closer to each other, but your acceptance eases my mind.*

We'll muddle through somehow. Pam's grin echoed back to her through the link like a benediction.

CHAPTER 58

SOLSTICE AND NEW DAY

R ex called the car about 22:10 on Friday night. "I need to go over there." It was late, he was barely home from the clinic himself, and still on a much-needed health leave. No one would think twice about it, if he curled up in his Corona Tower bedroom to sleep. But he needed to go. They were bringing Cinnamon out of re-gen tonight.

"I am coming with you." Shady's tone and body language brooked no dissent.

Do you want me to come? Charlie asked. He and Hildie had gone to a Solstice party in Precinct Ten. They'd been invited by Charlie's friend Eddie Chism, from STAT Blue Team.

No. Please. This is just a thing I feel I should do. Stay. Enjoy the party. I won't be long.

Charlie hesitated. Rex sensed through the link that his partner felt he ought come with him. To somehow protect him. But he also really didn't want to interrupt his evening with Hildie at the party.

Stay. Shady's coming with me. She won't let me do anything stupid. Or stay out too late.

The ripple of wry amusement that returned through the link also conveyed acquiescence. *Tell her I'm counting on her.*

"Charlie says it is up to you to keep me from doing anything stupid."

Shady snorted. "This whole excursion is probably stupid. Let us go."

Rex was already panting before he'd even reached the courtyard level. Since when did he lose his breath going *down* the stairs, for pity's sake? He stretched his jaws wide in a stress-yawn.

Since lung trauma, that's when, Charlie answered.

Rex growled. Rising frustration soured his stomach. His unwanted infirmities bottled him up. *I should be better by now.* He slept each night for ten or twelve hours, and also every afternoon. Some were normal sleeps, but many others were Healing Sleeps. And *still* he had no stamina.

It'll come. You'll note I'm now seven weeks out of the hospital, with augmentations, and I'm still on half-time work.

Rex flicked his ears. *I am not used to it taking so long.* He and Shady continued to the basement-level garage.

"If you go into Healing Sleep in the car, we are coming straight back home," Shady said.

"Understood."

Carma's door swung wide. He dragged his heavy body up inside. Stayed on the floor. He dozed, but startled awake often enough to stave off Healing Sleep. Eventually they rolled to a halt under Dr. Sandler's new security canopy.

The two automatic doors opened: clinic and car. They stood within centimeters of each other, and they'd stay open for as long as it took. Rex had only turned seven years old a few months back, but tonight he felt almost as geriatric as the white hairs on his face suggested he was.

The UPO at the front desk, Ax Gerwitz, had arrived for his regular night watch at the Clinic. He eyed Rex and Shady coming in. "Good evening. Everything all right?"

"Has Cinnamon come out of re-gen yet?" Rex asked.

Gerwitz shook his head. "They're in the beginning phases of

it now. Judging by how long it took them with you, it'll still be another hour or so till she's resting in a room."

"Where should we wait?"

"Liz and Razor just went down to Berwyn's room. Some of Berwyn's Family was here earlier. They had a little Solstice party, but they've gone home since then. Oh, and Shiv's been down there most of the day."

Rex accessed the calendar on his HUD. "That is right. I had forgotten. Today is the Solstice." He lolled his tongue and pictured LSA Wei, shaking his head and saying "Criminy!"

There wasn't much of a party atmosphere in Berwyn's room, just now.

Dr. Sandler had moved out clinic equipment and opened an acoustical airwall to create a suite that would accommodate a bed for Berwyn next to the re-gen chamber. But when Rex and Shady arrived, they found techs reconfiguring the place to install a hospital bed for Cinnamon.

No Berwyn, Shiv, Razor, or Liz.

"Retreat room across the hall," the tech with the tattoos said.

The retreat room across the hall was small, narrow, and pretty much maxed out, once three humans and three XK9s had squeezed themselves inside. The humans all smiled a greeting, while Razor wagged his tail.

"Rex. Shady. Wow," Berwyn said. "Would you like to observe the Solstice with us?"

"We came to wait with you," Rex said.

"Then please join us. I was explaining to the others ... What do you know about Solstice?"

"It is an astronomical phenomenon observable on many planets," Rex said. "If there are seasonal variations in the length of daylight and darkness, then the longest and shortest days are solstices, and the days which are divided equally between darkness and light are equinoxes."

Berwyn's smile held a trace of sadness. "You sound like Cinnamon, when I first explained it to her."

"We all attended the same planetary astronomy class," Shady said.

"Well, let me tell you about the way my Family observes the Solstice." He gestured toward a low table in the center of the room. Someone had placed a lighted, mostly-burned candle on it, next to a tall, new, unburned one. Both were the same brownish-dark-gray tone, with a spicy smell. Humans probably saw them as one of the colors XK9s couldn't distinguish. Between them, a small case pad ticked a silent countdown.

"My Family follows an ancient tradition that observed these variations on Mother Earth and found spiritual meaning in them. The shortest day—the longest darkness—takes place in a cold season there, when everything lies fallow. In the earliest ages, it was a time of privation, often of hunger, of death. A sort of nadir for the year." Berwyn stared at the flickering candle flame for a moment. "This year, I've been able to very personally relate. Almost losing Cinnamon has got to be one of the worst things I've ever gone through."

"Oh, man, I hear you!" Liz's eyes brimmed with tears. She reached over to squeeze Berwyn's shoulder. Shiv clasped Berwyn's hand. He did not speak, but he looked almost as haggard as Berwyn and Liz.

Rex's throat tightened. Having almost lost Charlie just a few weeks ago, he thought he understood some of what they must feel. Shady nuzzled him. Between her disagreement with Pam and his injuries, she'd likely had a pretty rough month, too.

"But at the end of every 'longest dark,' the light begins to return," Berwyn said. "It starts at that very moment when darkness and cold seem to conquer the world. The light comes back. The warmth begins to grow. New hope rises up, and the faith that things will get better."

He looked at Liz, Razor and Rex. "We will heal and grow stronger."

He met Shady's eyes. "We will rise again to new heights."

He turned to Shiv. "Unexpected new things may ... may dare

to take root." The fearful hope in both men's faces and scent factors filled Rex's heart with empathic, joyful yearning and set Shady's tail to thumping.

Berwyn drew in a breath, checked his HUD, then blinked. "Oh. It's already later than I thought. In my Family, it's our tradition to extinguish the old year's candle at 23:50, which is .... *now.*" He blew out the candle.

The Retreat room went pitch dark.

"Our tradition is to banish distractions, sit in silence, and let our minds find a centering peace."

No one answered. Six hearts beat quietly, although at different rhythms. Six presences breathed in and out. Rex noted that more than one ran a breathing pattern of the sort he'd learned from Charlie. Liz shifted in her seat. An itch prickled along his right shoulder blade. He lifted a hind paw to scratch it, then refrained. Stilled himself. The itch burned a moment or two longer, then died.

Darkness continued, and silence. Well, except for the movements across the hall.

Silent in here. Calmer, in here. They abided in silence.

Gradually, their breathing fell into a common rhythm. Their heartbeats slowly synchronized, too. The humans couldn't consciously hear it, but somehow they also attuned.

A deep calmness and peace fell over Rex. A sense of oneness with his companions, and of resting after strife. He abided in the moment, content.

Soft bells chimed. They grew louder, a growing carillon. They crescendoed into joyous, triumphant peals. The bells seemed to say, *Darkness is banished. Light will prevail. Things will get better! Rejoice!*

The sound broke over him, balm for his heart. Light and hope for his mind and spirit.

A *scratch* and a flare of flame. Sharp bite of burning struck his nose. Berwyn lit the new candle, then touched his case pad. The bells faded out. "Nadir has passed. The light is returning."

"The light is returning," Shiv murmured.

Berwyn straightened. "The light is returning, indeed." He sat back with a sigh and a smile. "Thank you. Thank you, *all* of you. I thought I'd be doing this alone." His dark eyes glistened with excess moisture.

Shiv shook his head. Gave Berwyn's hand a gentle squeeze. "Not alone. Not tonight."

"I know *I* needed to be here," Liz said. "Thank you. Thank you for sharing this with us."

Razor dipped his head. "Very much. That was amazing."

Shady looked Rex in the eye. "And not even a little bit stupid."

Dr. Sandler knocked tentatively at the door. "Sorry to intrude. But Cinnamon's re-gen is finished. She came through the transition well. Her scans look promising, and she's resting in normal Healing Sleep. I thought you'd want to know." She hesitated, met Berwyn's eye. "Solstice blessings, Berwyn."

"Solstice blessings to you, as well." Berwyn's gaze swept the room. "Solstice blessings abound." His focus stopped on Shiv.

Rex yawned a jaw-cracking yawn, all at once more than ready to sleep. "I think we should go home now."

Shady lolled her tongue. "I shall call the car."

THE NEXT DAY DAWNED MISTY, then shifted to clear and bright, just like every day did, without fail, on Rana Station.

Shady scored bacon at breakfast in the courtyard with the humans of Corona Tower, then came upstairs to share a Master Mix breakfast with Rex when he awoke at last. He'd had yet another Healing Sleep.

Once they'd eaten, Charlie, Hildie, Ted, and Mimi all converged on the inner balcony. Shady and Rex joined them, curious. The humans seemed unusually excited. They smelled of secrets and surprises.

"Okay," Shady said. "What gives?"

"We received a clearance from Chief Klein," Charlie said.

"And we made a special arrangement," Ted added.

"Would you please come down to the garage?" Mimi asked.
Hildie just smiled.

These humans were definitely up to something. Everyone
crowded into the elevator, then rode down to the garage-level.

Shady stepped out. Here was something new. "Carma," the
ugly, nondescript car they'd ridden to and from work for weeks,
was nowhere to be seen. A sleek, shiny-yellow Citron Flash
stood in Carma's customary parking slot.

Rex stepped out of the elevator and stopped. He stared at the
car. "What does this mean?"

Charlie smiled. "It means that Commodore Cornwell has
assured Chief Klein that Wisniewski's organization is in deep
disarray. None of their remaining agents are currently deployed
to Rana."

Rex made a little squeak. His body quivered with excitement,
and his tail began to wave. The bright, high-tone scents of his
reaction filled Shady with anticipation.

What's up, Shady? Pam asked through the link.

"That means no one is gunning for XK9s here, at least for
now." Mimi's grin stretched wide.

Rex's tail sped up. He pranced in place and uttered happy
squeaks.

Shady lolled her tongue. Her tail matched his beat-for-beat. *I
hope this means what I think!* She sensed Pam's chuckle through
the link.

"It means you can poke your head out the window and ride
without fear," Hildie said.

Now Rex's tail looked like a fan on 'high.' He pranced,
hopped, and made high-pitched squeals.

Shady danced and barked with him. *Yes! Yes!* She widened
the link for Pam.

"And I've rented 'Carmella' again," Ted concluded. "So you can ride in style. Consider it an early New Year's gift. You may run the switchbacks as many times as you like, with your heads outside the windows."

"We even got you eye protection." Charlie opened the yellow car's rear storage compartment, to retrieve goggles. "I'm told that when dogs wear these, they're called 'doggles.'" He helped the two XK9s put them on. It was hard to hold still long enough for him to fasten those "doggles."

Rex leaped into the auto-nav. "Carmella!" he commanded. "Lower windows." Down they went.

Shady needed no further invitation. She leaped inside too. The humans backed away.

"Close doors and take us down the switchbacks to Terrace One!" Rex commanded.

The vehicle's doors swung shut. It performed a three-point turn, emerged from the basement-level garage, turned onto Rim Eight Road and gained speed. A breeze from the car's movement fluttered their ears.

The wind brought a marvelous onrush of odors, borne by currents of morning air. *Oh! That's amazing!* Shady opened her mouth for more. The heady inflow of scents energized and astounded her. Who could imagine such a rush? They passed neighbor dogs, who barked at them from one side of their property to the other. This was *So! Incredibly! Smooth!*

Pam's laugh sparkled through the link. *Oh, that feels like fun.*

This is amazing!

So I gather. Well, enjoy!

Carmella took the ramp to bypass the train station. The swoop-and-turn-and-swoop-and-turn down forty switchbacks to the riverside exhilarated Shady in new and powerful ways. She'd never felt anything this wonderful!

The end of the switchbacks came far too soon. "Another?" she asked.

Rex lolled his tongue. It flapped sideways in the wind of their passing. "Yes! Yes! As many times as we like!"

As many times as we like ... turned out to be quite a lot.

-THE END-

WHAT HAPPENS NEXT?

If you enjoyed this novel, the very best way to support an author (other than **buying her book**) is writing a review!
Please rate and review this book!
Goodreads
Amazon

Stay in touch with the latest updates! Subscribe to Jan S. Gephardt's monthly newsletter (and get a FREE copy of *The Other Side of Fear*)!

Rex and his friends have more adventures in the works! Watch for *Bone of Contention: The 3rd book in the XK9 "Bones" Trilogy.*

XK9 Rex is a dog who dreams too big. Now he may lose everything.

Rex and his Packmates were bio-engineered and cyber-enhanced to be cutting edge law enforcement tools. But they're more than super-smart forensic tools with cold, wet noses and wagging tails. Their human allies on Rana Station claim the XK9s are sapient beings.

Rex and the Pack have begun to enjoy the freedom Ranans believe they deserve. But they also have work to do. They're hot on the trail of a murderous gang that explodes spaceships in the Black Void of space—killing all the souls onboard.

Mass murder in the Black Void is a hideous crime. But in the far-flung systems of the Alliance of the Peoples, trafficking in sapient beings is the most-reviled crime of all.

Inspectors from the Alliance of the Peoples are headed to Rana, to test the XK9s' sapience claim. The leaders of the XK9 Project that created Rex and his Pack deny wrongdoing. And the system-dominating Transmondian Government that sponsored the XK9 Project will do anything they must to protect themselves.

Even if it means destroying every XK9 in the universe.

Planned for release in 2022!

Stay in touch with the latest updates! Subscribe to Jan S. Gephardt's monthly newsletter (and get a FREE copy of *The Other Side of Fear*)!

And if you'd like a glimpse of a different Weird Sisters publication, we hope you'll enjoy Chapter One of G. S. Norwood's urban fantasy novelette, ***Deep Ellum Pawn*** at the end of this volume!

WHO'S WHO AND WHAT'S WHAT

CHARACTERS, SHIPS, ORGANIZATIONS,
PLACES, ACRONYMS AND ABBREVIATIONS
IN "A BONE TO PICK"

An Alphabetical Directory

Abhik "Abi" Bannerjee. (AH-beek BAN-er-jee) Hildie's younger brother, son of Pari and Dara. Significant of Smita Rostov. Abi, Smita, and Hildie share an apartment in Feliz Tower. (Pronouns: he, him.)

Adeyeme. (ah-DEE-yem) See *Elaine Adeyeme*.

Adelaide "Laidie" Perri. Director of the Station Bureau of Investigation. (Pronouns: she, her.)

Admiral Virendra. (vir-END-rah) See *Nolan Virendra*.

Afiq "Feek" Gonzalo. An unregistered resident of the Five-Ten. AKA "Dopey." (Pronouns: he, him.)

Agent Ayaana Chaten. (eye-YAWN-ah CHAY-den) An interrogation specialist from SDF Military Intelligence. (Pronouns: she, her.)

AI. Artificial Intelligence. On Rana, this means a Farricainan AI, Alliance-recognized as sapient cybernetic beings. An unusually large population of eight Farricainan AI "siblings" have chosen to locate their source nodes on Rana Station.

Ailani Idris. (eye-LAH-nee ID-riss) Mayor of Orangeboro. (Pronouns: she, her.)

Alliance of the Peoples. An interstellar alliance of sapient

536 | Who's Who and What's What

species whose treaties supersede all system-wide or national laws.

Alphonse Rami. (AL-fonce RAH-mee) A representative for the Orangeboro Safety Services Employees' Union. (Pronouns: he, him.)

Alyssa Hart. One of the two owners of the Heart-O-Howardsboro Veterinary Clinic, in Howardsboro, a mother-and-daughter team. The elder is Alyssa "Lissa" Hart, DVM. The younger is Alyssa "Allie" Hart, DVM. (Pronouns: she, her.)

Amare. (ah-MAH-ray) One of several types of relationships that are formally recognized on Rana Station. Amares are lovers in a Declared Relationship, who live together in a family-type unit.

Ambassador Nunzio. See *Ryder Nunzio*.

Amorous-Friend-of-Record. A beginning-level status for a nonbinary lover or one who eschews gender identity. It is official enough to affect leave eligibility and grant some privacy access to one's lover's personal information. See also: *Girlfriend-of-Record* and *Boyfriend-of-Record*.

Andrew "Andy" Lee Crannach. (CRAH-noch). Charlie's brother-in-law. Caro's husband, and Sophie and Lacey's father. (Pronouns: he, him.)

Anika Ogawa Chinbat. (AH-ni-ka a-GAH-wa chan-BAT) Orangeboro Medical Examiner, whose office is a unit of Borough Government that cooperates with law enforcement and legal systems but is subordinate to none of them. (Pronouns: she, her.)

Anne Kiuvidas. (key-YOU-vee-dass) an Inspector in the Kiuvidas Collective. (Pronouns: she, her.)

Annie Montoya Lee. (mon-TO-yah) Charlie's maternal grandmother, wife of Pedro Lee Montoya, daughter of Loretta Triola Lee, and official Head of Household for Corona Chartered Family. (Pronouns: she, her.)

Anthony. See *Lynne Anthony*.

Apodeddi Mamoor. Georgia Volkov's grandfather. *Apodeddi* means "Grandfather" in Mahusayan. (Pronouns: he, him.)

Archibald "Archy" Cody Danvir. (DAN-veer) A police captain. Aide and right-hand man to Chief Klein. (Pronouns: he, him.)

Archy. See *Captain Archibald "Archy" Cody Danvir.*

Asalatu. (as-ah-LAH-too) A spacecraft that slammed into the Orangeboro Docks.

Atilla "Till" Usher. An unregistered inhabitant of the Five-Ten. AKA "Greasy." (Pronouns: he, him.)

Axl "Ax" Gerwitz. An Orangeboro UPO assigned to Central HQ. (Pronouns: he, him.)

Babu. (BOB-oo) the eldest of Hildie's cousins. (Pronouns: he, him.)

Balchu Nowicki. (BAHL-chew) A Level Two Detective with the Orangeboro Police Department assigned to the Vice Unit at Central HQ. Pamela Gómez's Amare and Shady's housemate. (Pronouns: he, him.)

Beckett "Beck" Crombie. A field agent assigned to SIT Alpha. (Pronouns: he, him.)

Berwyn Yael. (BER-win yah-EL). Partner of XK9 Cinnamon "Cinnie" Lightfoot-Floss. A Level One Detective. (Pronouns: he, him.)

Beryl Lee Feininger. Pregnant wife of Charlie's cousin Germaine. (Pronouns: she, her.)

Betty Jean. The suspect "Dopey's" girlfriend. (Pronouns: she, her.)

Bill. See *William "Bill" Goldstein Sloane.*

Black Void. An old spacer term for the hard vacuum and expanses of space.

Blunder. See *Murder Brothers.* Blunder is the younger sibling. (Pronouns: he, him.)

Bonita. The Chartered Family that lives next door to Rex and Charlie's Corona Family.

Bonita Tower. The Bonita Family's residence, located on Starboard Hill Level Seven in the Ninth Precinct on Rana Station. It is the property directly leeward from Corona Tower.

Bordemer Canton. A Transmondian canton (like a state or province) immediately north of Solara City. It contains the suburban community Ensolay.

Boyfriend-of-Record. A beginning-level status for a male lover. It is official enough to affect leave eligibility and grant some privacy access to one's lover's personal information. See also: Girlfriend-of-Record, Amorous-Friend-of-Record.

Brenny. The pilot of Wisniewski's Dart. (Pronouns: they, them.)

Bridget Riordan Ryan. (RYE-or-dan) A DPO in Howardsboro. (Pronouns: she, her.)

Broaddus. See *Lt. Harrison Broaddus*

Brock Rivers. A friend of Charlie's, member of the STAT Team, and cousin of Eddie Chism. (Pronouns: he, him.)

Bruce Ibsen. Sheriff of Bordemer Canton in Transmondia. Mike and Elaine's friend. (Pronouns: he, him.)

Bureau. Station Bureau of Investigation (SBI).

CAP. Cybernetically-Assisted Perception. The implant-driven interface between an individual user and the Station Net.

Captain Hariri. Commanding officer of the OPD STAT Team. (Pronouns: he, him.)

Captain Treva "LaRock" LaRochelle. (TREE-vah la-row-SHELL). Commanding officer of Orangeboro's Emergency Rescue Team Base at the Hub. Hildie's boss. (Pronouns: he, him.)

Carma. The "name" of the pseudo-AI interface of an auto-nav vehicle from the OPD Motor Pool. (Pronoun: it.)

Carmella. The "name" of the pseudo-AI interface of a Citron Flash. (Pronoun: it.)

Carolyn "Caro" Crannach Lee. (CRAH-noch) Charlie's older sister. Wife of Andy, and mother of Sophie and Lacey. (Pronouns: she, her.)

Cecelia "Leeli" Tanaka. One of the Corona Tower children, Luther and Ari's daughter. (Pronouns: she, her.)

Central Plaza District. A neighborhood in Precinct Five, in the urban core of Orangeboro.

Charles "Charlie" Morgan. XK9 Rex Dieter-Nell's partner. A Detective Level One. (Pronouns: he, him.)

Chartered Family. Chartered Families are official entities of their own on Rana Station, with civic duties and special tax rates, among other things.

Chaten. See *Agent Ayaana Chaten.*

Chayko. (CHAY-koh) The human-inhabited planet that gives the Chayko System its name. It is the only planet in Alliance Space, other than Earth, that humans have been allowed to wholly claim.

Chief Klein. See *Kwame Odigo Klein.*

Chief Zhang. See *Lexie Zhang.*

Chinbat. See. *Anika Ogawa Chinbat.*

Cho. See *Frederika Cho.*

Cinnamon "Cinnie" Lightfoot-Floss. XK9 partner of Berwyn Yael. An explosives expert. (Pronouns: she, her.)

Civic Center. A large public building in Orangeboro's Central Plaza. Many Borough Government offices are located there, including OPD Central HQ. It also contains a large auditorium where public events are held.

Citron Flash. The model name of a stylish auto-nav sportscar on Rana Station.

Civic Center. See *Orangeboro Civic Center*

Class A, B, and C. Classes of microgravity certification on Rana Station, from basic through expert professional.

Clint. An assistant to Col. Wisniewski. (Pronouns: he, him.)

Clovis Kiuvidas. (klo-VEES key-YOU-vee-das) an Inspector in the Kiuvidas Collective. (Pronouns: he, him.)

Clumsy. The XK9s' placeholder nickname for a suspect in "Elmo's Group," identified only by scent profile. (Pronouns: he, him.)

Comets. A professional quiddo team.

Commodore Clarimonde Alvaro Montreaux. (CLAIR-ee-mond al-VAH-*rro*e mon-T*RR*UH) the administrator in charge of the SDF Wheel Two Base. (Pronouns: she, her.)

Commodore Farooq "Rooq" Tomoko Cornwell. (FAH-rook TOE-moe-ko) The spymaster in charge of Rana Station's SDF Military Intelligence. (Pronouns: he, him.)

Constance "Connie" Alkayev. (AL-kay-uv) XK9 Crystal Basho-Dancer's partner. A Detective Level One. (Pronouns: she, her.)

Cormac. Hildie's first cousin. Married to Maira. Their children are Jeliza and Bryan. (Pronouns: he, him.)

Corona Family. The Chartered Family that lives in Corona Tower (Charlie and Rex's family).

Corona Tower. The Corona Family's residence, located on Starboard Hill Terrace Eight in the Ninth Precinct on Rana Station.

Crozier Gulch Transit Terminal Station. (CROW-zher) A multi-level transportation hub located in the Crozier Gulch Neighborhood on Starboard Rim Seven in the Ninth Precinct. It includes commuter elevators linked to the Hub, a roadway passage between upper and lower switchbacks, a tramway stop, and a train station.

Crystal "Crys" Basho-Dancer. XK9 Partner of Connie Alkayev. An explosives expert. (Pronouns: she, her.)

CSU. Crime Scene Unit, the forensic evidence analysis unit of a law enforcement agency.

Danesh. See *Everett Danesh.*

Dara Bannerjee Gallagher. (DA-ra BAN-er-jee GAL-ah-gur) Hildie and Abi's mother, wife of Pari. (Pronouns: she, her.)

Darius Amin. Borough Treasurer for Orangeboro.

David "Dave" Santos. (SAN-tohs) A noted cyberneticist from Station Polytechnic University. (Pronouns: he, him.)

Detective Level One. Entry-level detective rank.

Devin. A member of Dr. Emily Rashidi's design team. (Pronouns: he, him.)

Dolan Brothers. Rufus and Neil Dolan, AKA "The Murder Brothers."

Dolph Gibson Sanger. A member of Corona Family and an

actor of System-wide repute. Technically, he's the husband of Charlie's first cousin once-removed (Ralph's brother Fred), but everyone in Charlie's generation calls the men of the previous generation "uncle," so to Charlie he's "Uncle Dolph." (Pronouns: he, him.)

Dominic "Dom" Wei. (WAY) A Lead Special Agent assigned to SIT Alpha. A sharpshooter. (Pronouns: he, him)

Dopey. The XK9s' placeholder nickname for a suspect in "Elmo's Group," identified only by scent profile. (Pronouns: he, him.)

Doug. A UPO assigned to OPD Central HQ's Detention Center. (Pronouns: he, him.)

DPO. Detective Police Officer, a civilian police rank.

Eddie Sakai Chism. (sah-KYE CHIZZ-m) A friend of Charlie's, a member of the STAT Blue Team, and a cousin of Brock Rivers.

Eduardo Donovan. Partner of XK9 Victor Sam-Janet. A Detective Level One. (Pronouns: he, him.)

Edwina "Wina" Emshwiller. (ed-WEE-nah EM-shwill-er) A Special Agent assigned to SIT Delta. A forensic accounting specialist. (Pronouns: she, her.)

Elaine Adeyeme. (ah-DEE-yem) The Senior Special Agent who leads the SBI's SIT Delta, and the lead investigator on the *Izgubil* case. Significant of SSA Mike Santiago. (Pronouns: she, her.)

Elijah "Eli" Isaiah. A paramedic on the ERT, assigned to the *Triumph*. Hildie's partner. (Pronouns: he, him.)

Elizabeth "Liz" Antonopoulos. (ann-ton-OP-o-liss) Partner of XK9 Razor Liam-Blanca. As an XK9 partner-candidate, Liz was one of Pam Gómez's podmates. (Pronouns: she, her.)

Elle Finnian-Ella. (EL, *not* "EL-ee") XK9 partner of Mikhail "Misha" Flores and mate of Tuxedo Moondog-Carrie. (Pronouns: she, her.)

Ellen. An Emergency Rescue Squad MERS-V driver critically injured in the *Asalatu* wreck. (Pronouns: she, her.)

Elmo's group. A group of eight individuals, including Elmo Smart, who left a scent trail going into the *Izgubil* and then coming out again, about a week before the ship's destruction. They are on Rex's list of suspects for having rigged the explosives. Scent-differentiated by the Pack, but mostly not apprehended (except for Elmo).

Elmo Smart. A mugger whom Rex knows; a suspect in the *Izgubil* case. (Pronouns: he, him.)

Emer Bellamy. (EE-mer) Daughter of Sorcha Moran Bellamy and Hideki Bellamy Moran, and a member of the wealthy and respected Vinebrook Family. (Pronouns: she, her.)

Emily Rashidi. (rah-SHE-dee) A robotics engineering specialist from Station Polytechnic University. (Pronouns: she, her.)

Ensolay. A northern suburb of Solara City, Bordemer Canton, Transmondia. Home of Dr. Frederika Cho, XK9 Nell Dodger-Meena, and Sheriff Bruce Ibsen.

Ernest "Ernie" Porringer. (POUR-in-jer) a GR artist. (Pronouns: he, him.)

ERT. Emergency Rescue Team. Although this designation could be applied to any Safety Services rescue unit, it is generally used to mean the Emergency Rescue Teams that operate at the Hub to respond to emergencies in microgravity. Sometimes members of such a team are called "ERTs."

EStee. (ESS-tee) A combination electro-shock/tranquilizer weapon. The standard service weapon used by officers of the OPD.

Everett Danesh. (Dah-NESH) A Howardsboro police officer. (Pronouns: he, him.)

FA. Field Agent, a rank in the SBI. Generally, a younger, early-career agent. An FA does tasks often assigned to uniformed patrol officers in police departments.

Fahim. (fa-HEEM) one of Hildie's cousins. (Pronouns: he, him.)

Fatal Funnel. A choke point or narrow area where a person could be shot.

Fatima Smythe, (FA-di-ma SMEYE'th) Welder, member of Bonita Family. Friend of Charlie's sister Caro.

Fee. See *Fiametta Morgan Wang.*

Feek, or **Feek-Man.** See *Afiq "Feek" Gonzalo.* (Pronouns: he, him.)

Felicia. Charlie Morgan's ex-Amare. (Pronouns: she, her.)

Feliz Family. The Chartered Family that lives in Feliz Tower (Hildie's family).

Feliz Tower. The Feliz Family's residence, located on Port Hill Terrace Eight in the Ninth Precinct on Rana Station.

Fergus "Mac" Mac Dermott. Maintenance technician at the Hub base for the Orangeboro Emergency Rescue Team. An innovative wearer of customized prosthetic arms and hands. (Pronouns: he, him.)

Feyodor Bayarmaa Nowicki. (F'YO-der BUYER-mah no-WICK-ee) Husband of Tuya, father of Balchu Nowicki and Sarnai Bayarmaa. (Pronouns: he, him.)

Fiametta "Fee" Morgan Wang. An Inspection Officer of the Orangeboro Port Authority office, stationed at the Hub. Charlie's former Police Academy classmate, she's now married to Charlie's cousin, Manuel "Manny" Wang Morgan. Hakan is their son. (Pronouns: she, her.)

Finlay. See *Virgilia "Gillie" Finlay.*

Five-Ten. An infamous "underworld" part of Orangeboro on Sub-Level Ten.

Fowler. Knife-Woman's male partner, an enforcer for the Whisper Syndicate. (Pronouns: he, him.)

Francis "Frankie" Freas. (FREEZE) A Special Agent assigned to SIT Delta.

Frederika Cho. Dr. Cho is head of the XK9 Project's Scent Reference Lab. Partner to XK9 Nell Dodger-Meena, Rex's mother. (Pronouns: she, her.)

Fujimoto. See *Helmer Fujimoto.*

Georgia Volkov. (VOLE-cove) XK9 Tuxedo Moondog-Carrie's partner. A Detective Level One. (Pronouns: she, her.)

Germaine Feininger Lee. Charlie's first cousin. Ralph and Serafina's daughter, wife of Beryl. (Pronouns: she, her.)

Gerritsen. See *Reza Gerritsen.*

Glen Haven Transit Terminal Station. A multi-level transportation hub located in the Glen Haven Neighborhood on Starboard Rim Eight in the Ninth Precinct. It includes commuter elevators linked to the Hub, a roadway passage between upper and lower switchbacks, a tramway stop, and a train station.

Gil. A field agent assigned to SIT Alpha.

Gillie. See *Virgilia "Gillie" Finlay.*

Girlfriend-of-Record. A beginning-level status for a female lover. It is official enough to affect leave eligibility and grant some privacy access to one's lover's personal information. See also: Boyfriend-of-Record, Amorous-Friend-of-Record.

Global Reconstruction. A technique for crafting 3-dimensional visual recreations and/or animations of crime scenes, objects, and individuals.

Gloria Huddleston Gibson. One of Charlie's same-generation cousins. Dolph and Fred's daughter, Quinn's wife, and Grant and Owen's mother. (Pronouns: she, her.)

Glorioso Tower. The Glorioso Family's residence (Misha's Family), located on Starboard Hill Terrace Six in the Fourth Precinct on Rana Station.

GR. See *Global Reconstruction.*

GR Artist. A person trained and certified in Global Reconstruction.

Gran Annie. See *Annie Montoya Lee,*

Grandma Hestia. See *Hestia Saha Gallagher.* (Pronouns: she, her.)

Grant Huddleston. Son of Charlie's cousin Gloria and her husband Quinn. (Pronouns: he, him.)

Greasy. The XK9s' placeholder nickname for a suspect in

"Elmo's Group," identified only by scent profile. (Pronouns: he, him.)

Green Mountain University. A liberal arts university in Monteverde Borough on Wheel Two.

GR Unit. The facility where Global Reconstructions are made.

Gregory Ordovich. (ORE-doe-vitch) Director of the XK9 Project. Transmondian geneticist and dog breeder who used genetic engineering to create the XK9s. (Pronouns: he, him.)

GSR. Gunshot residue.

Hakan Morgan. (HOH-kan) Son of Charlie Morgan's first cousin Manuel "Manny" Wang Morgan and his wife Fiametta "Fee" Morgan Wang. (Pronouns: he, him.)

Hannah Morgan Chahine. (SHY-een) Charlie's aunt and wife of Hector Chahine Morgan. A named partner in a law firm that specializes in interstellar trade. (Pronouns: she, her.)

Harrison Broaddus. A detective lieutenant in OPD Internal Affairs. (Pronouns: he, him.)

Head-of-Household. An official title on Rana Station. The designated chief executive of a Chartered Family.

Healing Sleep. The deep, trancelike sleep-state into which XK9 metabolisms revert after an injury, in which healing is dramatically accelerated.

Heart-O-Howardsboro Veterinary Clinic. The veterinary clinic in suburban Howardsboro that takes care of the Howardsboro PD K-9s. Owned and operated by the Drs. Hart, mother and daughter.

Hector Chahine Morgan. (SHY-een) Charlie's uncle. An inventor. (Pronouns: he, him.)

Hectorvault Security. Hector Chahine Morgan's security equipment corporation.

Helmer Fujimoto (HEL-mer fu-ji-MO-do) A veteran OPD detective. Balchu Nowicki's Field Training Officer. (Pronouns: he, him.)

Henry Sevencrows. Partner of UPO Lynne Anthony. A patrol officer assigned to the Five-Ten. (Pronouns: he, him.)

Hestia Saha Gallagher. (HESS-tee-uh SAH-ha GAL-ah-gur) Hildie's maternal grandmother, official Head of Household for Feliz Chartered Family. She is the head of agricultural operations for Feliz Tower. (Pronouns: she, her.)

Hideki Bellamy Moran. (hee-DAY-key) A member of Orangeboro's prominent Vinebrook Family, husband of Sorcha Moran Bellamy, and father of Emer and Orla Bellamy. (Pronouns: he, him.)

Hildegaard "Hildie" ("Hils") Gallagher. (HILL-dee-guard GAL-ah-gur) Girlfriend-of-Record to Charlie Morgan. A paramedic on the Orangeboro Emergency Rescue Team at Topside Base. Daughter of Pari and Dara, Abhik's big sister. (Pronouns: she, her.)

Howardsboro. A Ranan Borough on Wheel Three.

Hub. The central structure that serves as a "spine" or "axle" around which the habitat wheels of Rana Station turn. The Hub is also the location of the space docks and some space-based manufacturing. It is entirely a microgravity environment.

HUD. Heads-up Display. Among Ranans, this is an implant-driven internal system that creates a visual interface with the Station Net.

Hunter. See *SA Melynn Hunter.*

I.A.. Internal Affairs.

ICU. Intensive Care Unit.

Idris. Ailani Idris. (eye-LAH-nee ID-riss) Mayor of Orangeboro. (Pronouns: she, her).

Imre. See *Melisende Imre*

Institutes of Ascended Contemplation. An ozzirikkian university located on Wheel Five.

Internal Affairs. The intra-departmental self-policing arm of the OPD. In charge of investigating any potential irregularities within the OPD.

Iruka Jones. (EE-ru-kah) A detective with the Orangeboro Bureau of Missing Persons. (Pronouns: she, her.)

Iskander. See *Premier Eliana Iskander.*

IVs. Intravenous drip feeds.

Izgubil. (izz-GYOU-bill) A space barque that served as a mobile base of operations, brothel, and gambling casino for the Whisper Syndicate, a criminal organization on Rana Station before it was "explosively deconstructed" at the Orangeboro docks.

Jack Evanovich. A field agent assigned to SIT Alpha. (Pronouns: he, him.)

Jackson Wisniewski. (wizz-NEW-skee) The colonel in charge of Ranan Intelligence Operations for the Transmondian Intelligence Service. (Pronouns: he, him.)

Jalani Sanjaya. (ja-LAH-nee san-JAH-yah) Kristen's big brother, son of Charlie Morgan's cousin Marilyn and her husband Kimba. (Pronouns: he, him.)

Jeliza. (ja-LIE-zah) Eldest daughter of Hildie's first cousin Cormac and his wife Maira. Her little brother's name is Bryan.

Jenny Evans. a GR artist. (Pronouns: she, her.)

Jill Sandler. A Specialist Veterinarian in charge of XK9 health in Orangeboro. She owns the Sandler Clinic, a veterinary facility modified for XK9s. (Pronouns: she, her.)

Jimmy. A child who lives in Trondheim (TROND-hime) Tower, a neighbor of Corona Tower. (Pronouns: he, him.)

Joseph "Joe" Raach. (ROCK) An SBI Tech Specialist who holds a Ph. D. in Explosives Technology from the Wheel Three Institute of Technology. (Pronouns: he, him.)

Kabira Kiuvidas. (kah-BEE-rah key-YOU-vee-dass) a Lead Inspector in the Kiuvidas Collective. (Pronouns: she, her.)

Kalan Ministo. (KAY-lan mean-EEZ-doe) a senior member of Ministobrila Collective. (Pronouns: he, him.)

Kali. Hildie Gallagher's small calico cat. (Pronouns: she, her.)

Kee. A boy who lives in the Five-Ten. (Pronouns: he, him.)

Keya. (KAY-ah) Hildie's aunt. (Pronouns: she, her.)

Kieran O'Boyle. A suspect in "Elmo's Group," identified via DNA match because he is a Ranan Citizen. Son of Ostra Import Export Emporium manager Turlach O'Boyle, a known Whisper operative in the Five-Ten. (Pronouns: he, him.)

Kiuvidas Security Collective. (key-YOU-vee-dass) A Mahusayan collective that specializes in detective work.

Knife Woman. A Whisper Syndicate enforcer.

Kristen Lee. Jalani's little sister, daughter of Charlie Morgan's cousin Marilyn Sanjaya Lee and her husband Kimba Lee Sanjaya. (Pronouns: she, her.)

Kwame Odigo Klein. (KWAH-may OH-di-go KLINE) Orangeboro Chief of Police. (Pronouns: he, him.)

Lacey Lee. Daughter of Caro Cranach Lee and Andy Lee Cranach. (Pronouns: he, him.)

LaRochelle/"LaRock". See *Captain Treva LaRochelle.*

LEO's Grill. A restaurant in Central Plaza that caters to law enforcement officers. It is uniquely designed with mirrors and aligned passageways, so every seat is a corner booth, no one's back is exposed, and all the sightlines are clear.

Leeli See *Cecilia "Leeli" Tanaka.*

Lewis "Lou" Penny. An OPD homicide detective. (Pronouns: he, him.)

Lexie Zhang, MD. (JZHONG) Orangeboro Chief of Emergency Medical Services (a position of equal rank to Police Chief and Fire Marshal within the Orangeboro Safety Services Department). (Pronouns: she, her.)

Listener. A Ranan psychologist, commissioned through the Social Services Office of the Department of the Common Good.

Liz. See *Elizabeth "Liz" Antonopoulos.*

Lorena. A civilian property supervisor for the OPD at the Hub. (Pronouns: she, her.)

Loretta Triola Lee. (tree-OH-la LEE) Charlie's great-grandmother. Co-founder of Corona Chartered Family. (Pronouns: she, her.)

LSA. Lead Special Agent, a rank in the SBI. The Primary LSA (there normally are at least two) is second-in-command to the Senior Special Agent in charge.

Lynne Anthony. Partner of UPO Henry Sevencrows. A patrol officer assigned to the infamous Five-Ten. (Pronouns: she, her.)

Mac. See *Fergus "Mac" Mac Dermott.*

Mahusay Station. (MAH-hoo-say) A space station in the Chayko System, located in part of the asteroid belt. A sovereign political entity.

Mahusayan. (mah-hoo-SAY-un) From Mahusay Station.

Manuel "Manny" Wang Morgan. Charlie's first cousin. Hector and Hannah's son. A sous chef. Married to Fiametta "Fee" Morgan Wang. Hakan is their son. (Pronouns: he, him.)

Maria "Mimi" Morgan Lee. Charlie's mother. Wife of Theodore "Ted" Lee Morgan. (Pronouns: she, her.)

Marisol Patel. (MAIR-i-zol pa-TELL) An OPD detective lieutenant. (Pronouns: she, her.)

Marya Seaton. A UPO assigned to Ninth Precinct. (Pronouns: she, her.)

Martin. A MERS-V driver on the ERT. Assigned to the *Triumph.* (Pronouns: he, him.)

Master Mix. The nutritionally balanced, high-performance dog kibble designed by the XK9 Project for working XK9s.

Mayor Idris. See *Ailani Idris.*

Medal of Valor. Rana Station's highest recognition of honor for courage.

Melisende Imre. (MEL-lis-end EM-ray) CFO, Associate Head Geneticist, and XK9 Breeding Coordinator for the XK9 Project in Transmondia. (Pronouns: she, her.)

Melissa "Missy" Cranston. Director of the Orangeboro GR Unit. Secretary Oma Pandra's sister. (Pronouns: she, her.)

Melynn Hunter. (meh-LYN) a Special Agent assigned to SIT Delta. (Pronouns: she, her.)

MERS-V. – Multipurpose Emergency Response Space-Vehicle. A small, space-based vehicle designed to retrieve victims who have been "spaced" (ejected into the vacuum of space, usually by accident, where they have only 90 seconds to be rescued alive).

Mid-Levels. An educational level on Rana Station that is equivalent to Middle School. The evaluation for graduation to Upper Levels is referred to as "taking one's Mid-Levels."

Mike Santiago. The Senior Special Agent who leads the SBI's SIT Alpha, and the Station's leading law enforcement expert on the Whisper Syndicate. Significant of SSA Elaine Adeyeme. (Pronouns: he, him.)

Mikhail "Misha" Flores. (MEE-khah-yool "MEE-shah" FLO-race) XK9 Elle Finnian-Ella's partner. A Detective Level One. (Pronouns: he, him.)

Ministo Lulak. (mean-EEZ-doe LOO-lock) A Mahusayan mining spacecraft.

Ministobrila Collective. (mean-EEZ-doe-bree-lah) The Mahusayan collective unit that owns the *Ministo Lulak.*

Misha. See *Mikhail "Misha" Flores.*

Missy. See *Melissa Cranston.*

Monteverde Borough. (mon-tay-VAIR-day BUR-row) One of four Boroughs on Rana Station's Wheel Two. The other three are Petranova, Pueblo, and Orangeboro.

Montreaux. See *Commodore Clarimonde Alvaro Montreaux.*

MPs. Military Police Officers.

MUPATS. Multi-Passenger Transit Shuttle. A vehicle used to transport personnel and equipment in the microgravity inside the Hub.

Murder Brothers. Two men (siblings) who left a dead female in Warehouse 226 and fled to the *Izgubil* on the night of the Dock Breach. Since they are identified only by scent profile, the XK9s gave them the "placeholder nicknames" of Thud and Blunder, the Murder Brothers.

Nanda Errapel, MSN. (NAHN-dah EH-rah-pell) A nurse in the Re-Gen Unit at Orangeboro Medical Center. (Pronouns: he, him.)

Neil Dolan. The younger "Murder Brother," AKA "Blunder."

Nell Dodger-Meena. Rex's mother. Partnered with Dr. Frederika Cho. Together, they directed the XK9 Scent Reference Lab. (Pronouns: she, her.)

Nicole Oyunbileg. (oh-YOON-bill-egg) XK9 Scout Sam-Shana's partner. A Detective Level One. (Pronouns: she, her.)

Nolan Virendra. (vir-END-rah) An Admiral in the SDF. (Pronouns: he, him.)

NTA. "No Target Acquired," a readout on a MERS-V targeting rangefinder.

Nura Al-Masri. (NYOU-rah all-MAZ-ree) A child from Bonita Tower. Part of Owen's school project group. (Pronouns: she, her.)

Oma Peralta Pandra. (OH-ma per-ALL-ta PAN-drah) Secretary of Public Safety. Missy Cranston's brother. (Pronouns: he, him.)

OPD. Orangeboro Police Department.

OPD Central HQ. The administrative headquarters of the Orangeboro Police Department.

Orangeboro Civic Center. The building complex in Central Plaza that houses most Borough governmental departments and headquarters for their service administrations, and the Civic Center Auditorium.

Orangeboro Medical Center. The largest hospital in Orangeboro.

Orangeboro Police Department. The Borough's law enforcement agency. See also: *OPD*

Orangeboro Safety Services Department. A cabinet-level bureau of the Ranan Government. It includes Police, Fire, and Emergency Medical Services.

Orangeboro. (ORANGE-bur-row) One of four Boroughs on Rana Station's Wheel Two. The other three are Petranova, Pueblo, and Monteverde.

Ordovich. (ORE-dough-vitch). See *Gregory Ordovich*.

Osmond "Oz" Meredith. A Squad Commander of MERS-V drivers on the ERT, assigned to the *Triumph*.

Ostra Import-Export Emporium. (OH-straw) A storefront and shell corporation in the Five-Ten used by the Whisper Syndicate and managed by Turlach O'Boyle.

Owen Huddleston. Son of Charlie's cousin Gloria and her husband Quinn. (Pronouns: he, him.)

Ozzirikkians. (oz-zi-RICK-ee-uns) A non-terrestrial sapient species with a minority population that lives in Ranan Wheels Five and Six. Ranan ozzirikkians have all the same rights as other citizen-sapient beings on Rana Station.

Pack. As a group, all ten XK9s (large, intelligent, genetically engineered dogs) in the Orangeboro Police Department.

Pamela "Pam" Gómez. XK9 Shady Jacob-Belle's partner. A Detective Level One. Balchu Nowicki's Amare. (Learn more of her background in *The Other Side of Fear*, of which she's the protagonist.) (Pronouns: she, her.)

Pandra. See *Oma Peralta Pandra*.

Pari Gallagher Bannerjee. (PA-ree GAL-ah-gur BAN-er-jee) Hildie and Abi's father. Husband of Dara. (Pronouns: he, him.)

Pascal Jennings. (pass-KAL JEN-ings) Charlie's Personnel Assistance Liaison. (Pronouns: he, him.)

Pat Cornwell. An SBI Tech Specialist in signals intel attached to SIT Alpha. Nephew of SDF Commodore Farooq Cornwell. (Pronouns: he, him.)

Patel. See *Marisol Patel*.

Pedro "Gran Pepe" Lee Montoya. (PAY-dro "GRAN PAY-pay" mon-TO-yah). Charlie's maternal grandfather. Husband of Annie Montoya Lee, son-in-law of Loretta, father of Mimi and Serafina. Co-founder of Corona Chartered Family. (Pronouns: he, him.)

Penny. See *Lewis "Lew" Penny*.

Pepe. See *Pedro "Gran Pepe" Lee Montoya*.

Perri. See *Adelaide "Laidie" Perri*.

Petunia Yeller-Melody. XK9 partner of Walter Ejiamike. (Pronouns: she, her.)

Peynirci. See *Rona Peynirci*.

Poopy. The XK9s' placeholder nickname for a suspect in "Elmo's Group," identified only by scent profile. (Pronouns: he, him.)

Premier Eliana Iskander, (ell-ee-AHN-ah ISS-kin-der), The elected chief executive of Rana Station and a member of the Commonwealth Party.

Premier. The Ranan head of state. An elected position that may be filled by either a human or an ozzirikkian.

Primerans. People from Primero Station.

PTV. Personnel Transport Vehicle. A large 1-G-based government agency vehicle like a bus, designed primarily to transport people and their gear.

Purdy. See *Wayne Purdy.*

Purple Palace. The disparaging nickname the *Triumph* crew gave Charlie's apartment when it was decorated according to Felicia's taste.

Quiddo. A sport played in microgravity on maneuverable micrograv sleds.

Quinn Gibson Huddleston. Husband of Charlie's cousin Gloria, and father of Grant and Owen. (Pronouns: he, him.)

Raghnall Wall. (RAD-nal) A Saoirse Front member. AKA "Clumsy." (Pronouns: he, him.)

Ralph Lee Gibson. Charlie's uncle. Husband of Serafina Gibson Lee. A Certified Agricultural Technician, he is the head of agricultural operations for Corona Tower. (Pronouns: he, him.)

RAMoD. (RA-mod) Robotic Assisted Mobility Device. Hospital equipment used at Orangeboro Medical Center.

Ramón. A MERS-V driver on the ERT. Assigned to the *Triumph.* (Pronouns: he, him.)

Rana Habitat Space Station. (RAH-nah) One of six space-based megastructures in the Chayko System, and the sovereign government that controls it.

Razor Liam-Blanca. XK9 partner of Liz Antonopoulos. (Pronouns: he, him.)

Realiciné. An immersive, full-sensory-input cinema-arts entertainment experience.

Re-gen. Medical Regeneration, a therapeutic technique for re-growing or fortifying the healing process after tissue damage or catastrophic injury, including growing new organs or limbs.

Reihan Khan Al-Masri. (ray-HAHN con all-MAZ-ree) A Certified Agricultural Technician, she is the head of agricultural operations for Bonita Tower. (Pronouns: she, her.)

Rex Dieter-Nell. XK9 partner of Charlie Morgan. XK9 Shady Jacob-Belle's mate. (Pronouns: he, him.)

Reza Gerritsen. A Special Agent assigned to SIT Delta. (Pronouns: he, him.)

Ricardo "Ric." A child who lives in Fairleigh Tower, a neighbor of Corona Tower. (Pronouns: he, him.)

Rim Eight Road. The road that runs along the outer edge of Terrace Eight, including Corona Tower on Starboard Hill, and Feliz Tower on Port Hill.

Robert "Bob" Wells. A UPO assigned to Ninth Precinct. (Pronouns: he, him.)

Rona Peynirci. (ROW-nah pa-NEAR-see) Ninth Precinct representative on Orangeboro's Borough Council (Pronouns: she, her.)

Ronin Guerrero. A long-haul freighter spaceship.

Rooq. See *Commodore Farooq "Rooq" Tomoko Cornwell.*

Rory Fredericks. A former graduate student of Dr. SCISCO, whose doctoral project appears to have formed the basis for the explosives that destroyed the Izgubil. He has been missing for a year and a half. Former Amare of Emer Bellamy. (Pronouns: he, him.)

Rose Lavigne. (LA-veen) Amare of Sarnai Bayarmaa. (Pronouns: she, her.)

Rowan Glenn. Berwyn Yael's sister. (Pronouns: she, her.)

Rufus Dolan. The elder "Murder Brother," AKA "Thud."

Ryan. See *Bridget Riordan Ryan.*

Ryder Nunzio. (RYE-dur NOON-zee-oh) Transmondian

Ambassador to Rana Station. (Pronouns: he, him.)

S-3-9. Also *Central S-3-9*. Sub-Level Three, Section Nine, a secured location underneath OPD Central HQ.

S-Poly. Station Polytechnic, a university of technology in Orangeboro.

SA. Special Agent, a rank in the SBI.

Sair. A girl who lives in the Five-Ten. (Pronouns: she, her.)

Sally. A MERS-V driver on the ERT. Assigned to the *Triumph*. (Pronouns: she, her.)

Sandler Clinic. The specialized veterinary clinic run by Dr. Jill Sandler, DVM, an expert in the medical needs of XK9s.

Saoirse Front. (SEER-sha) A violent nationalist group from Uladh Nua, with ties to the Whisper Syndicate. Members often wear distinctive, Celtic-knot tattoos on their arms to proclaim their affiliation.

Sarnai Bayarmaa. (SAR-nah BUYER-mah) Balchu Nowicki's sister, daughter of Tuya and Feyodor, and Amare of Rose Lavigne. (Pronouns: she, her.)

SBI. Station Bureau of Investigation.

SCISCO 3750 (SHEES-koh) A Farricainan Artificial Intelligence who is a professor of explosives technology at Station Polytechnic University. (Pronouns: ne, nir.)

Scout Sam-Shana. XK9 partner of Nicole Oyunbileg. XK9 Victor Sam-Janet's half-brother. (Pronouns: he, him.)

SDF. Station Defense Force, the military arm of the Ranan Government.

Seaton. See *Marya Seaton*.

Serafina Gibson Lee. Charlie's aunt, Mimi's sister, Ralph's wife, mother of Germaine and Marilyn. (Pronouns: she, her.)

Sevencrows. See *Henry Sevencrows*.

Shady Jacob-Belle. XK9 partner of Pamela Gómez. XK9 Rex Dieter-Nell's mate. (Pronouns: she, her.)

Shawnee Kramer. Junior LSA of SIT Delta. She is nominally third-in command to Adeyeme and Shimon, but normally functions as Shimon's equal. (Pronouns: she, her.)

Sheriff Ibsen. See *Bruce Ibsen.*

Shik'ki-dok'tuum. (she-kee-DOCK-toom) The Learned Shik'ki-dok'tuum is a robotics engineering specialist from Wheel Five's Institutes of Ascended Contemplation. An ozzirikkian. (Pronouns: ti, tin.)

Shimon. (shee-MOWN) See *Shiva "Shiv" Shimon.*

Shiva "Shiv" Shimon. (SHEE-va "SHEEV" sheem-OWN) Primary Senior LSA of SIT Delta. He is second-in-command to SSA Adeyeme. (Pronouns: he, him.)

Shomari Hondo. Charlie's defense attorney. (Pronouns: he, him.)

Significant. A Domestic Partner on Rana Station. Domestic Partnerships are more legally binding than an Amare relationship.

Sionainn. (shon-INN) A sub-level area in Howardsboro, similar in type to the Five-Ten.

Sirius Valley. (SEAR-ee-us) The land on either side of the Sirius River, the waterway that runs in an endless circle down the middle of Rana Station's Wheel Two.

SIT. Special Investigations Team, an elite investigative unit of the SBI.

Smita Rostov. Significant of Abhik "Abi" Bannerjee. She and Abi share an apartment in Feliz Tower with Abi's older sister Hildie. (Pronouns: she, her.)

Solara City. The capitol of Transmondia.

Sophie Lee. Daughter of Caro Cranach Lee and Andy Lee Cranach. (Pronouns: she, her.)

Sound Tech Samuels. An OPD sound technician.

S-Poly. See *Station Polytechnic University.*

Spinward 32. An experimental paddy for Feliz Family to use for testing new rice varietals.

SSA. Senior Special Agent, a rank in the SBI. Senior Special Agents are the commanding officers of the Bureau's Special Investigative units, and of Borough or Timi'i offices.

STAT Team. Special Tools and Techniques Team, a Safety

Services Department unit that includes specialists in hostage negotiation, bomb disposal, rescue and recovery, and high-risk tactical operations.

Station Polytechnic University. A university of technology in Orangeboro on Wheel Two. See also *S-Poly.*

Stinky. The XK9s' placeholder nickname for a suspect in "Elmo's Group," identified only by scent profile. (Pronouns: he, him.)

Stubbs. A human captive of Col. Wisniewski. (Pronouns: he, him.)

Sweaty. The XK9s' placeholder nickname for a suspect in "Elmo's Group," identified only by scent profile. (Pronouns: he, him.)

Taios Collective. (DIE-ohs) a collective that works with Ministobrila Collective in the Mahusayan part of the Chaykoan asteroid belt.

Takhiachono Marines of Primero. (tack-hee-ah-CHO-no; pree-MAIR-oh) the most celebrated military cadre in the Human Diaspora, reputed to be the toughest human fighting unit in history.

Tech Specialist. A rating in the SBI or SDF. An expert in a particular technical specialty, such as explosives or signals technology. See also *TS.*

Tech with the tattoos. A veterinary technologist. (Pronouns: they/them.)

Theodore "Ted" Lee Morgan. Charlie's father and husband of Maria "Mimi" Morgan Lee. (Pronouns: he, him.)

Theresa Socorro. (tay-RAY-sa so-CORR-oh) A paramedic on the ERT, assigned to the *Triumph.* Hildie Gallagher's friend. (Pronouns: she, her.)

Thud. See *Murder Brothers.* Thud is the elder sibling.

Till. See *Atilla "Till" Usher.*

TIS. Transmondian Intelligence Service.

Toop. A boy who lives in the Five-Ten. (Pronouns: he, him.)

Town Cars On Call. An auto-nav vehicle rental and leasing business, with which Corona Family maintains an account.

Transmondian Republic. (trans-MON-dee-ahn) The dominant country on Monlandia, the largest landform on Planet Chayko.

Triumph. A rescue runner (small space vehicle) operated by the Emergency Rescue Team at the Ranan Hub.

TS. Tech Specialist, a rank in the SBI or SDF. An expert in a particular technical specialty, such as explosives or signals technology.

Turlach O'Boyle. Manager of Ostra Import Export Emporium in the Five-Ten. A known Whisper operative. (Pronouns: he, him.)

Tuuri. (TOO-ree)An Emergency Rescue Squad MERS-V driver killed in the *Asalatu* wreck. (Pronouns: he, him.)

Tuxedo "Tux" Moondog-Carrie. XK9 partner of Georgia Volkov and mate of Elle Finnian-Ella. An explosives expert. (Pronouns: he, him.)

Tuya Nowicki Bayarmaa. (TOO-yuh no-WICK-ee BUYER-mah) Balchu's mother. (Pronouns: she/her.)

Uncle Dolph. See *Dolph Gibson Sanger.*

Ullach. From Uladh Nua.

Uladh Nua. (ULL-ud NYOU-ah) A country in the northwestern quadrant of Monlandia.

Upper-Levels. An educational level on Rana Station that is equivalent to High School. The evaluation for graduation to Upper Levels is referred to as "taking one's Upper-Levels."

UPO. Uniformed Police Officer, a civilian police rank.

UPO Marya Seaton. A Uniformed Police Officer who works a patrol beat in Precinct Nine. (Pronouns: she, her.)

UPO Wells. A Uniformed Police Officer (Pronouns: he, him.)

Victor Sam-Janet. XK9 partner of Eduardo Donovan. Half-brother of Scout Sam-Shana. (Pronouns: he, him.)

Virendra. See *Nolan Virendra.*

Virgilia "Gillie" Finlay. A Special Agent assigned to SIT Delta. A forensic accounting specialist. (Pronouns: she, her.)

Walter Ejiamike. (edge-EE-a-meek) XK9 Petunia Yeller-Melody's partner. A Detective Level One. (Pronouns: he, him.)

Wayne Purdy. An unregistered resident of the Five-Ten, AKA "Stinky." (Pronouns: he, him.)

Wei. See *Dominic Wei.*

Wells. See *Robert "Bob" Wells.*

Whisper Syndicate. A powerful criminal organization on Rana Station, as well as on the most closely adjacent asteroids to Rana and Mahusay Stations.

William "Bill" Goldstein Sloane. An OPD Corporal. Rex's friend. (Pronouns: he, him.)

Willow. A cousin of Berwyn Yael and his sister Rowan. A new mother. (Pronouns: she, her.)

Wina. (WEE-nah) See *Edwina Emshwiller.*

Wisniewski. See *Jackson Wisniewski.*

Wu "Yo-yo" Guanyu. Maintenance technician at the Hub base for the Orangeboro Emergency Rescue Team. An innovative wearer of customized prosthetic arms and hands. (Pronouns: he, him.)

XK9 Project. A Transmondian corporation that produces genetically engineered dogs called XK9s. It has close ties to the Transmondian Intelligence Service.

XK9s. An acronym adopted by the XK9 Project to identify specially-bred, genetically-modified, cybernetically-enhanced canines with extraordinary memories, olfactory capabilities, and verbal acuity.

XK9 Special Investigations Unit. A proposed new group Chief Klein proposes to create within the OPD.

Yo-yo. See *Wu "Yo-yo" Guanyu.*

Zane. A field agent assigned to SIT Alpha. (Pronouns: he, him.)

Zhixizzixi. (ZHICK-zee-*zick*-zee) An annual festival celebrated by Ranan ozzirikkians at the turn of the calendar year.

Zuni. Dr. Mika Zuni (MY-ca ZOO-nee), a renowned re-gen specialist. (Pronouns: he, him.)

ACKNOWLEDGMENTS

Every book is its own journey, and this one took me down a much longer, more winding road than I expected. I hope and believe it's a better book than it otherwise would have been, thanks to that journey and all who helped me along the way. But it definitely challenged the perseverance of all involved.

Many of the mainstays who got me through earlier books were essential to this one as well. I am most particularly indebted to my faithful Brain Trust, **Lucy A. Synk, Dora Furlong,** and **G. S. Norwood**. By the end of this process, they had become the most patient, honest, and absolutely essential of partners. This book could not have happened (at least not in this form) without their invaluable guidance and advice.

I have a new writers' group to thank, hosted both in person and virtually as the need arose, by **Dyann Love Barr**; her husband, Zoom wizard **Dennis Barr**; and **Cathy Morrison**. Other indispensable regulars include **Rod Galindo, Edwin Frownfelter, Becky Lynn**, and **Karin Gastreich**, as well as **Dora Furlong, Lynette M. Burrows, Deb Branson**, and many more who cycled through from time to time.

I also want to acknowledge my deeply-valued beta-readers. They took time to not only read my half-baked efforts, but offered comments to help me improve: **Margaret Middleton, Robin Wayne Bailey, Diana J. Bailey, Janice Raach, Don McCann, Mike Whitney, P.R.** and **Tina Adams,** and **Karin L. Frank.**

Extra-special thanks to **Paula Helm Murray** and **Ann Vanderlaan!** I also want to acknowledge **Dr. Jill Sandler, DVM, Joseph Raach,** and **Tyrell E. Gephardt.**

As readers of my blog are aware, I owe an extra-fervent thank you to my amazing (both patient and persistent, as well as brilliantly gifted) illustrator, **Jody A. Lee.** And where would I be without the Essential Polish of my intrepid proofreader, **Deb Branson?**

My bedrock, as ever, is my Beloved, **Pascal Gephardt,** who has been my "patron of the arts" for well over 40 years. And I'm forever grateful to my sister and partner-in-publishing, **G. S. Norwood.**

I love you all.

ABOUT THE AUTHOR

Jan S. Gephardt commutes daily between her Kansas City metro area home in the United States and Rana Station, a habitat space station the size of New York City, a very long way from Earth and several hundred years in the future.

Writer, artist, and longtime science fiction fan, Jan's been a teacher, a journalist, an illustrator, a graphic designer, an art director, a book designer, a marketing specialist, and an art agent, all while rearing two children and honing the writer's craft for several decades.

Her fine-art paper sculpture has been featured in regionally-exhibited one-person shows, juried into national exhibitions all over the United States, and is on display wherever she travels to science fiction conventions. She lives with her family, which *always* includes animals.

in g f a y

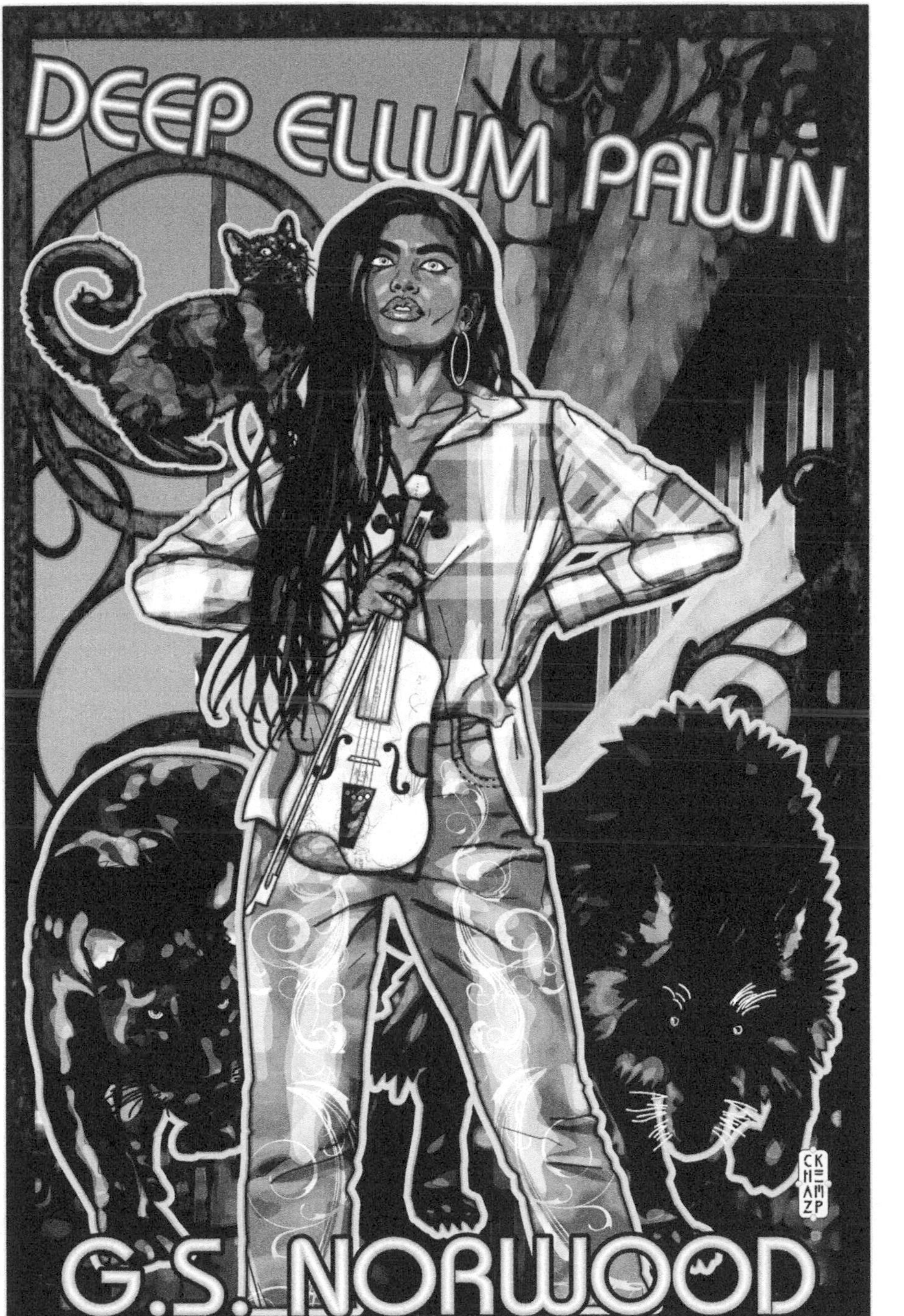
DEEP ELLUM PAWN
G.S. NORWOOD

CHAPTER ONE OF "DEEP ELLUM PAWN"

AN URBAN FANTASY NOVELETTE SET IN
TEXAS

Chapter One: GOLDEN FIDDLE

The guy on the other side of the counter shifted from foot to foot, taking quick swipes at his streaming nose with the cuff of his beige flannel shirt. His eyes, half-hidden by greasy blond bangs, darted from side to side, as if he was afraid Hell Hounds would appear at any moment, hot on his trail.

God knows, the Hounds wouldn't have any trouble following his scent. He reeked of sweat, adrenaline, and old urine.

I looked from him to the battered violin case he'd shoved across my sales counter toward me. I was pretty sure what I'd find inside.

"Two hundred bucks," I said.

"You haven't even looked at it!"

"One fifty."

"But it's *gold*!"

Of course it was. "One hundred. Take it or leave it."

"That's not fair! It's worth lots more than that! You don't understand!"

I did understand. I understood that all his hopes and fears were in that case. Maybe even his life's meaning. I understood that he wanted his lost dreams and wasted talent to be worth more than one hundred measly dollars. I also understood that he was really, really bad at striking bargains.

"Look, buddy." I leaned closer despite the waves of meth sweat wafting off of him. "You used to be a musician, right?"

"I AM a musician!" He tried to stand up straighter, but some old pain caught him between the shoulder blades and he hunched over again. "I played with the Dallas Symphony."

"Uh-huh. And you were pretty good. Then some guy challenged you to a fiddling contest, which you won, and he gave you his fiddle as the prize." I rested my hand on the duct tape that covered the violin case. "This fiddle, which is made of solid gold."

Heat, and a faint vibration, rose up from the case as if the instrument inside was alive.

"It has no resonance. The strings screech like damned souls. And ever since you got it, you've had horrible nightmares about giant, slavering bloodhounds with eyes red as fire, tracking you down to carry your soul to Hell."

My gaze held his as the color leached from his face.

"The booze didn't help, and neither did the pills." I counted down the steps. "So you tried the harder stuff. You lost your chair at the symphony, then your cushy apartment, your equally cushy girlfriend, and now even your mother won't accept your calls. Maybe I'm a sap, but I will take this cursed instrument off your hands and give you dreamless sleep, room to breathe, and one last chance to turn your life around. Plus fifty bucks."

He blinked. "Fifty bucks?"

"That's enough to buy you something to eat and a cab to the rehab facility of your choice. I'm giving you your freedom, asshole. You should be paying me."

He nodded once, and took a step back as I counted out the bills. His fingers didn't touch mine as he snatched his money and bolted out the door.

He didn't need to run. The Hell Hounds were my problem now.

A brisk wind kicked a shower of red-gold leaves down the street as he disappeared into the swirl of hipsters and hucksters who called Deep Ellum home.

At two o'clock on a cool fall afternoon, the lunch crowd had pretty much disappeared from my little pocket of Dallas. The pub crawlers had yet to show up, but the natives were out in their usual force. A steady parade of beards, body piercings, green hair, and tattoo sleeves surged past my pawn shop windows.

I looked tame in comparison. These days I wore my hair longer, without a hint of purple or pink, and favored trim jeans and loose flannel shirts to the flamboyantly patterned leggings and mini-skirts the Deep Ellum fashionistas preferred. No makeup, so anyone who cared to look could see the full, rich blend of black, Native American, and anglo written boldly across my face.

It was a face that reflected the neighborhood. A century ago Deep Ellum had been the heart of Dallas' black business community, and pawn shops had lined every block. Today, mine was the only pawn shop left, wedged in amongst the pizza parlors, leather shops, and music clubs. The people were a more diverse mix, but Deep Ellum was still a place you could find just about any type of trouble you wanted to get into.

The legendary bluesman, Robert Johnson, had recorded his song about Hell Hounds on his trail just a few blocks west of here. I looked down at the ragged violin case on my counter. "What kind of song are you trying to sing?" I asked the fiddle softly.

Rather than speculate, I dug my utility knife out of my back pocket and got to work. Duct tape all but mummified the case.

Its former owner had used far more than was necessary if he just wanted to keep the case from falling open. No. He'd wanted to make sure the thing stayed shut.

With a little effort, I peeled back enough layers of tape to get a look at the case itself. It was made of wood, covered by leather, and there were scorch marks along the seam where the top met the bottom, as if there had once been a fire inside.

"Great," I muttered as I pried it open. I should have worn gloves. My fingers were already sticking together.

But there it was, just as I remembered it. The fiddle was heartbreakingly beautiful and light as a feather, despite being made of solid gold. As I lifted it out of the case, a stray afternoon sunbeam broke through the burglar bars on my front window to dance along the silver strings.

There was a matching bow, perfectly balanced, that seemed to adjust itself to my hand as I held it over the strings. Ripples of energy passed between the two, all but begging me to touch bow to fiddle and make some music. Any music. Irish jigs, bluegrass breakdowns, classical sonatas, Iron Maiden covers; whatever I chose, it would be glorious.

"Fat chance, fiddle freak." I said the words aloud, with a snarl of contempt, just in case anyone was listening. Nobody needed to know how strongly I was tempted.

I put bow and fiddle back in the case and closed the lid, then stepped away. Took a deep breath and let it out slowly as my gaze wandered over my pawn shop. It was kind of a jumble, as pawn shops get to be. Everything from gas-powered weed eaters to old videotapes— even a prosthetic leg—filled the shelves in the center of the room. A dozen guitars and a couple of fiddles hung from the wall to my right, with amps, drums, and a symphonic gong arranged neatly underneath.

Two glass cases of jewelry—mostly wedding rings—stood against the wall to my left. I kept some guns in a display case on the end wall, with the rest locked in a safe behind it.

You'd think anyone who wanted to rob a pawn shop would

go for the guns or the jewelry, but the only thing ever stolen from my place was this damn golden fiddle. Three times, in fact. And the hell of it was, people just kept bringing it back.

Something brushed against my leg and I looked down into the green eyes of a small black cat.

"Hey, Tid," I greeted her. "Where you been? The fiddle is back."

I'd rescued Tidbit, along with her brother, Morsel, from the dumpster behind the 7- Eleven several years back. They were full-time residents of the pawn shop, just like me. Morsel spent his days roaming the alleys and wasting his charm on the girls from the charter school over on Elm. Tid stayed closer to home, focusing her efforts on keeping my shop free of rats and mice. I liked that in a cat.

She leapt up onto the counter with the easy grace of one who wastes no time on nonsense like golden violins. Butted her head into my hand. This meant that she loved me, but her bowl was empty, and if I loved her, I'd attend to it right away.

I did love her, so I stretched my arms above my head, rolled my shoulders to work out the tension, then followed Tid back to the kitchen in the private part of the shop. I left the violin case on the counter—a straight shot in from the door. No way you could miss it if you happened to glance in from the street. Maybe someone else would steal it.

I should be so lucky.

If you'd like to read more, get the story on Amazon!